Archie at RIVERDALE HIGH®

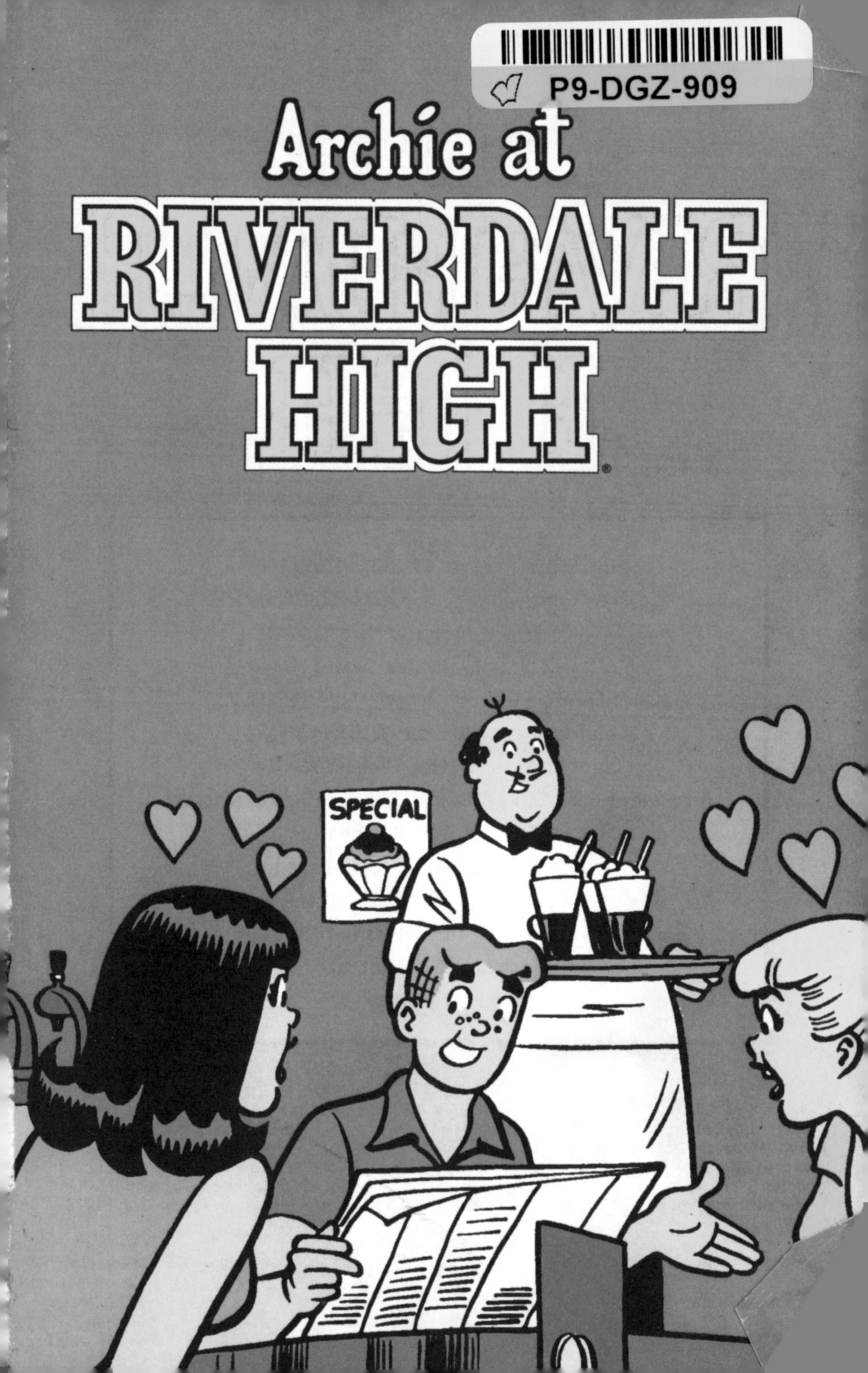
SPECIAL

Archie at RIVERDALE HIGH

Publisher / Co-CEO: Jon Goldwater
Co-President / Editor-In-Chief: Victor Gorelick
Co-President: Mike Pellerito
Co-President: Alex Segura
Chief Creative Officer: Roberto Aguirre-Sacasa
Chief Operating Officer: William Mooar
Chief Financial Officer: Robert Wintle
Director of Book Sales & Operations: Jonathan Betancourt
Art Director: Vincent Lovallo
Production Manager: Stephen Oswald
Lead Designer: Kari McLachlan
Associate Editor: Carlos Antunes
Editor: Jamie Lee Rotante
Co-CEO: Nancy Silberkleit

Printed in USA. First Printing. ISBN: 978-1-68255-819-5

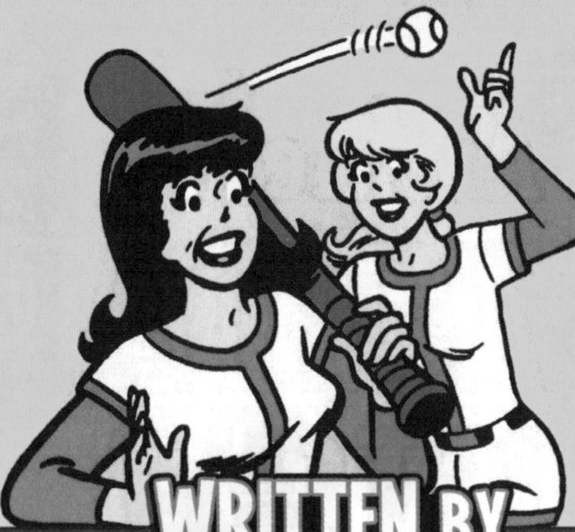

WRITTEN BY

George Gladir, Frank Doyle,
Dick Malmgren & Mike Pellowski

ART BY

Bob Bolling, Stan Goldberg, Dan DeCarlo,
Dan DeCarlo Jr., Harry Lucey, Samm Schwartz, Rudy Lapick,
Jon D'Agostino, Chic Stone, Jimmy DeCarlo, Alison Flood,
Bob Smith, Bill Yoshida, Vince DeCarlo & Barry Grossman

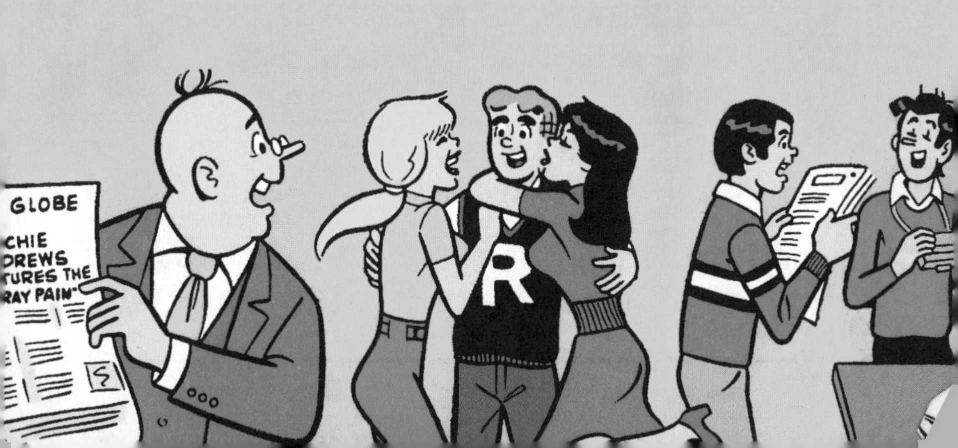
GLOBE

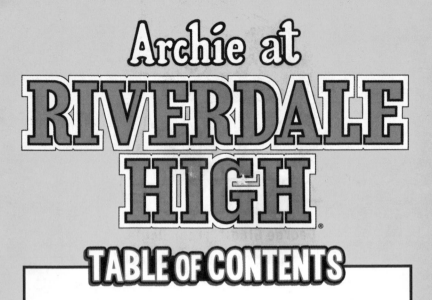

Archie at RIVERDALE HIGH®

TABLE OF CONTENTS

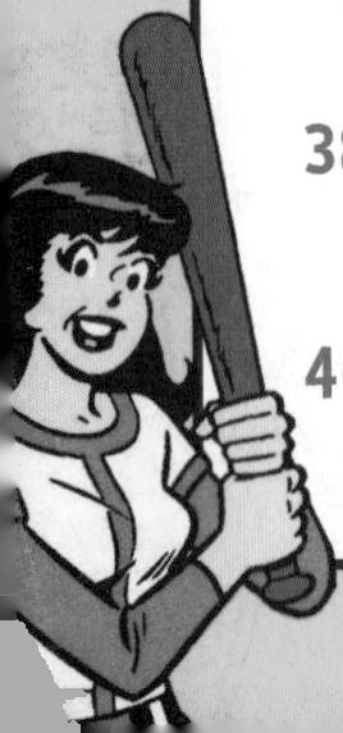

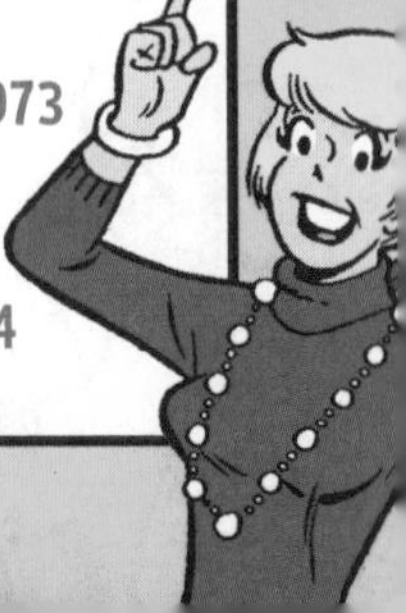

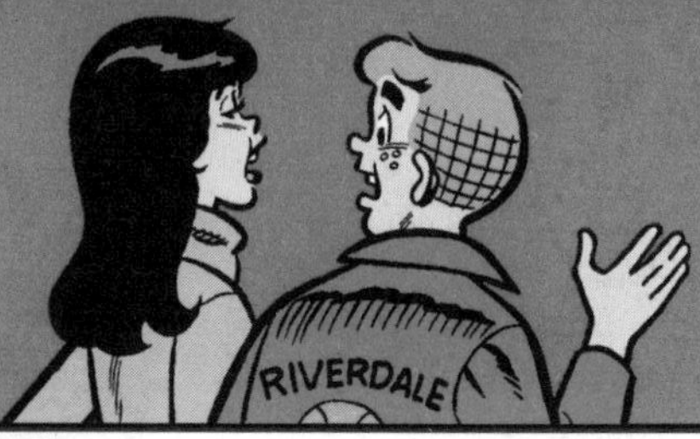
RIVERDALE
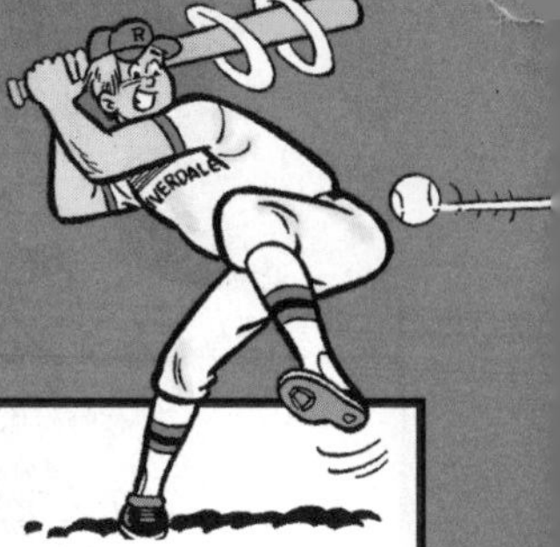
RIVERDALE

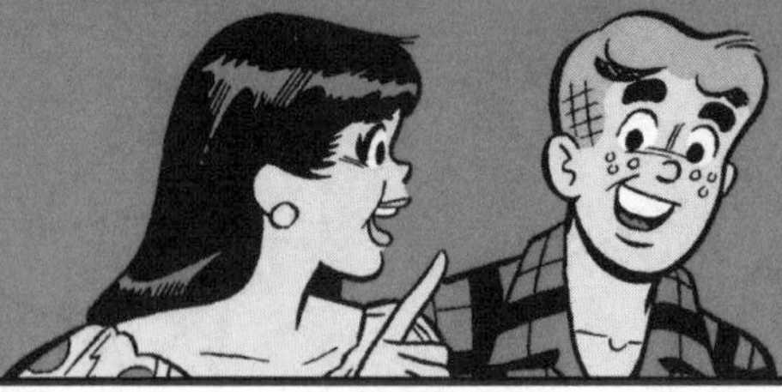

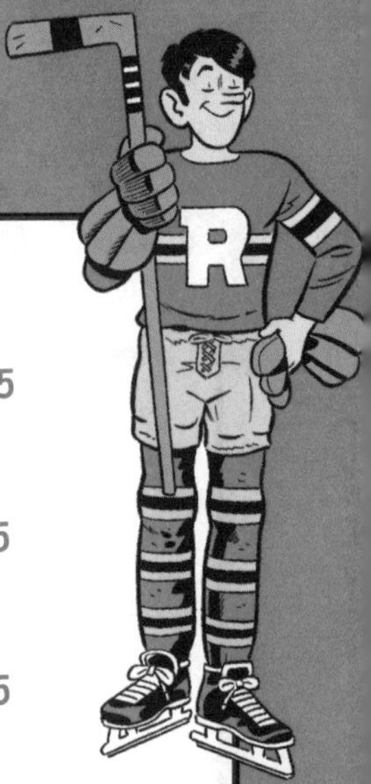

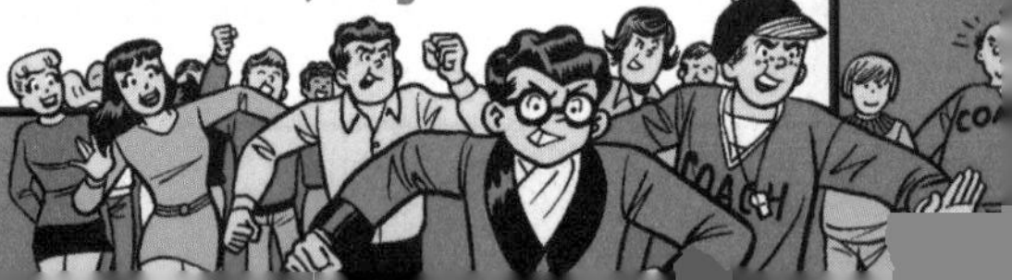

COACH

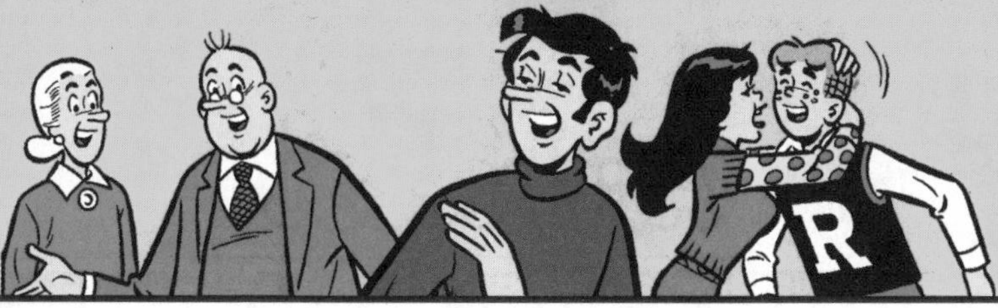

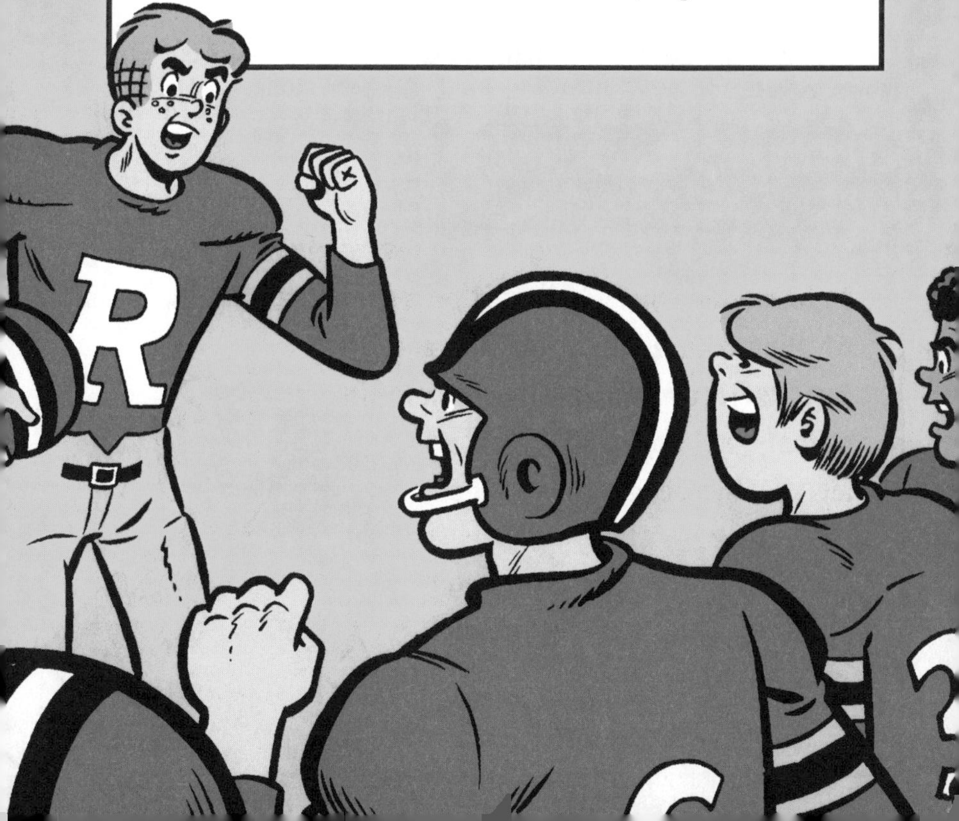

Archie at RIVERDALE HIGH

Welcome back, for another installment of entertaining and fun tales from the 1970s series ARCHIE AT RIVERDALE HIGH!

One thing that hasn't changed in the many decades since Archie's creation is that a lot of wild things take place in Riverdale--namely at Riverdale High.

This second book highlights stories ranging from thrilling to heartwarming; whether it be a thief roaming the halls of Riverdale High or Archie and the Gang reflecting on how much their high school--and especially their principal, Mr. Weatherbee--means to them.

Now, turn the page to begin studying just why Riverdale High is so special!

Archie at Riverdale High in GHOSTS

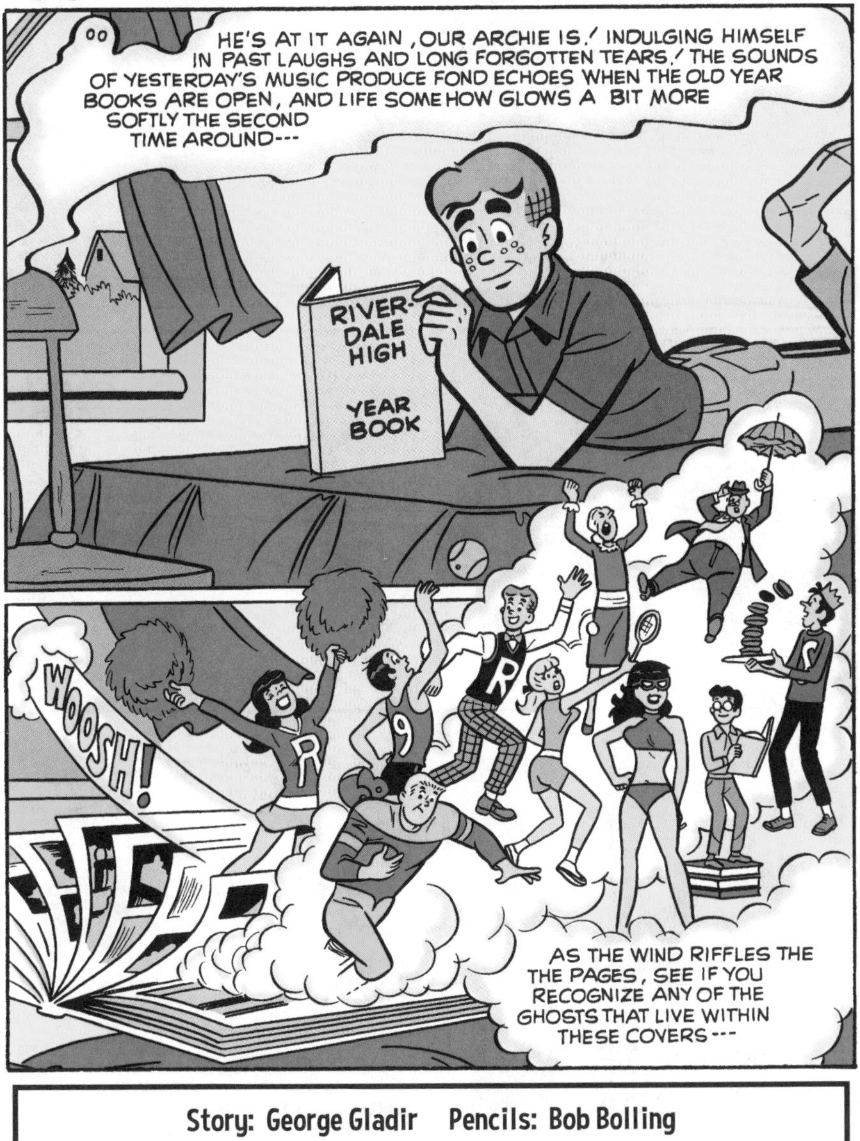
HE'S AT IT AGAIN, OUR ARCHIE IS! INDULGING HIMSELF IN PAST LAUGHS AND LONG FORGOTTEN TEARS! THE SOUNDS OF YESTERDAY'S MUSIC PRODUCE FOND ECHOES WHEN THE OLD YEAR BOOKS ARE OPEN, AND LIFE SOME HOW GLOWS A BIT MORE SOFTLY THE SECOND TIME AROUND---
RIVER-DALE HIGH YEAR BOOK
WOOSH!
AS THE WIND RIFFLES THE THE PAGES, SEE IF YOU RECOGNIZE ANY OF THE GHOSTS THAT LIVE WITHIN THESE COVERS---

Story: George Gladir   Pencils: Bob Bolling
Inks: Rudy Lapick   Letters: Bill Yoshida

Originally printed in ARCHIE AT RIVERDALE HIGH #7, JUNE 1973

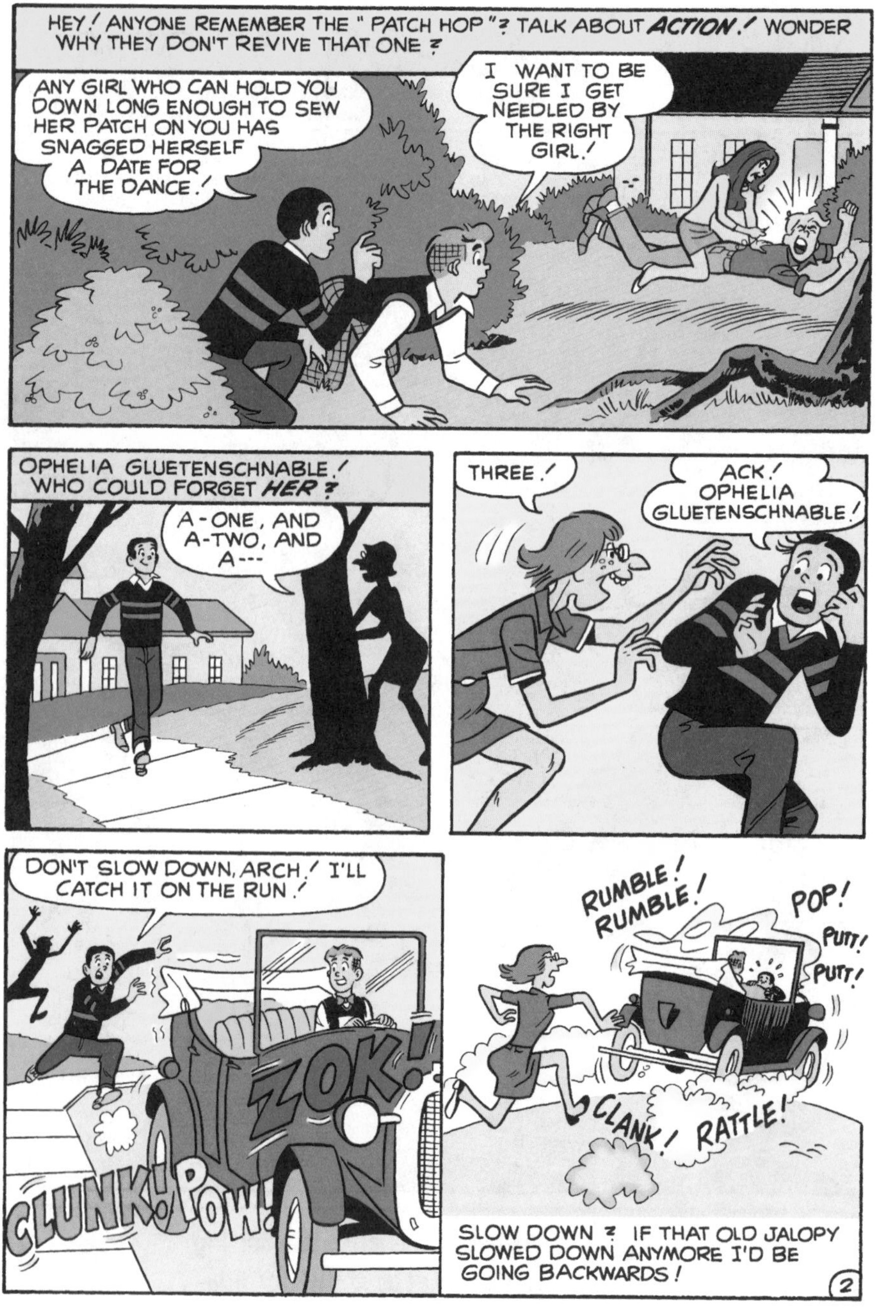
HEY! ANYONE REMEMBER THE " PATCH HOP "? TALK ABOUT ACTION! WONDER WHY THEY DON'T REVIVE THAT ONE?
ANY GIRL WHO CAN HOLD YOU DOWN LONG ENOUGH TO SEW HER PATCH ON YOU HAS SNAGGED HERSELF A DATE FOR THE DANCE!
I WANT TO BE SURE I GET NEEDLED BY THE RIGHT GIRL!
OPHELIA GLUETENSCHNABLE! WHO COULD FORGET HER?
A-ONE, AND A-TWO, AND A---
THREE!
ACK! OPHELIA GLUETENSCHNABLE!
DON'T SLOW DOWN, ARCH! I'LL CATCH IT ON THE RUN!
ZOK!
CLUNK! POW!
RUMBLE! RUMBLE!
POP!
PUTT! PUTT!
CLANK! RATTLE!
SLOW DOWN? IF THAT OLD JALOPY SLOWED DOWN ANYMORE I'D BE GOING BACKWARDS!
2

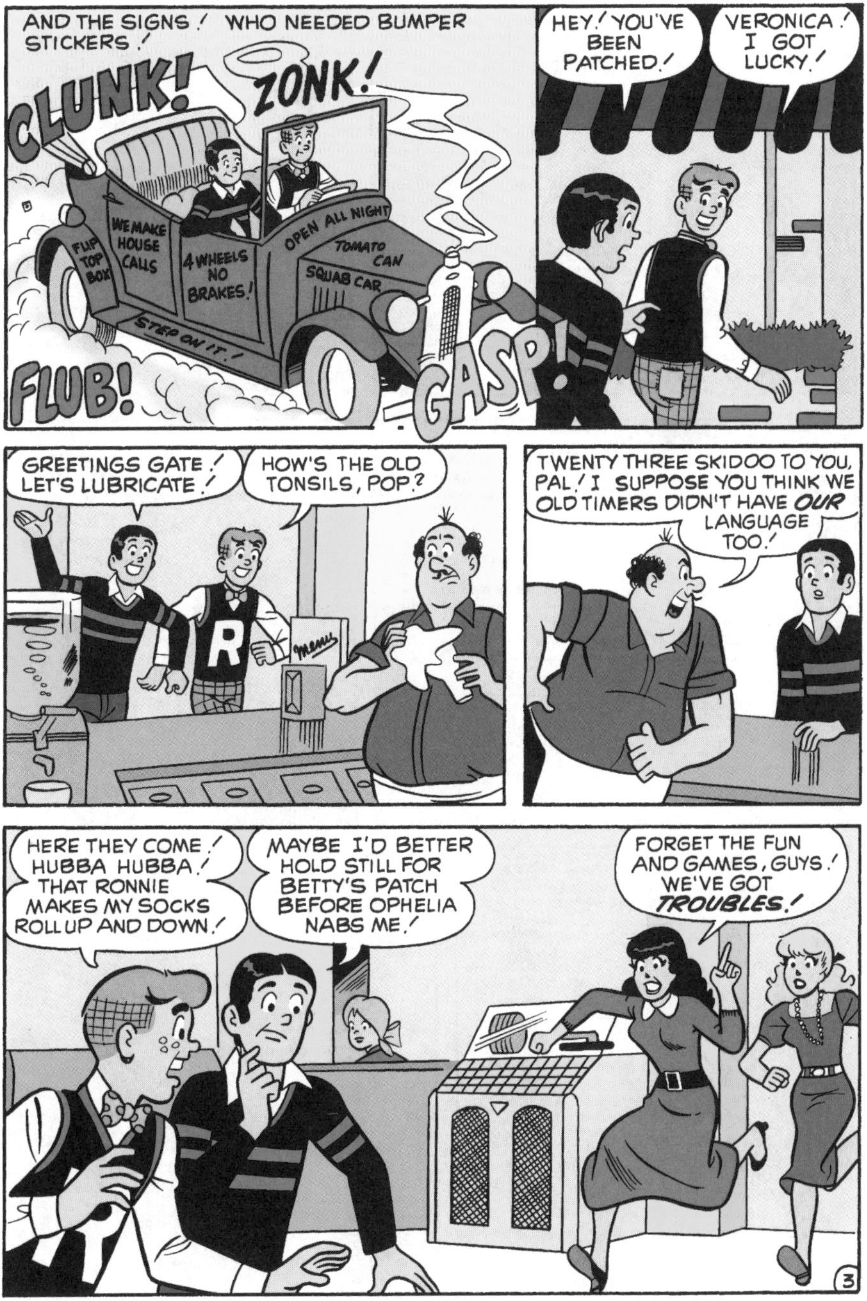
AND THE SIGNS! WHO NEEDED BUMPER STICKERS!
CLUNK!
ZONK!
FLIP TOP BOX
WE MAKE HOUSE CALLS
4 WHEELS NO BRAKES!
OPEN ALL NIGHT
TOMATO CAN
SQUAB CAR
STEP ON IT!
FLUB!
GASP!
HEY! YOU'VE BEEN PATCHED!
VERONICA! I GOT LUCKY!
GREETINGS GATE! LET'S LUBRICATE!
HOW'S THE OLD TONSILS, POP?
TWENTY THREE SKIDOO TO YOU, PAL! I SUPPOSE YOU THINK WE OLD TIMERS DIDN'T HAVE OUR LANGUAGE TOO!
HERE THEY COME! HUBBA HUBBA! THAT RONNIE MAKES MY SOCKS ROLL UP AND DOWN!
MAYBE I'D BETTER HOLD STILL FOR BETTY'S PATCH BEFORE OPHELIA NABS ME!
FORGET THE FUN AND GAMES, GUYS! WE'VE GOT TROUBLES!
3

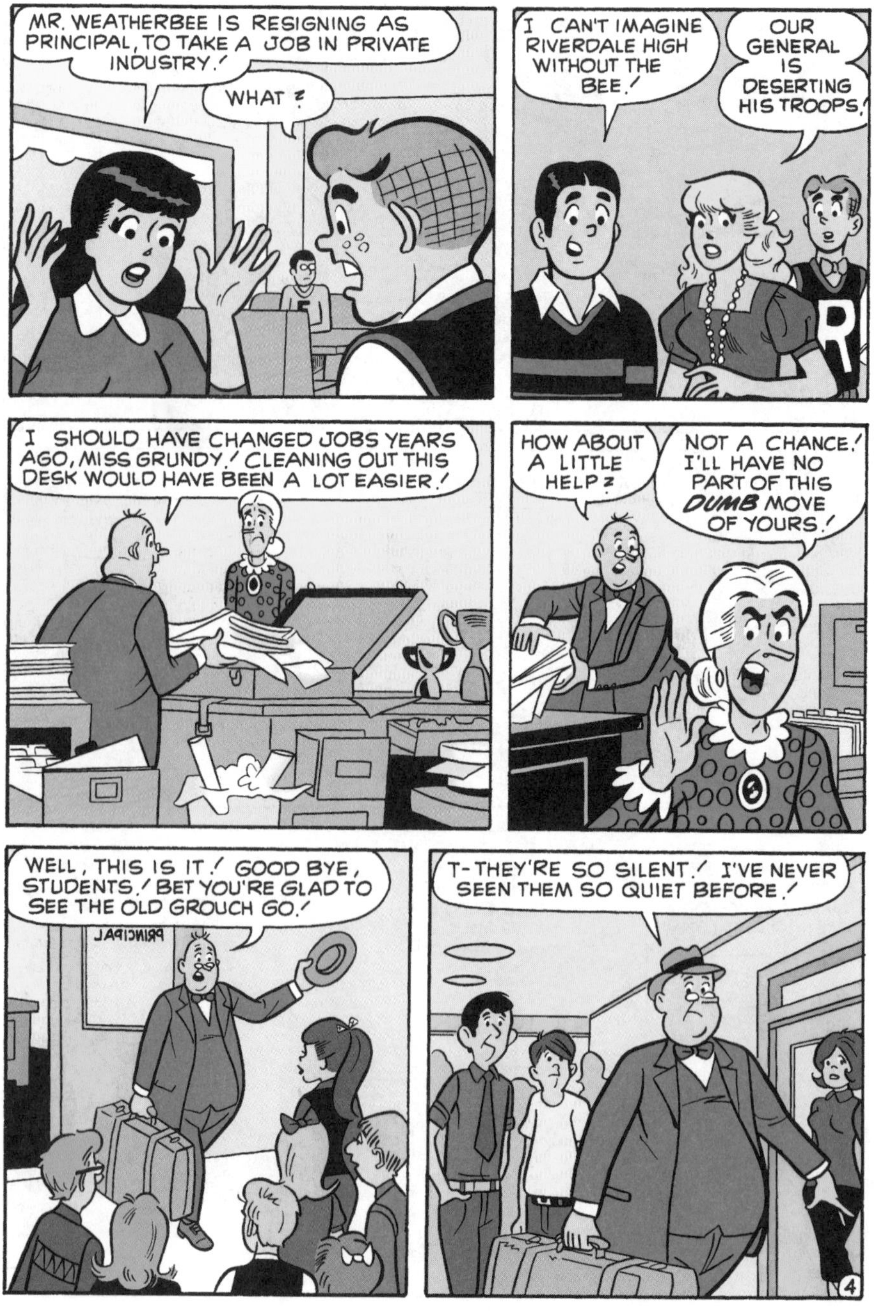
MR. WEATHERBEE IS RESIGNING AS PRINCIPAL, TO TAKE A JOB IN PRIVATE INDUSTRY!
WHAT ?
I CAN'T IMAGINE RIVERDALE HIGH WITHOUT THE BEE!
OUR GENERAL IS DESERTING HIS TROOPS!
I SHOULD HAVE CHANGED JOBS YEARS AGO, MISS GRUNDY! CLEANING OUT THIS DESK WOULD HAVE BEEN A LOT EASIER!
HOW ABOUT A LITTLE HELP ?
NOT A CHANCE! I'LL HAVE NO PART OF THIS DUMB MOVE OF YOURS!
WELL, THIS IS IT! GOOD BYE, STUDENTS! BET YOU'RE GLAD TO SEE THE OLD GROUCH GO!
PRINCIPAL
T-THEY'RE SO SILENT! I'VE NEVER SEEN THEM SO QUIET BEFORE!
4

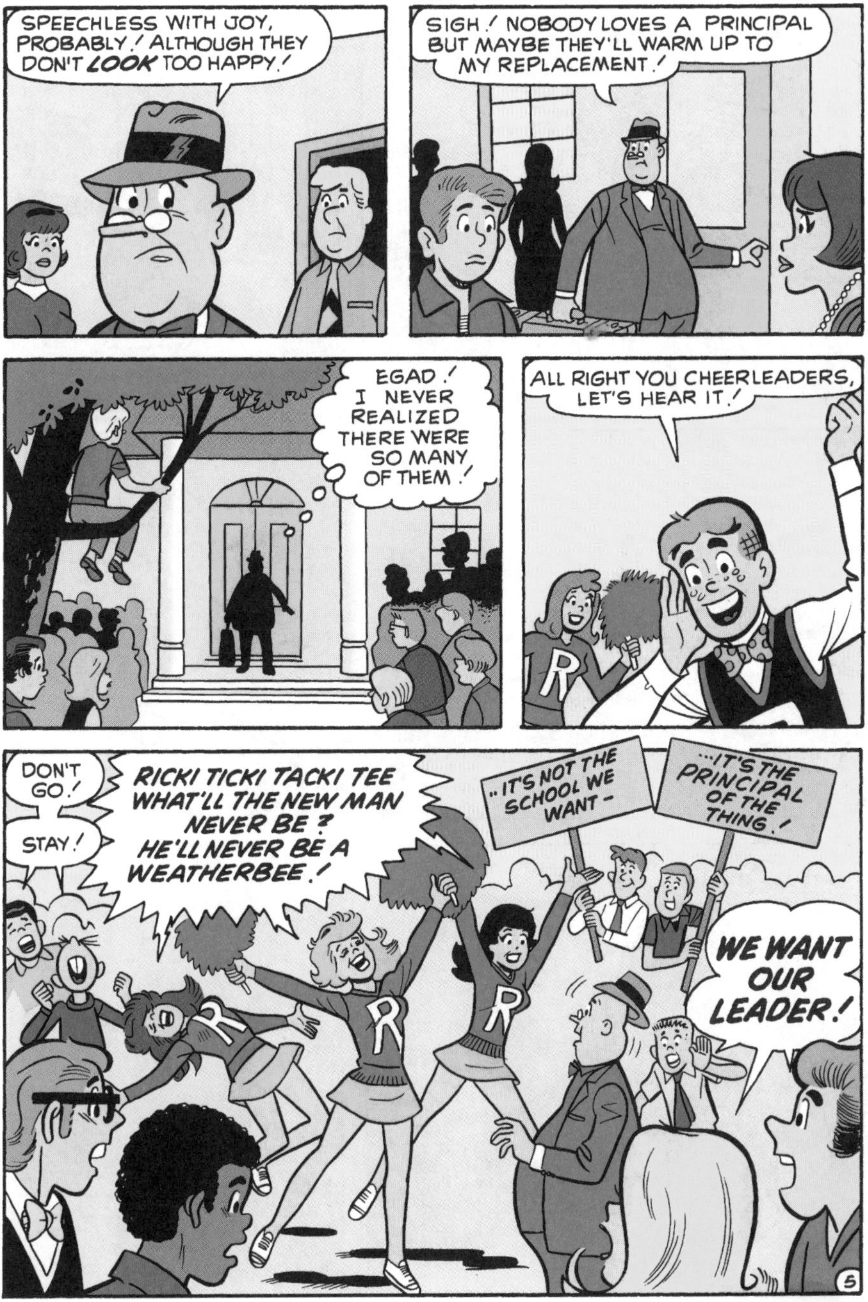
SPEECHLESS WITH JOY, PROBABLY! ALTHOUGH THEY DON'T LOOK TOO HAPPY!
SIGH! NOBODY LOVES A PRINCIPAL BUT MAYBE THEY'LL WARM UP TO MY REPLACEMENT!
EGAD! I NEVER REALIZED THERE WERE SO MANY OF THEM!
ALL RIGHT YOU CHEERLEADERS, LET'S HEAR IT!
DON'T GO!
STAY!
RICKI TICKI TACKI TEE WHAT'LL THE NEW MAN NEVER BE? HE'LL NEVER BE A WEATHERBEE!
..IT'S NOT THE SCHOOL WE WANT -
...IT'S THE PRINCIPAL OF THE THING!
WE WANT OUR LEADER!
5

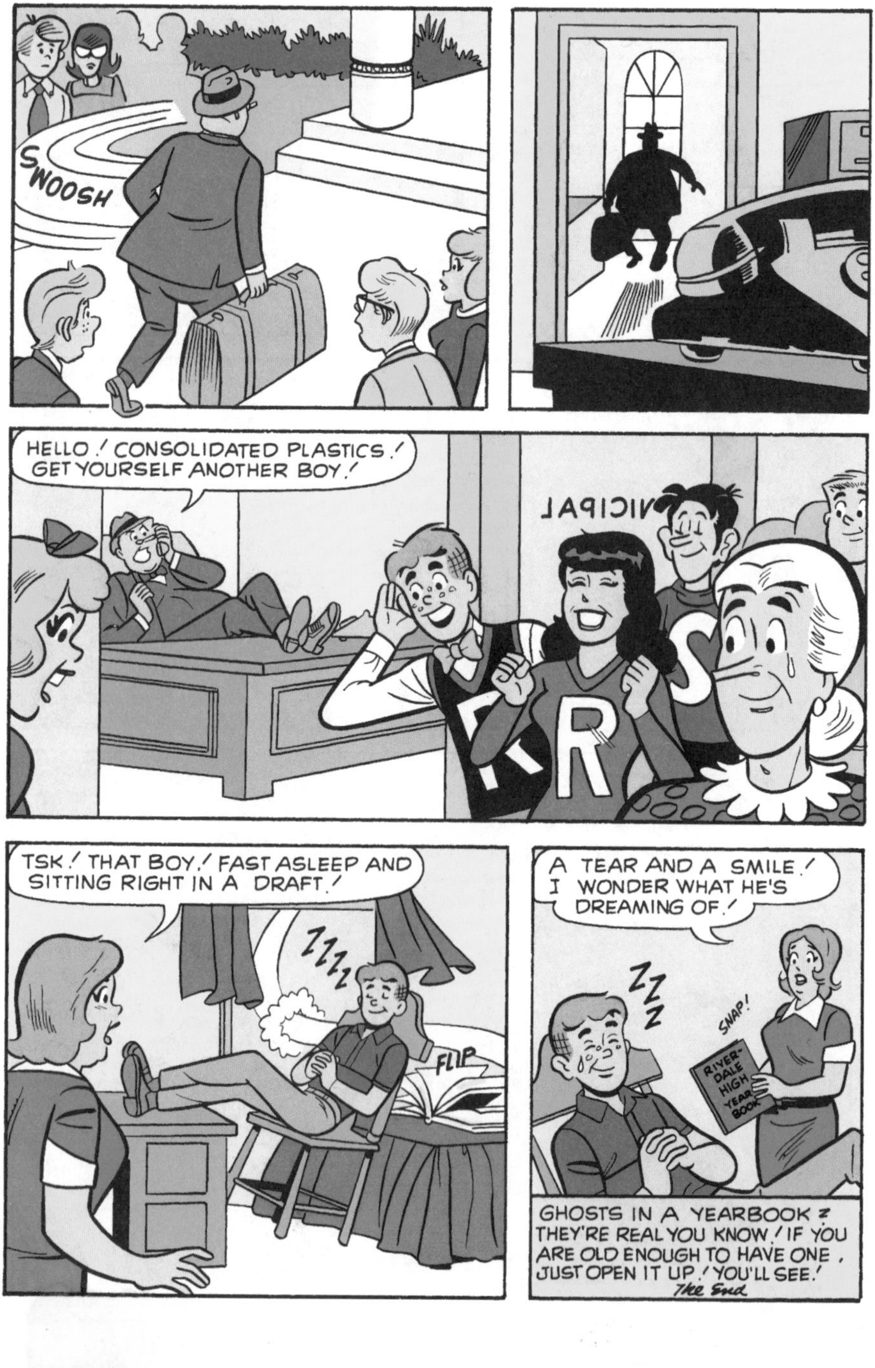
SWOOSH
HELLO! CONSOLIDATED PLASTICS! GET YOURSELF ANOTHER BOY!
VICIPAL
TSK! THAT BOY! FAST ASLEEP AND SITTING RIGHT IN A DRAFT!
ZZZZ
FLIP
A TEAR AND A SMILE! I WONDER WHAT HE'S DREAMING OF!
ZZZ
SNAP!
RIVER-DALE HIGH YEAR BOOK
GHOSTS IN A YEARBOOK? THEY'RE REAL YOU KNOW! IF YOU ARE OLD ENOUGH TO HAVE ONE, JUST OPEN IT UP! YOU'LL SEE!
The End

Archie at RIVERDALE in "The Last Farewell"

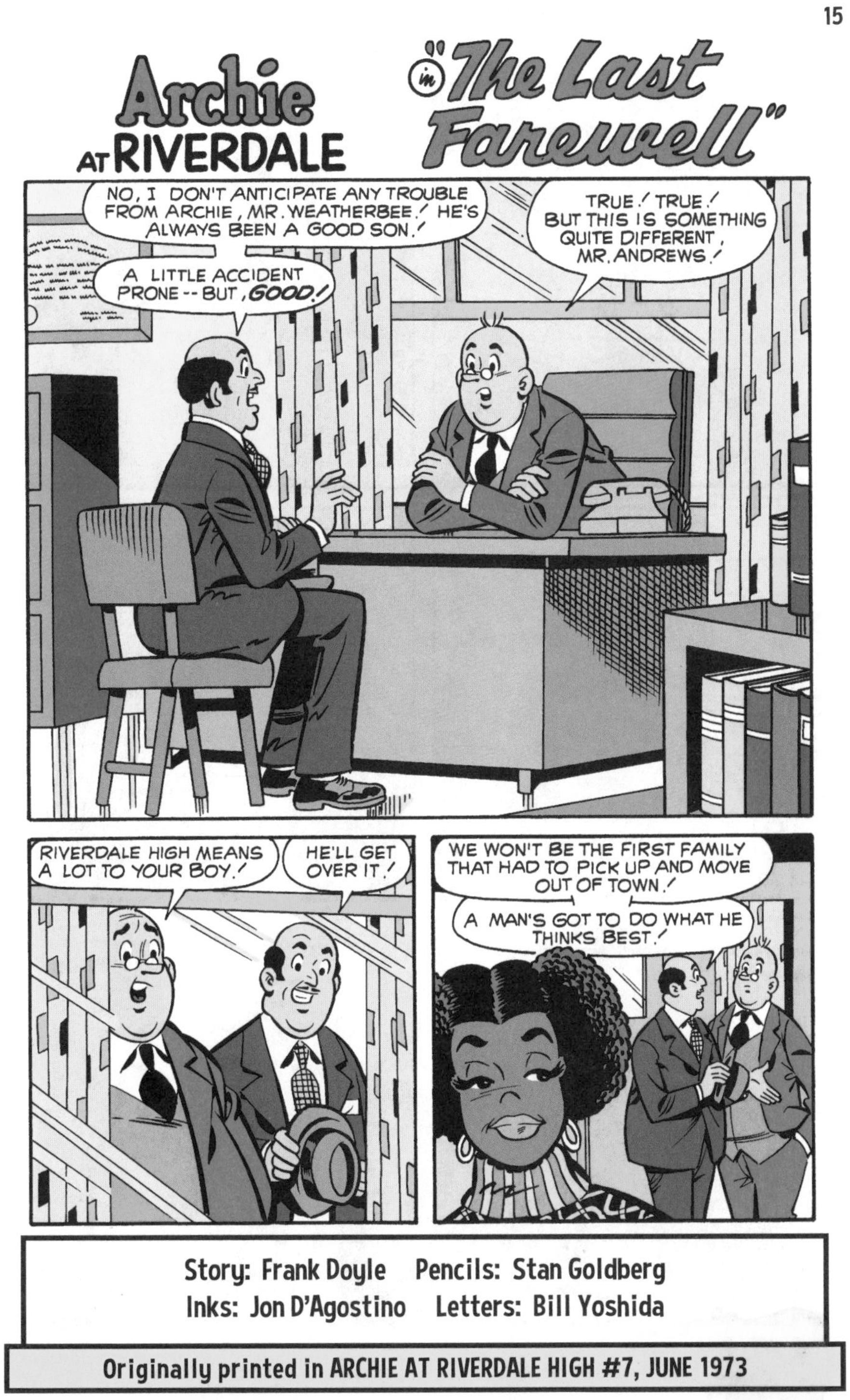
NO, I DON'T ANTICIPATE ANY TROUBLE FROM ARCHIE, MR. WEATHERBEE! HE'S ALWAYS BEEN A GOOD SON!
A LITTLE ACCIDENT PRONE -- BUT, GOOD!
TRUE! TRUE! BUT THIS IS SOMETHING QUITE DIFFERENT, MR. ANDREWS!
RIVERDALE HIGH MEANS A LOT TO YOUR BOY!
HE'LL GET OVER IT!
WE WON'T BE THE FIRST FAMILY THAT HAD TO PICK UP AND MOVE OUT OF TOWN!
A MAN'S GOT TO DO WHAT HE THINKS BEST!

Story: Frank Doyle **Pencils:** Stan Goldberg
Inks: Jon D'Agostino **Letters:** Bill Yoshida

Originally printed in ARCHIE AT RIVERDALE HIGH #7, JUNE 1973

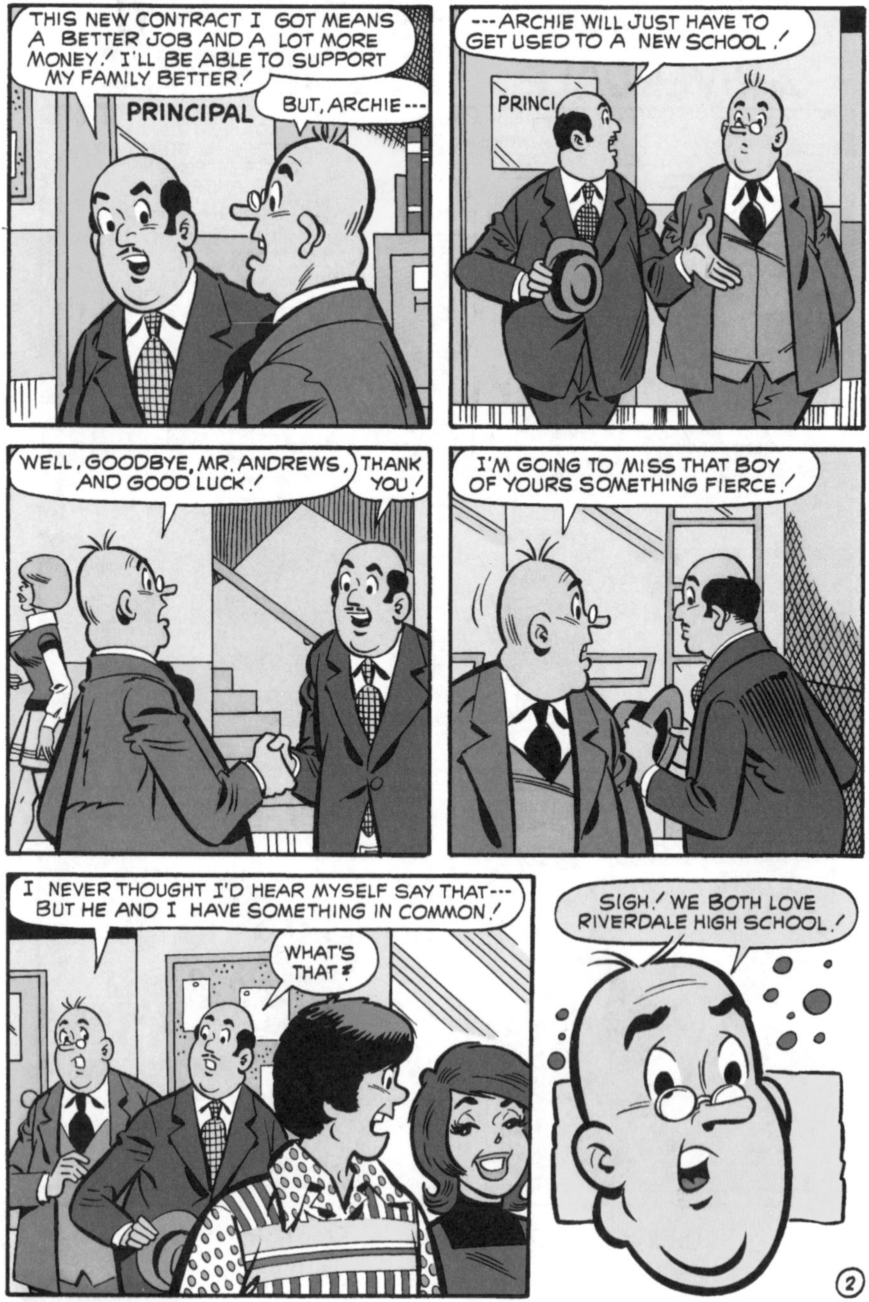
THIS NEW CONTRACT I GOT MEANS A BETTER JOB AND A LOT MORE MONEY! I'LL BE ABLE TO SUPPORT MY FAMILY BETTER!
PRINCIPAL
BUT, ARCHIE---
---ARCHIE WILL JUST HAVE TO GET USED TO A NEW SCHOOL!
PRINCI
WELL, GOODBYE, MR. ANDREWS, AND GOOD LUCK!
THANK YOU!
I'M GOING TO MISS THAT BOY OF YOURS SOMETHING FIERCE!
I NEVER THOUGHT I'D HEAR MYSELF SAY THAT--- BUT HE AND I HAVE SOMETHING IN COMMON!
WHAT'S THAT?
SIGH! WE BOTH LOVE RIVERDALE HIGH SCHOOL!
2

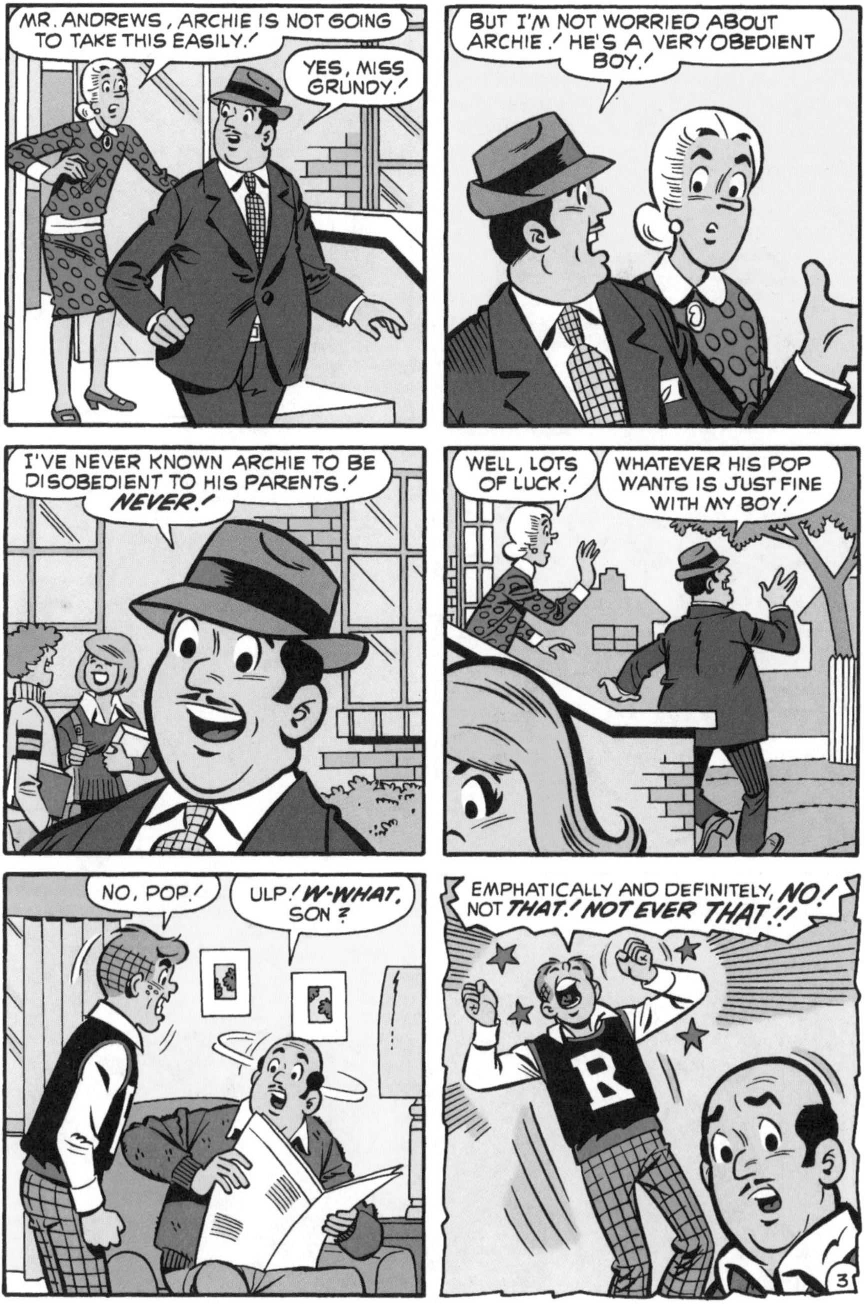
MR. ANDREWS, ARCHIE IS NOT GOING TO TAKE THIS EASILY.!
YES, MISS GRUNDY.!
BUT I'M NOT WORRIED ABOUT ARCHIE.! HE'S A VERY OBEDIENT BOY.!
I'VE NEVER KNOWN ARCHIE TO BE DISOBEDIENT TO HIS PARENTS.! NEVER.!
WELL, LOTS OF LUCK.!
WHATEVER HIS POP WANTS IS JUST FINE WITH MY BOY.!
NO, POP.!
ULP.! W-WHAT, SON?
EMPHATICALLY AND DEFINITELY, NO.! NOT THAT.! NOT EVER THAT.!!
3

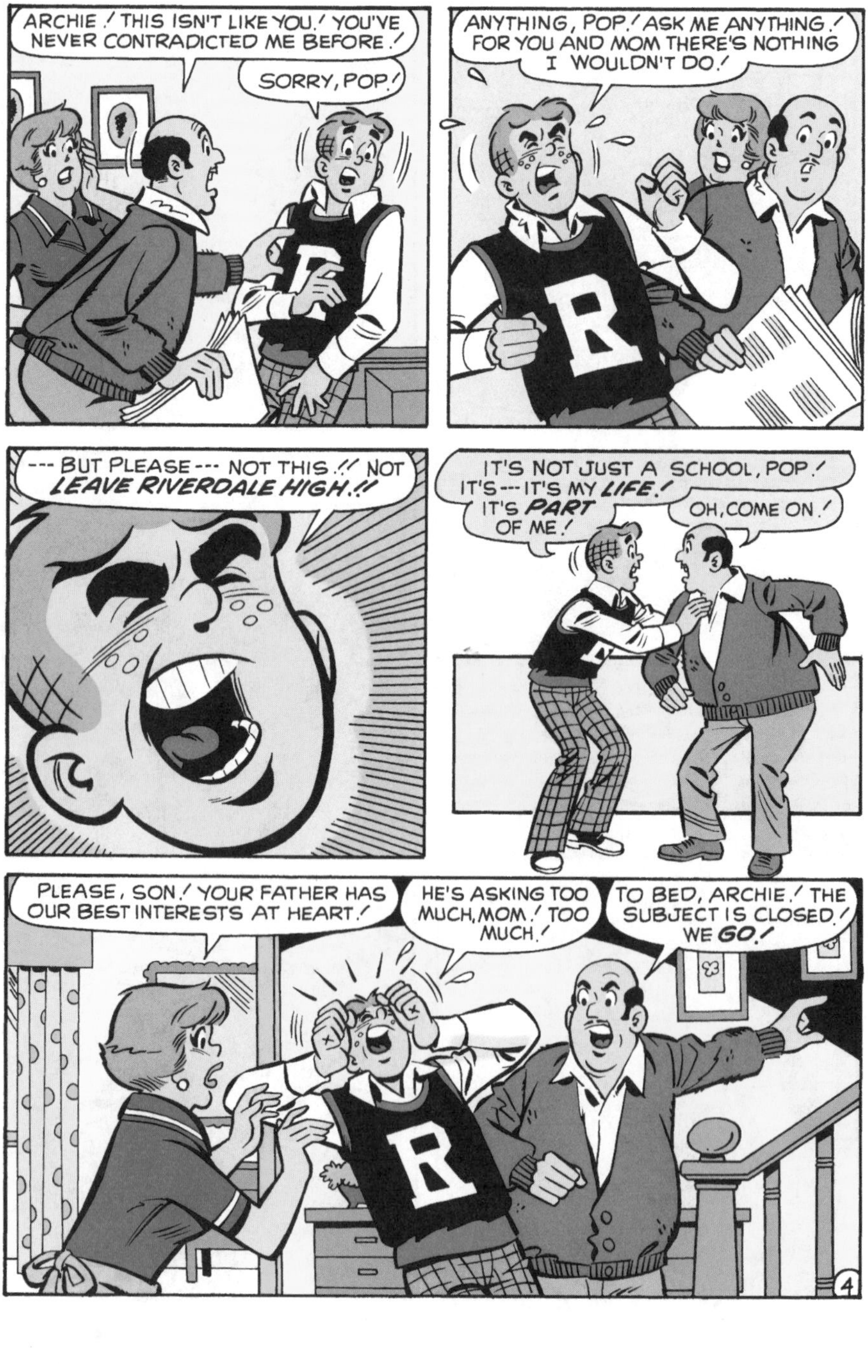
ARCHIE! THIS ISN'T LIKE YOU! YOU'VE NEVER CONTRADICTED ME BEFORE!
SORRY, POP!
ANYTHING, POP! ASK ME ANYTHING! FOR YOU AND MOM THERE'S NOTHING I WOULDN'T DO!
--- BUT PLEASE --- NOT THIS!! NOT LEAVE RIVERDALE HIGH!!
IT'S NOT JUST A SCHOOL, POP! IT'S --- IT'S MY LIFE! IT'S PART OF ME!
OH, COME ON!
PLEASE, SON! YOUR FATHER HAS OUR BEST INTERESTS AT HEART!
HE'S ASKING TOO MUCH, MOM! TOO MUCH!
TO BED, ARCHIE! THE SUBJECT IS CLOSED! WE GO!
4

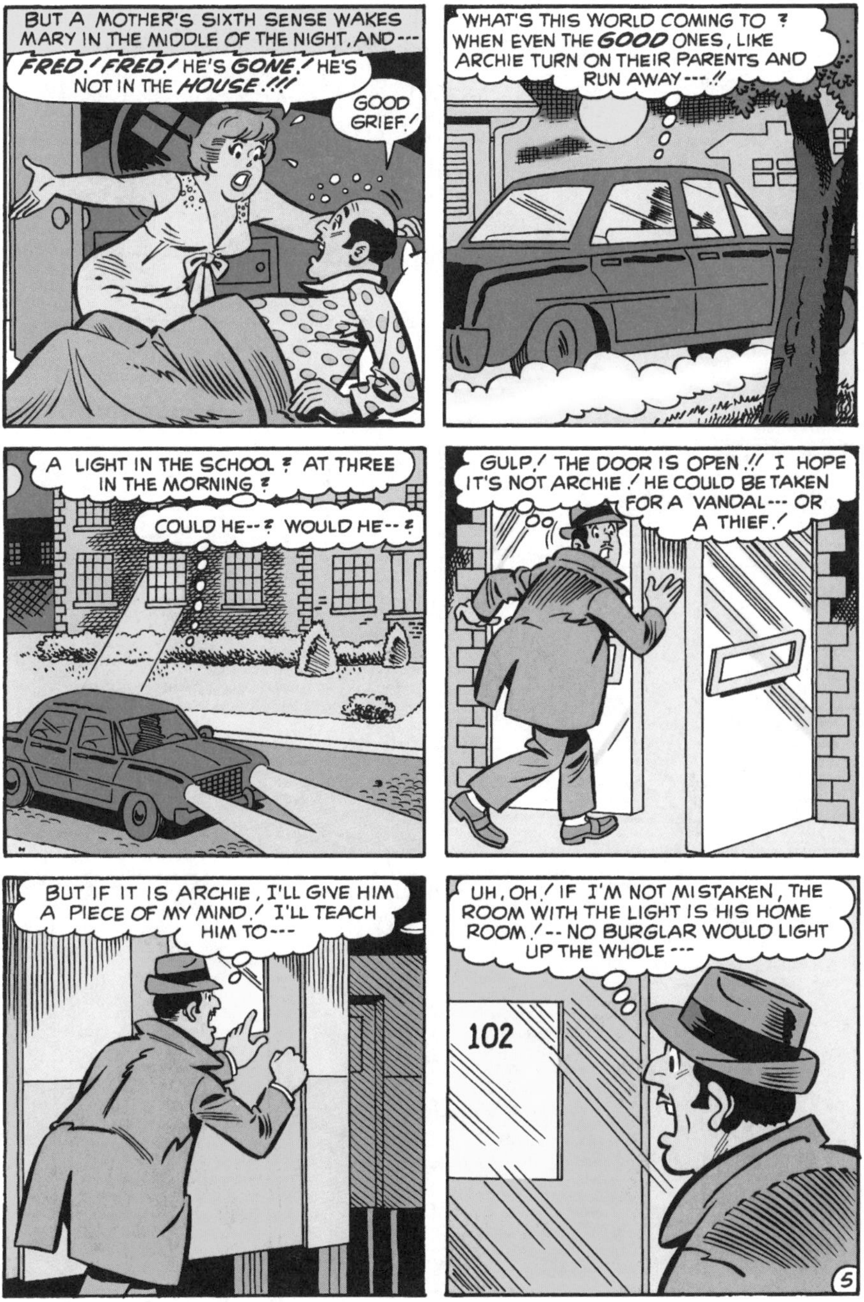
BUT A MOTHER'S SIXTH SENSE WAKES MARY IN THE MIDDLE OF THE NIGHT, AND---
FRED! FRED! HE'S GONE! HE'S NOT IN THE HOUSE!!!
GOOD GRIEF!
WHAT'S THIS WORLD COMING TO? WHEN EVEN THE GOOD ONES, LIKE ARCHIE TURN ON THEIR PARENTS AND RUN AWAY---!!
A LIGHT IN THE SCHOOL? AT THREE IN THE MORNING?
COULD HE--? WOULD HE--?
GULP! THE DOOR IS OPEN!! I HOPE IT'S NOT ARCHIE! HE COULD BE TAKEN FOR A VANDAL--- OR A THIEF!
BUT IF IT IS ARCHIE, I'LL GIVE HIM A PIECE OF MY MIND! I'LL TEACH HIM TO---
UH, OH! IF I'M NOT MISTAKEN, THE ROOM WITH THE LIGHT IS HIS HOME ROOM!--NO BURGLAR WOULD LIGHT UP THE WHOLE---
102
5

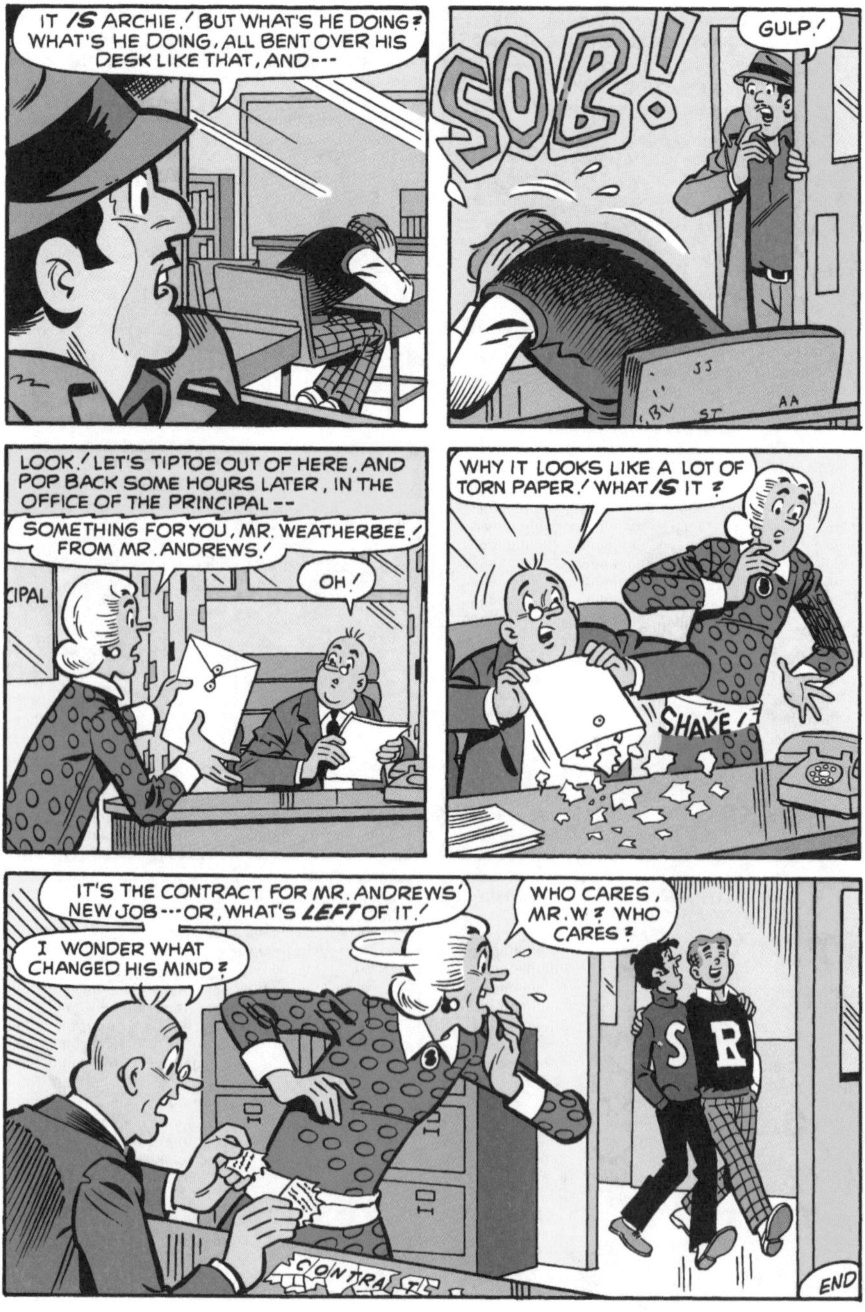
IT IS ARCHIE! BUT WHAT'S HE DOING? WHAT'S HE DOING, ALL BENT OVER HIS DESK LIKE THAT, AND---
SOB!
GULP!
JJ
BV
ST
AA
LOOK! LET'S TIPTOE OUT OF HERE, AND POP BACK SOME HOURS LATER, IN THE OFFICE OF THE PRINCIPAL--
SOMETHING FOR YOU, MR. WEATHERBEE! FROM MR. ANDREWS!
OH!
CIPAL
WHY IT LOOKS LIKE A LOT OF TORN PAPER! WHAT IS IT?
SHAKE!
IT'S THE CONTRACT FOR MR. ANDREWS' NEW JOB---OR, WHAT'S LEFT OF IT!
I WONDER WHAT CHANGED HIS MIND?
WHO CARES, MR. W? WHO CARES?
S
R
CONTRA
END

Archie at RIVERDALE in "THE FALSE ALARM"

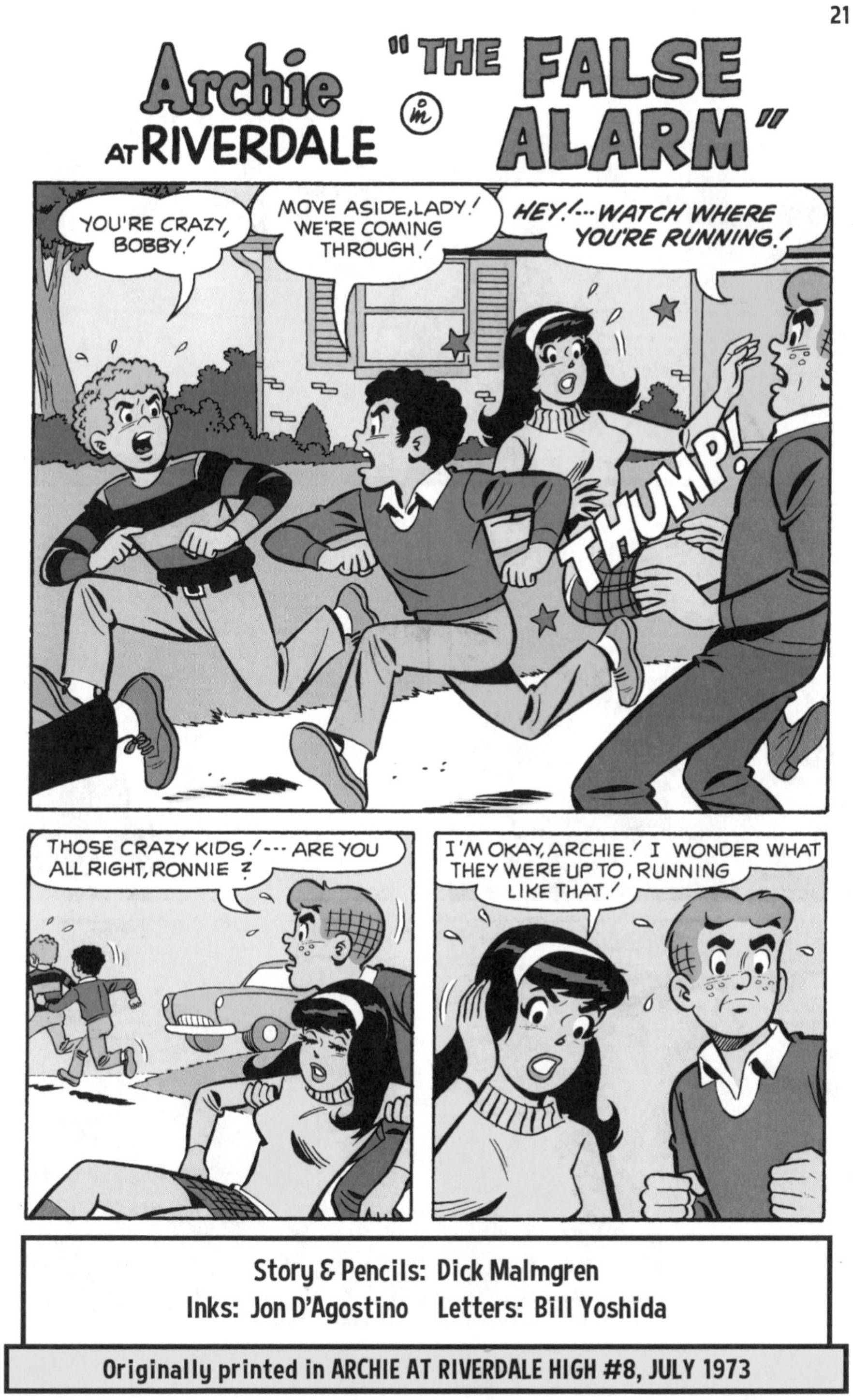
YOU'RE CRAZY, BOBBY!
MOVE ASIDE, LADY! WE'RE COMING THROUGH!
HEY!... WATCH WHERE YOU'RE RUNNING!
THUMP!
THOSE CRAZY KIDS!--- ARE YOU ALL RIGHT, RONNIE?
I'M OKAY, ARCHIE! I WONDER WHAT THEY WERE UP TO, RUNNING LIKE THAT!

Story & Pencils: Dick Malmgren
Inks: Jon D'Agostino Letters: Bill Yoshida

Originally printed in ARCHIE AT RIVERDALE HIGH #8, JULY 1973

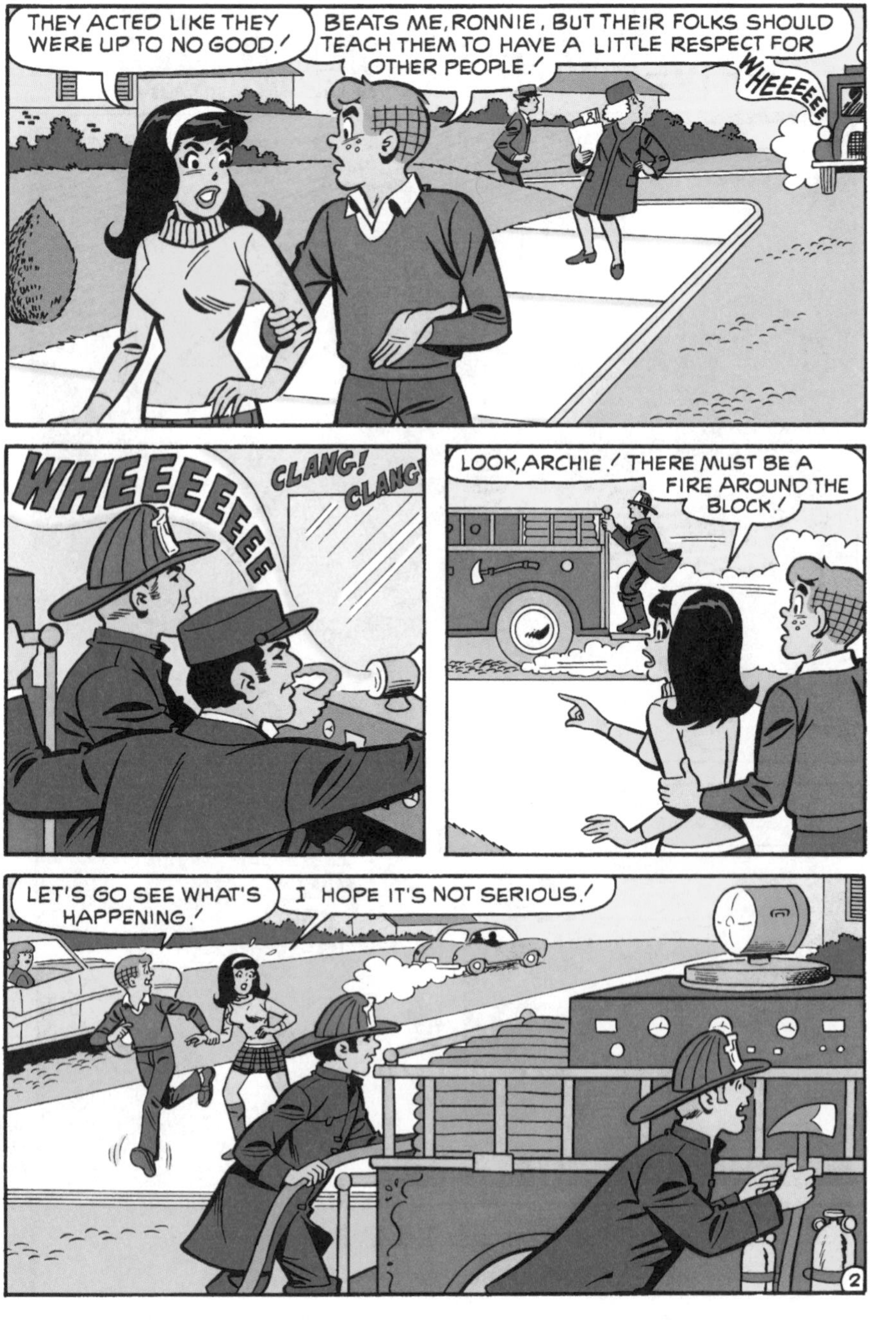
THEY ACTED LIKE THEY WERE UP TO NO GOOD.!
BEATS ME, RONNIE, BUT THEIR FOLKS SHOULD TEACH THEM TO HAVE A LITTLE RESPECT FOR OTHER PEOPLE.!
WHEEEEEE
WHEEEEEEEEE
CLANG! CLANG!
LOOK, ARCHIE! THERE MUST BE A FIRE AROUND THE BLOCK!
LET'S GO SEE WHAT'S HAPPENING!
I HOPE IT'S NOT SERIOUS!
2

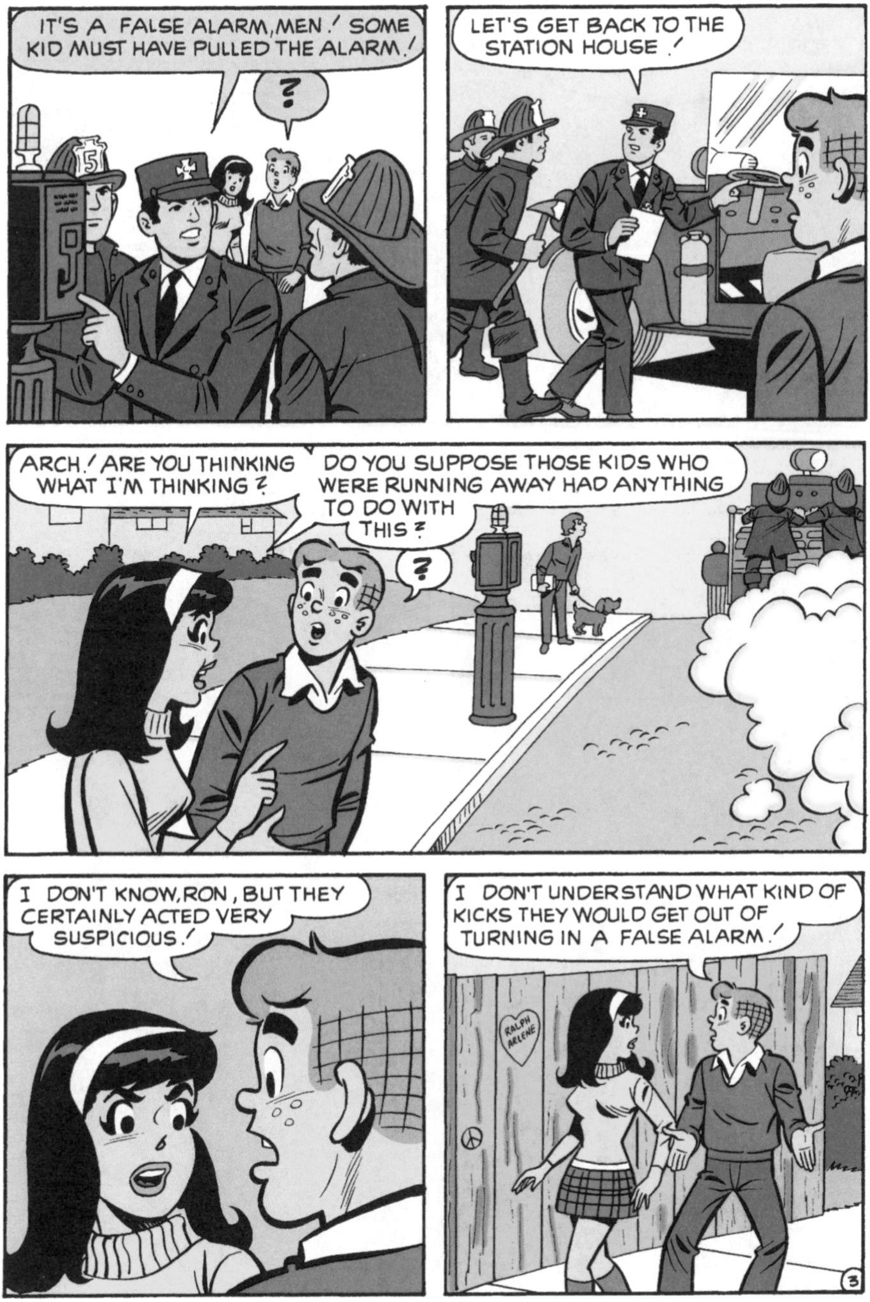
IT'S A FALSE ALARM, MEN! SOME KID MUST HAVE PULLED THE ALARM!
?
LET'S GET BACK TO THE STATION HOUSE!
ARCH! ARE YOU THINKING WHAT I'M THINKING?
DO YOU SUPPOSE THOSE KIDS WHO WERE RUNNING AWAY HAD ANYTHING TO DO WITH THIS?
?
I DON'T KNOW, RON, BUT THEY CERTAINLY ACTED VERY SUSPICIOUS!
I DON'T UNDERSTAND WHAT KIND OF KICKS THEY WOULD GET OUT OF TURNING IN A FALSE ALARM!
RALPH
ARLENE

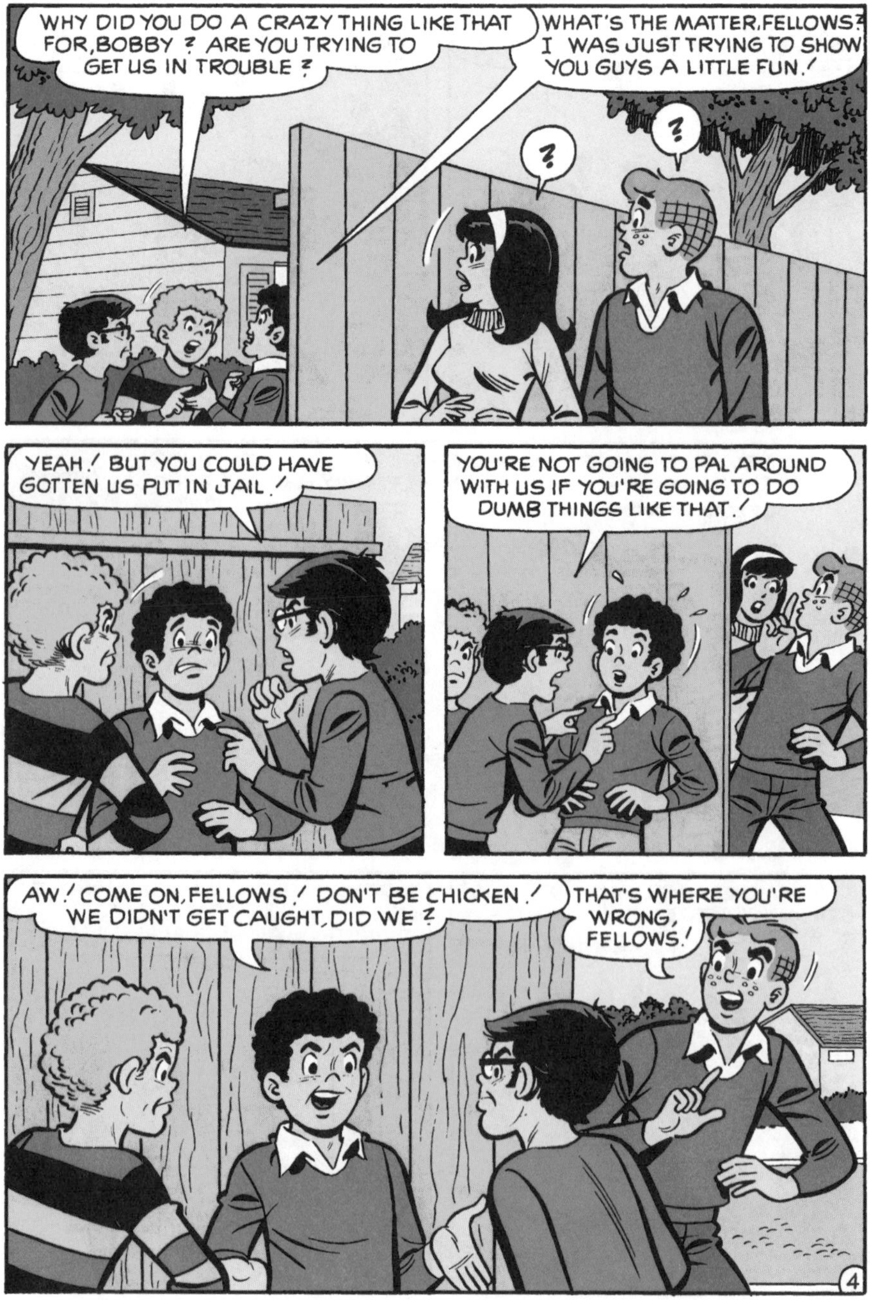
WHY DID YOU DO A CRAZY THING LIKE THAT FOR, BOBBY? ARE YOU TRYING TO GET US IN TROUBLE?
WHAT'S THE MATTER, FELLOWS? I WAS JUST TRYING TO SHOW YOU GUYS A LITTLE FUN!
?
?
YEAH! BUT YOU COULD HAVE GOTTEN US PUT IN JAIL!
YOU'RE NOT GOING TO PAL AROUND WITH US IF YOU'RE GOING TO DO DUMB THINGS LIKE THAT!
AW! COME ON, FELLOWS! DON'T BE CHICKEN! WE DIDN'T GET CAUGHT, DID WE?
THAT'S WHERE YOU'RE WRONG, FELLOWS!
4

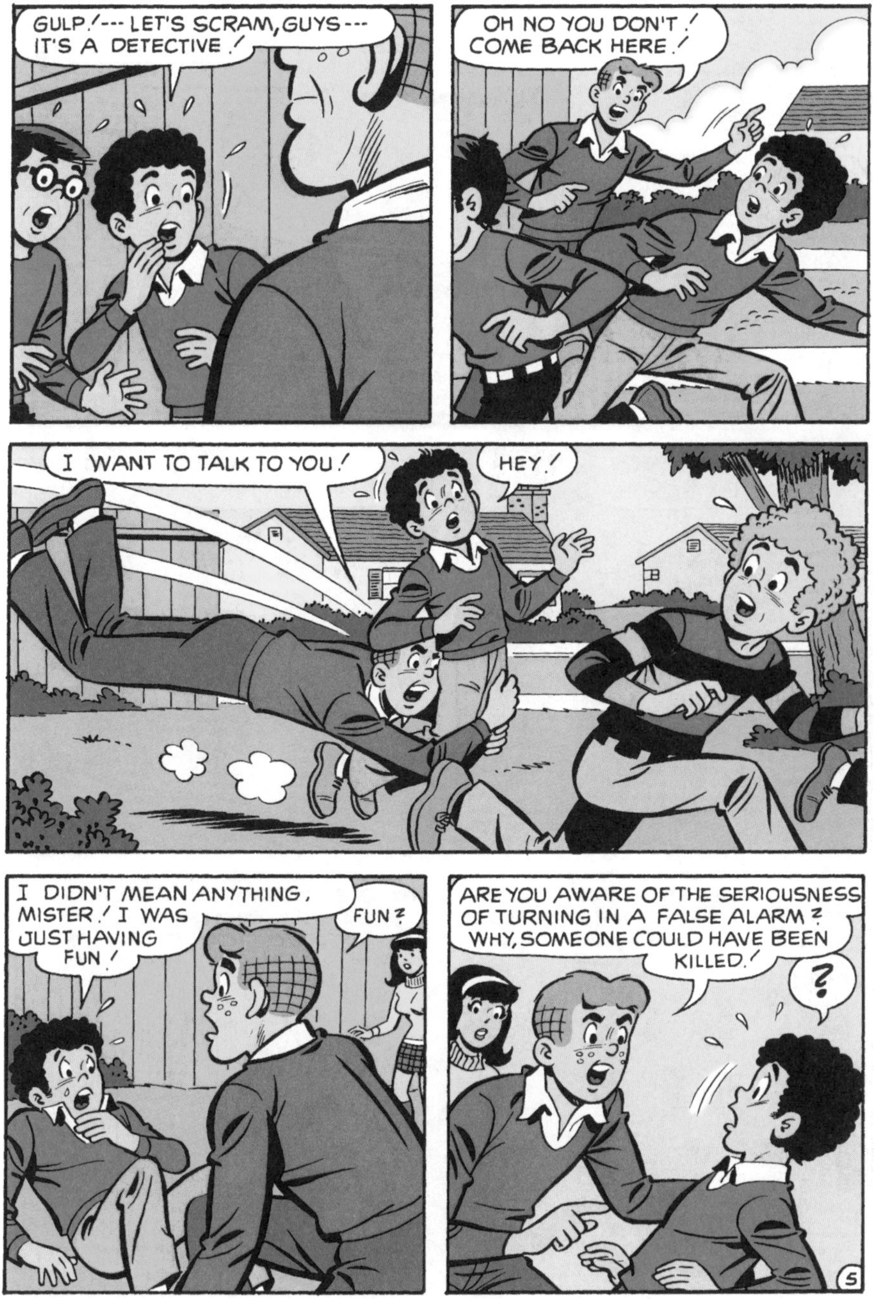
GULP! --- LET'S SCRAM, GUYS --- IT'S A DETECTIVE!
OH NO YOU DON'T! COME BACK HERE!
I WANT TO TALK TO YOU!
HEY!
I DIDN'T MEAN ANYTHING, MISTER! I WAS JUST HAVING FUN!
FUN?
ARE YOU AWARE OF THE SERIOUSNESS OF TURNING IN A FALSE ALARM? WHY, SOMEONE COULD HAVE BEEN KILLED!
?
5

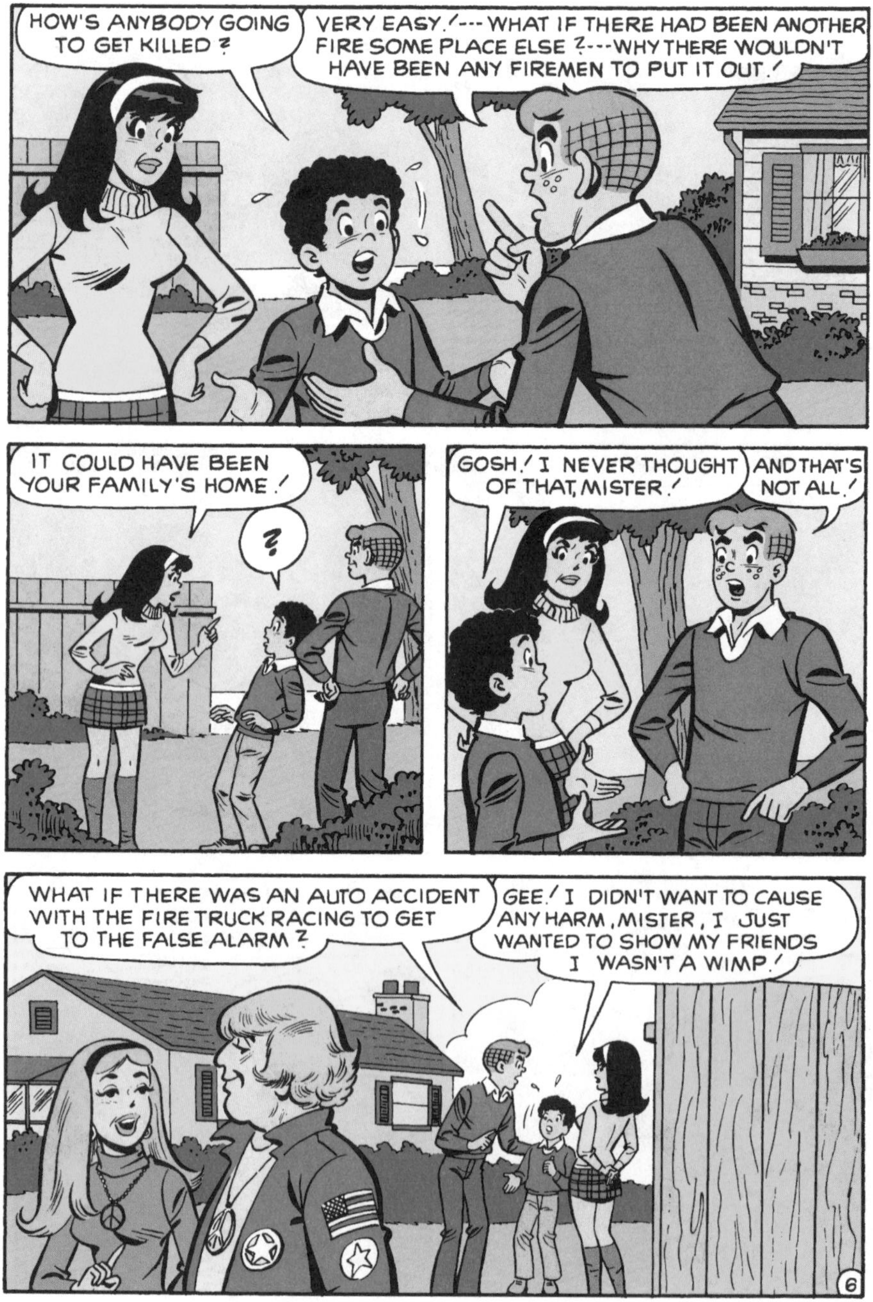
HOW'S ANYBODY GOING TO GET KILLED?
VERY EASY!--- WHAT IF THERE HAD BEEN ANOTHER FIRE SOME PLACE ELSE?---WHY THERE WOULDN'T HAVE BEEN ANY FIREMEN TO PUT IT OUT!
IT COULD HAVE BEEN YOUR FAMILY'S HOME!
?
GOSH! I NEVER THOUGHT OF THAT, MISTER!
AND THAT'S NOT ALL!
WHAT IF THERE WAS AN AUTO ACCIDENT WITH THE FIRE TRUCK RACING TO GET TO THE FALSE ALARM?
GEE! I DIDN'T WANT TO CAUSE ANY HARM, MISTER, I JUST WANTED TO SHOW MY FRIENDS I WASN'T A WIMP!
6

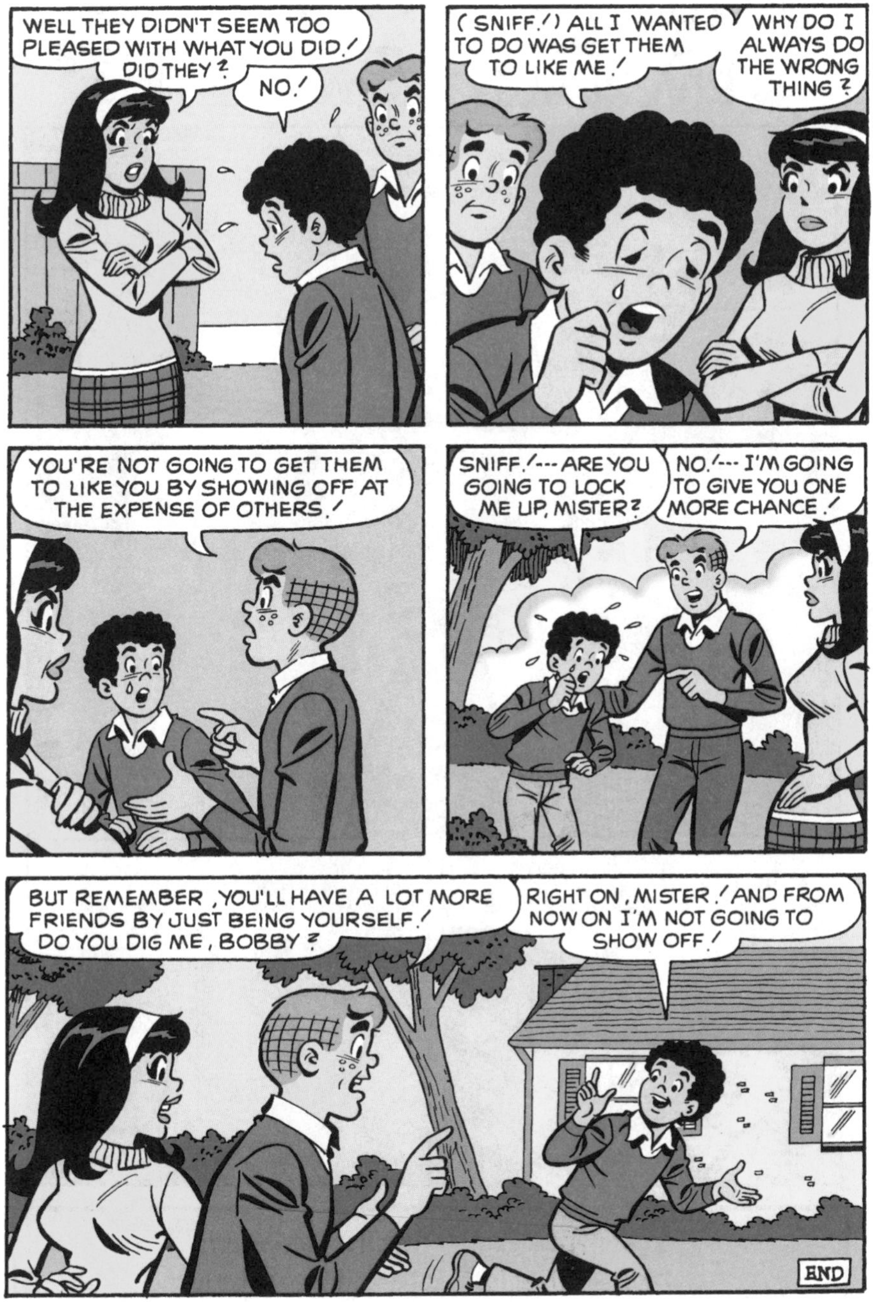
WELL THEY DIDN'T SEEM TOO PLEASED WITH WHAT YOU DID! DID THEY?
NO!
(SNIFF!) ALL I WANTED TO DO WAS GET THEM TO LIKE ME!
WHY DO I ALWAYS DO THE WRONG THING?
YOU'RE NOT GOING TO GET THEM TO LIKE YOU BY SHOWING OFF AT THE EXPENSE OF OTHERS!
SNIFF!--- ARE YOU GOING TO LOCK ME UP, MISTER?
NO!--- I'M GOING TO GIVE YOU ONE MORE CHANCE!
BUT REMEMBER, YOU'LL HAVE A LOT MORE FRIENDS BY JUST BEING YOURSELF! DO YOU DIG ME, BOBBY?
RIGHT ON, MISTER! AND FROM NOW ON I'M NOT GOING TO SHOW OFF!
END

Archie at Riverdale in "The Whole Picture"

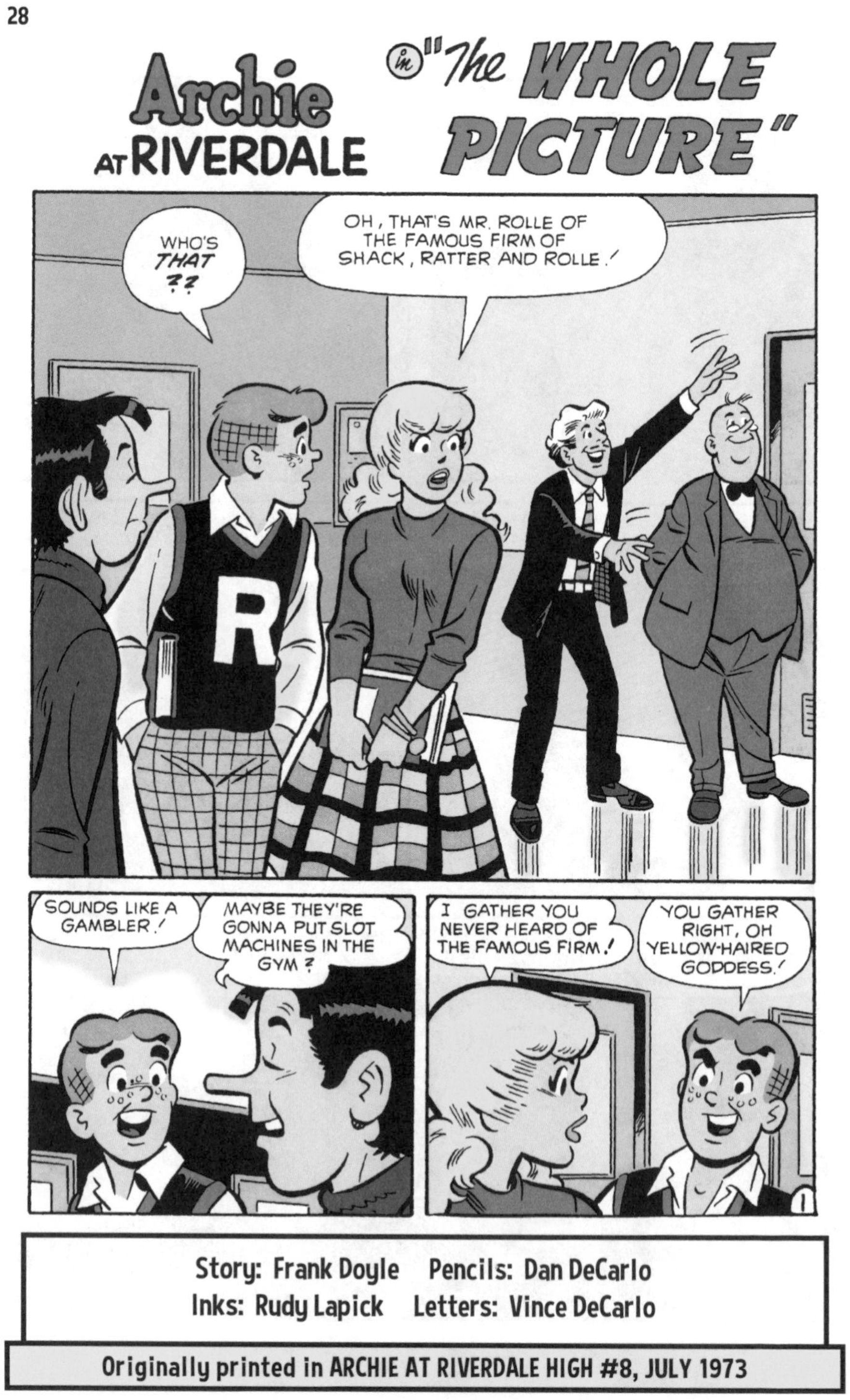
WHO'S THAT ??
OH, THAT'S MR. ROLLE OF THE FAMOUS FIRM OF SHACK, RATTER AND ROLLE!
SOUNDS LIKE A GAMBLER!
MAYBE THEY'RE GONNA PUT SLOT MACHINES IN THE GYM?
I GATHER YOU NEVER HEARD OF THE FAMOUS FIRM!
YOU GATHER RIGHT, OH YELLOW-HAIRED GODDESS!
1

Story: Frank Doyle Pencils: Dan DeCarlo
Inks: Rudy Lapick Letters: Vince DeCarlo

Originally printed in ARCHIE AT RIVERDALE HIGH #8, JULY 1973

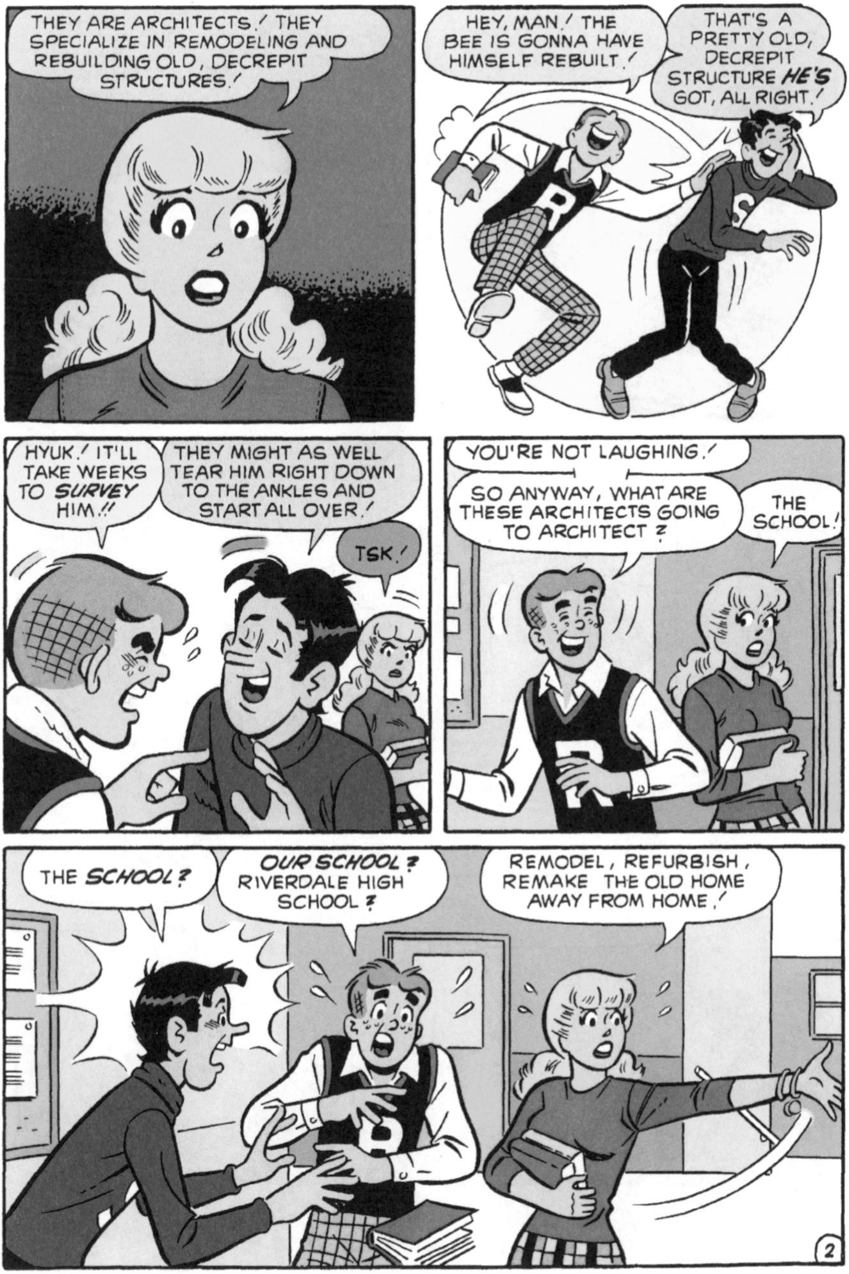
THEY ARE ARCHITECTS! THEY SPECIALIZE IN REMODELING AND REBUILDING OLD, DECREPIT STRUCTURES!
HEY, MAN! THE BEE IS GONNA HAVE HIMSELF REBUILT!
THAT'S A PRETTY OLD, DECREPIT STRUCTURE HE'S GOT, ALL RIGHT!
HYUK! IT'LL TAKE WEEKS TO SURVEY HIM!!
THEY MIGHT AS WELL TEAR HIM RIGHT DOWN TO THE ANKLES AND START ALL OVER!
TSK!
YOU'RE NOT LAUGHING!
SO ANYWAY, WHAT ARE THESE ARCHITECTS GOING TO ARCHITECT?
THE SCHOOL!
THE SCHOOL?
OUR SCHOOL? RIVERDALE HIGH SCHOOL?
REMODEL, REFURBISH, REMAKE THE OLD HOME AWAY FROM HOME!
2

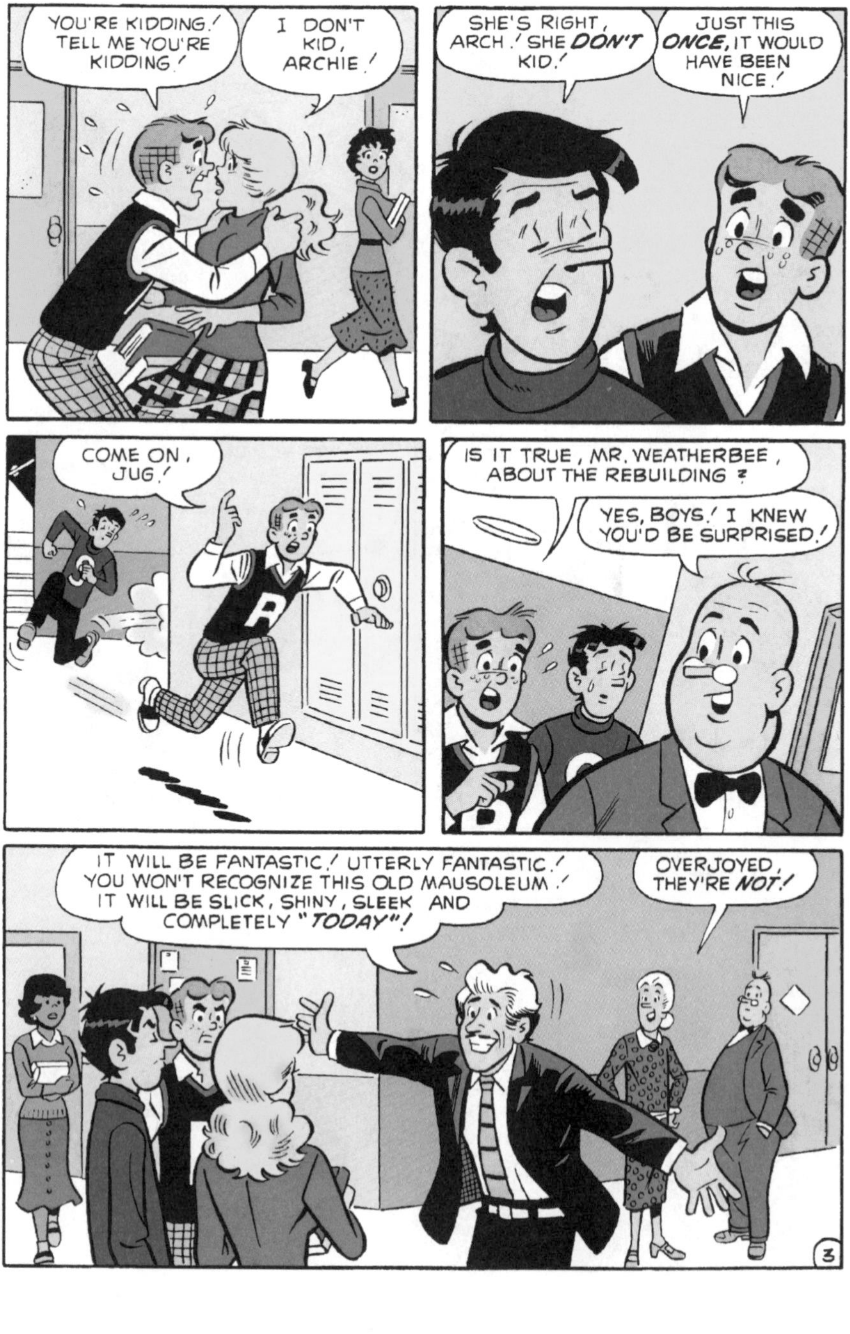
YOU'RE KIDDING! TELL ME YOU'RE KIDDING!
I DON'T KID, ARCHIE!
SHE'S RIGHT, ARCH! SHE DON'T KID!
JUST THIS ONCE, IT WOULD HAVE BEEN NICE!
COME ON, JUG!
IS IT TRUE, MR. WEATHERBEE, ABOUT THE REBUILDING?
YES, BOYS! I KNEW YOU'D BE SURPRISED!
IT WILL BE FANTASTIC! UTTERLY FANTASTIC! YOU WON'T RECOGNIZE THIS OLD MAUSOLEUM! IT WILL BE SLICK, SHINY, SLEEK AND COMPLETELY "TODAY"!
OVERJOYED, THEY'RE NOT!
3

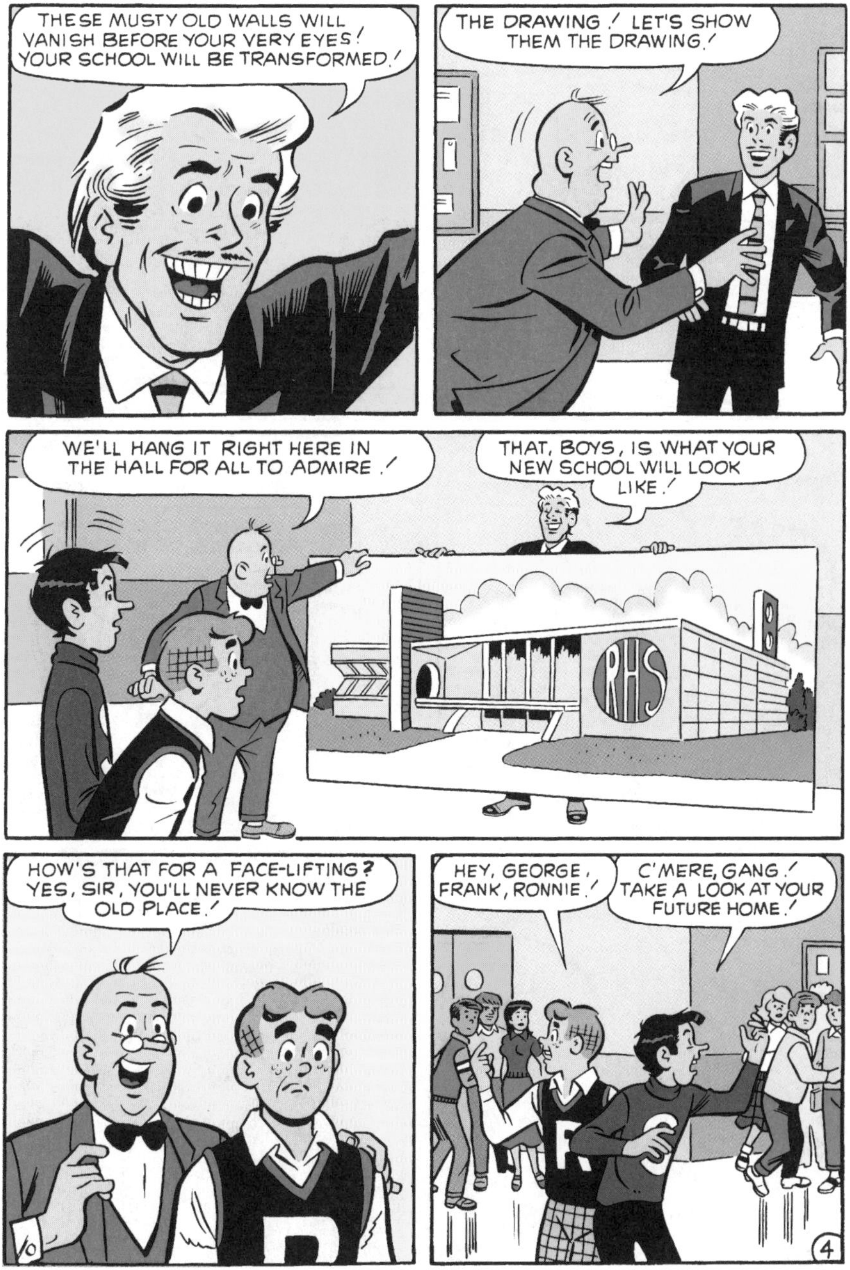
THESE MUSTY OLD WALLS WILL VANISH BEFORE YOUR VERY EYES! YOUR SCHOOL WILL BE TRANSFORMED!
THE DRAWING! LET'S SHOW THEM THE DRAWING!
WE'LL HANG IT RIGHT HERE IN THE HALL FOR ALL TO ADMIRE!
THAT, BOYS, IS WHAT YOUR NEW SCHOOL WILL LOOK LIKE!
RHS
HOW'S THAT FOR A FACE-LIFTING? YES, SIR, YOU'LL NEVER KNOW THE OLD PLACE!
HEY, GEORGE, FRANK, RONNIE!
C'MERE, GANG! TAKE A LOOK AT YOUR FUTURE HOME!
4

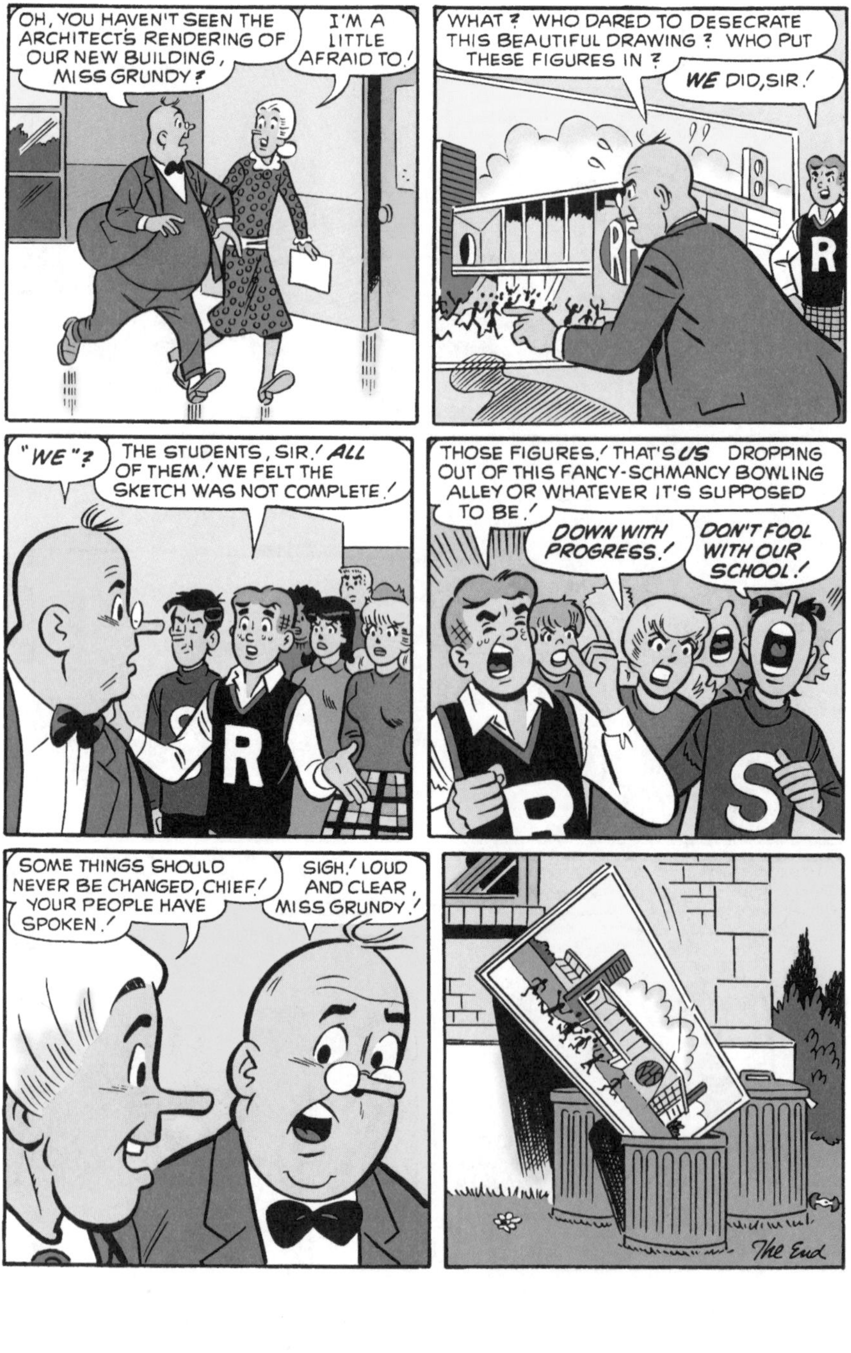
OH, YOU HAVEN'T SEEN THE ARCHITECT'S RENDERING OF OUR NEW BUILDING, MISS GRUNDY?
I'M A LITTLE AFRAID TO!
WHAT? WHO DARED TO DESECRATE THIS BEAUTIFUL DRAWING? WHO PUT THESE FIGURES IN?
WE DID, SIR!
"WE"?
THE STUDENTS, SIR! ALL OF THEM! WE FELT THE SKETCH WAS NOT COMPLETE!
THOSE FIGURES! THAT'S US DROPPING OUT OF THIS FANCY-SCHMANCY BOWLING ALLEY OR WHATEVER IT'S SUPPOSED TO BE!
DOWN WITH PROGRESS!
DON'T FOOL WITH OUR SCHOOL!
SOME THINGS SHOULD NEVER BE CHANGED, CHIEF! YOUR PEOPLE HAVE SPOKEN!
SIGH! LOUD AND CLEAR, MISS GRUNDY!
The End

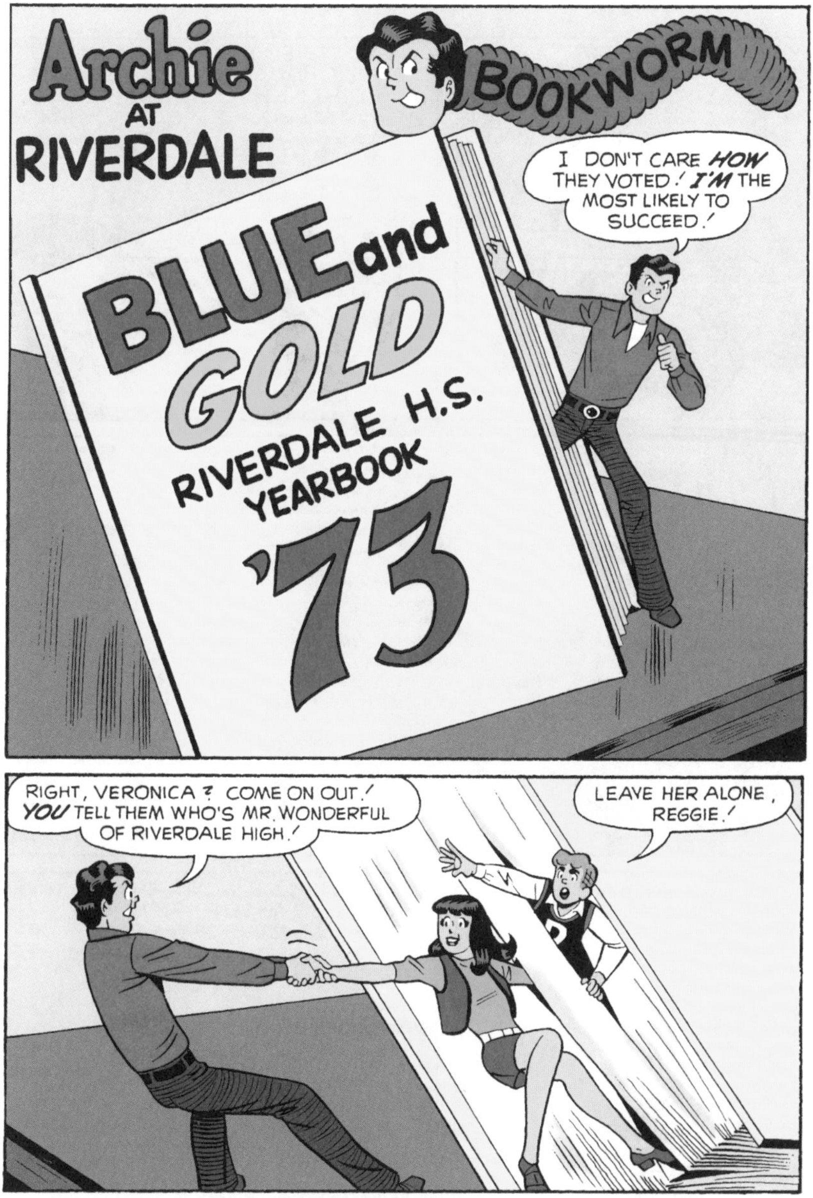
Archie AT RIVERDALE
BOOKWORM
BLUE and GOLD
RIVERDALE H.S.
RIVERDALE YEARBOOK
'73
I DON'T CARE *HOW* THEY VOTED! *I'M* THE MOST LIKELY TO SUCCEED!
RIGHT, VERONICA? COME ON OUT! *YOU* TELL THEM WHO'S MR. WONDERFUL OF RIVERDALE HIGH!
LEAVE HER ALONE, REGGIE!

Story: Frank Doyle   Pencils: Harry Lucey
Letters: Bill Yoshida

Originally printed in ARCHIE AT RIVERDALE HIGH #8, JULY 1973

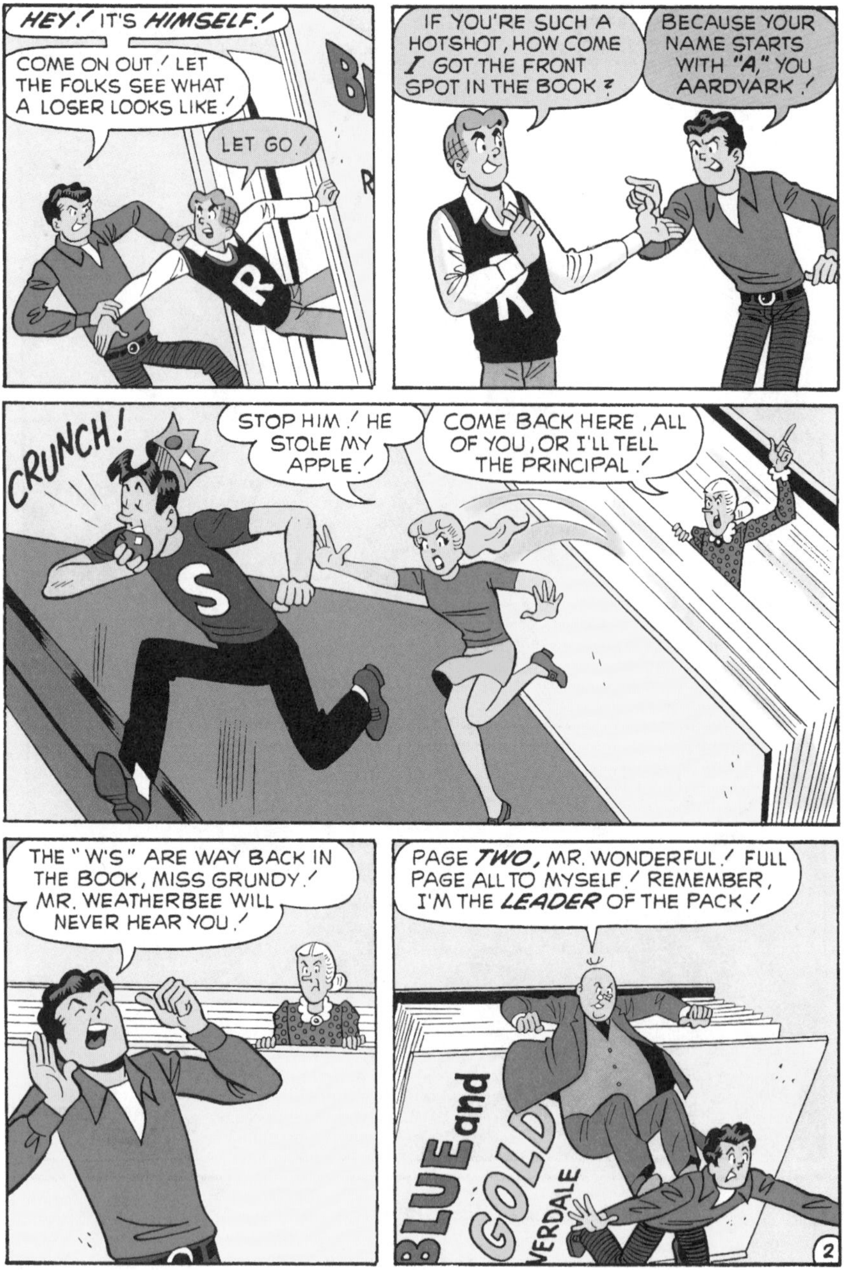
HEY! IT'S HIMSELF!
COME ON OUT! LET THE FOLKS SEE WHAT A LOSER LOOKS LIKE!
LET GO!
IF YOU'RE SUCH A HOTSHOT, HOW COME I GOT THE FRONT SPOT IN THE BOOK?
BECAUSE YOUR NAME STARTS WITH "A," YOU AARDVARK!
CRUNCH!
STOP HIM! HE STOLE MY APPLE!
COME BACK HERE, ALL OF YOU, OR I'LL TELL THE PRINCIPAL!
THE "W'S" ARE WAY BACK IN THE BOOK, MISS GRUNDY! MR. WEATHERBEE WILL NEVER HEAR YOU!
PAGE TWO, MR. WONDERFUL! FULL PAGE ALL TO MYSELF! REMEMBER, I'M THE LEADER OF THE PACK!
BLUE and GOLD
VERDALE
2

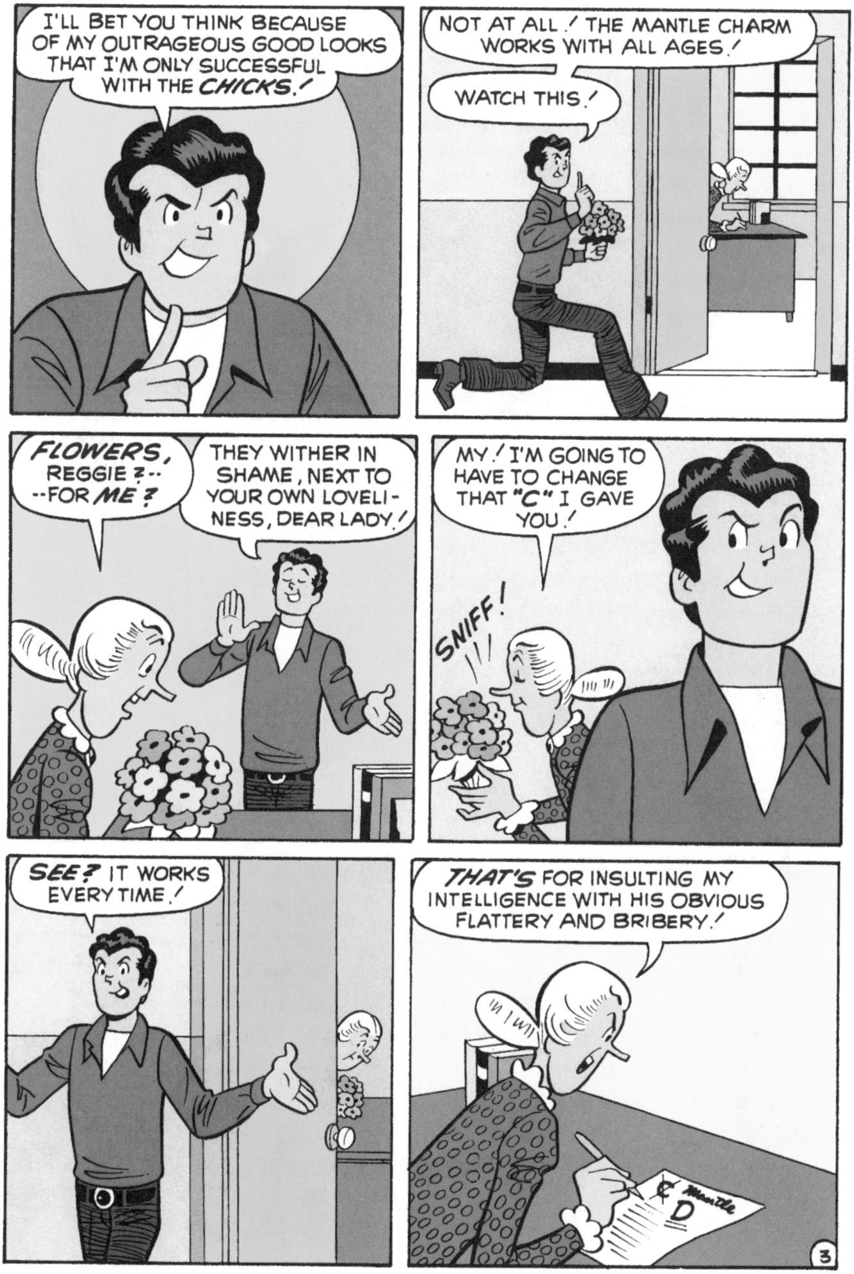
I'LL BET YOU THINK BECAUSE OF MY OUTRAGEOUS GOOD LOOKS THAT I'M ONLY SUCCESSFUL WITH THE CHICKS!
NOT AT ALL! THE MANTLE CHARM WORKS WITH ALL AGES!
WATCH THIS!
FLOWERS, REGGIE?-- --FOR ME?
THEY WITHER IN SHAME, NEXT TO YOUR OWN LOVELI-NESS, DEAR LADY!
MY! I'M GOING TO HAVE TO CHANGE THAT "C" I GAVE YOU!
SNIFF!
SEE? IT WORKS EVERY TIME!
THAT'S FOR INSULTING MY INTELLIGENCE WITH HIS OBVIOUS FLATTERY AND BRIBERY!
C
Mantle
D
3

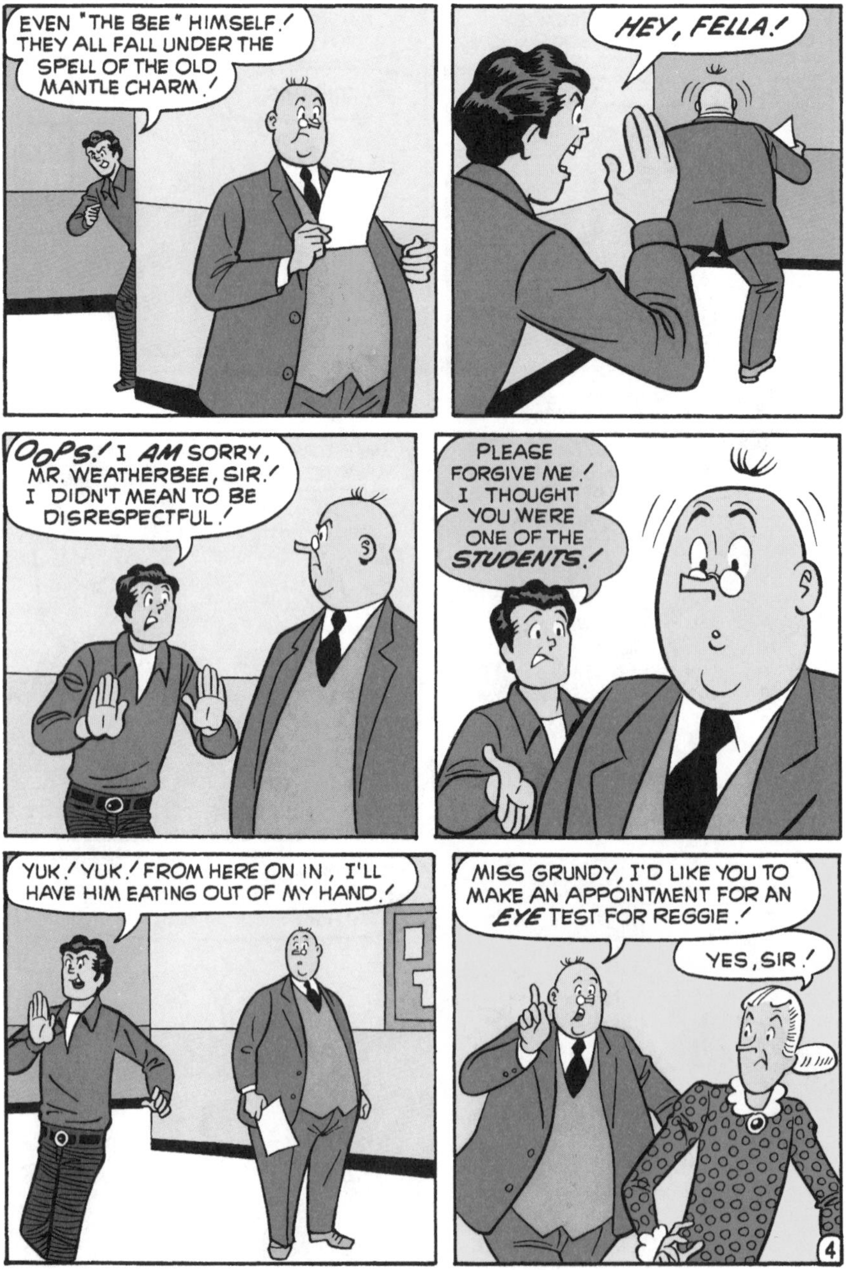
EVEN "THE BEE" HIMSELF! THEY ALL FALL UNDER THE SPELL OF THE OLD MANTLE CHARM!
HEY, FELLA!
OOPS! I AM SORRY, MR. WEATHERBEE, SIR! I DIDN'T MEAN TO BE DISRESPECTFUL!
PLEASE FORGIVE ME! I THOUGHT YOU WERE ONE OF THE STUDENTS!
YUK! YUK! FROM HERE ON IN, I'LL HAVE HIM EATING OUT OF MY HAND!
MISS GRUNDY, I'D LIKE YOU TO MAKE AN APPOINTMENT FOR AN EYE TEST FOR REGGIE!
YES, SIR!
4

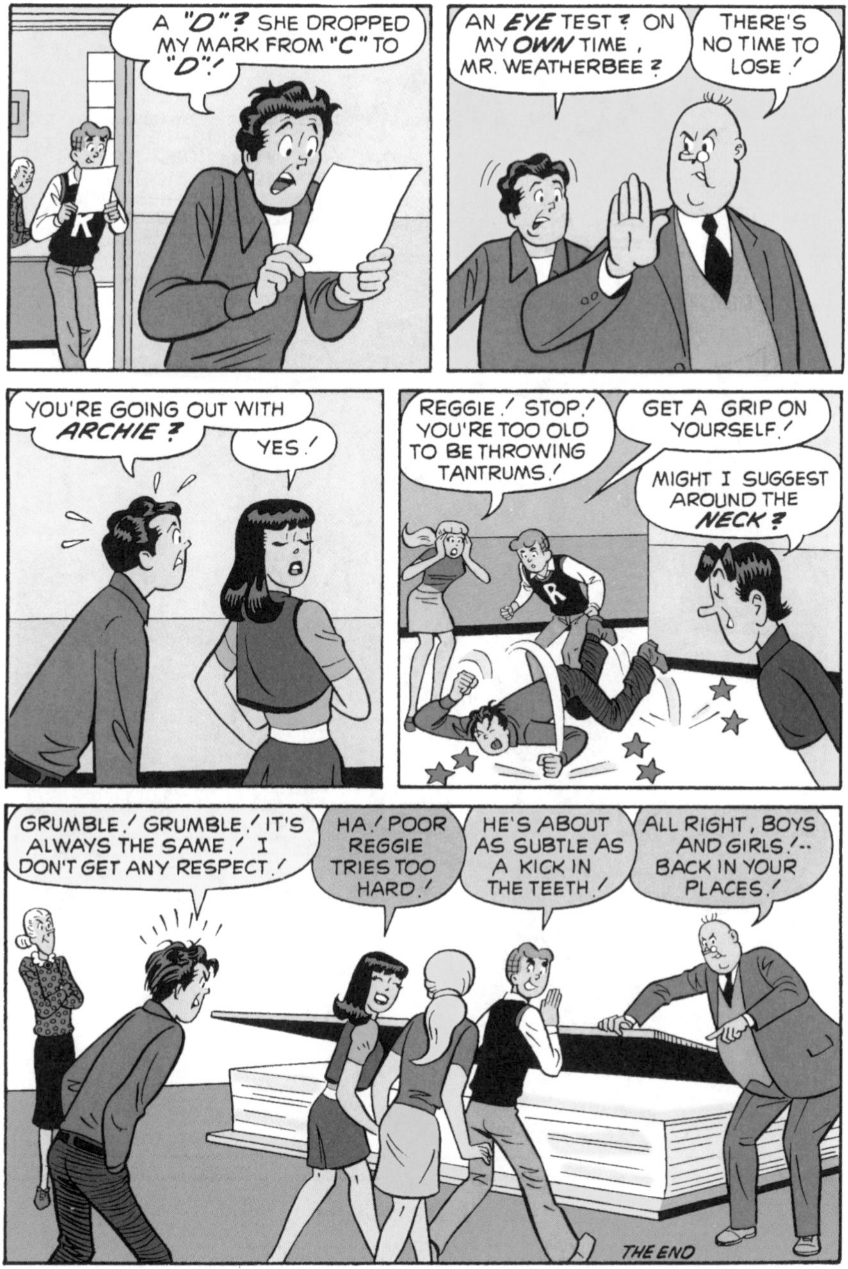
A "D"? SHE DROPPED MY MARK FROM "C" TO "D"!
AN EYE TEST? ON MY OWN TIME, MR. WEATHERBEE?
THERE'S NO TIME TO LOSE!
YOU'RE GOING OUT WITH ARCHIE?
YES!
REGGIE! STOP! YOU'RE TOO OLD TO BE THROWING TANTRUMS!
GET A GRIP ON YOURSELF!
MIGHT I SUGGEST AROUND THE NECK?
GRUMBLE! GRUMBLE! IT'S ALWAYS THE SAME! I DON'T GET ANY RESPECT!
HA! POOR REGGIE TRIES TOO HARD!
HE'S ABOUT AS SUBTLE AS A KICK IN THE TEETH!
ALL RIGHT, BOYS AND GIRLS!-- BACK IN YOUR PLACES!
THE END

Archie at Riverdale

PERILS FROM THE PAST

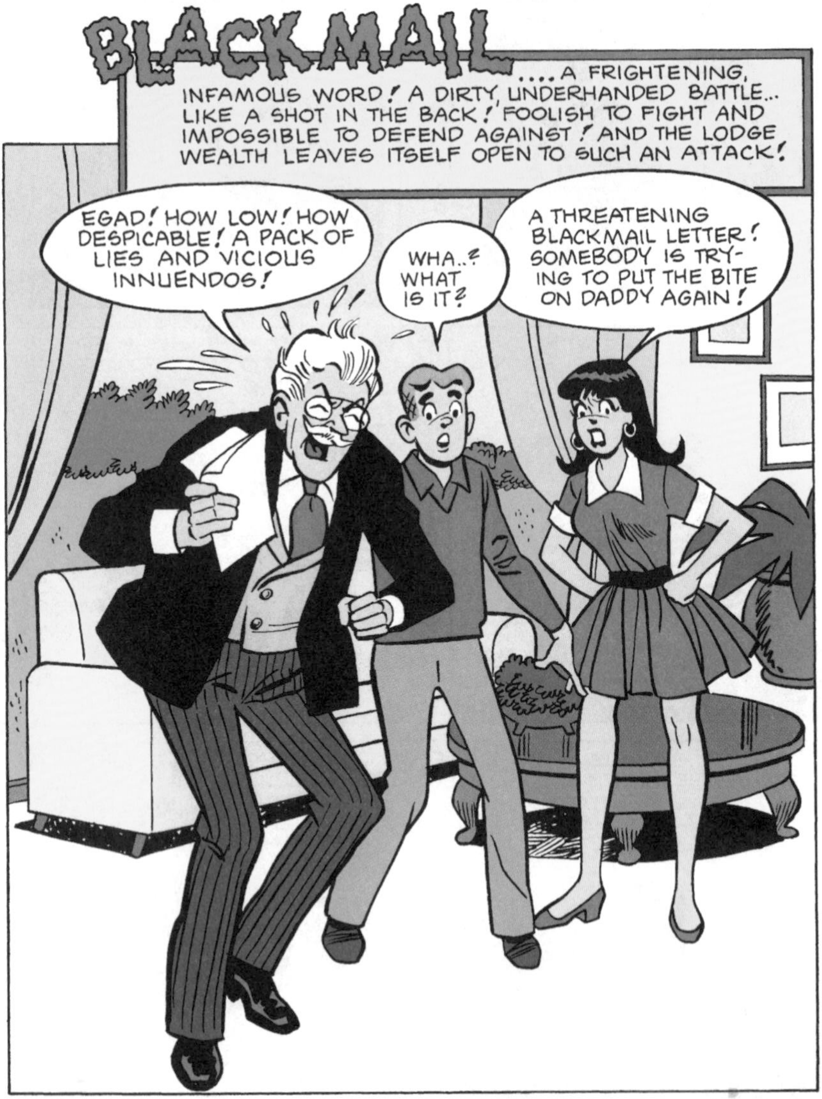
BLACKMAIL
....A FRIGHTENING, INFAMOUS WORD! A DIRTY, UNDERHANDED BATTLE... LIKE A SHOT IN THE BACK! FOOLISH TO FIGHT AND IMPOSSIBLE TO DEFEND AGAINST! AND THE LODGE WEALTH LEAVES ITSELF OPEN TO SUCH AN ATTACK!
EGAD! HOW LOW! HOW DESPICABLE! A PACK OF LIES AND VICIOUS INNUENDOS!
WHA..? WHAT IS IT?
A THREATENING BLACKMAIL LETTER! SOMEBODY IS TRYING TO PUT THE BITE ON DADDY AGAIN!

Story: Frank Doyle
Art & Letters: Samm Schwartz

Originally printed in ARCHIE AT RIVERDALE HIGH #10, SEPTEMBER 1973

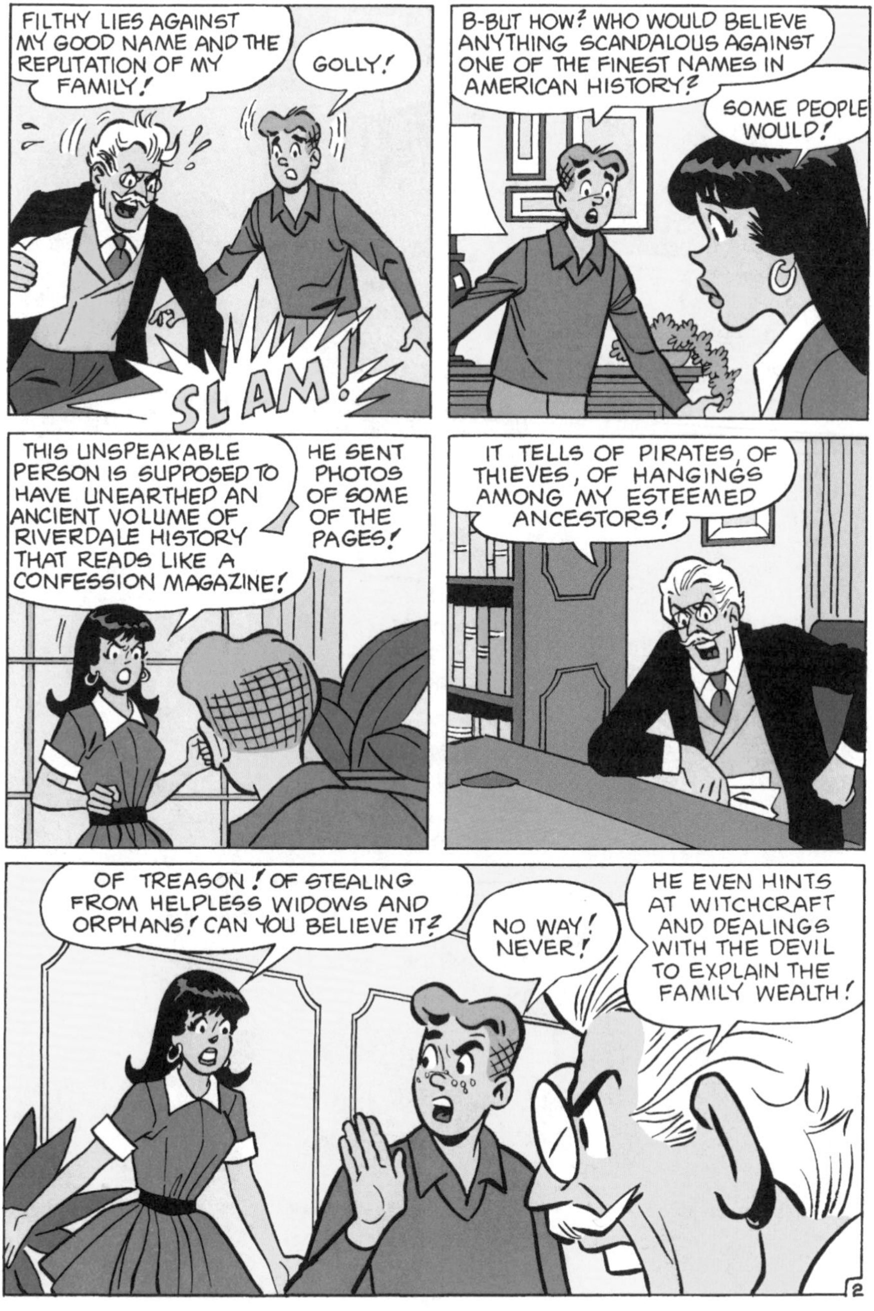
FILTHY LIES AGAINST MY GOOD NAME AND THE REPUTATION OF MY FAMILY!
GOLLY!
SLAM!
B-BUT HOW? WHO WOULD BELIEVE ANYTHING SCANDALOUS AGAINST ONE OF THE FINEST NAMES IN AMERICAN HISTORY?
SOME PEOPLE WOULD!
THIS UNSPEAKABLE PERSON IS SUPPOSED TO HAVE UNEARTHED AN ANCIENT VOLUME OF RIVERDALE HISTORY THAT READS LIKE A CONFESSION MAGAZINE!
HE SENT PHOTOS OF SOME OF THE PAGES!
IT TELLS OF PIRATES, OF THIEVES, OF HANGINGS AMONG MY ESTEEMED ANCESTORS!
OF TREASON! OF STEALING FROM HELPLESS WIDOWS AND ORPHANS! CAN YOU BELIEVE IT?
NO WAY! NEVER!
HE EVEN HINTS AT WITCHCRAFT AND DEALINGS WITH THE DEVIL TO EXPLAIN THE FAMILY WEALTH!
2

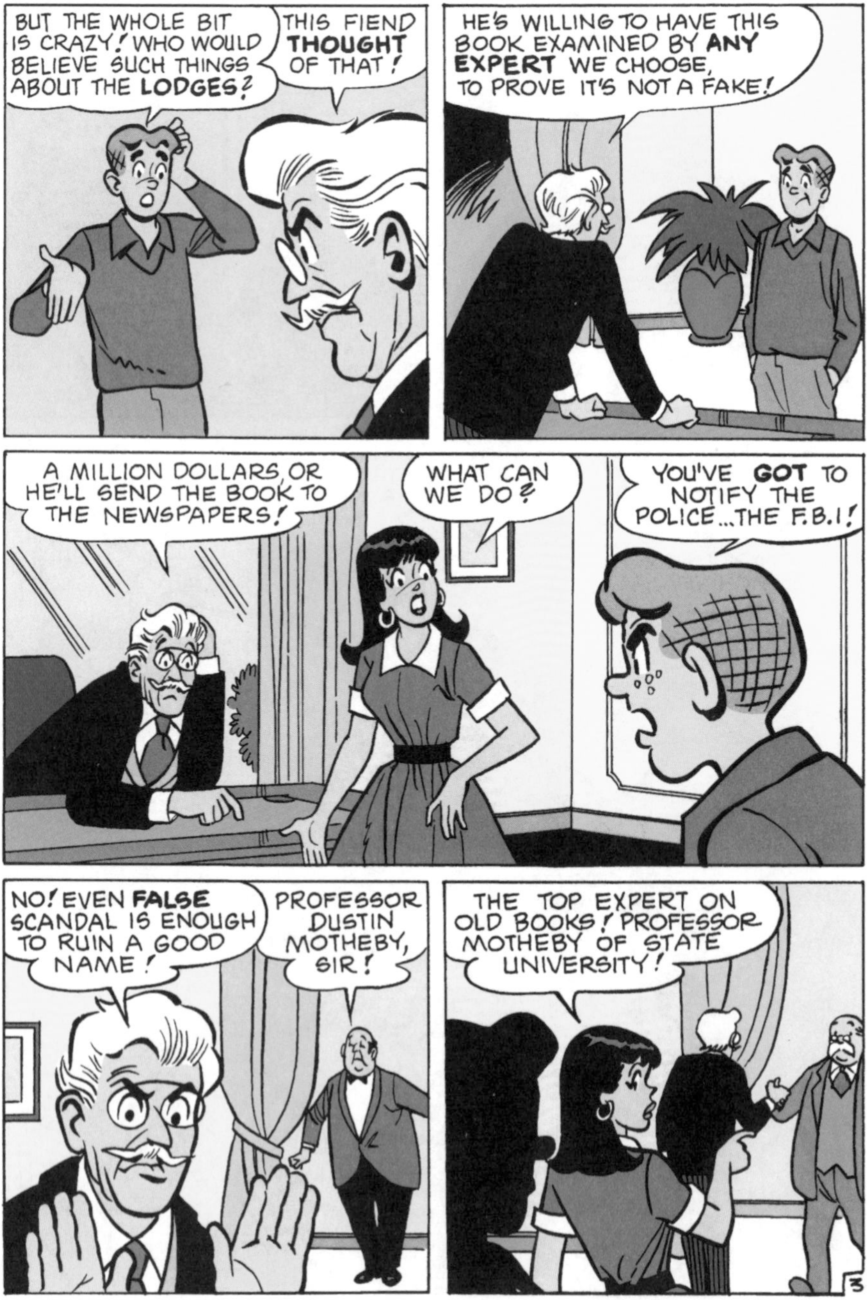
BUT THE WHOLE BIT IS CRAZY! WHO WOULD BELIEVE SUCH THINGS ABOUT THE **LODGES**?
THIS FIEND **THOUGHT** OF THAT!
HE'S WILLING TO HAVE THIS BOOK EXAMINED BY **ANY EXPERT** WE CHOOSE, TO PROVE IT'S NOT A FAKE!
A MILLION DOLLARS OR HE'LL SEND THE BOOK TO THE NEWSPAPERS!
WHAT CAN WE DO?
YOU'VE **GOT** TO NOTIFY THE POLICE...THE F.B.I!
NO! EVEN **FALSE** SCANDAL IS ENOUGH TO RUIN A GOOD NAME!
PROFESSOR DUSTIN MOTHEBY, SIR!
THE TOP EXPERT ON OLD BOOKS! PROFESSOR MOTHEBY OF STATE UNIVERSITY!
3

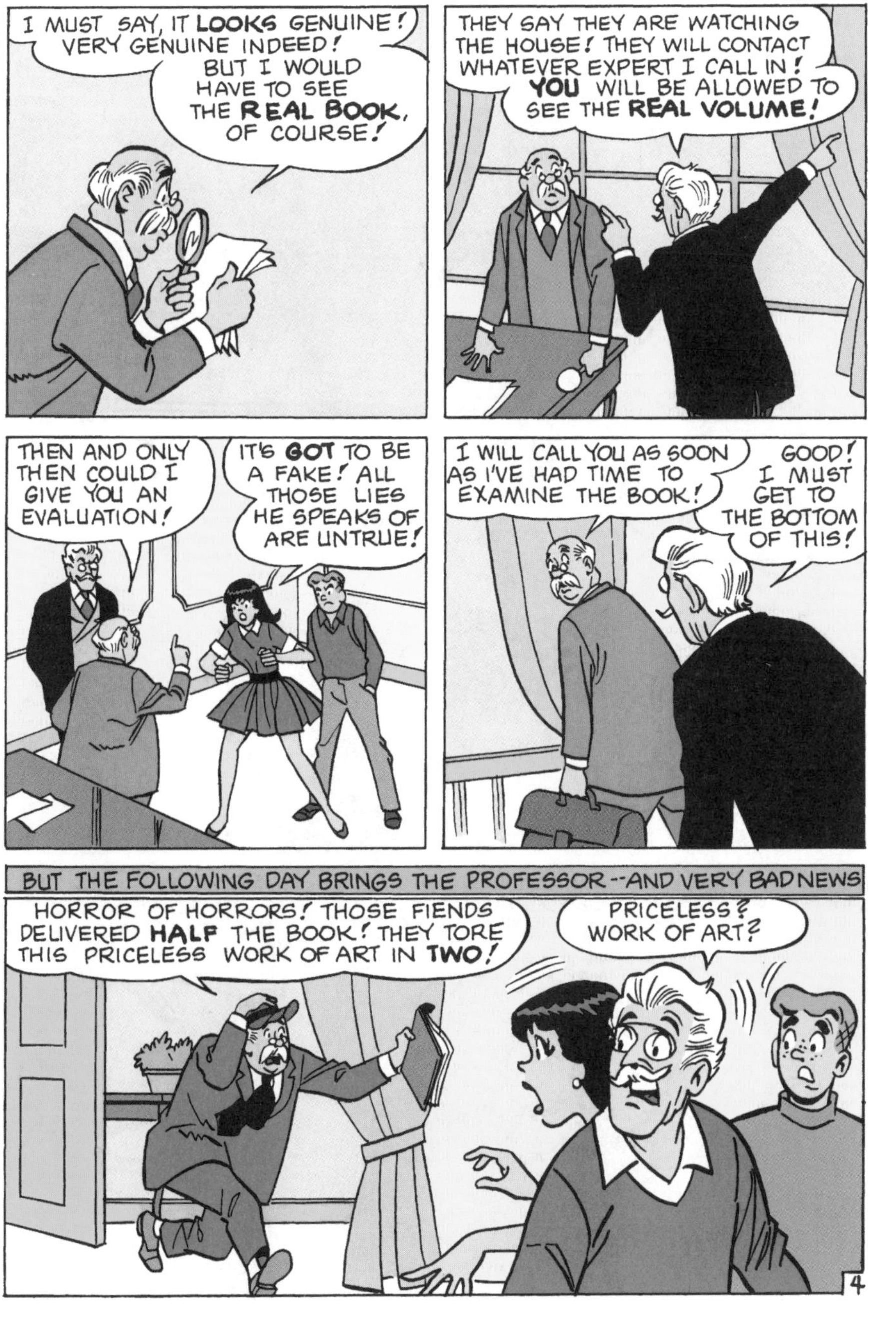
I MUST SAY, IT LOOKS GENUINE! VERY GENUINE INDEED!
BUT I WOULD HAVE TO SEE THE REAL BOOK, OF COURSE!
THEY SAY THEY ARE WATCHING THE HOUSE! THEY WILL CONTACT WHATEVER EXPERT I CALL IN! YOU WILL BE ALLOWED TO SEE THE REAL VOLUME!
THEN AND ONLY THEN COULD I GIVE YOU AN EVALUATION!
IT'S GOT TO BE A FAKE! ALL THOSE LIES HE SPEAKS OF ARE UNTRUE!
I WILL CALL YOU AS SOON AS I'VE HAD TIME TO EXAMINE THE BOOK!
GOOD! I MUST GET TO THE BOTTOM OF THIS!
BUT THE FOLLOWING DAY BRINGS THE PROFESSOR--AND VERY BAD NEWS
HORROR OF HORRORS! THOSE FIENDS DELIVERED HALF THE BOOK! THEY TORE THIS PRICELESS WORK OF ART IN TWO!
PRICELESS? WORK OF ART?
4

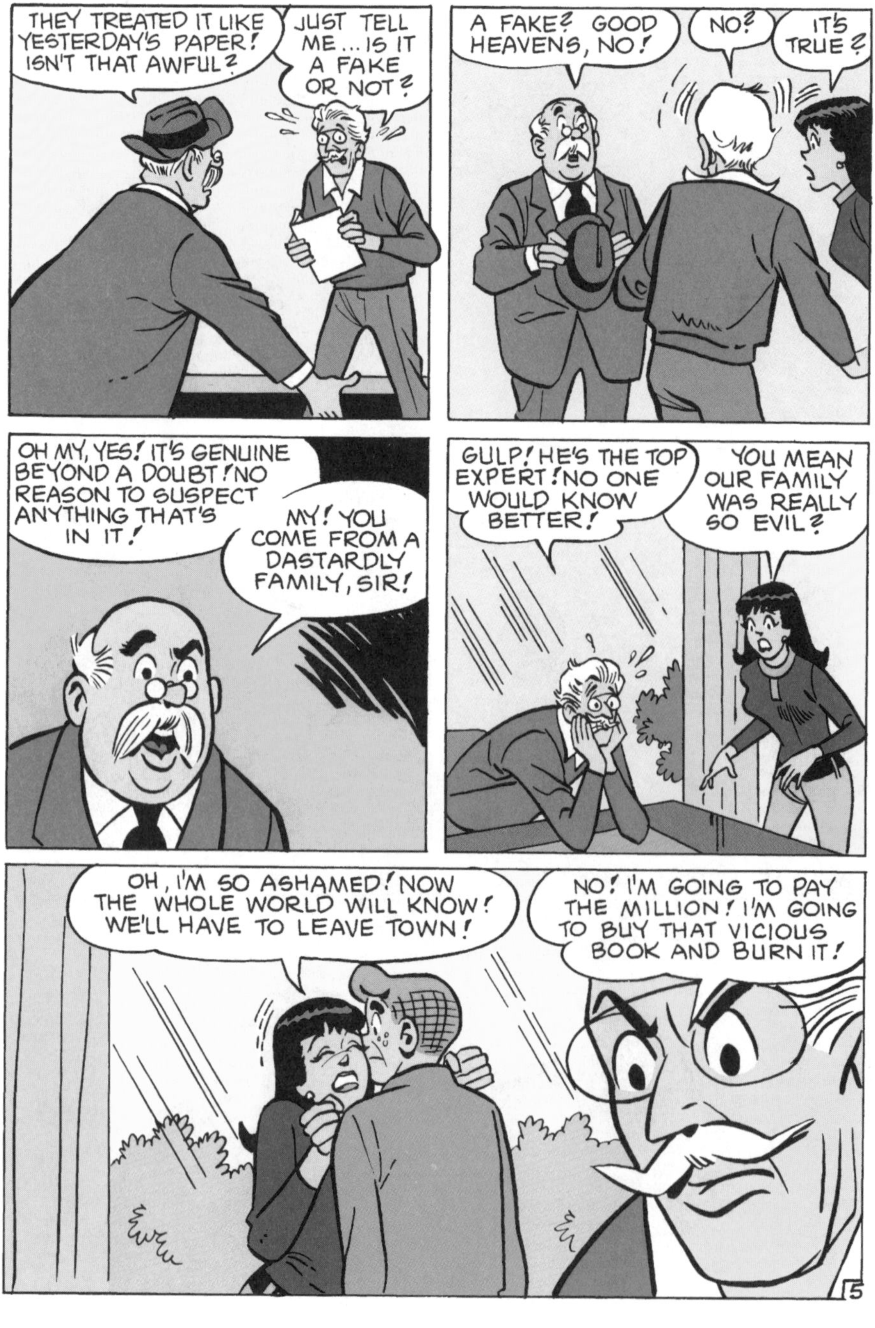
THEY TREATED IT LIKE YESTERDAY'S PAPER! ISN'T THAT AWFUL?
JUST TELL ME... IS IT A FAKE OR NOT?
A FAKE? GOOD HEAVENS, NO!
NO?
IT'S TRUE?
OH MY, YES! IT'S GENUINE BEYOND A DOUBT! NO REASON TO SUSPECT ANYTHING THAT'S IN IT!
MY! YOU COME FROM A DASTARDLY FAMILY, SIR!
GULP! HE'S THE TOP EXPERT! NO ONE WOULD KNOW BETTER!
YOU MEAN OUR FAMILY WAS REALLY SO EVIL?
OH, I'M SO ASHAMED! NOW THE WHOLE WORLD WILL KNOW! WE'LL HAVE TO LEAVE TOWN!
NO! I'M GOING TO PAY THE MILLION! I'M GOING TO BUY THAT VICIOUS BOOK AND BURN IT!
5

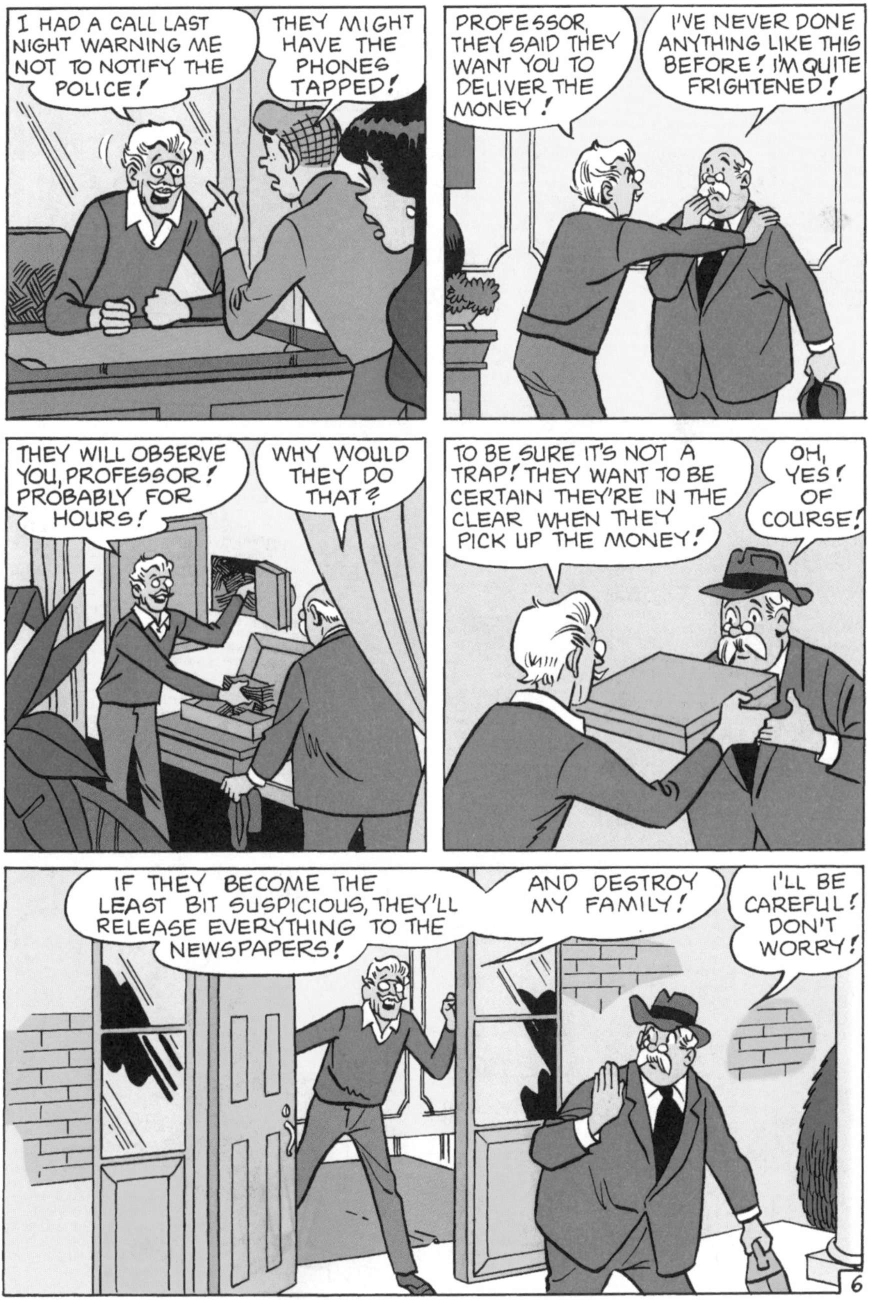
I HAD A CALL LAST NIGHT WARNING ME NOT TO NOTIFY THE POLICE!
THEY MIGHT HAVE THE PHONES TAPPED!
PROFESSOR, THEY SAID THEY WANT YOU TO DELIVER THE MONEY!
I'VE NEVER DONE ANYTHING LIKE THIS BEFORE! I'M QUITE FRIGHTENED!
THEY WILL OBSERVE YOU, PROFESSOR! PROBABLY FOR HOURS!
WHY WOULD THEY DO THAT?
TO BE SURE IT'S NOT A TRAP! THEY WANT TO BE CERTAIN THEY'RE IN THE CLEAR WHEN THEY PICK UP THE MONEY!
OH, YES! OF COURSE!
IF THEY BECOME THE LEAST BIT SUSPICIOUS, THEY'LL RELEASE EVERYTHING TO THE NEWSPAPERS!
AND DESTROY MY FAMILY!
I'LL BE CAREFUL! DON'T WORRY!
6

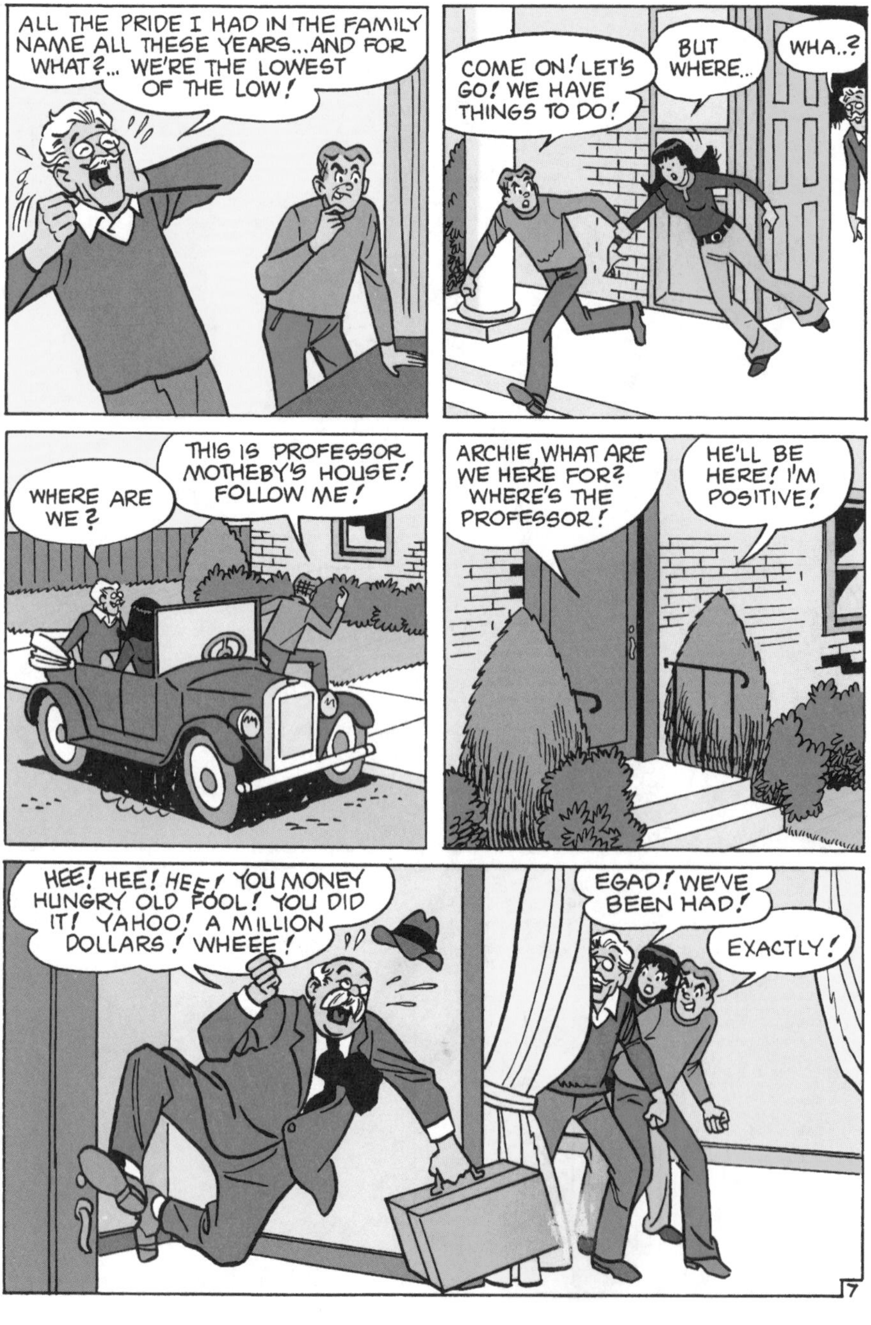
ALL THE PRIDE I HAD IN THE FAMILY NAME ALL THESE YEARS...AND FOR WHAT?... WE'RE THE LOWEST OF THE LOW!
COME ON! LET'S GO! WE HAVE THINGS TO DO!
BUT WHERE...
WHA..?
WHERE ARE WE?
THIS IS PROFESSOR MOTHEBY'S HOUSE! FOLLOW ME!
ARCHIE, WHAT ARE WE HERE FOR? WHERE'S THE PROFESSOR!
HE'LL BE HERE! I'M POSITIVE!
HEE! HEE! HEE! YOU MONEY HUNGRY OLD FOOL! YOU DID IT! YAHOO! A MILLION DOLLARS! WHEEE!
EGAD! WE'VE BEEN HAD!
EXACTLY!
7

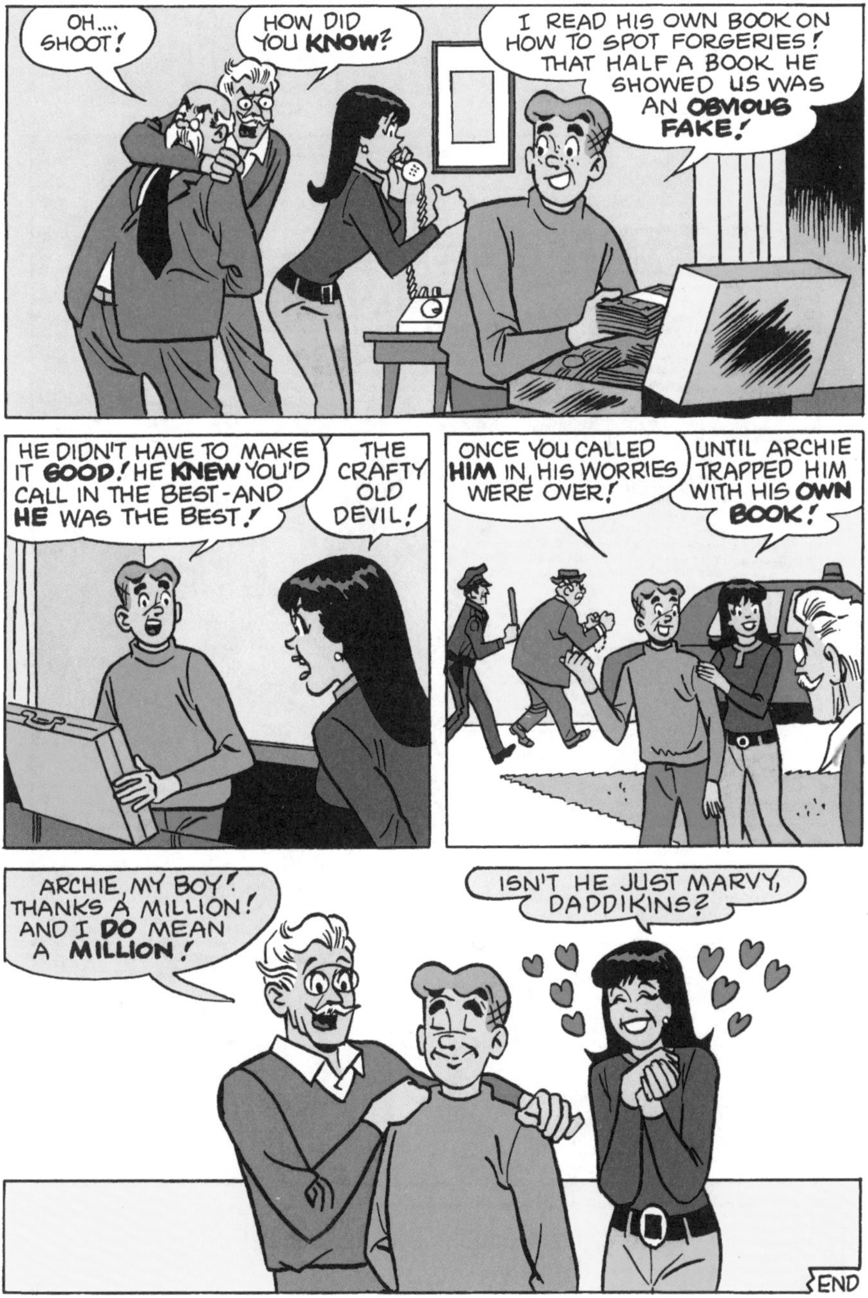
OH...., SHOOT!
HOW DID YOU KNOW?
I READ HIS OWN BOOK ON HOW TO SPOT FORGERIES! THAT HALF A BOOK HE SHOWED US WAS AN OBVIOUS FAKE!
HE DIDN'T HAVE TO MAKE IT GOOD! HE KNEW YOU'D CALL IN THE BEST-AND HE WAS THE BEST!
THE CRAFTY OLD DEVIL!
ONCE YOU CALLED HIM IN, HIS WORRIES WERE OVER!
UNTIL ARCHIE TRAPPED HIM WITH HIS OWN BOOK!
ARCHIE, MY BOY! THANKS A MILLION! AND I DO MEAN A MILLION!
ISN'T HE JUST MARVY, DADDIKINS?
END

Archie at Riverdale in "The ACCOUNT"

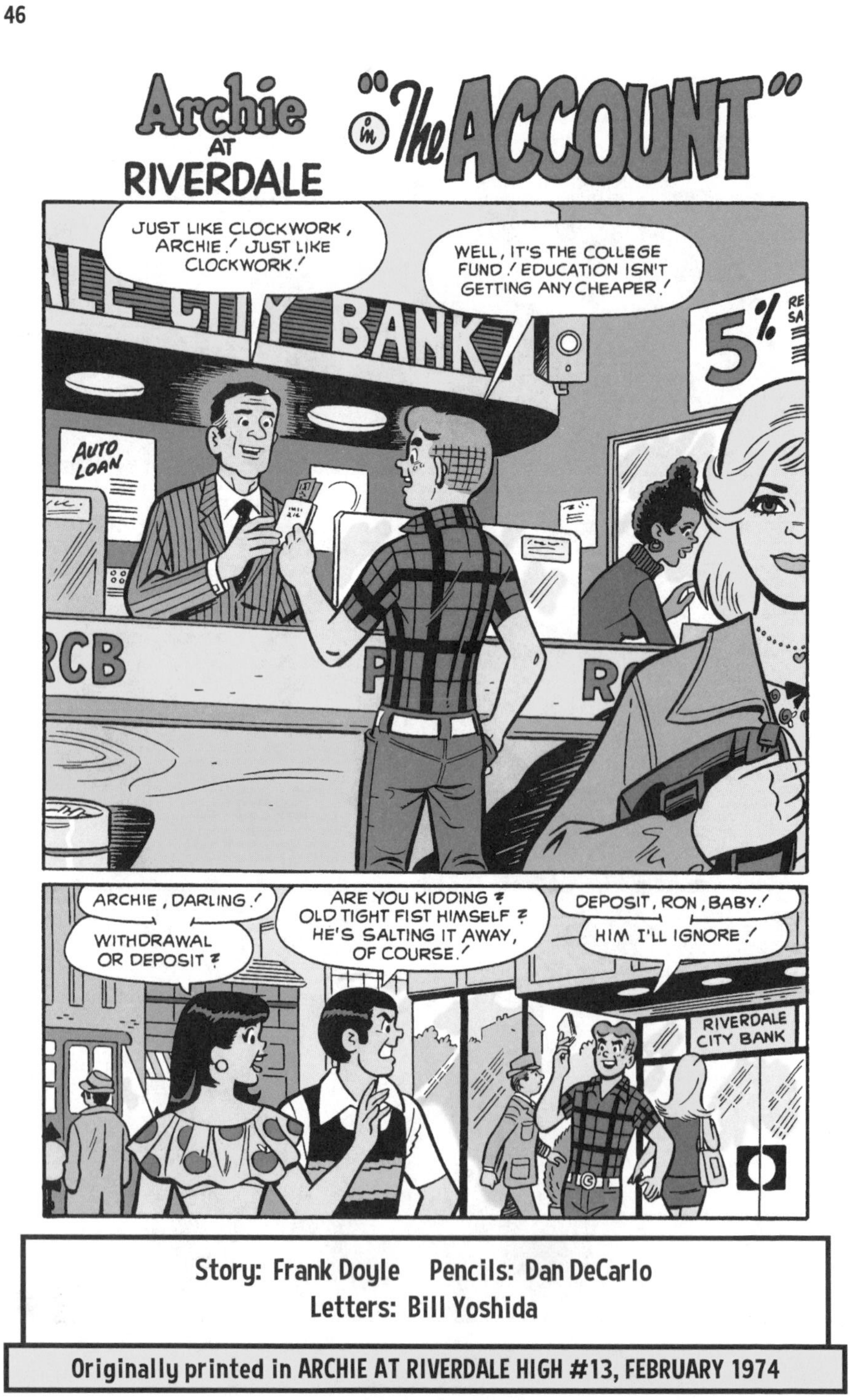
JUST LIKE CLOCKWORK, ARCHIE! JUST LIKE CLOCKWORK!
WELL, IT'S THE COLLEGE FUND! EDUCATION ISN'T GETTING ANY CHEAPER!
BANK
5%
AUTO LOAN
RCB
ARCHIE, DARLING!
WITHDRAWAL OR DEPOSIT?
ARE YOU KIDDING? OLD TIGHT FIST HIMSELF? HE'S SALTING IT AWAY, OF COURSE!
DEPOSIT, RON, BABY!
HIM I'LL IGNORE!
RIVERDALE CITY BANK

Story: Frank Doyle **Pencils:** Dan DeCarlo
Letters: Bill Yoshida

Originally printed in ARCHIE AT RIVERDALE HIGH #13, FEBRUARY 1974

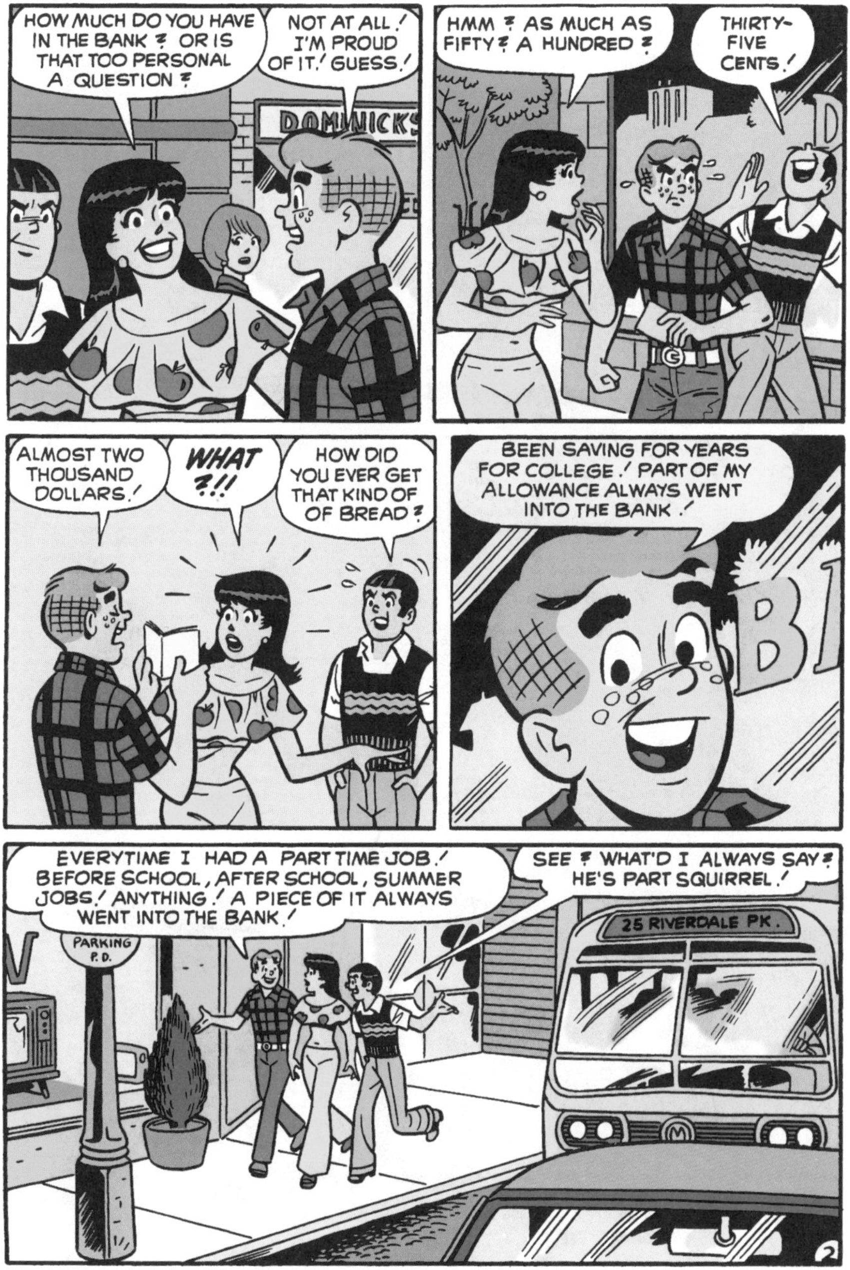
HOW MUCH DO YOU HAVE IN THE BANK ? OR IS THAT TOO PERSONAL A QUESTION ?
NOT AT ALL! I'M PROUD OF IT! GUESS!
DOMINICKS
HMM ? AS MUCH AS FIFTY ? A HUNDRED ?
THIRTY-FIVE CENTS!
ALMOST TWO THOUSAND DOLLARS!
WHAT ?!!
HOW DID YOU EVER GET THAT KIND OF OF BREAD ?
BEEN SAVING FOR YEARS FOR COLLEGE! PART OF MY ALLOWANCE ALWAYS WENT INTO THE BANK!
EVERYTIME I HAD A PART TIME JOB! BEFORE SCHOOL, AFTER SCHOOL, SUMMER JOBS! ANYTHING! A PIECE OF IT ALWAYS WENT INTO THE BANK!
SEE ? WHAT'D I ALWAYS SAY ? HE'S PART SQUIRREL!
PARKING P.D.
25 RIVERDALE PK.
2

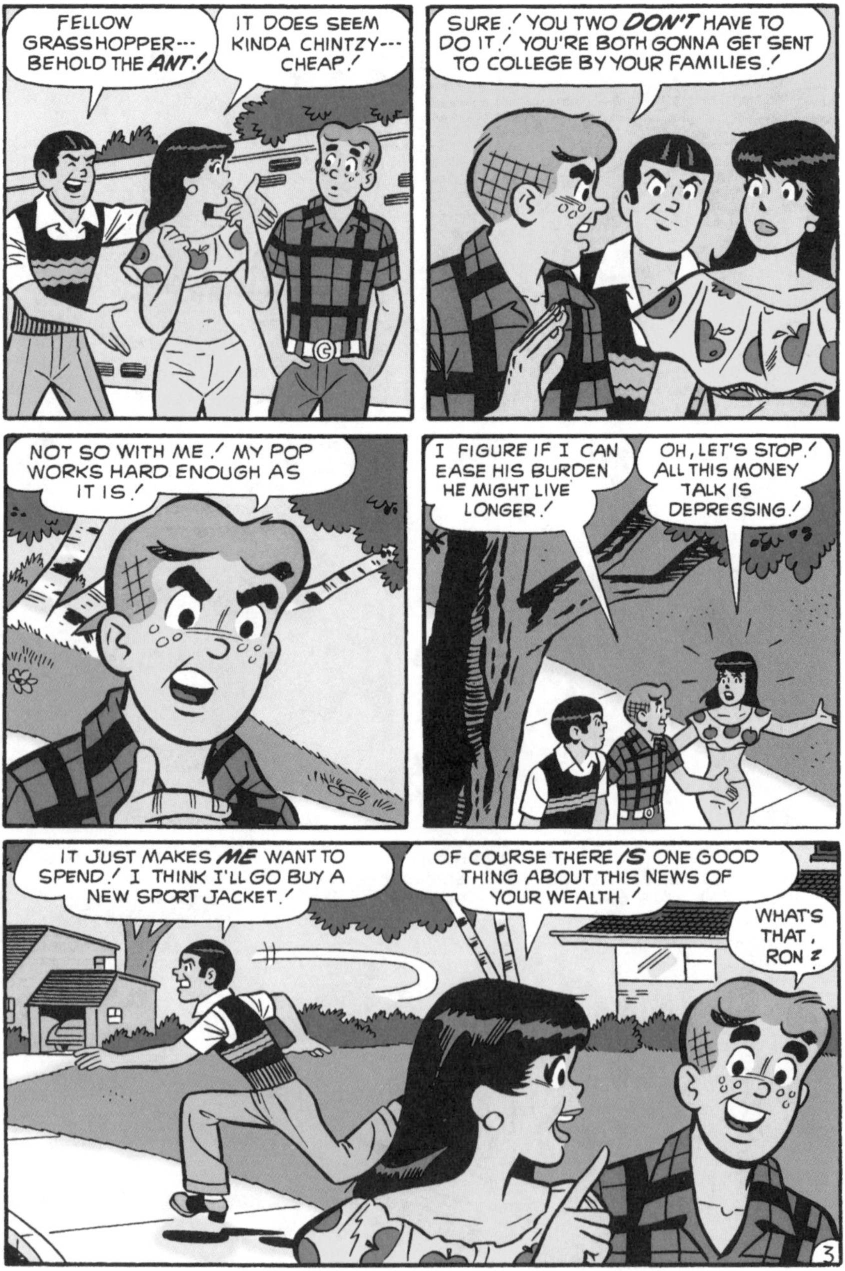
FELLOW GRASSHOPPER--- BEHOLD THE ANT!
IT DOES SEEM KINDA CHINTZY--- CHEAP!
SURE! YOU TWO DON'T HAVE TO DO IT! YOU'RE BOTH GONNA GET SENT TO COLLEGE BY YOUR FAMILIES!
NOT SO WITH ME! MY POP WORKS HARD ENOUGH AS IT IS!
I FIGURE IF I CAN EASE HIS BURDEN HE MIGHT LIVE LONGER!
OH, LET'S STOP! ALL THIS MONEY TALK IS DEPRESSING!
IT JUST MAKES ME WANT TO SPEND! I THINK I'LL GO BUY A NEW SPORT JACKET!
OF COURSE THERE IS ONE GOOD THING ABOUT THIS NEWS OF YOUR WEALTH!
WHAT'S THAT, RON?
3

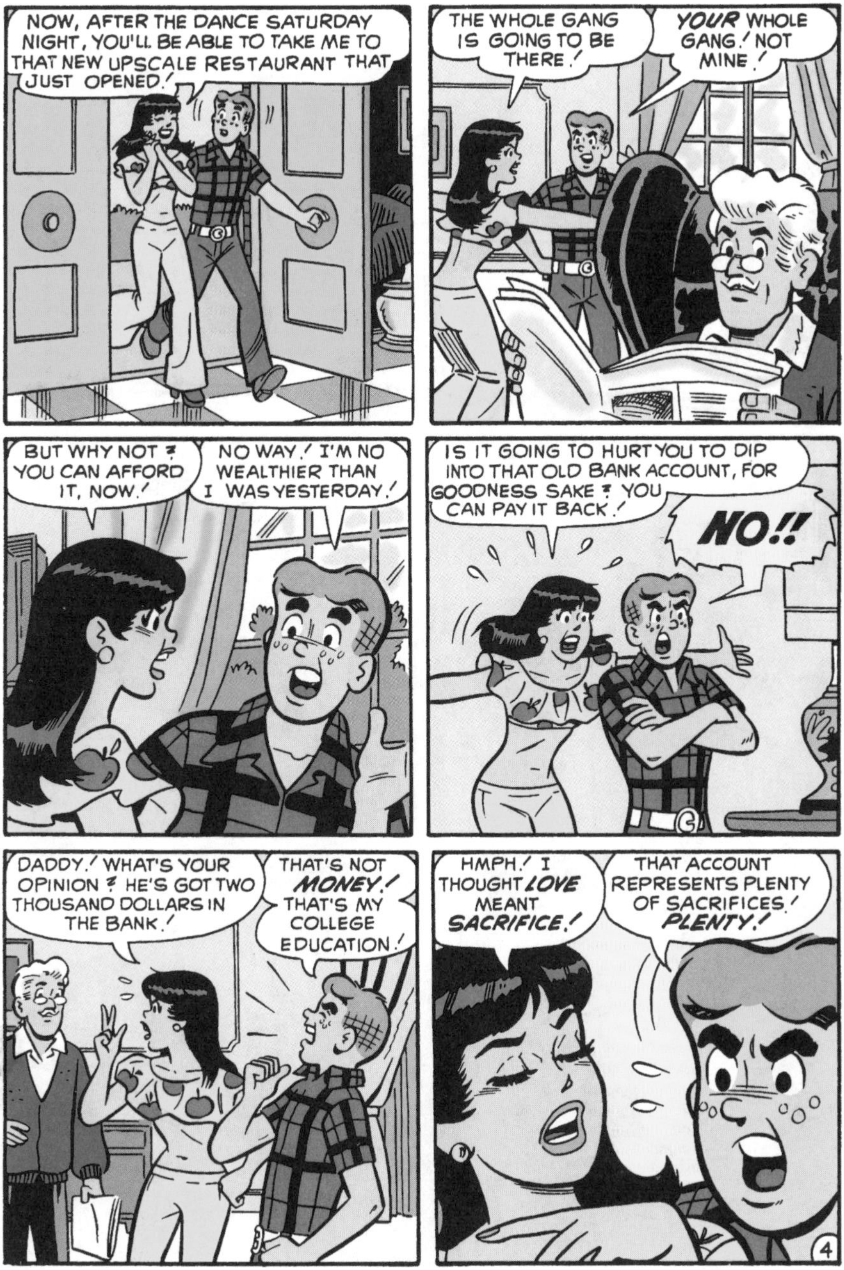
NOW, AFTER THE DANCE SATURDAY NIGHT, YOU'LL BE ABLE TO TAKE ME TO THAT NEW UPSCALE RESTAURANT THAT JUST OPENED!
THE WHOLE GANG IS GOING TO BE THERE!
YOUR WHOLE GANG! NOT MINE!
BUT WHY NOT? YOU CAN AFFORD IT, NOW!
NO WAY! I'M NO WEALTHIER THAN I WAS YESTERDAY!
IS IT GOING TO HURT YOU TO DIP INTO THAT OLD BANK ACCOUNT, FOR GOODNESS SAKE? YOU CAN PAY IT BACK!
NO!!
DADDY! WHAT'S YOUR OPINION? HE'S GOT TWO THOUSAND DOLLARS IN THE BANK!
THAT'S NOT MONEY! THAT'S MY COLLEGE EDUCATION!
HMPH! I THOUGHT LOVE MEANT SACRIFICE!
THAT ACCOUNT REPRESENTS PLENTY OF SACRIFICES! PLENTY!
4

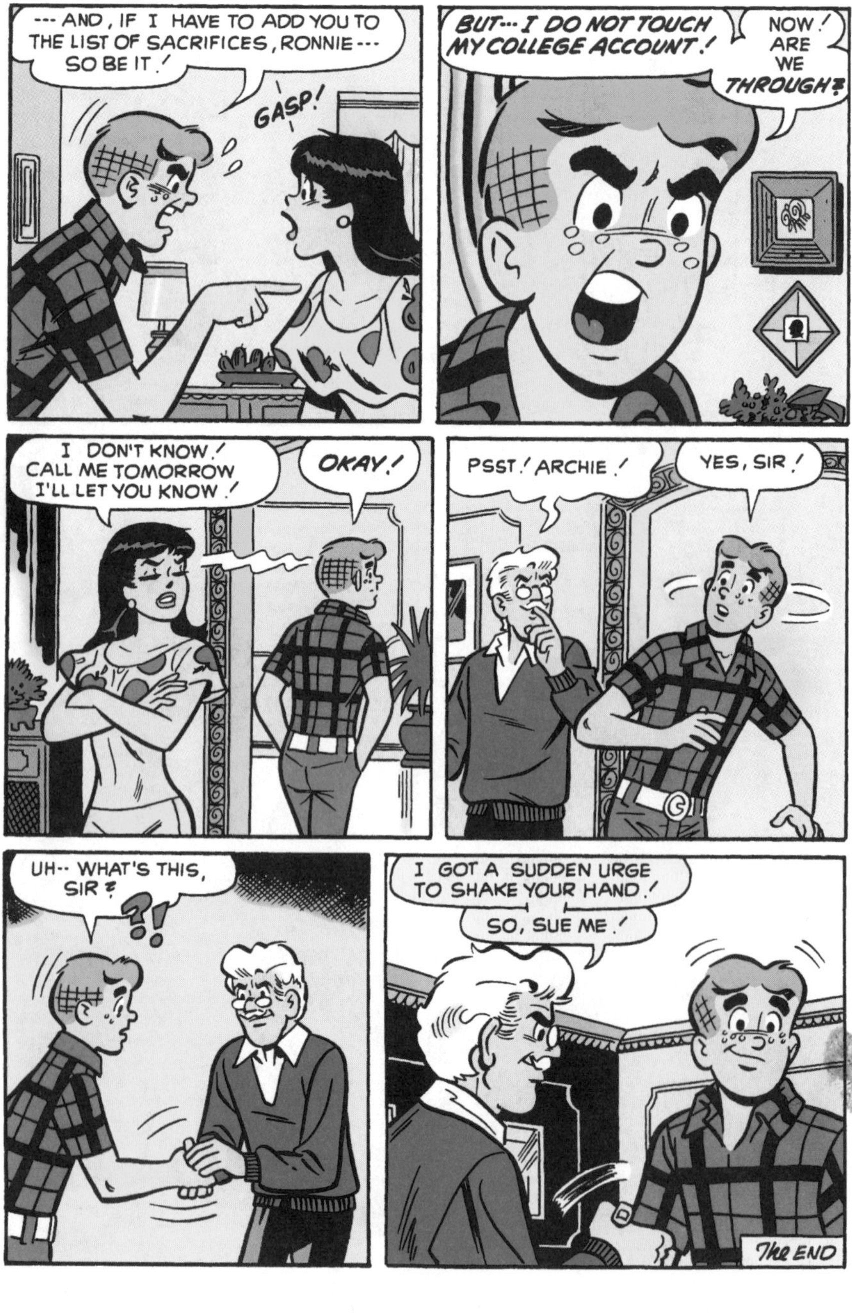
--- AND, IF I HAVE TO ADD YOU TO THE LIST OF SACRIFICES, RONNIE --- SO BE IT!
GASP!
BUT--- I DO NOT TOUCH MY COLLEGE ACCOUNT!
NOW! ARE WE THROUGH?
I DON'T KNOW! CALL ME TOMORROW I'LL LET YOU KNOW!
OKAY!
PSST! ARCHIE!
YES, SIR!
UH-- WHAT'S THIS, SIR?
?!
I GOT A SUDDEN URGE TO SHAKE YOUR HAND!
SO, SUE ME!
The END

Archie at RIVERDALE in "SOPHOMORE SCANDAL"

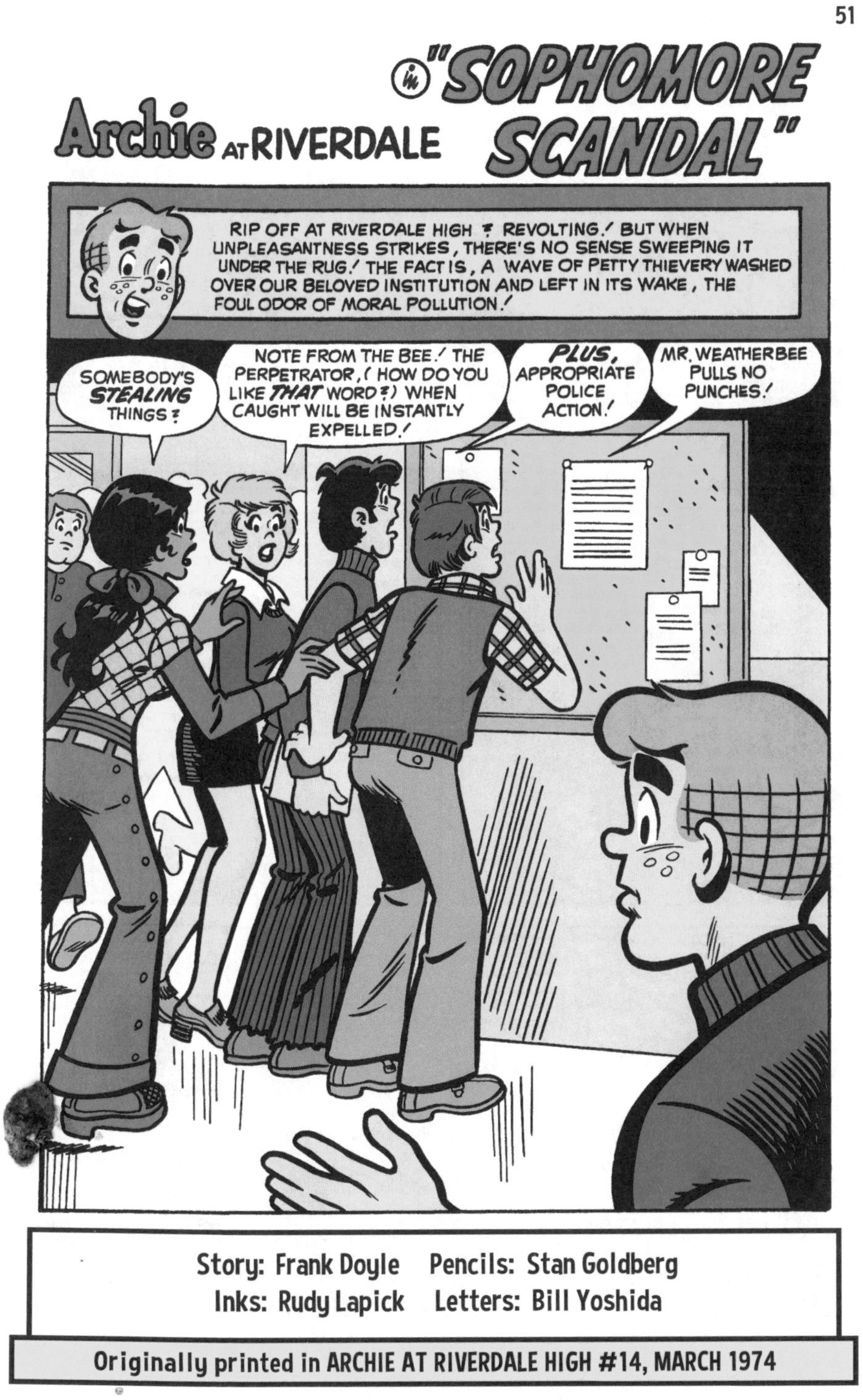
RIP OFF AT RIVERDALE HIGH ?! REVOLTING! BUT WHEN UNPLEASANTNESS STRIKES, THERE'S NO SENSE SWEEPING IT UNDER THE RUG! THE FACT IS, A WAVE OF PETTY THIEVERY WASHED OVER OUR BELOVED INSTITUTION AND LEFT IN ITS WAKE, THE FOUL ODOR OF MORAL POLLUTION!
SOMEBODY'S *STEALING* THINGS ?!
NOTE FROM THE BEE! THE PERPETRATOR, (HOW DO YOU LIKE *THAT* WORD ?!) WHEN CAUGHT WILL BE INSTANTLY EXPELLED!
PLUS, APPROPRIATE POLICE ACTION!
MR. WEATHERBEE PULLS NO PUNCHES!

Story: Frank Doyle **Pencils:** Stan Goldberg
Inks: Rudy Lapick **Letters:** Bill Yoshida

Originally printed in ARCHIE AT RIVERDALE HIGH #14, MARCH 1974

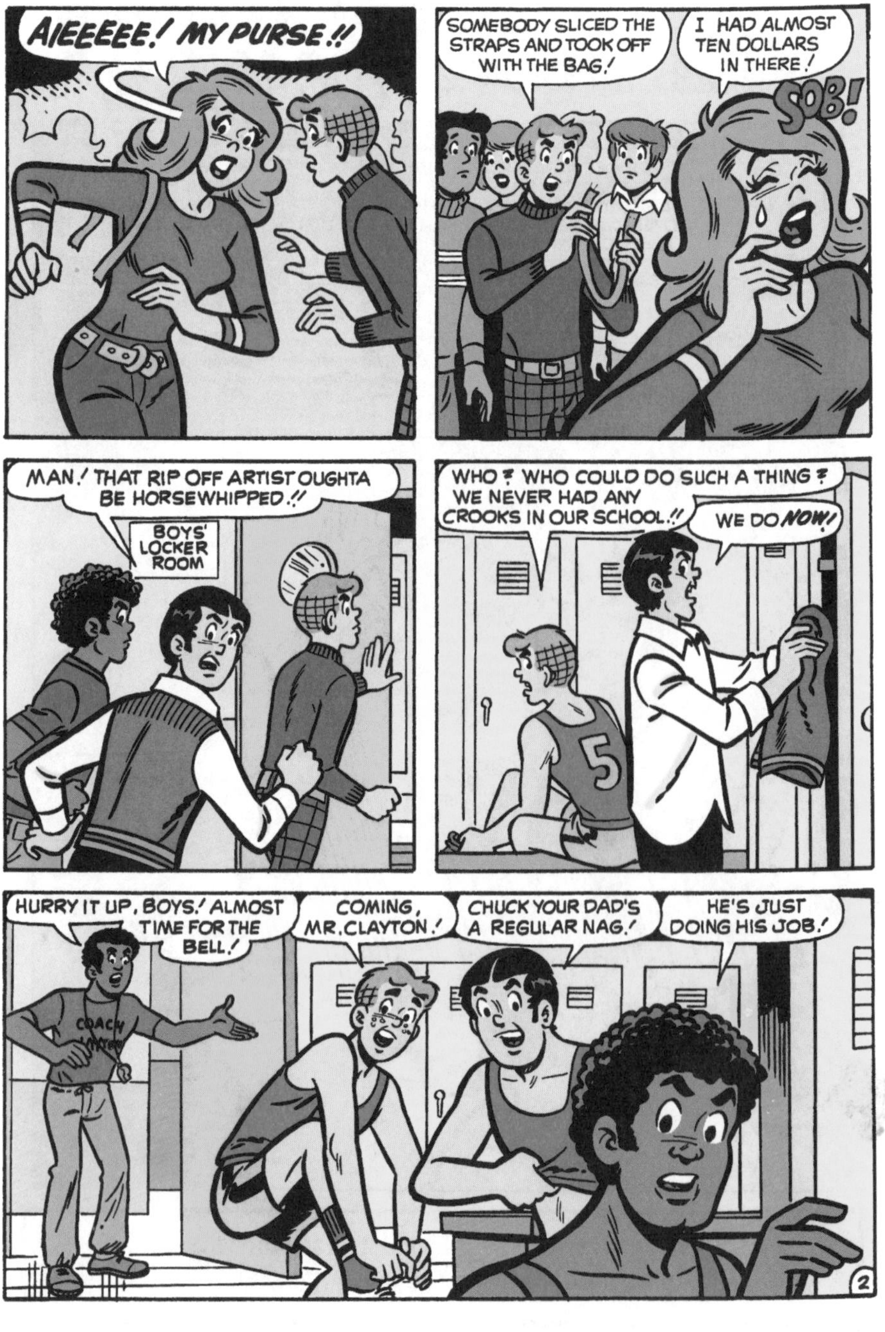
AIEEEEE! MY PURSE!!
SOMEBODY SLICED THE STRAPS AND TOOK OFF WITH THE BAG!
I HAD ALMOST TEN DOLLARS IN THERE!
SOB!
MAN! THAT RIP OFF ARTIST OUGHTA BE HORSEWHIPPED!!
BOYS' LOCKER ROOM
WHO? WHO COULD DO SUCH A THING? WE NEVER HAD ANY CROOKS IN OUR SCHOOL!!
WE DO NOW!
HURRY IT UP, BOYS! ALMOST TIME FOR THE BELL!
COMING, MR. CLAYTON!
CHUCK YOUR DAD'S A REGULAR NAG!
HE'S JUST DOING HIS JOB!
COACH
2

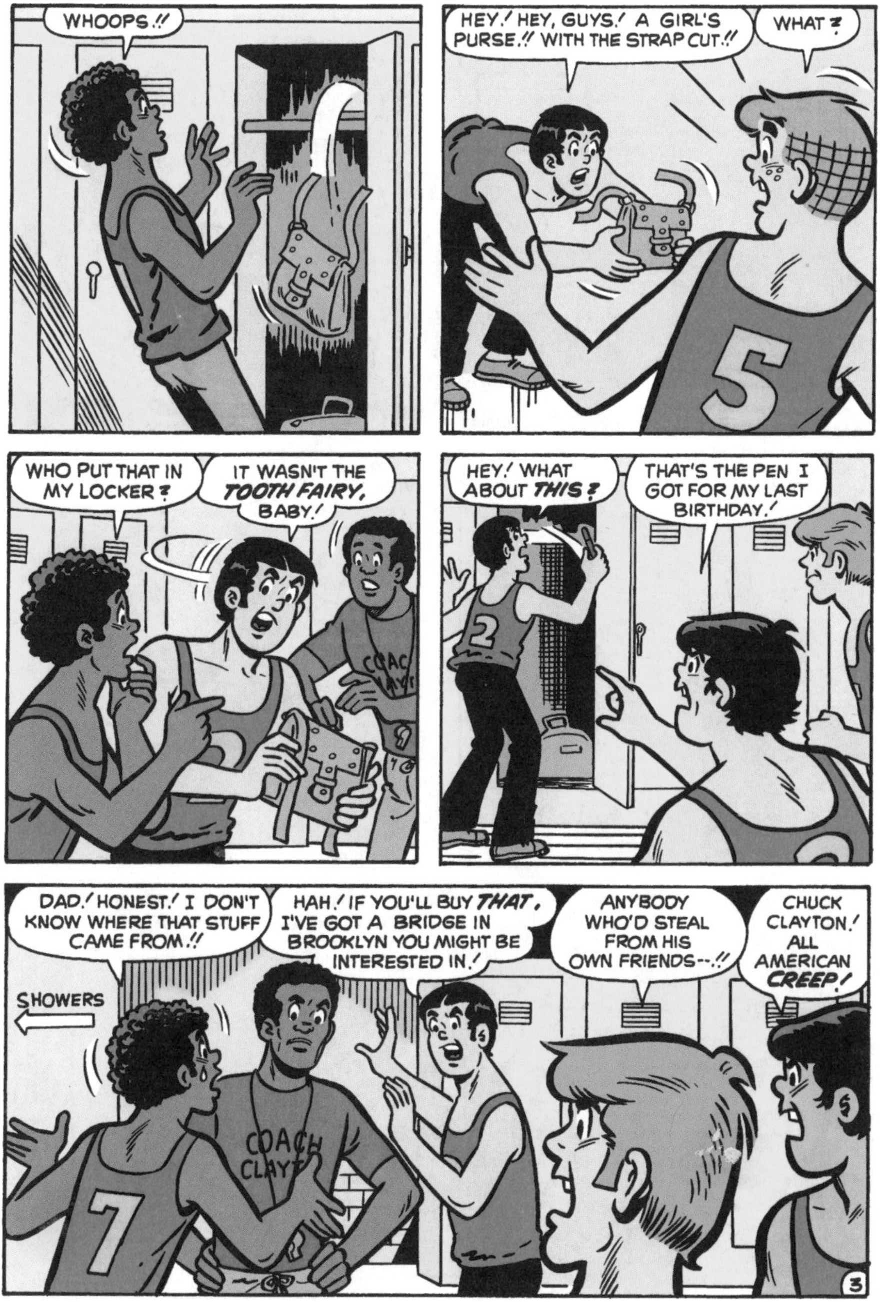
WHOOPS.!!
HEY.! HEY, GUYS.! A GIRL'S PURSE.!! WITH THE STRAP CUT.!!
WHAT?
WHO PUT THAT IN MY LOCKER?
IT WASN'T THE TOOTH FAIRY, BABY.!
HEY.! WHAT ABOUT THIS?
THAT'S THE PEN I GOT FOR MY LAST BIRTHDAY.!
DAD.! HONEST.! I DON'T KNOW WHERE THAT STUFF CAME FROM.!!
HAH.! IF YOU'LL BUY THAT, I'VE GOT A BRIDGE IN BROOKLYN YOU MIGHT BE INTERESTED IN.!
ANYBODY WHO'D STEAL FROM HIS OWN FRIENDS--.!!
CHUCK CLAYTON.! ALL AMERICAN CREEP!
SHOWERS
3

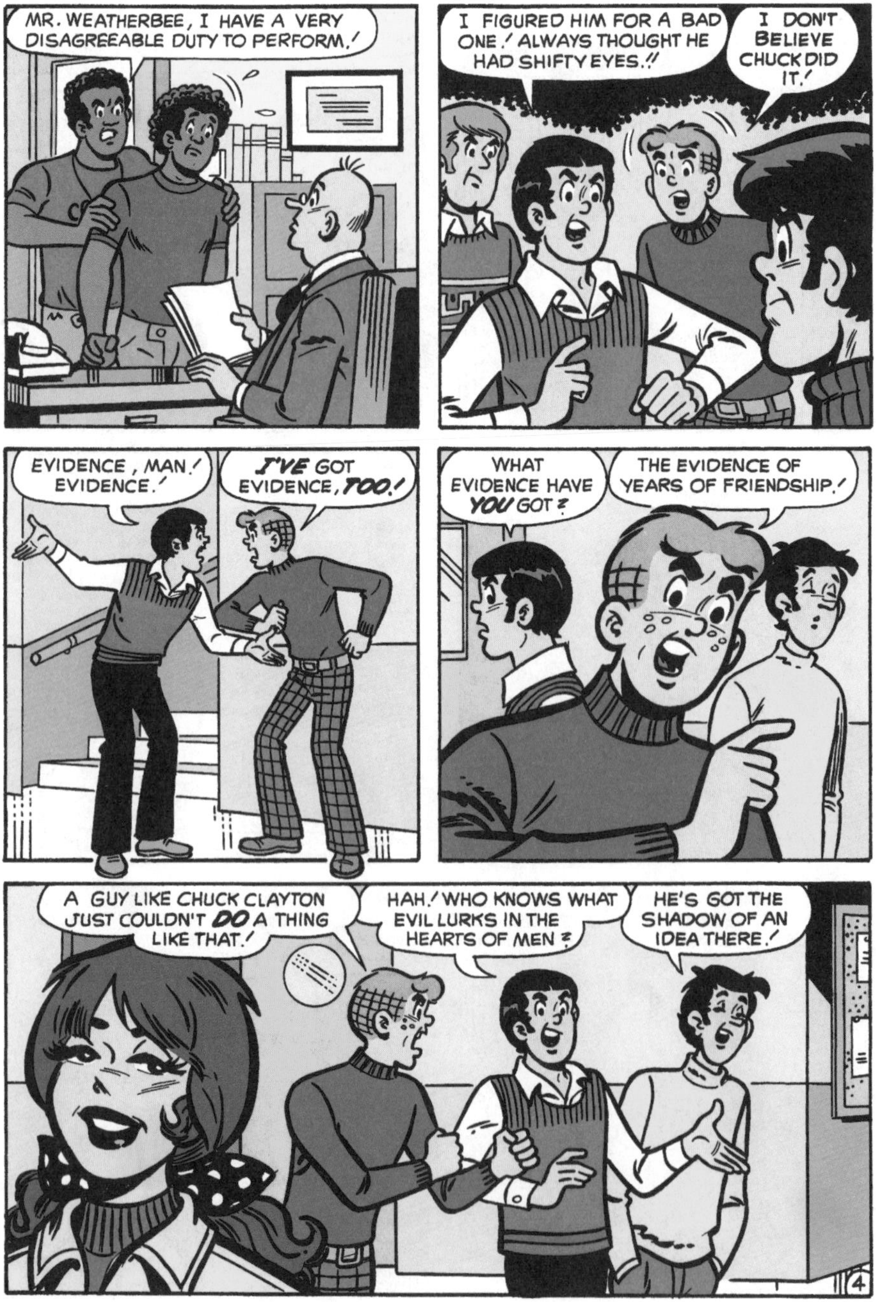
MR. WEATHERBEE, I HAVE A VERY DISAGREEABLE DUTY TO PERFORM.!
I FIGURED HIM FOR A BAD ONE.! ALWAYS THOUGHT HE HAD SHIFTY EYES.!!
I DON'T BELIEVE CHUCK DID IT.!
EVIDENCE, MAN.! EVIDENCE.!
I'VE GOT EVIDENCE, TOO.!
WHAT EVIDENCE HAVE YOU GOT?
THE EVIDENCE OF YEARS OF FRIENDSHIP.!
A GUY LIKE CHUCK CLAYTON JUST COULDN'T DO A THING LIKE THAT.!
HAH.! WHO KNOWS WHAT EVIL LURKS IN THE HEARTS OF MEN?
HE'S GOT THE SHADOW OF AN IDEA THERE.!
4

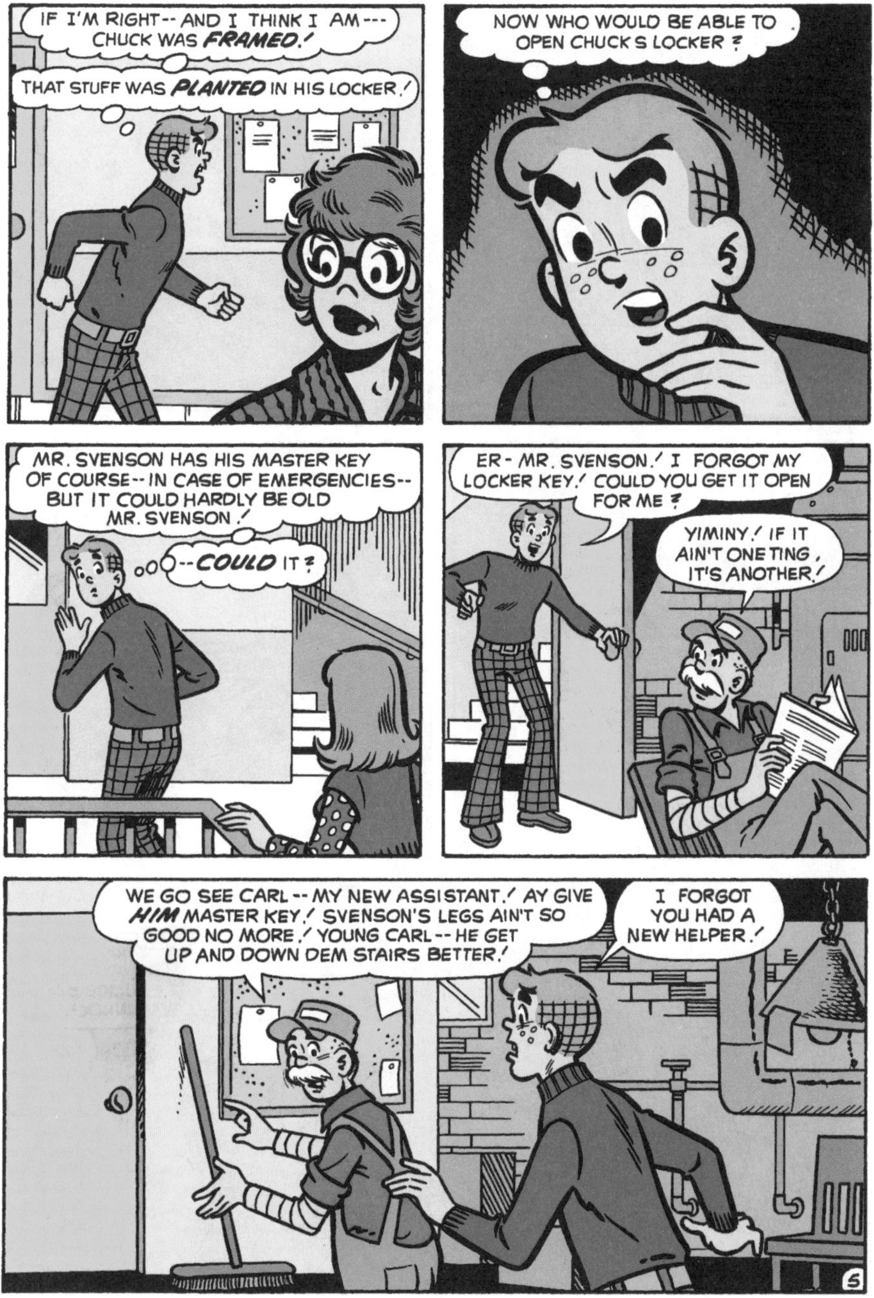
IF I'M RIGHT-- AND I THINK I AM--- CHUCK WAS FRAMED!
THAT STUFF WAS PLANTED IN HIS LOCKER!
NOW WHO WOULD BE ABLE TO OPEN CHUCK'S LOCKER?
MR. SVENSON HAS HIS MASTER KEY OF COURSE-- IN CASE OF EMERGENCIES-- BUT IT COULD HARDLY BE OLD MR. SVENSON!
--COULD IT?
ER- MR. SVENSON! I FORGOT MY LOCKER KEY! COULD YOU GET IT OPEN FOR ME?
YIMINY! IF IT AIN'T ONE TING, IT'S ANOTHER!
WE GO SEE CARL-- MY NEW ASSISTANT! AY GIVE HIM MASTER KEY! SVENSON'S LEGS AIN'T SO GOOD NO MORE! YOUNG CARL-- HE GET UP AND DOWN DEM STAIRS BETTER!
I FORGOT YOU HAD A NEW HELPER!
5

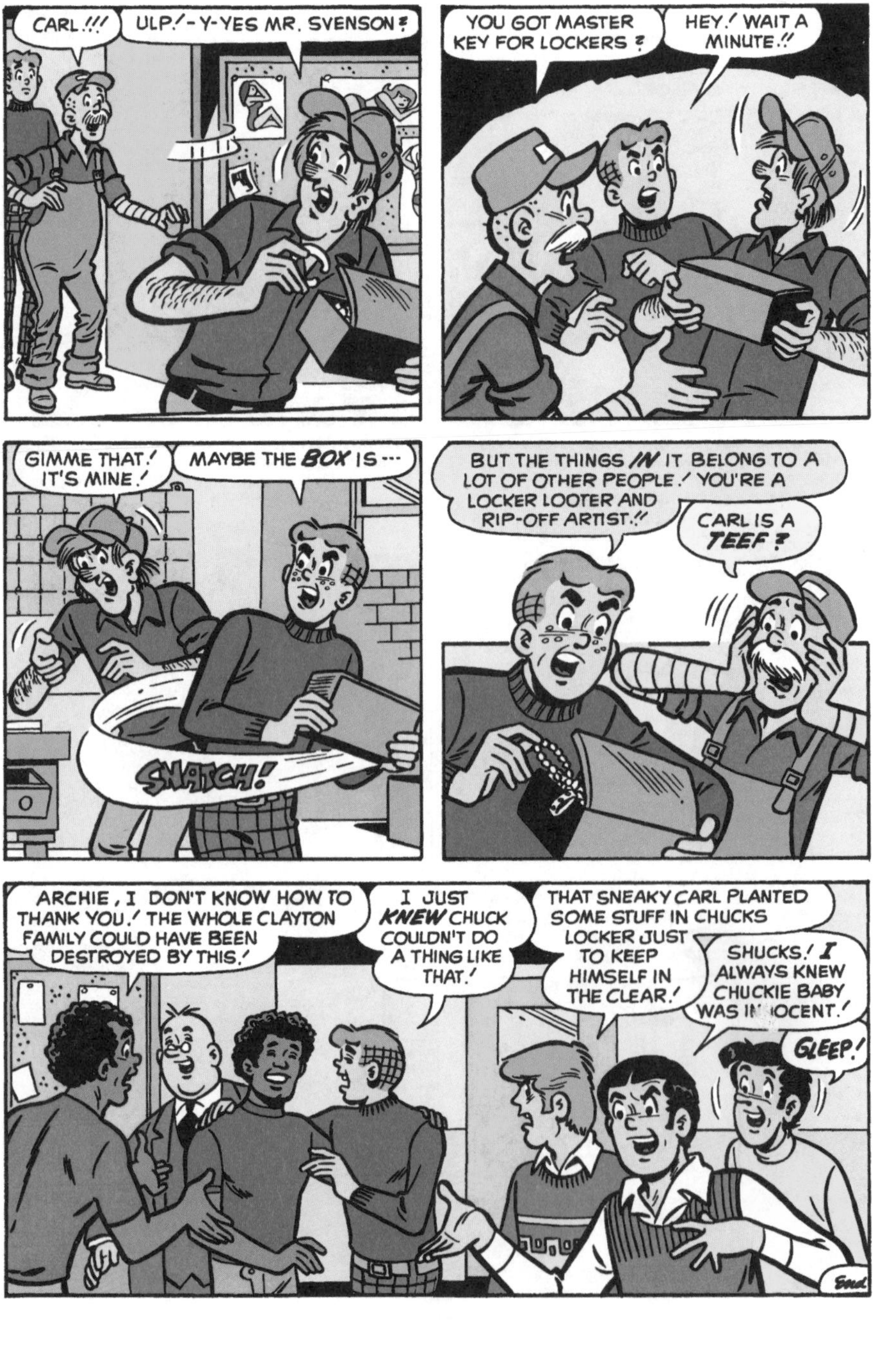
CARL!!!
ULP!-Y-YES MR. SVENSON?
YOU GOT MASTER KEY FOR LOCKERS?
HEY! WAIT A MINUTE!!
GIMME THAT! IT'S MINE!
MAYBE THE BOX IS---
SNATCH!
BUT THE THINGS IN IT BELONG TO A LOT OF OTHER PEOPLE! YOU'RE A LOCKER LOOTER AND RIP-OFF ARTIST!!
CARL IS A TEEF?
ARCHIE, I DON'T KNOW HOW TO THANK YOU! THE WHOLE CLAYTON FAMILY COULD HAVE BEEN DESTROYED BY THIS!
I JUST KNEW CHUCK COULDN'T DO A THING LIKE THAT!
THAT SNEAKY CARL PLANTED SOME STUFF IN CHUCKS LOCKER JUST TO KEEP HIMSELF IN THE CLEAR!
SHUCKS! I ALWAYS KNEW CHUCKIE BABY WAS INNOCENT!
GLEEP!
End

Archie at Riverdale in Stick Shift

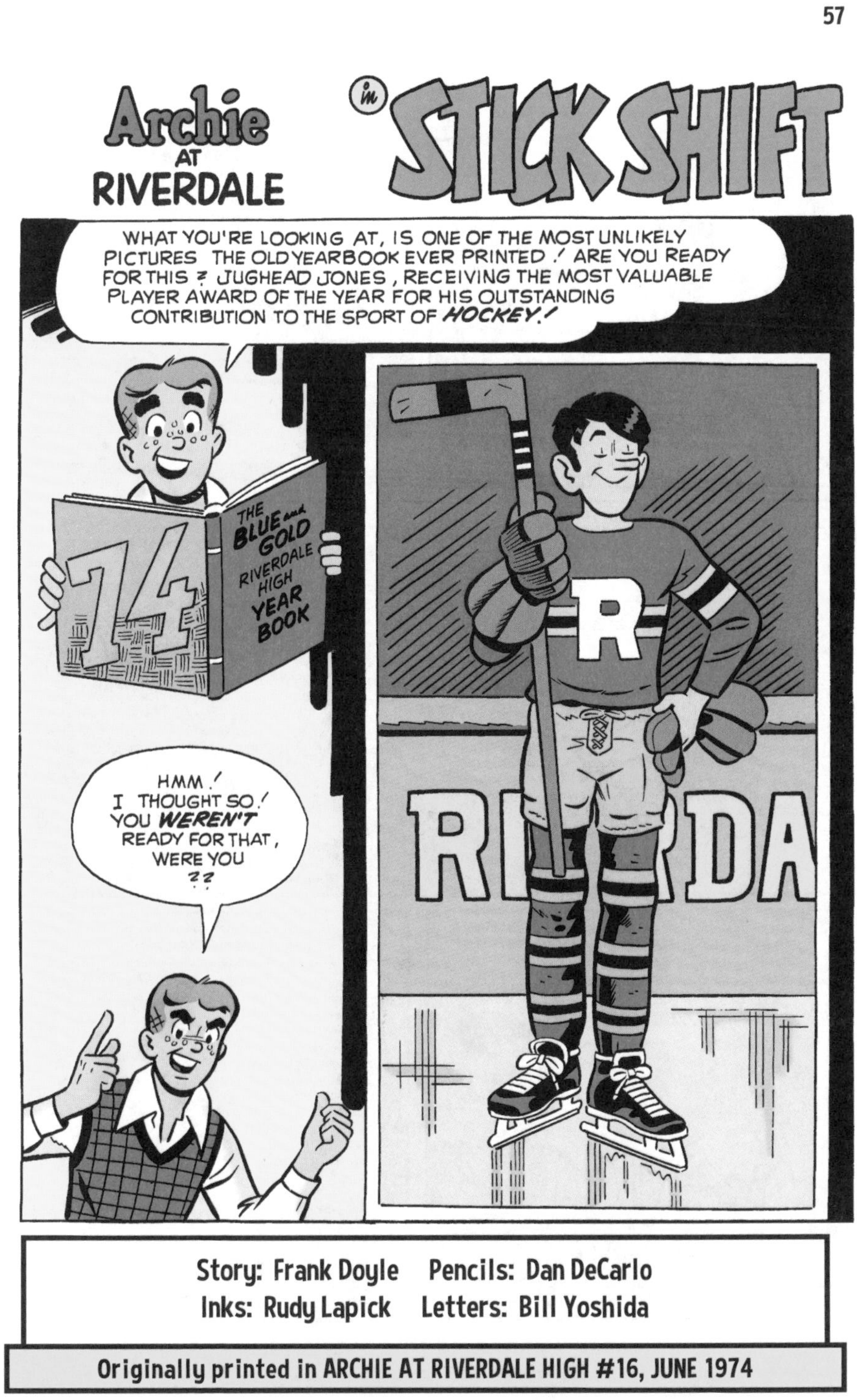
WHAT YOU'RE LOOKING AT, IS ONE OF THE MOST UNLIKELY PICTURES THE OLD YEARBOOK EVER PRINTED! ARE YOU READY FOR THIS ? JUGHEAD JONES, RECEIVING THE MOST VALUABLE PLAYER AWARD OF THE YEAR FOR HIS OUTSTANDING CONTRIBUTION TO THE SPORT OF HOCKEY!
74
THE BLUE and GOLD RIVERDALE HIGH YEAR BOOK
R
HMM! I THOUGHT SO! YOU WEREN'T READY FOR THAT, WERE YOU ??
RI DA

Story: Frank Doyle Pencils: Dan DeCarlo
Inks: Rudy Lapick Letters: Bill Yoshida

Originally printed in ARCHIE AT RIVERDALE HIGH #16, JUNE 1974

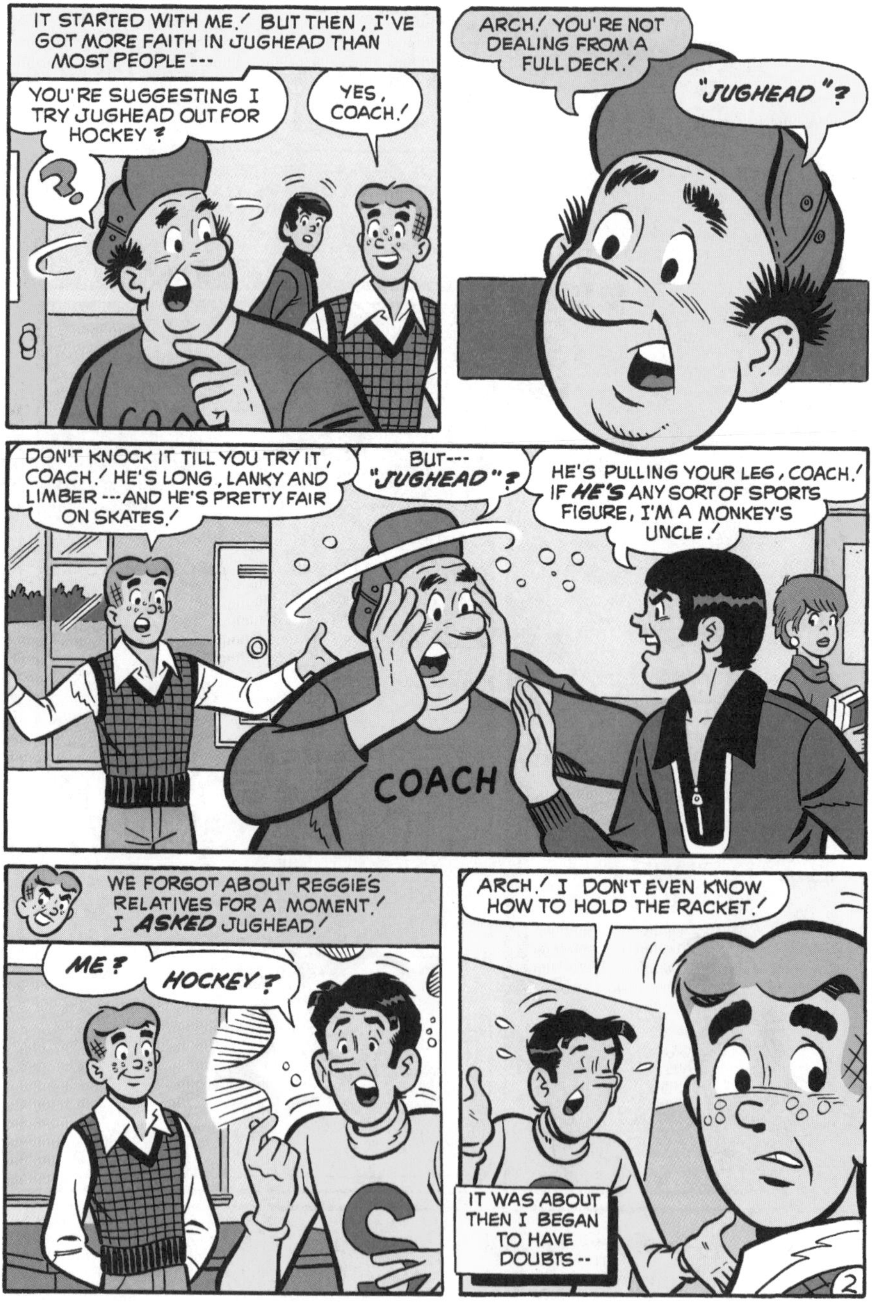
IT STARTED WITH ME! BUT THEN, I'VE GOT MORE FAITH IN JUGHEAD THAN MOST PEOPLE ---
YOU'RE SUGGESTING I TRY JUGHEAD OUT FOR HOCKEY ?
YES, COACH!
?
ARCH! YOU'RE NOT DEALING FROM A FULL DECK!
"JUGHEAD"?
COACH
DON'T KNOCK IT TILL YOU TRY IT, COACH! HE'S LONG, LANKY AND LIMBER --- AND HE'S PRETTY FAIR ON SKATES!
BUT--- "JUGHEAD"?
HE'S PULLING YOUR LEG, COACH! IF HE'S ANY SORT OF SPORTS FIGURE, I'M A MONKEY'S UNCLE!
COACH
WE FORGOT ABOUT REGGIE'S RELATIVES FOR A MOMENT! I ASKED JUGHEAD!
ME?
HOCKEY?
ARCH! I DON'T EVEN KNOW HOW TO HOLD THE RACKET!
IT WAS ABOUT THEN I BEGAN TO HAVE DOUBTS --
2

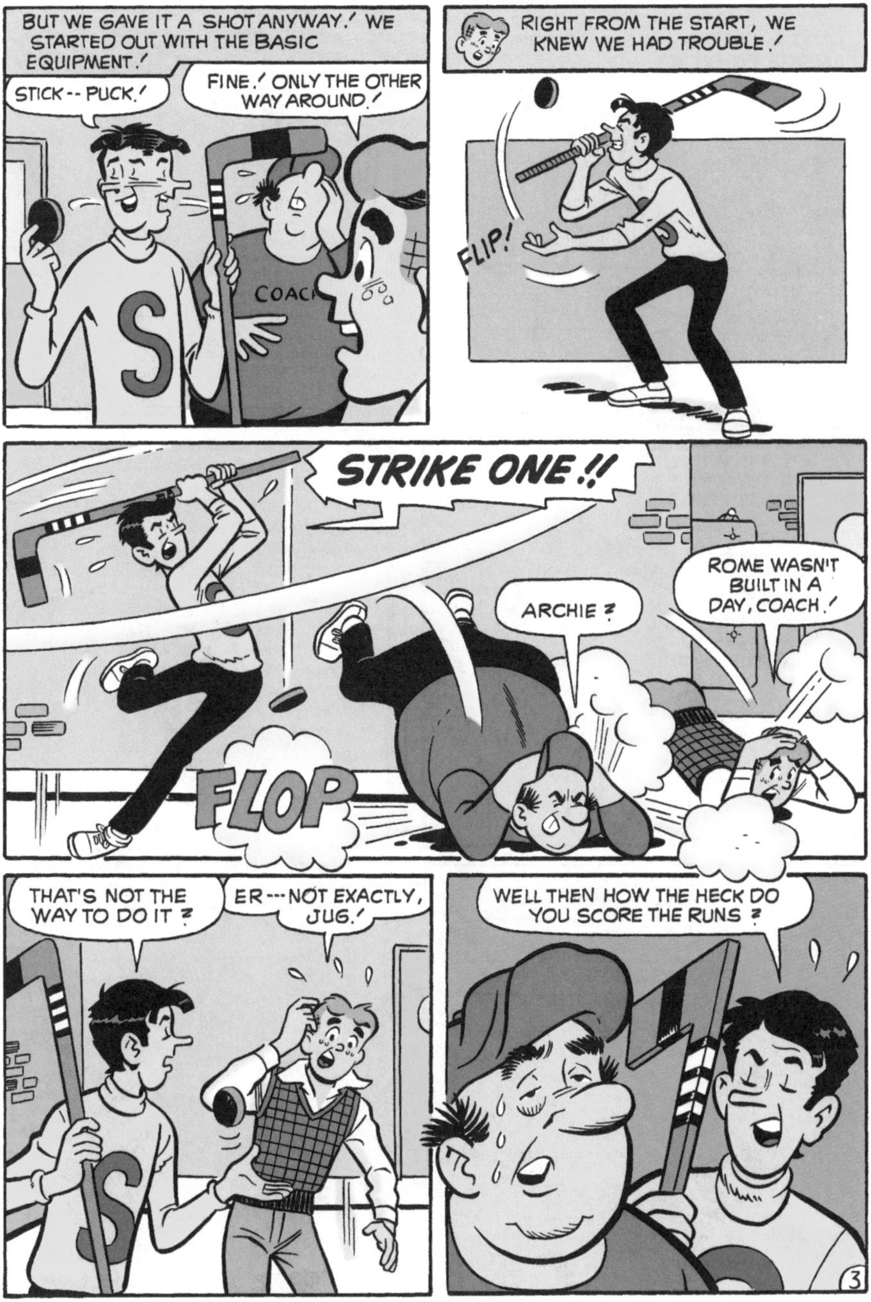
BUT WE GAVE IT A SHOT ANYWAY! WE STARTED OUT WITH THE BASIC EQUIPMENT!
STICK -- PUCK!
FINE! ONLY THE OTHER WAY AROUND!
COACH
RIGHT FROM THE START, WE KNEW WE HAD TROUBLE!
FLIP!
STRIKE ONE!!
ARCHIE?
ROME WASN'T BUILT IN A DAY, COACH!
FLOP
THAT'S NOT THE WAY TO DO IT?
ER --- NOT EXACTLY, JUG!
WELL THEN HOW THE HECK DO YOU SCORE THE RUNS?
3

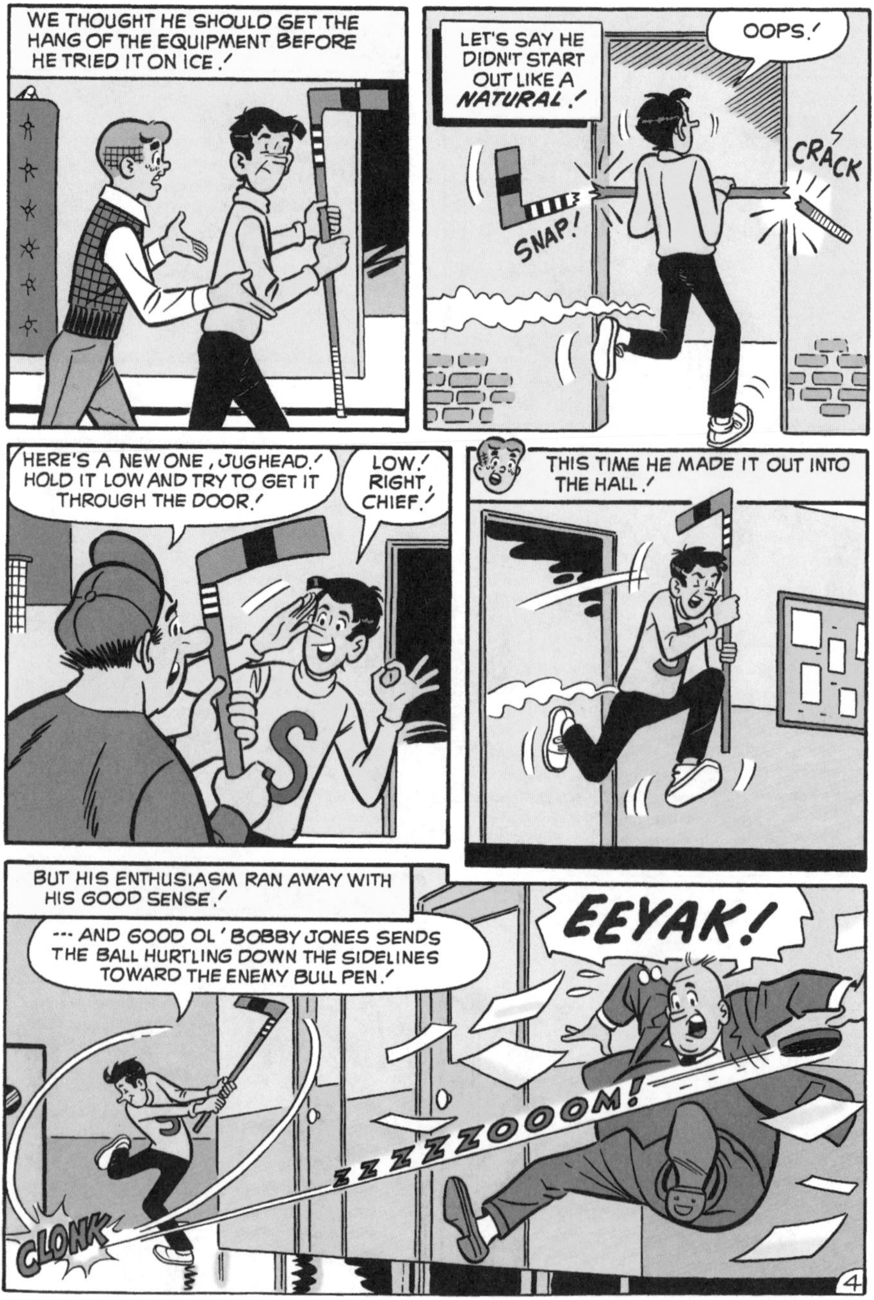
WE THOUGHT HE SHOULD GET THE HANG OF THE EQUIPMENT BEFORE HE TRIED IT ON ICE!
LET'S SAY HE DIDN'T START OUT LIKE A NATURAL!
OOPS!
SNAP!
CRACK
HERE'S A NEW ONE, JUGHEAD! HOLD IT LOW AND TRY TO GET IT THROUGH THE DOOR!
LOW! RIGHT, CHIEF!
THIS TIME HE MADE IT OUT INTO THE HALL!
BUT HIS ENTHUSIASM RAN AWAY WITH HIS GOOD SENSE!
--- AND GOOD OL' BOBBY JONES SENDS THE BALL HURTLING DOWN THE SIDELINES TOWARD THE ENEMY BULL PEN!
EEYAK!
CLONK
ZZZZZZOOOOOM!
4

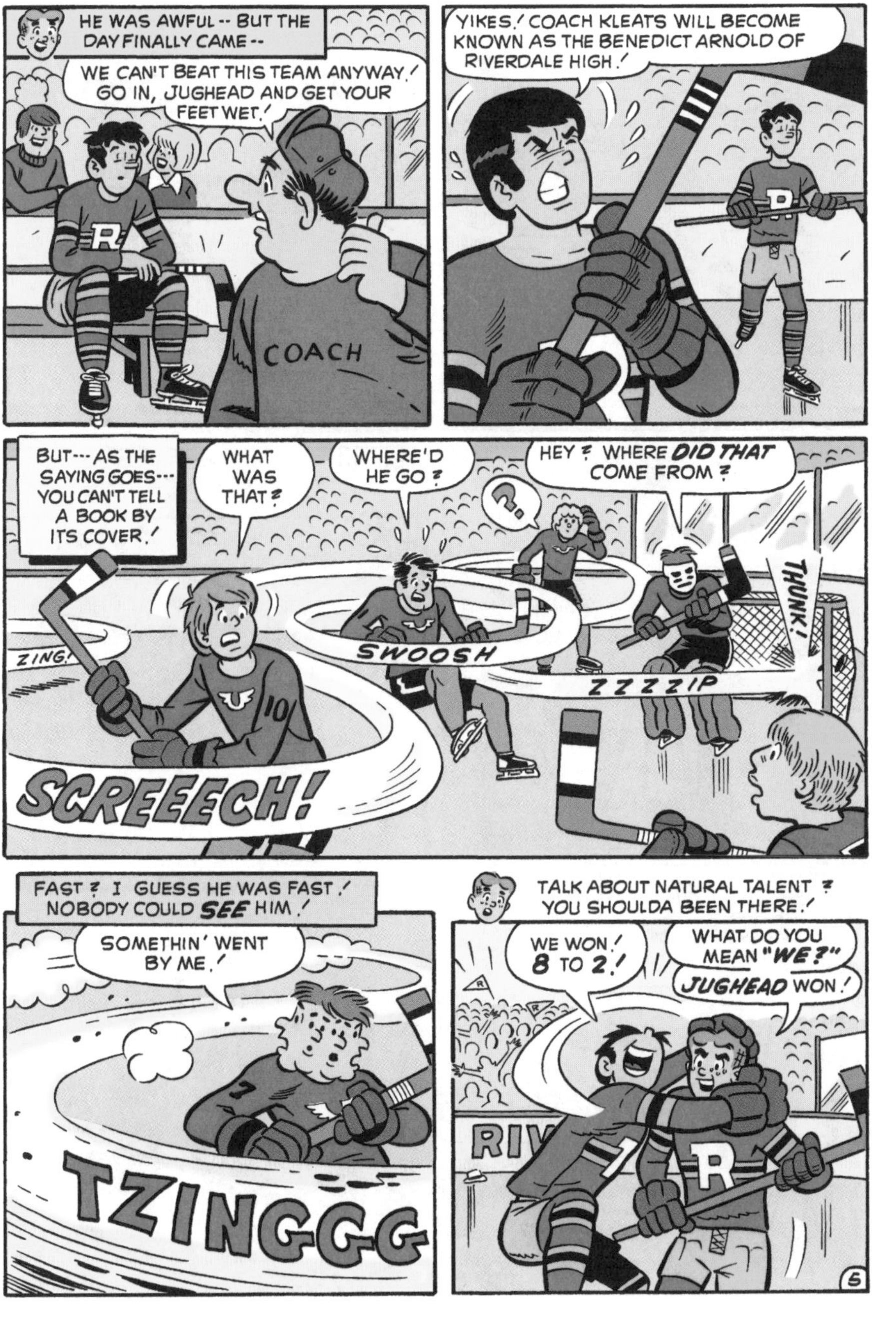
HE WAS AWFUL -- BUT THE DAY FINALLY CAME --
WE CAN'T BEAT THIS TEAM ANYWAY! GO IN, JUGHEAD AND GET YOUR FEET WET!
COACH
YIKES! COACH KLEATS WILL BECOME KNOWN AS THE BENEDICT ARNOLD OF RIVERDALE HIGH!
BUT--- AS THE SAYING GOES--- YOU CAN'T TELL A BOOK BY ITS COVER!
WHAT WAS THAT?
WHERE'D HE GO?
HEY? WHERE DID THAT COME FROM?
THUNK!
ZING!
SWOOSH
ZZZZIP
SCREEECH!
FAST? I GUESS HE WAS FAST! NOBODY COULD SEE HIM!
SOMETHIN' WENT BY ME!
TZINGGG
TALK ABOUT NATURAL TALENT? YOU SHOULDA BEEN THERE!
WE WON! 8 TO 2!
WHAT DO YOU MEAN "WE?" JUGHEAD WON!
RIV
5

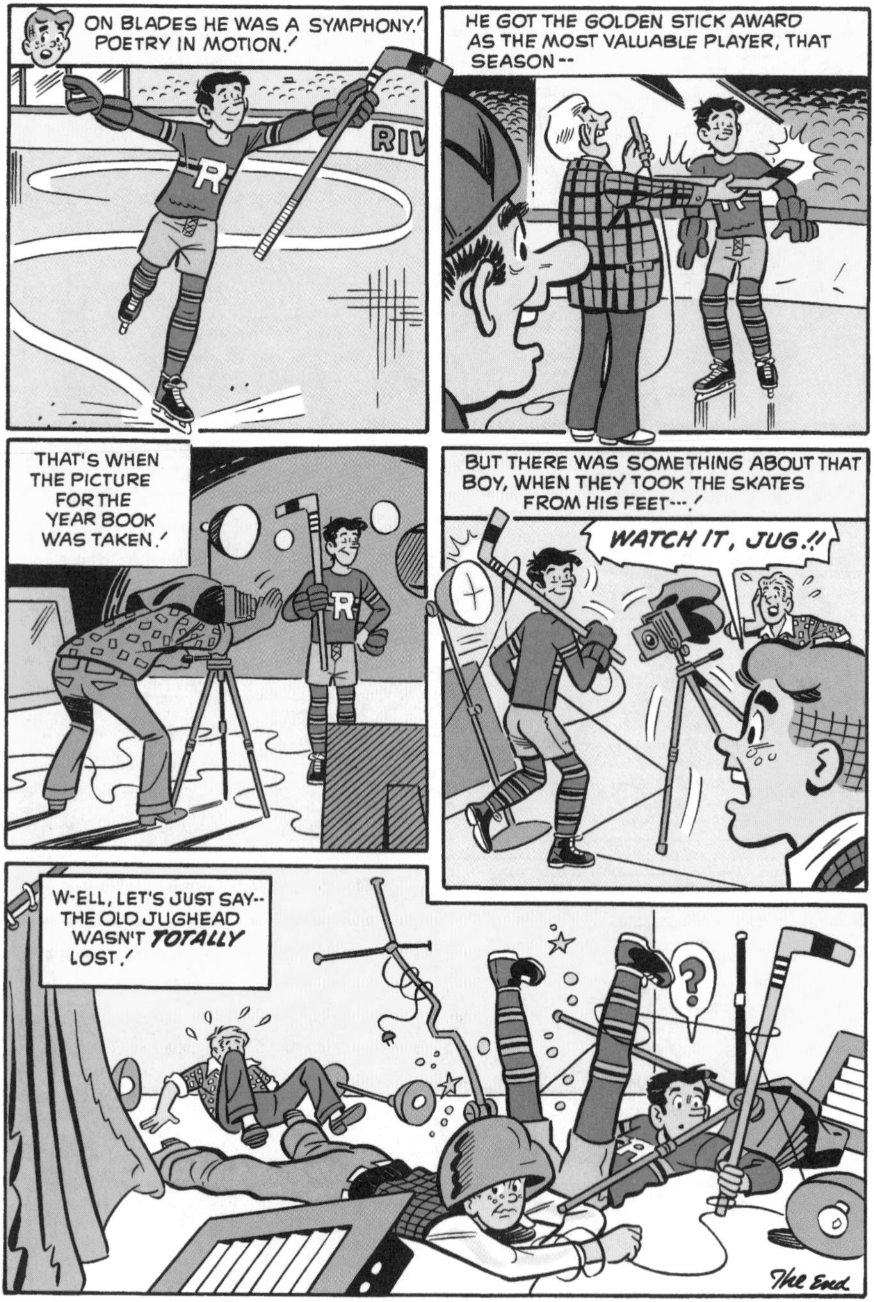
ON BLADES HE WAS A SYMPHONY! POETRY IN MOTION!
RIV
HE GOT THE GOLDEN STICK AWARD AS THE MOST VALUABLE PLAYER, THAT SEASON --
THAT'S WHEN THE PICTURE FOR THE YEAR BOOK WAS TAKEN!
BUT THERE WAS SOMETHING ABOUT THAT BOY, WHEN THEY TOOK THE SKATES FROM HIS FEET---!
WATCH IT, JUG!!
W-ELL, LET'S JUST SAY-- THE OLD JUGHEAD WASN'T TOTALLY LOST!
?
The End

Archie at RIVERDALE in "LAUGH CLOWN LAUGH"

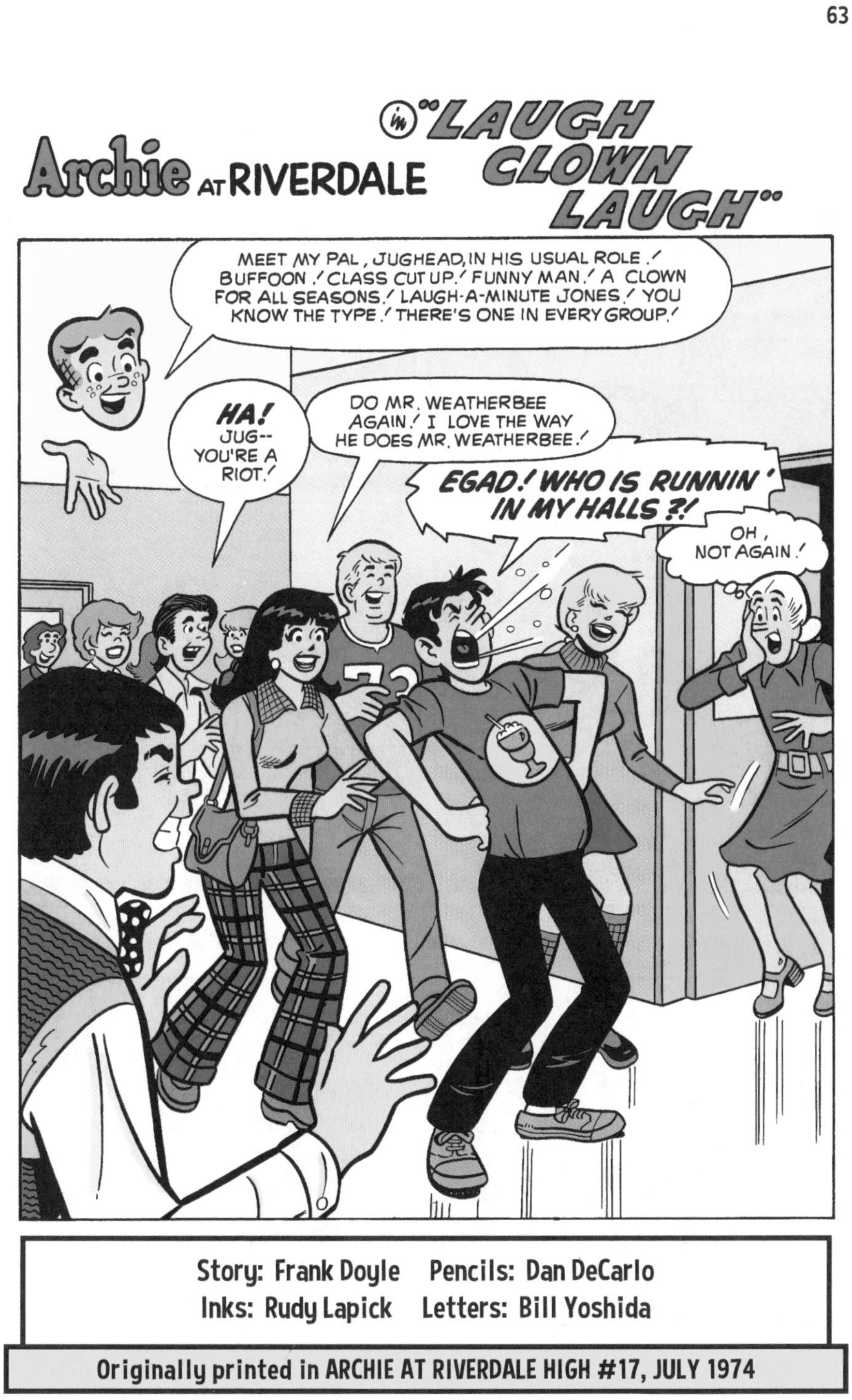
MEET MY PAL, JUGHEAD, IN HIS USUAL ROLE.! BUFFOON.! CLASS CUT UP.! FUNNY MAN.! A CLOWN FOR ALL SEASONS.! LAUGH-A-MINUTE JONES.! YOU KNOW THE TYPE.! THERE'S ONE IN EVERY GROUP.!
HA! JUG-- YOU'RE A RIOT.!
DO MR. WEATHERBEE AGAIN.! I LOVE THE WAY HE DOES MR. WEATHERBEE.!
EGAD.! WHO IS RUNNIN' IN MY HALLS ?!
OH, NOT AGAIN.!

Story: Frank Doyle Pencils: Dan DeCarlo
Inks: Rudy Lapick Letters: Bill Yoshida

Originally printed in ARCHIE AT RIVERDALE HIGH #17, JULY 1974

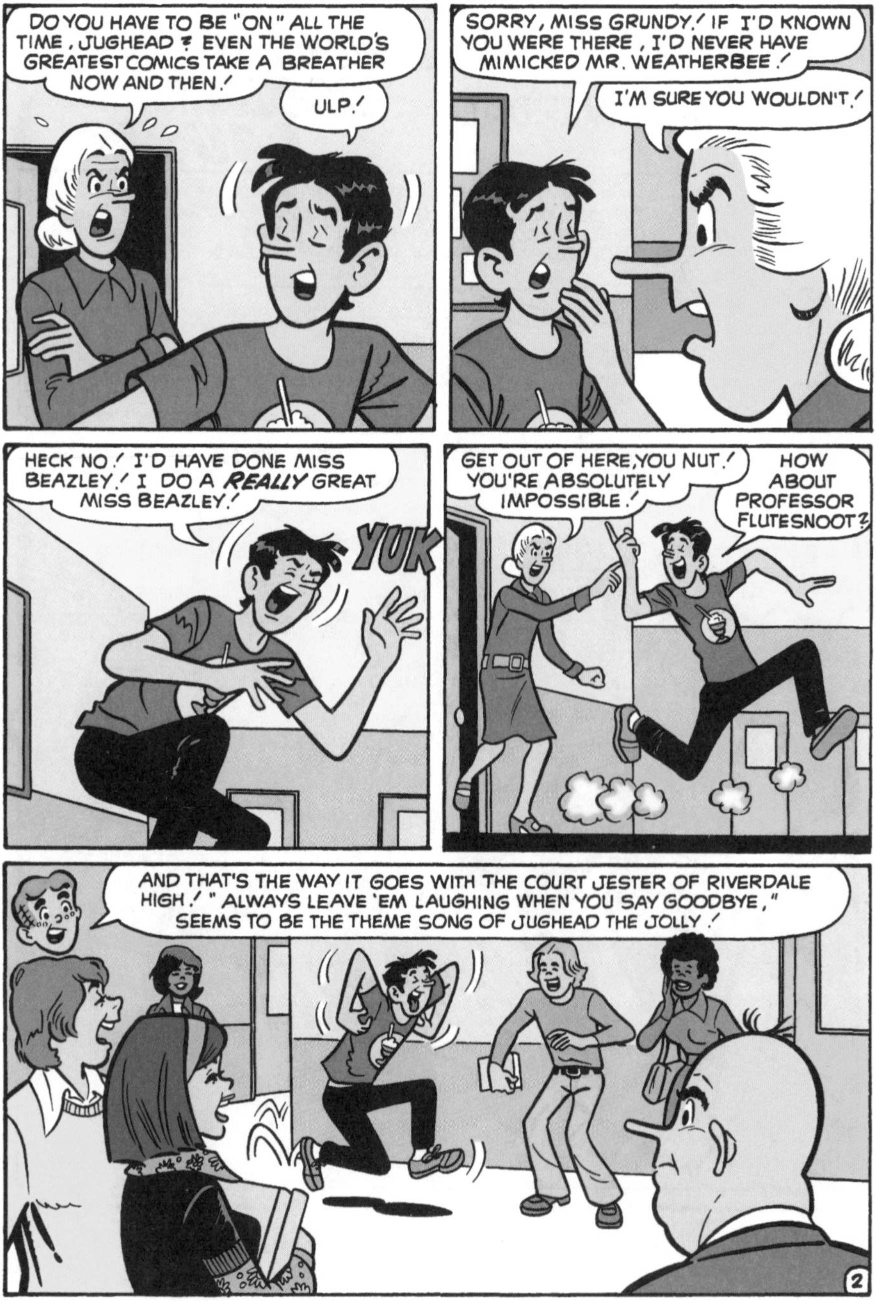
DO YOU HAVE TO BE "ON" ALL THE TIME, JUGHEAD? EVEN THE WORLD'S GREATEST COMICS TAKE A BREATHER NOW AND THEN!
ULP!
SORRY, MISS GRUNDY! IF I'D KNOWN YOU WERE THERE, I'D NEVER HAVE MIMICKED MR. WEATHERBEE!
I'M SURE YOU WOULDN'T!
HECK NO! I'D HAVE DONE MISS BEAZLEY! I DO A REALLY GREAT MISS BEAZLEY!
YUK
GET OUT OF HERE, YOU NUT! YOU'RE ABSOLUTELY IMPOSSIBLE!
HOW ABOUT PROFESSOR FLUTESNOOT?
AND THAT'S THE WAY IT GOES WITH THE COURT JESTER OF RIVERDALE HIGH! "ALWAYS LEAVE 'EM LAUGHING WHEN YOU SAY GOODBYE," SEEMS TO BE THE THEME SONG OF JUGHEAD THE JOLLY!
2

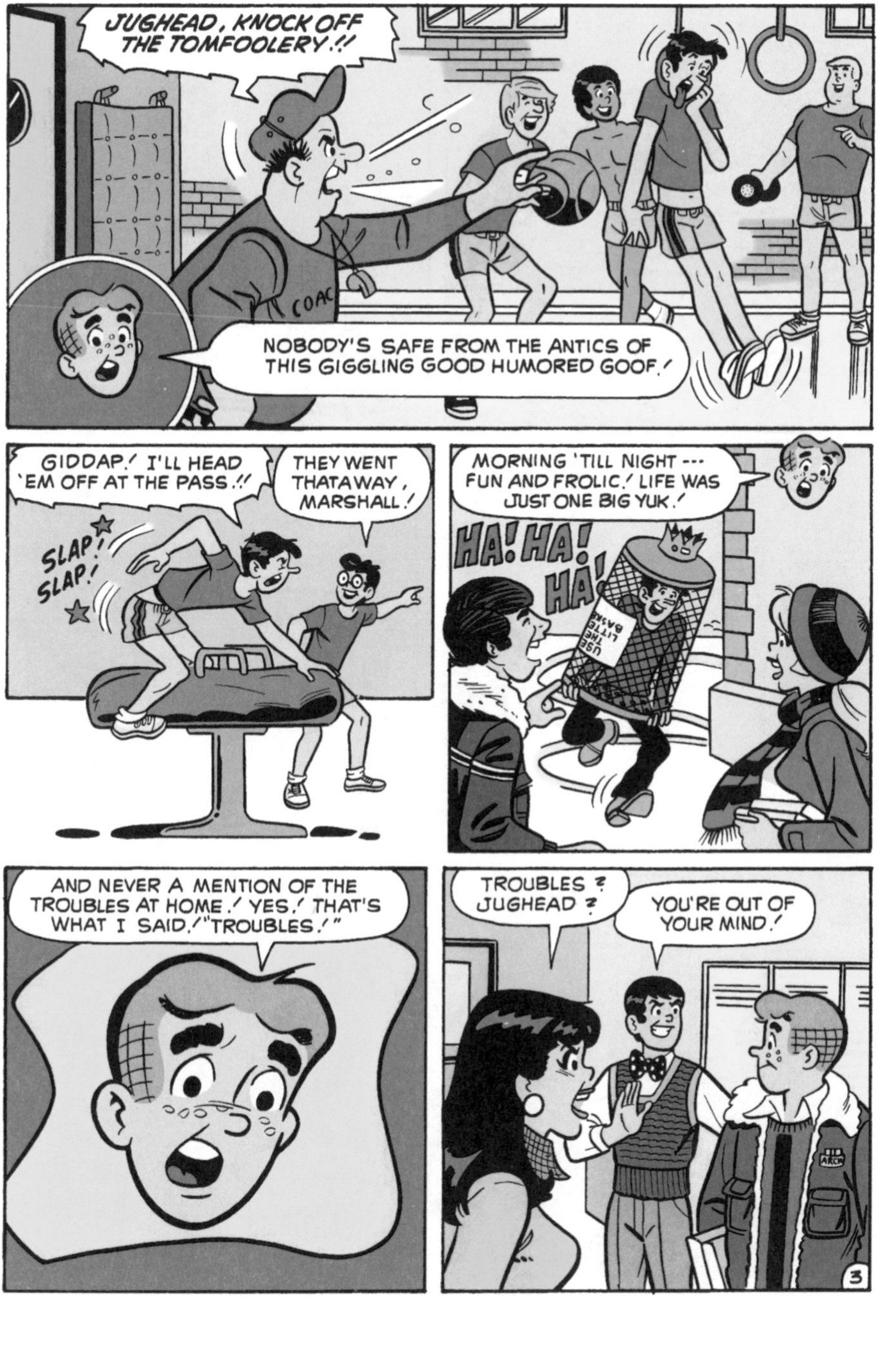
JUGHEAD, KNOCK OFF THE TOMFOOLERY!!
NOBODY'S SAFE FROM THE ANTICS OF THIS GIGGLING GOOD HUMORED GOOF!
GIDDAP! I'LL HEAD 'EM OFF AT THE PASS!!
THEY WENT THATAWAY, MARSHALL!
SLAP! SLAP!
MORNING 'TILL NIGHT --- FUN AND FROLIC! LIFE WAS JUST ONE BIG YUK!
HA! HA! HA!
AND NEVER A MENTION OF THE TROUBLES AT HOME! YES! THAT'S WHAT I SAID! "TROUBLES!"
TROUBLES? JUGHEAD?
YOU'RE OUT OF YOUR MIND!

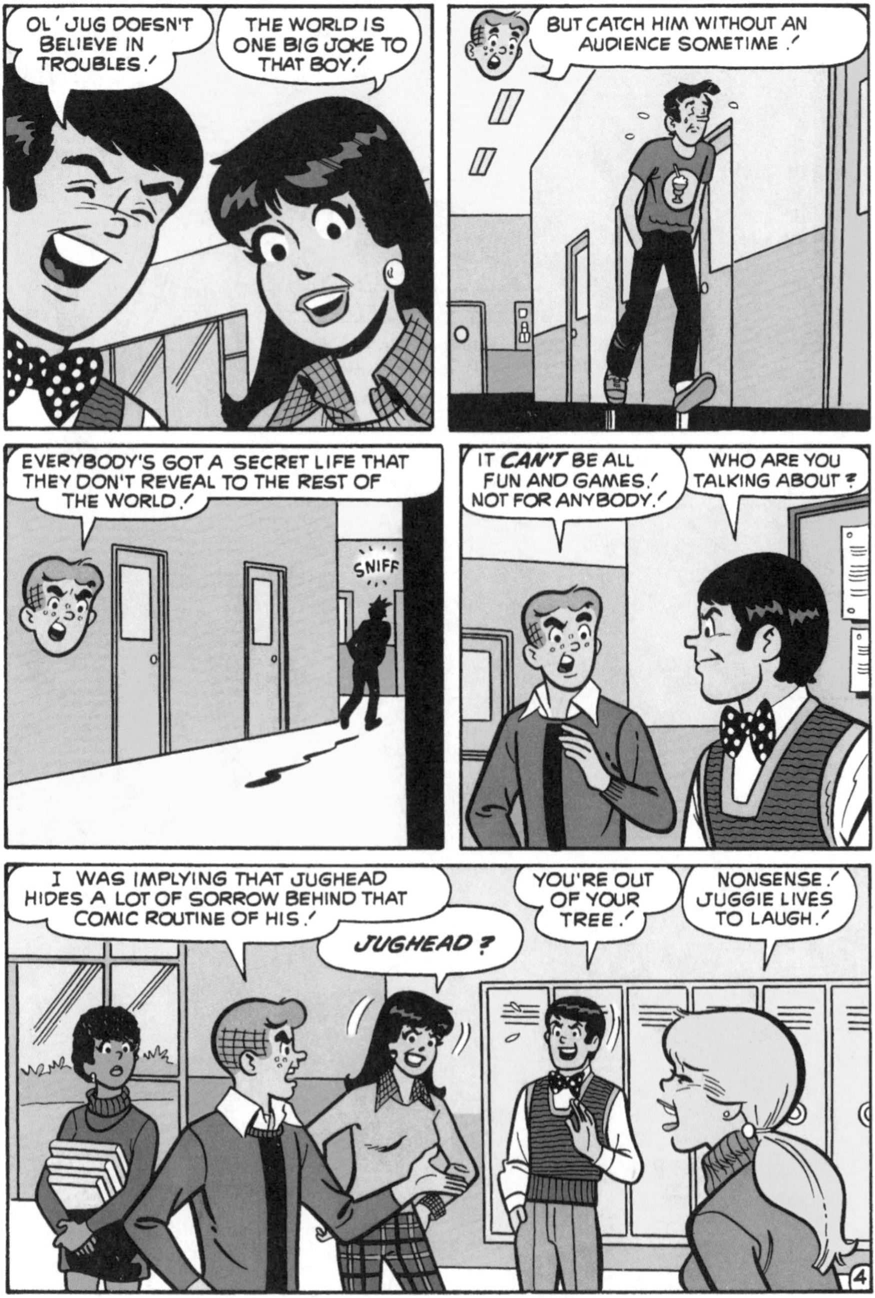
OL' JUG DOESN'T BELIEVE IN TROUBLES.!
THE WORLD IS ONE BIG JOKE TO THAT BOY.!
BUT CATCH HIM WITHOUT AN AUDIENCE SOMETIME.!
EVERYBODY'S GOT A SECRET LIFE THAT THEY DON'T REVEAL TO THE REST OF THE WORLD.!
SNIFF
IT CAN'T BE ALL FUN AND GAMES.! NOT FOR ANYBODY.!
WHO ARE YOU TALKING ABOUT?
I WAS IMPLYING THAT JUGHEAD HIDES A LOT OF SORROW BEHIND THAT COMIC ROUTINE OF HIS.!
JUGHEAD?
YOU'RE OUT OF YOUR TREE.!
NONSENSE.! JUGGIE LIVES TO LAUGH.!
4

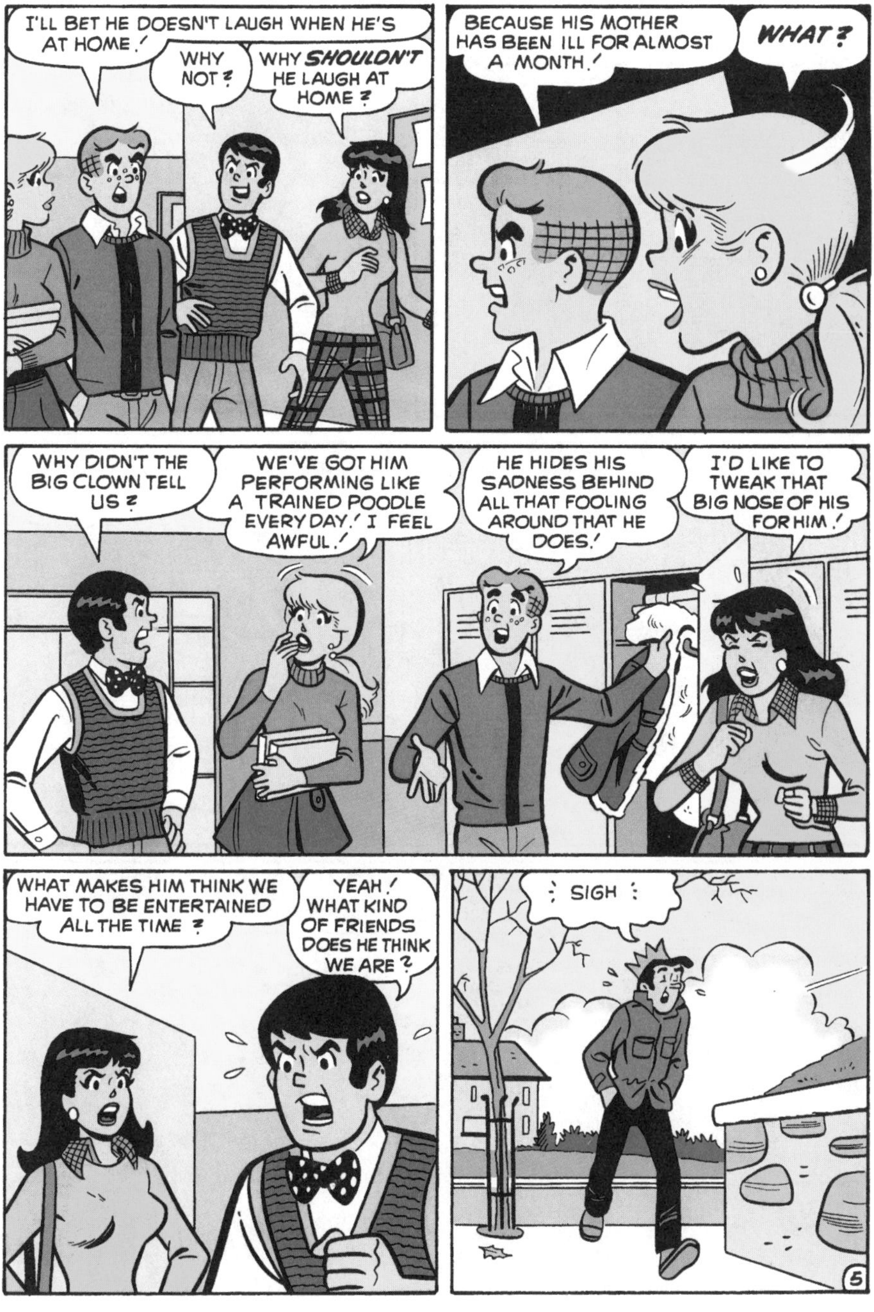
I'LL BET HE DOESN'T LAUGH WHEN HE'S AT HOME!
WHY NOT?
WHY SHOULDN'T HE LAUGH AT HOME?
BECAUSE HIS MOTHER HAS BEEN ILL FOR ALMOST A MONTH!
WHAT?
WHY DIDN'T THE BIG CLOWN TELL US?
WE'VE GOT HIM PERFORMING LIKE A TRAINED POODLE EVERY DAY! I FEEL AWFUL!
HE HIDES HIS SADNESS BEHIND ALL THAT FOOLING AROUND THAT HE DOES!
I'D LIKE TO TWEAK THAT BIG NOSE OF HIS FOR HIM!
WHAT MAKES HIM THINK WE HAVE TO BE ENTERTAINED ALL THE TIME?
YEAH! WHAT KIND OF FRIENDS DOES HE THINK WE ARE?
SIGH
5

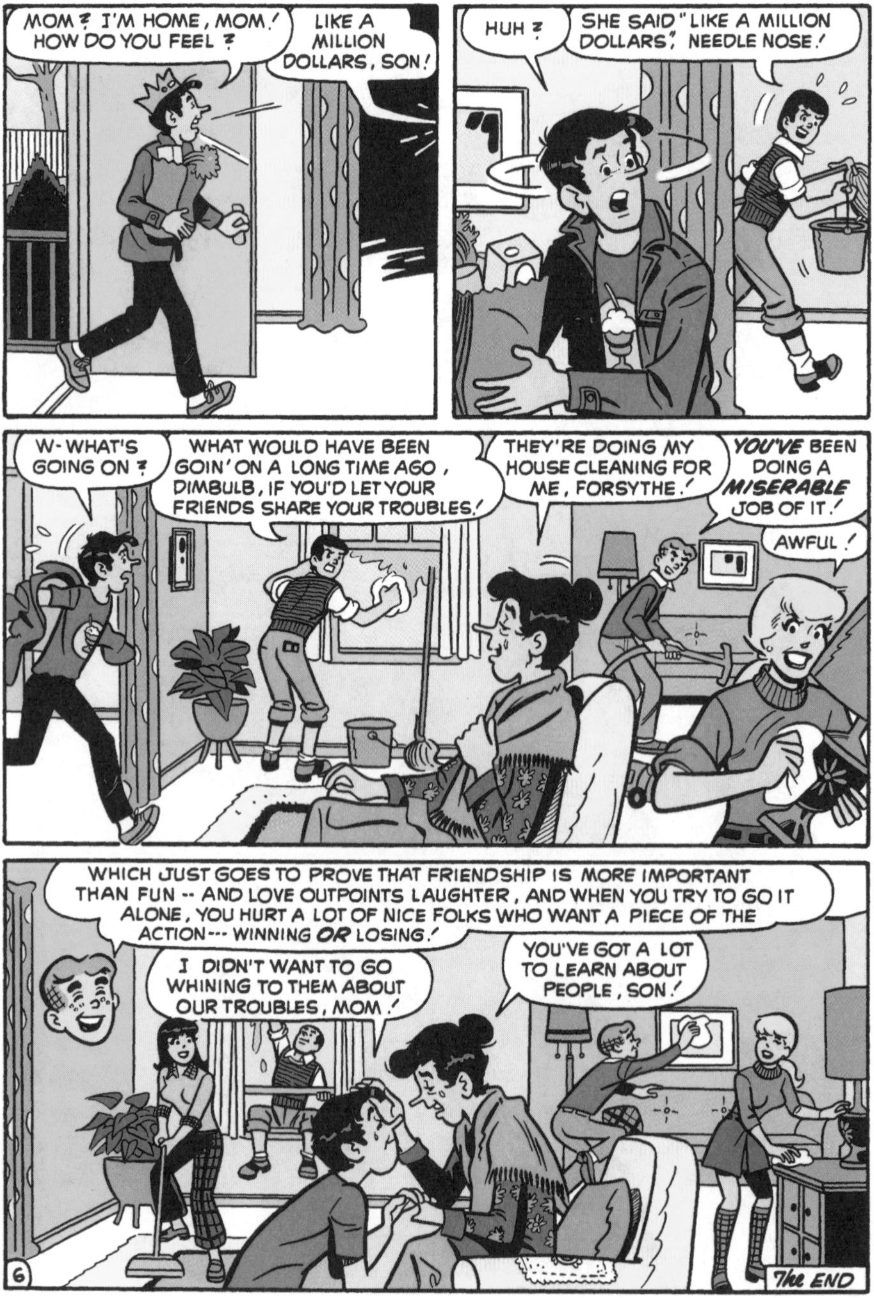
MOM? I'M HOME, MOM! HOW DO YOU FEEL?
LIKE A MILLION DOLLARS, SON!
HUH?
SHE SAID "LIKE A MILLION DOLLARS", NEEDLE NOSE!
W-WHAT'S GOING ON?
WHAT WOULD HAVE BEEN GOIN' ON A LONG TIME AGO, DIMBULB, IF YOU'D LET YOUR FRIENDS SHARE YOUR TROUBLES!
THEY'RE DOING MY HOUSE CLEANING FOR ME, FORSYTHE!
YOU'VE BEEN DOING A MISERABLE JOB OF IT!
AWFUL!
WHICH JUST GOES TO PROVE THAT FRIENDSHIP IS MORE IMPORTANT THAN FUN -- AND LOVE OUTPOINTS LAUGHTER, AND WHEN YOU TRY TO GO IT ALONE, YOU HURT A LOT OF NICE FOLKS WHO WANT A PIECE OF THE ACTION--- WINNING OR LOSING!
I DIDN'T WANT TO GO WHINING TO THEM ABOUT OUR TROUBLES, MOM!
YOU'VE GOT A LOT TO LEARN ABOUT PEOPLE, SON!
6
The END

Archie at Riverdale in PEP RALLY

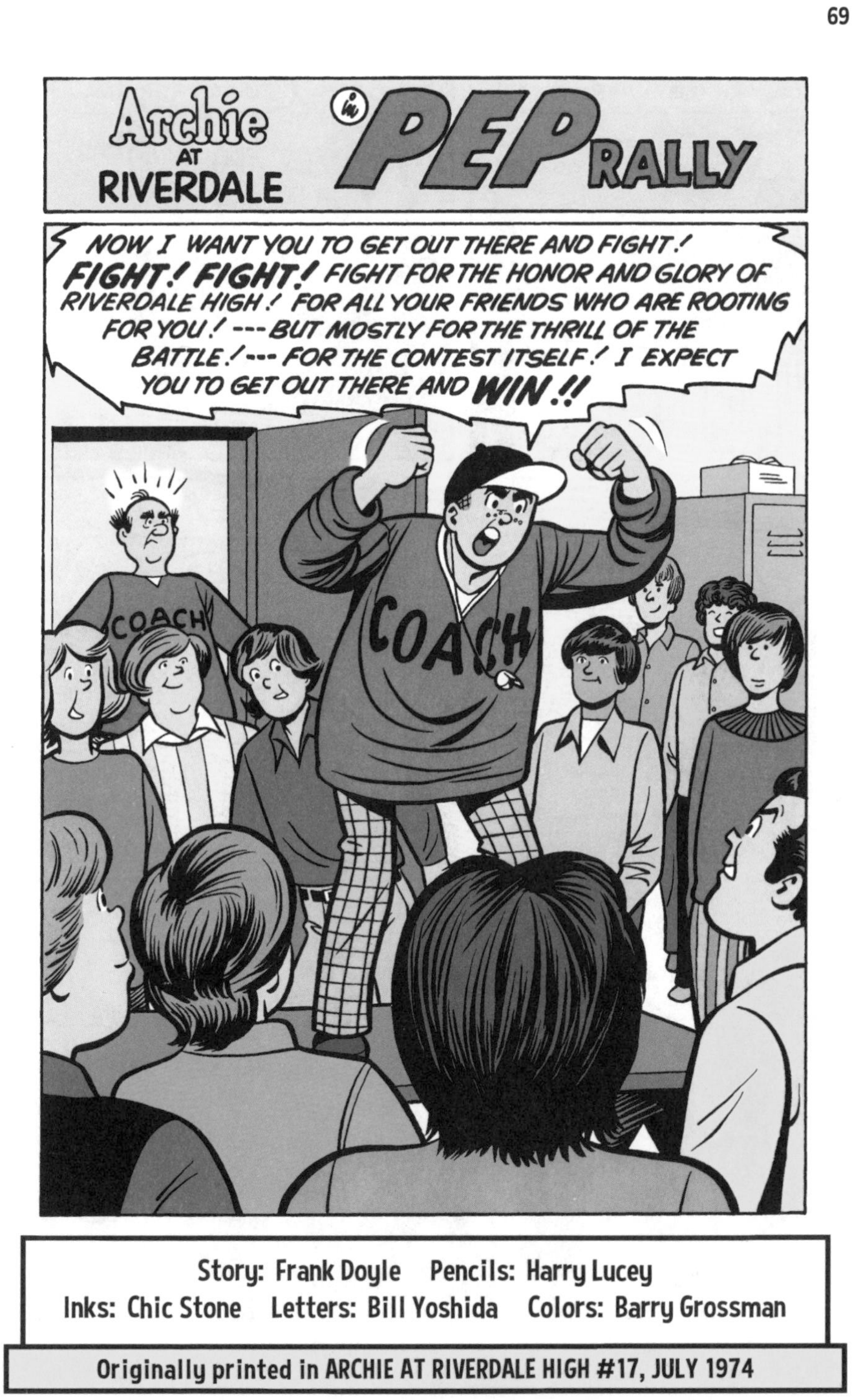
NOW I WANT YOU TO GET OUT THERE AND FIGHT! FIGHT! FIGHT! FIGHT FOR THE HONOR AND GLORY OF RIVERDALE HIGH! FOR ALL YOUR FRIENDS WHO ARE ROOTING FOR YOU! ---BUT MOSTLY FOR THE THRILL OF THE BATTLE! --- FOR THE CONTEST ITSELF! I EXPECT YOU TO GET OUT THERE AND WIN!!
COACH
COACH

Story: Frank Doyle Pencils: Harry Lucey
Inks: Chic Stone Letters: Bill Yoshida Colors: Barry Grossman

Originally printed in ARCHIE AT RIVERDALE HIGH #17, JULY 1974

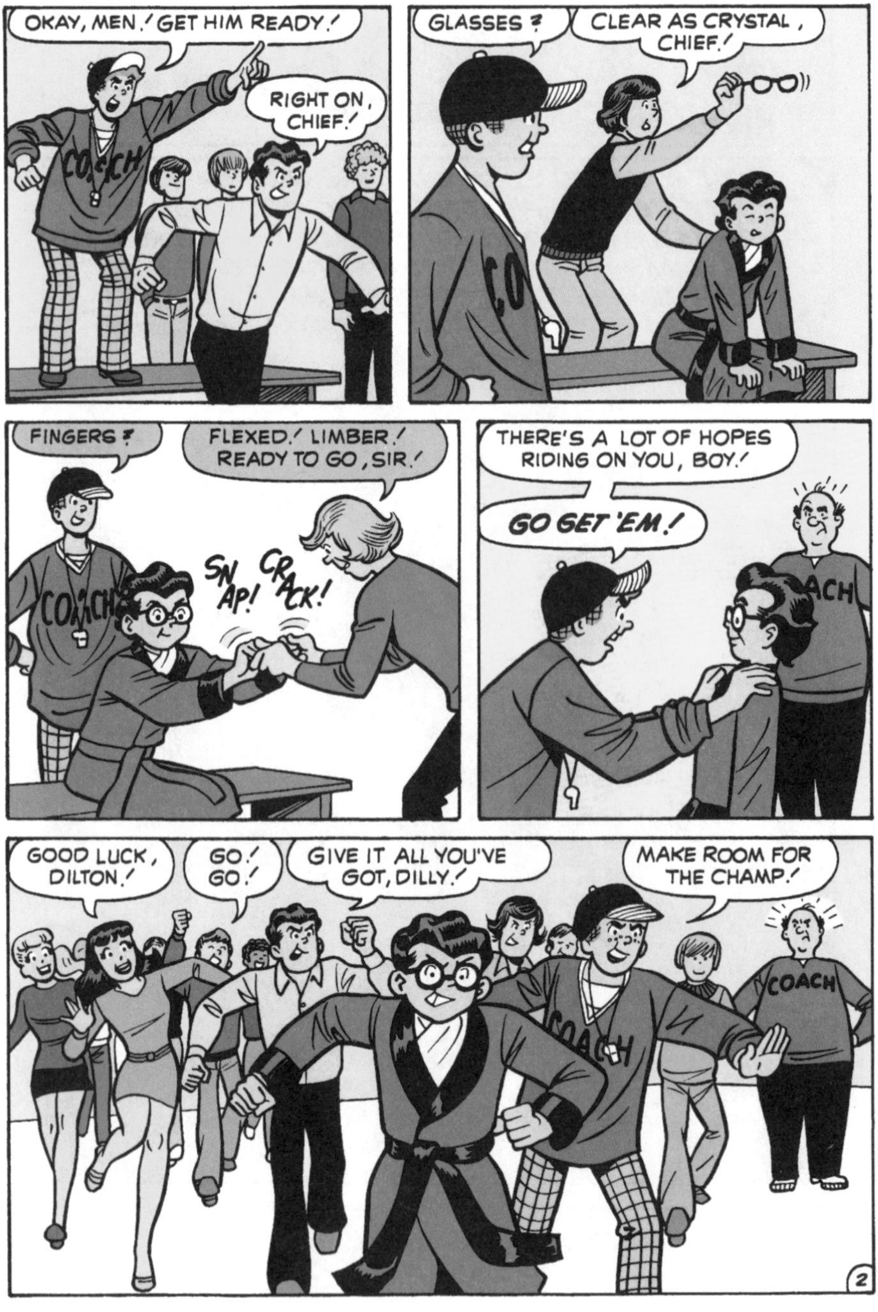
OKAY, MEN! GET HIM READY!
RIGHT ON, CHIEF!
GLASSES ?
CLEAR AS CRYSTAL, CHIEF!
FINGERS ?
FLEXED! LIMBER! READY TO GO, SIR!
SNAP! CRACK!
THERE'S A LOT OF HOPES RIDING ON YOU, BOY!
GO GET 'EM!
ACH
GOOD LUCK, DILTON!
GO! GO!
GIVE IT ALL YOU'VE GOT, DILLY!
MAKE ROOM FOR THE CHAMP!
COACH
2

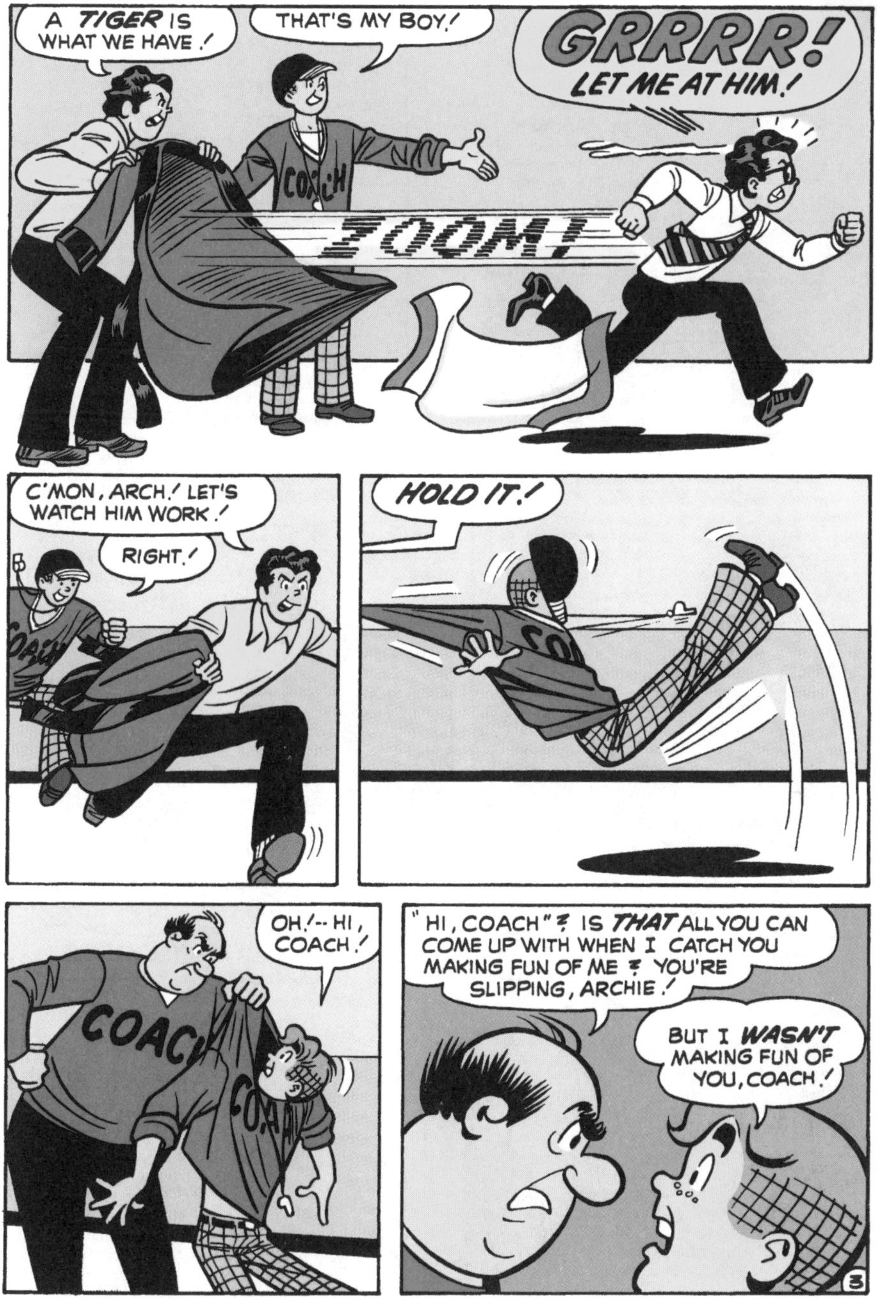
A TIGER IS WHAT WE HAVE!
THAT'S MY BOY!
GRRRR! LET ME AT HIM!
ZOOM!
C'MON, ARCH! LET'S WATCH HIM WORK!
RIGHT!
HOLD IT!
OH!-- HI, COACH!
"HI, COACH"? IS THAT ALL YOU CAN COME UP WITH WHEN I CATCH YOU MAKING FUN OF ME? YOU'RE SLIPPING, ARCHIE!
BUT I WASN'T MAKING FUN OF YOU, COACH!
3

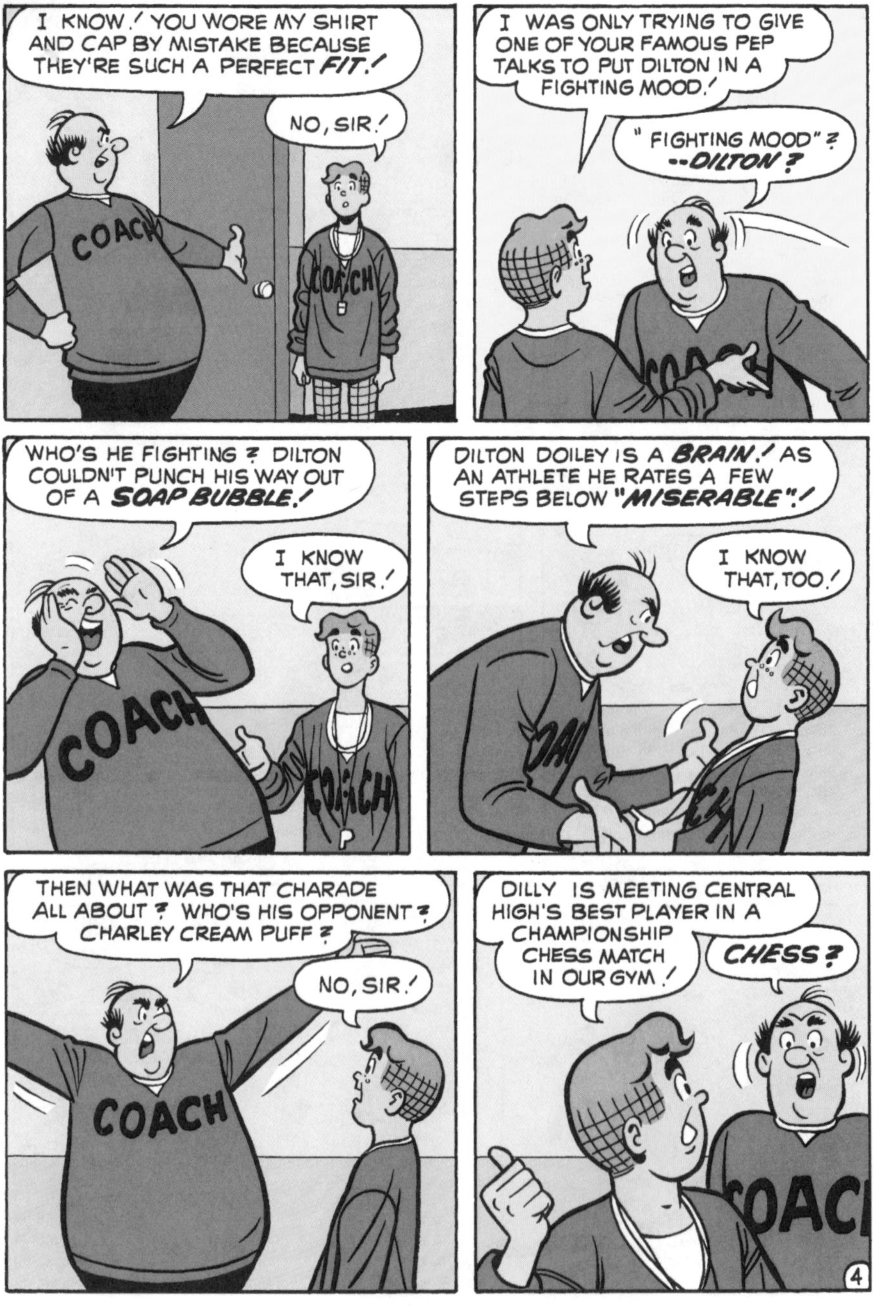
I KNOW! YOU WORE MY SHIRT AND CAP BY MISTAKE BECAUSE THEY'RE SUCH A PERFECT FIT!
NO, SIR!
COACH
COACH
I WAS ONLY TRYING TO GIVE ONE OF YOUR FAMOUS PEP TALKS TO PUT DILTON IN A FIGHTING MOOD!
" FIGHTING MOOD"? --DILTON?
WHO'S HE FIGHTING? DILTON COULDN'T PUNCH HIS WAY OUT OF A SOAP BUBBLE!
I KNOW THAT, SIR!
COACH
COACH
DILTON DOILEY IS A BRAIN! AS AN ATHLETE HE RATES A FEW STEPS BELOW "MISERABLE"!
I KNOW THAT, TOO!
THEN WHAT WAS THAT CHARADE ALL ABOUT? WHO'S HIS OPPONENT? CHARLEY CREAM PUFF?
NO, SIR!
COACH
DILLY IS MEETING CENTRAL HIGH'S BEST PLAYER IN A CHAMPIONSHIP CHESS MATCH IN OUR GYM!
CHESS?
4

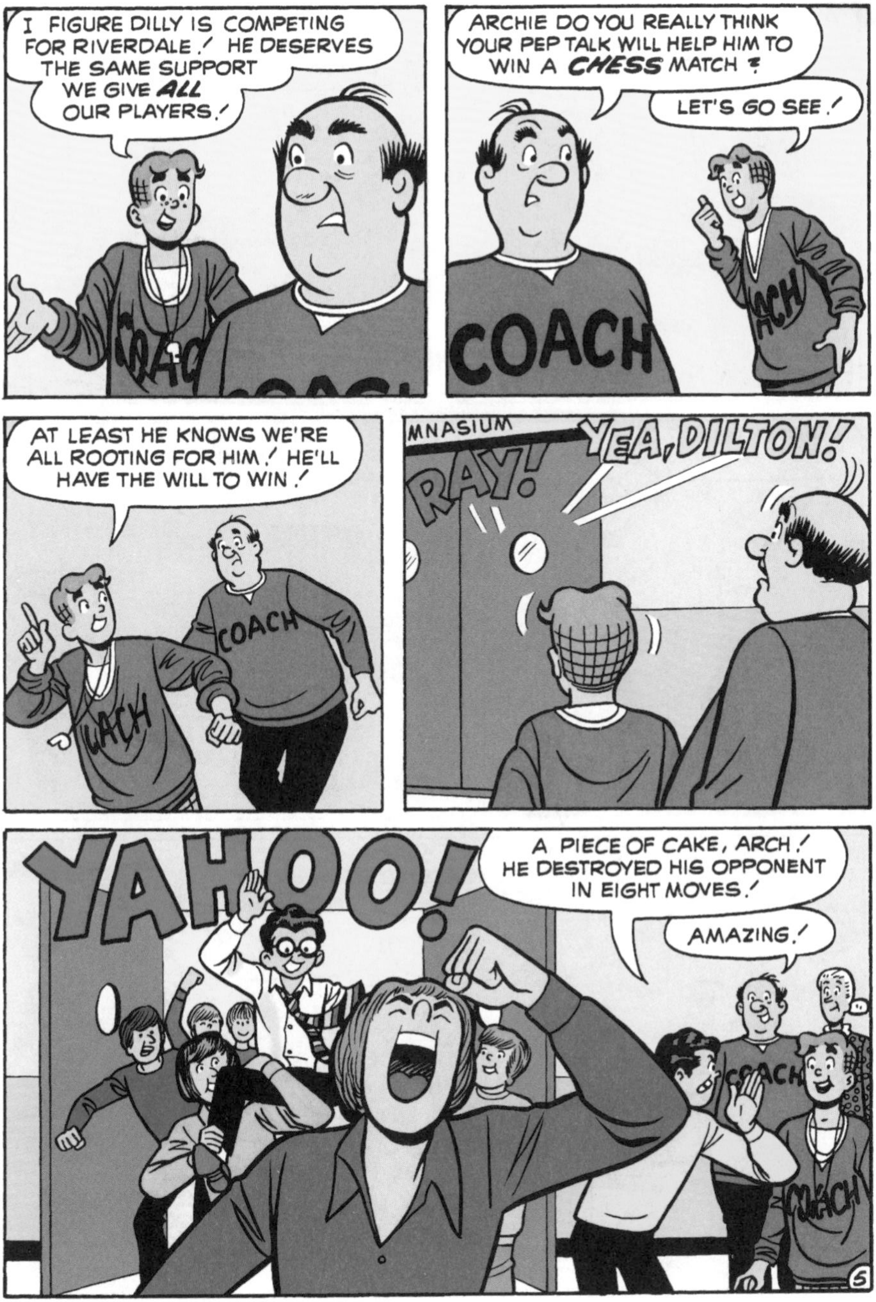
I FIGURE DILLY IS COMPETING FOR RIVERDALE! HE DESERVES THE SAME SUPPORT WE GIVE ALL OUR PLAYERS!
COACH
ARCHIE DO YOU REALLY THINK YOUR PEP TALK WILL HELP HIM TO WIN A CHESS MATCH?
LET'S GO SEE!
COACH
AT LEAST HE KNOWS WE'RE ALL ROOTING FOR HIM! HE'LL HAVE THE WILL TO WIN!
COACH
MNASIUM
YEA, DILTON!
RAY!
YAHOO!
A PIECE OF CAKE, ARCH! HE DESTROYED HIS OPPONENT IN EIGHT MOVES!
AMAZING!
COACH
5

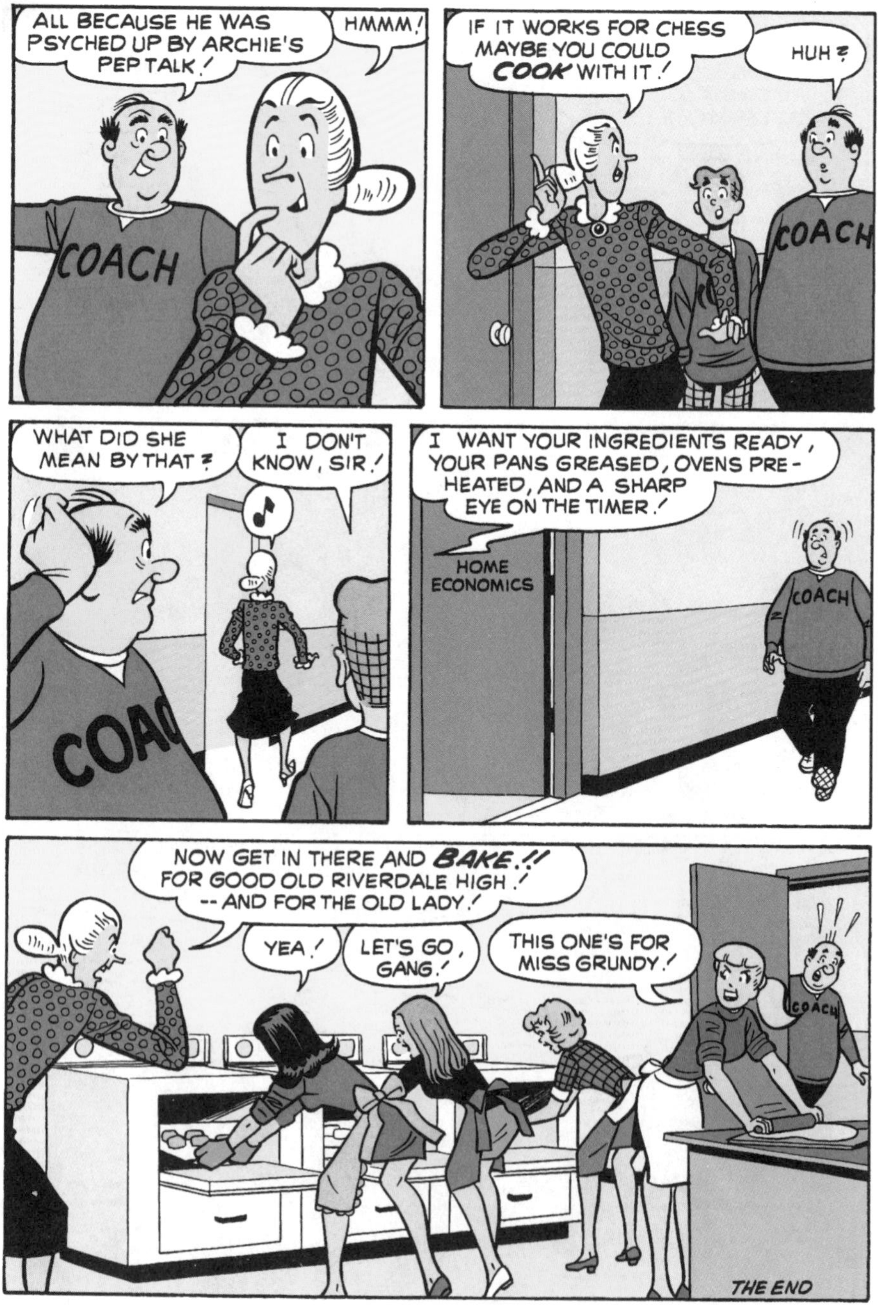
ALL BECAUSE HE WAS PSYCHED UP BY ARCHIE'S PEP TALK!
HMMM!
IF IT WORKS FOR CHESS MAYBE YOU COULD COOK WITH IT!
HUH?
WHAT DID SHE MEAN BY THAT?
I DON'T KNOW, SIR!
I WANT YOUR INGREDIENTS READY, YOUR PANS GREASED, OVENS PRE-HEATED, AND A SHARP EYE ON THE TIMER!
HOME ECONOMICS
COACH
NOW GET IN THERE AND BAKE!! FOR GOOD OLD RIVERDALE HIGH! -- AND FOR THE OLD LADY!
YEA!
LET'S GO, GANG!
THIS ONE'S FOR MISS GRUNDY!
THE END

Archie at RIVERDALE in "The CENTER RING"

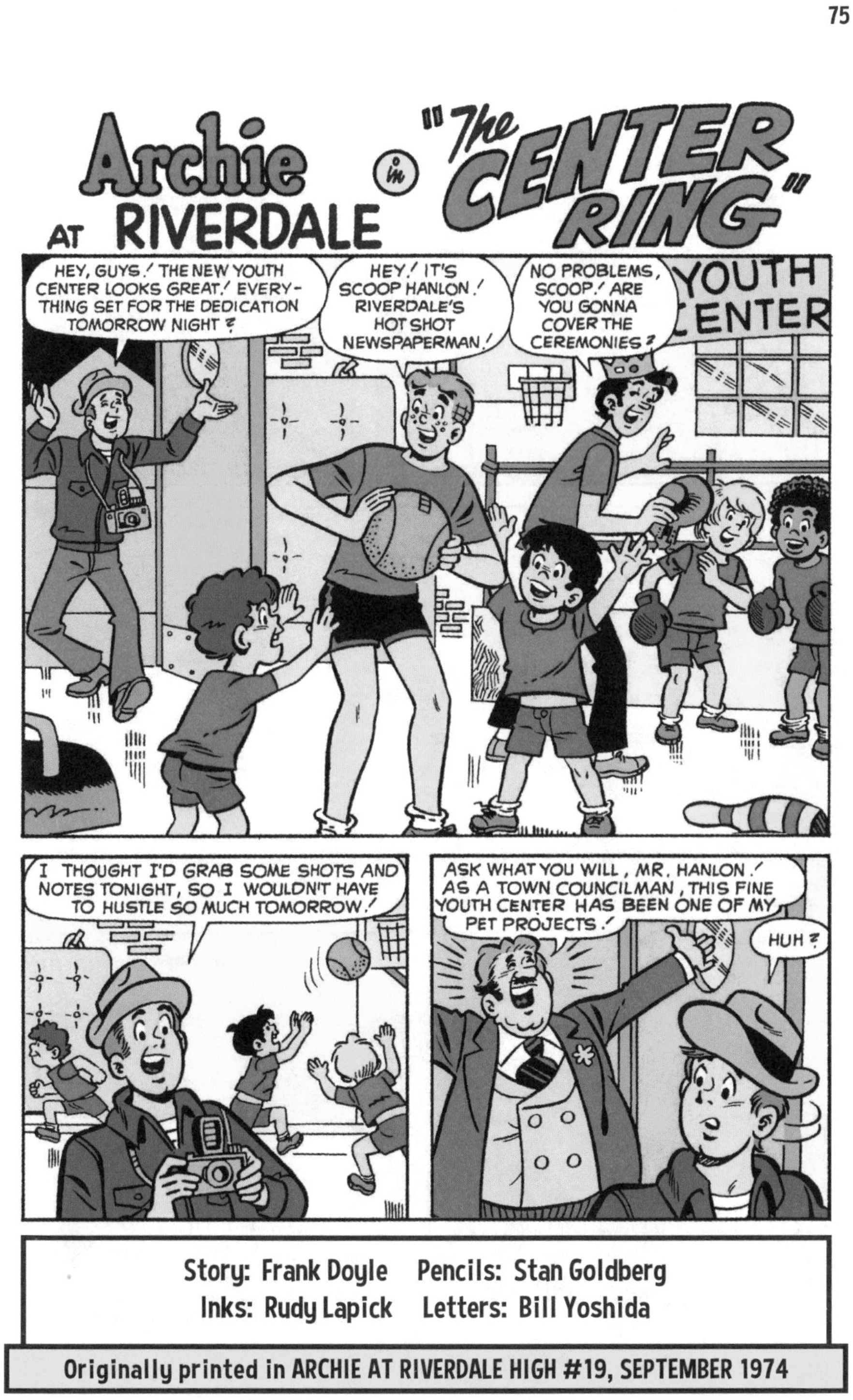
HEY, GUYS! THE NEW YOUTH CENTER LOOKS GREAT! EVERY-THING SET FOR THE DEDICATION TOMORROW NIGHT?
HEY! IT'S SCOOP HANLON! RIVERDALE'S HOT SHOT NEWSPAPERMAN!
NO PROBLEMS, SCOOP! ARE YOU GONNA COVER THE CEREMONIES?
YOUTH CENTER
I THOUGHT I'D GRAB SOME SHOTS AND NOTES TONIGHT, SO I WOULDN'T HAVE TO HUSTLE SO MUCH TOMORROW!
ASK WHAT YOU WILL, MR. HANLON! AS A TOWN COUNCILMAN, THIS FINE YOUTH CENTER HAS BEEN ONE OF MY PET PROJECTS!
HUH?

Story: Frank Doyle Pencils: Stan Goldberg
Inks: Rudy Lapick Letters: Bill Yoshida

Originally printed in ARCHIE AT RIVERDALE HIGH #19, SEPTEMBER 1974

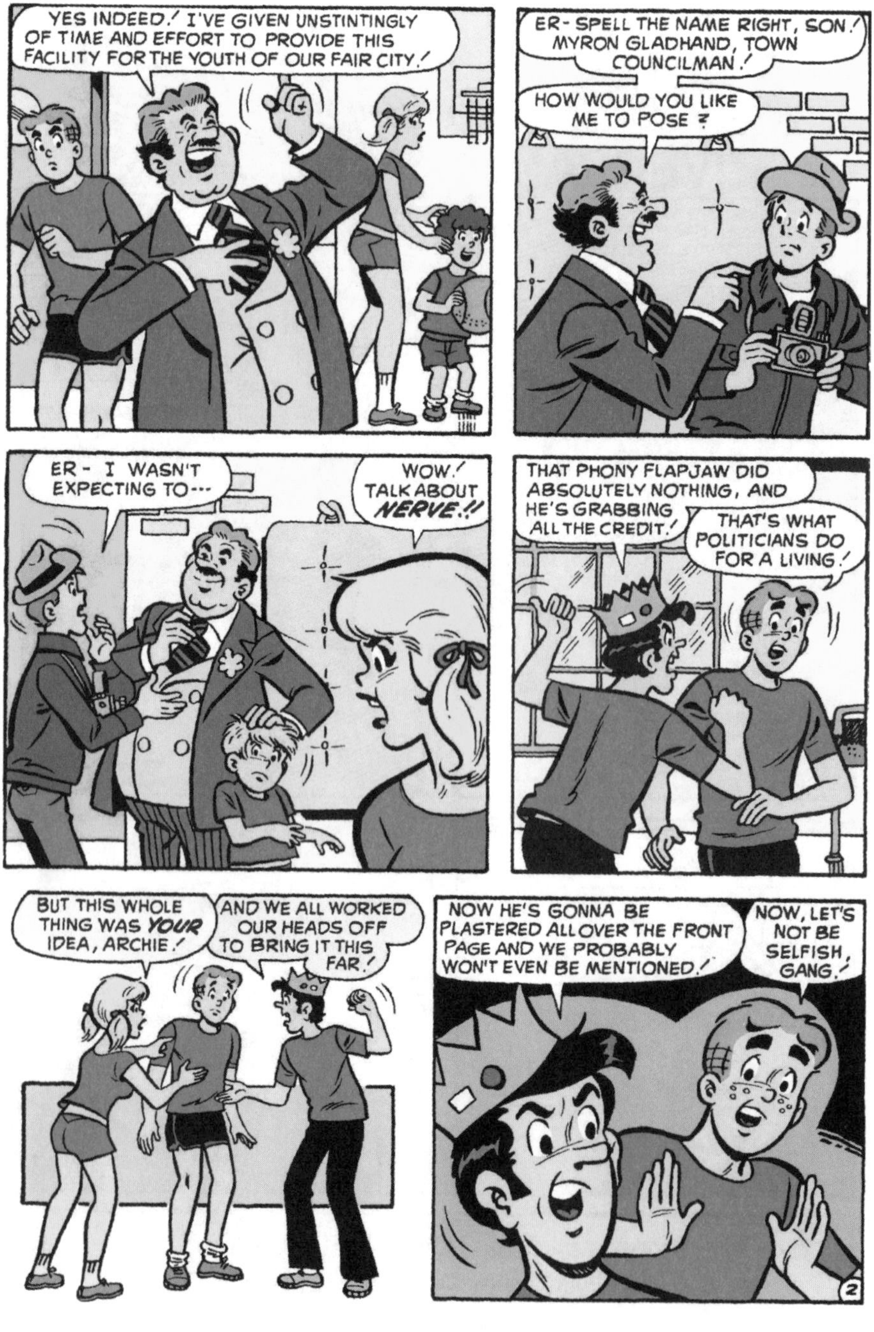
YES INDEED! I'VE GIVEN UNSTINTINGLY OF TIME AND EFFORT TO PROVIDE THIS FACILITY FOR THE YOUTH OF OUR FAIR CITY!
ER- SPELL THE NAME RIGHT, SON! MYRON GLADHAND, TOWN COUNCILMAN!
HOW WOULD YOU LIKE ME TO POSE ?
ER- I WASN'T EXPECTING TO---
WOW! TALK ABOUT NERVE!!
THAT PHONY FLAPJAW DID ABSOLUTELY NOTHING, AND HE'S GRABBING ALL THE CREDIT!
THAT'S WHAT POLITICIANS DO FOR A LIVING!
BUT THIS WHOLE THING WAS YOUR IDEA, ARCHIE!
AND WE ALL WORKED OUR HEADS OFF TO BRING IT THIS FAR!
NOW HE'S GONNA BE PLASTERED ALL OVER THE FRONT PAGE AND WE PROBABLY WON'T EVEN BE MENTIONED!
NOW, LET'S NOT BE SELFISH, GANG!
2

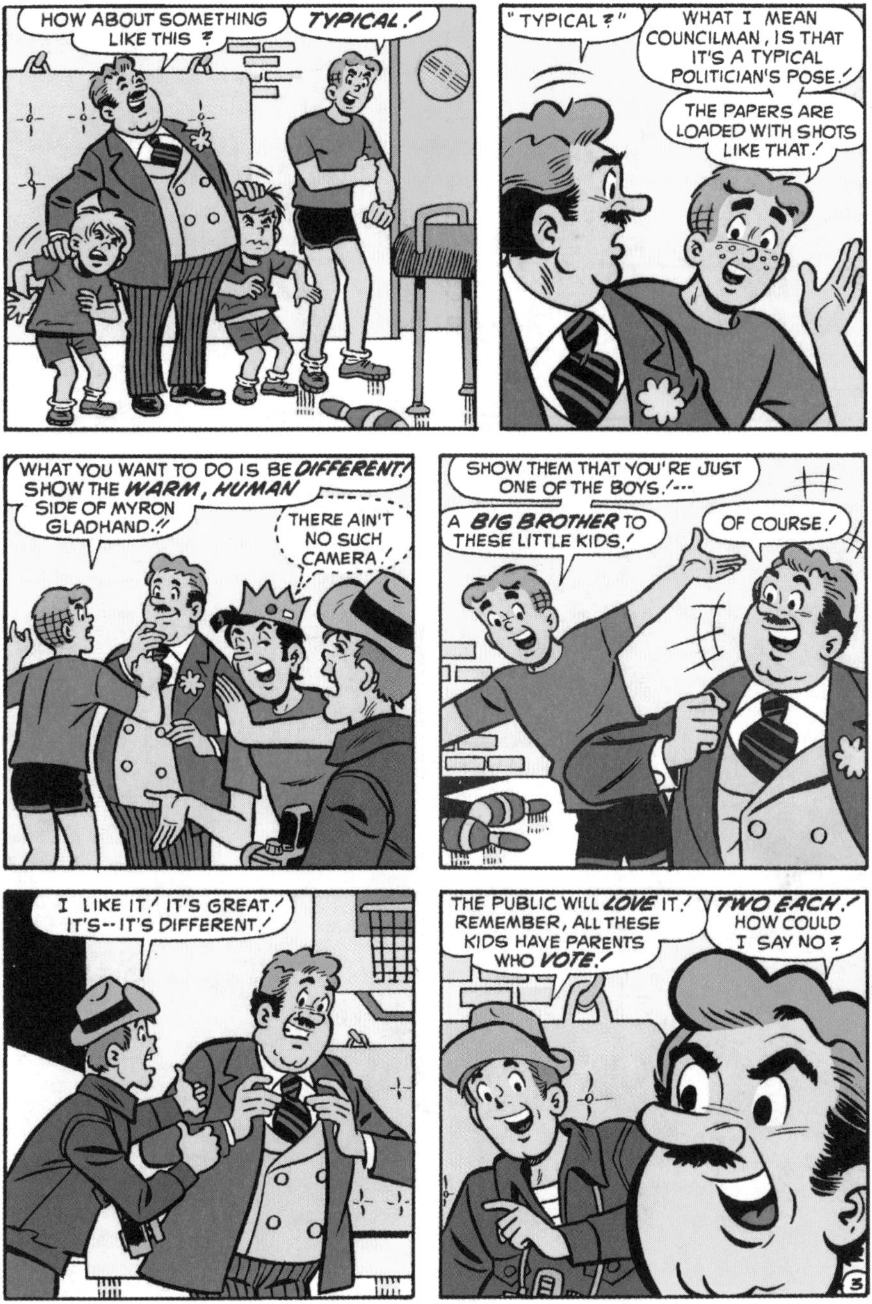
HOW ABOUT SOMETHING LIKE THIS ?
TYPICAL!
"TYPICAL ?"
WHAT I MEAN COUNCILMAN, IS THAT IT'S A TYPICAL POLITICIAN'S POSE!
THE PAPERS ARE LOADED WITH SHOTS LIKE THAT!
WHAT YOU WANT TO DO IS BE DIFFERENT! SHOW THE WARM, HUMAN SIDE OF MYRON GLADHAND!!
THERE AIN'T NO SUCH CAMERA!
SHOW THEM THAT YOU'RE JUST ONE OF THE BOYS!---
A BIG BROTHER TO THESE LITTLE KIDS!
OF COURSE!
I LIKE IT! IT'S GREAT! IT'S--IT'S DIFFERENT!
THE PUBLIC WILL LOVE IT! REMEMBER, ALL THESE KIDS HAVE PARENTS WHO VOTE!
TWO EACH! HOW COULD I SAY NO ?
3

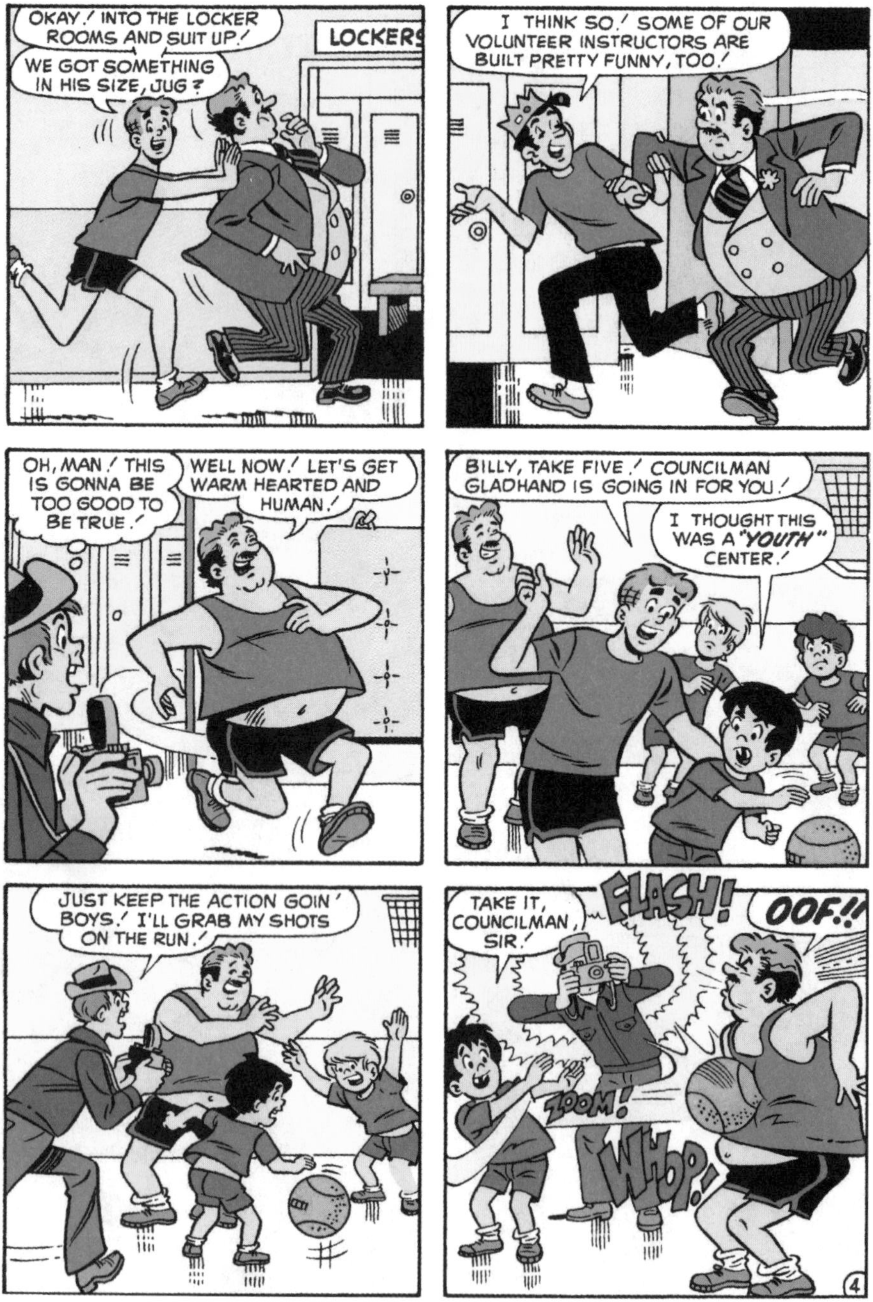
OKAY! INTO THE LOCKER ROOMS AND SUIT UP!
WE GOT SOMETHING IN HIS SIZE, JUG?
LOCKERS
I THINK SO! SOME OF OUR VOLUNTEER INSTRUCTORS ARE BUILT PRETTY FUNNY, TOO!
OH, MAN! THIS IS GONNA BE TOO GOOD TO BE TRUE!
WELL NOW! LET'S GET WARM HEARTED AND HUMAN!
BILLY, TAKE FIVE! COUNCILMAN GLADHAND IS GOING IN FOR YOU!
I THOUGHT THIS WAS A "YOUTH" CENTER!
JUST KEEP THE ACTION GOIN' BOYS! I'LL GRAB MY SHOTS ON THE RUN!
TAKE IT, COUNCILMAN, SIR!
FLASH!
OOF!!
ZOOM!
WHOP!
4

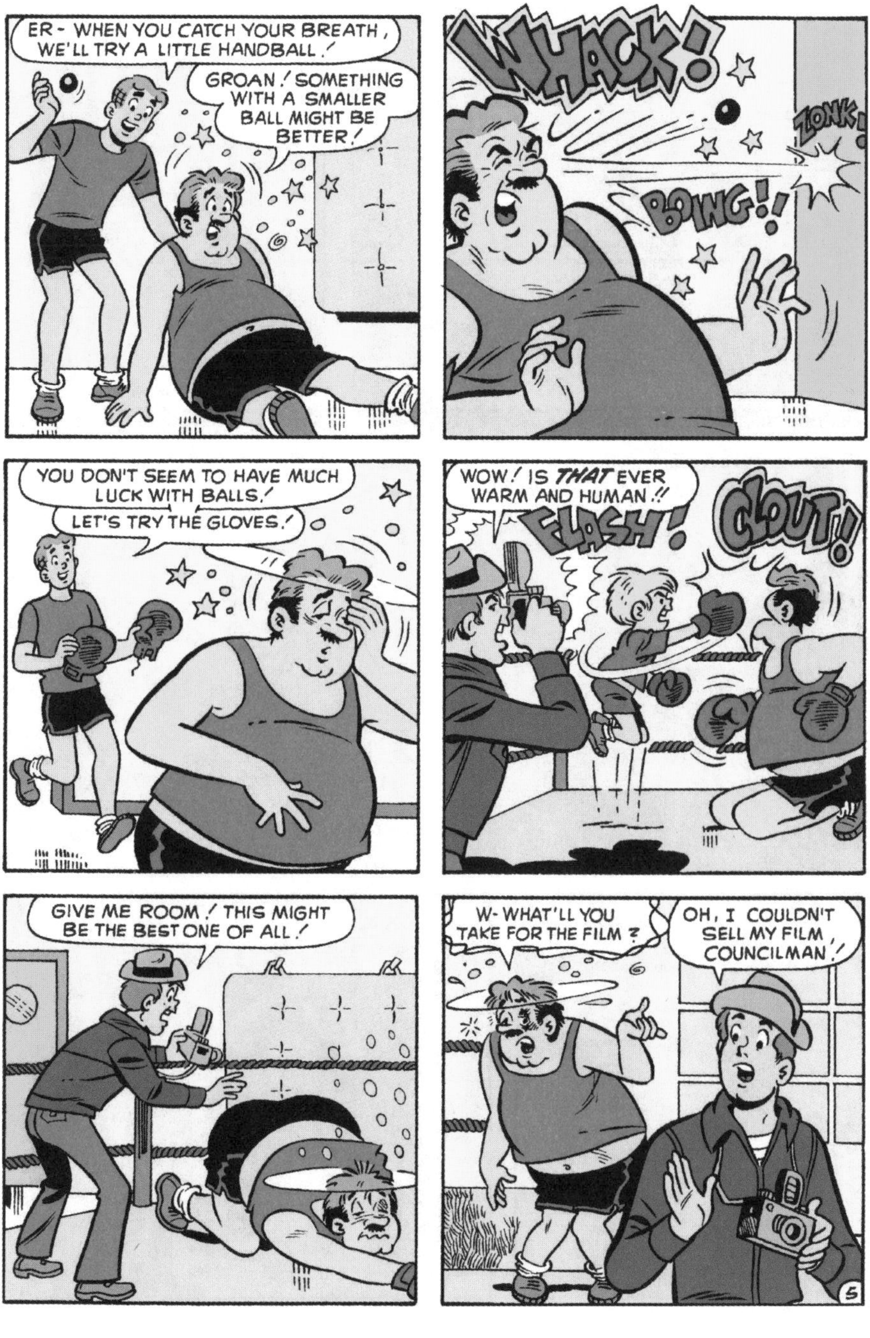
ER- WHEN YOU CATCH YOUR BREATH, WE'LL TRY A LITTLE HANDBALL.!
GROAN! SOMETHING WITH A SMALLER BALL MIGHT BE BETTER!
WHACK!
ZONK!
BOING!!
YOU DON'T SEEM TO HAVE MUCH LUCK WITH BALLS!
LET'S TRY THE GLOVES!
WOW! IS THAT EVER WARM AND HUMAN!!
FLASH!
CLOUT!!
GIVE ME ROOM! THIS MIGHT BE THE BEST ONE OF ALL!
W-WHAT'LL YOU TAKE FOR THE FILM?
OH, I COULDN'T SELL MY FILM, COUNCILMAN!
5

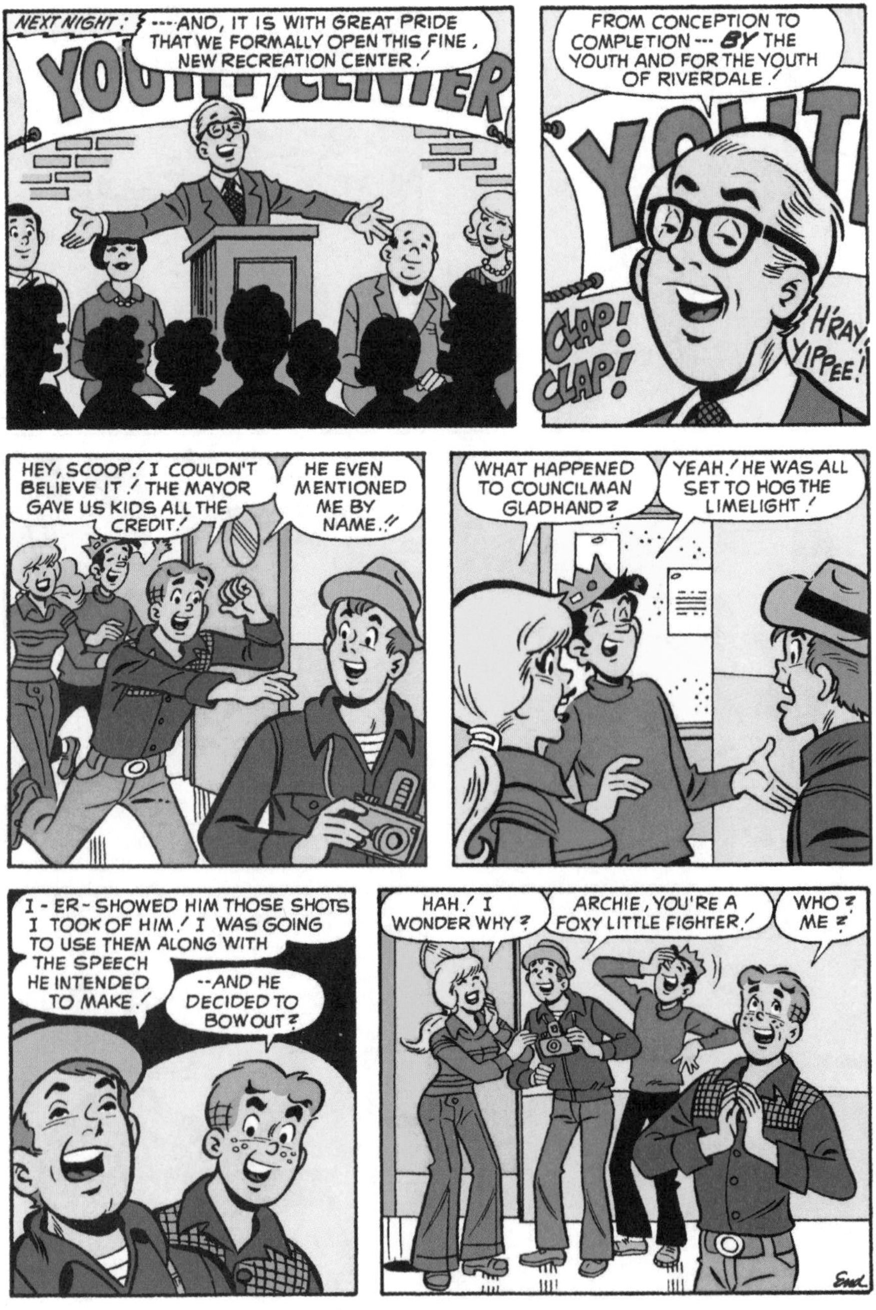
NEXT NIGHT:
---AND, IT IS WITH GREAT PRIDE THAT WE FORMALLY OPEN THIS FINE, NEW RECREATION CENTER!
YOUTH CENTER
FROM CONCEPTION TO COMPLETION --- BY THE YOUTH AND FOR THE YOUTH OF RIVERDALE!
CLAP! CLAP!
H'RAY! YIPPEE!
HEY, SCOOP! I COULDN'T BELIEVE IT! THE MAYOR GAVE US KIDS ALL THE CREDIT!
HE EVEN MENTIONED ME BY NAME.!!
WHAT HAPPENED TO COUNCILMAN GLADHAND?
YEAH! HE WAS ALL SET TO HOG THE LIMELIGHT!
I - ER - SHOWED HIM THOSE SHOTS I TOOK OF HIM! I WAS GOING TO USE THEM ALONG WITH THE SPEECH HE INTENDED TO MAKE!
--AND HE DECIDED TO BOW OUT?
HAH! I WONDER WHY?
ARCHIE, YOU'RE A FOXY LITTLE FIGHTER!
WHO? ME?
End

Archie at RIVERDALE in Truck 32

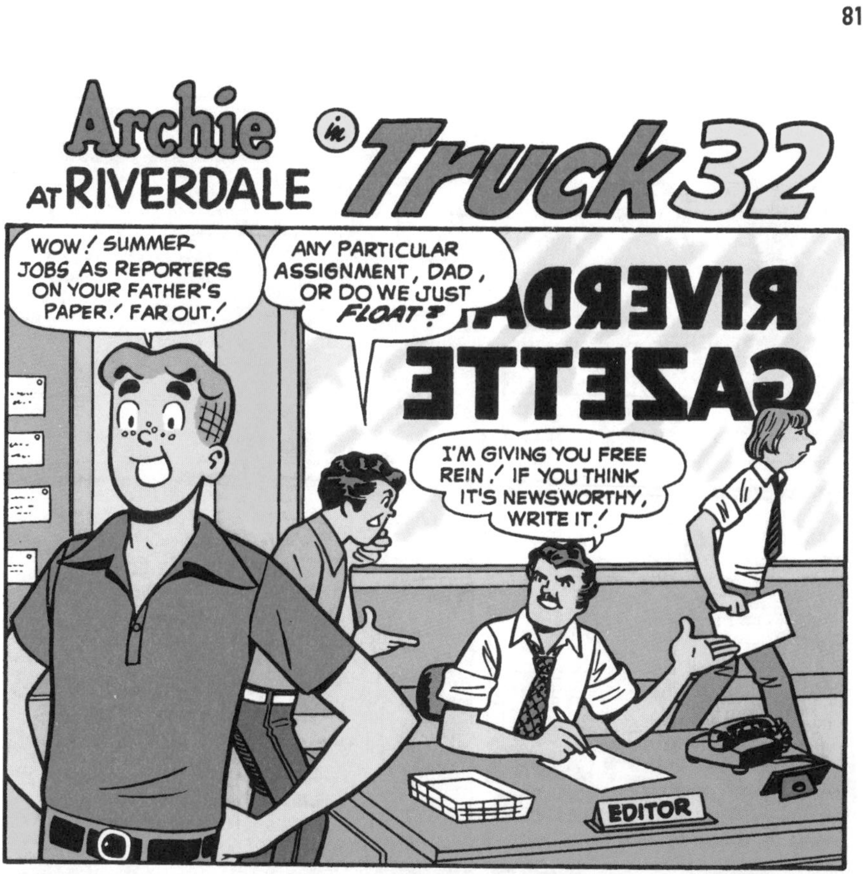
WOW! SUMMER JOBS AS REPORTERS ON YOUR FATHER'S PAPER! FAR OUT!
ANY PARTICULAR ASSIGNMENT, DAD, OR DO WE JUST FLOAT?
I'M GIVING YOU FREE REIN! IF YOU THINK IT'S NEWSWORTHY, WRITE IT!
EDITOR

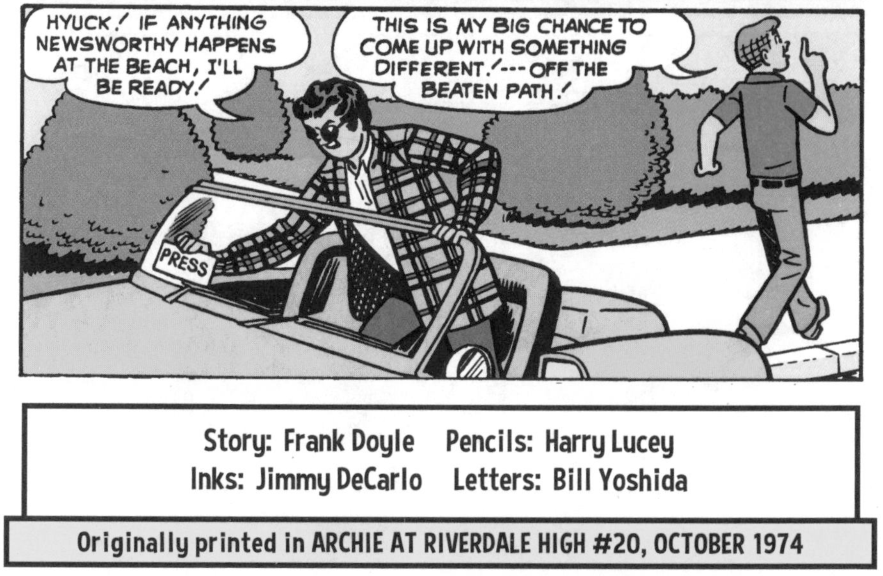
HYUCK! IF ANYTHING NEWSWORTHY HAPPENS AT THE BEACH, I'LL BE READY!
THIS IS MY BIG CHANCE TO COME UP WITH SOMETHING DIFFERENT!--- OFF THE BEATEN PATH!
PRESS

Story: Frank Doyle Pencils: Harry Lucey
Inks: Jimmy DeCarlo Letters: Bill Yoshida

Originally printed in ARCHIE AT RIVERDALE HIGH #20, OCTOBER 1974

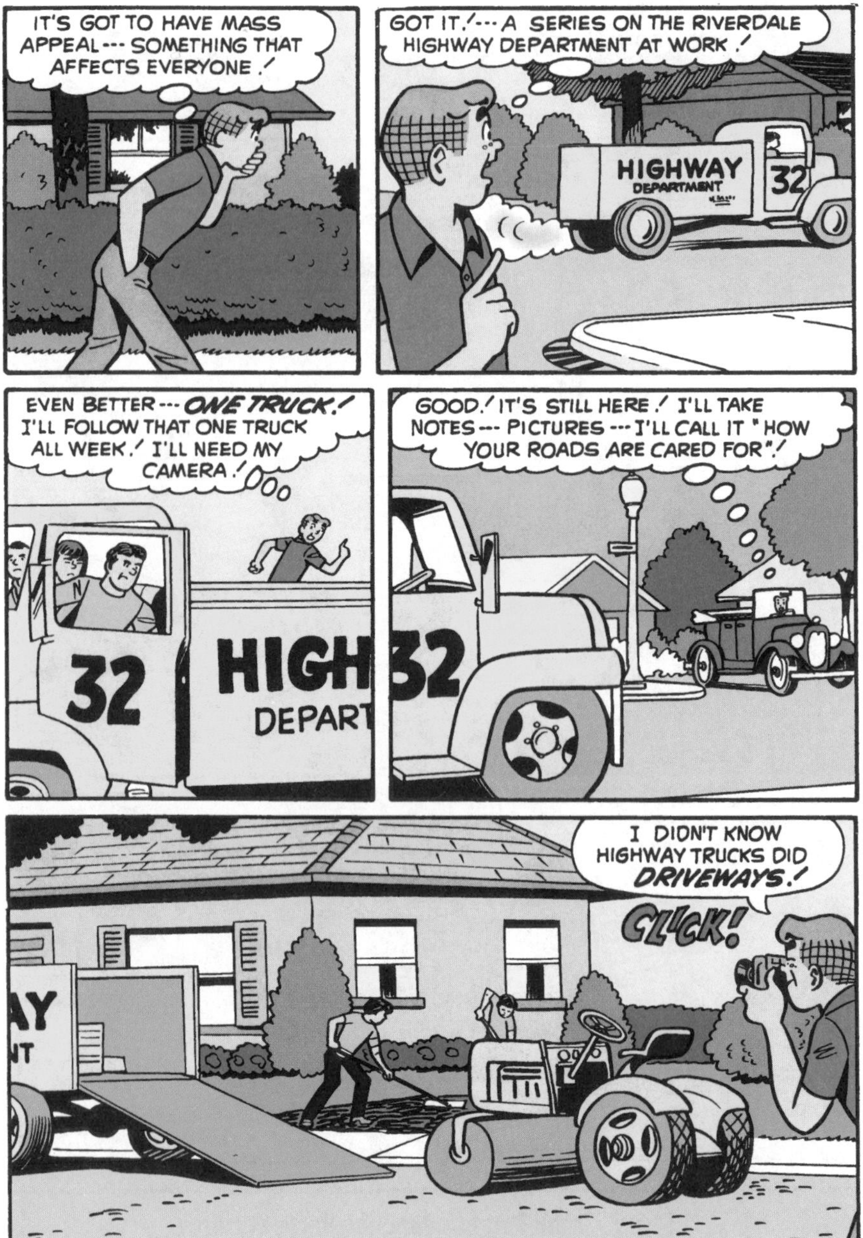
IT'S GOT TO HAVE MASS APPEAL --- SOMETHING THAT AFFECTS EVERYONE !
GOT IT ! --- A SERIES ON THE RIVERDALE HIGHWAY DEPARTMENT AT WORK !
HIGHWAY DEPARTMENT
32
EVEN BETTER --- ONE TRUCK ! I'LL FOLLOW THAT ONE TRUCK ALL WEEK ! I'LL NEED MY CAMERA !
32
HIGH
DEPART
GOOD ! IT'S STILL HERE ! I'LL TAKE NOTES --- PICTURES --- I'LL CALL IT " HOW YOUR ROADS ARE CARED FOR" !
32
I DIDN'T KNOW HIGHWAY TRUCKS DID DRIVEWAYS !
CLICK!
AY
NT
2

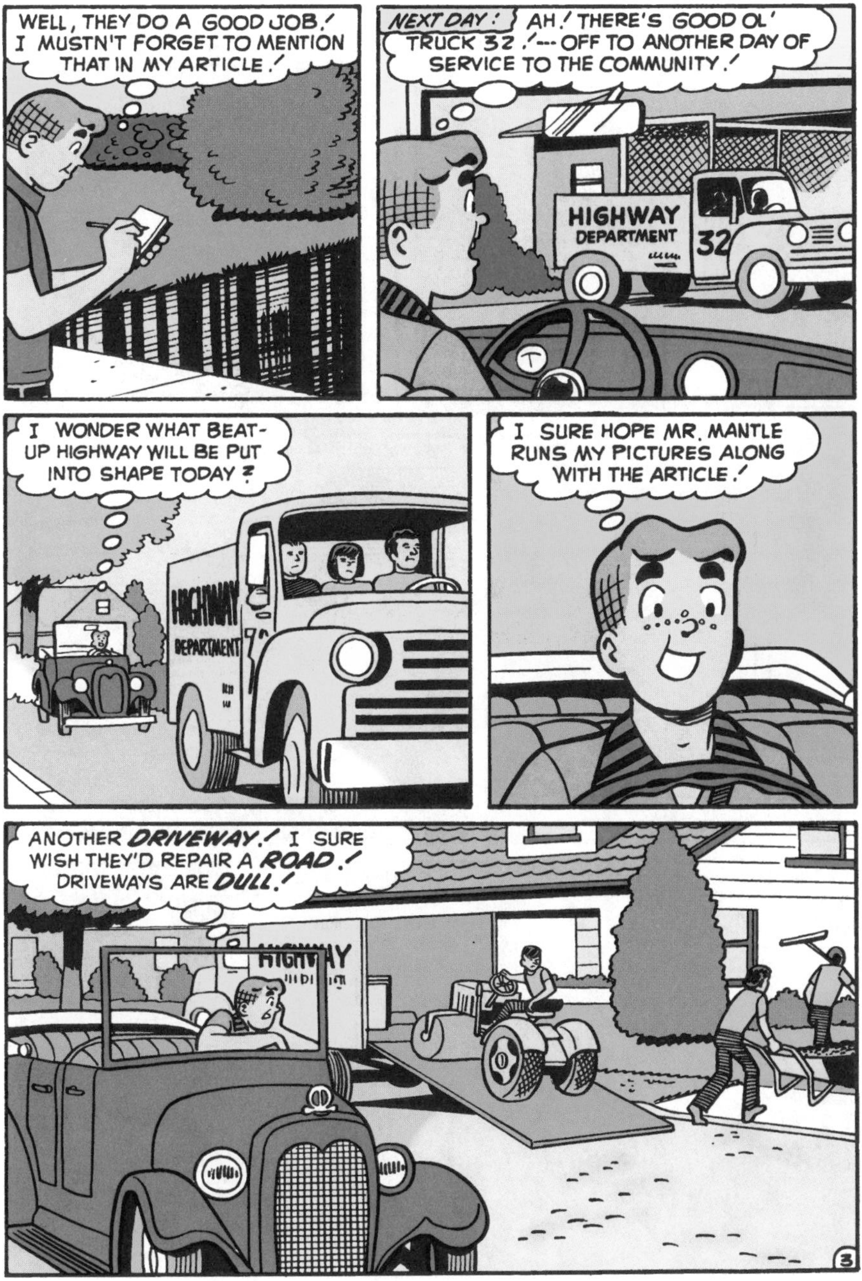
WELL, THEY DO A GOOD JOB! I MUSTN'T FORGET TO MENTION THAT IN MY ARTICLE!
NEXT DAY:
AH! THERE'S GOOD OL' TRUCK 32!--- OFF TO ANOTHER DAY OF SERVICE TO THE COMMUNITY!
HIGHWAY DEPARTMENT 32
I WONDER WHAT BEAT-UP HIGHWAY WILL BE PUT INTO SHAPE TODAY?
HIGHWAY DEPARTMENT
I SURE HOPE MR. MANTLE RUNS MY PICTURES ALONG WITH THE ARTICLE!
ANOTHER DRIVEWAY! I SURE WISH THEY'D REPAIR A ROAD! DRIVEWAYS ARE DULL!
3

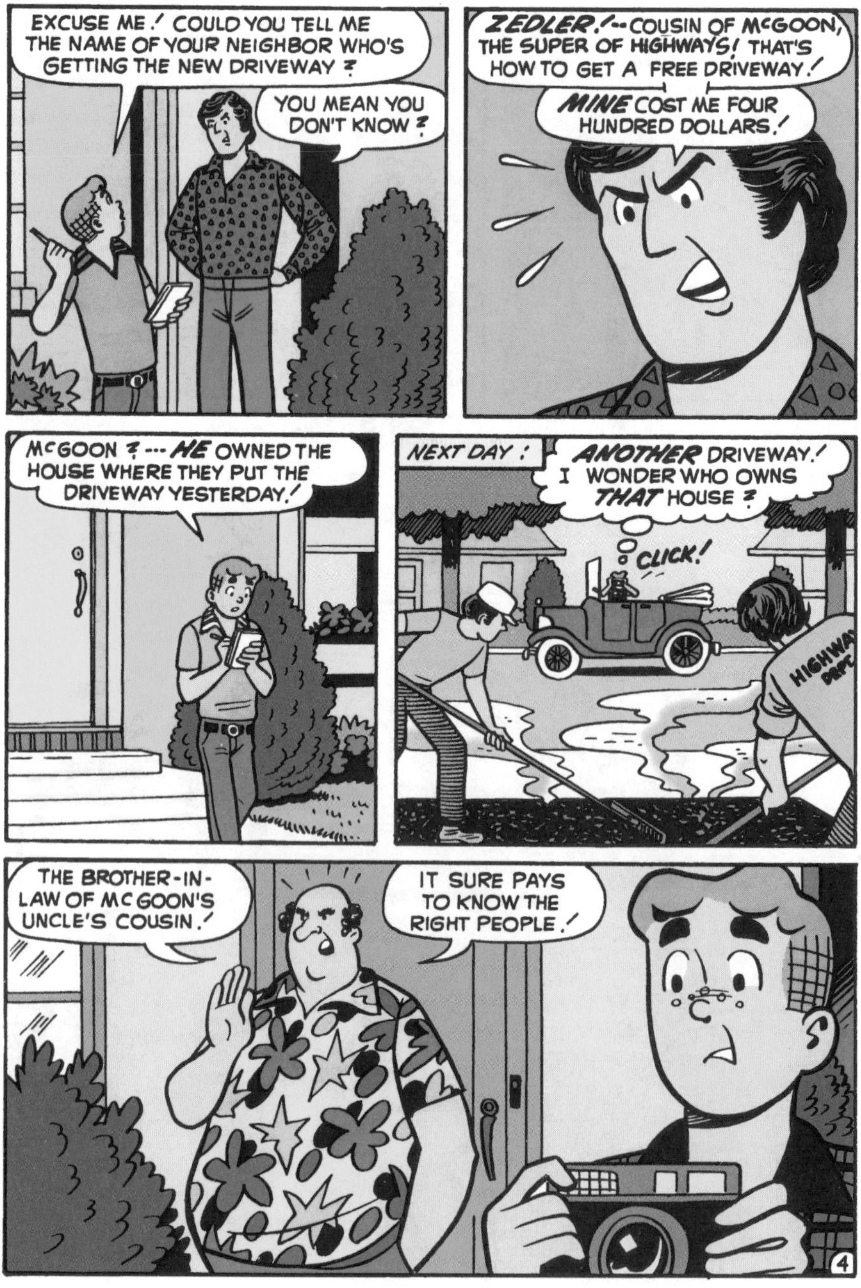
EXCUSE ME! COULD YOU TELL ME THE NAME OF YOUR NEIGHBOR WHO'S GETTING THE NEW DRIVEWAY ?
YOU MEAN YOU DON'T KNOW ?
ZEDLER!--COUSIN OF McGOON, THE SUPER OF HIGHWAYS! THAT'S HOW TO GET A FREE DRIVEWAY!
MINE COST ME FOUR HUNDRED DOLLARS!
McGOON ?--- HE OWNED THE HOUSE WHERE THEY PUT THE DRIVEWAY YESTERDAY!
NEXT DAY :
ANOTHER DRIVEWAY! I WONDER WHO OWNS THAT HOUSE ?
CLICK!
HIGHWAY DEPT.
THE BROTHER-IN-LAW OF McGOON'S UNCLE'S COUSIN!
IT SURE PAYS TO KNOW THE RIGHT PEOPLE!
4

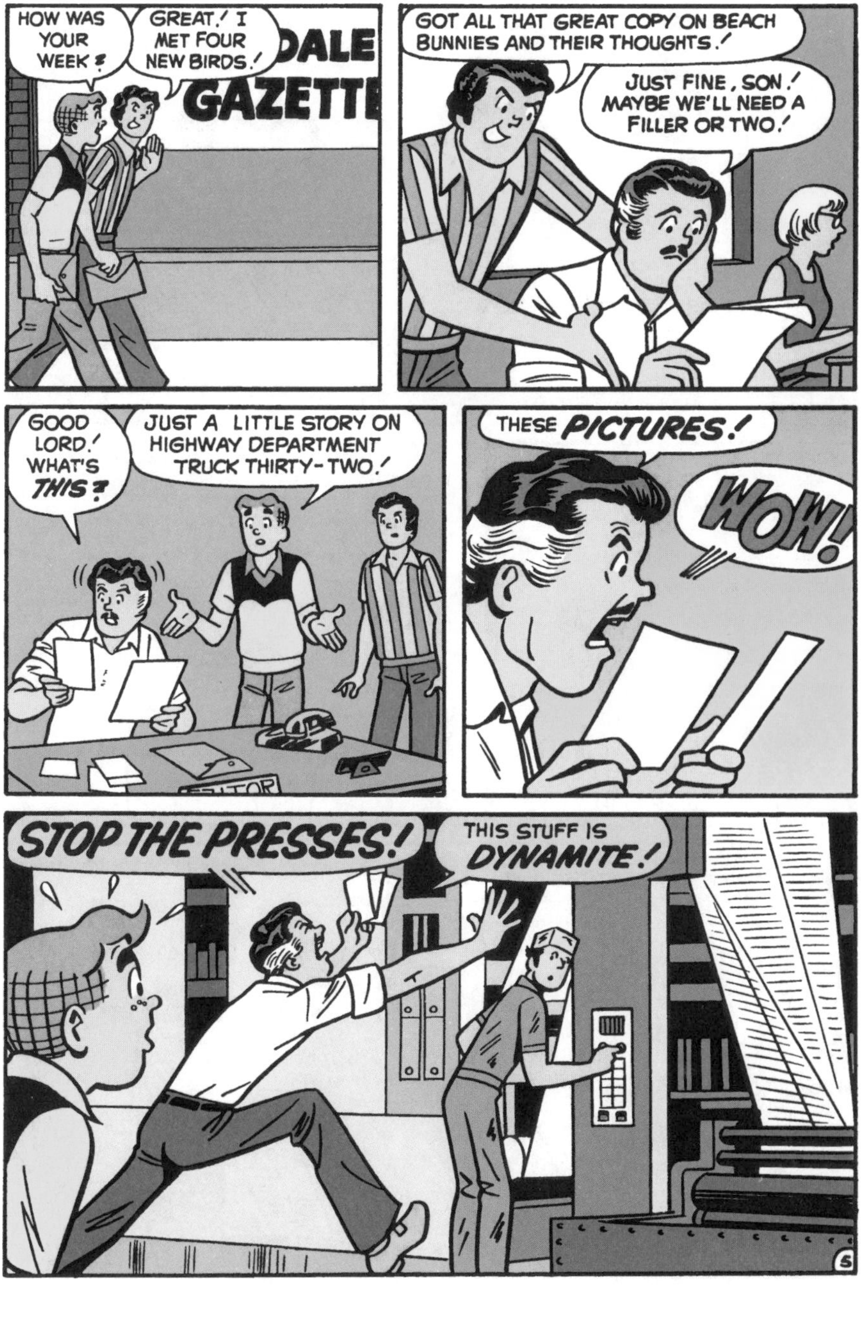
HOW WAS YOUR WEEK?
GREAT! I MET FOUR NEW BIRDS!
DALE GAZETT
GOT ALL THAT GREAT COPY ON BEACH BUNNIES AND THEIR THOUGHTS!
JUST FINE, SON! MAYBE WE'LL NEED A FILLER OR TWO!
GOOD LORD! WHAT'S THIS?
JUST A LITTLE STORY ON HIGHWAY DEPARTMENT TRUCK THIRTY-TWO!
THESE PICTURES!
WOW!
STOP THE PRESSES!
THIS STUFF IS DYNAMITE!
5

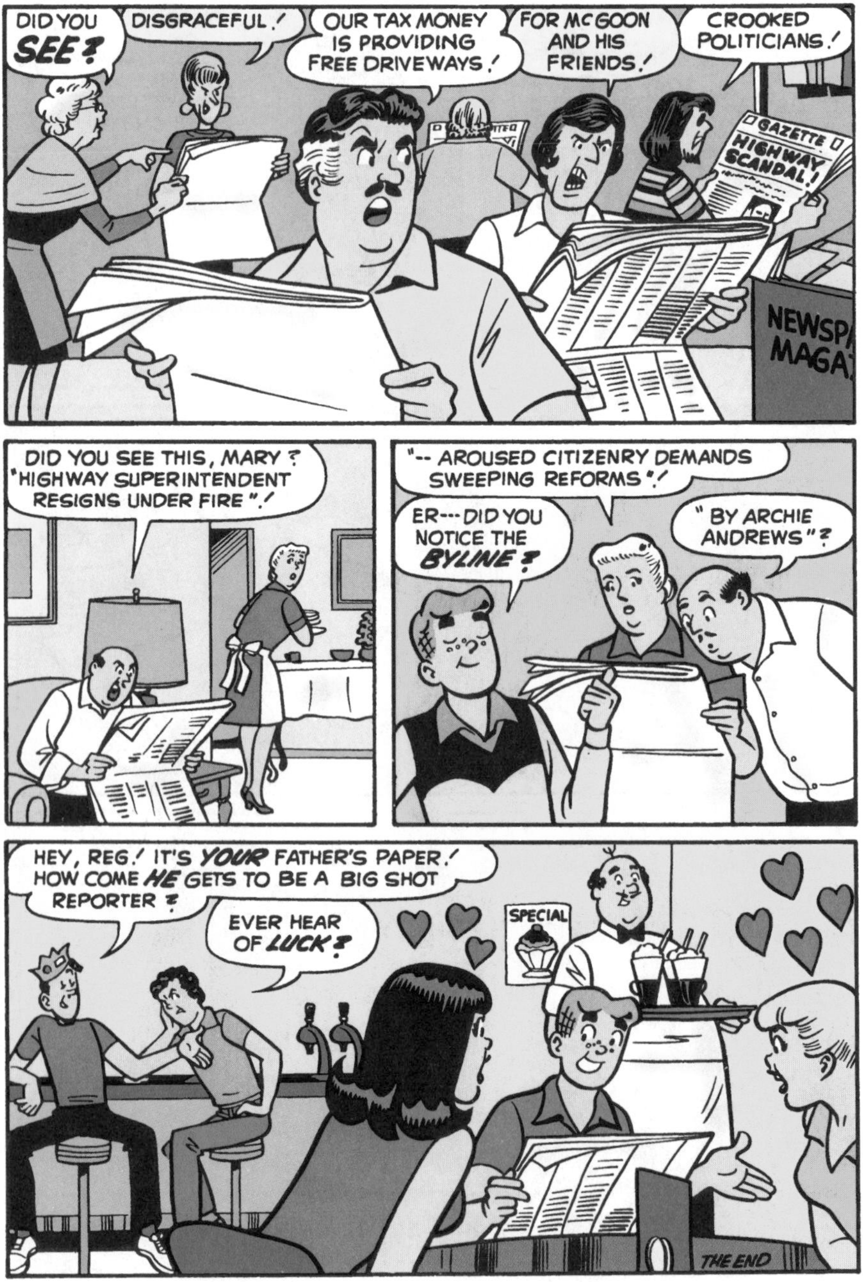
DID YOU SEE?
DISGRACEFUL!
OUR TAX MONEY IS PROVIDING FREE DRIVEWAYS!
FOR McGOON AND HIS FRIENDS!
CROOKED POLITICIANS!
GAZETTE
HIGHWAY SCANDAL!
NEWSPA
MAGA
DID YOU SEE THIS, MARY? "HIGHWAY SUPERINTENDENT RESIGNS UNDER FIRE"!
"-- AROUSED CITIZENRY DEMANDS SWEEPING REFORMS"!
ER--- DID YOU NOTICE THE BYLINE?
"BY ARCHIE ANDREWS"?
HEY, REG! IT'S YOUR FATHER'S PAPER! HOW COME HE GETS TO BE A BIG SHOT REPORTER?
EVER HEAR OF LUCK?
SPECIAL
THE END

Archie at Riverdale in "Spy Guy"

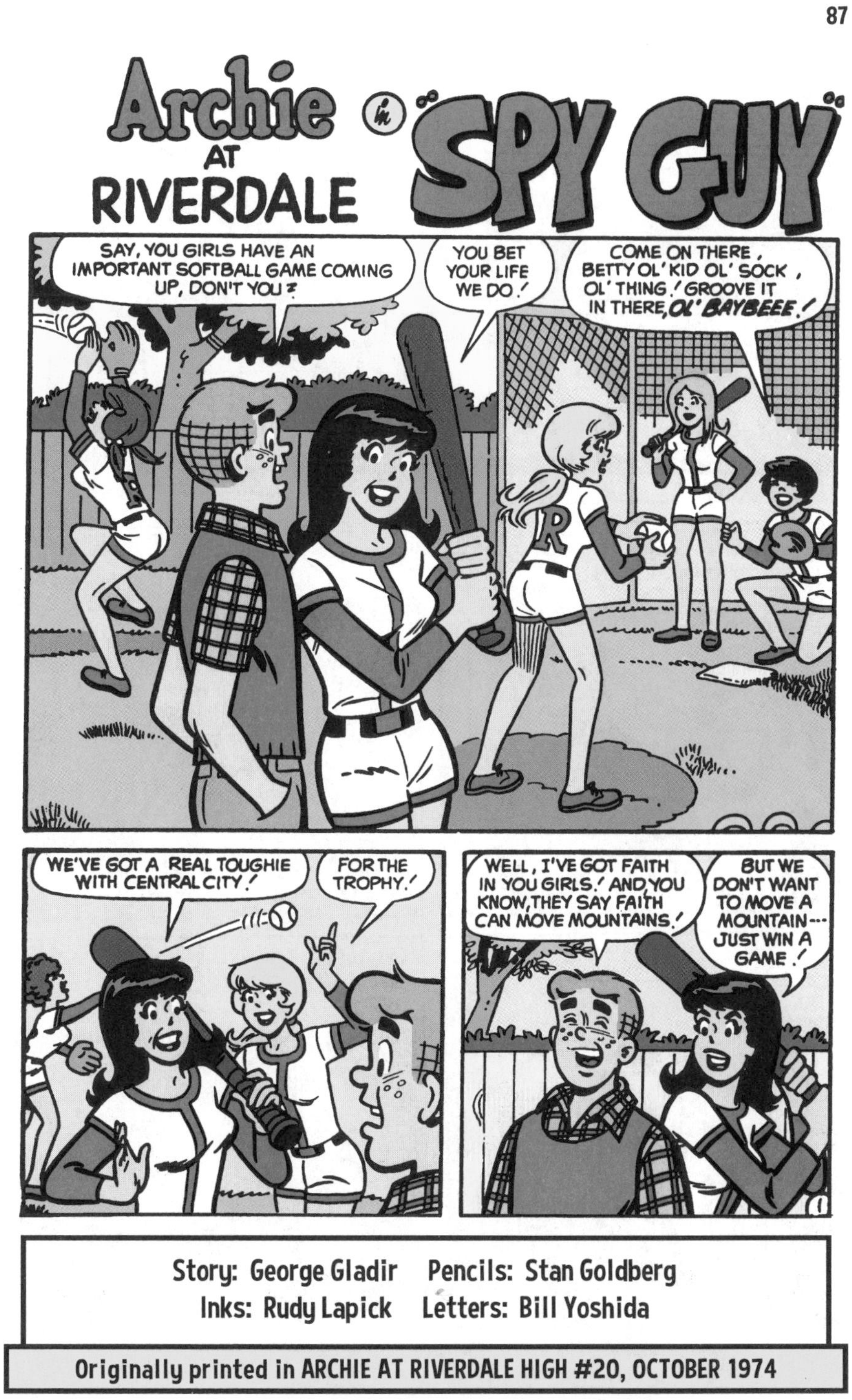
SAY, YOU GIRLS HAVE AN IMPORTANT SOFTBALL GAME COMING UP, DON'T YOU?
YOU BET YOUR LIFE WE DO!
COME ON THERE, BETTY OL' KID OL' SOCK, OL' THING! GROOVE IT IN THERE, OL' BAYBEEE!
WE'VE GOT A REAL TOUGHIE WITH CENTRAL CITY!
FOR THE TROPHY!
WELL, I'VE GOT FAITH IN YOU GIRLS! AND, YOU KNOW, THEY SAY FAITH CAN MOVE MOUNTAINS!
BUT WE DON'T WANT TO MOVE A MOUNTAIN--- JUST WIN A GAME!

Story: George Gladir Pencils: Stan Goldberg
Inks: Rudy Lapick Letters: Bill Yoshida

Originally printed in ARCHIE AT RIVERDALE HIGH #20, OCTOBER 1974

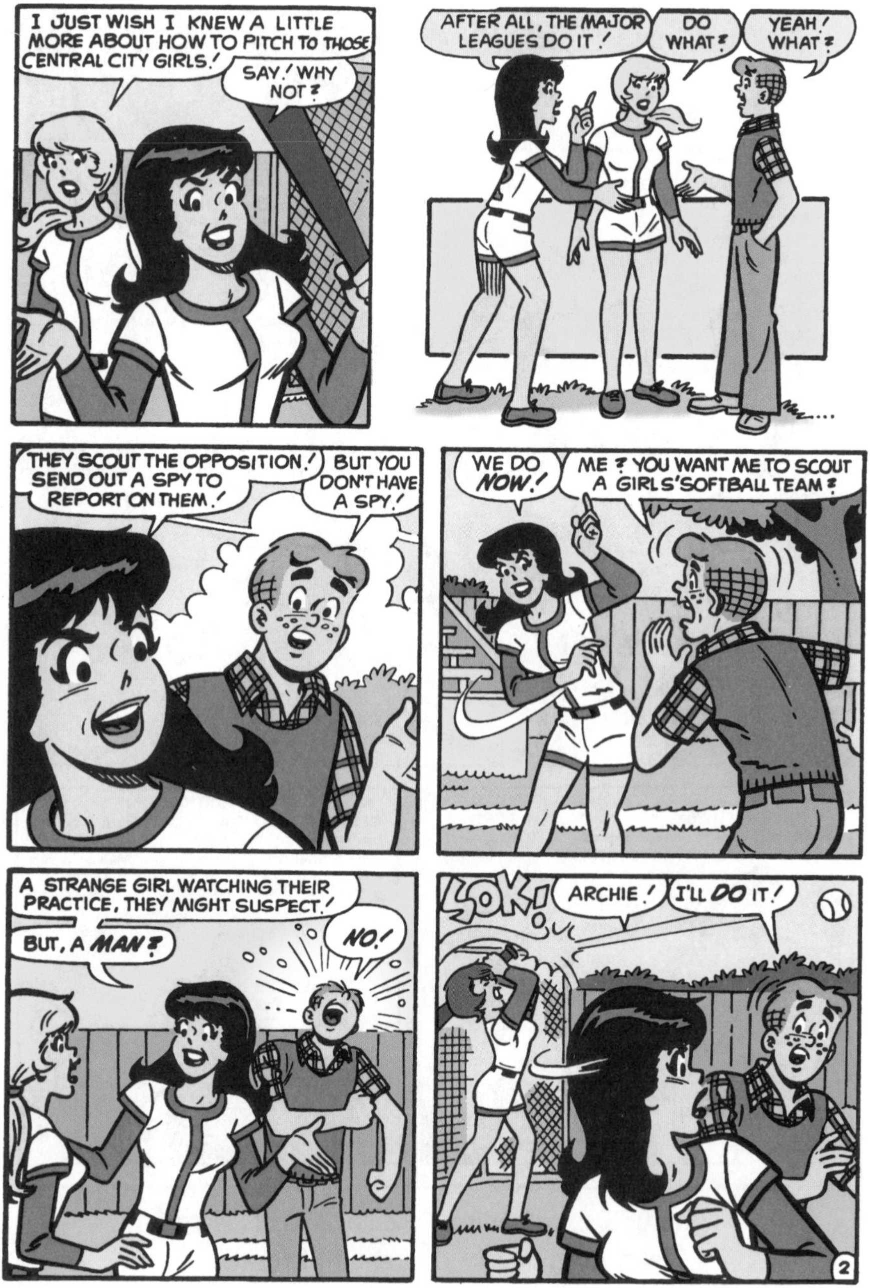
I JUST WISH I KNEW A LITTLE MORE ABOUT HOW TO PITCH TO THOSE CENTRAL CITY GIRLS!
SAY! WHY NOT?
AFTER ALL, THE MAJOR LEAGUES DO IT!
DO WHAT?
YEAH! WHAT?
THEY SCOUT THE OPPOSITION! SEND OUT A SPY TO REPORT ON THEM!
BUT YOU DON'T HAVE A SPY!
WE DO NOW!
ME? YOU WANT ME TO SCOUT A GIRLS' SOFTBALL TEAM?
A STRANGE GIRL WATCHING THEIR PRACTICE, THEY MIGHT SUSPECT!
BUT, A MAN?
NO!
SOK!
ARCHIE!
I'LL DO IT!
2

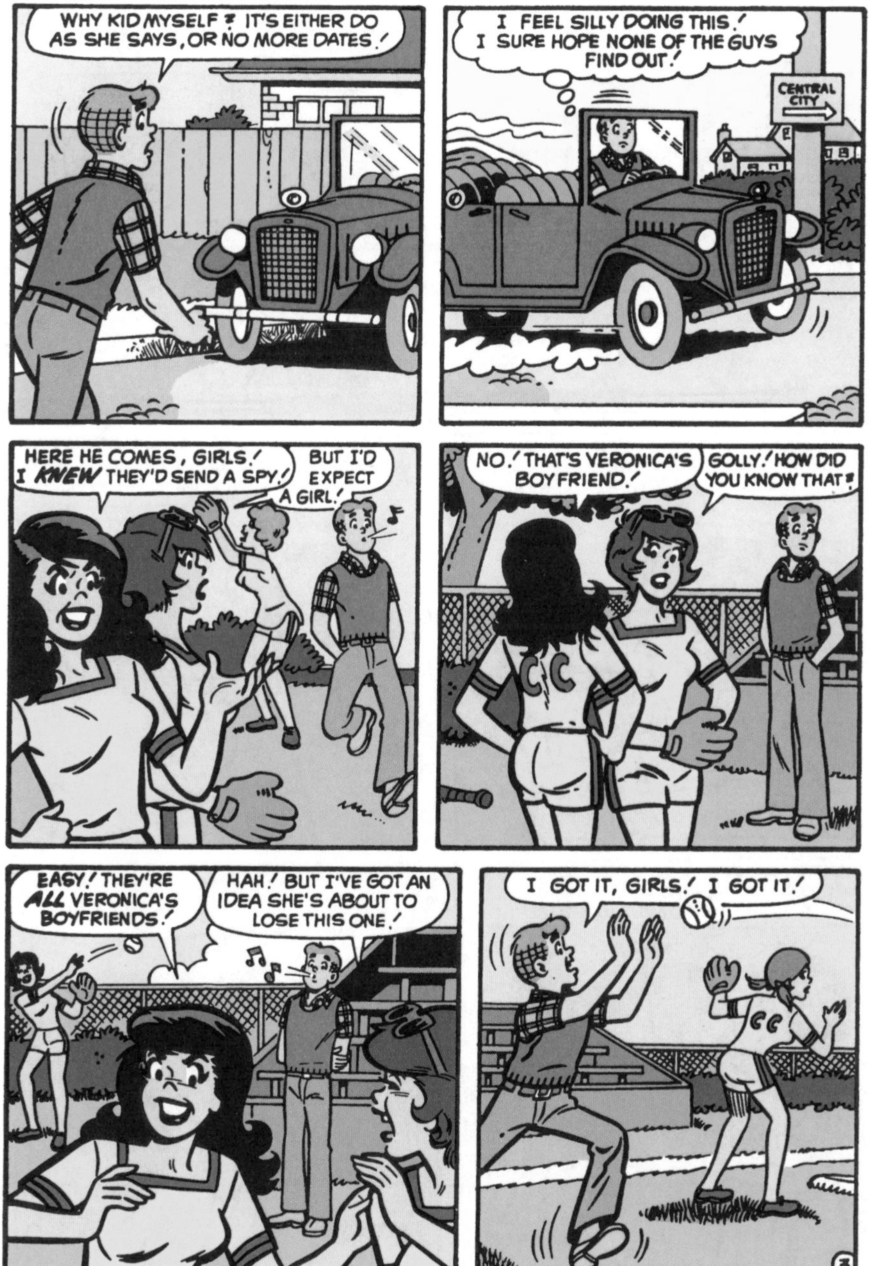
WHY KID MYSELF? IT'S EITHER DO AS SHE SAYS, OR NO MORE DATES!
I FEEL SILLY DOING THIS! I SURE HOPE NONE OF THE GUYS FIND OUT!
CENTRAL CITY
HERE HE COMES, GIRLS! I KNEW THEY'D SEND A SPY!
BUT I'D EXPECT A GIRL!
NO! THAT'S VERONICA'S BOYFRIEND!
GOLLY! HOW DID YOU KNOW THAT?
EASY! THEY'RE ALL VERONICA'S BOYFRIENDS!
HAH! BUT I'VE GOT AN IDEA SHE'S ABOUT TO LOSE THIS ONE!
I GOT IT, GIRLS! I GOT IT!
3

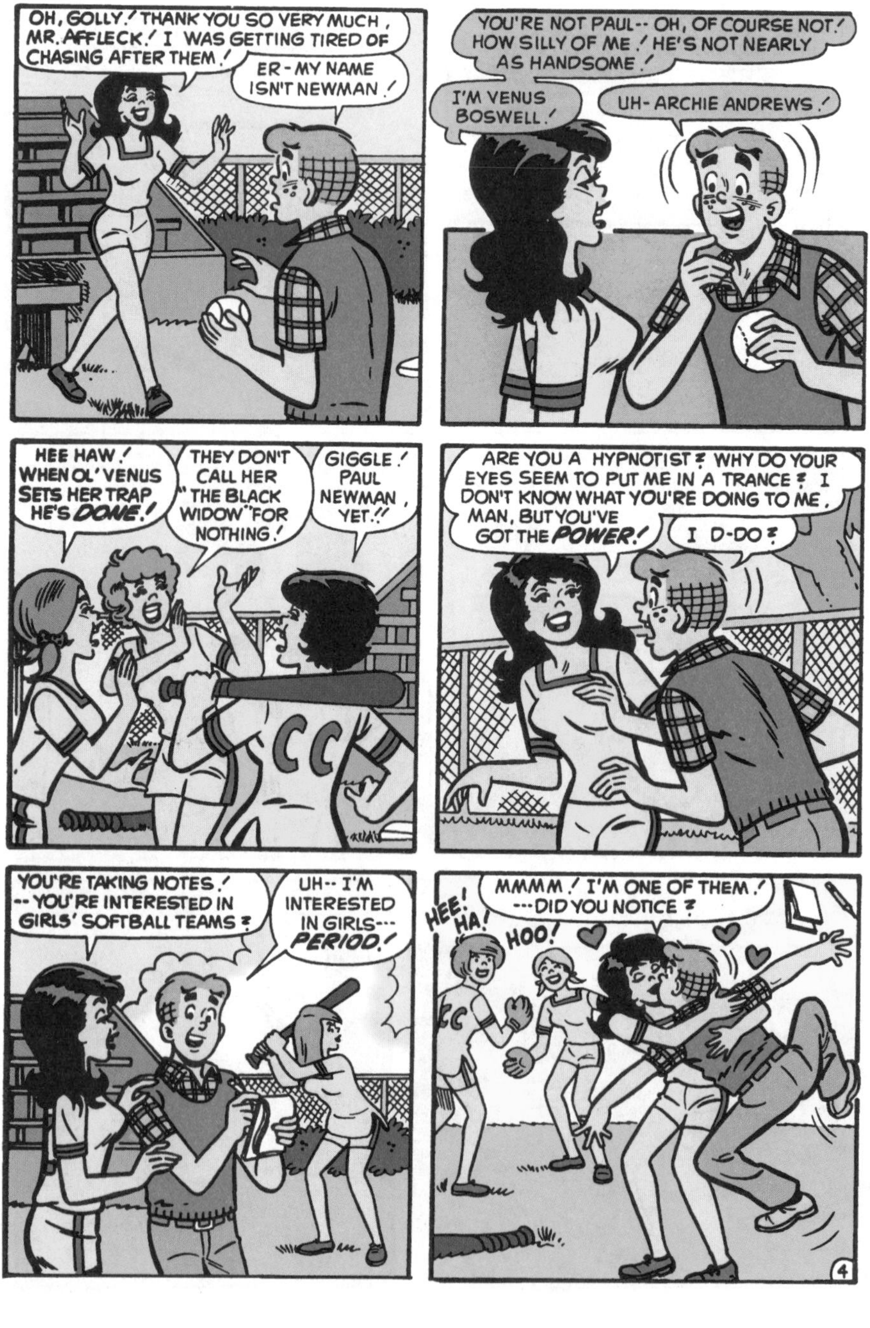
OH, GOLLY! THANK YOU SO VERY MUCH, MR. AFFLECK! I WAS GETTING TIRED OF CHASING AFTER THEM!
ER-MY NAME ISN'T NEWMAN!
YOU'RE NOT PAUL-- OH, OF COURSE NOT! HOW SILLY OF ME! HE'S NOT NEARLY AS HANDSOME!
I'M VENUS BOSWELL!
UH- ARCHIE ANDREWS!
HEE HAW! WHEN OL' VENUS SETS HER TRAP HE'S DONE!
THEY DON'T CALL HER "THE BLACK WIDOW" FOR NOTHING!
GIGGLE! PAUL NEWMAN, YET!!
ARE YOU A HYPNOTIST? WHY DO YOUR EYES SEEM TO PUT ME IN A TRANCE? I DON'T KNOW WHAT YOU'RE DOING TO ME, MAN, BUT YOU'VE GOT THE POWER!
I D-DO?
YOU'RE TAKING NOTES! -- YOU'RE INTERESTED IN GIRLS' SOFTBALL TEAMS?
UH-- I'M INTERESTED IN GIRLS--- PERIOD!
MMMM! I'M ONE OF THEM! ---DID YOU NOTICE?
HEE! HA! HOO!
4

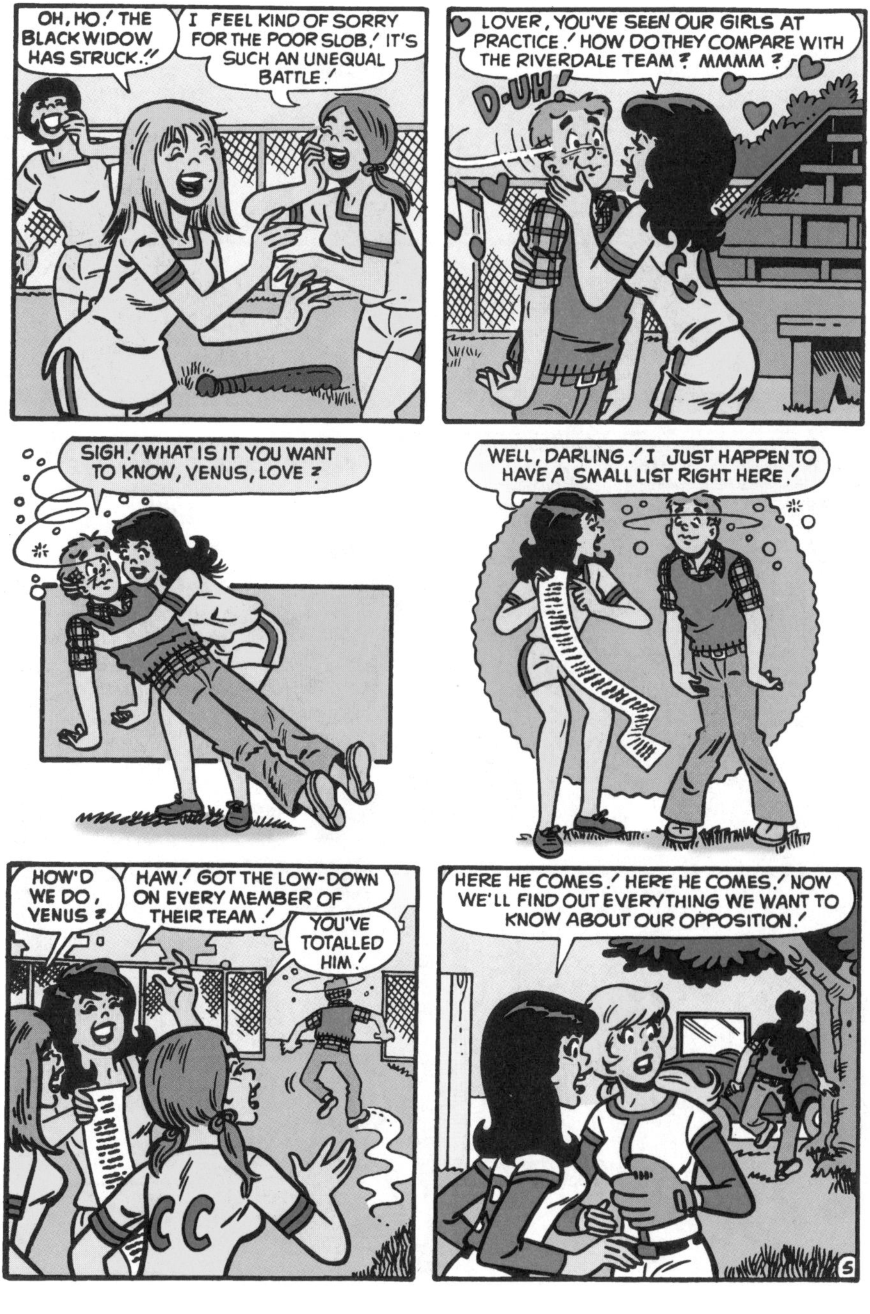
OH, HO! THE BLACK WIDOW HAS STRUCK.!!
I FEEL KIND OF SORRY FOR THE POOR SLOB! IT'S SUCH AN UNEQUAL BATTLE!
LOVER, YOU'VE SEEN OUR GIRLS AT PRACTICE! HOW DO THEY COMPARE WITH THE RIVERDALE TEAM? MMMM?
D-UH!
SIGH! WHAT IS IT YOU WANT TO KNOW, VENUS, LOVE?
WELL, DARLING! I JUST HAPPEN TO HAVE A SMALL LIST RIGHT HERE!
HOW'D WE DO, VENUS?
HAW! GOT THE LOW-DOWN ON EVERY MEMBER OF THEIR TEAM!
YOU'VE TOTALLED HIM!
HERE HE COMES! HERE HE COMES! NOW WE'LL FIND OUT EVERYTHING WE WANT TO KNOW ABOUT OUR OPPOSITION!
5

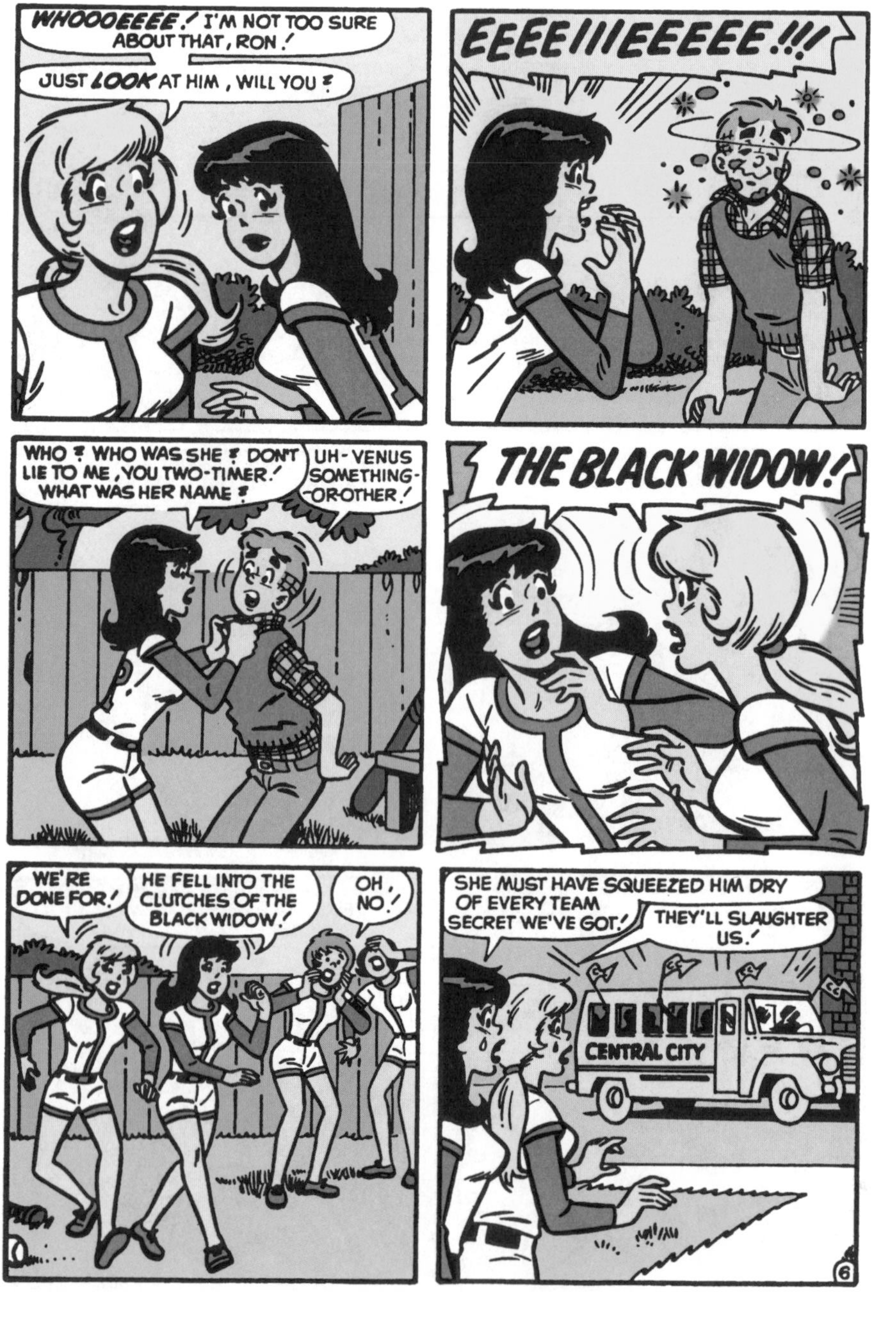
WHOOOEEEE! I'M NOT TOO SURE ABOUT THAT, RON!
JUST LOOK AT HIM, WILL YOU?
EEEEIIIEEEEEE!!!
WHO? WHO WAS SHE? DON'T LIE TO ME, YOU TWO-TIMER! WHAT WAS HER NAME?
UH-VENUS SOMETHING-OR-OTHER!
THE BLACK WIDOW!
WE'RE DONE FOR!
HE FELL INTO THE CLUTCHES OF THE BLACK WIDOW!
OH, NO!
SHE MUST HAVE SQUEEZED HIM DRY OF EVERY TEAM SECRET WE'VE GOT!
THEY'LL SLAUGHTER US!
CENTRAL CITY
6

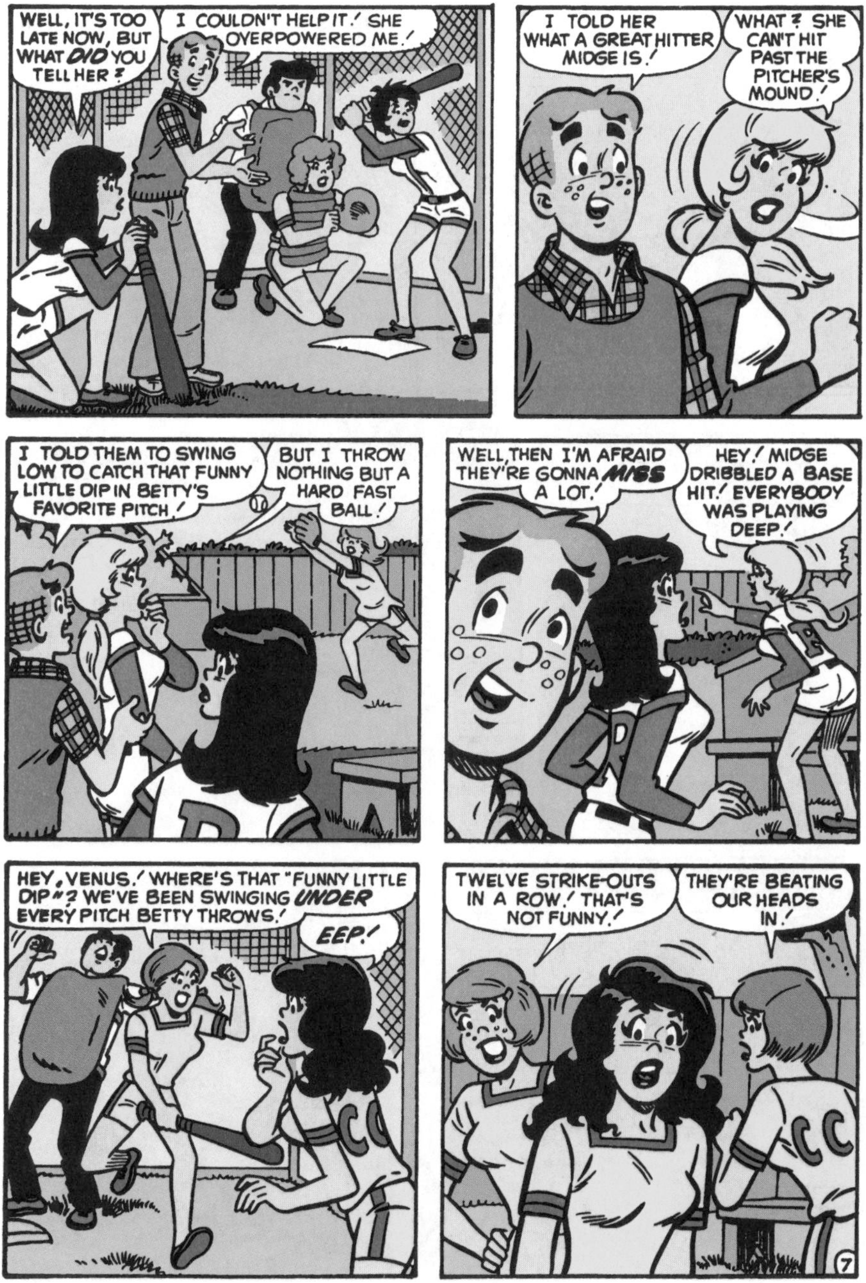
WELL, IT'S TOO LATE NOW, BUT WHAT DID YOU TELL HER ?
I COULDN'T HELP IT.! SHE OVERPOWERED ME.!
I TOLD HER WHAT A GREAT HITTER MIDGE IS.!
WHAT ? SHE CAN'T HIT PAST THE PITCHER'S MOUND.!
I TOLD THEM TO SWING LOW TO CATCH THAT FUNNY LITTLE DIP IN BETTY'S FAVORITE PITCH.!
BUT I THROW NOTHING BUT A HARD FAST BALL.!
WELL, THEN I'M AFRAID THEY'RE GONNA MISS A LOT.!
HEY.! MIDGE DRIBBLED A BASE HIT.! EVERYBODY WAS PLAYING DEEP.!
HEY, VENUS.! WHERE'S THAT "FUNNY LITTLE DIP"? WE'VE BEEN SWINGING UNDER EVERY PITCH BETTY THROWS.!
EEP!
TWELVE STRIKE-OUTS IN A ROW.! THAT'S NOT FUNNY.!
THEY'RE BEATING OUR HEADS IN.!
7

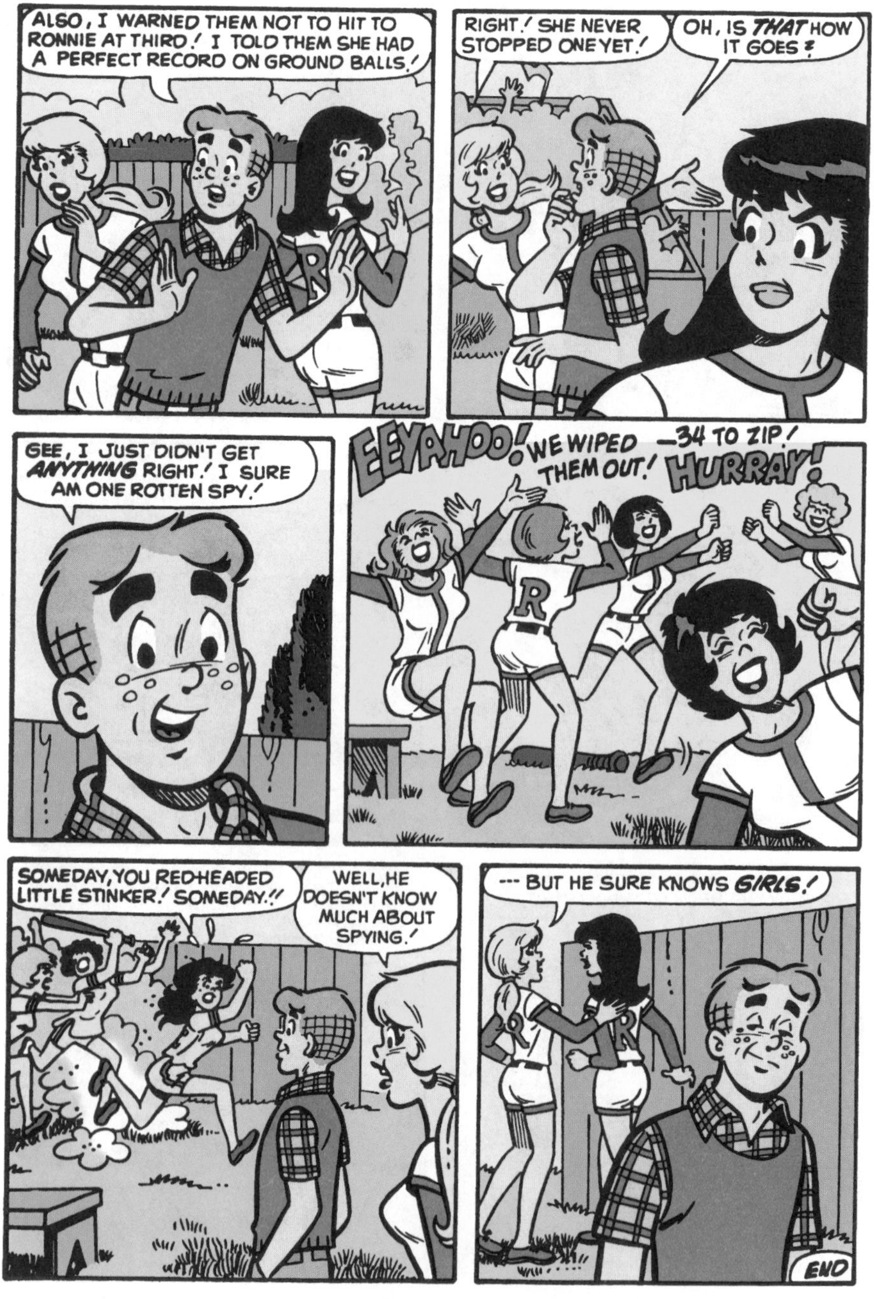
ALSO, I WARNED THEM NOT TO HIT TO RONNIE AT THIRD! I TOLD THEM SHE HAD A PERFECT RECORD ON GROUND BALLS!
RIGHT! SHE NEVER STOPPED ONE YET!
OH, IS *THAT* HOW IT GOES?
GEE, I JUST DIDN'T GET *ANYTHING* RIGHT! I SURE AM ONE ROTTEN SPY!
EEYAHOO!
WE WIPED THEM OUT!
—34 TO ZIP!
HURRAY!
SOMEDAY, YOU RED-HEADED LITTLE STINKER! SOMEDAY!!
WELL, HE DOESN'T KNOW MUCH ABOUT SPYING!
--- BUT HE SURE KNOWS *GIRLS*!
END

Archie at Riverdale in "The Hidden Talent"

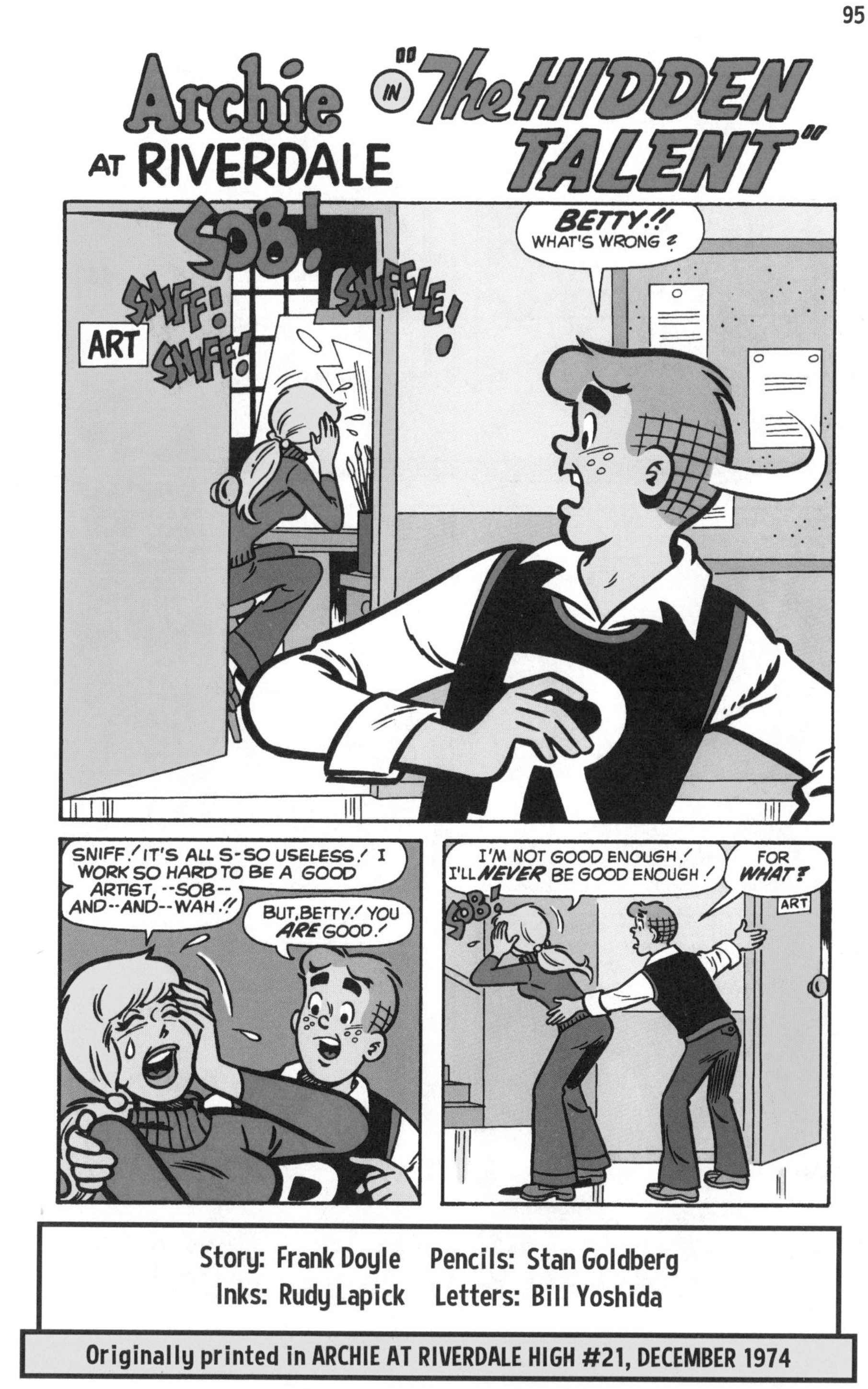
SOB!
SNIFF!
SNIFFLE!
SNIFF!
ART
BETTY!! WHAT'S WRONG?
SNIFF! IT'S ALL S-SO USELESS! I WORK SO HARD TO BE A GOOD ARTIST, --SOB-- AND--AND--WAH!!
BUT, BETTY! YOU ARE GOOD!
SOB!
I'M NOT GOOD ENOUGH! I'LL NEVER BE GOOD ENOUGH!
FOR WHAT?
ART

Story: Frank Doyle Pencils: Stan Goldberg
Inks: Rudy Lapick Letters: Bill Yoshida

Originally printed in ARCHIE AT RIVERDALE HIGH #21, DECEMBER 1974

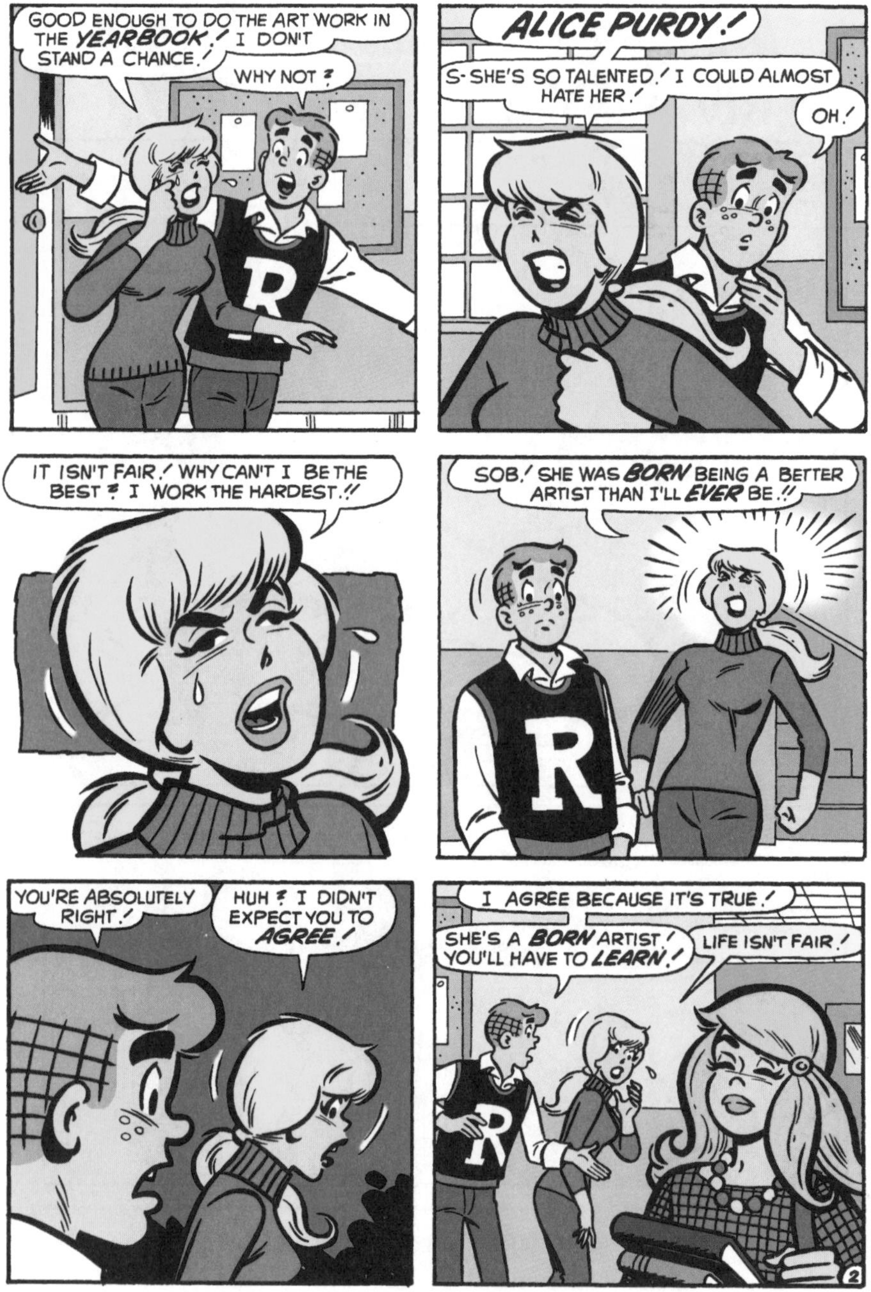
GOOD ENOUGH TO DO THE ART WORK IN THE YEARBOOK! I DON'T STAND A CHANCE!
WHY NOT?
ALICE PURDY!
S-SHE'S SO TALENTED! I COULD ALMOST HATE HER!
OH!
IT ISN'T FAIR! WHY CAN'T I BE THE BEST? I WORK THE HARDEST!!
SOB! SHE WAS BORN BEING A BETTER ARTIST THAN I'LL EVER BE!!
YOU'RE ABSOLUTELY RIGHT!
HUH? I DIDN'T EXPECT YOU TO AGREE!
I AGREE BECAUSE IT'S TRUE!
SHE'S A BORN ARTIST! YOU'LL HAVE TO LEARN!
LIFE ISN'T FAIR!
2

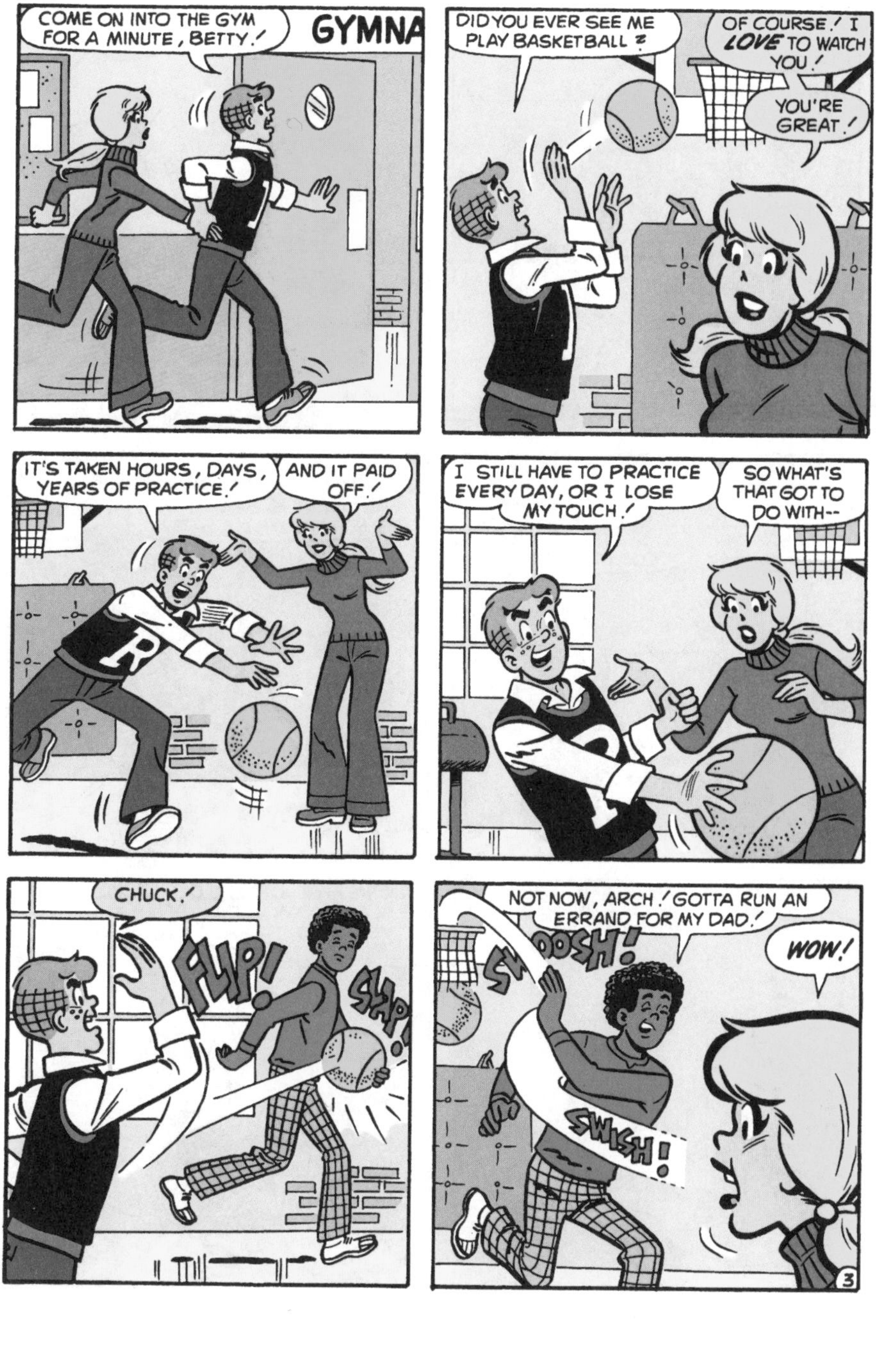
COME ON INTO THE GYM FOR A MINUTE, BETTY!
GYMNA
DID YOU EVER SEE ME PLAY BASKETBALL?
OF COURSE! I LOVE TO WATCH YOU!
YOU'RE GREAT!
IT'S TAKEN HOURS, DAYS, YEARS OF PRACTICE!
AND IT PAID OFF!
I STILL HAVE TO PRACTICE EVERY DAY, OR I LOSE MY TOUCH!
SO WHAT'S THAT GOT TO DO WITH--
CHUCK!
FLIP!
SLAP!
NOT NOW, ARCH! GOTTA RUN AN ERRAND FOR MY DAD!
WOW!
SWOOSH!
SWISH!
3

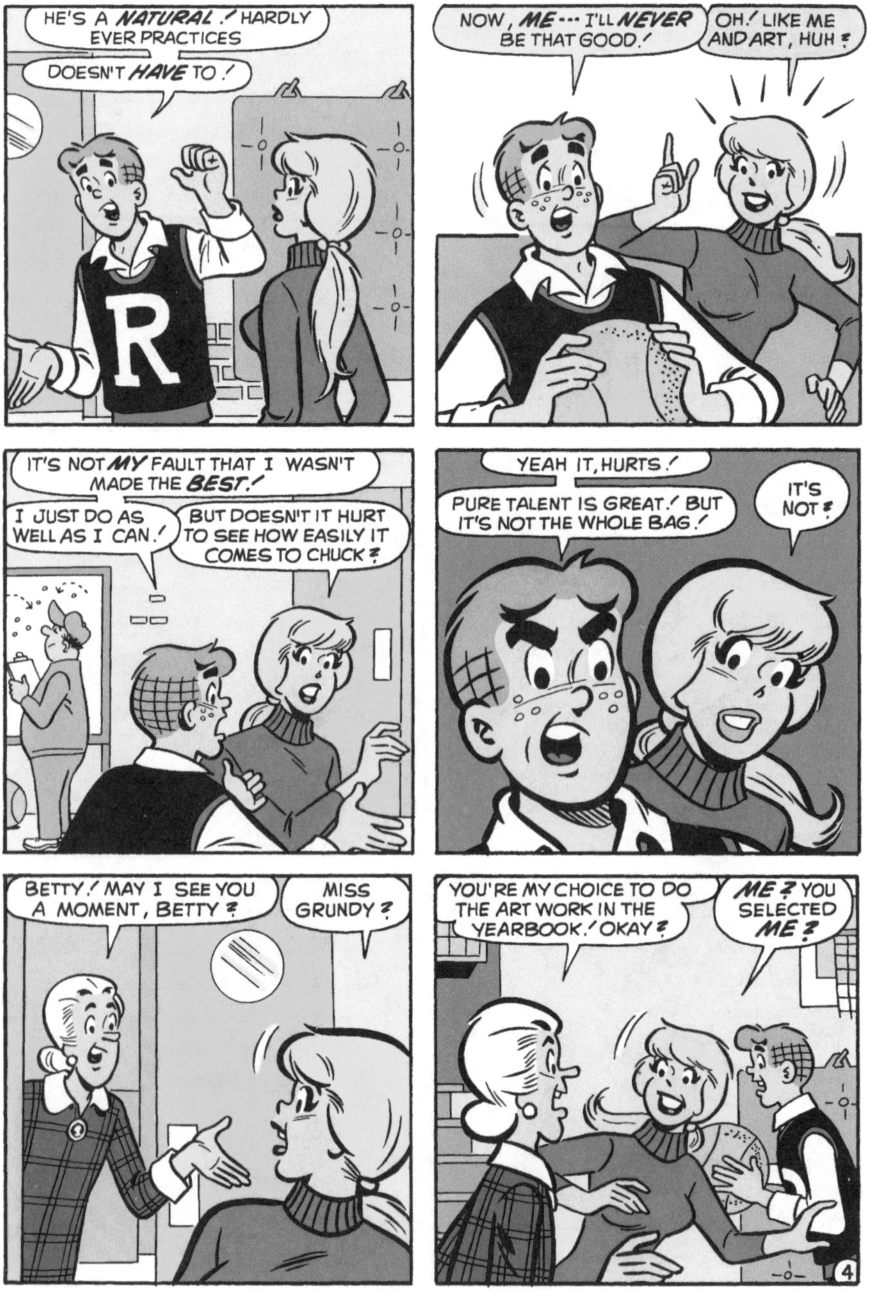
HE'S A NATURAL! HARDLY EVER PRACTICES
DOESN'T HAVE TO!
NOW, ME··· I'LL NEVER BE THAT GOOD!
OH! LIKE ME AND ART, HUH?
IT'S NOT MY FAULT THAT I WASN'T MADE THE BEST!
I JUST DO AS WELL AS I CAN!
BUT DOESN'T IT HURT TO SEE HOW EASILY IT COMES TO CHUCK?
YEAH IT, HURTS!
PURE TALENT IS GREAT! BUT IT'S NOT THE WHOLE BAG!
IT'S NOT?
BETTY! MAY I SEE YOU A MOMENT, BETTY?
MISS GRUNDY?
YOU'RE MY CHOICE TO DO THE ART WORK IN THE YEARBOOK! OKAY?
ME? YOU SELECTED ME?
4

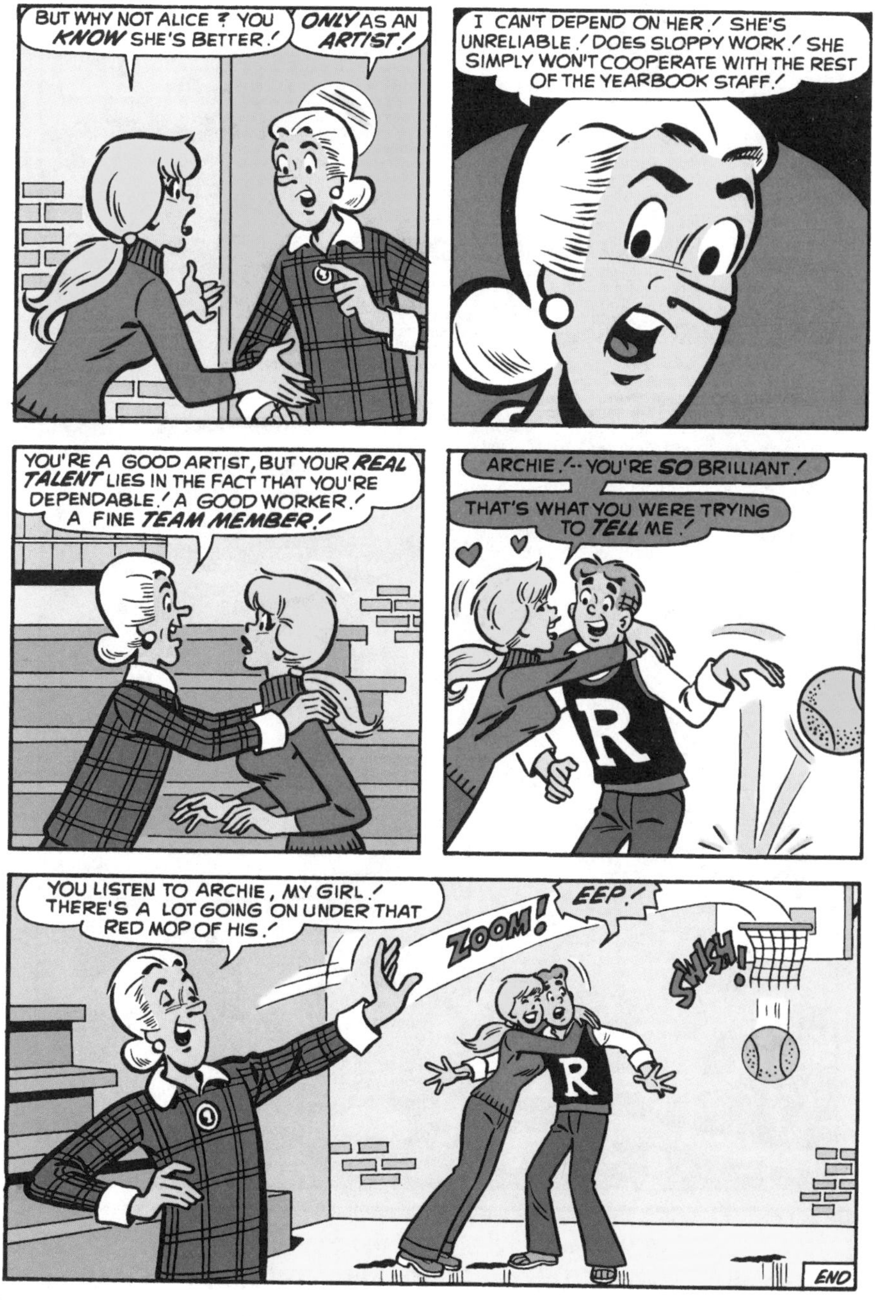
BUT WHY NOT ALICE ? YOU KNOW SHE'S BETTER!
ONLY AS AN ARTIST!
I CAN'T DEPEND ON HER! SHE'S UNRELIABLE! DOES SLOPPY WORK! SHE SIMPLY WON'T COOPERATE WITH THE REST OF THE YEARBOOK STAFF!
YOU'RE A GOOD ARTIST, BUT YOUR REAL TALENT LIES IN THE FACT THAT YOU'RE DEPENDABLE! A GOOD WORKER! A FINE TEAM MEMBER!
ARCHIE!-- YOU'RE SO BRILLIANT!
THAT'S WHAT YOU WERE TRYING TO TELL ME!
R
YOU LISTEN TO ARCHIE, MY GIRL! THERE'S A LOT GOING ON UNDER THAT RED MOP OF HIS!
ZOOM!
EEP!
SWISH!
R
END

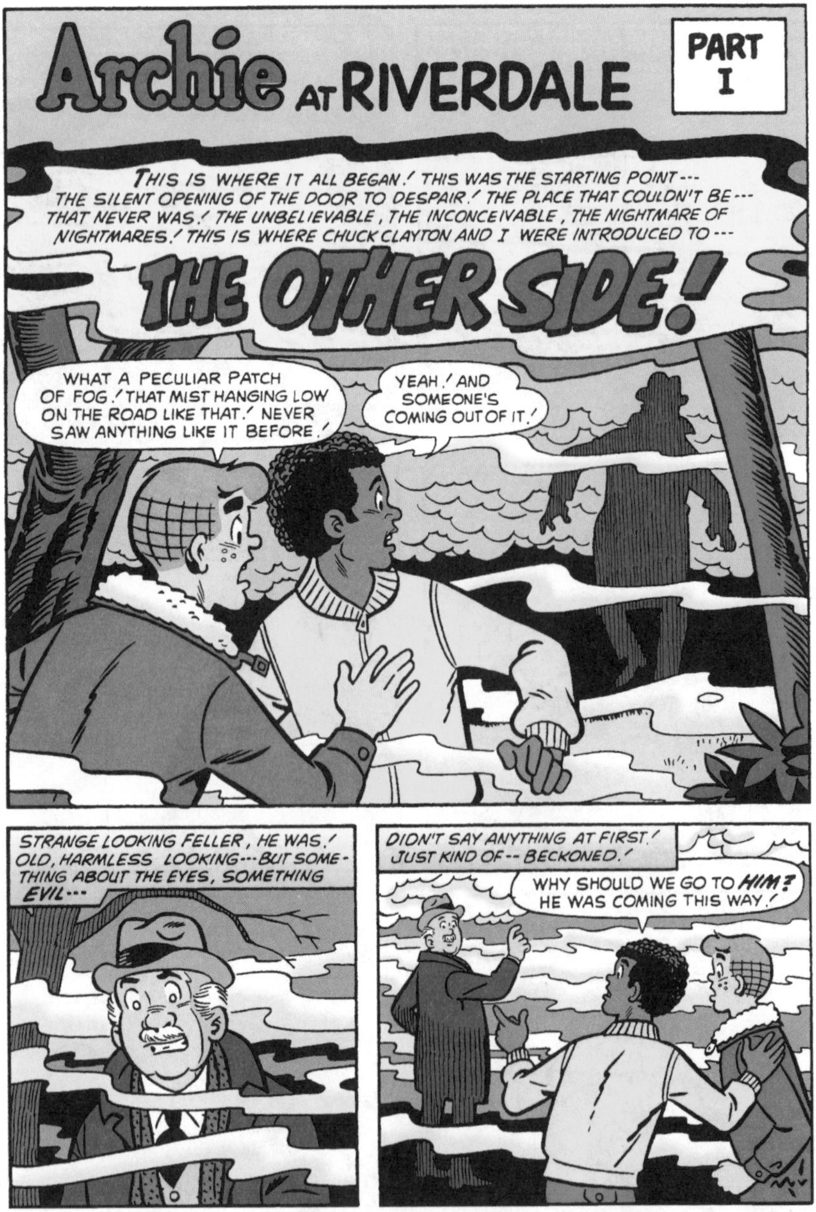
Archie AT RIVERDALE
PART I
THIS IS WHERE IT ALL BEGAN! THIS WAS THE STARTING POINT--- THE SILENT OPENING OF THE DOOR TO DESPAIR! THE PLACE THAT COULDN'T BE--- THAT NEVER WAS! THE UNBELIEVABLE, THE INCONCEIVABLE, THE NIGHTMARE OF NIGHTMARES! THIS IS WHERE CHUCK CLAYTON AND I WERE INTRODUCED TO---
THE OTHER SIDE!
WHAT A PECULIAR PATCH OF FOG! THAT MIST HANGING LOW ON THE ROAD LIKE THAT! NEVER SAW ANYTHING LIKE IT BEFORE!
YEAH! AND SOMEONE'S COMING OUT OF IT!
STRANGE LOOKING FELLER, HE WAS! OLD, HARMLESS LOOKING---BUT SOMETHING ABOUT THE EYES, SOMETHING EVIL---
DIDN'T SAY ANYTHING AT FIRST! JUST KIND OF--BECKONED!
WHY SHOULD WE GO TO HIM? HE WAS COMING THIS WAY!

Story: Frank Doyle **Pencils:** Stan Goldberg
Inks: Jon D'Agostino **Letters:** Bill Yoshida **Colors:** Barry Grossman

Originally printed in ARCHIE AT RIVERDALE HIGH #24, APRIL 1975

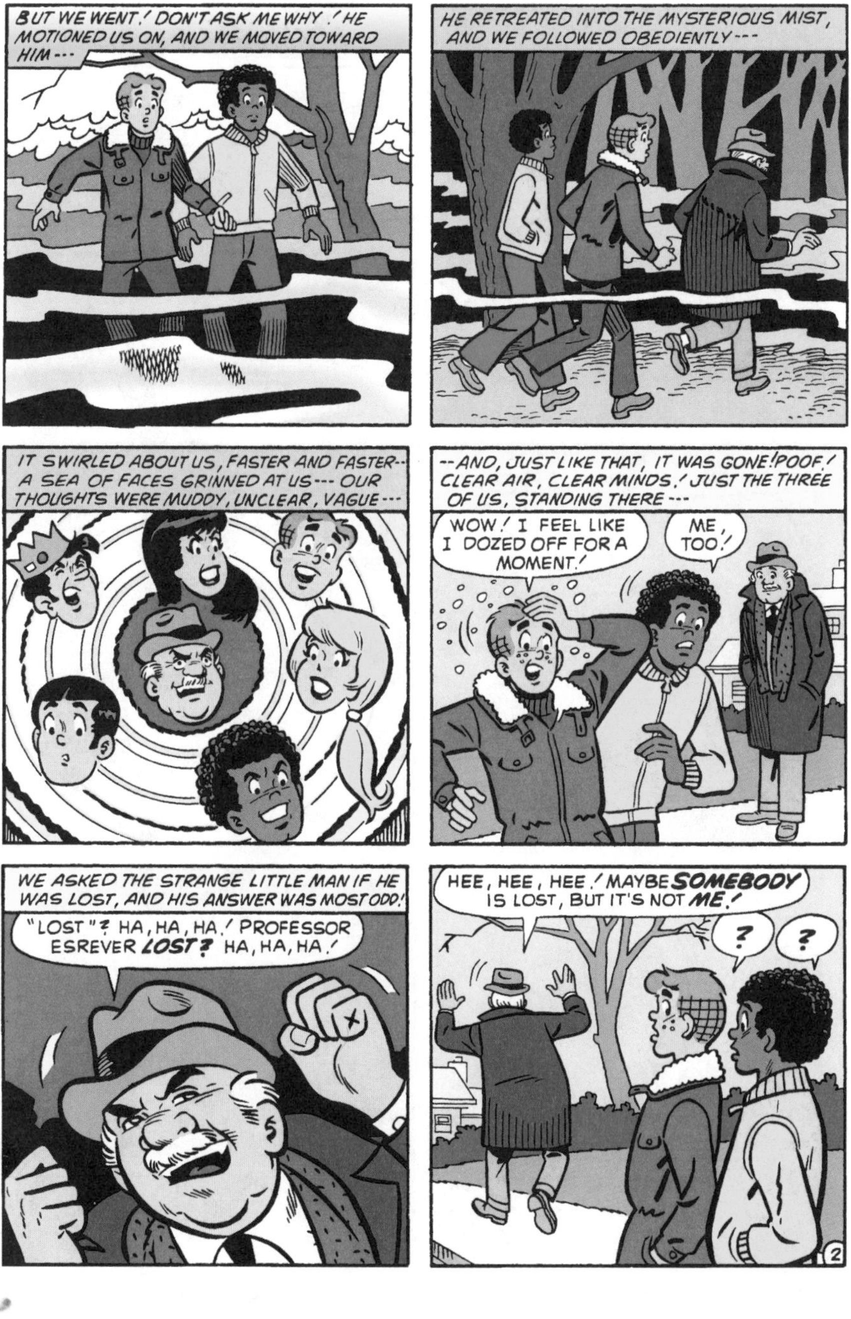
BUT WE WENT! DON'T ASK ME WHY! HE MOTIONED US ON, AND WE MOVED TOWARD HIM---
HE RETREATED INTO THE MYSTERIOUS MIST, AND WE FOLLOWED OBEDIENTLY---
IT SWIRLED ABOUT US, FASTER AND FASTER-- A SEA OF FACES GRINNED AT US--- OUR THOUGHTS WERE MUDDY, UNCLEAR, VAGUE---
--AND, JUST LIKE THAT, IT WAS GONE! POOF! CLEAR AIR, CLEAR MINDS! JUST THE THREE OF US, STANDING THERE---
WOW! I FEEL LIKE I DOZED OFF FOR A MOMENT!
ME, TOO!
WE ASKED THE STRANGE LITTLE MAN IF HE WAS LOST, AND HIS ANSWER WAS MOST ODD!
"LOST"? HA, HA, HA! PROFESSOR ESREVER LOST? HA, HA, HA!
HEE, HEE, HEE! MAYBE SOMEBODY IS LOST, BUT IT'S NOT ME!
?
?
2

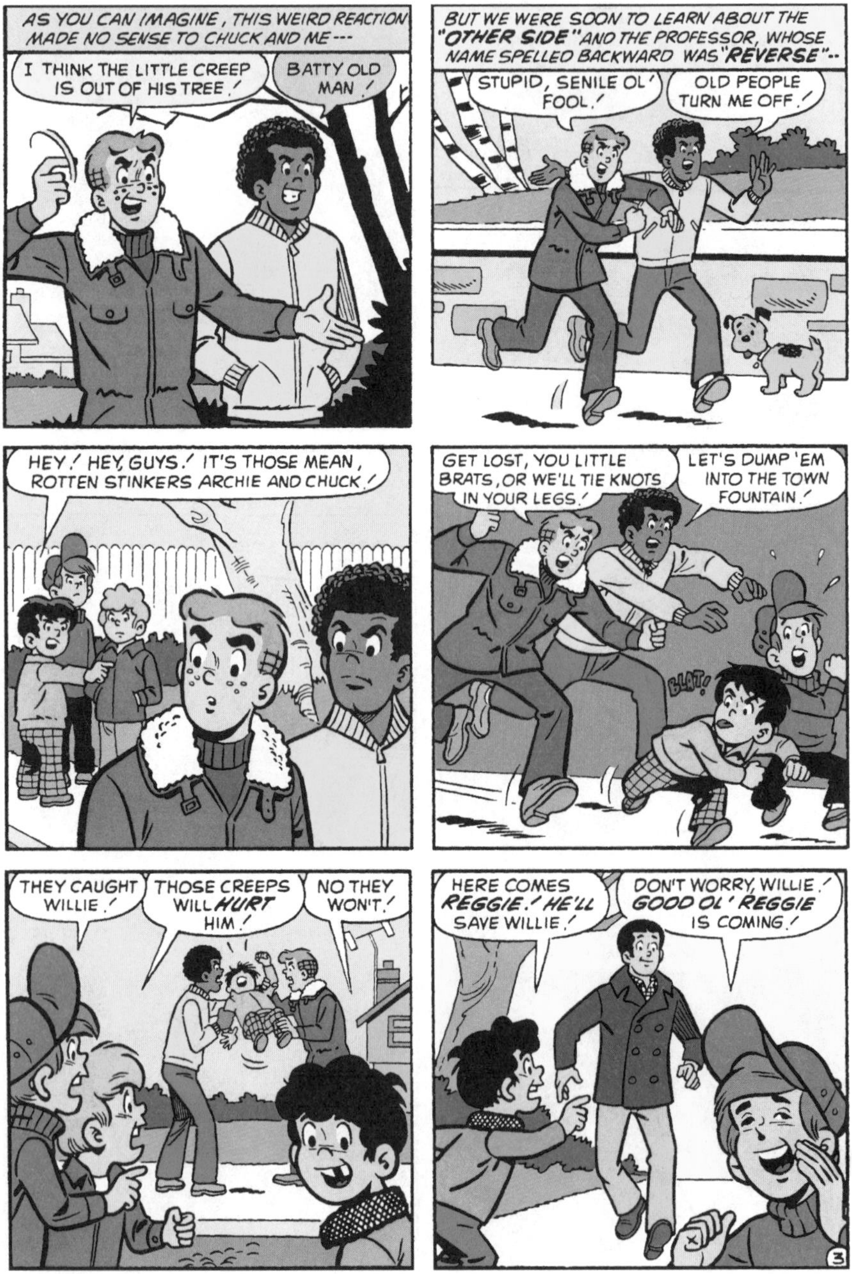
AS YOU CAN IMAGINE, THIS WEIRD REACTION MADE NO SENSE TO CHUCK AND ME---
I THINK THE LITTLE CREEP IS OUT OF HIS TREE!
BATTY OLD MAN!
BUT WE WERE SOON TO LEARN ABOUT THE "OTHER SIDE" AND THE PROFESSOR, WHOSE NAME SPELLED BACKWARD WAS "REVERSE"--
STUPID, SENILE OL' FOOL!
OLD PEOPLE TURN ME OFF!
HEY! HEY, GUYS! IT'S THOSE MEAN, ROTTEN STINKERS ARCHIE AND CHUCK!
GET LOST, YOU LITTLE BRATS, OR WE'LL TIE KNOTS IN YOUR LEGS!
LET'S DUMP 'EM INTO THE TOWN FOUNTAIN!
BLAT!
THEY CAUGHT WILLIE!
THOSE CREEPS WILL HURT HIM!
NO THEY WON'T!
HERE COMES REGGIE! HE'LL SAVE WILLIE!
DON'T WORRY, WILLIE! GOOD OL' REGGIE IS COMING!
3

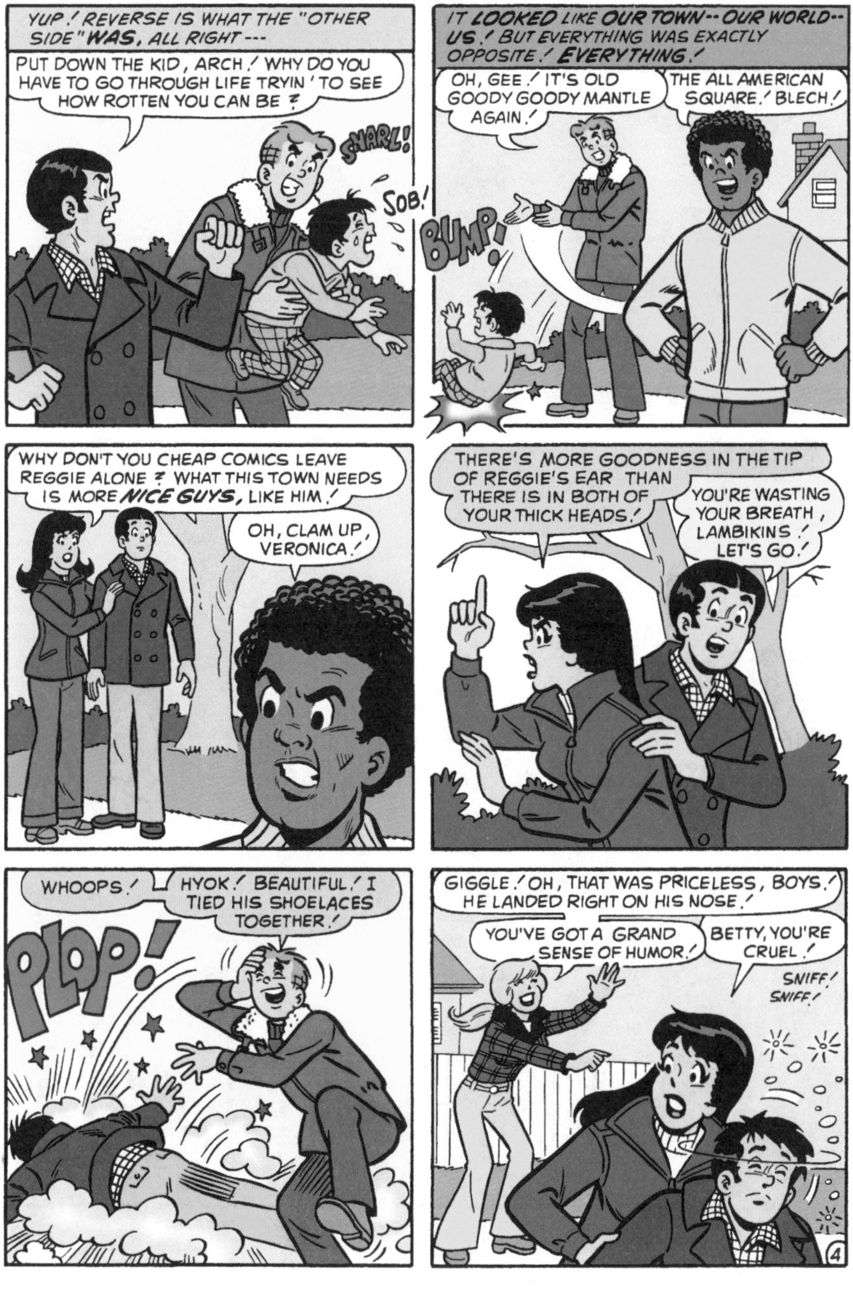
YUP! REVERSE IS WHAT THE "OTHER SIDE" WAS, ALL RIGHT---
PUT DOWN THE KID, ARCH! WHY DO YOU HAVE TO GO THROUGH LIFE TRYIN' TO SEE HOW ROTTEN YOU CAN BE?
SNARL!
SOB!
IT LOOKED LIKE OUR TOWN--OUR WORLD--US! BUT EVERYTHING WAS EXACTLY OPPOSITE! EVERYTHING!
OH, GEE! IT'S OLD GOODY GOODY MANTLE AGAIN!
THE ALL AMERICAN SQUARE! BLECH!
BUMP!
WHY DON'T YOU CHEAP COMICS LEAVE REGGIE ALONE? WHAT THIS TOWN NEEDS IS MORE NICE GUYS, LIKE HIM!
OH, CLAM UP, VERONICA!
THERE'S MORE GOODNESS IN THE TIP OF REGGIE'S EAR THAN THERE IS IN BOTH OF YOUR THICK HEADS!
YOU'RE WASTING YOUR BREATH, LAMBIKINS! LET'S GO!
WHOOPS!
HYOK! BEAUTIFUL! I TIED HIS SHOELACES TOGETHER!
PLOP!
GIGGLE! OH, THAT WAS PRICELESS, BOYS! HE LANDED RIGHT ON HIS NOSE!
YOU'VE GOT A GRAND SENSE OF HUMOR!
BETTY, YOU'RE CRUEL!
SNIFF! SNIFF!
4

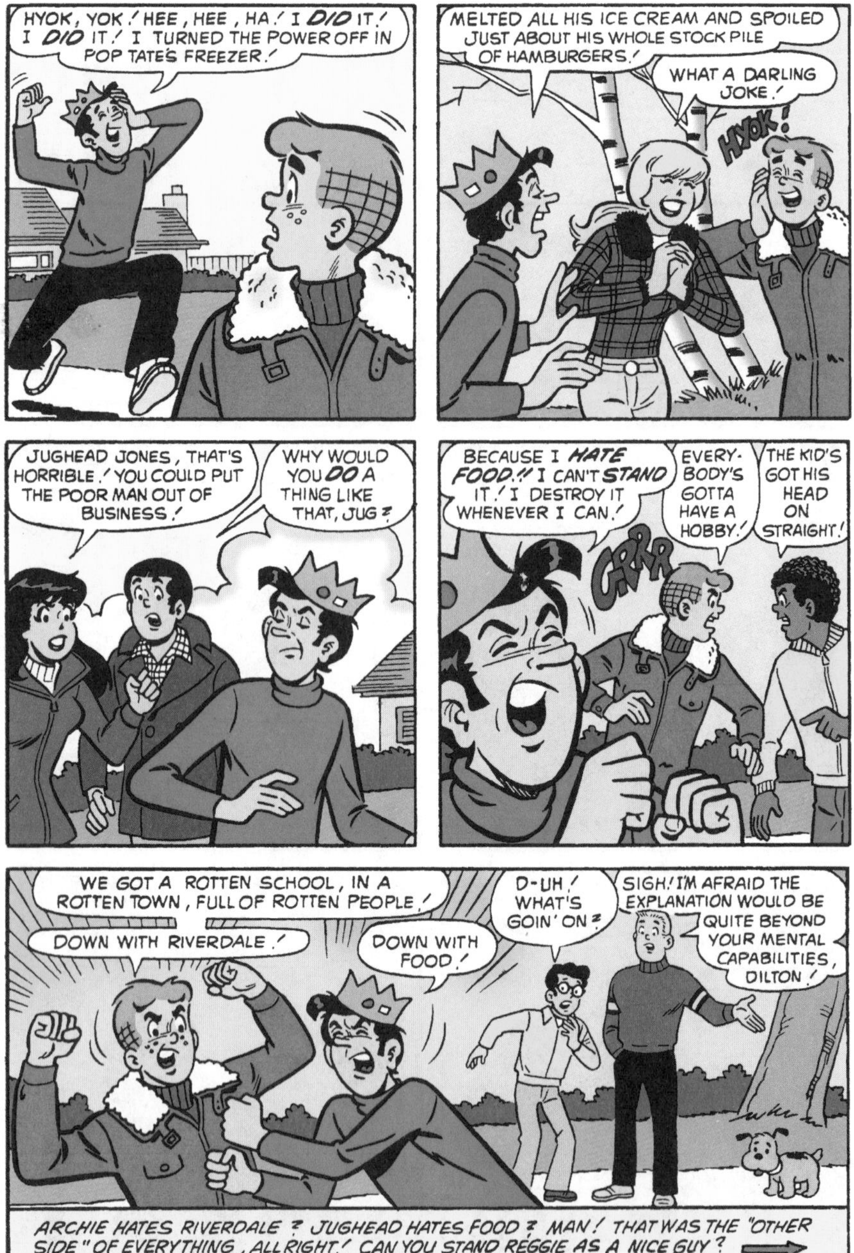
HYOK, YOK! HEE, HEE, HA! I DID IT! I DID IT! I TURNED THE POWER OFF IN POP TATE'S FREEZER!
MELTED ALL HIS ICE CREAM AND SPOILED JUST ABOUT HIS WHOLE STOCK PILE OF HAMBURGERS!
WHAT A DARLING JOKE!
HYOK!
JUGHEAD JONES, THAT'S HORRIBLE! YOU COULD PUT THE POOR MAN OUT OF BUSINESS!
WHY WOULD YOU DO A THING LIKE THAT, JUG?
BECAUSE I HATE FOOD!! I CAN'T STAND IT! I DESTROY IT WHENEVER I CAN!
EVERY-BODY'S GOTTA HAVE A HOBBY!
THE KID'S GOT HIS HEAD ON STRAIGHT!
GRRR
WE GOT A ROTTEN SCHOOL, IN A ROTTEN TOWN, FULL OF ROTTEN PEOPLE!
DOWN WITH RIVERDALE!
DOWN WITH FOOD!
D-UH! WHAT'S GOIN' ON?
SIGH! I'M AFRAID THE EXPLANATION WOULD BE QUITE BEYOND YOUR MENTAL CAPABILITIES, DILTON!
ARCHIE HATES RIVERDALE? JUGHEAD HATES FOOD? MAN! THAT WAS THE "OTHER SIDE" OF EVERYTHING, ALL RIGHT! CAN YOU STAND REGGIE AS A NICE GUY?

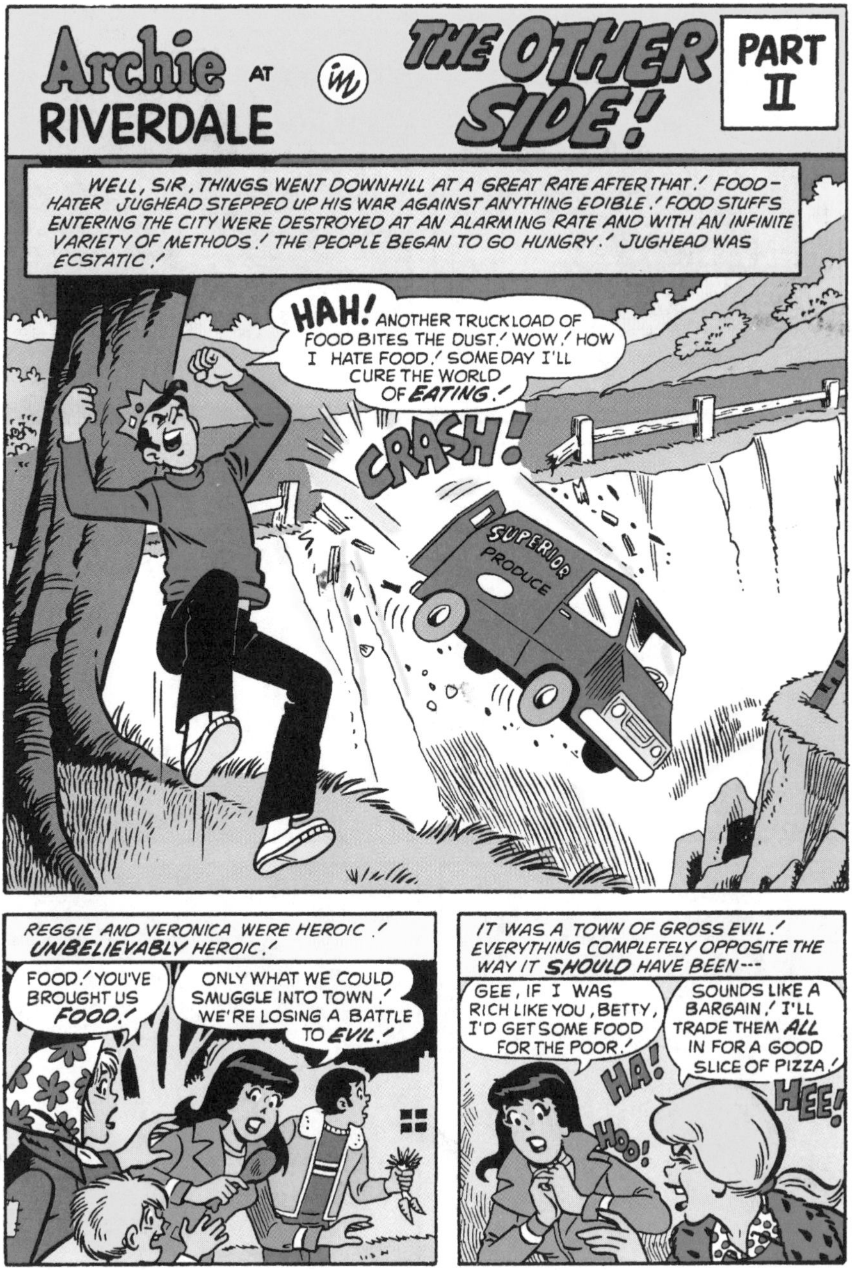
Archie AT RIVERDALE
in
THE OTHER SIDE!
PART II
WELL, SIR, THINGS WENT DOWNHILL AT A GREAT RATE AFTER THAT! FOOD-HATER JUGHEAD STEPPED UP HIS WAR AGAINST ANYTHING EDIBLE! FOOD STUFFS ENTERING THE CITY WERE DESTROYED AT AN ALARMING RATE AND WITH AN INFINITE VARIETY OF METHODS! THE PEOPLE BEGAN TO GO HUNGRY! JUGHEAD WAS ECSTATIC!
HAH! ANOTHER TRUCKLOAD OF FOOD BITES THE DUST! WOW! HOW I HATE FOOD! SOMEDAY I'LL CURE THE WORLD OF EATING!
CRASH!
SUPERIOR PRODUCE
REGGIE AND VERONICA WERE HEROIC! UNBELIEVABLY HEROIC!
FOOD! YOU'VE BROUGHT US FOOD!
ONLY WHAT WE COULD SMUGGLE INTO TOWN! WE'RE LOSING A BATTLE TO EVIL!
IT WAS A TOWN OF GROSS EVIL! EVERYTHING COMPLETELY OPPOSITE THE WAY IT SHOULD HAVE BEEN---
GEE, IF I WAS RICH LIKE YOU, BETTY, I'D GET SOME FOOD FOR THE POOR!
SOUNDS LIKE A BARGAIN! I'LL TRADE THEM ALL IN FOR A GOOD SLICE OF PIZZA!
HA!
HOO!
HEE!

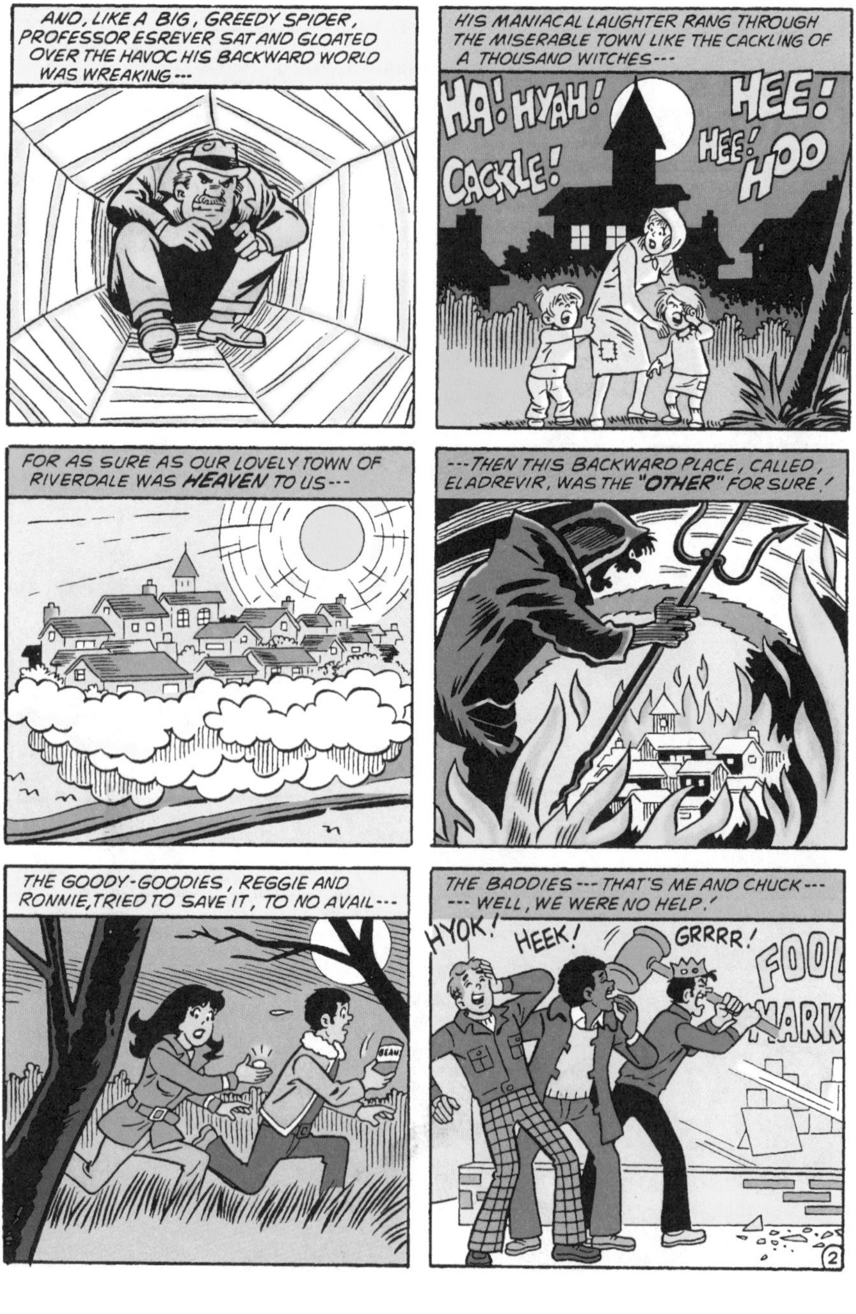
AND, LIKE A BIG, GREEDY SPIDER, PROFESSOR ESREVER SAT AND GLOATED OVER THE HAVOC HIS BACKWARD WORLD WAS WREAKING---
HIS MANIACAL LAUGHTER RANG THROUGH THE MISERABLE TOWN LIKE THE CACKLING OF A THOUSAND WITCHES---
HA! HYAH!
HEE!
CACKLE!
HEE! HOO
FOR AS SURE AS OUR LOVELY TOWN OF RIVERDALE WAS HEAVEN TO US---
---THEN THIS BACKWARD PLACE, CALLED, ELADREVIR, WAS THE "OTHER" FOR SURE!
THE GOODY-GOODIES, REGGIE AND RONNIE, TRIED TO SAVE IT, TO NO AVAIL---
THE BADDIES---THAT'S ME AND CHUCK--- ---WELL, WE WERE NO HELP!
HYOK!
HEEK!
GRRRR!
2

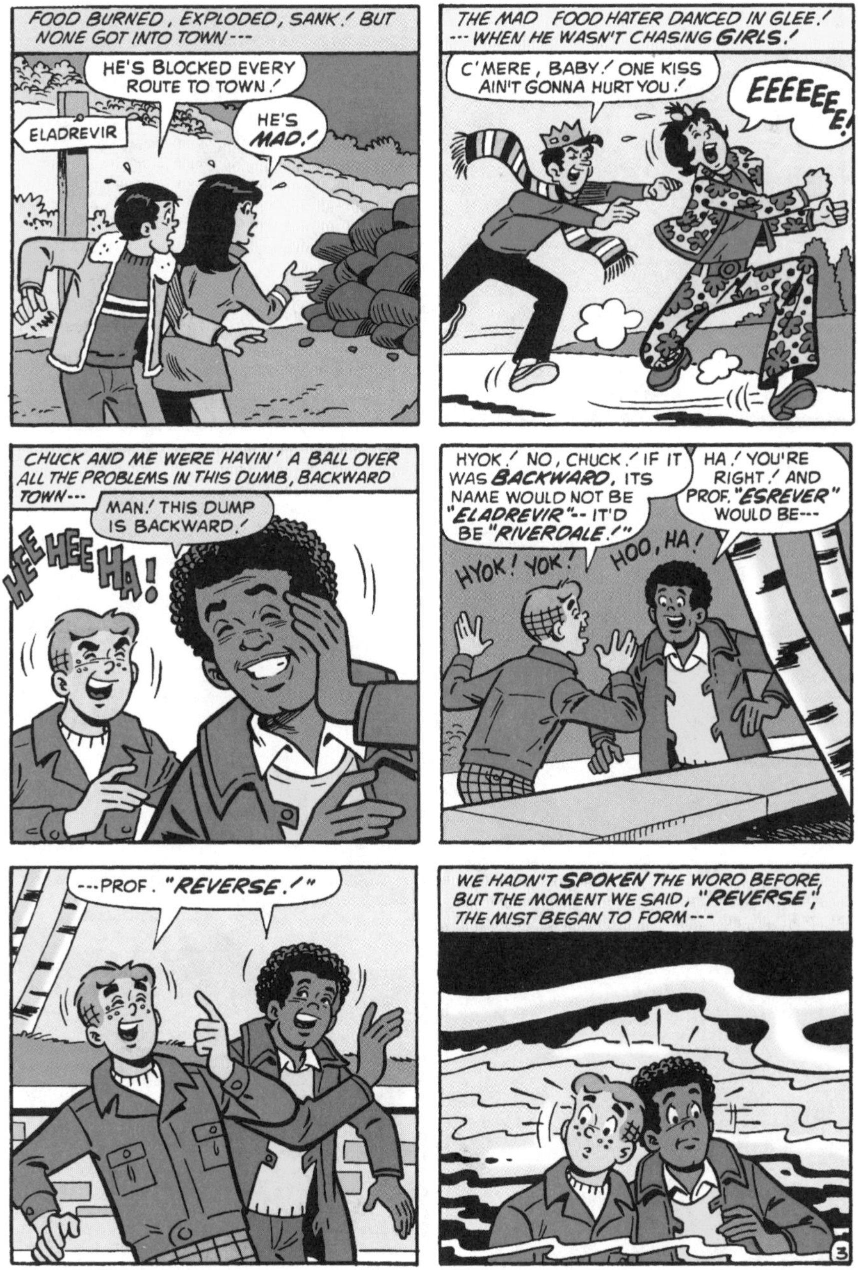
FOOD BURNED, EXPLODED, SANK! BUT NONE GOT INTO TOWN---
HE'S BLOCKED EVERY ROUTE TO TOWN!
ELADREVIR
HE'S MAD!
THE MAD FOOD HATER DANCED IN GLEE! --- WHEN HE WASN'T CHASING GIRLS!
C'MERE, BABY! ONE KISS AIN'T GONNA HURT YOU!
EEEEEEE!
CHUCK AND ME WERE HAVIN' A BALL OVER ALL THE PROBLEMS IN THIS DUMB, BACKWARD TOWN---
MAN! THIS DUMP IS BACKWARD!
HEE HEE HA!
HYOK! NO, CHUCK! IF IT WAS BACKWARD, ITS NAME WOULD NOT BE "ELADREVIR"-- IT'D BE "RIVERDALE!"
HA! YOU'RE RIGHT! AND PROF. "ESREVER" WOULD BE---
HYOK! YOK!
HOO, HA!
---PROF. "REVERSE!"
WE HADN'T SPOKEN THE WORD BEFORE, BUT THE MOMENT WE SAID, "REVERSE", THE MIST BEGAN TO FORM---
3

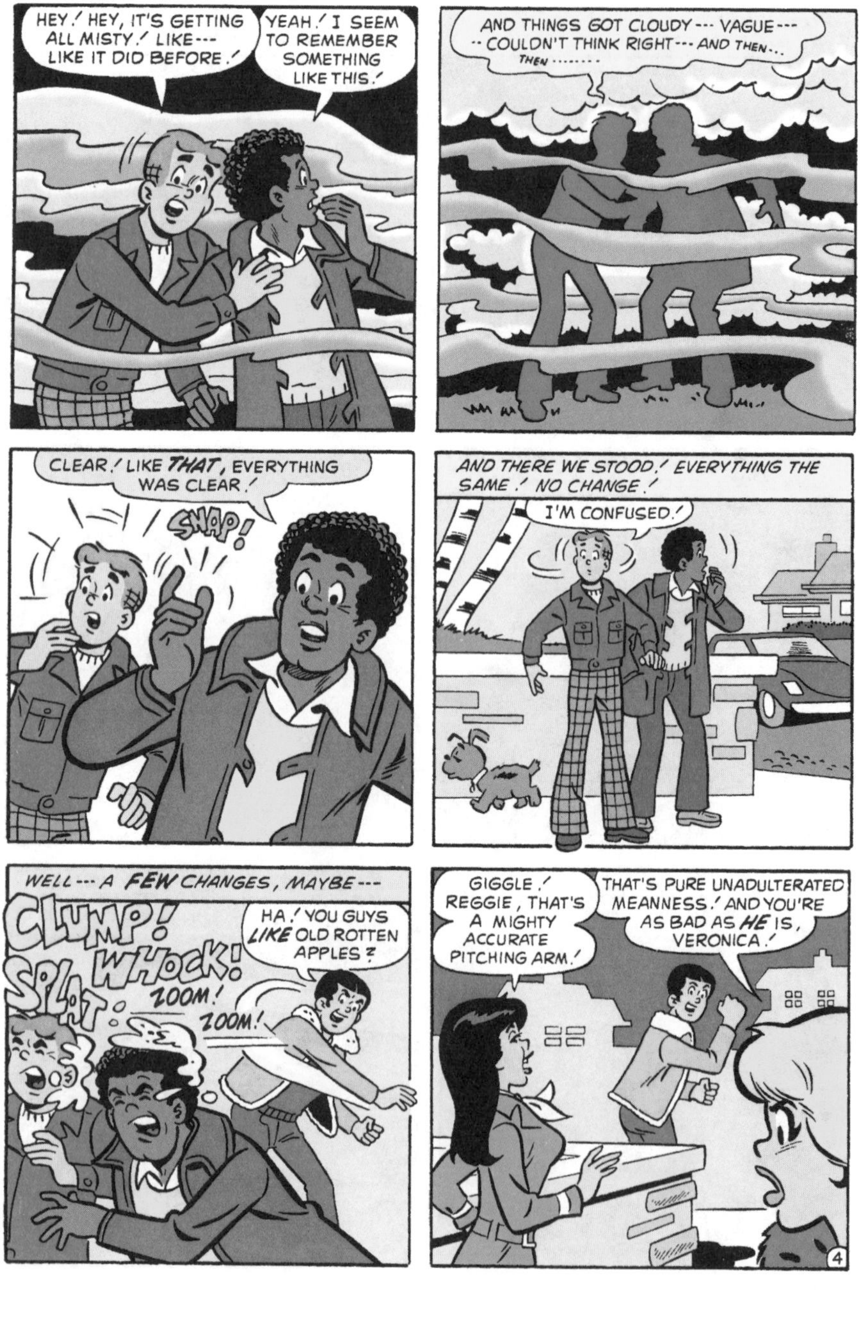
HEY! HEY, IT'S GETTING ALL MISTY! LIKE--- LIKE IT DID BEFORE!
YEAH! I SEEM TO REMEMBER SOMETHING LIKE THIS!
AND THINGS GOT CLOUDY --- VAGUE --- -- COULDN'T THINK RIGHT --- AND THEN... THEN ....
CLEAR! LIKE THAT, EVERYTHING WAS CLEAR!
SNAP!
AND THERE WE STOOD! EVERYTHING THE SAME! NO CHANGE!
I'M CONFUSED!
WELL --- A FEW CHANGES, MAYBE ---
CLUMP!
WHOCK!
SPLAT
ZOOM!
ZOOM!
HA! YOU GUYS LIKE OLD ROTTEN APPLES?
GIGGLE! REGGIE, THAT'S A MIGHTY ACCURATE PITCHING ARM!
THAT'S PURE UNADULTERATED MEANNESS! AND YOU'RE AS BAD AS HE IS, VERONICA!
4

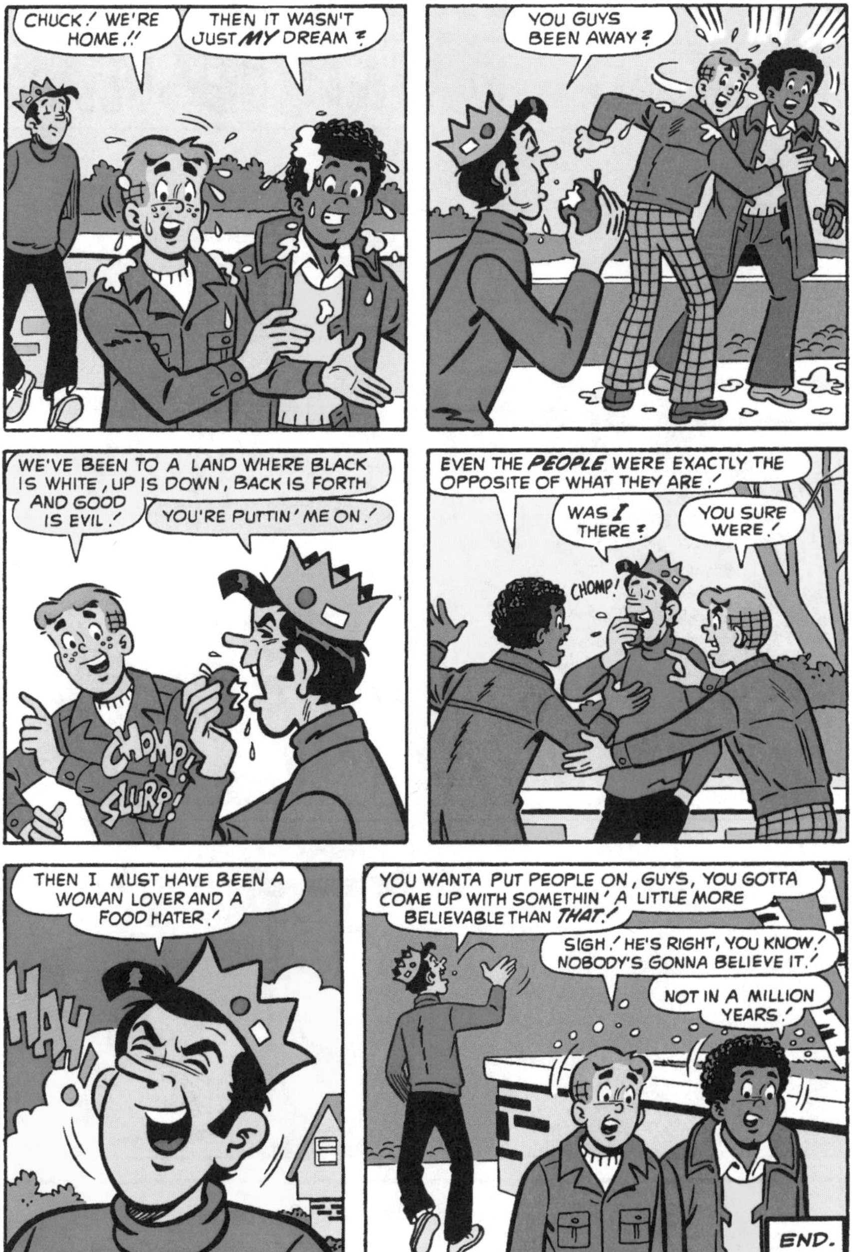
CHUCK! WE'RE HOME!!
THEN IT WASN'T JUST MY DREAM?
YOU GUYS BEEN AWAY?
WE'VE BEEN TO A LAND WHERE BLACK IS WHITE, UP IS DOWN, BACK IS FORTH AND GOOD IS EVIL!
YOU'RE PUTTIN' ME ON!
CHOMP! SLURP!
EVEN THE PEOPLE WERE EXACTLY THE OPPOSITE OF WHAT THEY ARE!
WAS I THERE?
YOU SURE WERE!
CHOMP!
THEN I MUST HAVE BEEN A WOMAN LOVER AND A FOOD HATER!
HAW!
YOU WANTA PUT PEOPLE ON, GUYS, YOU GOTTA COME UP WITH SOMETHIN' A LITTLE MORE BELIEVABLE THAN THAT!
SIGH! HE'S RIGHT, YOU KNOW! NOBODY'S GONNA BELIEVE IT!
NOT IN A MILLION YEARS!
END.

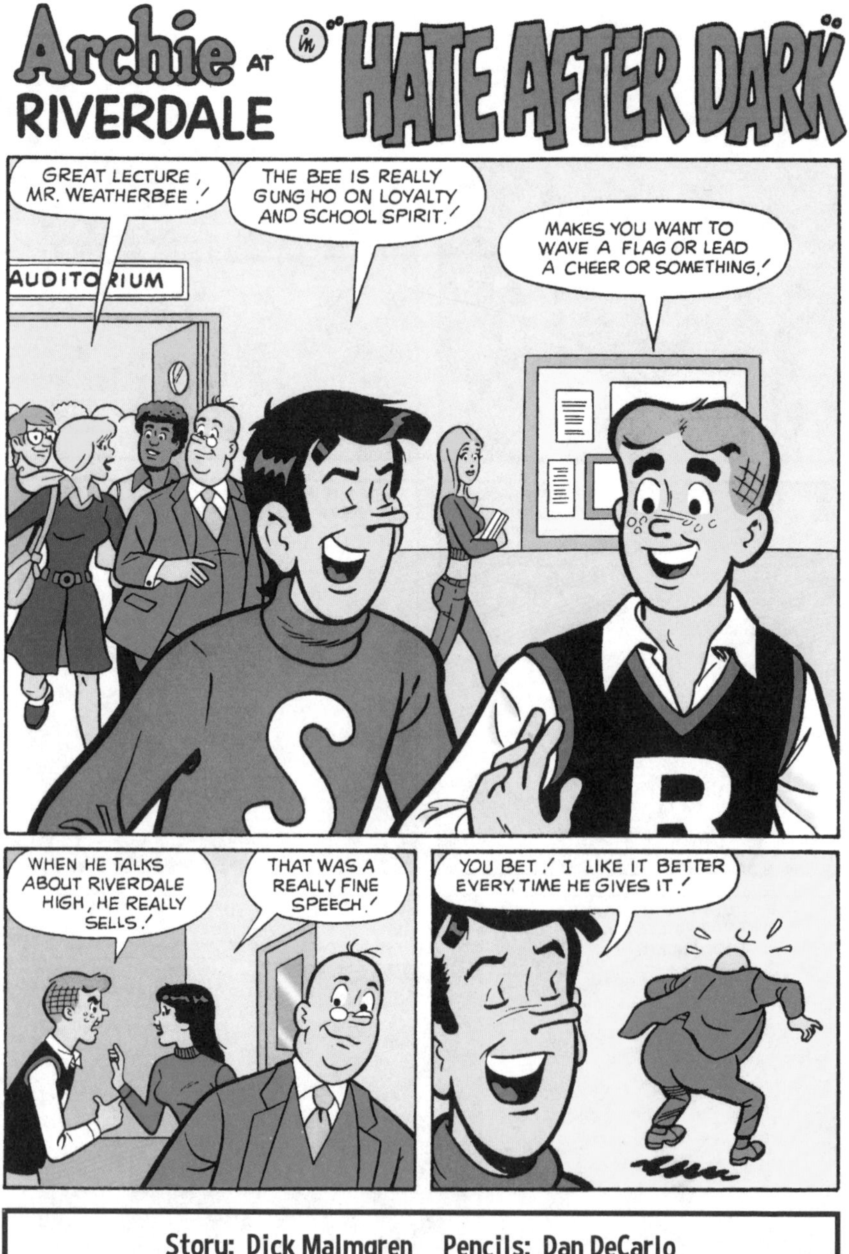
Archie AT RIVERDALE
in "HATE AFTER DARK"
GREAT LECTURE, MR. WEATHERBEE!
THE BEE IS REALLY GUNG HO ON LOYALTY AND SCHOOL SPIRIT!
AUDITORIUM
MAKES YOU WANT TO WAVE A FLAG OR LEAD A CHEER OR SOMETHING!
WHEN HE TALKS ABOUT RIVERDALE HIGH, HE REALLY SELLS!
THAT WAS A REALLY FINE SPEECH!
YOU BET! I LIKE IT BETTER EVERY TIME HE GIVES IT!

Story: Dick Malmgren Pencils: Dan DeCarlo
Inks: Alison Flood Letters: Bill Yoshida Colors: Barry Grossman

Originally printed in ARCHIE AT RIVERDALE HIGH #24, APRIL 1975

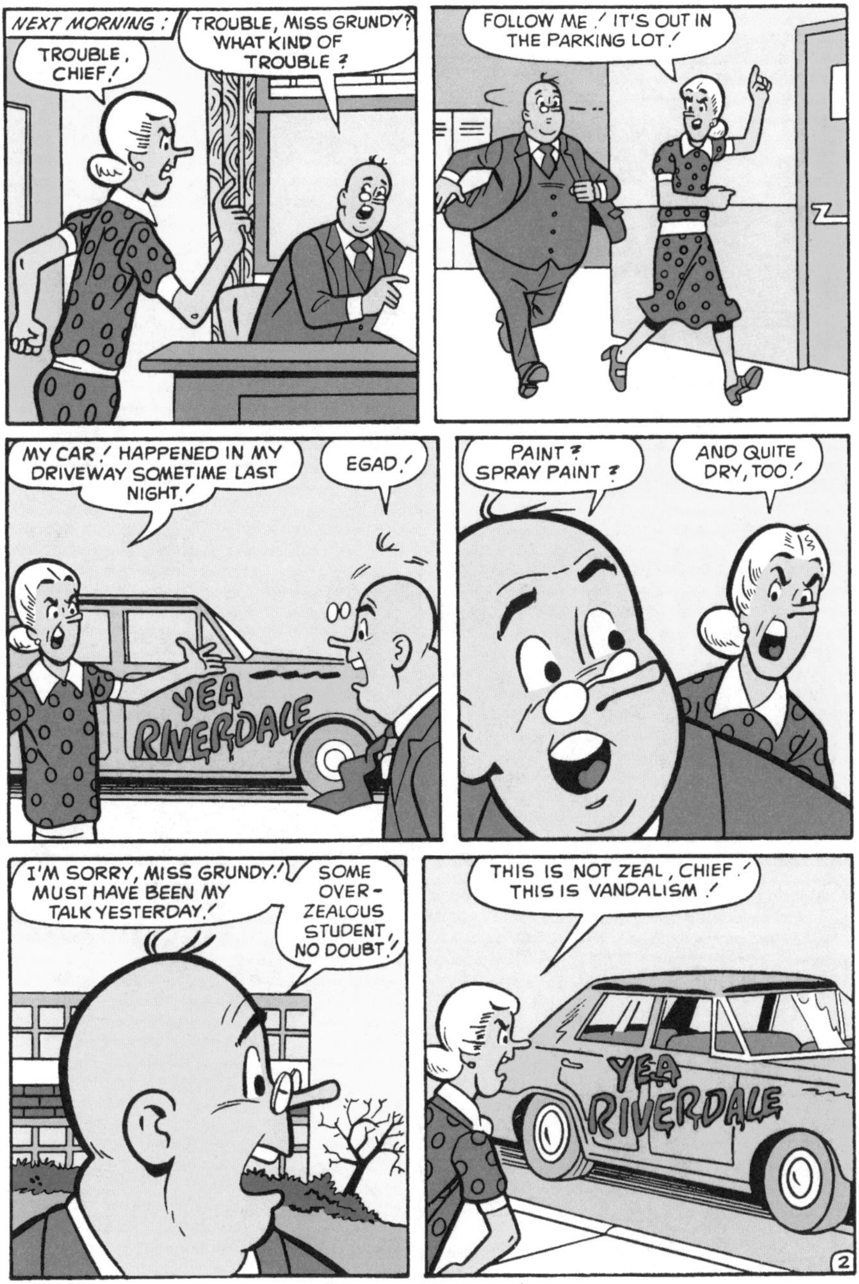
NEXT MORNING :
TROUBLE, CHIEF!
TROUBLE, MISS GRUNDY? WHAT KIND OF TROUBLE ?
FOLLOW ME! IT'S OUT IN THE PARKING LOT!
MY CAR! HAPPENED IN MY DRIVEWAY SOMETIME LAST NIGHT!
EGAD!
YEA RIVERDALE
PAINT ? SPRAY PAINT ?
AND QUITE DRY, TOO!
I'M SORRY, MISS GRUNDY! MUST HAVE BEEN MY TALK YESTERDAY!
SOME OVER-ZEALOUS STUDENT, NO DOUBT!
THIS IS NOT ZEAL, CHIEF! THIS IS VANDALISM!
YEA RIVERDALE
2

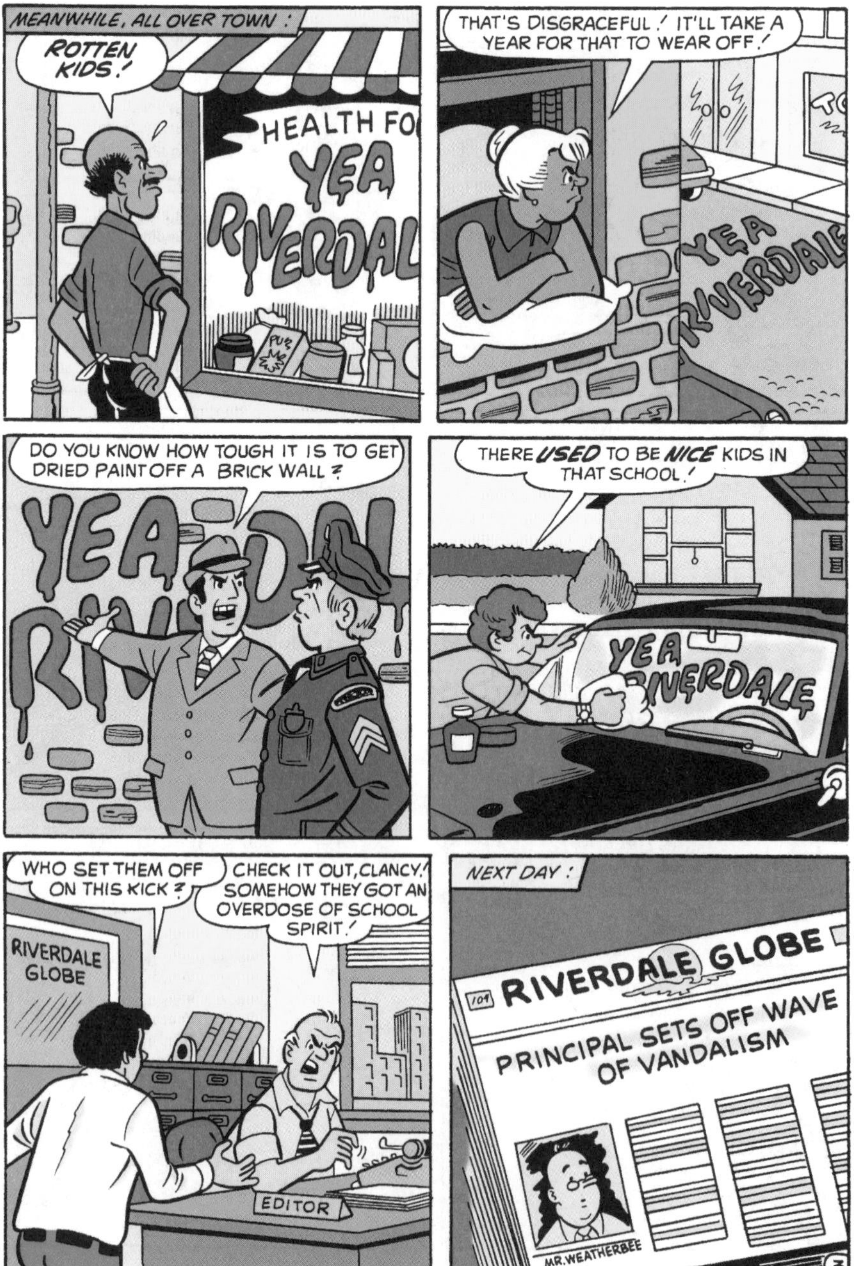
MEANWHILE, ALL OVER TOWN :
ROTTEN KIDS.!
HEALTH FO
YEA RIVERDAL
THAT'S DISGRACEFUL.! IT'LL TAKE A YEAR FOR THAT TO WEAR OFF.!
YEA RIVERDALE
DO YOU KNOW HOW TOUGH IT IS TO GET DRIED PAINT OFF A BRICK WALL ?
THERE USED TO BE NICE KIDS IN THAT SCHOOL.!
YEA RIVERDALE
WHO SET THEM OFF ON THIS KICK ?
CHECK IT OUT, CLANCY.! SOMEHOW THEY GOT AN OVERDOSE OF SCHOOL SPIRIT.!
RIVERDALE GLOBE
EDITOR
NEXT DAY :
RIVERDALE GLOBE
PRINCIPAL SETS OFF WAVE OF VANDALISM
MR. WEATHERBEE
3

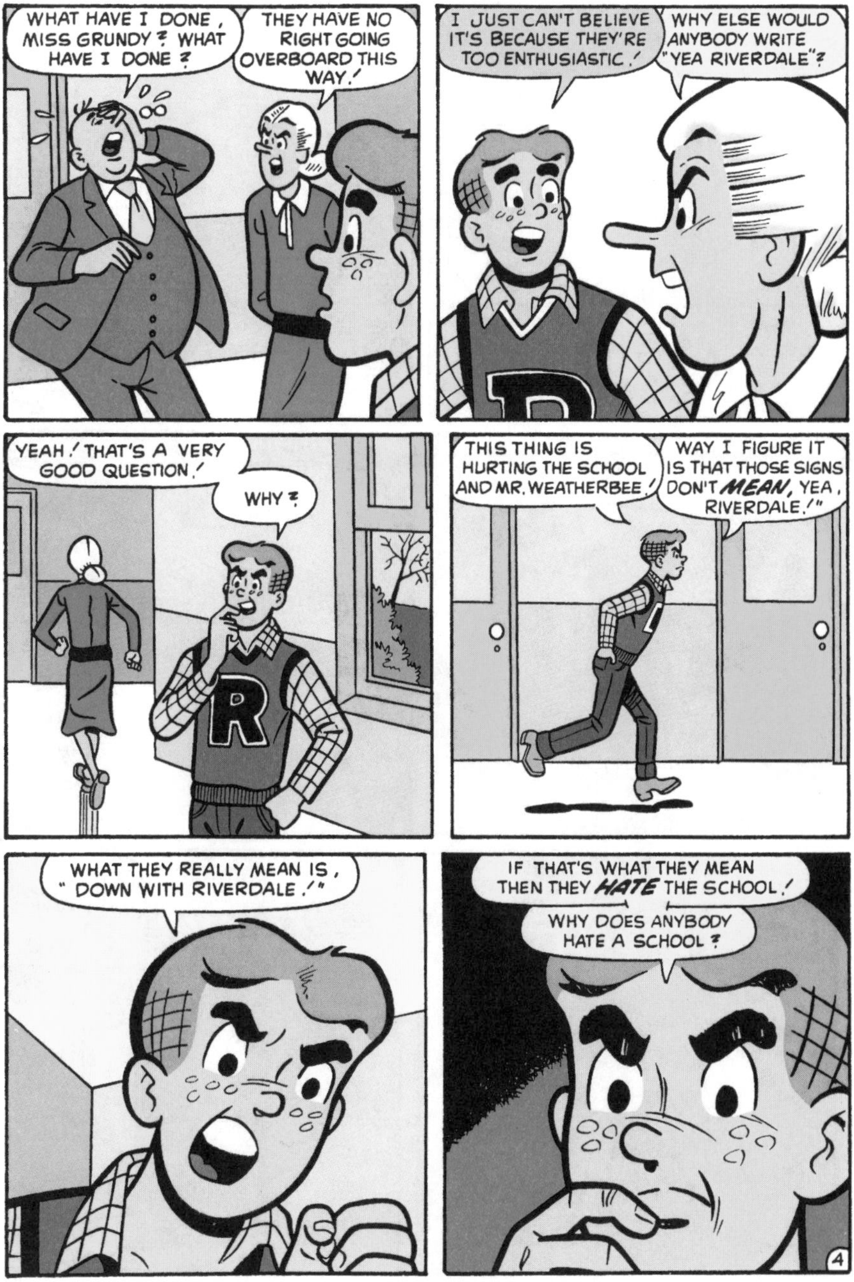
WHAT HAVE I DONE, MISS GRUNDY? WHAT HAVE I DONE?
THEY HAVE NO RIGHT GOING OVERBOARD THIS WAY.!
I JUST CAN'T BELIEVE IT'S BECAUSE THEY'RE TOO ENTHUSIASTIC.!
WHY ELSE WOULD ANYBODY WRITE "YEA RIVERDALE"?
YEAH! THAT'S A VERY GOOD QUESTION!
WHY?
THIS THING IS HURTING THE SCHOOL AND MR. WEATHERBEE!
WAY I FIGURE IT IS THAT THOSE SIGNS DON'T *MEAN*, YEA, RIVERDALE!"
WHAT THEY REALLY MEAN IS, "DOWN WITH RIVERDALE!"
IF THAT'S WHAT THEY MEAN THEN THEY *HATE* THE SCHOOL!
WHY DOES ANYBODY HATE A SCHOOL?
4

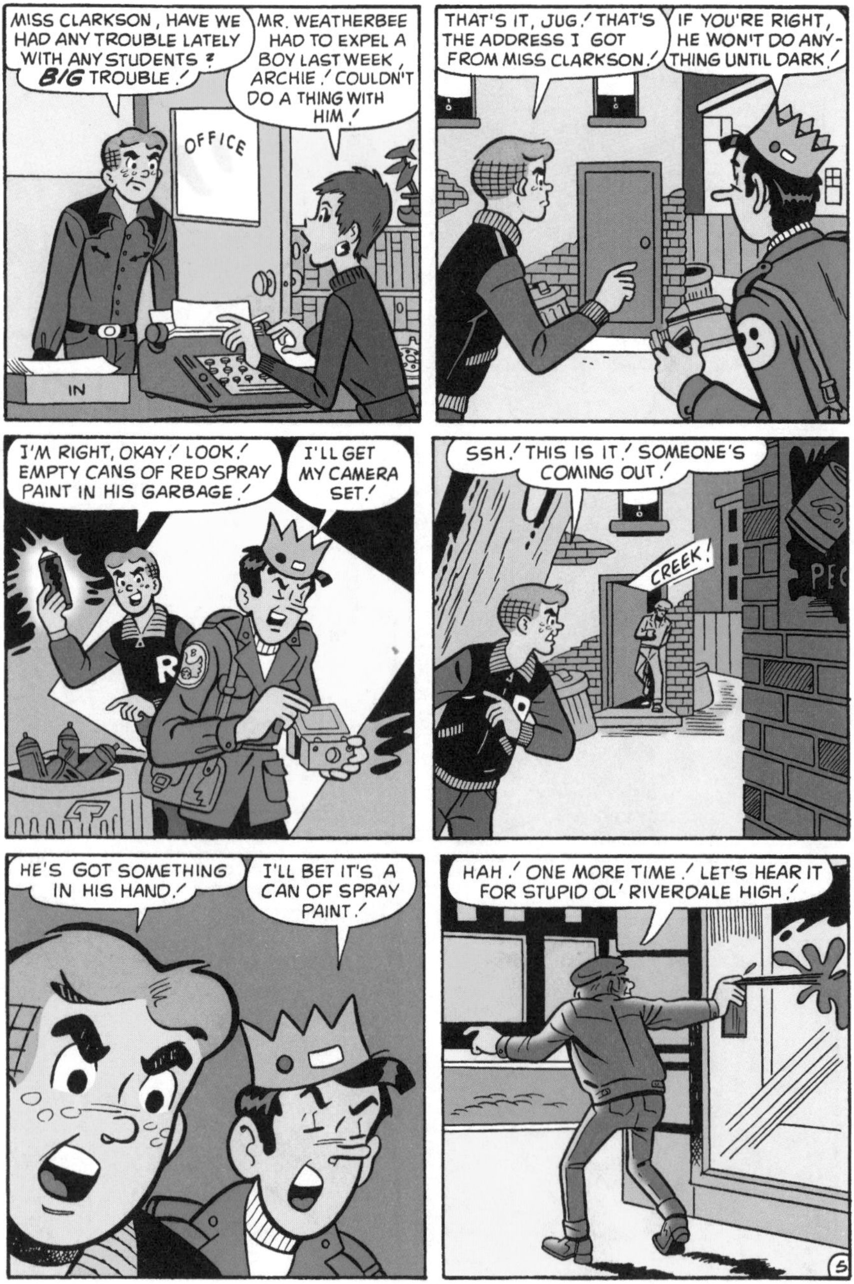
MISS CLARKSON, HAVE WE HAD ANY TROUBLE LATELY WITH ANY STUDENTS? BIG TROUBLE!
MR. WEATHERBEE HAD TO EXPEL A BOY LAST WEEK, ARCHIE! COULDN'T DO A THING WITH HIM!
OFFICE
IN
THAT'S IT, JUG! THAT'S THE ADDRESS I GOT FROM MISS CLARKSON!
IF YOU'RE RIGHT, HE WON'T DO ANYTHING UNTIL DARK!
I'M RIGHT, OKAY! LOOK! EMPTY CANS OF RED SPRAY PAINT IN HIS GARBAGE!
I'LL GET MY CAMERA SET!
SSH! THIS IS IT! SOMEONE'S COMING OUT!
CREEK!
HE'S GOT SOMETHING IN HIS HAND!
I'LL BET IT'S A CAN OF SPRAY PAINT!
HAH! ONE MORE TIME! LET'S HEAR IT FOR STUPID OL' RIVERDALE HIGH!
5

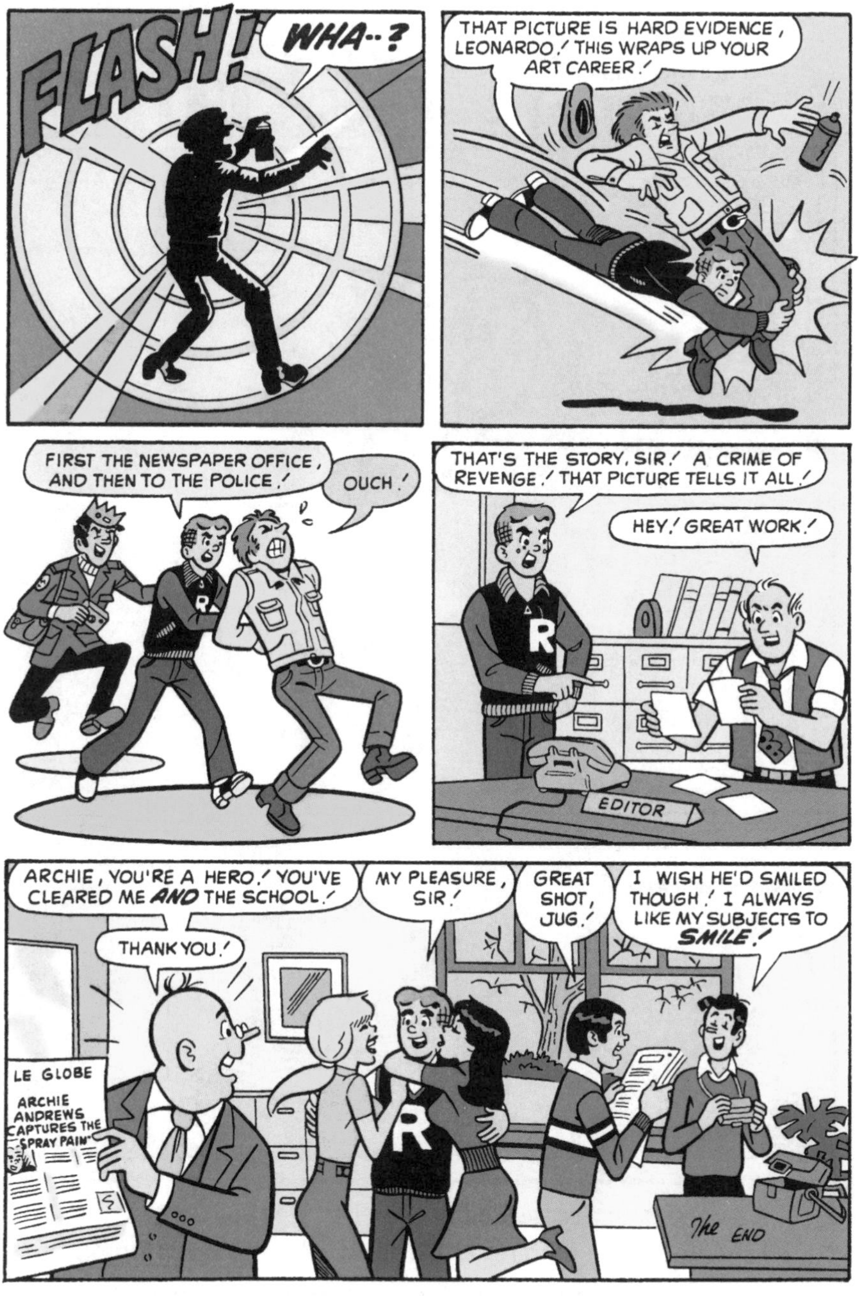
FLASH!
WHA-- ?
THAT PICTURE IS HARD EVIDENCE, LEONARDO! THIS WRAPS UP YOUR ART CAREER!
FIRST THE NEWSPAPER OFFICE, AND THEN TO THE POLICE!
OUCH!
THAT'S THE STORY, SIR! A CRIME OF REVENGE! THAT PICTURE TELLS IT ALL!
HEY! GREAT WORK!
EDITOR
ARCHIE, YOU'RE A HERO! YOU'VE CLEARED ME AND THE SCHOOL!
THANK YOU!
MY PLEASURE, SIR!
GREAT SHOT, JUG!
I WISH HE'D SMILED THOUGH! I ALWAYS LIKE MY SUBJECTS TO SMILE!
LE GLOBE
ARCHIE ANDREWS CAPTURES THE "SPRAY PAIN"
The END

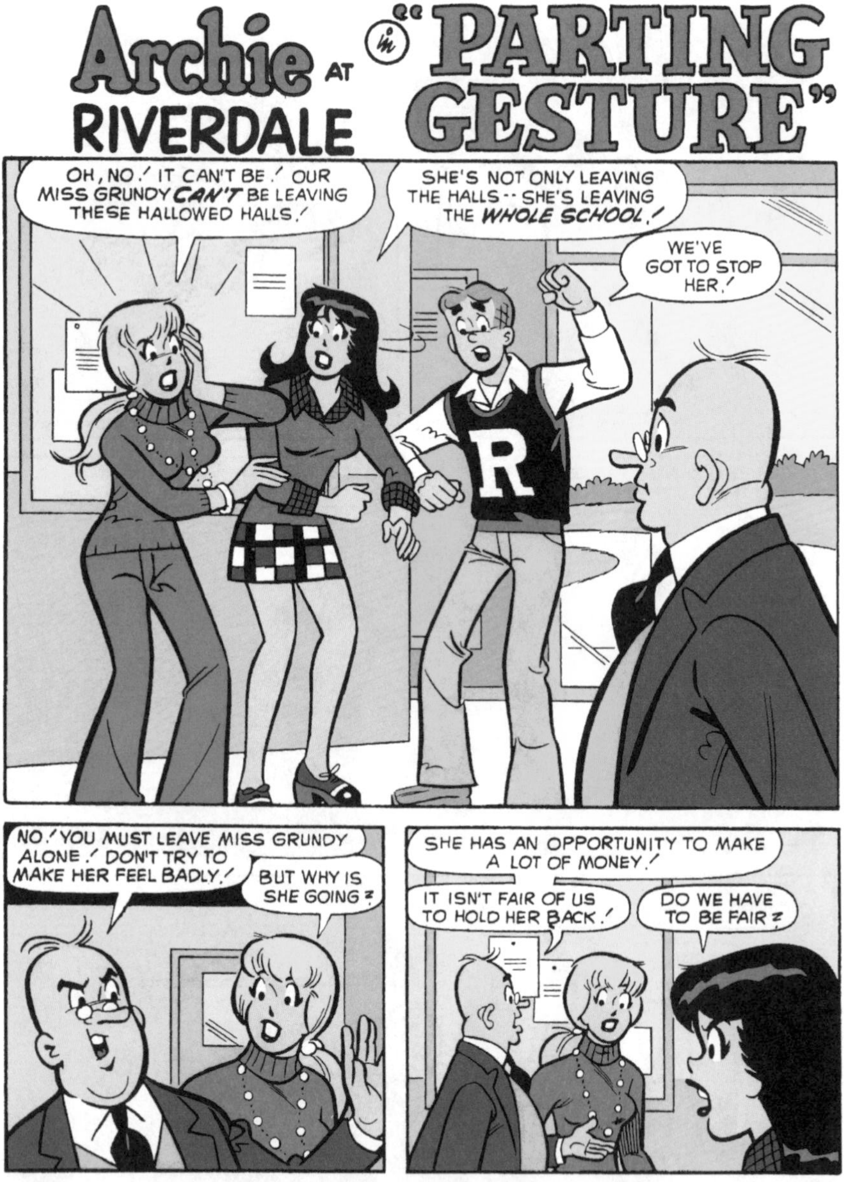
Archie AT RIVERDALE
in
"PARTING GESTURE"
OH, NO! IT CAN'T BE! OUR MISS GRUNDY CAN'T BE LEAVING THESE HALLOWED HALLS!
SHE'S NOT ONLY LEAVING THE HALLS -- SHE'S LEAVING THE WHOLE SCHOOL!
WE'VE GOT TO STOP HER!
R
NO! YOU MUST LEAVE MISS GRUNDY ALONE! DON'T TRY TO MAKE HER FEEL BADLY!
BUT WHY IS SHE GOING?
SHE HAS AN OPPORTUNITY TO MAKE A LOT OF MONEY!
IT ISN'T FAIR OF US TO HOLD HER BACK!
DO WE HAVE TO BE FAIR?

Story: George Gladir **Pencils:** Stan Goldberg
Inks: Chic Stone **Letters:** Bill Yoshida **Colors:** Barry Grossman

Originally printed in ARCHIE AT RIVERDALE HIGH #25, JUNE 1975

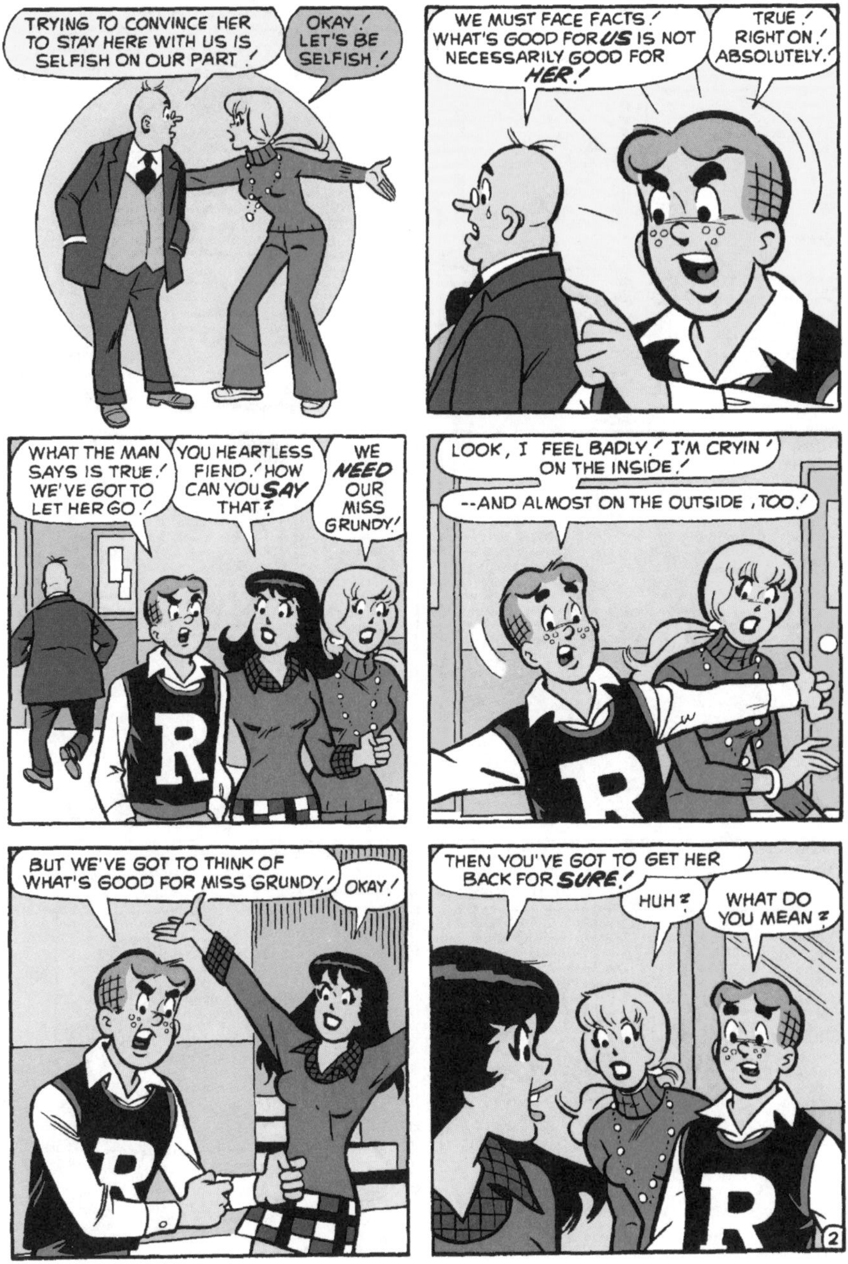
TRYING TO CONVINCE HER TO STAY HERE WITH US IS SELFISH ON OUR PART!
OKAY! LET'S BE SELFISH!
WE MUST FACE FACTS! WHAT'S GOOD FOR US IS NOT NECESSARILY GOOD FOR HER!
TRUE! RIGHT ON! ABSOLUTELY!
WHAT THE MAN SAYS IS TRUE! WE'VE GOT TO LET HER GO!
YOU HEARTLESS FIEND! HOW CAN YOU SAY THAT?
WE NEED OUR MISS GRUNDY!
LOOK, I FEEL BADLY! I'M CRYIN' ON THE INSIDE!
--AND ALMOST ON THE OUTSIDE, TOO!
BUT WE'VE GOT TO THINK OF WHAT'S GOOD FOR MISS GRUNDY!
OKAY!
THEN YOU'VE GOT TO GET HER BACK FOR SURE!
HUH?
WHAT DO YOU MEAN?
2

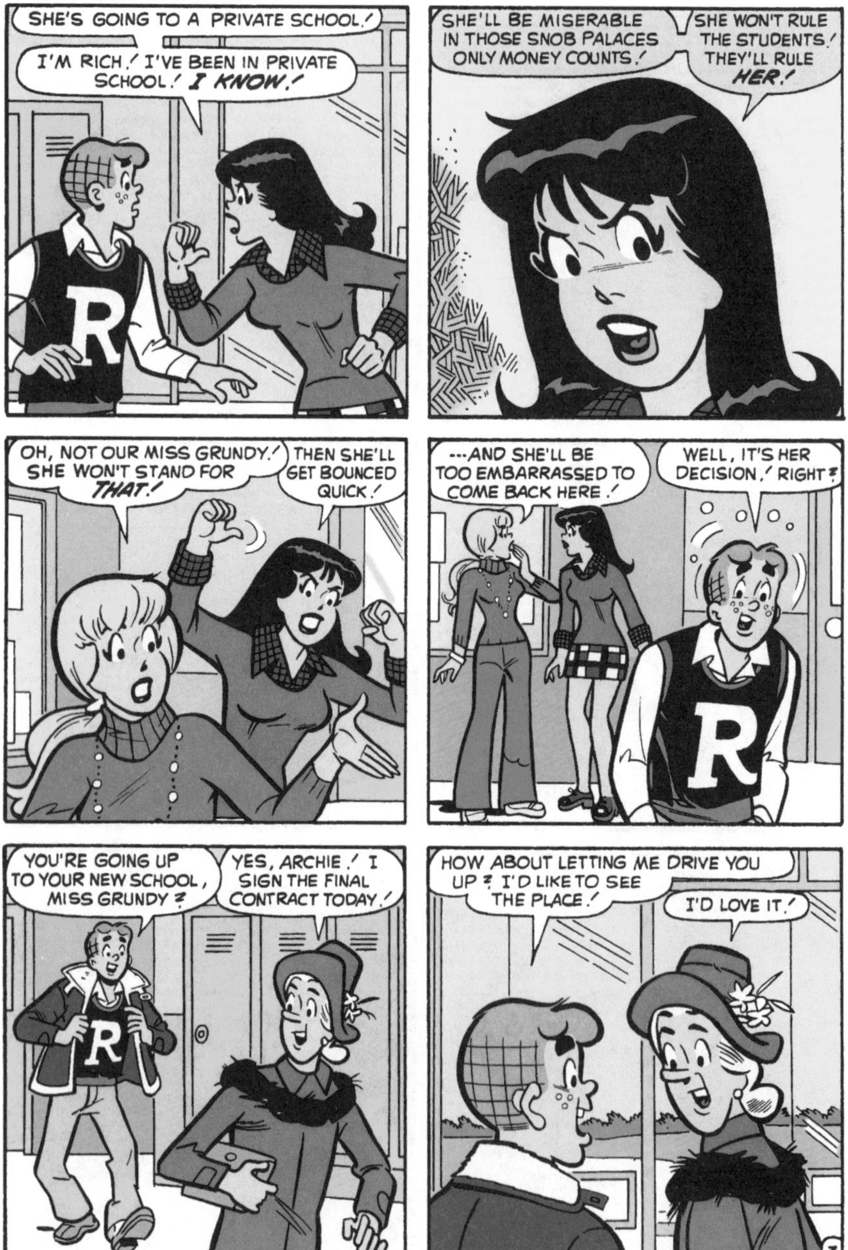
SHE'S GOING TO A PRIVATE SCHOOL!
I'M RICH! I'VE BEEN IN PRIVATE SCHOOL! I KNOW!
SHE'LL BE MISERABLE IN THOSE SNOB PALACES ONLY MONEY COUNTS!
SHE WON'T RULE THE STUDENTS! THEY'LL RULE HER!
OH, NOT OUR MISS GRUNDY! SHE WON'T STAND FOR THAT!
THEN SHE'LL GET BOUNCED QUICK!
---AND SHE'LL BE TOO EMBARRASSED TO COME BACK HERE!
WELL, IT'S HER DECISION! RIGHT?
YOU'RE GOING UP TO YOUR NEW SCHOOL, MISS GRUNDY?
YES, ARCHIE! I SIGN THE FINAL CONTRACT TODAY!
HOW ABOUT LETTING ME DRIVE YOU UP? I'D LIKE TO SEE THE PLACE!
I'D LOVE IT!
3

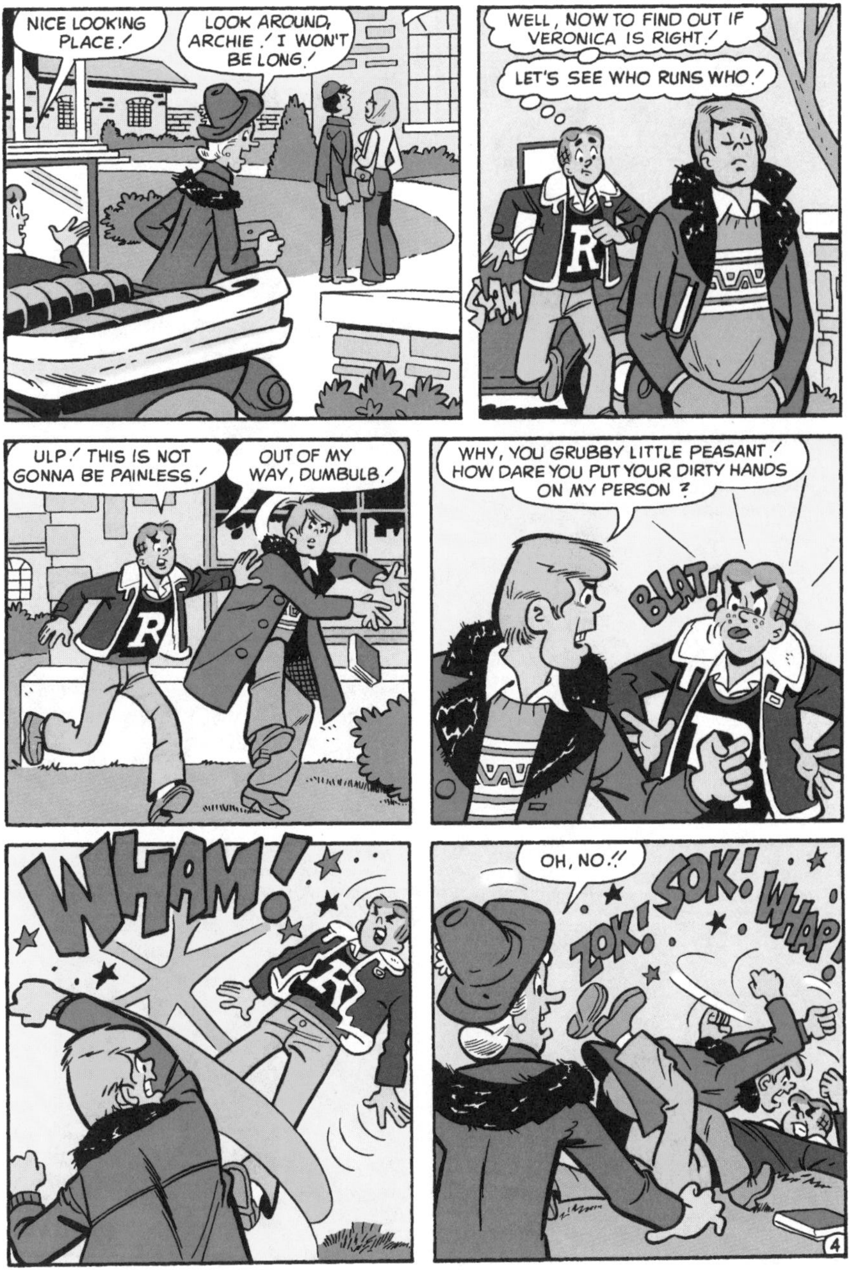
NICE LOOKING PLACE.!
LOOK AROUND, ARCHIE.! I WON'T BE LONG.!
WELL, NOW TO FIND OUT IF VERONICA IS RIGHT.!
LET'S SEE WHO RUNS WHO.!
SLAM
ULP.! THIS IS NOT GONNA BE PAINLESS.!
OUT OF MY WAY, DUMBULB.!
WHY, YOU GRUBBY LITTLE PEASANT.! HOW DARE YOU PUT YOUR DIRTY HANDS ON MY PERSON ?
BLAT!
WHAM!
OH, NO.!!
ZOK!
SOK!
WHAP!
4

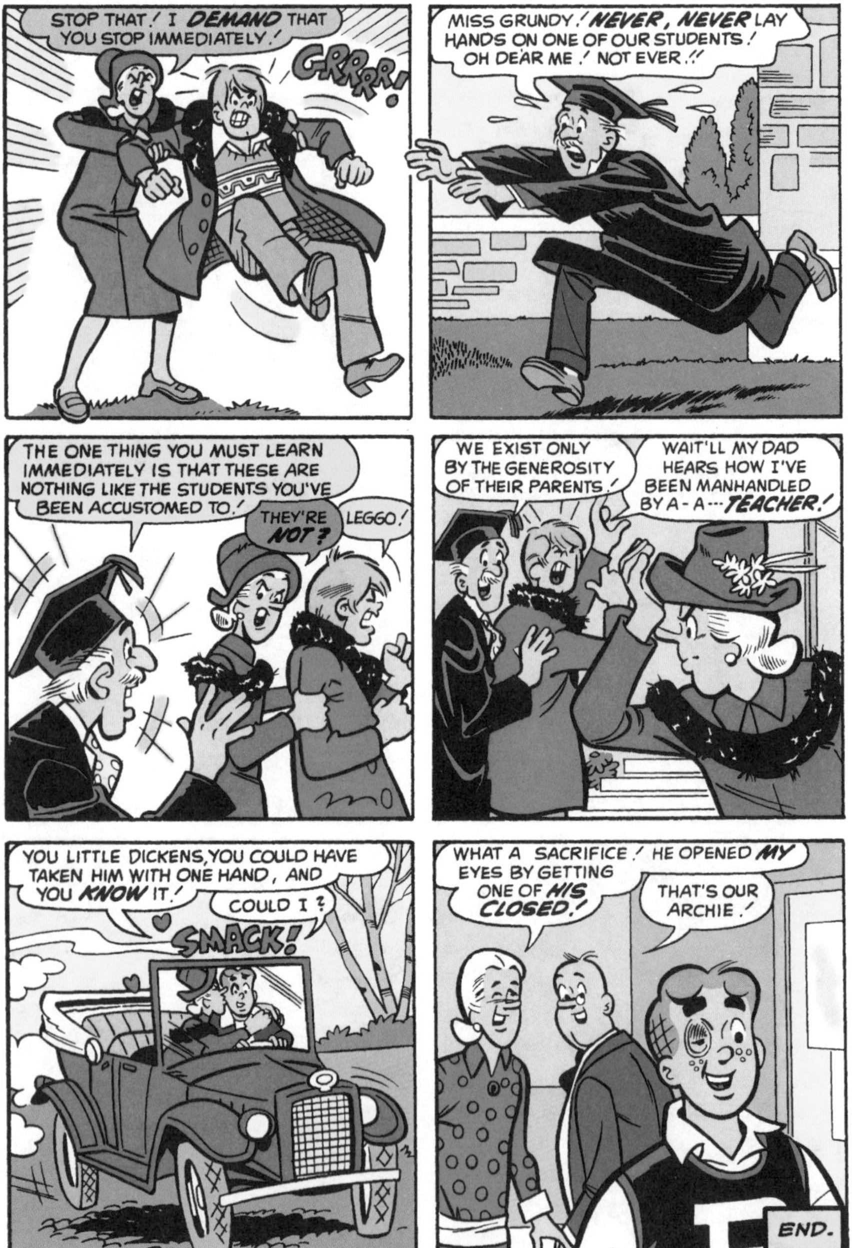
STOP THAT! I DEMAND THAT YOU STOP IMMEDIATELY!
GRRRR!
MISS GRUNDY! NEVER, NEVER LAY HANDS ON ONE OF OUR STUDENTS! OH DEAR ME! NOT EVER!!
THE ONE THING YOU MUST LEARN IMMEDIATELY IS THAT THESE ARE NOTHING LIKE THE STUDENTS YOU'VE BEEN ACCUSTOMED TO!
THEY'RE NOT?
LEGGO!
WE EXIST ONLY BY THE GENEROSITY OF THEIR PARENTS!
WAIT'LL MY DAD HEARS HOW I'VE BEEN MANHANDLED BY A-A--- TEACHER!
YOU LITTLE DICKENS, YOU COULD HAVE TAKEN HIM WITH ONE HAND, AND YOU KNOW IT!
COULD I?
SMACK!
WHAT A SACRIFICE! HE OPENED MY EYES BY GETTING ONE OF HIS CLOSED!
THAT'S OUR ARCHIE!
END.

Archie AT RIVERDALE in "BASIC TRAINING"

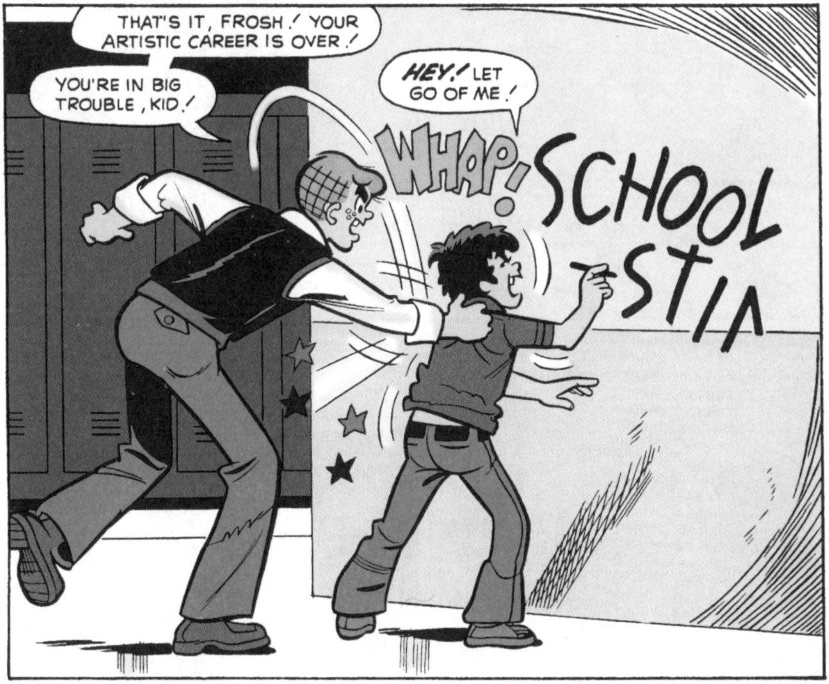
THAT'S IT, FROSH! YOUR ARTISTIC CAREER IS OVER!
YOU'RE IN BIG TROUBLE, KID!
HEY! LET GO OF ME!
WHAP!
SCHOOL STI

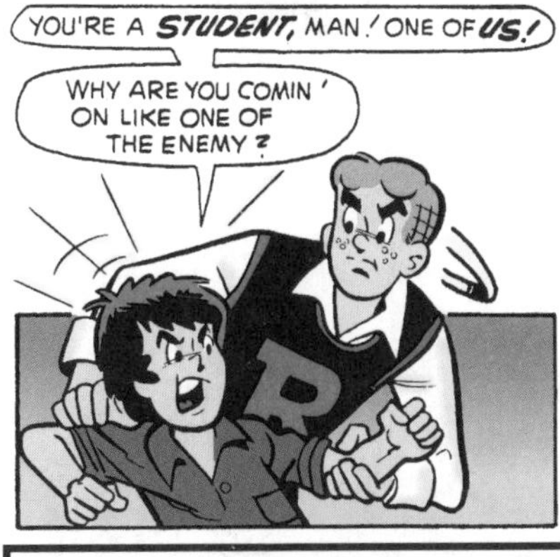
YOU'RE A STUDENT, MAN! ONE OF US!
WHY ARE YOU COMIN' ON LIKE ONE OF THE ENEMY?

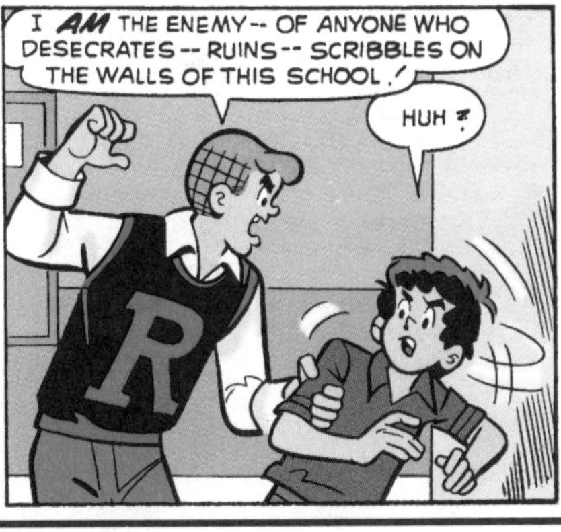
I AM THE ENEMY-- OF ANYONE WHO DESECRATES -- RUINS -- SCRIBBLES ON THE WALLS OF THIS SCHOOL!
HUH?

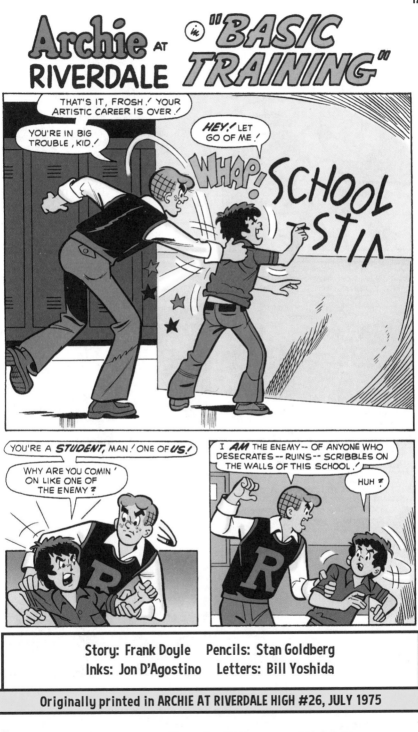

Story: Frank Doyle Pencils: Stan Goldberg
Inks: Jon D'Agostino Letters: Bill Yoshida

Originally printed in ARCHIE AT RIVERDALE HIGH #26, JULY 1975

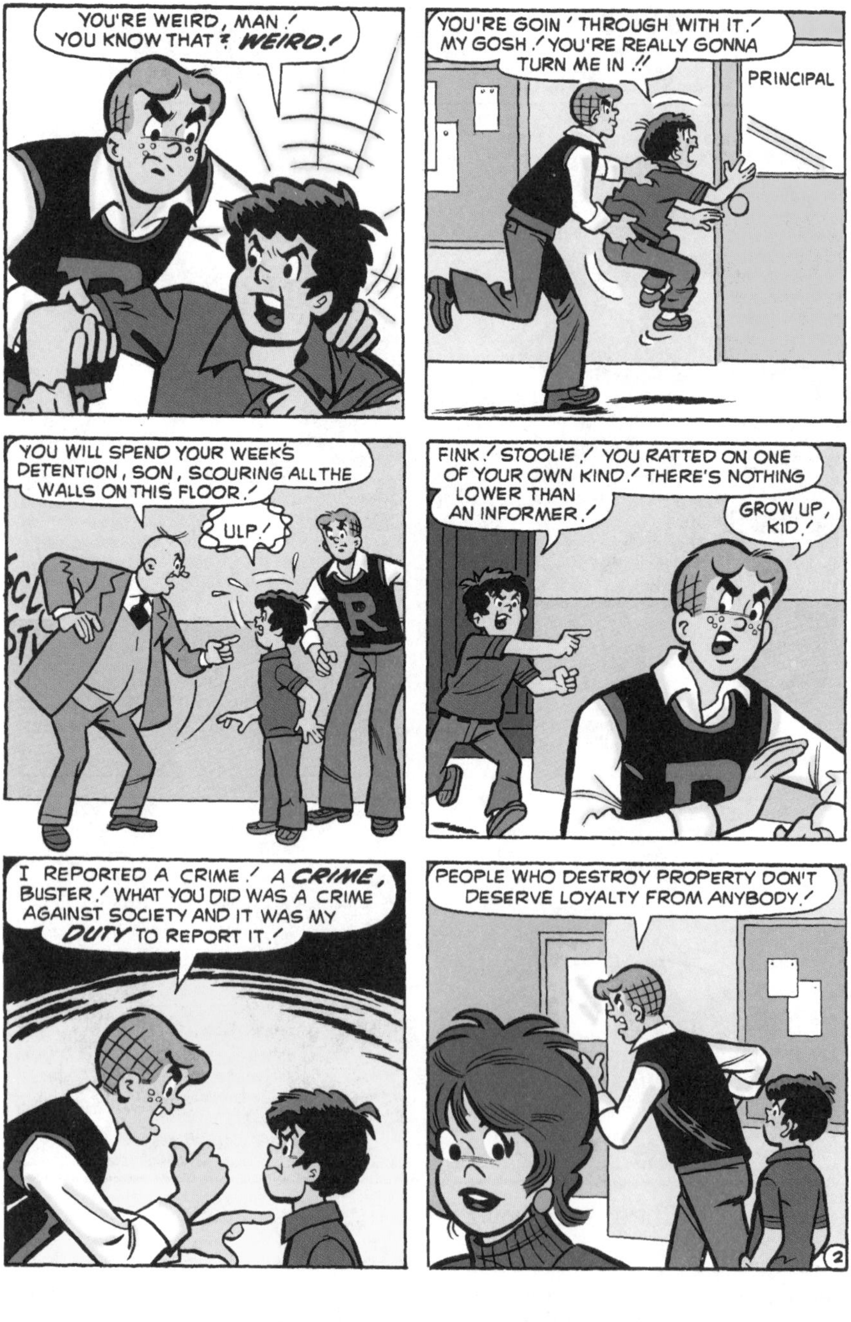
YOU'RE WEIRD, MAN! YOU KNOW THAT? WEIRD!
YOU'RE GOIN' THROUGH WITH IT! MY GOSH! YOU'RE REALLY GONNA TURN ME IN!!
PRINCIPAL
YOU WILL SPEND YOUR WEEK'S DETENTION, SON, SCOURING ALL THE WALLS ON THIS FLOOR!
ULP!
FINK! STOOLIE! YOU RATTED ON ONE OF YOUR OWN KIND! THERE'S NOTHING LOWER THAN AN INFORMER!
GROW UP, KID!
I REPORTED A CRIME! A CRIME, BUSTER! WHAT YOU DID WAS A CRIME AGAINST SOCIETY AND IT WAS MY DUTY TO REPORT IT!
PEOPLE WHO DESTROY PROPERTY DON'T DESERVE LOYALTY FROM ANYBODY!
2

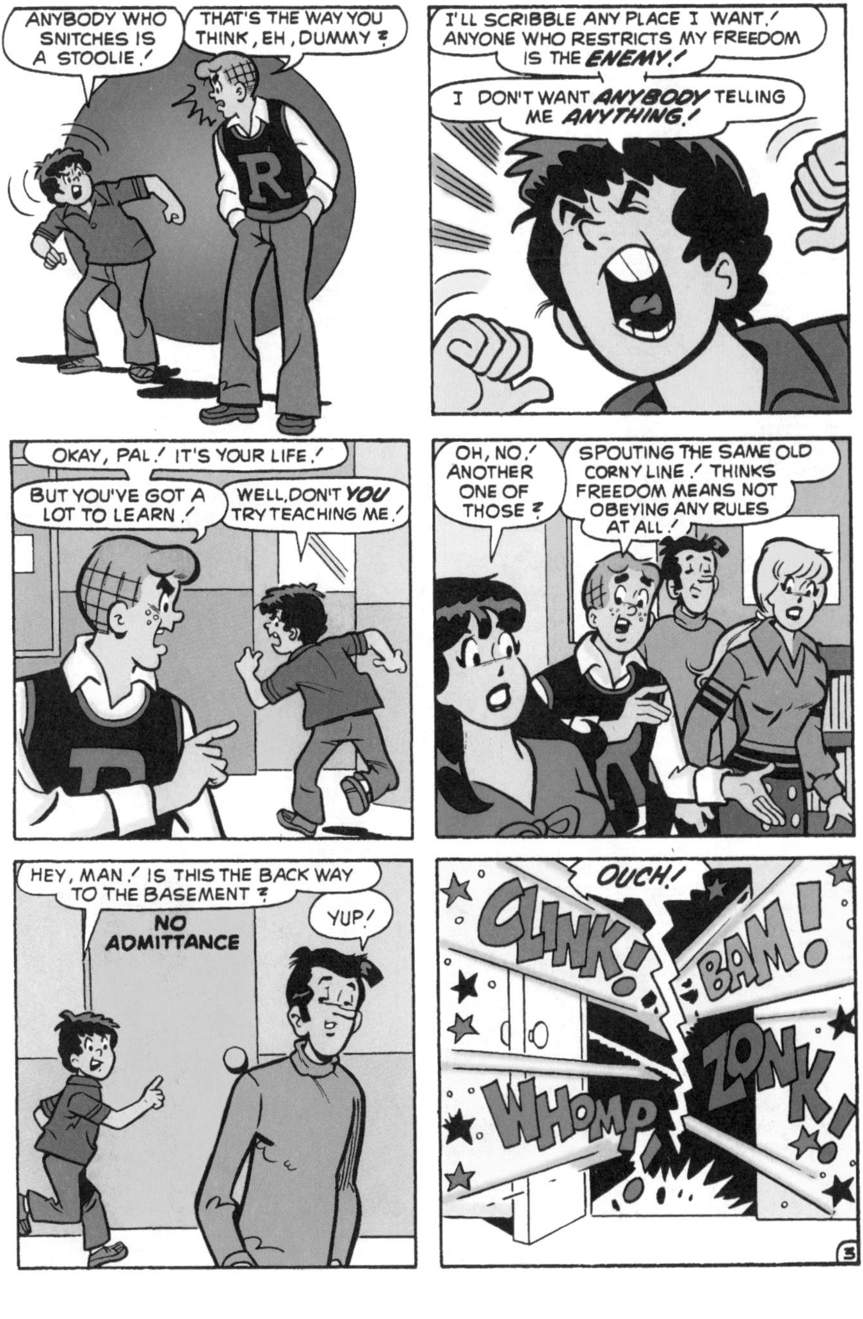
ANYBODY WHO SNITCHES IS A STOOLIE!
THAT'S THE WAY YOU THINK, EH, DUMMY?
I'LL SCRIBBLE ANY PLACE I WANT! ANYONE WHO RESTRICTS MY FREEDOM IS THE ENEMY!
I DON'T WANT ANYBODY TELLING ME ANYTHING!
OKAY, PAL! IT'S YOUR LIFE!
BUT YOU'VE GOT A LOT TO LEARN!
WELL, DON'T YOU TRY TEACHING ME!
OH, NO! ANOTHER ONE OF THOSE?
SPOUTING THE SAME OLD CORNY LINE! THINKS FREEDOM MEANS NOT OBEYING ANY RULES AT ALL!
HEY, MAN! IS THIS THE BACK WAY TO THE BASEMENT?
NO ADMITTANCE
YUP!
OUCH!
CLINK!
BAM!
WHOMP!
ZONK!
3

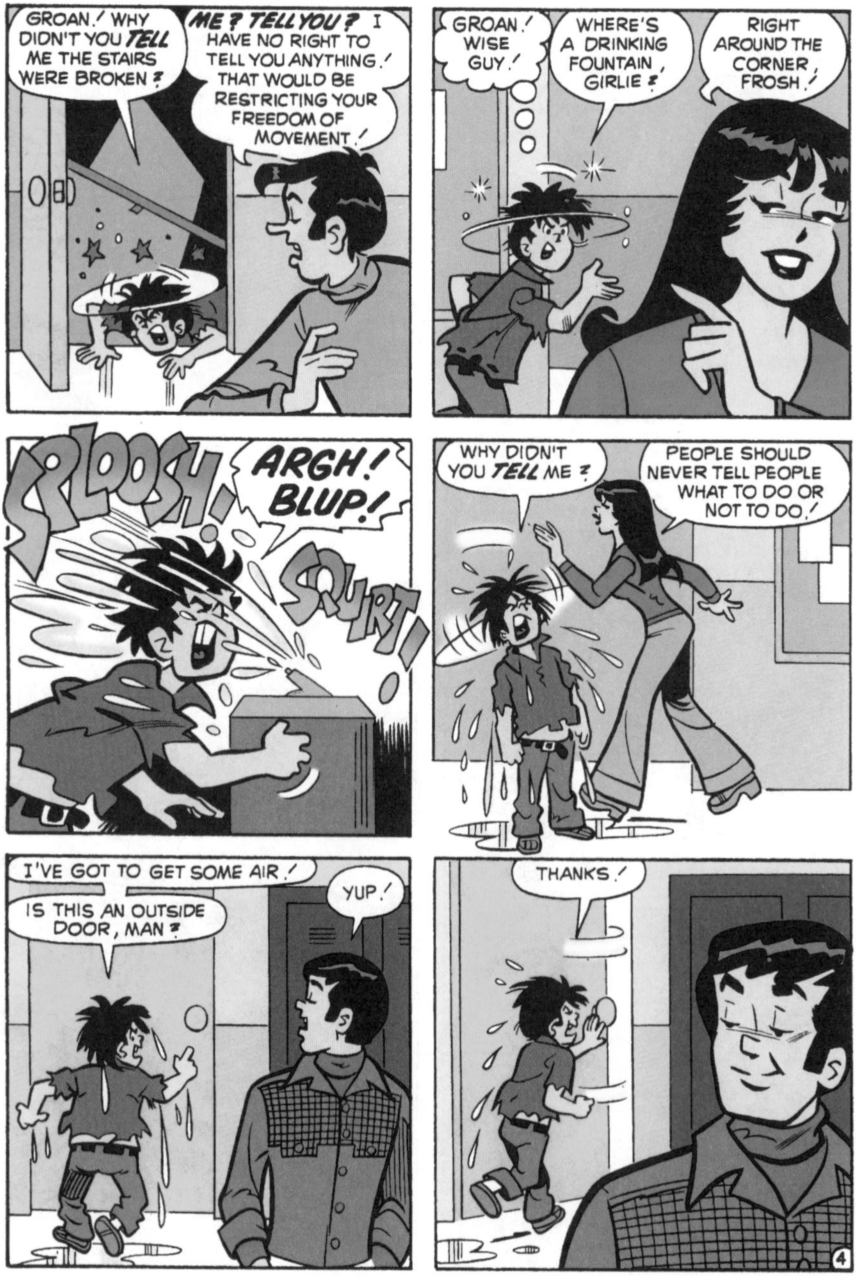
GROAN! WHY DIDN'T YOU TELL ME THE STAIRS WERE BROKEN ?
ME ? TELL YOU ? I HAVE NO RIGHT TO TELL YOU ANYTHING! THAT WOULD BE RESTRICTING YOUR FREEDOM OF MOVEMENT!
GROAN! WISE GUY!
WHERE'S A DRINKING FOUNTAIN, GIRLIE ?
RIGHT AROUND THE CORNER, FROSH!
SPLOOSH!
ARGH! BLUP!
SQURT!
WHY DIDN'T YOU TELL ME ?
PEOPLE SHOULD NEVER TELL PEOPLE WHAT TO DO OR NOT TO DO!
I'VE GOT TO GET SOME AIR!
IS THIS AN OUTSIDE DOOR, MAN ?
YUP!
THANKS!
4

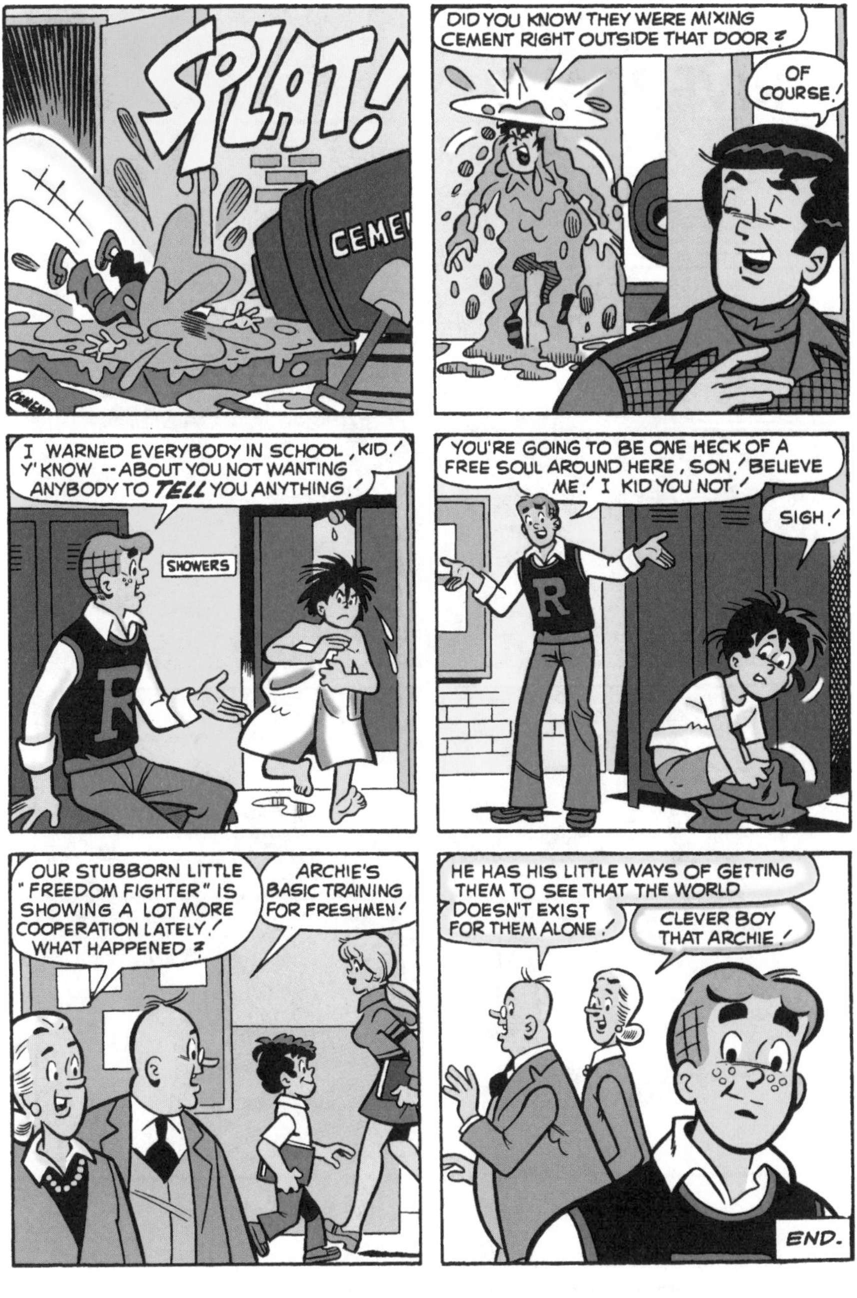
SPLAT!
CEMENT
DID YOU KNOW THEY WERE MIXING CEMENT RIGHT OUTSIDE THAT DOOR?
OF COURSE!
I WARNED EVERYBODY IN SCHOOL, KID! Y'KNOW -- ABOUT YOU NOT WANTING ANYBODY TO TELL YOU ANYTHING!
SHOWERS
YOU'RE GOING TO BE ONE HECK OF A FREE SOUL AROUND HERE, SON! BELIEVE ME! I KID YOU NOT!
SIGH!
OUR STUBBORN LITTLE "FREEDOM FIGHTER" IS SHOWING A LOT MORE COOPERATION LATELY! WHAT HAPPENED?
ARCHIE'S BASIC TRAINING FOR FRESHMEN!
HE HAS HIS LITTLE WAYS OF GETTING THEM TO SEE THAT THE WORLD DOESN'T EXIST FOR THEM ALONE!
CLEVER BOY THAT ARCHIE!
END.

Archie at Riverdale in "Cheer Up"

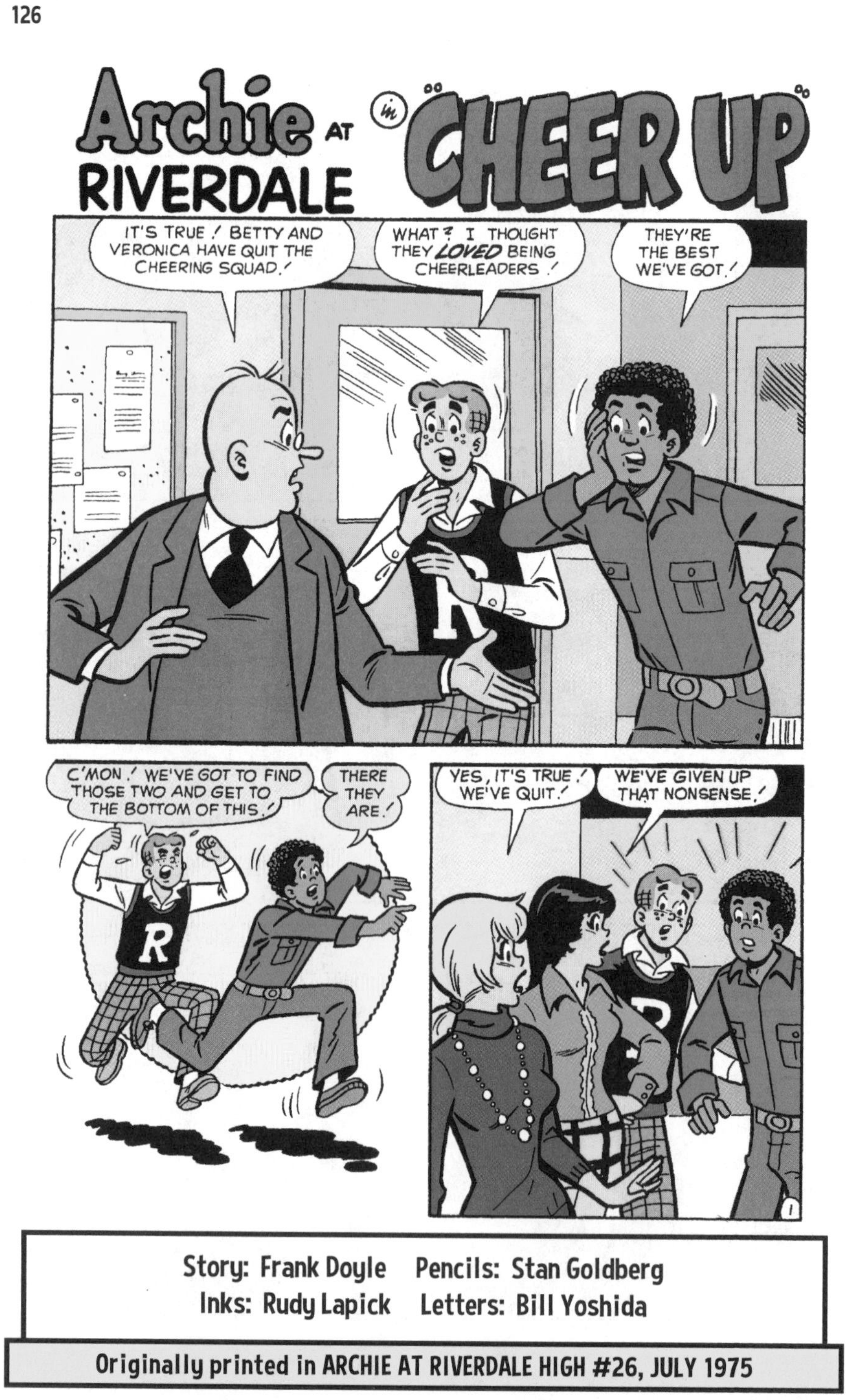
IT'S TRUE! BETTY AND VERONICA HAVE QUIT THE CHEERING SQUAD!
WHAT? I THOUGHT THEY LOVED BEING CHEERLEADERS!
THEY'RE THE BEST WE'VE GOT!
C'MON! WE'VE GOT TO FIND THOSE TWO AND GET TO THE BOTTOM OF THIS!
THERE THEY ARE!
YES, IT'S TRUE! WE'VE QUIT!
WE'VE GIVEN UP THAT NONSENSE!
1

Story: Frank Doyle Pencils: Stan Goldberg
Inks: Rudy Lapick Letters: Bill Yoshida

Originally printed in ARCHIE AT RIVERDALE HIGH #26, JULY 1975

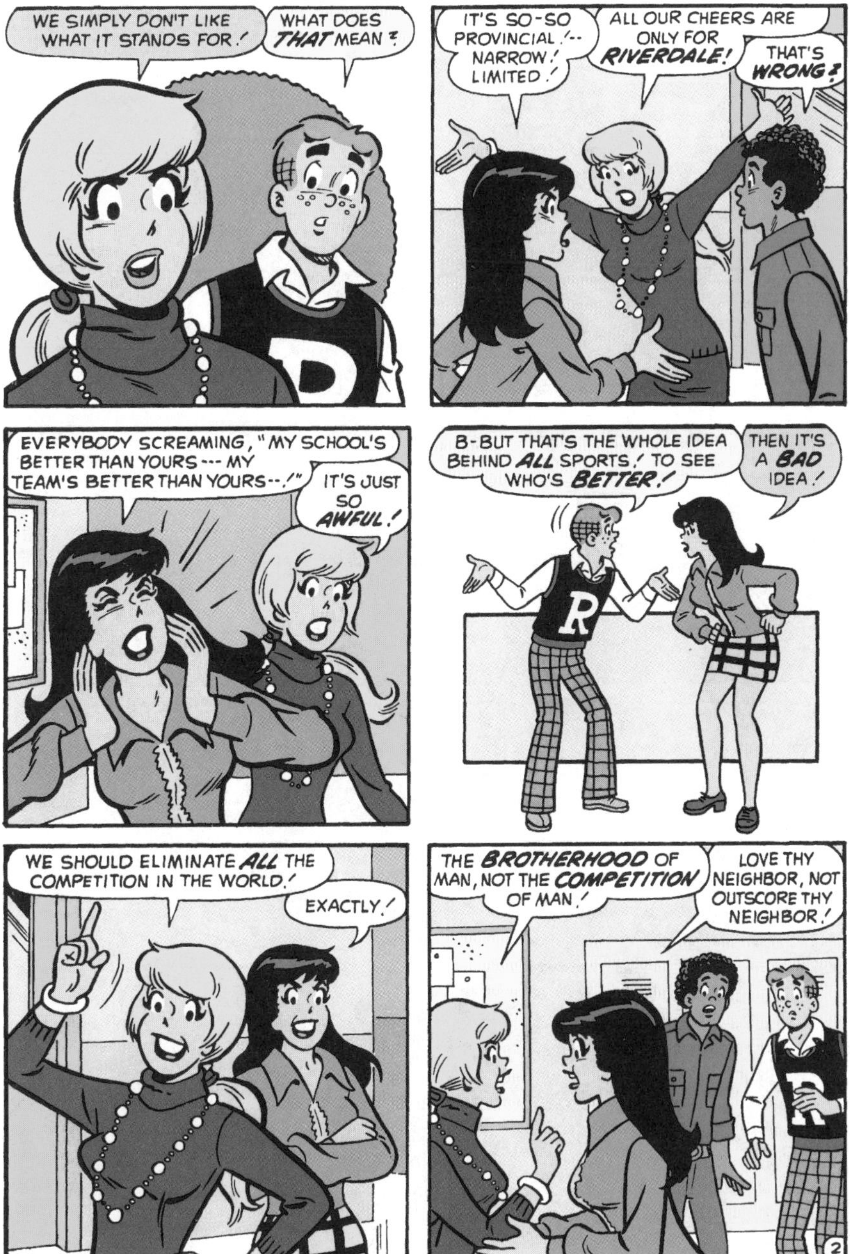
WE SIMPLY DON'T LIKE WHAT IT STANDS FOR!
WHAT DOES THAT MEAN?
IT'S SO-SO PROVINCIAL!-- NARROW! LIMITED!
ALL OUR CHEERS ARE ONLY FOR RIVERDALE!
THAT'S WRONG!
EVERYBODY SCREAMING, "MY SCHOOL'S BETTER THAN YOURS --- MY TEAM'S BETTER THAN YOURS--!"
IT'S JUST SO AWFUL!
B-BUT THAT'S THE WHOLE IDEA BEHIND ALL SPORTS! TO SEE WHO'S BETTER!
THEN IT'S A BAD IDEA!
WE SHOULD ELIMINATE ALL THE COMPETITION IN THE WORLD!
EXACTLY!
THE BROTHERHOOD OF MAN, NOT THE COMPETITION OF MAN!
LOVE THY NEIGHBOR, NOT OUTSCORE THY NEIGHBOR!
2

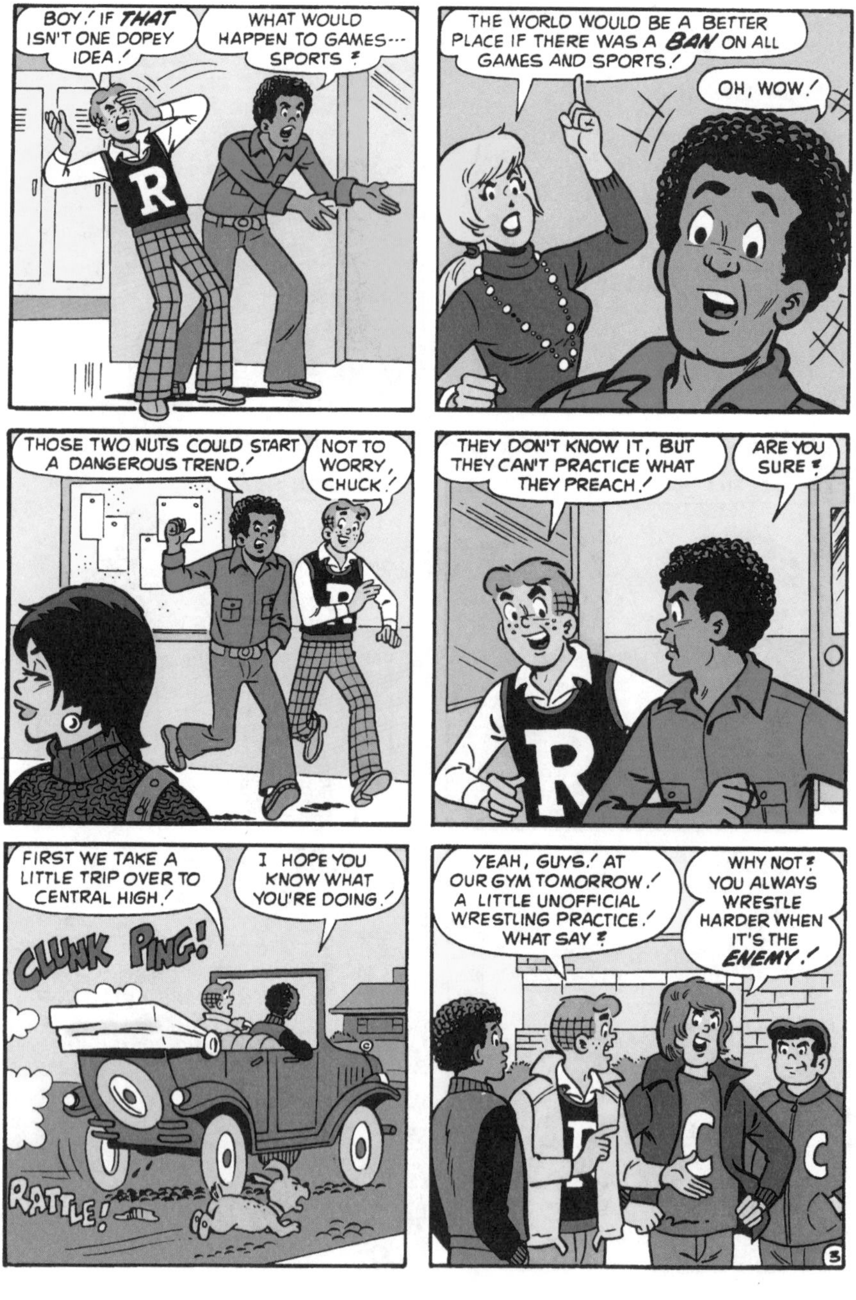
BOY! IF THAT ISN'T ONE DOPEY IDEA!
WHAT WOULD HAPPEN TO GAMES--- SPORTS?
THE WORLD WOULD BE A BETTER PLACE IF THERE WAS A BAN ON ALL GAMES AND SPORTS!
OH, WOW!
THOSE TWO NUTS COULD START A DANGEROUS TREND!
NOT TO WORRY, CHUCK!
THEY DON'T KNOW IT, BUT THEY CAN'T PRACTICE WHAT THEY PREACH!
ARE YOU SURE?
FIRST WE TAKE A LITTLE TRIP OVER TO CENTRAL HIGH!
I HOPE YOU KNOW WHAT YOU'RE DOING!
CLUNK PING!
RATTLE!
YEAH, GUYS! AT OUR GYM TOMORROW! A LITTLE UNOFFICIAL WRESTLING PRACTICE! WHAT SAY?
WHY NOT? YOU ALWAYS WRESTLE HARDER WHEN IT'S THE ENEMY!
3

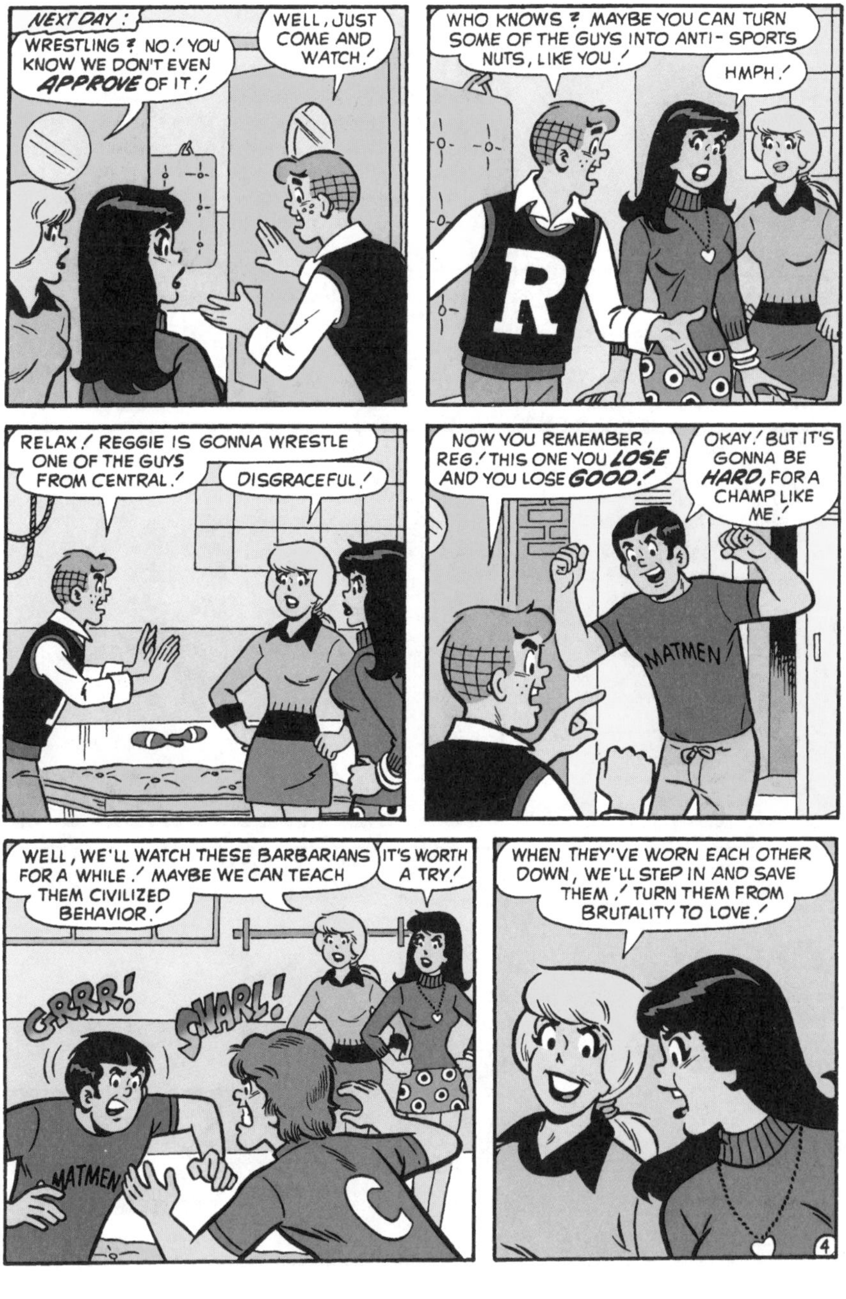
NEXT DAY :
WRESTLING ? NO.! YOU KNOW WE DON'T EVEN APPROVE OF IT.!
WELL, JUST COME AND WATCH.!
WHO KNOWS ? MAYBE YOU CAN TURN SOME OF THE GUYS INTO ANTI-SPORTS NUTS, LIKE YOU.!
HMPH.!
RELAX.! REGGIE IS GONNA WRESTLE ONE OF THE GUYS FROM CENTRAL.!
DISGRACEFUL.!
NOW YOU REMEMBER, REG.! THIS ONE YOU LOSE AND YOU LOSE GOOD.!
OKAY.! BUT IT'S GONNA BE HARD, FOR A CHAMP LIKE ME.!
MATMEN
WELL, WE'LL WATCH THESE BARBARIANS FOR A WHILE.! MAYBE WE CAN TEACH THEM CIVILIZED BEHAVIOR.!
IT'S WORTH A TRY.!
GRRR!
SNARL!
MATMEN
WHEN THEY'VE WORN EACH OTHER DOWN, WE'LL STEP IN AND SAVE THEM.! TURN THEM FROM BRUTALITY TO LOVE.!
4

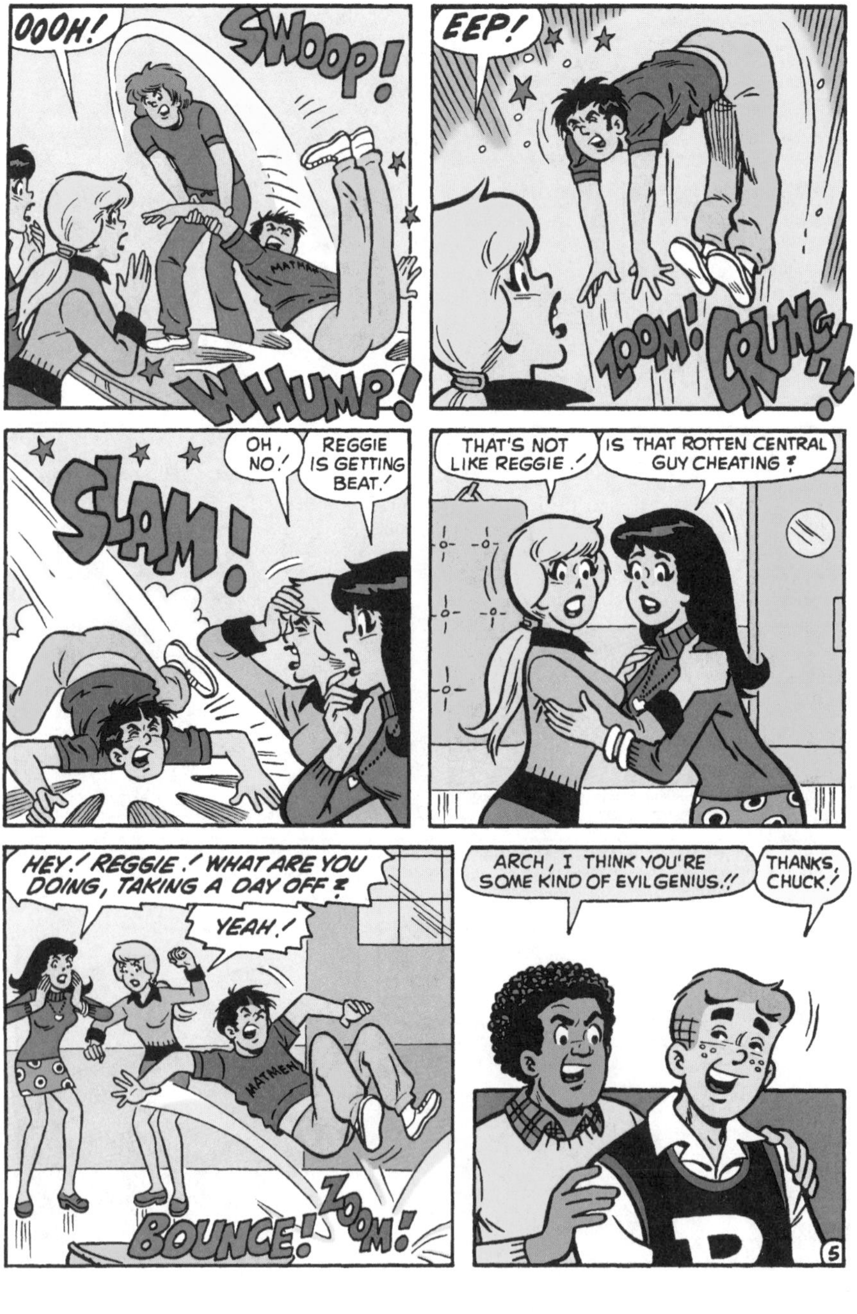
OOOH!
SWOOP!
WHUMP!
EEP!
ZOOM! CRUNCH!
SLAM!
OH, NO!
REGGIE IS GETTING BEAT!
THAT'S NOT LIKE REGGIE!
IS THAT ROTTEN CENTRAL GUY CHEATING?
HEY! REGGIE! WHAT ARE YOU DOING, TAKING A DAY OFF?
YEAH!
BOUNCE! ZOOM!
ARCH, I THINK YOU'RE SOME KIND OF EVIL GENIUS!!
THANKS, CHUCK!
5

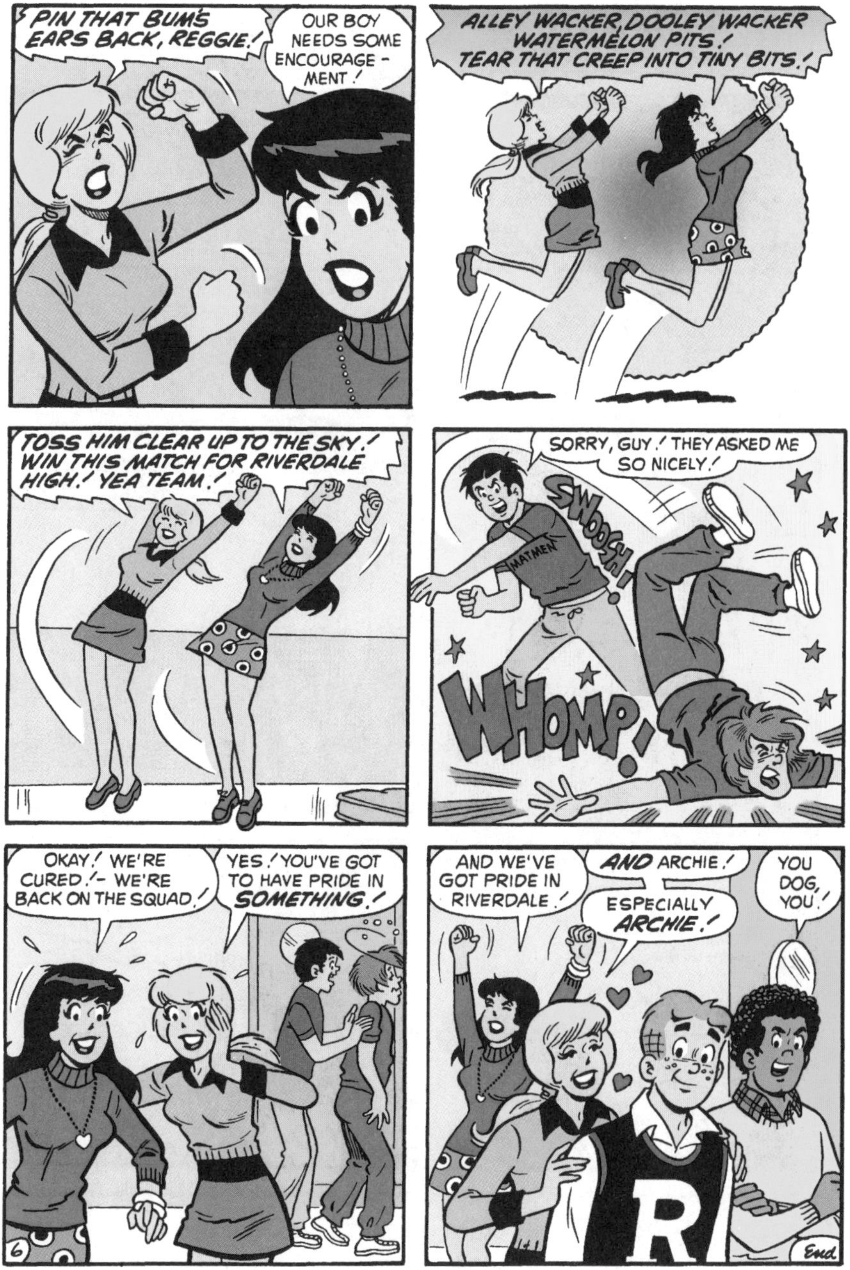
PIN THAT BUM'S EARS BACK, REGGIE!
OUR BOY NEEDS SOME ENCOURAGE - MENT!
ALLEY WACKER, DOOLEY WACKER WATERMELON PITS! TEAR THAT CREEP INTO TINY BITS!
TOSS HIM CLEAR UP TO THE SKY! WIN THIS MATCH FOR RIVERDALE HIGH! YEA TEAM!
SORRY, GUY! THEY ASKED ME SO NICELY!
MATMEN
SWOOSH!
WHOMP!
OKAY! WE'RE CURED!- WE'RE BACK ON THE SQUAD!
YES! YOU'VE GOT TO HAVE PRIDE IN SOMETHING!
6
AND WE'VE GOT PRIDE IN RIVERDALE!
AND ARCHIE!
ESPECIALLY ARCHIE!
YOU DOG, YOU!
R
End

Archie at Riverdale in "The Two-Edged Ax"

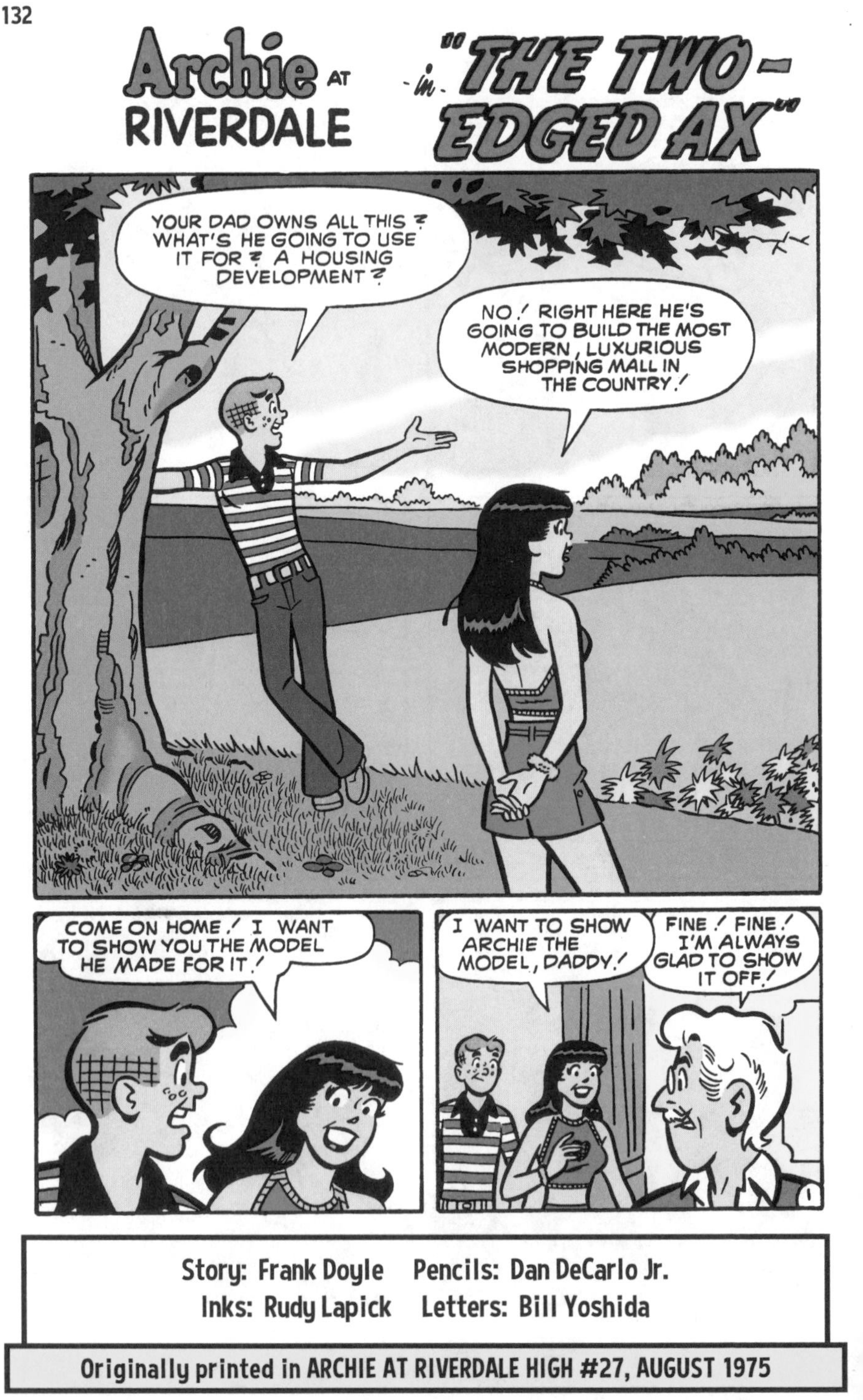
YOUR DAD OWNS ALL THIS? WHAT'S HE GOING TO USE IT FOR? A HOUSING DEVELOPMENT?
NO! RIGHT HERE HE'S GOING TO BUILD THE MOST MODERN, LUXURIOUS SHOPPING MALL IN THE COUNTRY!
COME ON HOME! I WANT TO SHOW YOU THE MODEL HE MADE FOR IT!
I WANT TO SHOW ARCHIE THE MODEL, DADDY!
FINE! FINE! I'M ALWAYS GLAD TO SHOW IT OFF!
1

Story: Frank Doyle Pencils: Dan DeCarlo Jr.
Inks: Rudy Lapick Letters: Bill Yoshida

Originally printed in ARCHIE AT RIVERDALE HIGH #27, AUGUST 1975

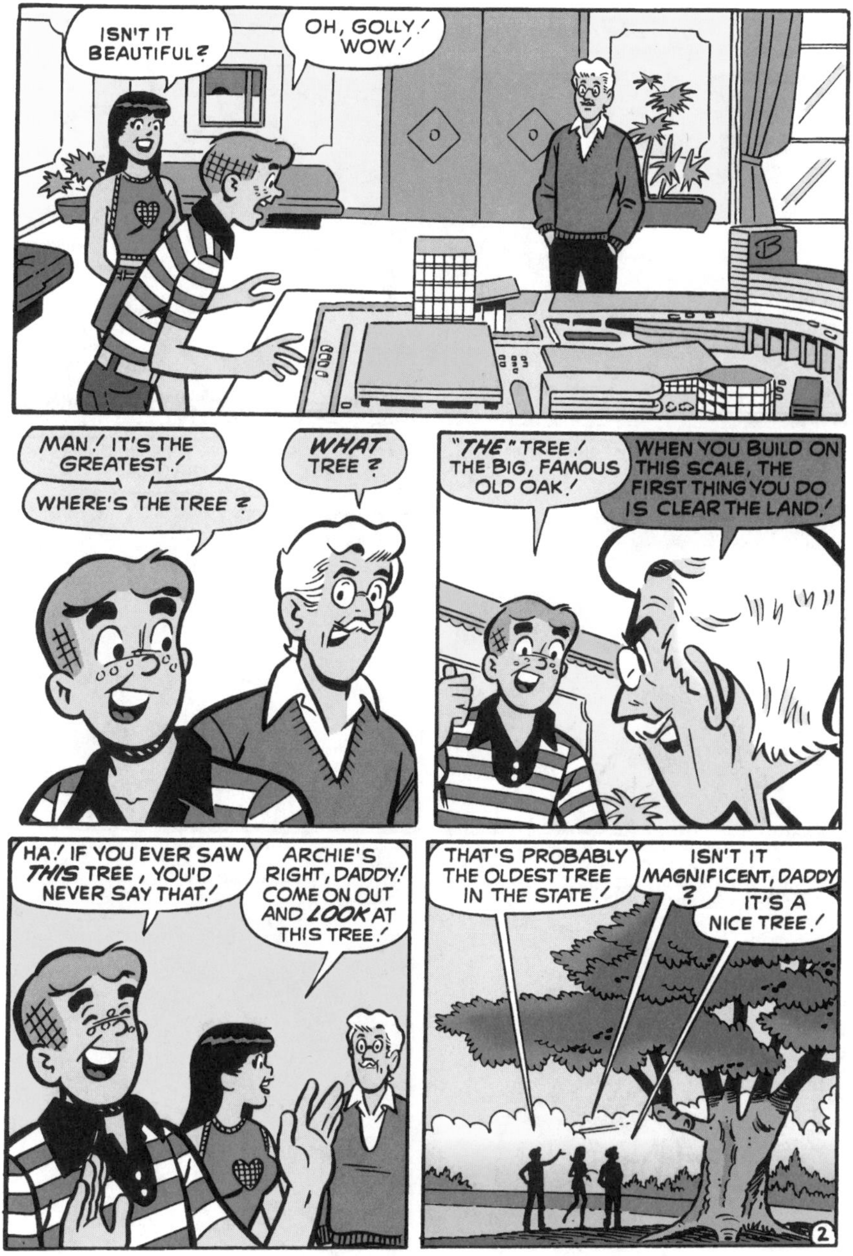
ISN'T IT BEAUTIFUL?
OH, GOLLY! WOW!
MAN! IT'S THE GREATEST!
WHERE'S THE TREE?
WHAT TREE?
"*THE*" TREE! THE BIG, FAMOUS OLD OAK!
WHEN YOU BUILD ON THIS SCALE, THE FIRST THING YOU DO IS CLEAR THE LAND!
HA! IF YOU EVER SAW *THIS* TREE, YOU'D NEVER SAY THAT!
ARCHIE'S RIGHT, DADDY! COME ON OUT AND *LOOK* AT THIS TREE!
THAT'S PROBABLY THE OLDEST TREE IN THE STATE!
ISN'T IT MAGNIFICENT, DADDY?
IT'S A NICE TREE!
2

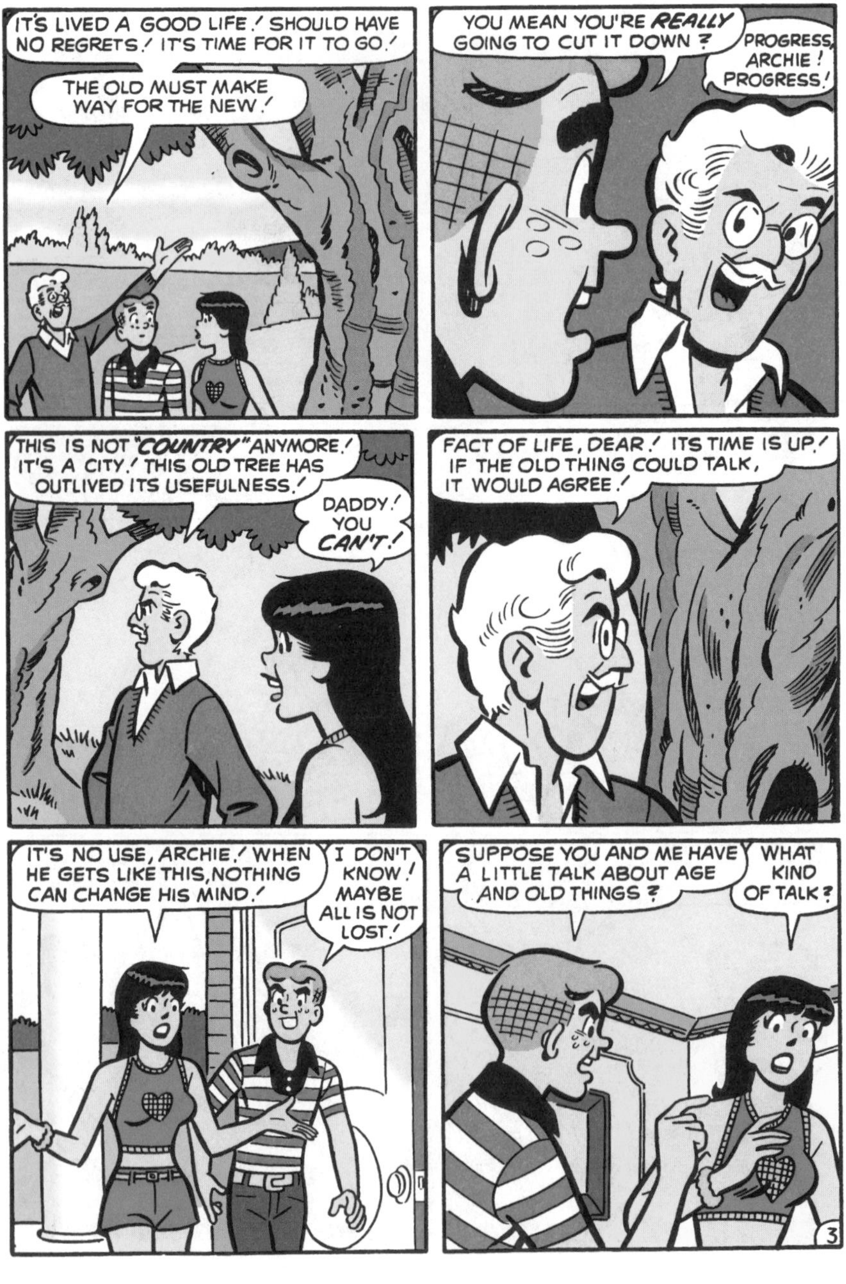
IT'S LIVED A GOOD LIFE! SHOULD HAVE NO REGRETS! IT'S TIME FOR IT TO GO!
THE OLD MUST MAKE WAY FOR THE NEW!
YOU MEAN YOU'RE REALLY GOING TO CUT IT DOWN?
PROGRESS, ARCHIE! PROGRESS!
THIS IS NOT "COUNTRY" ANYMORE! IT'S A CITY! THIS OLD TREE HAS OUTLIVED ITS USEFULNESS!
DADDY! YOU CAN'T!
FACT OF LIFE, DEAR! ITS TIME IS UP! IF THE OLD THING COULD TALK, IT WOULD AGREE!
IT'S NO USE, ARCHIE! WHEN HE GETS LIKE THIS, NOTHING CAN CHANGE HIS MIND!
I DON'T KNOW! MAYBE ALL IS NOT LOST!
SUPPOSE YOU AND ME HAVE A LITTLE TALK ABOUT AGE AND OLD THINGS?
WHAT KIND OF TALK?
3

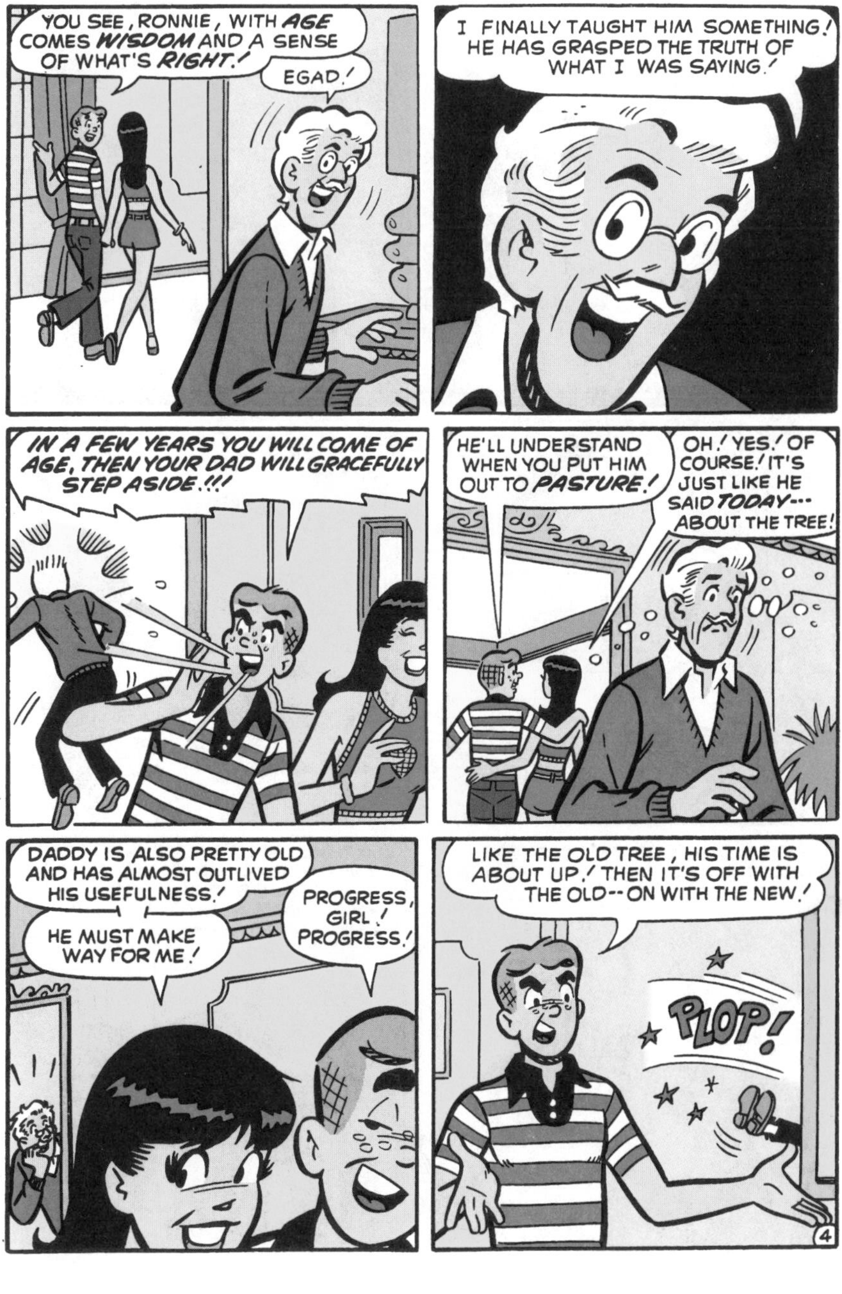
YOU SEE, RONNIE, WITH AGE COMES WISDOM AND A SENSE OF WHAT'S RIGHT!
EGAD!
I FINALLY TAUGHT HIM SOMETHING! HE HAS GRASPED THE TRUTH OF WHAT I WAS SAYING!
IN A FEW YEARS YOU WILL COME OF AGE, THEN YOUR DAD WILL GRACEFULLY STEP ASIDE!!!
HE'LL UNDERSTAND WHEN YOU PUT HIM OUT TO PASTURE!
OH! YES! OF COURSE! IT'S JUST LIKE HE SAID TODAY--- ABOUT THE TREE!
DADDY IS ALSO PRETTY OLD AND HAS ALMOST OUTLIVED HIS USEFULNESS!
HE MUST MAKE WAY FOR ME!
PROGRESS, GIRL! PROGRESS!
LIKE THE OLD TREE, HIS TIME IS ABOUT UP! THEN IT'S OFF WITH THE OLD--ON WITH THE NEW!
PLOP!
4

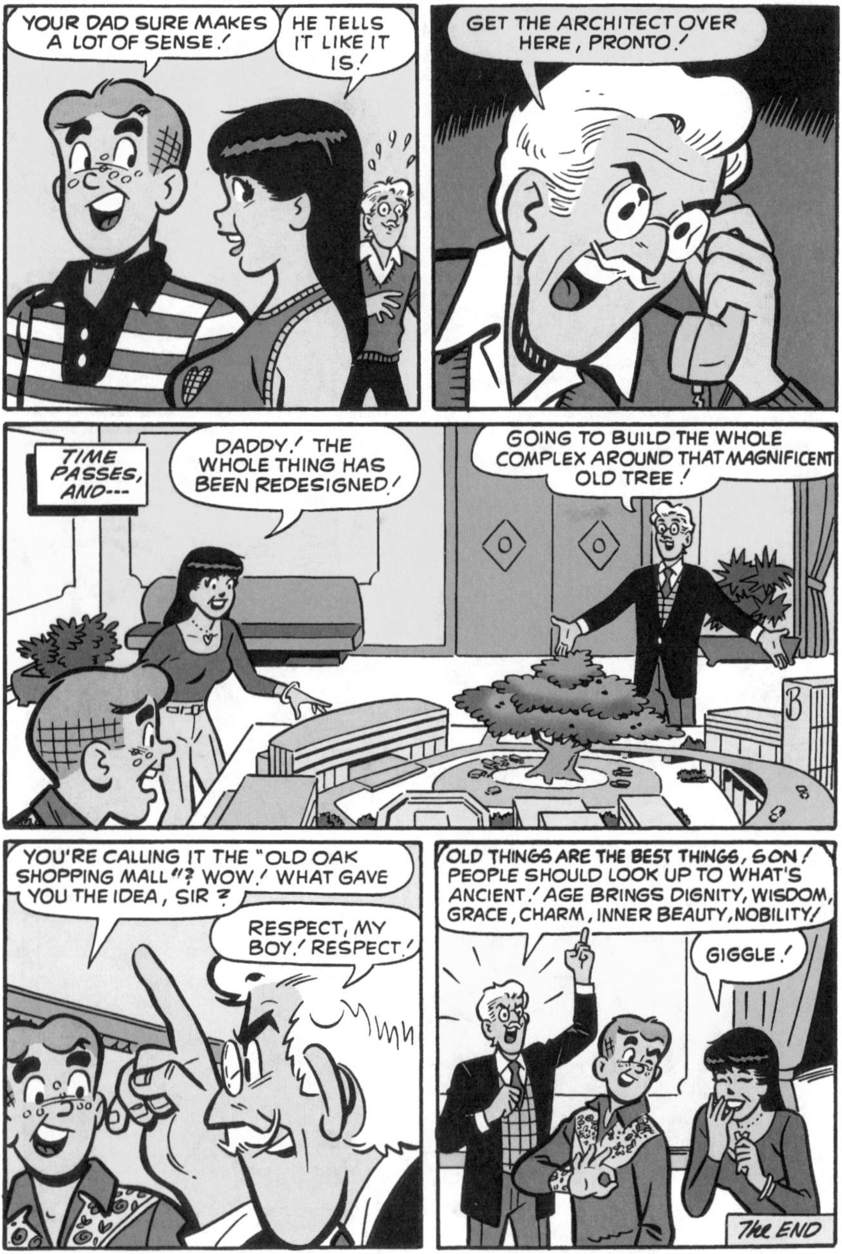
YOUR DAD SURE MAKES A LOT OF SENSE!
HE TELLS IT LIKE IT IS!
GET THE ARCHITECT OVER HERE, PRONTO!
TIME PASSES, AND---
DADDY! THE WHOLE THING HAS BEEN REDESIGNED!
GOING TO BUILD THE WHOLE COMPLEX AROUND THAT MAGNIFICENT OLD TREE!
YOU'RE CALLING IT THE "OLD OAK SHOPPING MALL"? WOW! WHAT GAVE YOU THE IDEA, SIR?
RESPECT, MY BOY! RESPECT!
OLD THINGS ARE THE BEST THINGS, SON! PEOPLE SHOULD LOOK UP TO WHAT'S ANCIENT! AGE BRINGS DIGNITY, WISDOM, GRACE, CHARM, INNER BEAUTY, NOBILITY!
GIGGLE!
The END

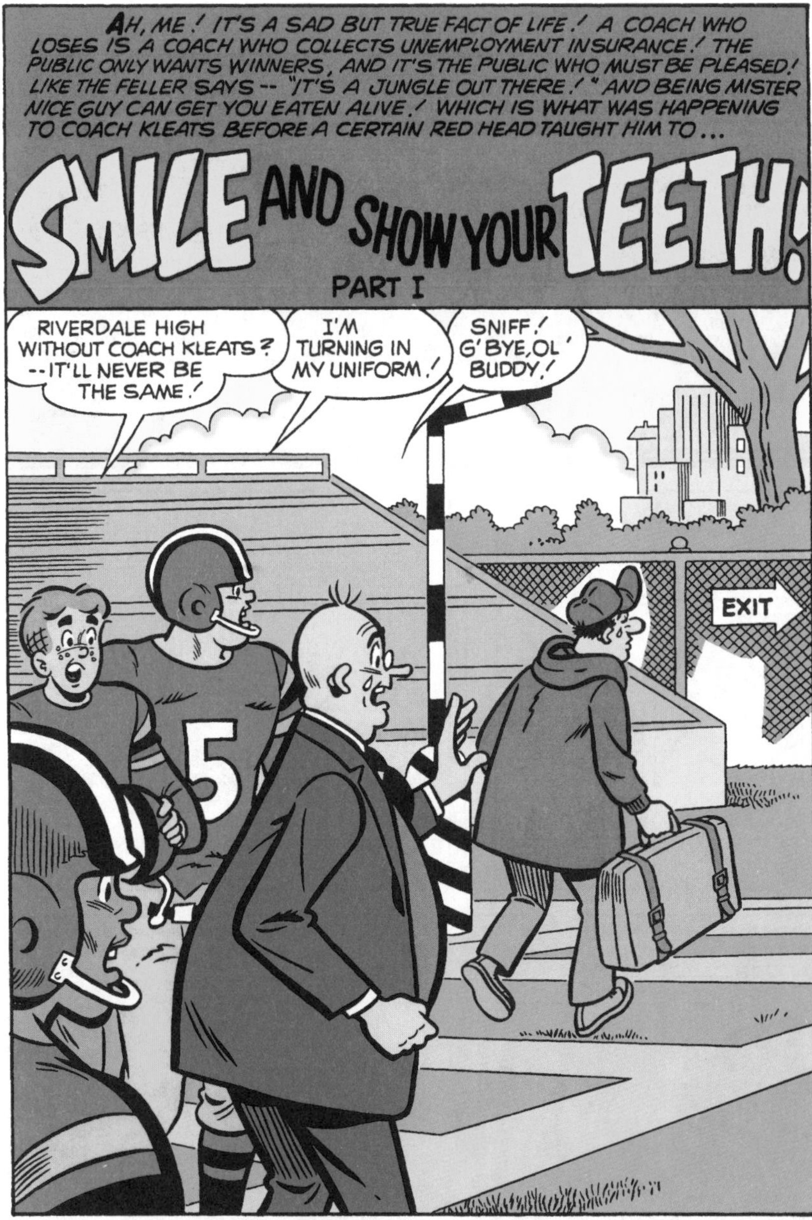
AH, ME! IT'S A SAD BUT TRUE FACT OF LIFE! A COACH WHO LOSES IS A COACH WHO COLLECTS UNEMPLOYMENT INSURANCE! THE PUBLIC ONLY WANTS WINNERS, AND IT'S THE PUBLIC WHO MUST BE PLEASED! LIKE THE FELLER SAYS -- "IT'S A JUNGLE OUT THERE!" AND BEING MISTER NICE GUY CAN GET YOU EATEN ALIVE! WHICH IS WHAT WAS HAPPENING TO COACH KLEATS BEFORE A CERTAIN RED HEAD TAUGHT HIM TO...
SMILE AND SHOW YOUR TEETH!
PART I
RIVERDALE HIGH WITHOUT COACH KLEATS? --IT'LL NEVER BE THE SAME!
I'M TURNING IN MY UNIFORM!
SNIFF! G'BYE, OL' BUDDY!
EXIT
5

Story: George Gladir Pencils: Stan Goldberg
Inks: Jon D'Agostino Letters: Bill Yoshida

Originally printed in ARCHIE AT RIVERDALE HIGH #36, JUNE 1976

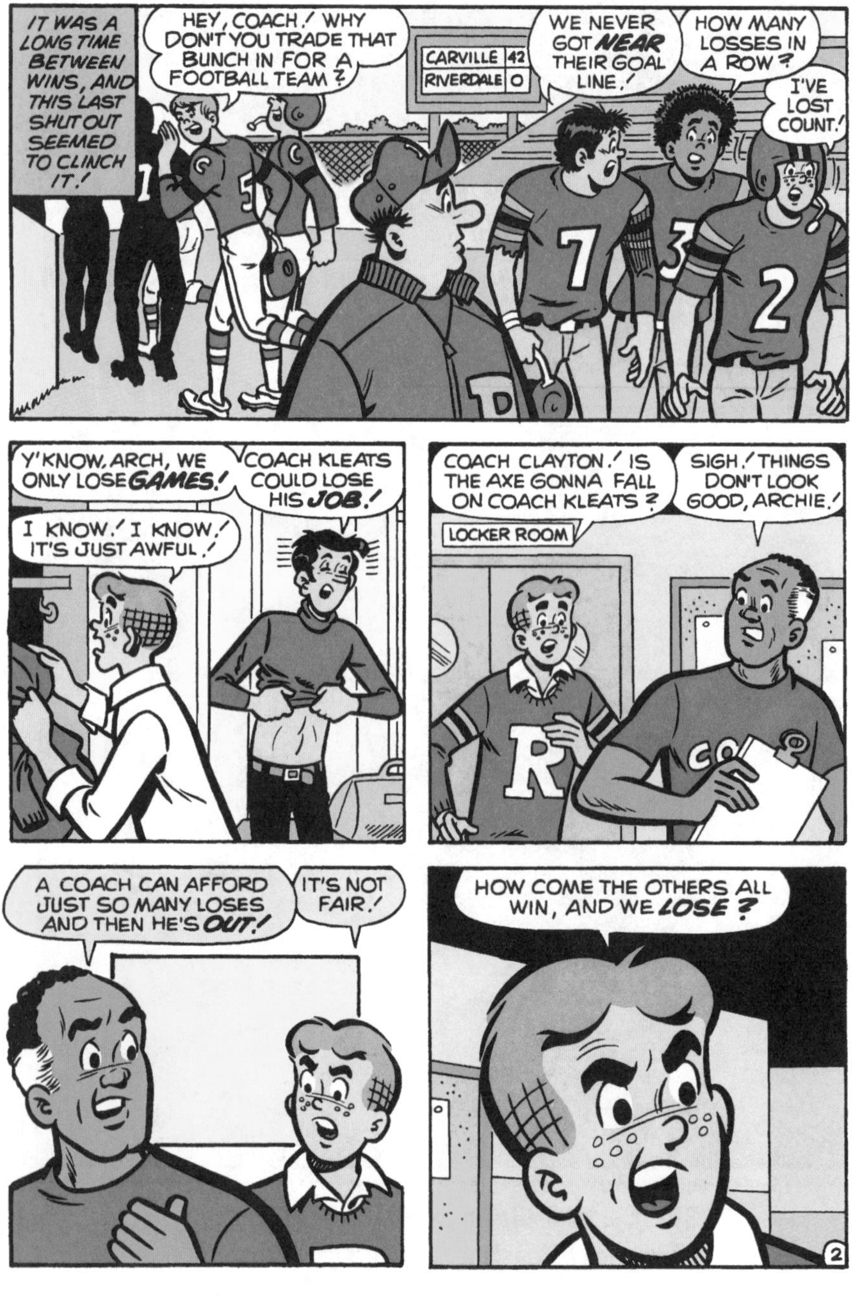
IT WAS A LONG TIME BETWEEN WINS, AND THIS LAST SHUTOUT SEEMED TO CLINCH IT!
HEY, COACH! WHY DON'T YOU TRADE THAT BUNCH IN FOR A FOOTBALL TEAM?
CARVILLE 42
RIVERDALE 0
WE NEVER GOT NEAR THEIR GOAL LINE!
HOW MANY LOSSES IN A ROW?
I'VE LOST COUNT!
Y'KNOW, ARCH, WE ONLY LOSE GAMES!
COACH KLEATS COULD LOSE HIS JOB!
I KNOW! I KNOW! IT'S JUST AWFUL!
COACH CLAYTON! IS THE AXE GONNA FALL ON COACH KLEATS?
SIGH! THINGS DON'T LOOK GOOD, ARCHIE!
LOCKER ROOM
A COACH CAN AFFORD JUST SO MANY LOSES AND THEN HE'S OUT!
IT'S NOT FAIR!
HOW COME THE OTHERS ALL WIN, AND WE LOSE?
2

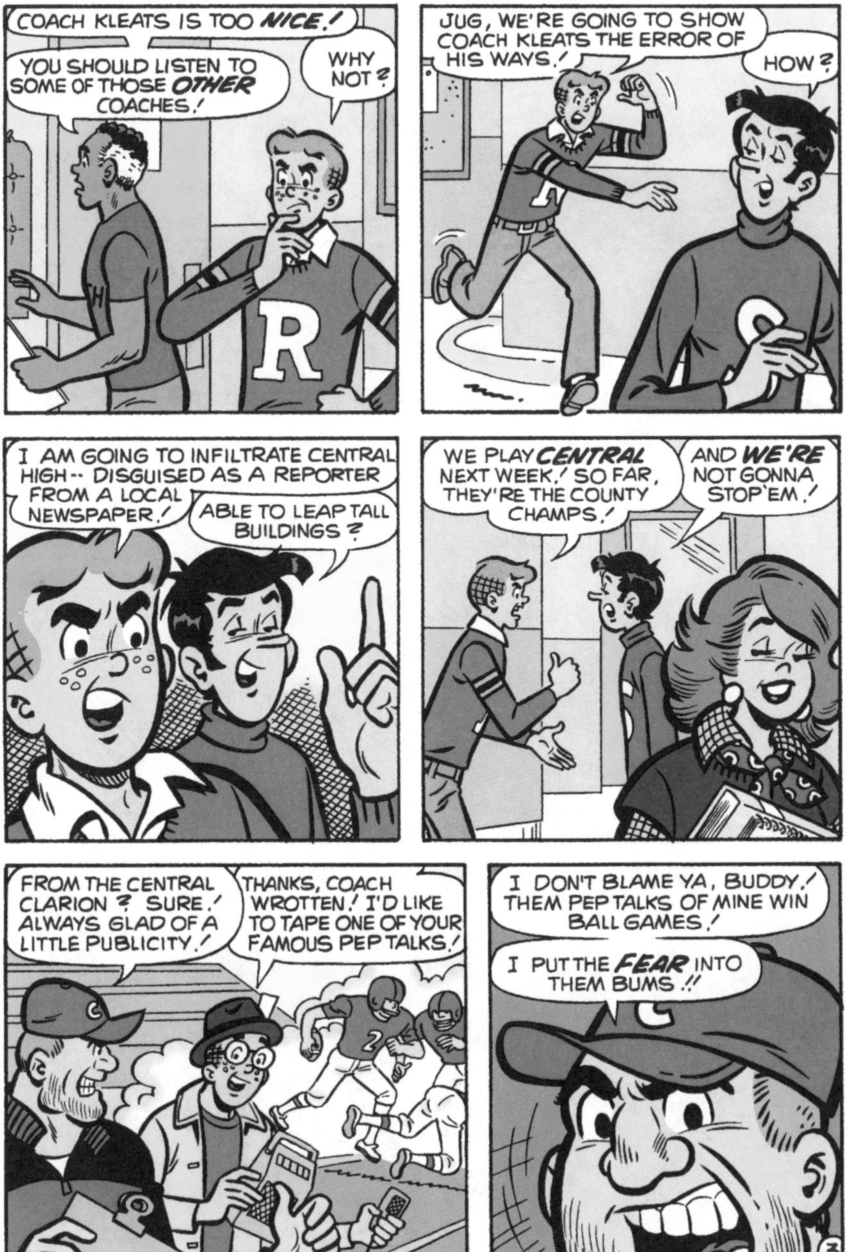
COACH KLEATS IS TOO NICE!
YOU SHOULD LISTEN TO SOME OF THOSE OTHER COACHES!
WHY NOT?
JUG, WE'RE GOING TO SHOW COACH KLEATS THE ERROR OF HIS WAYS!
HOW?
I AM GOING TO INFILTRATE CENTRAL HIGH -- DISGUISED AS A REPORTER FROM A LOCAL NEWSPAPER!
ABLE TO LEAP TALL BUILDINGS?
WE PLAY CENTRAL NEXT WEEK! SO FAR, THEY'RE THE COUNTY CHAMPS!
AND WE'RE NOT GONNA STOP 'EM!
FROM THE CENTRAL CLARION? SURE! ALWAYS GLAD OF A LITTLE PUBLICITY!
THANKS, COACH WROTTEN! I'D LIKE TO TAPE ONE OF YOUR FAMOUS PEP TALKS!
I DON'T BLAME YA, BUDDY! THEM PEP TALKS OF MINE WIN BALL GAMES!
I PUT THE FEAR INTO THEM BUMS!!
3

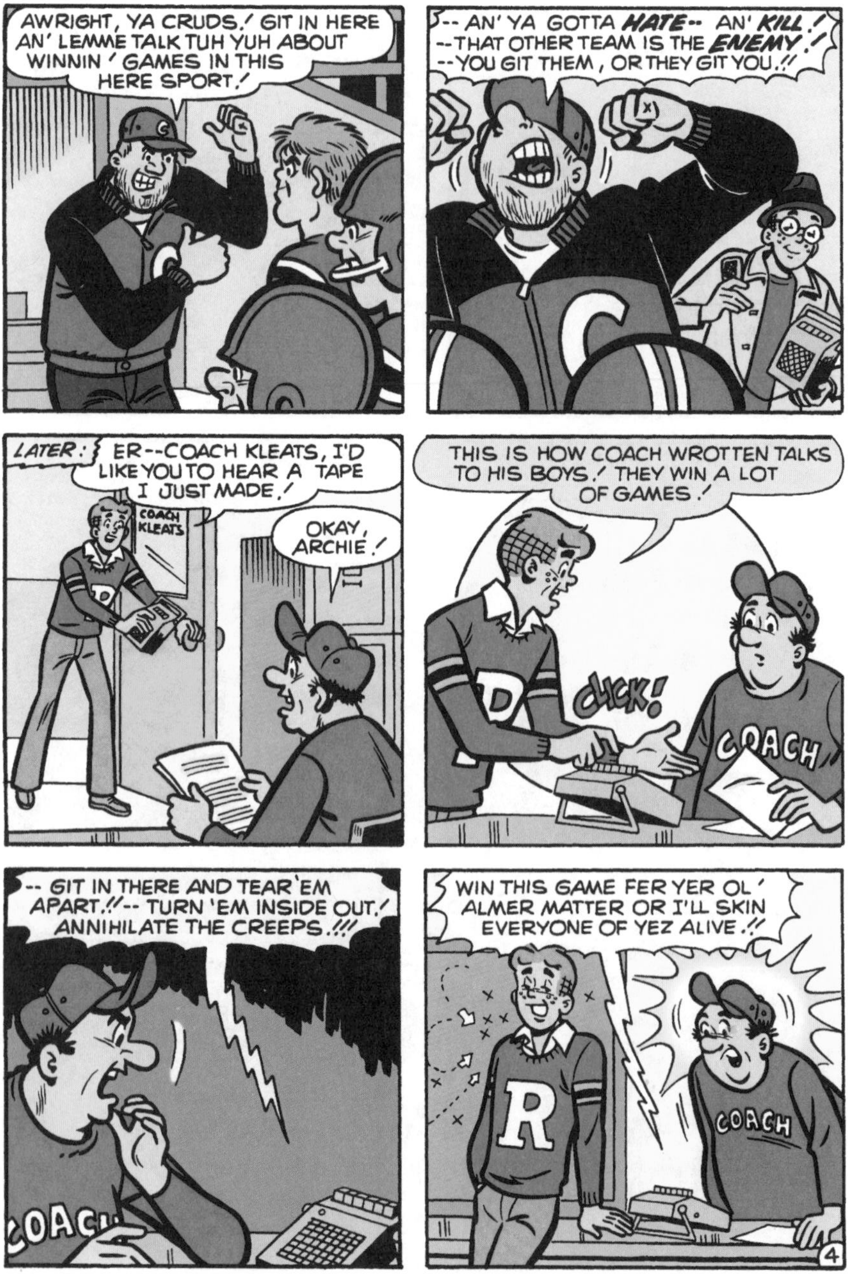
AWRIGHT, YA CRUDS.! GIT IN HERE AN' LEMME TALK TUH YUH ABOUT WINNIN' GAMES IN THIS HERE SPORT.!
-- AN' YA GOTTA HATE-- AN' KILL.! --THAT OTHER TEAM IS THE ENEMY.! --YOU GIT THEM, OR THEY GIT YOU.!!
LATER:
ER--COACH KLEATS, I'D LIKE YOU TO HEAR A TAPE I JUST MADE.!
COACH KLEATS
OKAY, ARCHIE.!
THIS IS HOW COACH WROTTEN TALKS TO HIS BOYS.! THEY WIN A LOT OF GAMES.!
CLICK!
COACH
-- GIT IN THERE AND TEAR 'EM APART.!!-- TURN 'EM INSIDE OUT.! ANNIHILATE THE CREEPS.!!!
WIN THIS GAME FER YER OL' ALMER MATTER OR I'LL SKIN EVERYONE OF YEZ ALIVE.!!
R
COACH
4

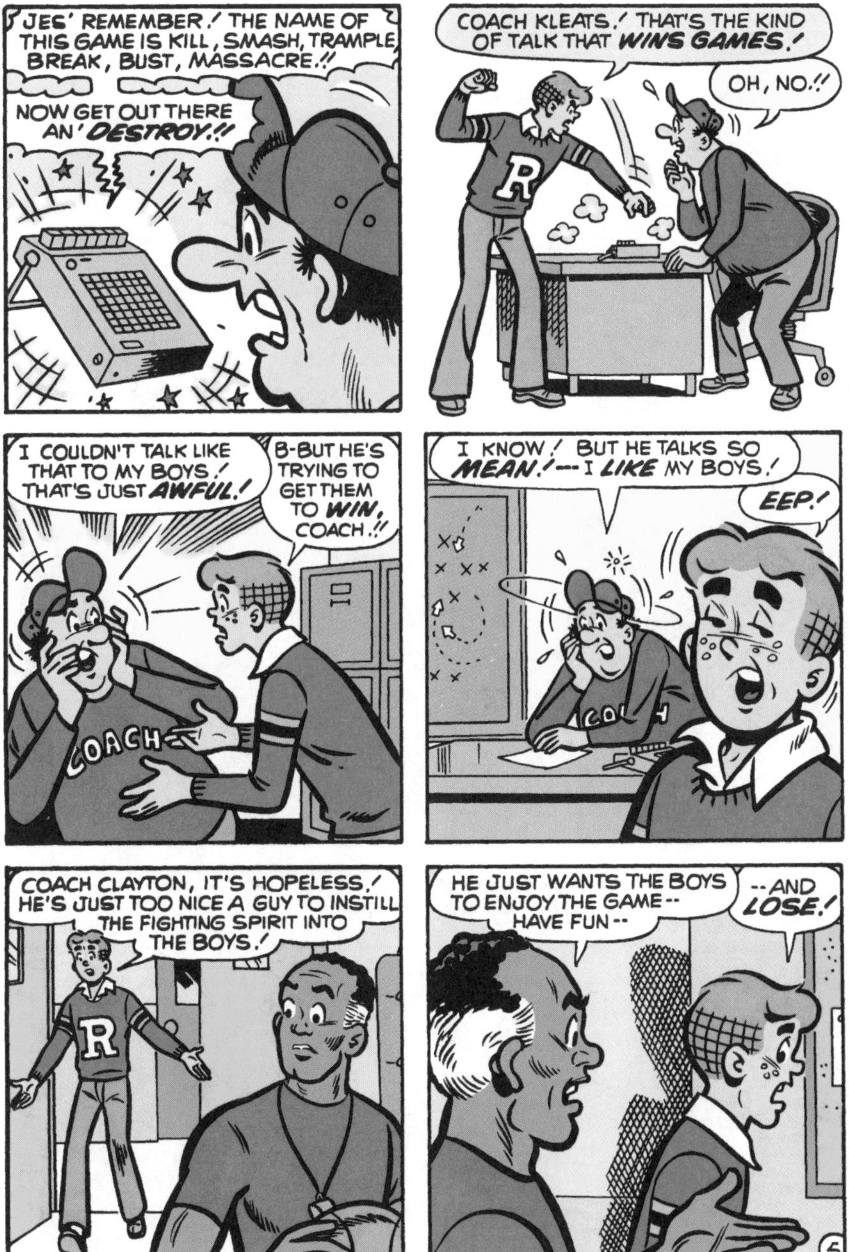
JES' REMEMBER! THE NAME OF THIS GAME IS KILL, SMASH, TRAMPLE, BREAK, BUST, MASSACRE!!
NOW GET OUT THERE AN' DESTROY!!
COACH KLEATS! THAT'S THE KIND OF TALK THAT WINS GAMES!
OH, NO!!
I COULDN'T TALK LIKE THAT TO MY BOYS! THAT'S JUST AWFUL!
B-BUT HE'S TRYING TO GET THEM TO WIN, COACH!!
COACH
I KNOW! BUT HE TALKS SO MEAN! --- I LIKE MY BOYS!
EEP!
COACH CLAYTON, IT'S HOPELESS! HE'S JUST TOO NICE A GUY TO INSTILL THE FIGHTING SPIRIT INTO THE BOYS!
HE JUST WANTS THE BOYS TO ENJOY THE GAME -- HAVE FUN --
--AND LOSE!
5

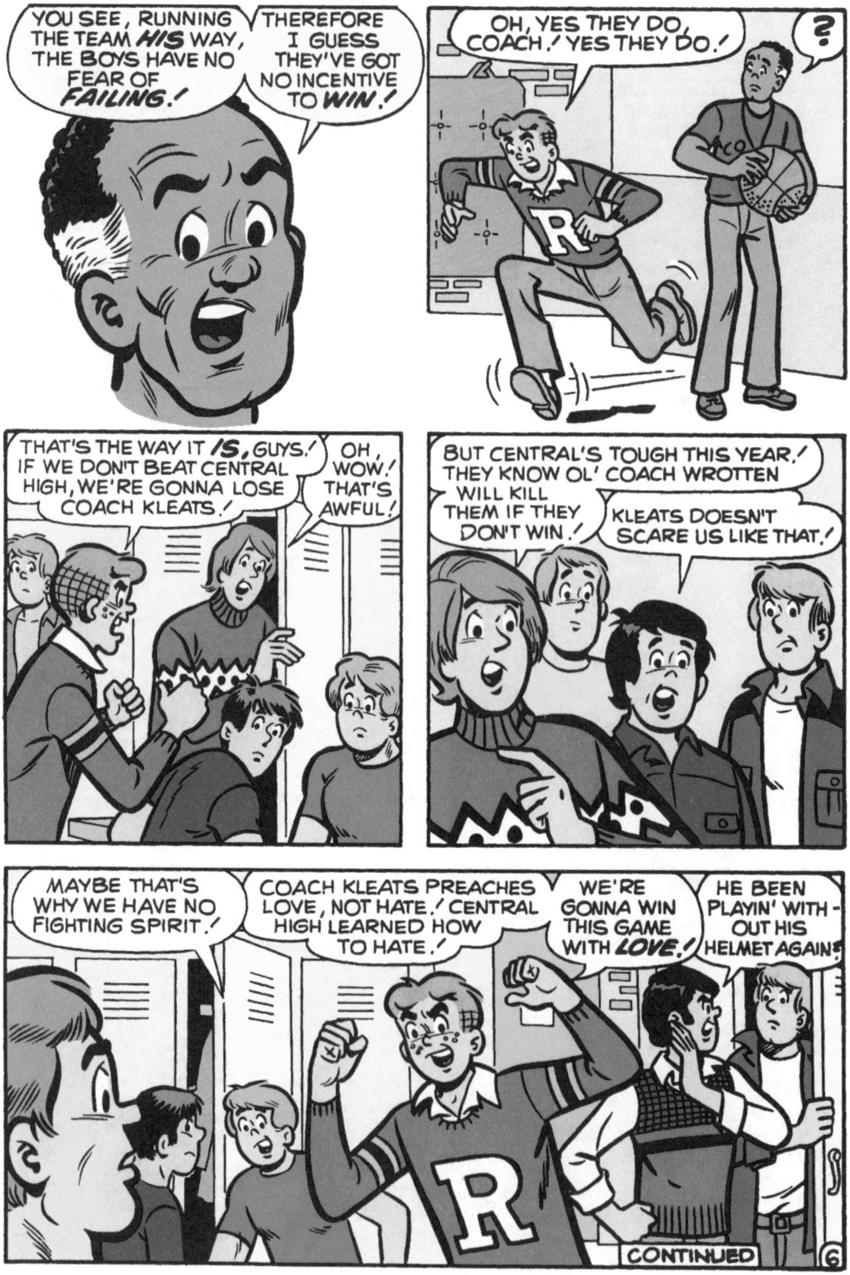
YOU SEE, RUNNING THE TEAM HIS WAY, THE BOYS HAVE NO FEAR OF FAILING.!
THEREFORE I GUESS THEY'VE GOT NO INCENTIVE TO WIN.!
OH, YES THEY DO, COACH.! YES THEY DO.!
?
THAT'S THE WAY IT IS, GUYS.! IF WE DON'T BEAT CENTRAL HIGH, WE'RE GONNA LOSE COACH KLEATS.!
OH, WOW.! THAT'S AWFUL.!
BUT CENTRAL'S TOUGH THIS YEAR.! THEY KNOW OL' COACH WROTTEN WILL KILL THEM IF THEY DON'T WIN.!
KLEATS DOESN'T SCARE US LIKE THAT.!
MAYBE THAT'S WHY WE HAVE NO FIGHTING SPIRIT.!
COACH KLEATS PREACHES LOVE, NOT HATE.! CENTRAL HIGH LEARNED HOW TO HATE.!
WE'RE GONNA WIN THIS GAME WITH LOVE.!
HE BEEN PLAYIN' WITH-OUT HIS HELMET AGAIN!
CONTINUED
6

Archie at Riverdale: Smile and Show Your Teeth! Part II

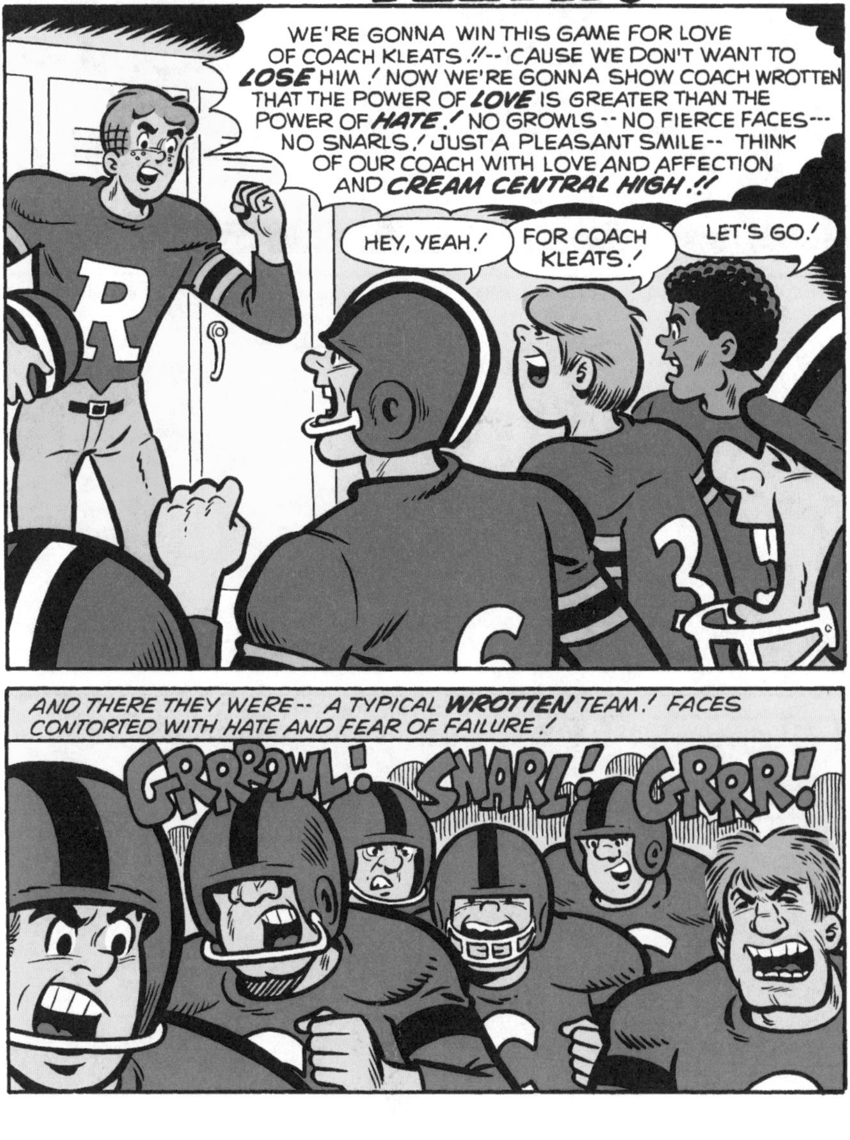
WE'RE GONNA WIN THIS GAME FOR LOVE OF COACH KLEATS.!!--'CAUSE WE DON'T WANT TO LOSE HIM.! NOW WE'RE GONNA SHOW COACH WROTTEN THAT THE POWER OF LOVE IS GREATER THAN THE POWER OF HATE.! NO GROWLS -- NO FIERCE FACES--- NO SNARLS.! JUST A PLEASANT SMILE-- THINK OF OUR COACH WITH LOVE AND AFFECTION AND CREAM CENTRAL HIGH.!!
HEY, YEAH.!
FOR COACH KLEATS.!
LET'S GO.!
AND THERE THEY WERE-- A TYPICAL WROTTEN TEAM.! FACES CONTORTED WITH HATE AND FEAR OF FAILURE.!
GRRROWL! SNARL! GRRRR!

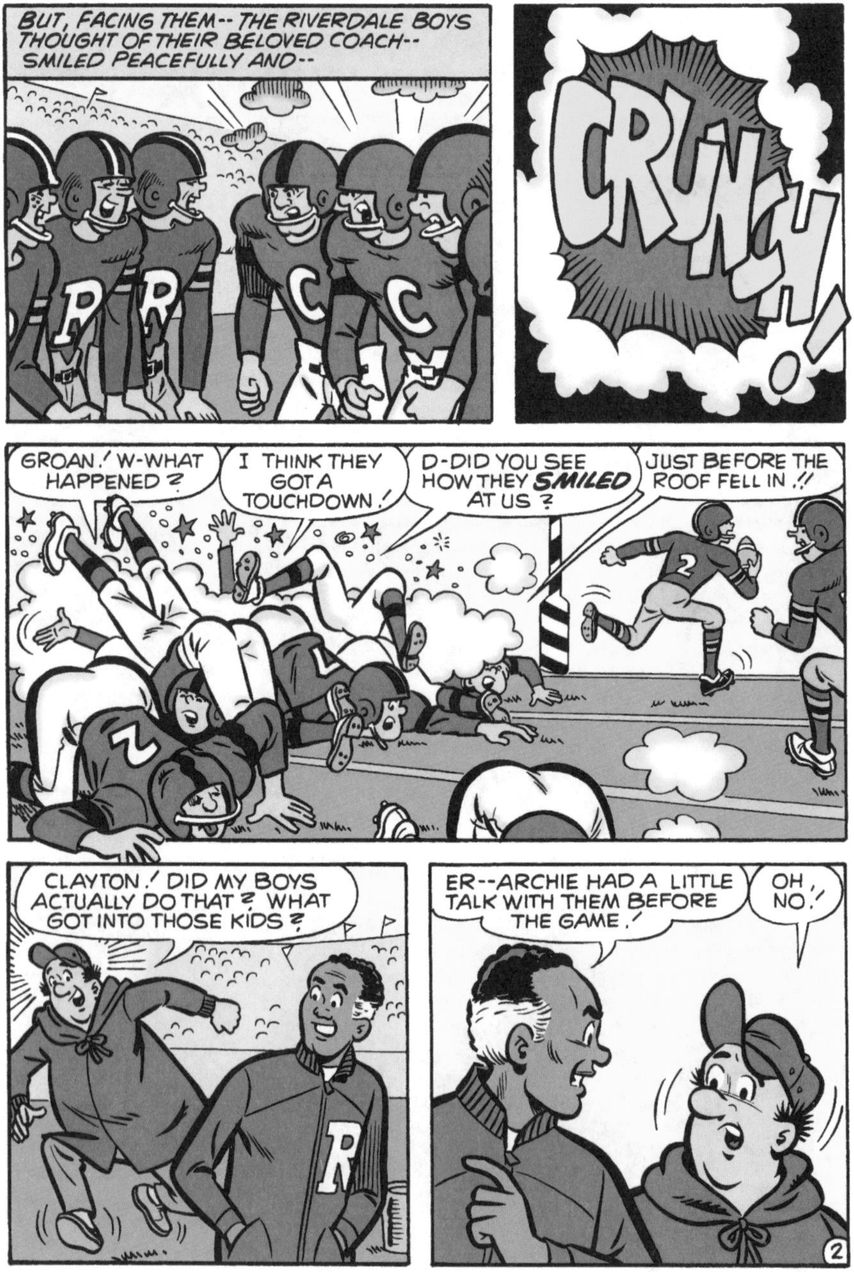
BUT, FACING THEM-- THE RIVERDALE BOYS THOUGHT OF THEIR BELOVED COACH-- SMILED PEACEFULLY AND--
CRUNCH!
GROAN! W-WHAT HAPPENED?
I THINK THEY GOT A TOUCHDOWN!
D-DID YOU SEE HOW THEY SMILED AT US?
JUST BEFORE THE ROOF FELL IN!!
CLAYTON! DID MY BOYS ACTUALLY DO THAT? WHAT GOT INTO THOSE KIDS?
ER--ARCHIE HAD A LITTLE TALK WITH THEM BEFORE THE GAME!
OH, NO!
2

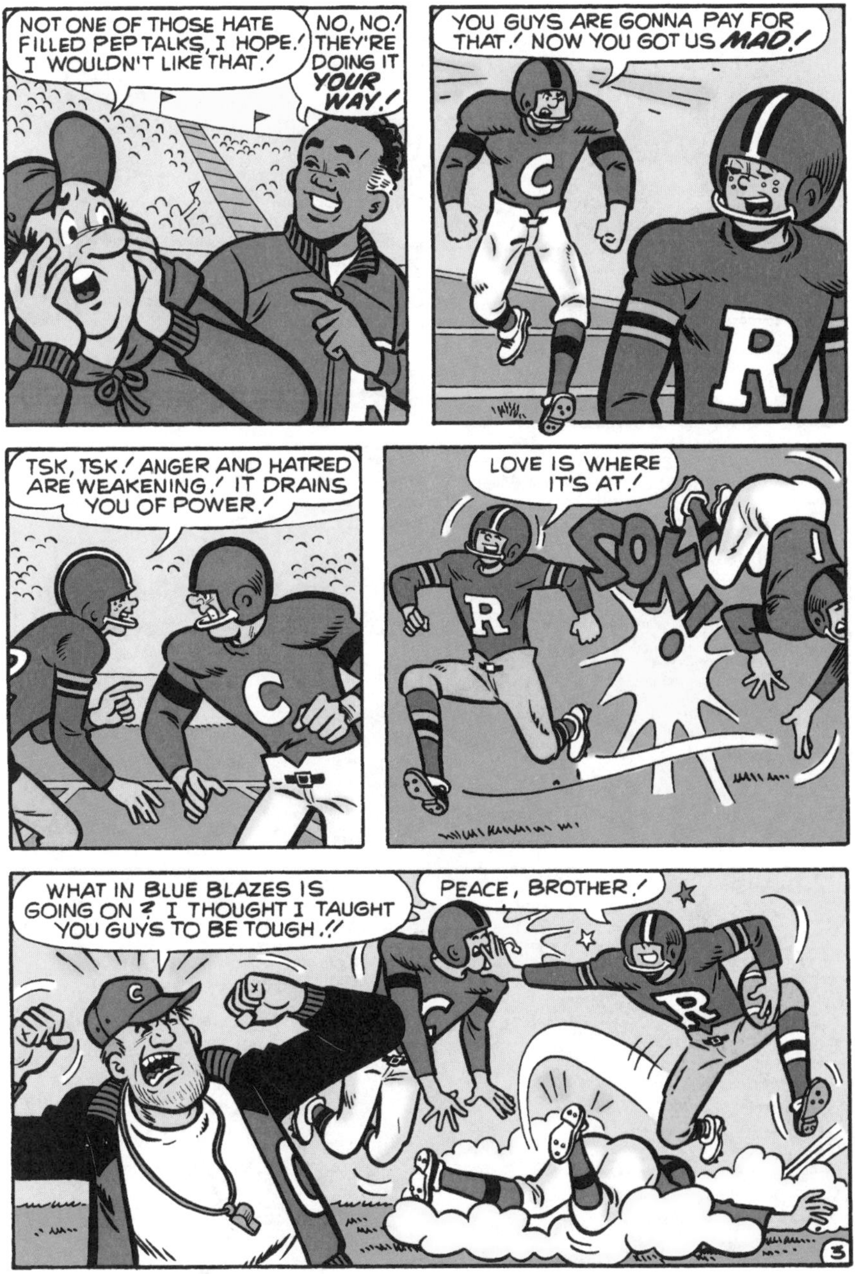
NOT ONE OF THOSE HATE FILLED PEP TALKS, I HOPE.! I WOULDN'T LIKE THAT.!
NO, NO.! THEY'RE DOING IT YOUR WAY.!
YOU GUYS ARE GONNA PAY FOR THAT.! NOW YOU GOT US MAD.!
TSK, TSK.! ANGER AND HATRED ARE WEAKENING.! IT DRAINS YOU OF POWER.!
LOVE IS WHERE IT'S AT.!
SOK!
WHAT IN BLUE BLAZES IS GOING ON ? I THOUGHT I TAUGHT YOU GUYS TO BE TOUGH.!!
PEACE, BROTHER.!
3

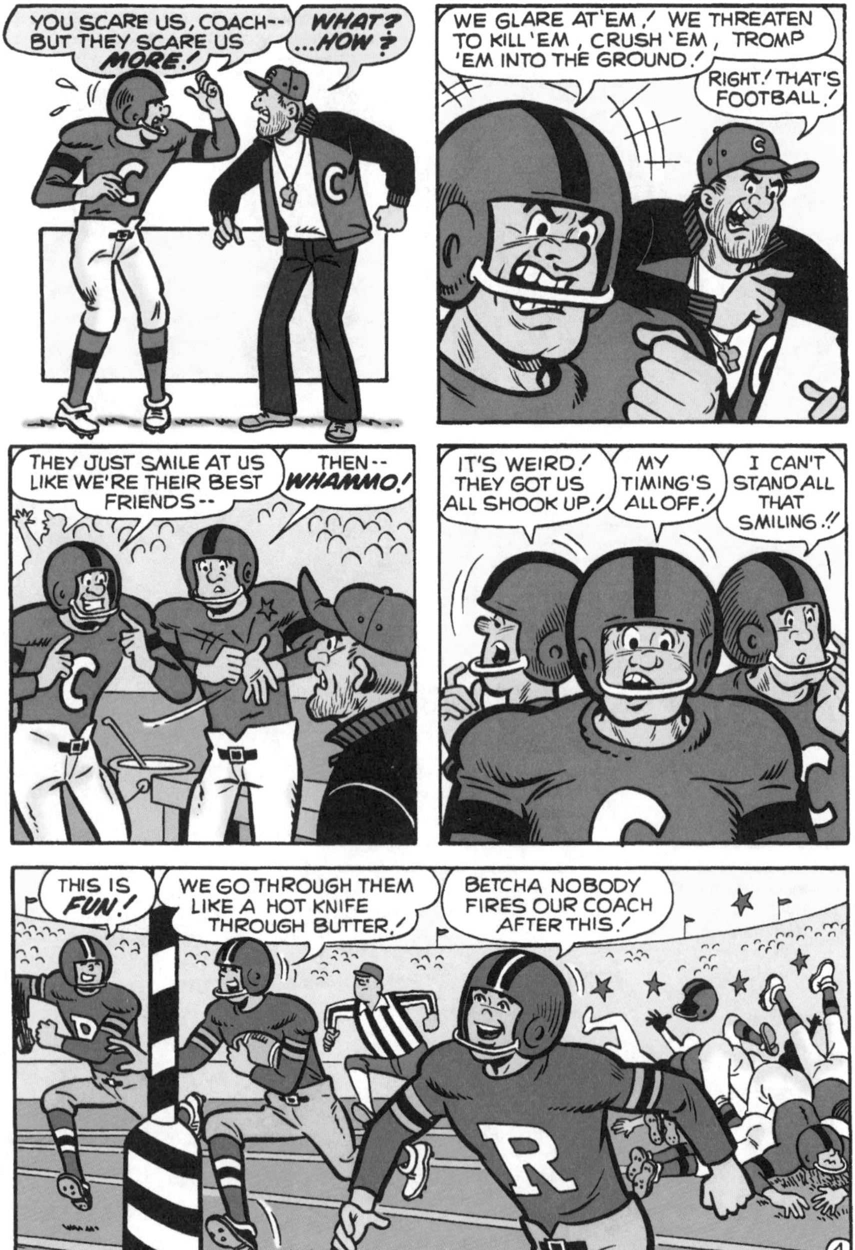

YOU SCARE US, COACH-- BUT THEY SCARE US MORE!
WHAT? ...HOW?
WE GLARE AT 'EM! WE THREATEN TO KILL 'EM, CRUSH 'EM, TROMP 'EM INTO THE GROUND!
RIGHT! THAT'S FOOTBALL!
THEY JUST SMILE AT US LIKE WE'RE THEIR BEST FRIENDS--
THEN-- WHAMMO!
IT'S WEIRD! THEY GOT US ALL SHOOK UP!
MY TIMING'S ALL OFF!
I CAN'T STAND ALL THAT SMILING!!
THIS IS FUN!
WE GO THROUGH THEM LIKE A HOT KNIFE THROUGH BUTTER!
BETCHA NOBODY FIRES OUR COACH AFTER THIS!
4

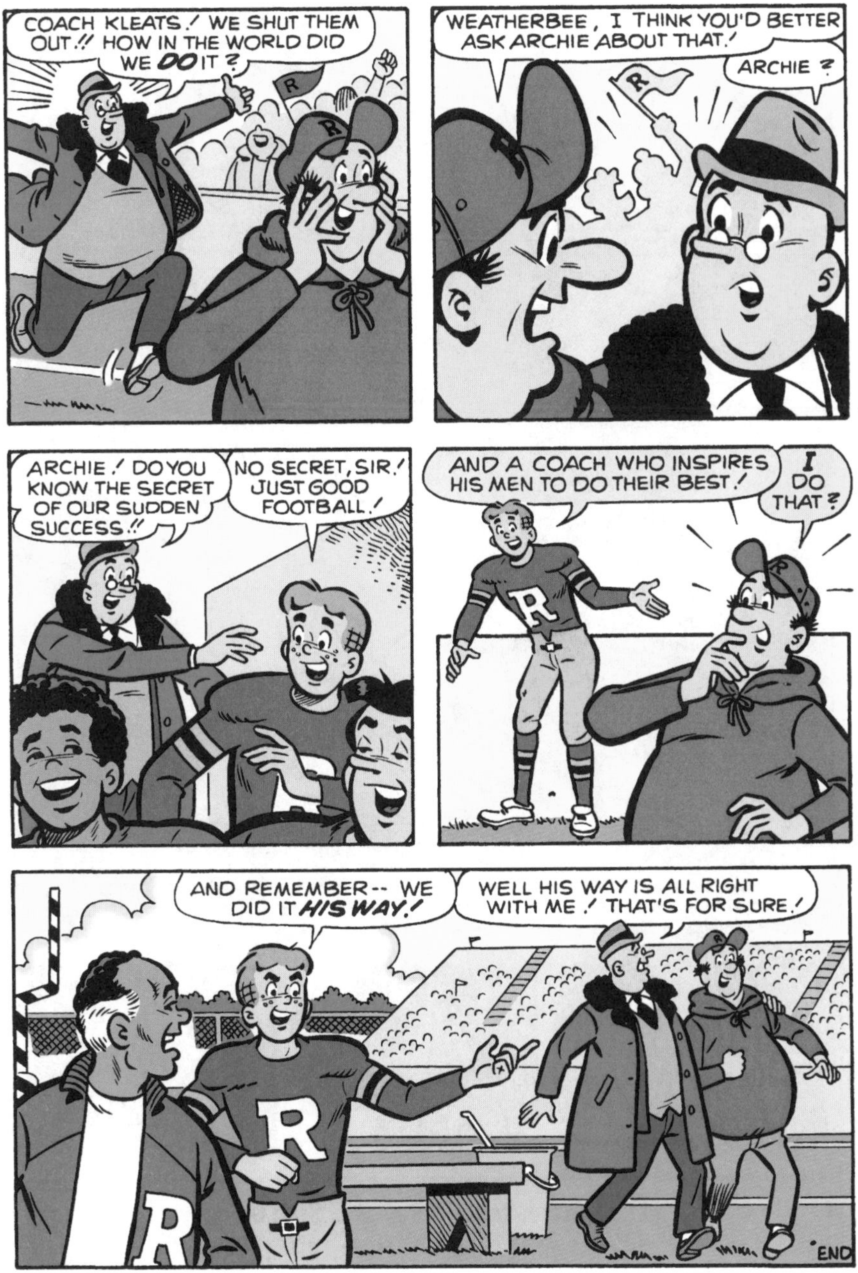
COACH KLEATS! WE SHUT THEM OUT!! HOW IN THE WORLD DID WE DO IT?
WEATHERBEE, I THINK YOU'D BETTER ASK ARCHIE ABOUT THAT!
ARCHIE?
ARCHIE! DO YOU KNOW THE SECRET OF OUR SUDDEN SUCCESS!!
NO SECRET, SIR! JUST GOOD FOOTBALL!
AND A COACH WHO INSPIRES HIS MEN TO DO THEIR BEST!
I DO THAT?
AND REMEMBER-- WE DID IT HIS WAY!
WELL HIS WAY IS ALL RIGHT WITH ME! THAT'S FOR SURE!
END

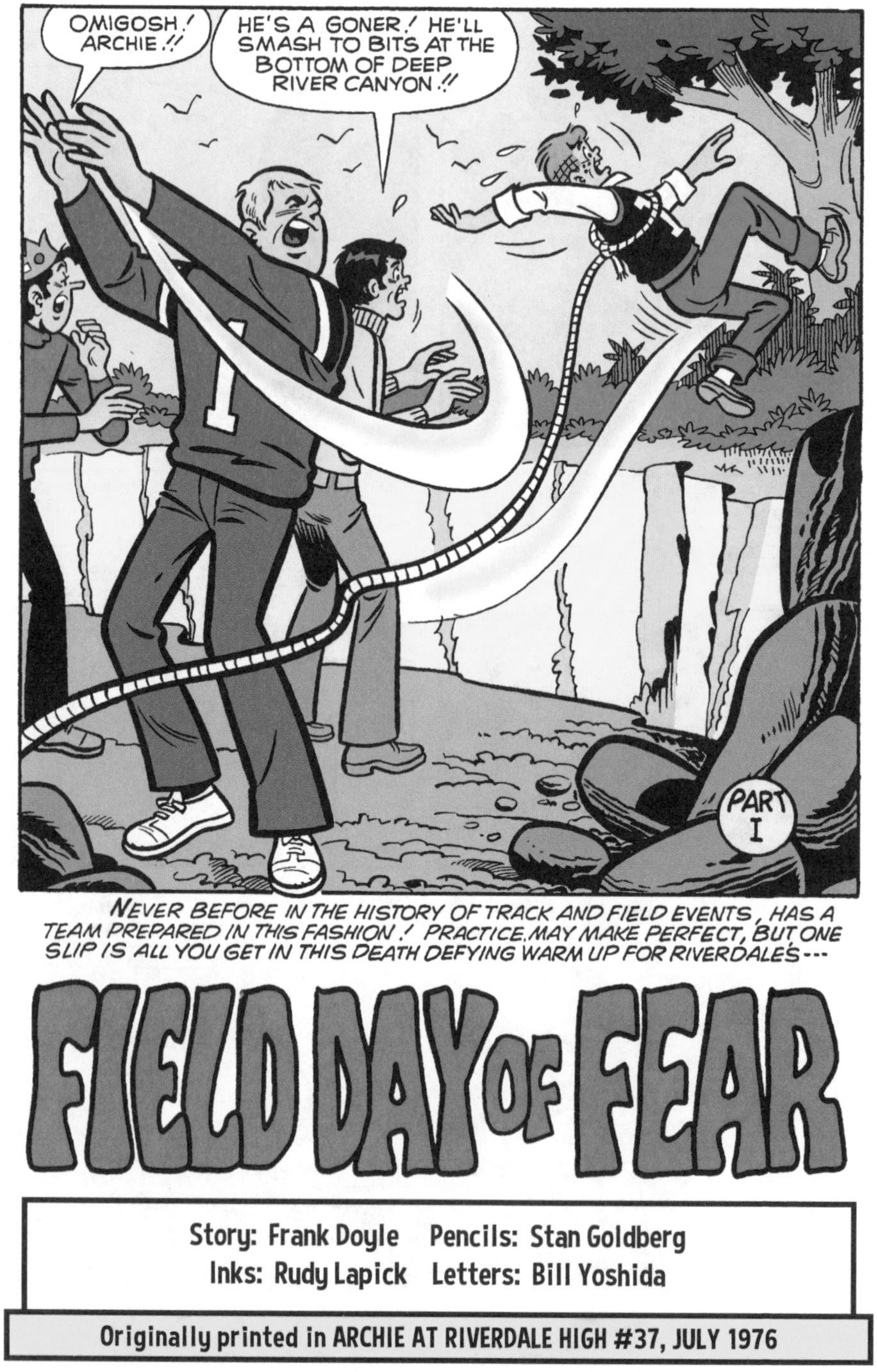
OMIGOSH! ARCHIE!!
HE'S A GONER! HE'LL SMASH TO BITS AT THE BOTTOM OF DEEP RIVER CANYON!!
PART I

NEVER BEFORE IN THE HISTORY OF TRACK AND FIELD EVENTS, HAS A TEAM PREPARED IN THIS FASHION! PRACTICE MAY MAKE PERFECT, BUT ONE SLIP IS ALL YOU GET IN THIS DEATH DEFYING WARM UP FOR RIVERDALE'S---

FIELD DAY OF FEAR

Story: Frank Doyle Pencils: Stan Goldberg
Inks: Rudy Lapick Letters: Bill Yoshida

Originally printed in ARCHIE AT RIVERDALE HIGH #37, JULY 1976

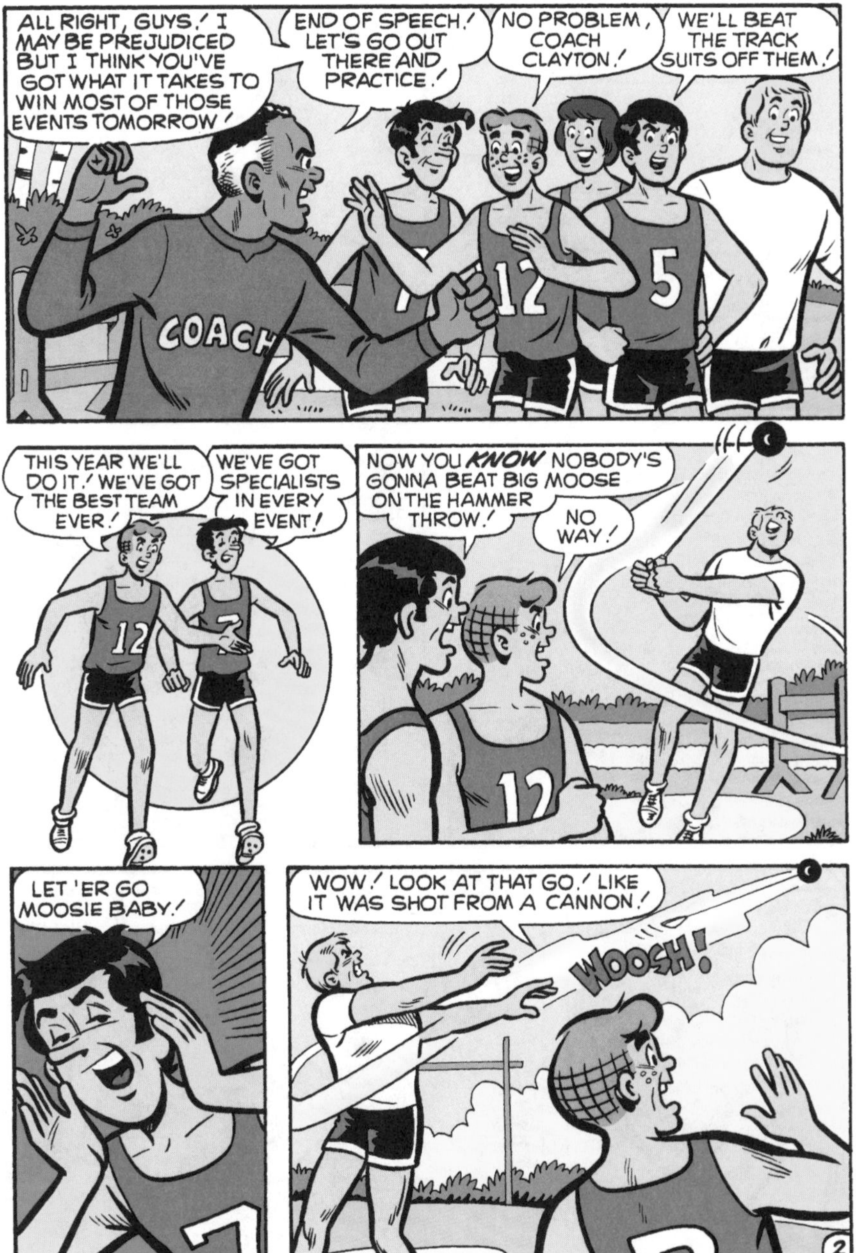
ALL RIGHT, GUYS! I MAY BE PREJUDICED BUT I THINK YOU'VE GOT WHAT IT TAKES TO WIN MOST OF THOSE EVENTS TOMORROW!
END OF SPEECH! LET'S GO OUT THERE AND PRACTICE!
NO PROBLEM, COACH CLAYTON!
WE'LL BEAT THE TRACK SUITS OFF THEM!
COACH
12
5
THIS YEAR WE'LL DO IT! WE'VE GOT THE BEST TEAM EVER!
WE'VE GOT SPECIALISTS IN EVERY EVENT!
12
NOW YOU KNOW NOBODY'S GONNA BEAT BIG MOOSE ON THE HAMMER THROW!
NO WAY!
12
LET 'ER GO MOOSIE BABY!
WOW! LOOK AT THAT GO! LIKE IT WAS SHOT FROM A CANNON!
WOOSH!
2

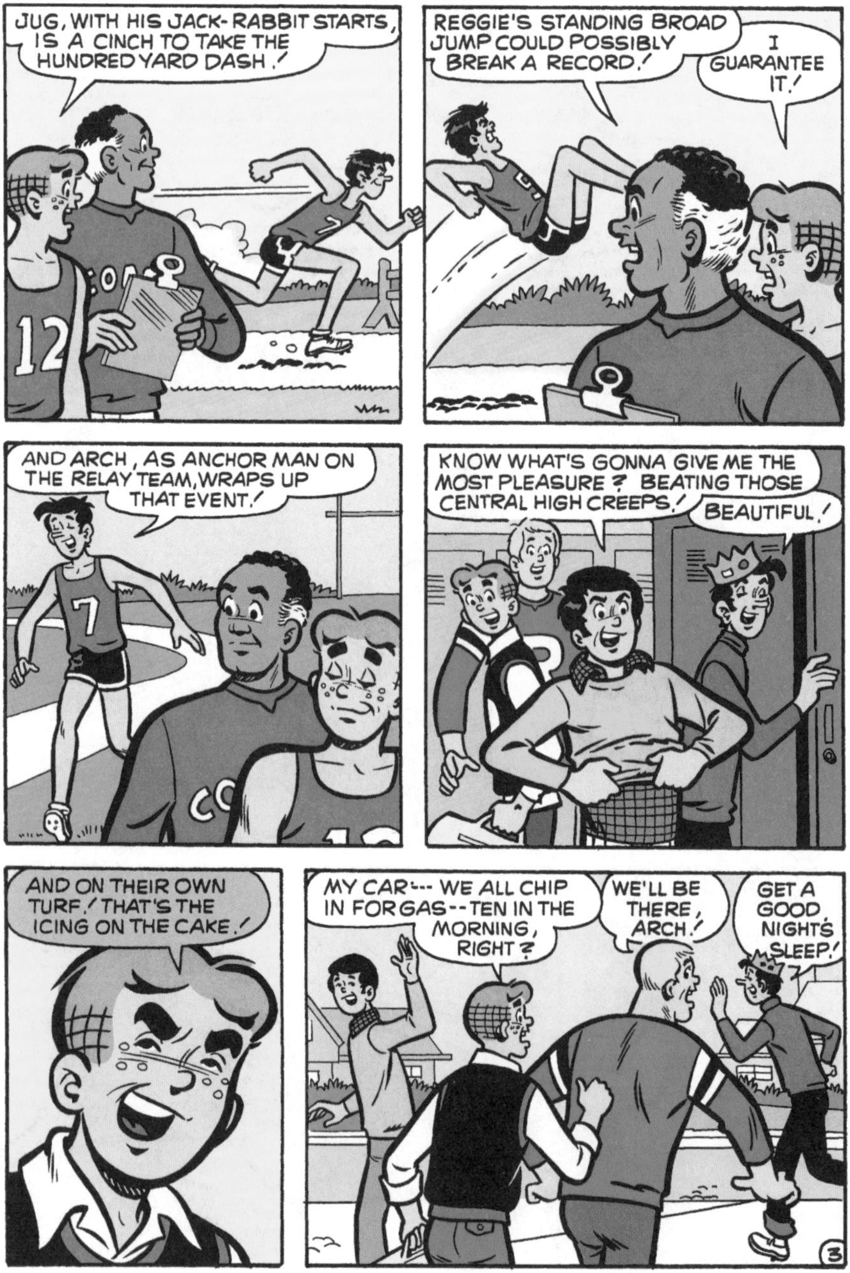
JUG, WITH HIS JACK-RABBIT STARTS, IS A CINCH TO TAKE THE HUNDRED YARD DASH.!
REGGIE'S STANDING BROAD JUMP COULD POSSIBLY BREAK A RECORD.!
I GUARANTEE IT.!
AND ARCH, AS ANCHOR MAN ON THE RELAY TEAM, WRAPS UP THAT EVENT.!
KNOW WHAT'S GONNA GIVE ME THE MOST PLEASURE? BEATING THOSE CENTRAL HIGH CREEPS!
BEAUTIFUL!
AND ON THEIR OWN TURF! THAT'S THE ICING ON THE CAKE!
MY CAR--- WE ALL CHIP IN FOR GAS--TEN IN THE MORNING, RIGHT?
WE'LL BE THERE, ARCH!
GET A GOOD NIGHT'S SLEEP!
3

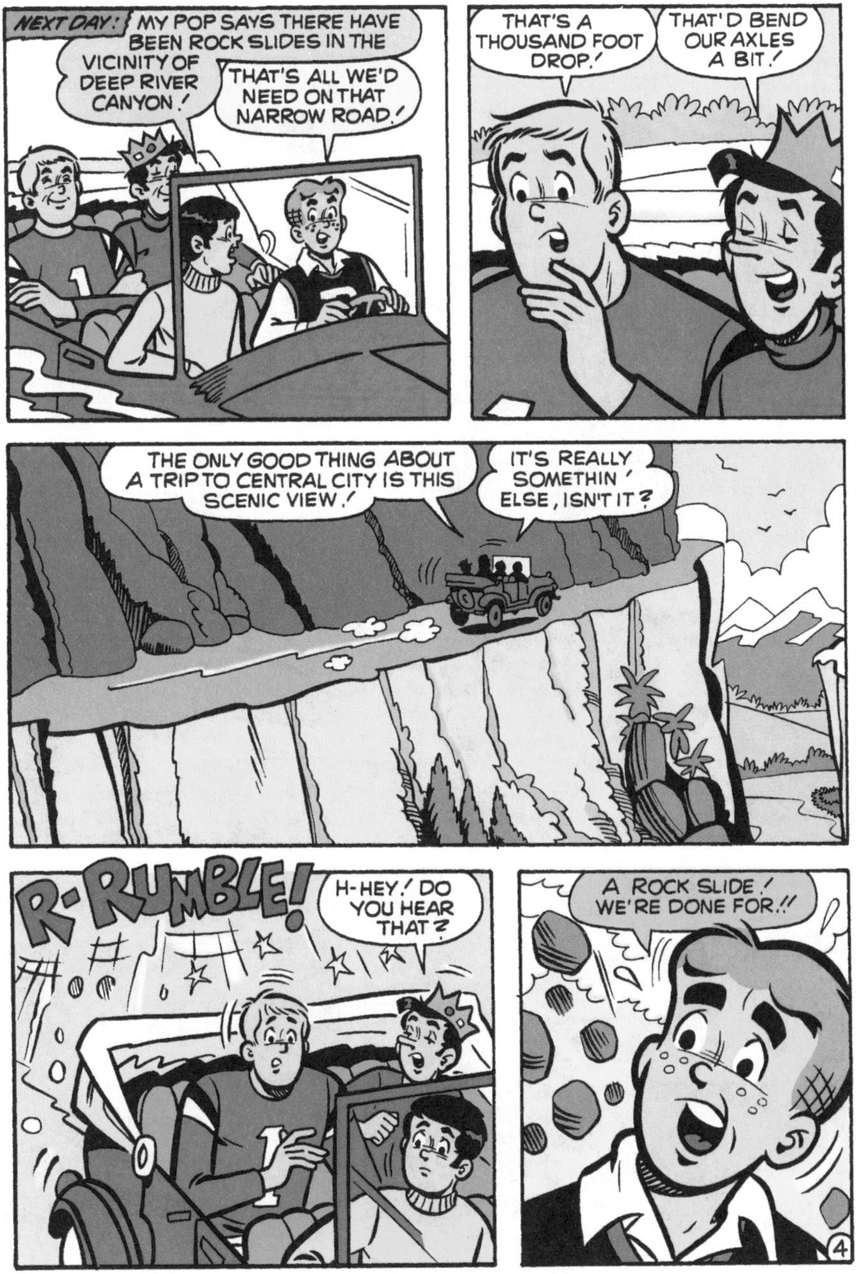
NEXT DAY:
MY POP SAYS THERE HAVE BEEN ROCK SLIDES IN THE VICINITY OF DEEP RIVER CANYON!
THAT'S ALL WE'D NEED ON THAT NARROW ROAD!
THAT'S A THOUSAND FOOT DROP!
THAT'D BEND OUR AXLES A BIT!
THE ONLY GOOD THING ABOUT A TRIP TO CENTRAL CITY IS THIS SCENIC VIEW!
IT'S REALLY SOMETHIN' ELSE, ISN'T IT?
R-RUMBLE!
H-HEY! DO YOU HEAR THAT?
A ROCK SLIDE! WE'RE DONE FOR!!
4

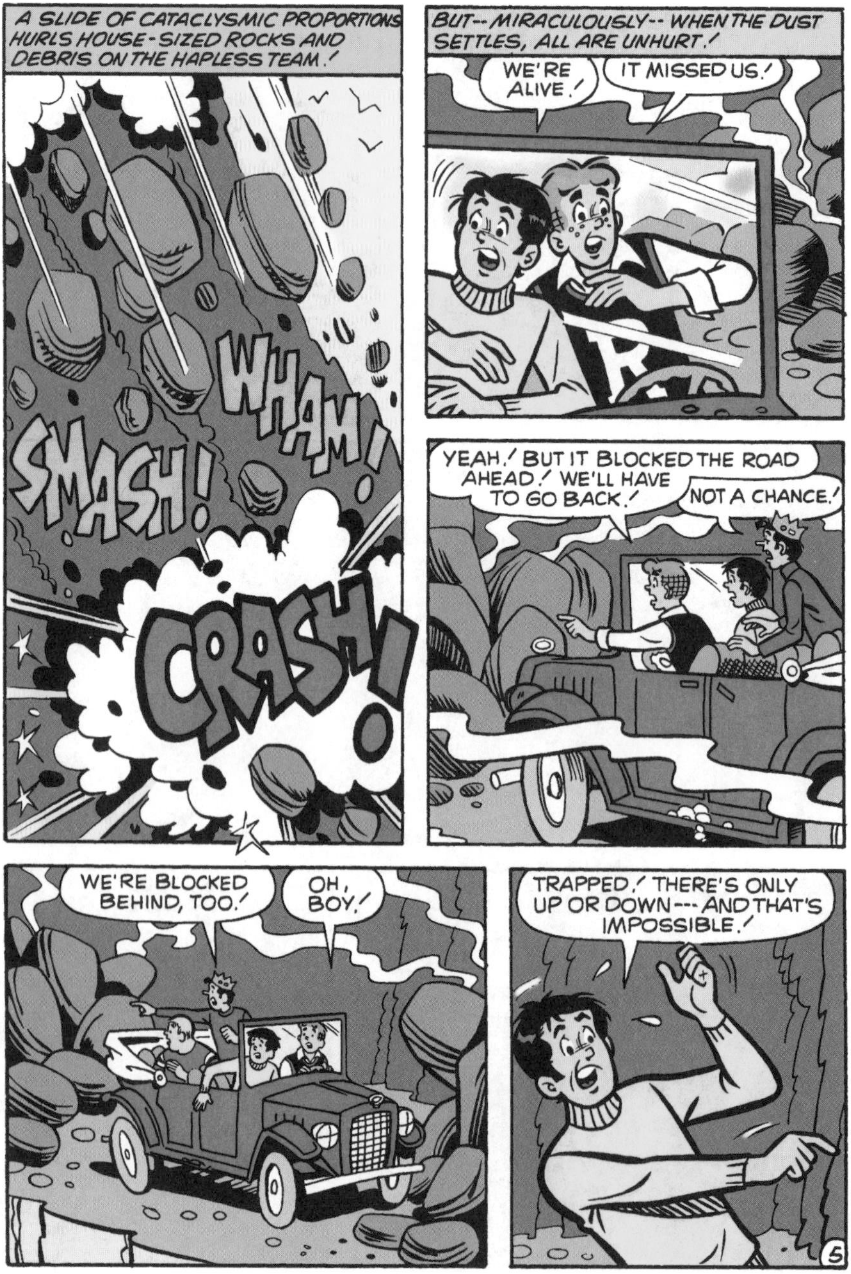
A SLIDE OF CATACLYSMIC PROPORTIONS HURLS HOUSE-SIZED ROCKS AND DEBRIS ON THE HAPLESS TEAM!
WHAM!
SMASH!
CRASH!
BUT-- MIRACULOUSLY-- WHEN THE DUST SETTLES, ALL ARE UNHURT!
WE'RE ALIVE!
IT MISSED US!
YEAH! BUT IT BLOCKED THE ROAD AHEAD! WE'LL HAVE TO GO BACK!
NOT A CHANCE!
WE'RE BLOCKED BEHIND, TOO!
OH, BOY!
TRAPPED! THERE'S ONLY UP OR DOWN --- AND THAT'S IMPOSSIBLE!
5

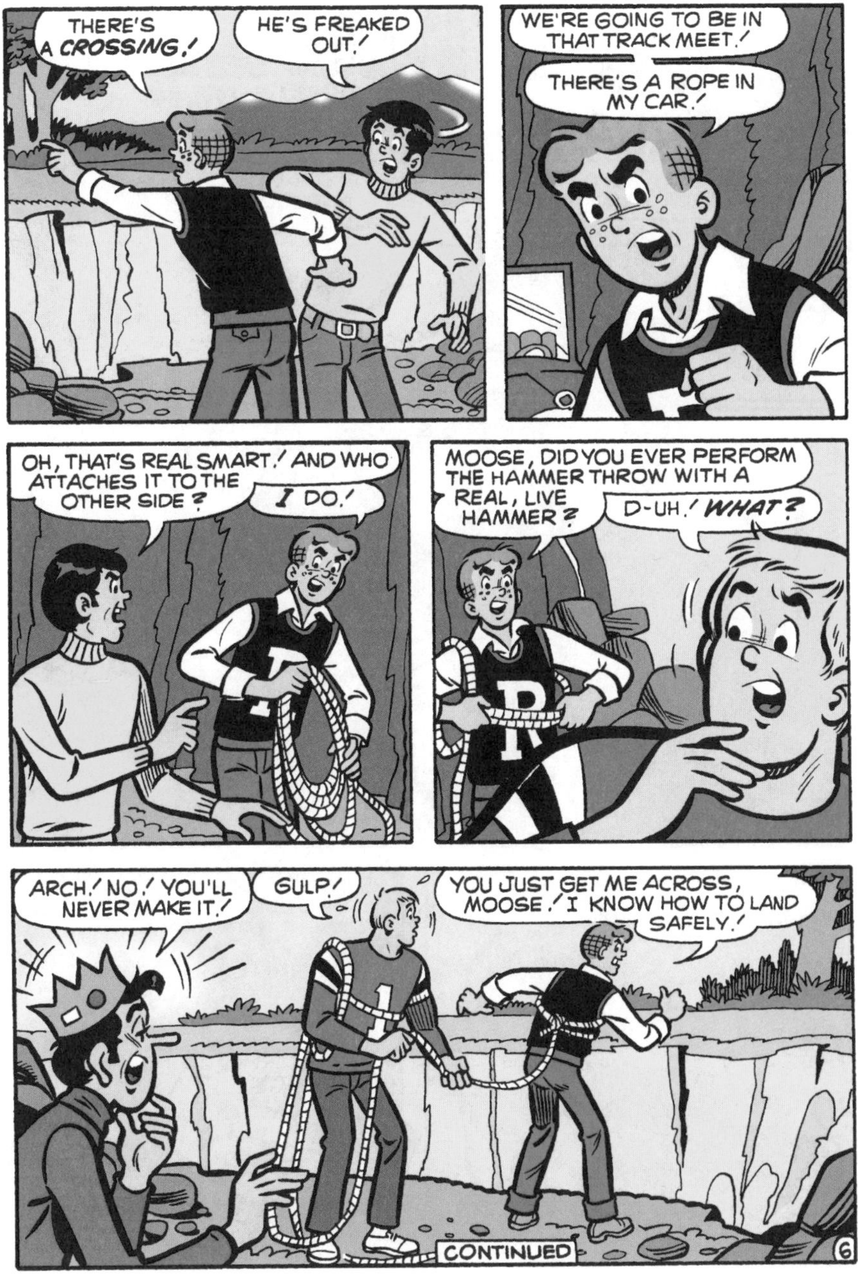
THERE'S A *CROSSING*!
HE'S FREAKED OUT!
WE'RE GOING TO BE IN THAT TRACK MEET!
THERE'S A ROPE IN MY CAR!
OH, THAT'S REAL SMART! AND WHO ATTACHES IT TO THE OTHER SIDE?
I DO!
MOOSE, DID YOU EVER PERFORM THE HAMMER THROW WITH A REAL, LIVE HAMMER?
D-UH! *WHAT?*
ARCH! NO! YOU'LL NEVER MAKE IT!
GULP!
YOU JUST GET ME ACROSS, MOOSE! I KNOW HOW TO LAND SAFELY!
CONTINUED
6

Archie at Riverdale "Field Day of Fear" Part II

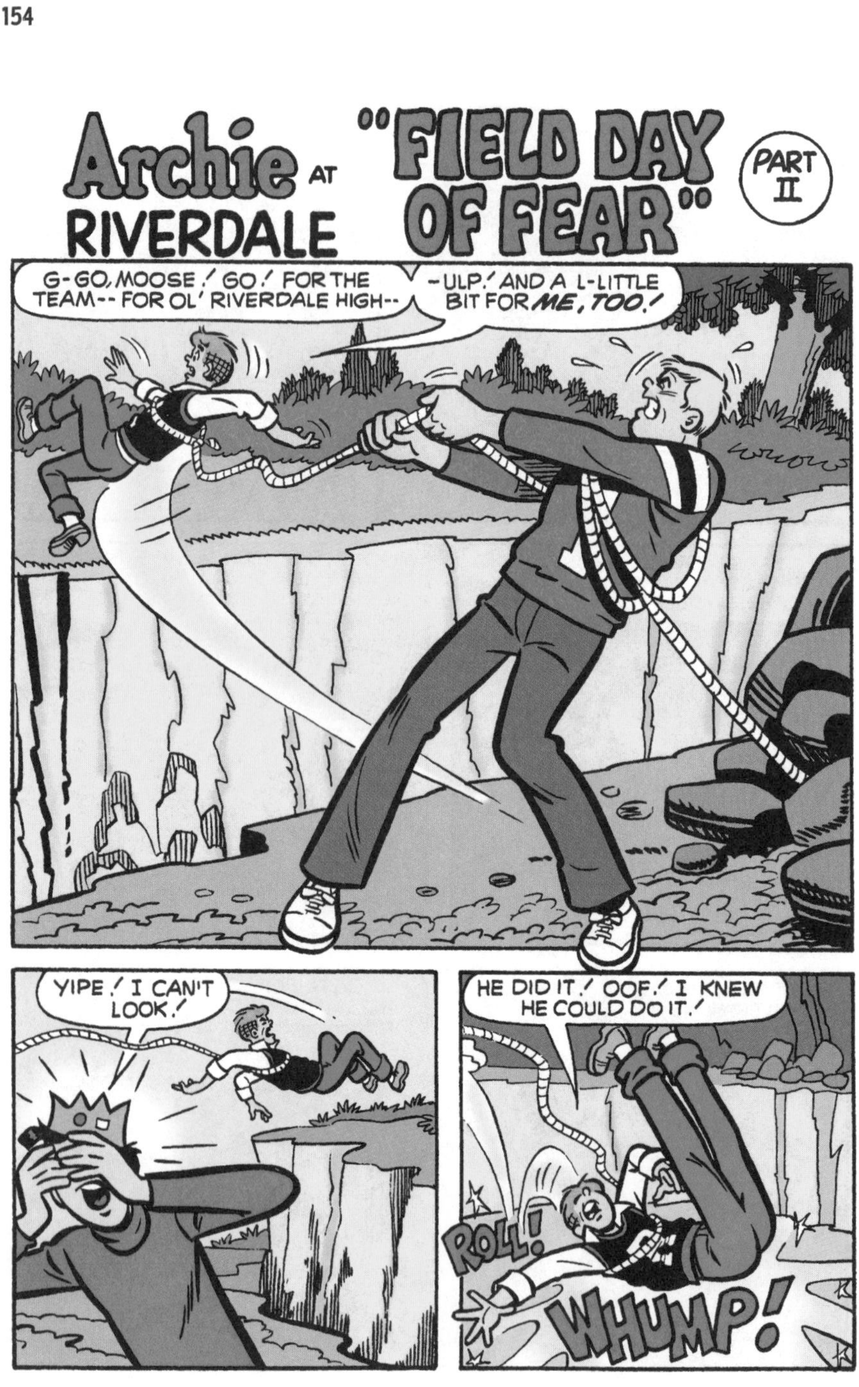
G-GO, MOOSE! GO! FOR THE TEAM-- FOR OL' RIVERDALE HIGH--
-ULP! AND A L-LITTLE BIT FOR ME, TOO!
YIPE! I CAN'T LOOK!
HE DID IT! OOF! I KNEW HE COULD DO IT!
ROLL!
WHUMP!

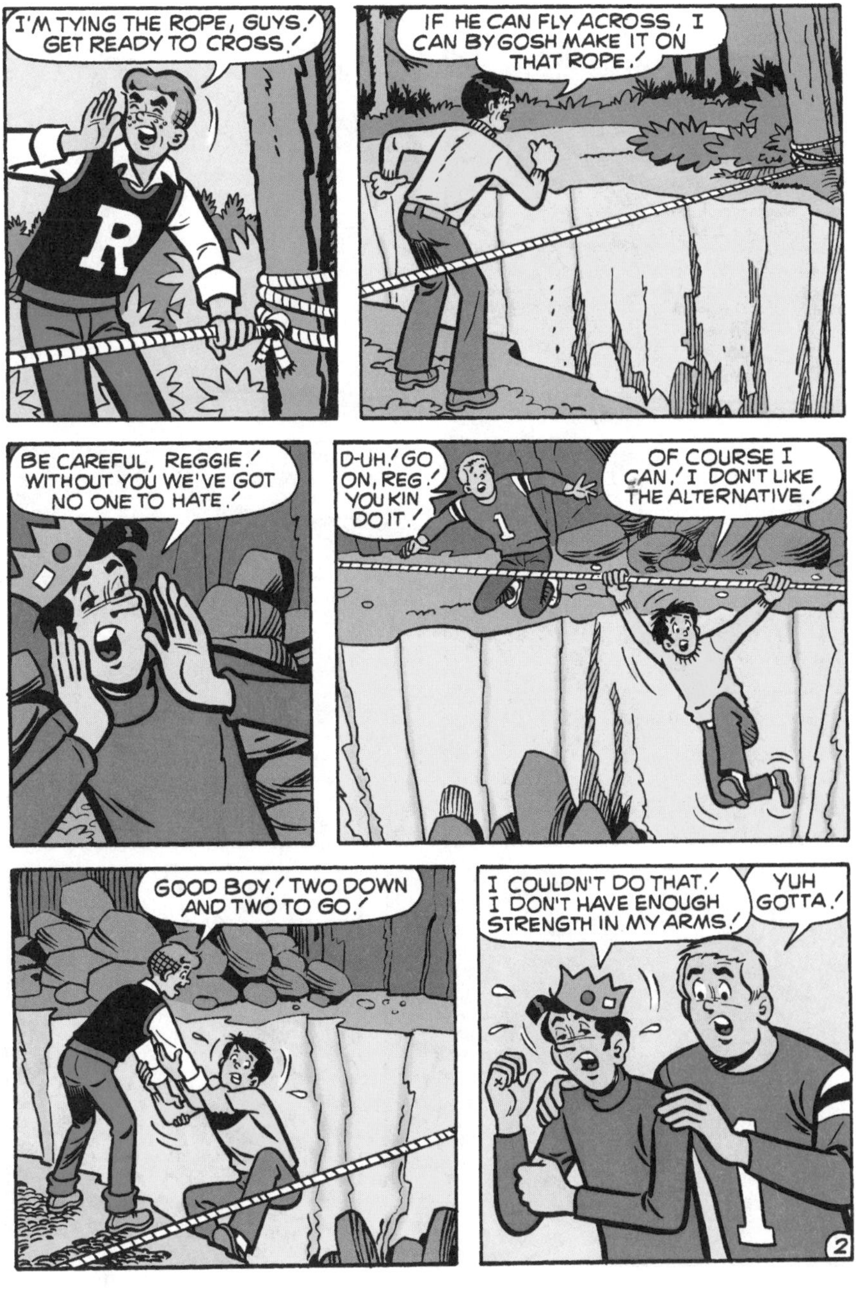
I'M TYING THE ROPE, GUYS! GET READY TO CROSS!
IF HE CAN FLY ACROSS, I CAN BY GOSH MAKE IT ON THAT ROPE!
BE CAREFUL, REGGIE! WITHOUT YOU WE'VE GOT NO ONE TO HATE!
D-UH! GO ON, REG! YOU KIN DO IT!
OF COURSE I CAN! I DON'T LIKE THE ALTERNATIVE!
GOOD BOY! TWO DOWN AND TWO TO GO!
I COULDN'T DO THAT! I DON'T HAVE ENOUGH STRENGTH IN MY ARMS!
YUH GOTTA!
2

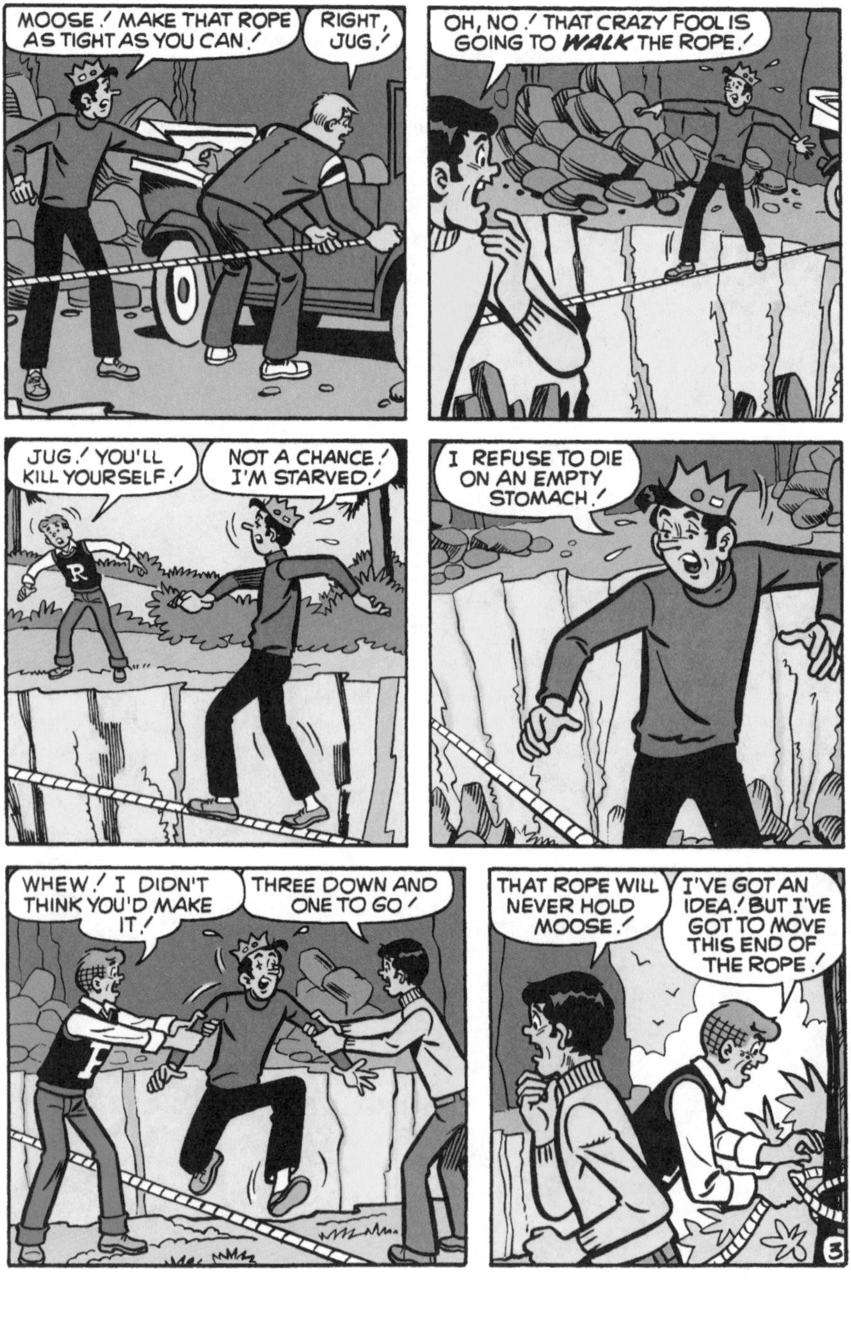
MOOSE! MAKE THAT ROPE AS TIGHT AS YOU CAN!
RIGHT, JUG!
OH, NO! THAT CRAZY FOOL IS GOING TO *WALK* THE ROPE!
JUG! YOU'LL KILL YOURSELF!
NOT A CHANCE! I'M STARVED!
I REFUSE TO DIE ON AN EMPTY STOMACH!
WHEW! I DIDN'T THINK YOU'D MAKE IT!
THREE DOWN AND ONE TO GO!
THAT ROPE WILL NEVER HOLD MOOSE!
I'VE GOT AN IDEA! BUT I'VE GOT TO MOVE THIS END OF THE ROPE!

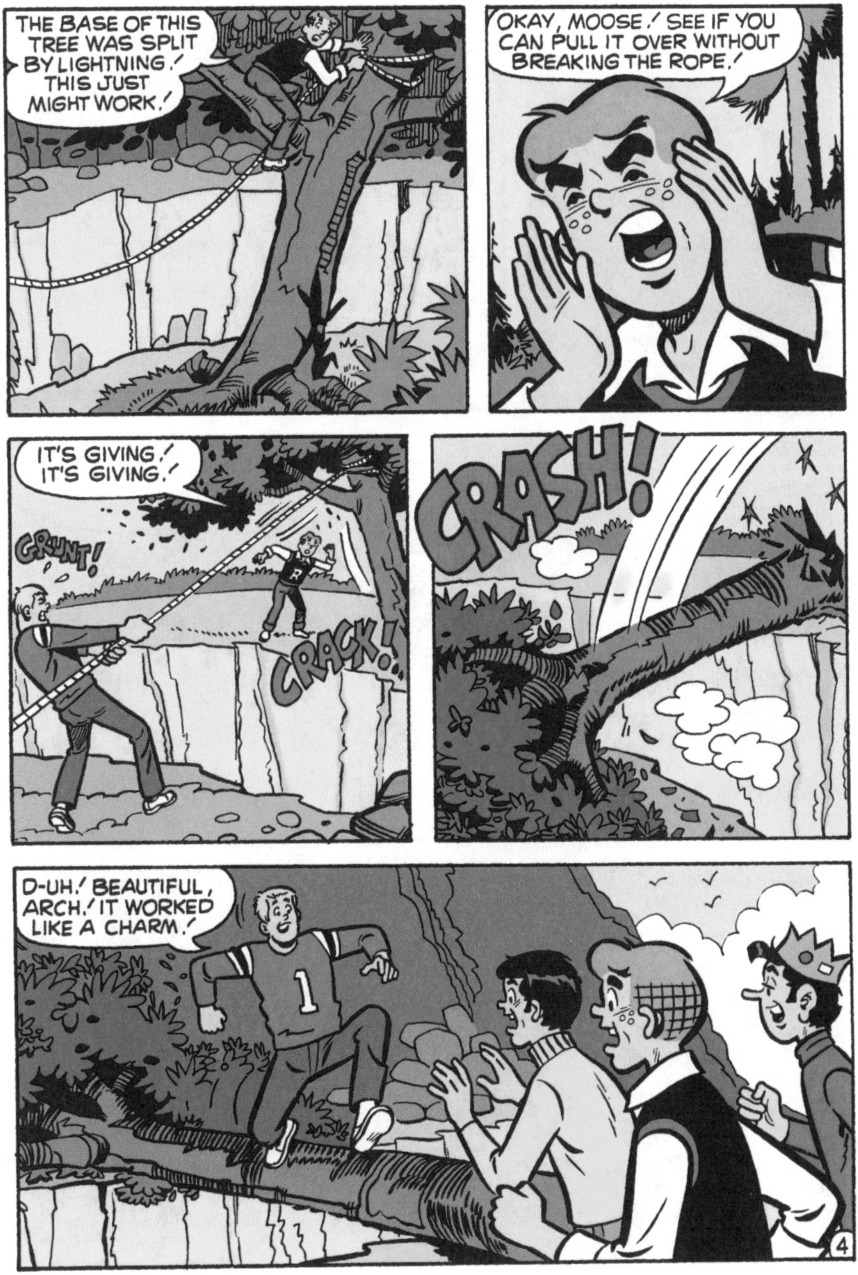
THE BASE OF THIS TREE WAS SPLIT BY LIGHTNING! THIS JUST MIGHT WORK!
OKAY, MOOSE! SEE IF YOU CAN PULL IT OVER WITHOUT BREAKING THE ROPE!
IT'S GIVING! IT'S GIVING!
GRUNT!
CRACK!
CRASH!
D-UH! BEAUTIFUL, ARCH! IT WORKED LIKE A CHARM!
4

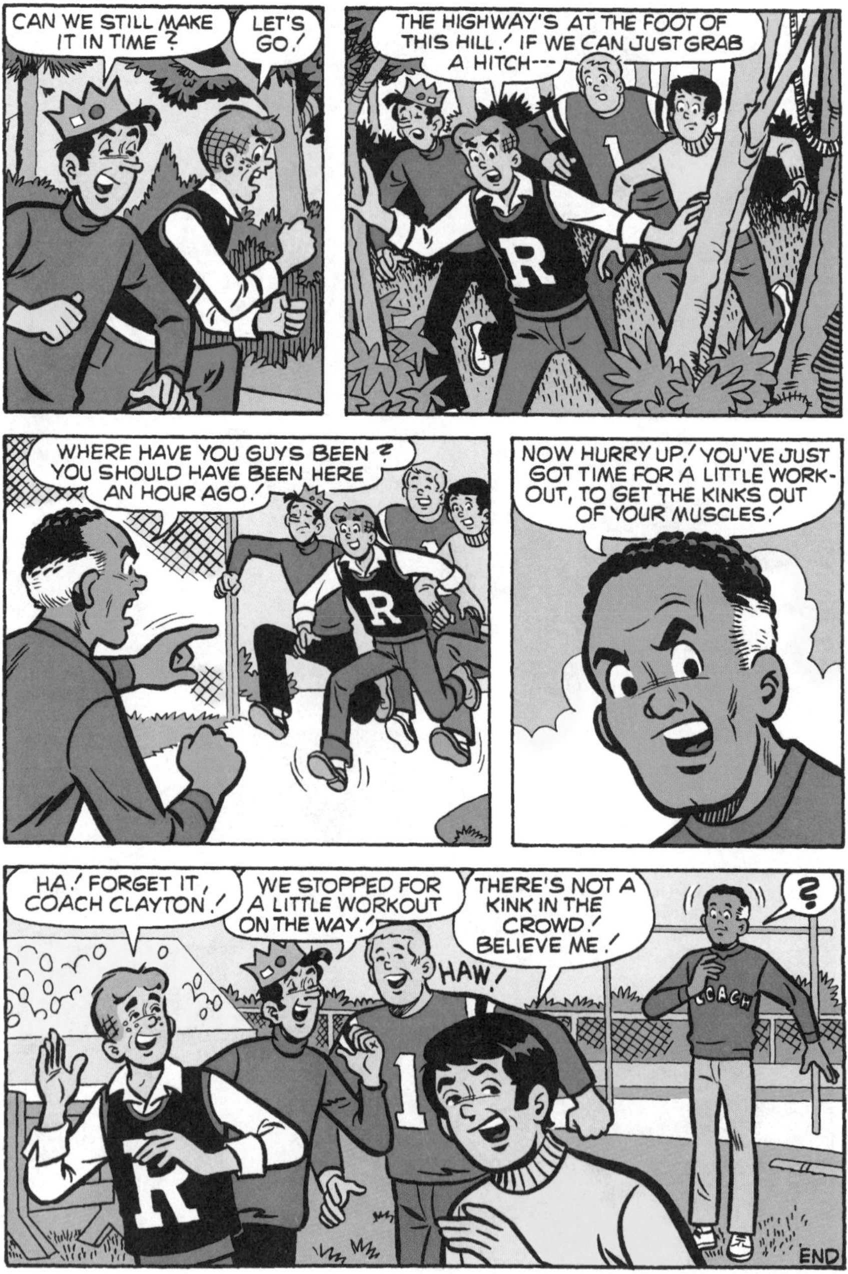
CAN WE STILL MAKE IT IN TIME ?
LET'S GO!
THE HIGHWAY'S AT THE FOOT OF THIS HILL! IF WE CAN JUST GRAB A HITCH---
WHERE HAVE YOU GUYS BEEN ? YOU SHOULD HAVE BEEN HERE AN HOUR AGO!
NOW HURRY UP! YOU'VE JUST GOT TIME FOR A LITTLE WORK-OUT, TO GET THE KINKS OUT OF YOUR MUSCLES!
HA! FORGET IT, COACH CLAYTON!
WE STOPPED FOR A LITTLE WORKOUT ON THE WAY!
HAW!
THERE'S NOT A KINK IN THE CROWD! BELIEVE ME!
?
COACH
END

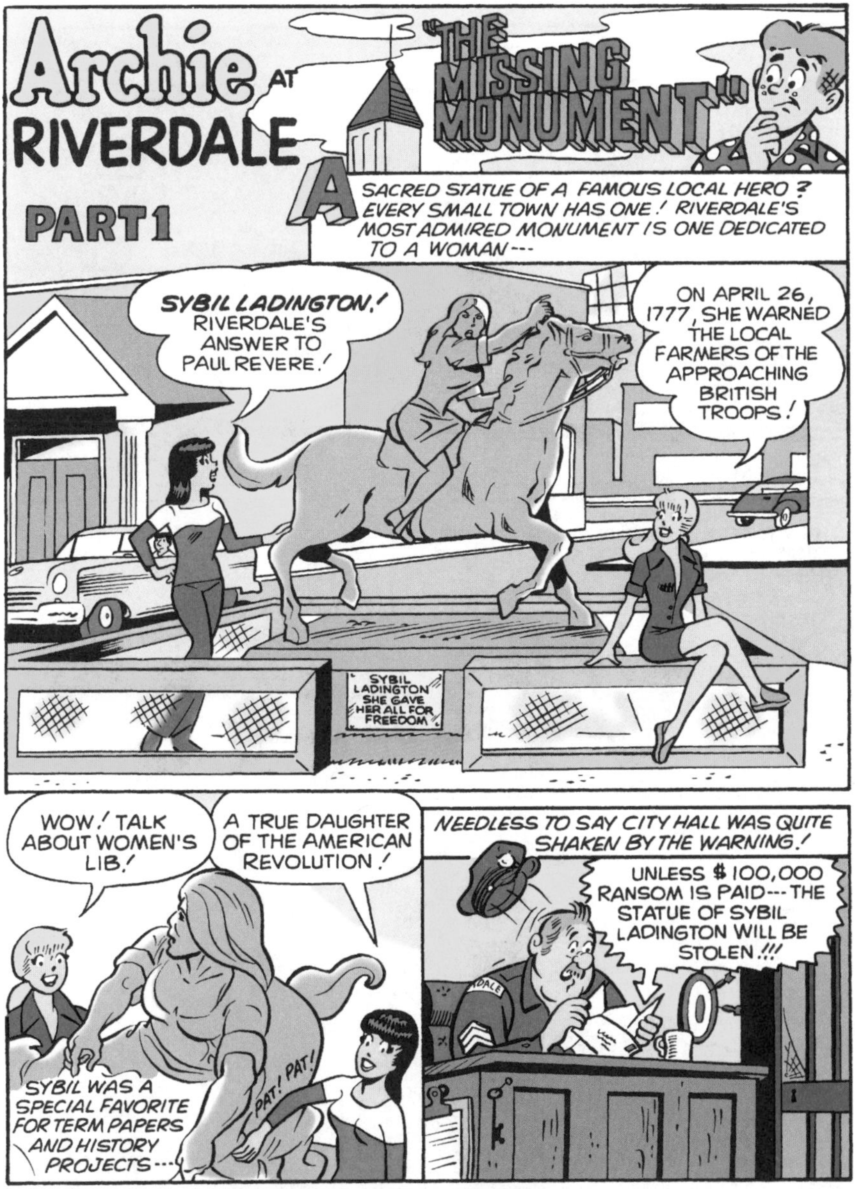
Archie AT RIVERDALE
"THE MISSING MONUMENT!"
PART 1
A SACRED STATUE OF A FAMOUS LOCAL HERO? EVERY SMALL TOWN HAS ONE! RIVERDALE'S MOST ADMIRED MONUMENT IS ONE DEDICATED TO A WOMAN---
SYBIL LADINGTON! RIVERDALE'S ANSWER TO PAUL REVERE!
ON APRIL 26, 1777, SHE WARNED THE LOCAL FARMERS OF THE APPROACHING BRITISH TROOPS!
SYBIL LADINGTON SHE GAVE HER ALL FOR FREEDOM
WOW! TALK ABOUT WOMEN'S LIB!
A TRUE DAUGHTER OF THE AMERICAN REVOLUTION!
PAT! PAT!
SYBIL WAS A SPECIAL FAVORITE FOR TERM PAPERS AND HISTORY PROJECTS---
NEEDLESS TO SAY CITY HALL WAS QUITE SHAKEN BY THE WARNING!
UNLESS $100,000 RANSOM IS PAID--- THE STATUE OF SYBIL LADINGTON WILL BE STOLEN!!!

Story: Frank Doyle Pencils: Bob Bolling
Inks: Bob Smith Letters: Bill Yoshida

Originally printed in ARCHIE AT RIVERDALE HIGH #37, JULY 1976

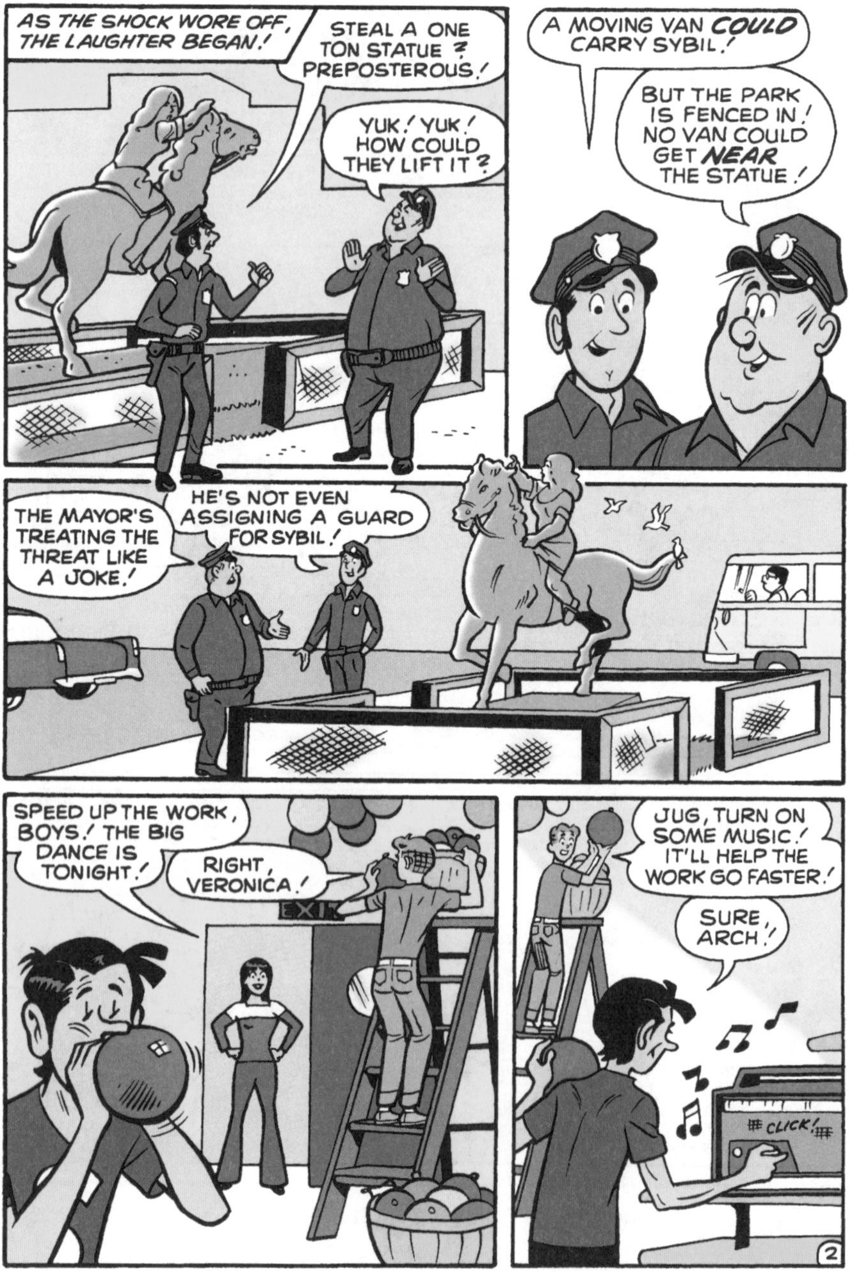
AS THE SHOCK WORE OFF, THE LAUGHTER BEGAN!
STEAL A ONE TON STATUE? PREPOSTEROUS!
YUK! YUK! HOW COULD THEY LIFT IT?
A MOVING VAN COULD CARRY SYBIL!
BUT THE PARK IS FENCED IN! NO VAN COULD GET NEAR THE STATUE!
THE MAYOR'S TREATING THE THREAT LIKE A JOKE!
HE'S NOT EVEN ASSIGNING A GUARD FOR SYBIL!
SPEED UP THE WORK, BOYS! THE BIG DANCE IS TONIGHT!
RIGHT, VERONICA!
EXIT
JUG, TURN ON SOME MUSIC! IT'LL HELP THE WORK GO FASTER!
SURE, ARCH!
CLICK!
2

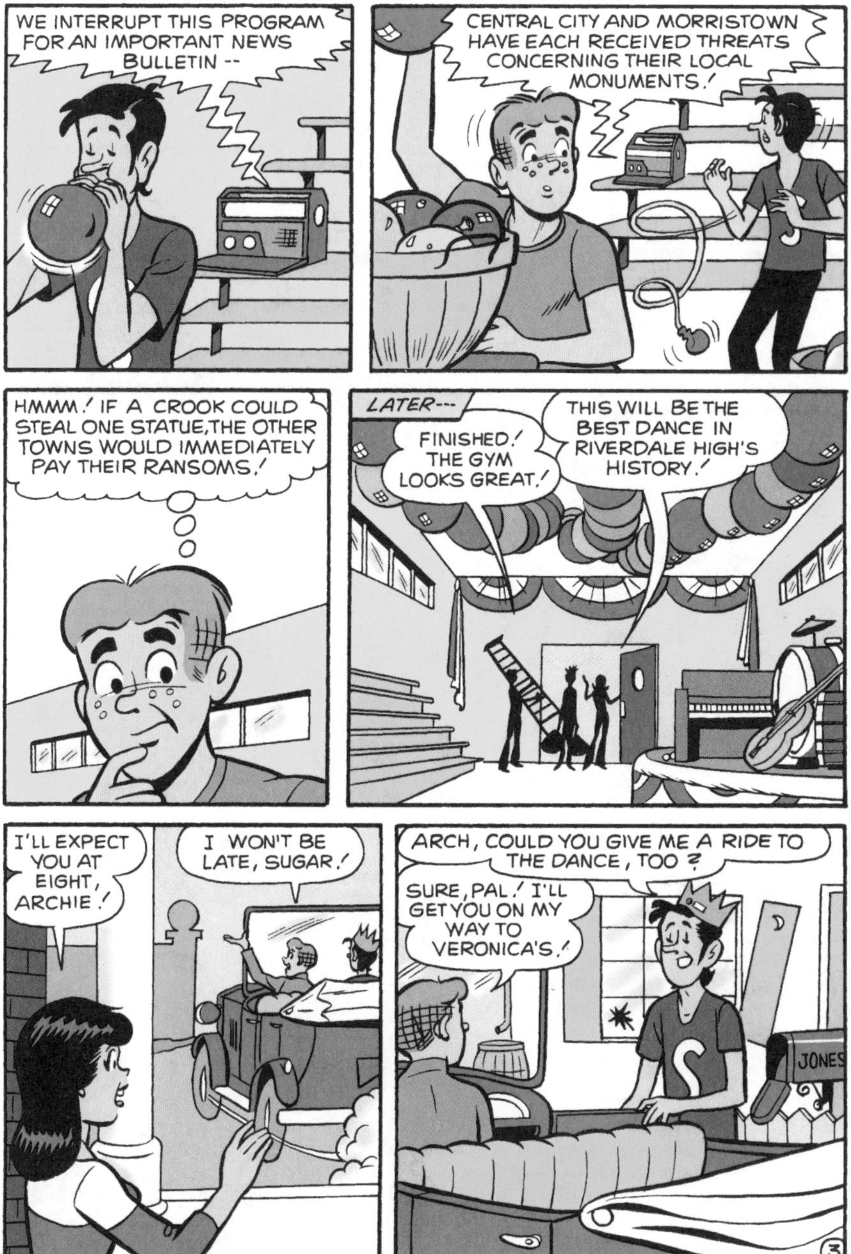
WE INTERRUPT THIS PROGRAM FOR AN IMPORTANT NEWS BULLETIN --
CENTRAL CITY AND MORRISTOWN HAVE EACH RECEIVED THREATS CONCERNING THEIR LOCAL MONUMENTS!
HMMM! IF A CROOK COULD STEAL ONE STATUE, THE OTHER TOWNS WOULD IMMEDIATELY PAY THEIR RANSOMS!
LATER---
FINISHED! THE GYM LOOKS GREAT!
THIS WILL BE THE BEST DANCE IN RIVERDALE HIGH'S HISTORY!
I'LL EXPECT YOU AT EIGHT, ARCHIE!
I WON'T BE LATE, SUGAR!
ARCH, COULD YOU GIVE ME A RIDE TO THE DANCE, TOO?
SURE, PAL! I'LL GET YOU ON MY WAY TO VERONICA'S!
JONES
3

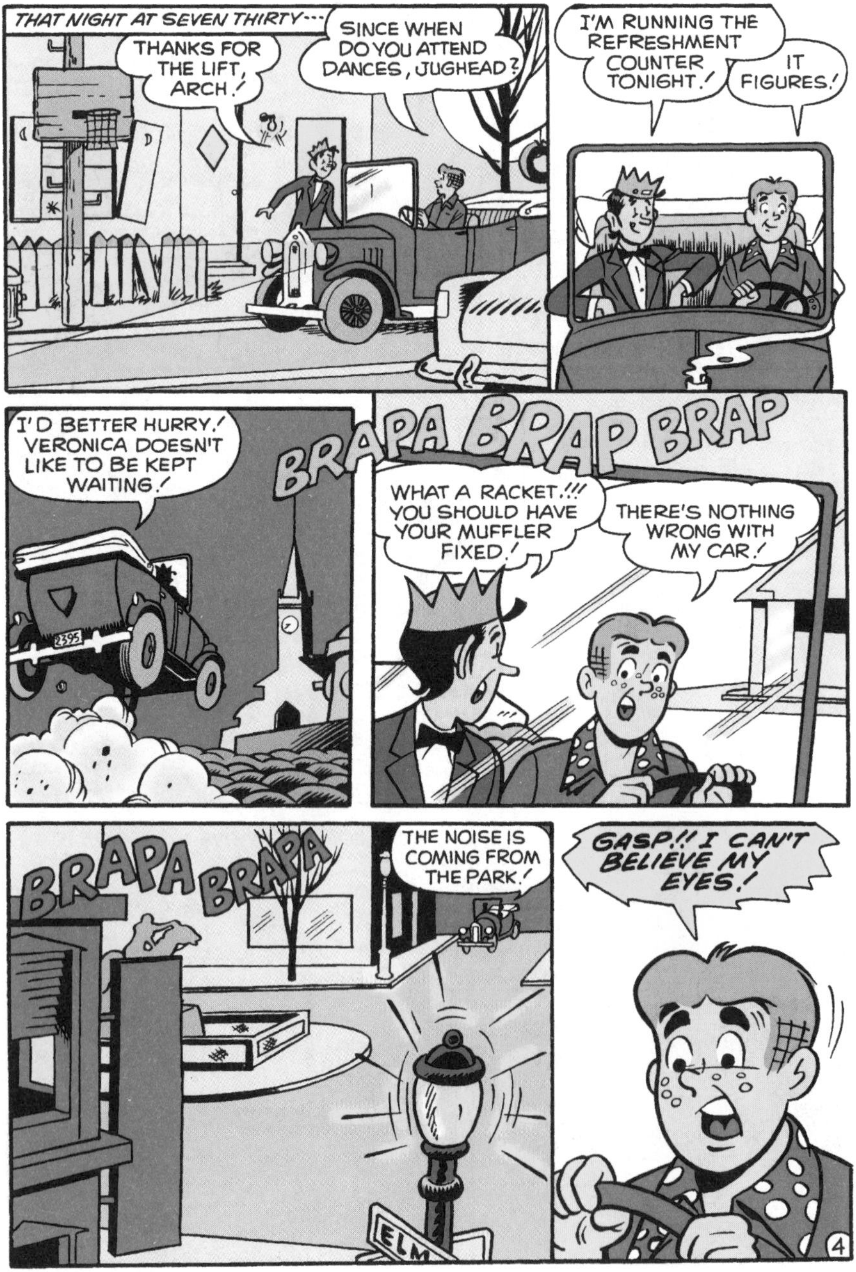
THAT NIGHT AT SEVEN THIRTY---
THANKS FOR THE LIFT, ARCH!
SINCE WHEN DO YOU ATTEND DANCES, JUGHEAD?
I'M RUNNING THE REFRESHMENT COUNTER TONIGHT!
IT FIGURES!
I'D BETTER HURRY! VERONICA DOESN'T LIKE TO BE KEPT WAITING!
BRAPA BRAP BRAP
WHAT A RACKET!!! YOU SHOULD HAVE YOUR MUFFLER FIXED!
THERE'S NOTHING WRONG WITH MY CAR!
BRAPA BRAPA
THE NOISE IS COMING FROM THE PARK!
GASP!! I CAN'T BELIEVE MY EYES!
ELM
4

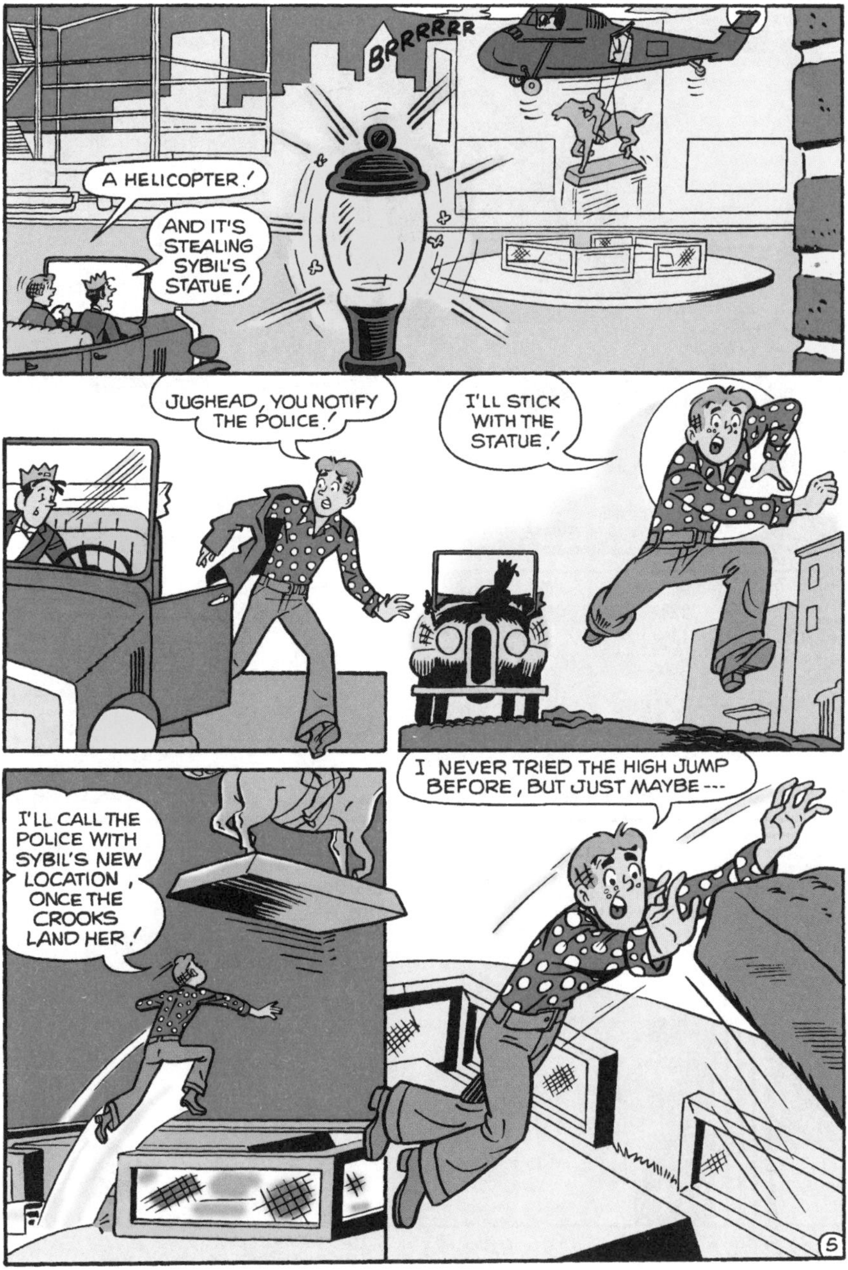
BRRRRRR
A HELICOPTER!
AND IT'S STEALING SYBIL'S STATUE!
JUGHEAD, YOU NOTIFY THE POLICE!
I'LL STICK WITH THE STATUE!
I NEVER TRIED THE HIGH JUMP BEFORE, BUT JUST MAYBE---
I'LL CALL THE POLICE WITH SYBIL'S NEW LOCATION, ONCE THE CROOKS LAND HER!
5

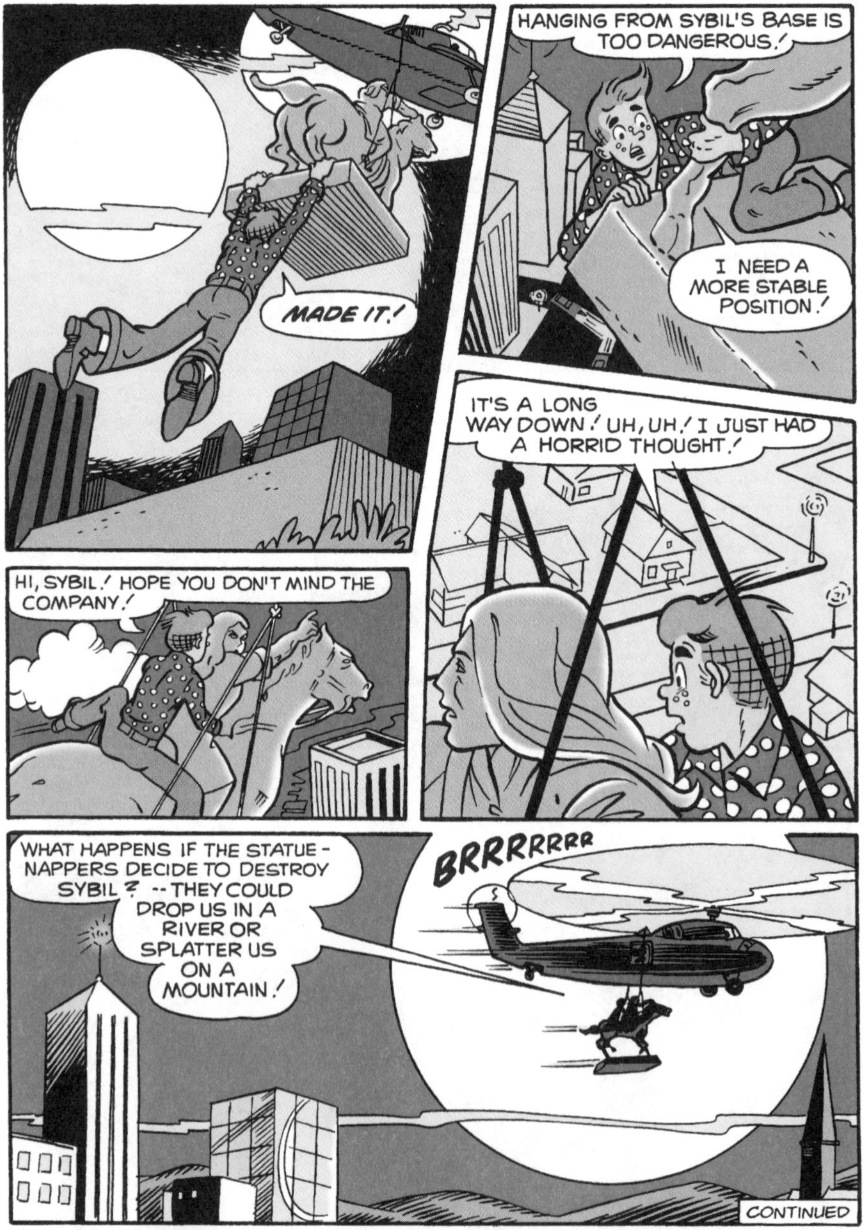
MADE IT!
HANGING FROM SYBIL'S BASE IS TOO DANGEROUS!
I NEED A MORE STABLE POSITION!
HI, SYBIL! HOPE YOU DON'T MIND THE COMPANY!
IT'S A LONG WAY DOWN! UH, UH! I JUST HAD A HORRID THOUGHT!
WHAT HAPPENS IF THE STATUE-NAPPERS DECIDE TO DESTROY SYBIL? --THEY COULD DROP US IN A RIVER OR SPLATTER US ON A MOUNTAIN!
BRRRRRRR
CONTINUED

WILL ARCHIE SUCCEED IN RESCUING RIVERDALE'S PRIZED MONUMENT? OR WILL HE BECOME PART OF THE COUNTRYSIDE? HURRY! PART 2 AWAITS--

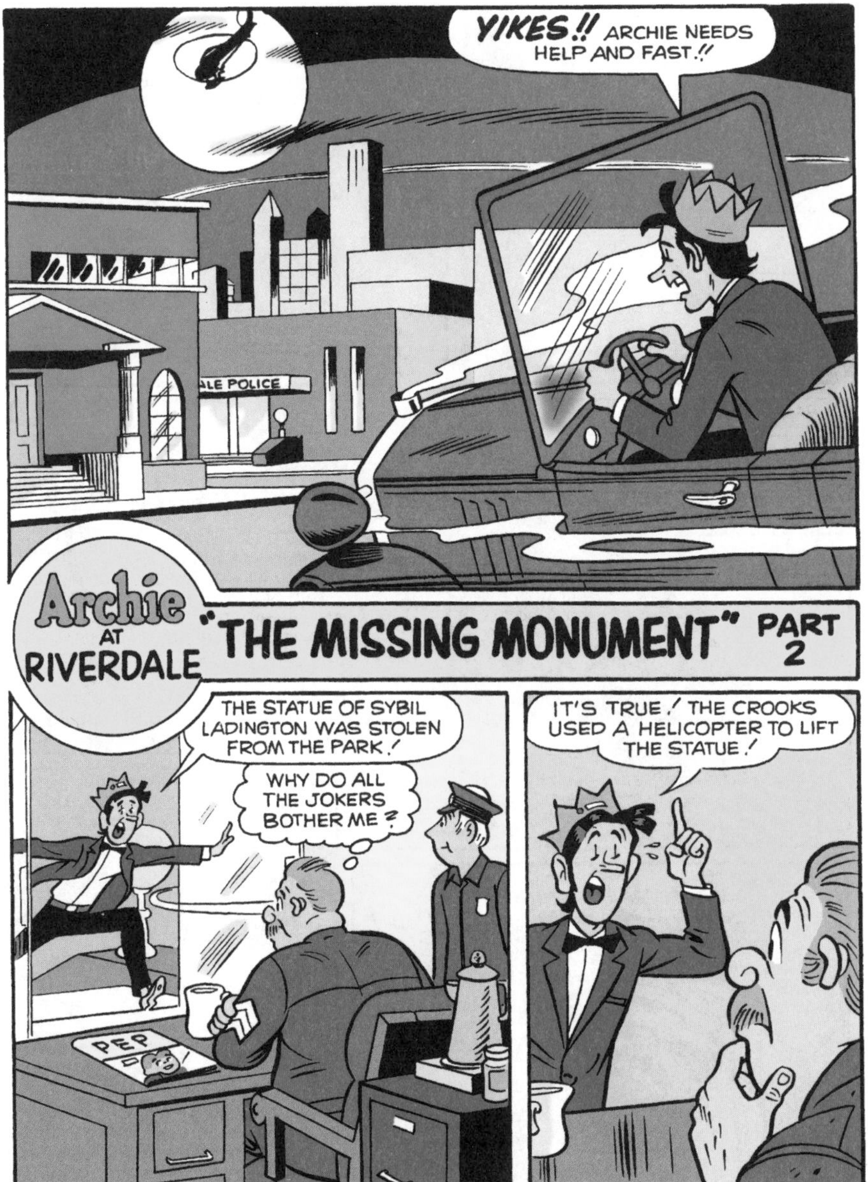
YIKES!! ARCHIE NEEDS HELP AND FAST!!
Archie AT RIVERDALE
"THE MISSING MONUMENT" PART 2
THE STATUE OF SYBIL LADINGTON WAS STOLEN FROM THE PARK!
WHY DO ALL THE JOKERS BOTHER ME?
IT'S TRUE! THE CROOKS USED A HELICOPTER TO LIFT THE STATUE!
PEP

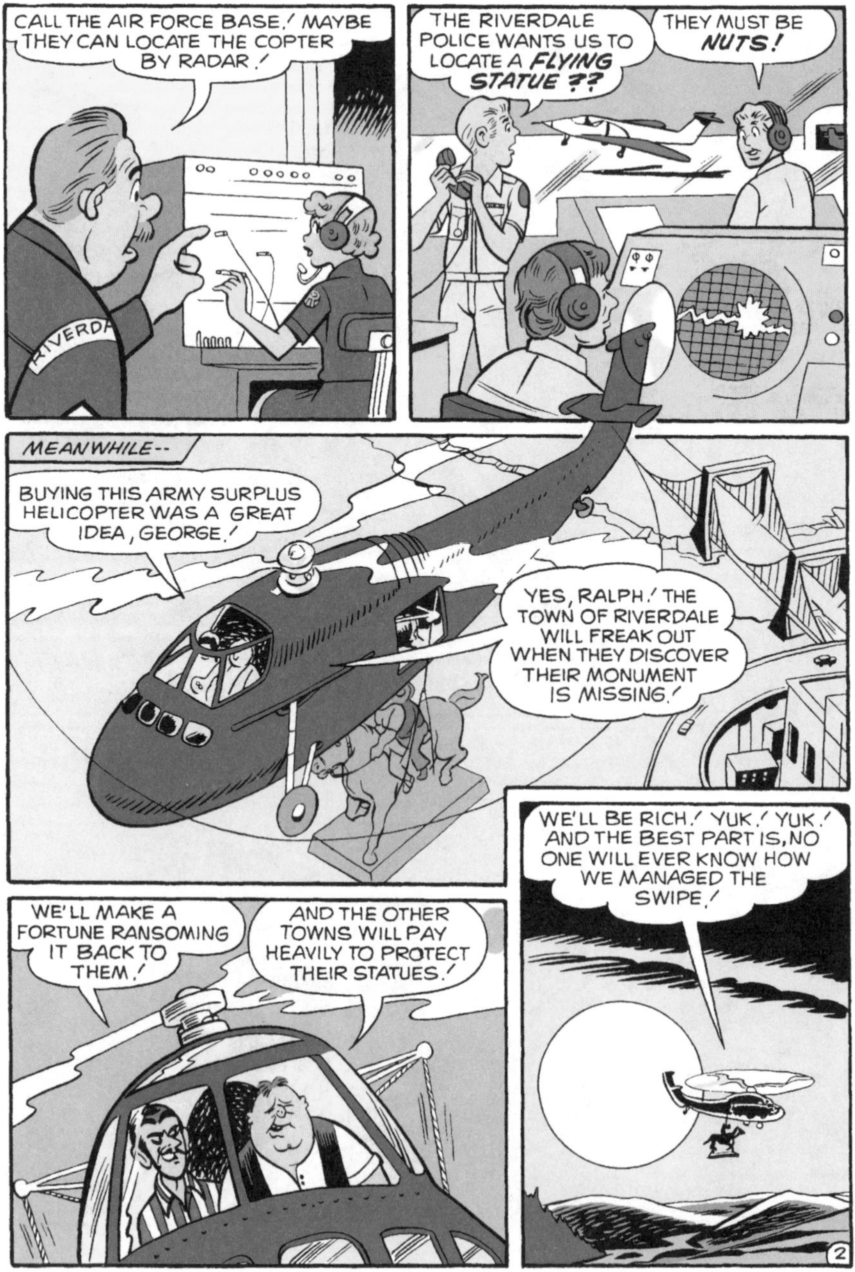
CALL THE AIR FORCE BASE! MAYBE THEY CAN LOCATE THE COPTER BY RADAR!
THE RIVERDALE POLICE WANTS US TO LOCATE A FLYING STATUE ??
THEY MUST BE NUTS!
MEANWHILE--
BUYING THIS ARMY SURPLUS HELICOPTER WAS A GREAT IDEA, GEORGE!
YES, RALPH! THE TOWN OF RIVERDALE WILL FREAK OUT WHEN THEY DISCOVER THEIR MONUMENT IS MISSING!
WE'LL MAKE A FORTUNE RANSOMING IT BACK TO THEM!
AND THE OTHER TOWNS WILL PAY HEAVILY TO PROTECT THEIR STATUES!
WE'LL BE RICH! YUK! YUK! AND THE BEST PART IS, NO ONE WILL EVER KNOW HOW WE MANAGED THE SWIPE!
2

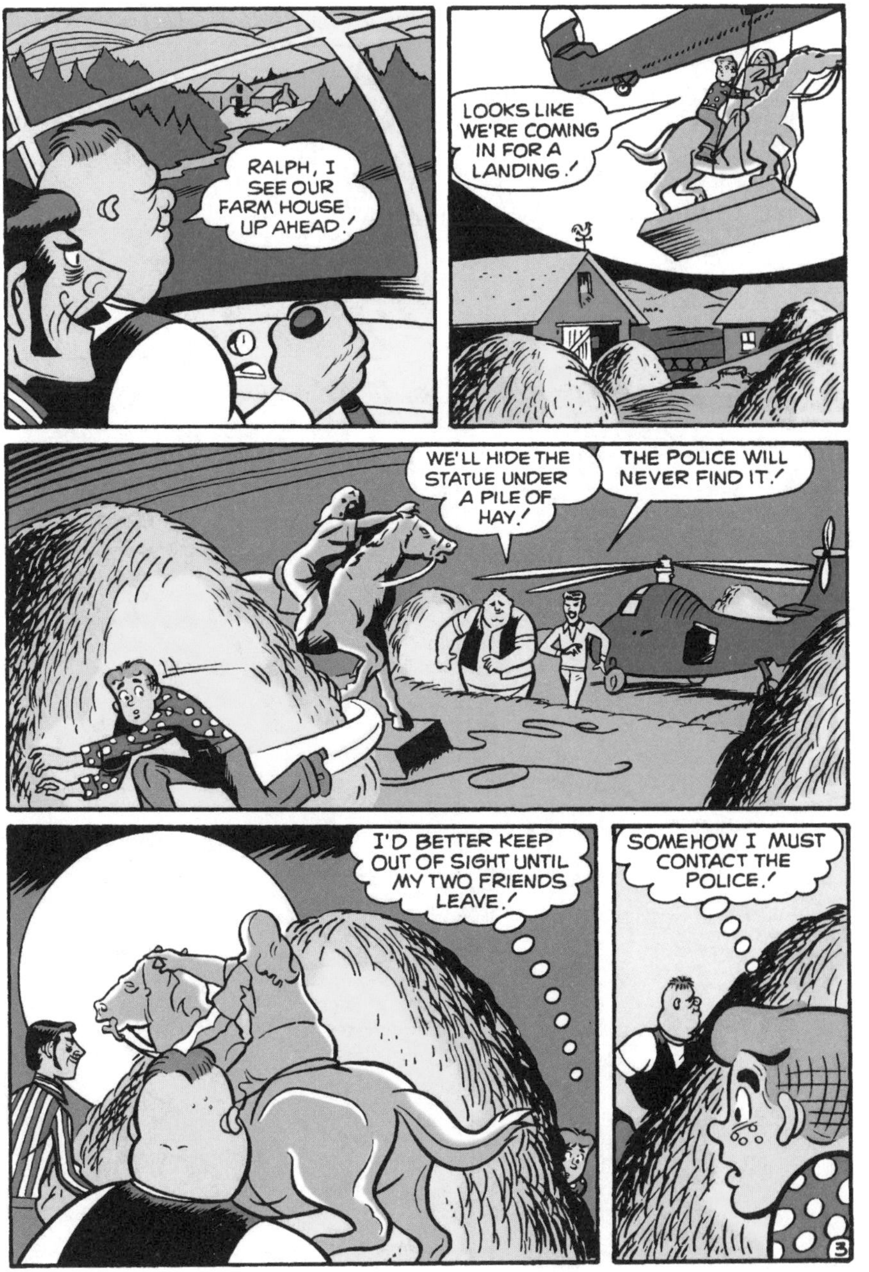
RALPH, I SEE OUR FARM HOUSE UP AHEAD!
LOOKS LIKE WE'RE COMING IN FOR A LANDING!
WE'LL HIDE THE STATUE UNDER A PILE OF HAY!
THE POLICE WILL NEVER FIND IT!
I'D BETTER KEEP OUT OF SIGHT UNTIL MY TWO FRIENDS LEAVE!
SOMEHOW I MUST CONTACT THE POLICE!
3

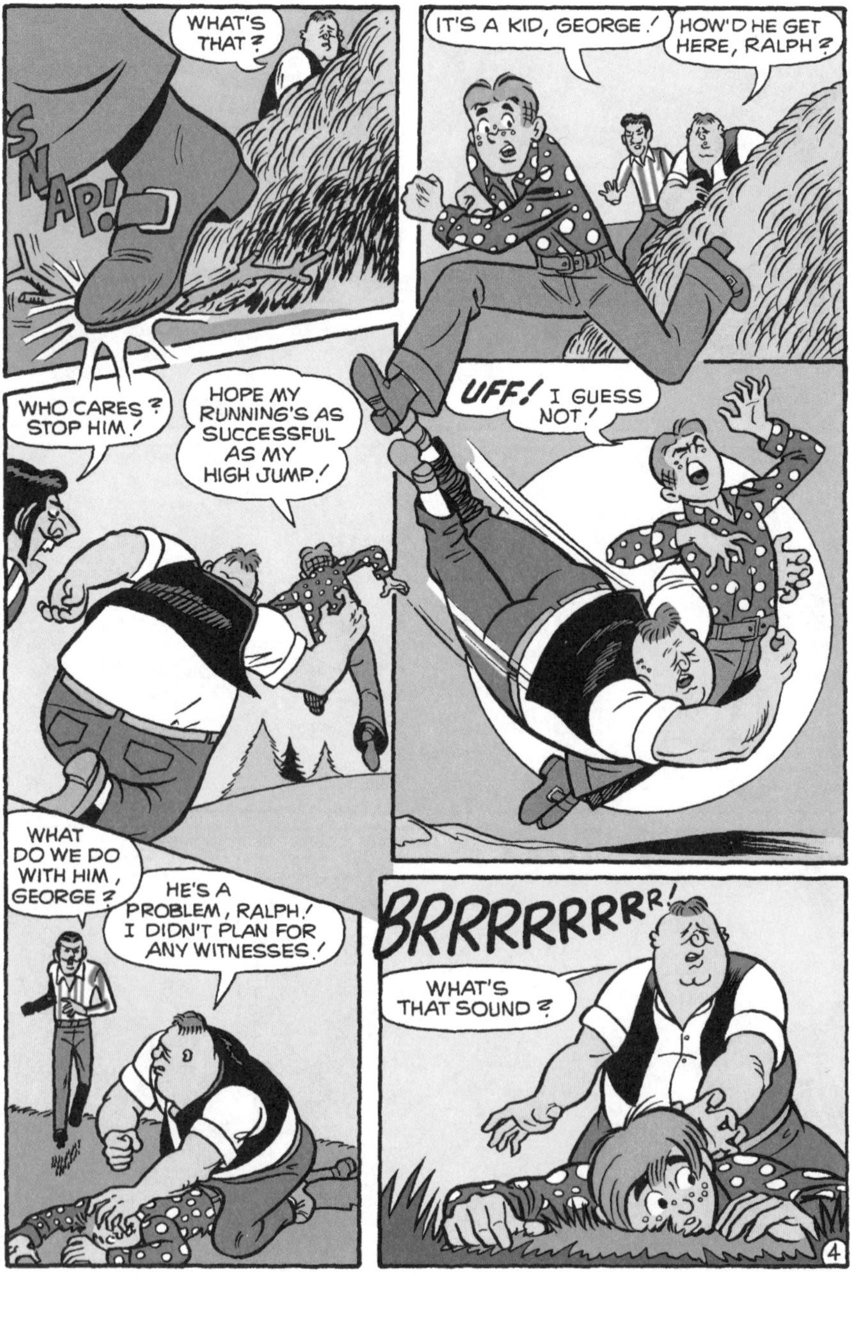
WHAT'S THAT?
SNAP!
IT'S A KID, GEORGE!
HOW'D HE GET HERE, RALPH?
WHO CARES? STOP HIM!
HOPE MY RUNNING'S AS SUCCESSFUL AS MY HIGH JUMP!
UFF! I GUESS NOT!
WHAT DO WE DO WITH HIM, GEORGE?
HE'S A PROBLEM, RALPH! I DIDN'T PLAN FOR ANY WITNESSES!
BRRRRRRRR!
WHAT'S THAT SOUND?
4

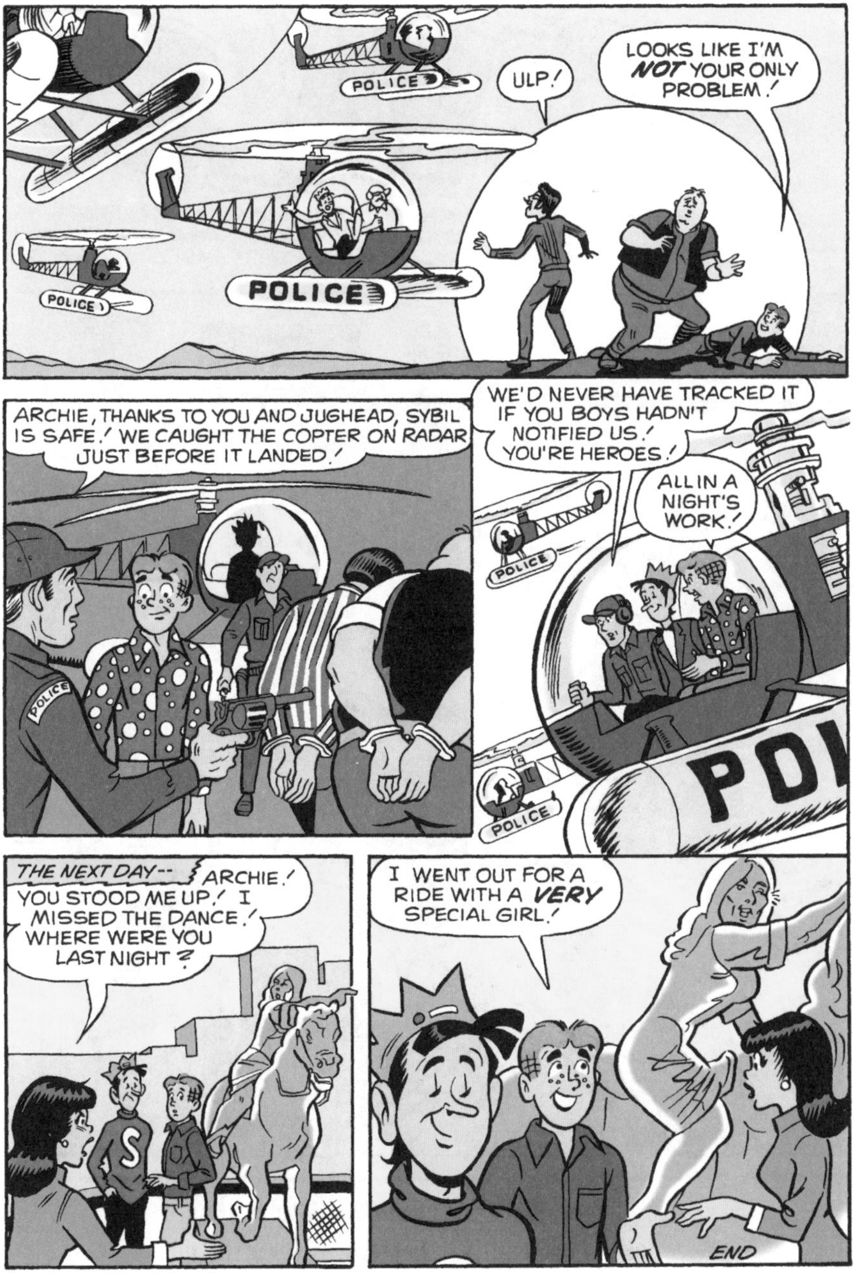
ULP!
LOOKS LIKE I'M NOT YOUR ONLY PROBLEM!
POLICE
POLICE
POLICE
ARCHIE, THANKS TO YOU AND JUGHEAD, SYBIL IS SAFE! WE CAUGHT THE COPTER ON RADAR JUST BEFORE IT LANDED!
POLICE
WE'D NEVER HAVE TRACKED IT IF YOU BOYS HADN'T NOTIFIED US! YOU'RE HEROES!
ALL IN A NIGHT'S WORK!
POLICE
POLICE
POL
THE NEXT DAY--
ARCHIE! YOU STOOD ME UP! I MISSED THE DANCE! WHERE WERE YOU LAST NIGHT?
I WENT OUT FOR A RIDE WITH A VERY SPECIAL GIRL!
END

"THE RIVALS" PART I

DO WE NEED TO REMIND YOU THAT RIVALRY RUNS RAMPANT BETWEEN RIVERDALE AND CENTRAL HIGH? WELL, AS IN MOST SCHOOLS, THERE ARE TREASURED REMINDERS OF PAST GLORIES AND HEROES OF BYGONE DAYS!

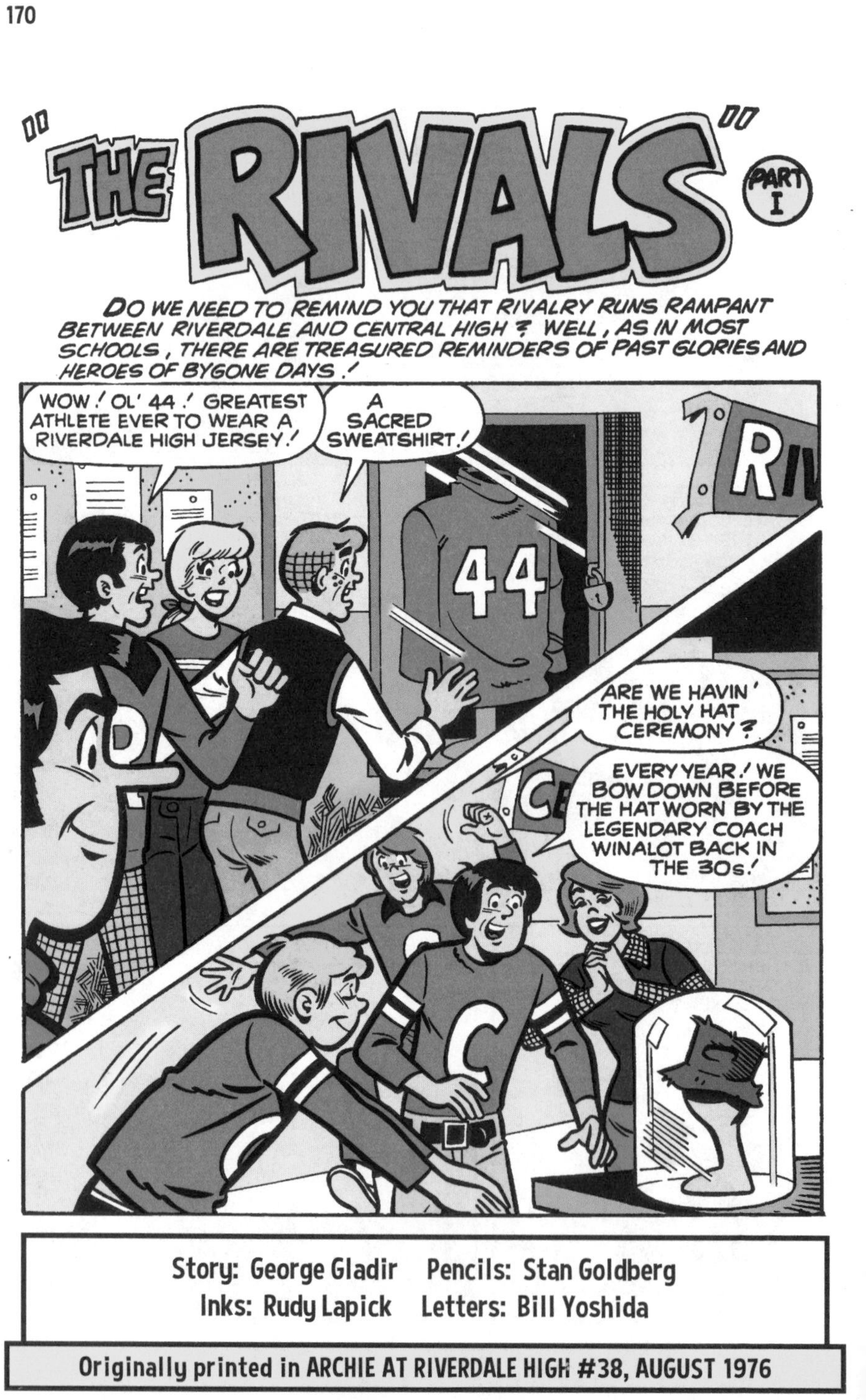

WOW! OL' 44! GREATEST ATHLETE EVER TO WEAR A RIVERDALE HIGH JERSEY!
A SACRED SWEATSHIRT!
44
RI
ARE WE HAVIN' THE HOLY HAT CEREMONY?
EVERY YEAR! WE BOW DOWN BEFORE THE HAT WORN BY THE LEGENDARY COACH WINALOT BACK IN THE 30s!
CE

Story: George Gladir Pencils: Stan Goldberg
Inks: Rudy Lapick Letters: Bill Yoshida

Originally printed in ARCHIE AT RIVERDALE HIGH #38, AUGUST 1976

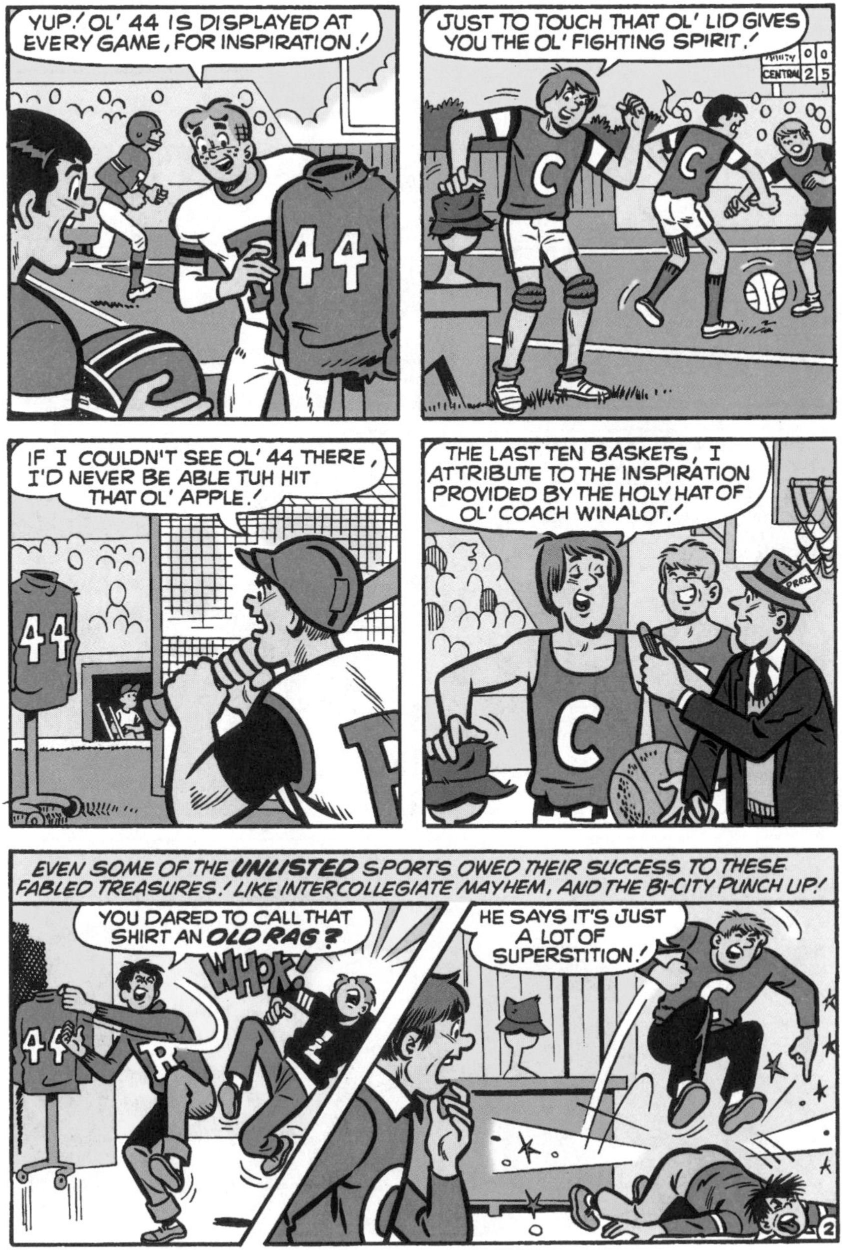
YUP.! OL' 44 IS DISPLAYED AT EVERY GAME, FOR INSPIRATION.!
JUST TO TOUCH THAT OL' LID GIVES YOU THE OL' FIGHTING SPIRIT.!
CENTRAL
IF I COULDN'T SEE OL' 44 THERE, I'D NEVER BE ABLE TUH HIT THAT OL' APPLE.!
THE LAST TEN BASKETS, I ATTRIBUTE TO THE INSPIRATION PROVIDED BY THE HOLY HAT OF OL' COACH WINALOT.!
PRESS
EVEN SOME OF THE UNLISTED SPORTS OWED THEIR SUCCESS TO THESE FABLED TREASURES.! LIKE INTERCOLLEGIATE MAYHEM, AND THE BI-CITY PUNCH UP!
YOU DARED TO CALL THAT SHIRT AN OLD RAG?
WHOK!
HE SAYS IT'S JUST A LOT OF SUPERSTITION.!
2

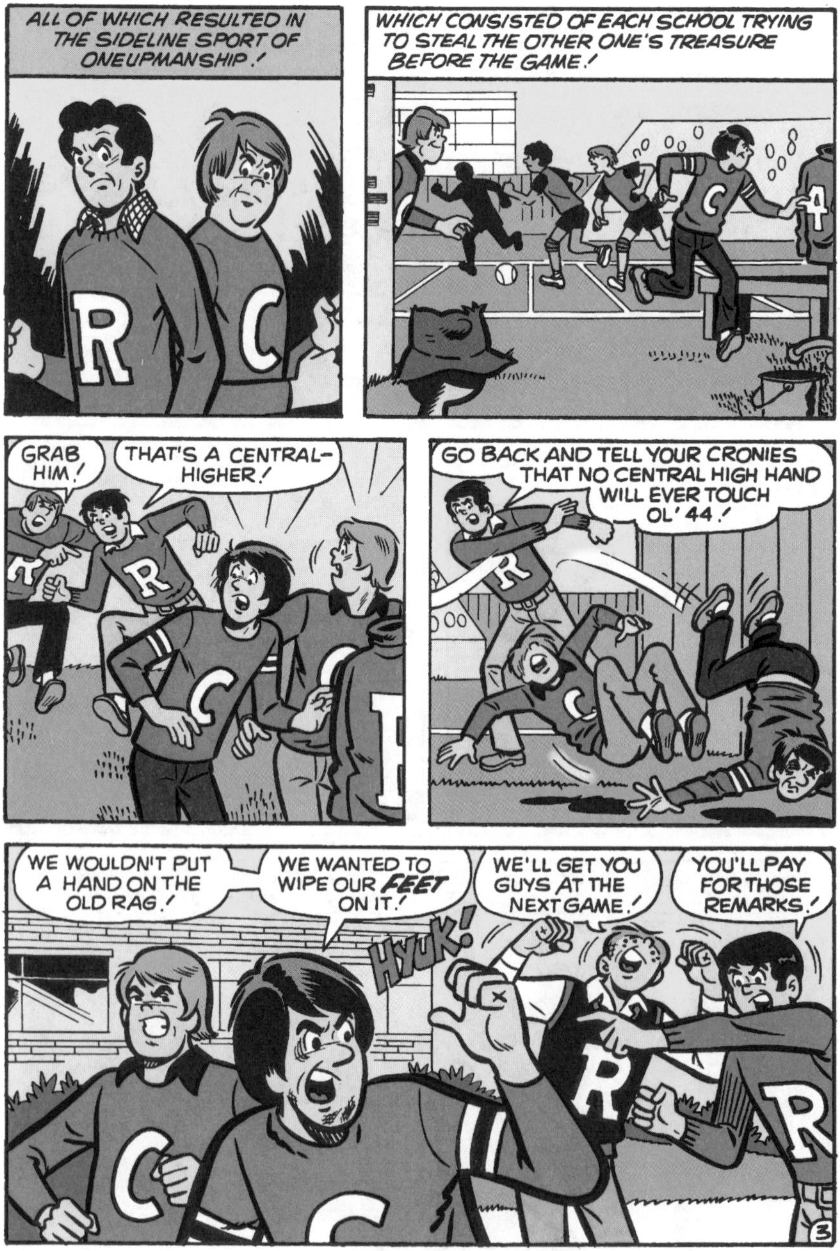
ALL OF WHICH RESULTED IN THE SIDELINE SPORT OF ONEUPMANSHIP.!
WHICH CONSISTED OF EACH SCHOOL TRYING TO STEAL THE OTHER ONE'S TREASURE BEFORE THE GAME.!
4
GRAB HIM.!
THAT'S A CENTRAL-HIGHER.!
GO BACK AND TELL YOUR CRONIES THAT NO CENTRAL HIGH HAND WILL EVER TOUCH OL' 44.!
WE WOULDN'T PUT A HAND ON THE OLD RAG.!
WE WANTED TO WIPE OUR FEET ON IT.!
HYUK!
WE'LL GET YOU GUYS AT THE NEXT GAME.!
YOU'LL PAY FOR THOSE REMARKS.!
3

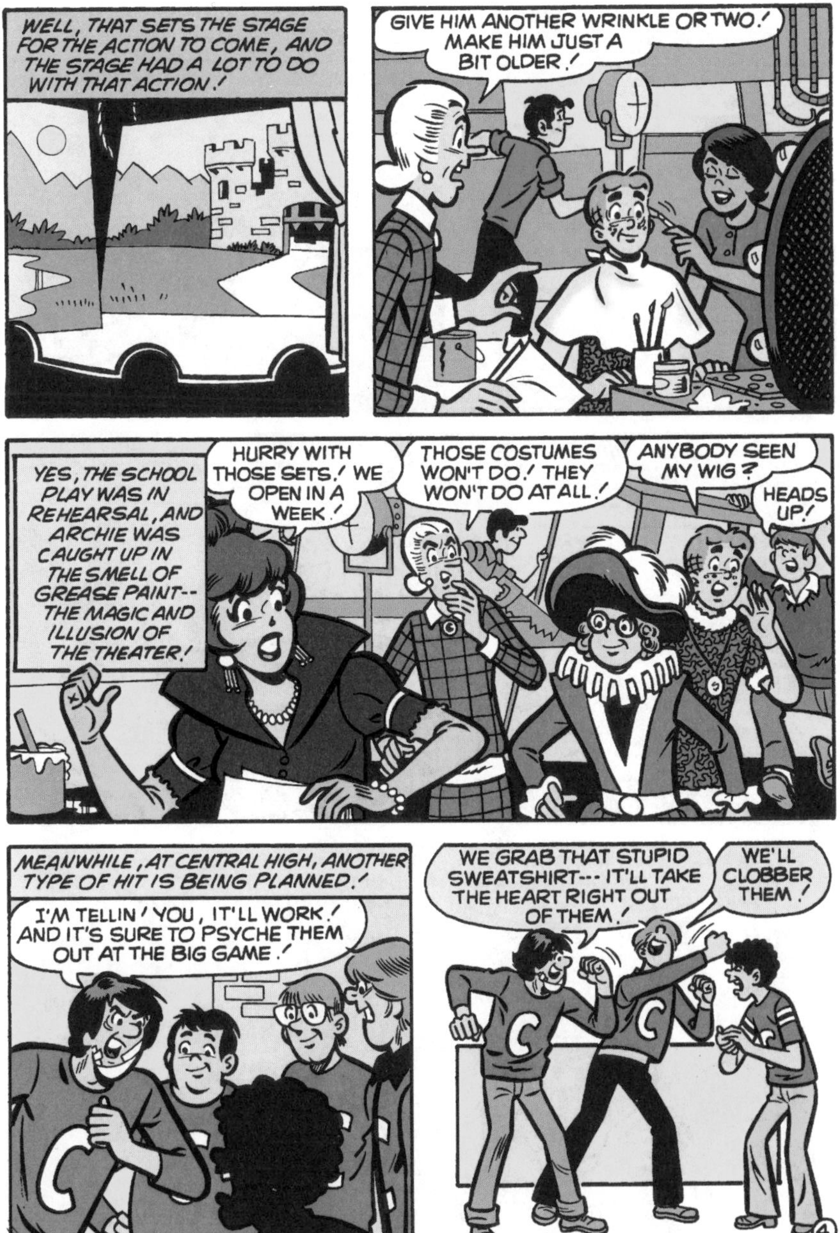
WELL, THAT SETS THE STAGE FOR THE ACTION TO COME, AND THE STAGE HAD A LOT TO DO WITH THAT ACTION!
GIVE HIM ANOTHER WRINKLE OR TWO! MAKE HIM JUST A BIT OLDER!
YES, THE SCHOOL PLAY WAS IN REHEARSAL, AND ARCHIE WAS CAUGHT UP IN THE SMELL OF GREASE PAINT-- THE MAGIC AND ILLUSION OF THE THEATER!
HURRY WITH THOSE SETS! WE OPEN IN A WEEK!
THOSE COSTUMES WON'T DO! THEY WON'T DO AT ALL!
ANYBODY SEEN MY WIG?
HEADS UP!
MEANWHILE, AT CENTRAL HIGH, ANOTHER TYPE OF HIT IS BEING PLANNED!
I'M TELLIN' YOU, IT'LL WORK! AND IT'S SURE TO PSYCHE THEM OUT AT THE BIG GAME!
WE GRAB THAT STUPID SWEATSHIRT--- IT'LL TAKE THE HEART RIGHT OUT OF THEM!
WE'LL CLOBBER THEM!
4

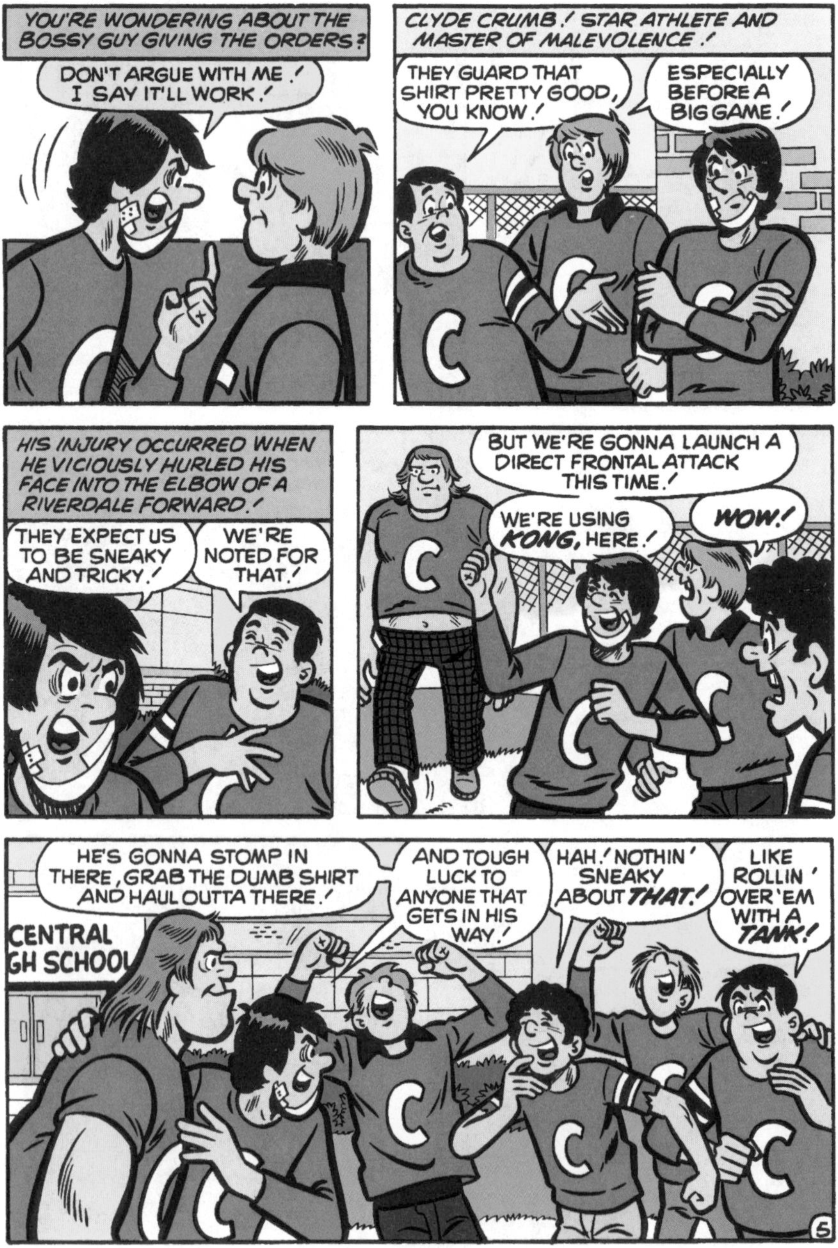
YOU'RE WONDERING ABOUT THE BOSSY GUY GIVING THE ORDERS?
DON'T ARGUE WITH ME! I SAY IT'LL WORK!
CLYDE CRUMB! STAR ATHLETE AND MASTER OF MALEVOLENCE!
THEY GUARD THAT SHIRT PRETTY GOOD, YOU KNOW!
ESPECIALLY BEFORE A BIG GAME!
HIS INJURY OCCURRED WHEN HE VICIOUSLY HURLED HIS FACE INTO THE ELBOW OF A RIVERDALE FORWARD!
THEY EXPECT US TO BE SNEAKY AND TRICKY!
WE'RE NOTED FOR THAT!
BUT WE'RE GONNA LAUNCH A DIRECT FRONTAL ATTACK THIS TIME!
WE'RE USING KONG, HERE!
WOW!
HE'S GONNA STOMP IN THERE, GRAB THE DUMB SHIRT AND HAUL OUTTA THERE!
AND TOUGH LUCK TO ANYONE THAT GETS IN HIS WAY!
HAH! NOTHIN' SNEAKY ABOUT THAT!
LIKE ROLLIN' OVER 'EM WITH A TANK!
CENTRAL
GH SCHOO
5

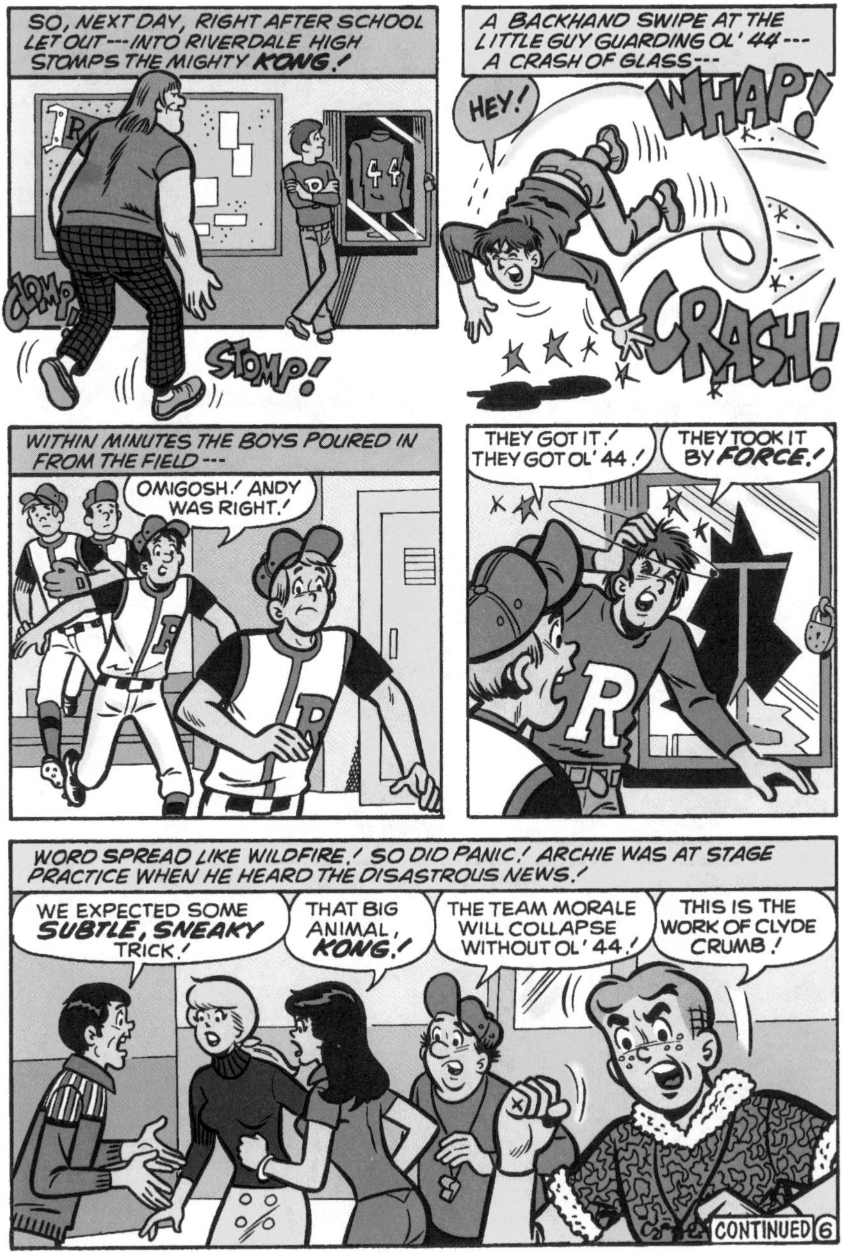
SO, NEXT DAY, RIGHT AFTER SCHOOL LET OUT---INTO RIVERDALE HIGH STOMPS THE MIGHTY KONG.!
CLOMP!
STOMP!
A BACKHAND SWIPE AT THE LITTLE GUY GUARDING OL' 44--- A CRASH OF GLASS---
HEY!
WHAP!
CRASH!
WITHIN MINUTES THE BOYS POURED IN FROM THE FIELD---
OMIGOSH! ANDY WAS RIGHT!
THEY GOT IT! THEY GOT OL' 44!
THEY TOOK IT BY FORCE!
WORD SPREAD LIKE WILDFIRE! SO DID PANIC! ARCHIE WAS AT STAGE PRACTICE WHEN HE HEARD THE DISASTROUS NEWS!
WE EXPECTED SOME SUBTLE, SNEAKY TRICK!
THAT BIG ANIMAL, KONG!
THE TEAM MORALE WILL COLLAPSE WITHOUT OL' 44!
THIS IS THE WORK OF CLYDE CRUMB!
CONTINUED 6

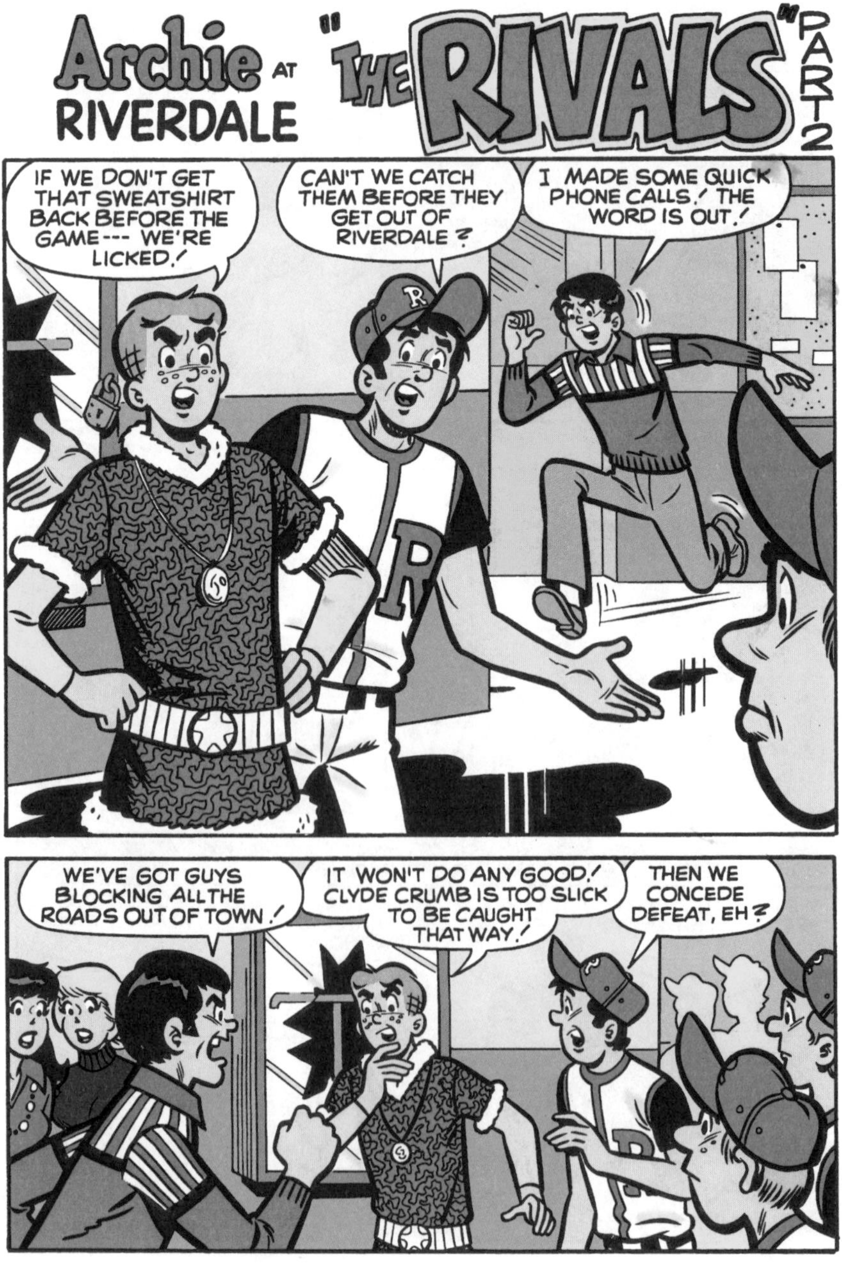
Archie AT RIVERDALE
"THE RIVALS" PART 2
IF WE DON'T GET THAT SWEATSHIRT BACK BEFORE THE GAME--- WE'RE LICKED!
CAN'T WE CATCH THEM BEFORE THEY GET OUT OF RIVERDALE?
I MADE SOME QUICK PHONE CALLS! THE WORD IS OUT!
WE'VE GOT GUYS BLOCKING ALL THE ROADS OUT OF TOWN!
IT WON'T DO ANY GOOD! CLYDE CRUMB IS TOO SLICK TO BE CAUGHT THAT WAY!
THEN WE CONCEDE DEFEAT, EH?

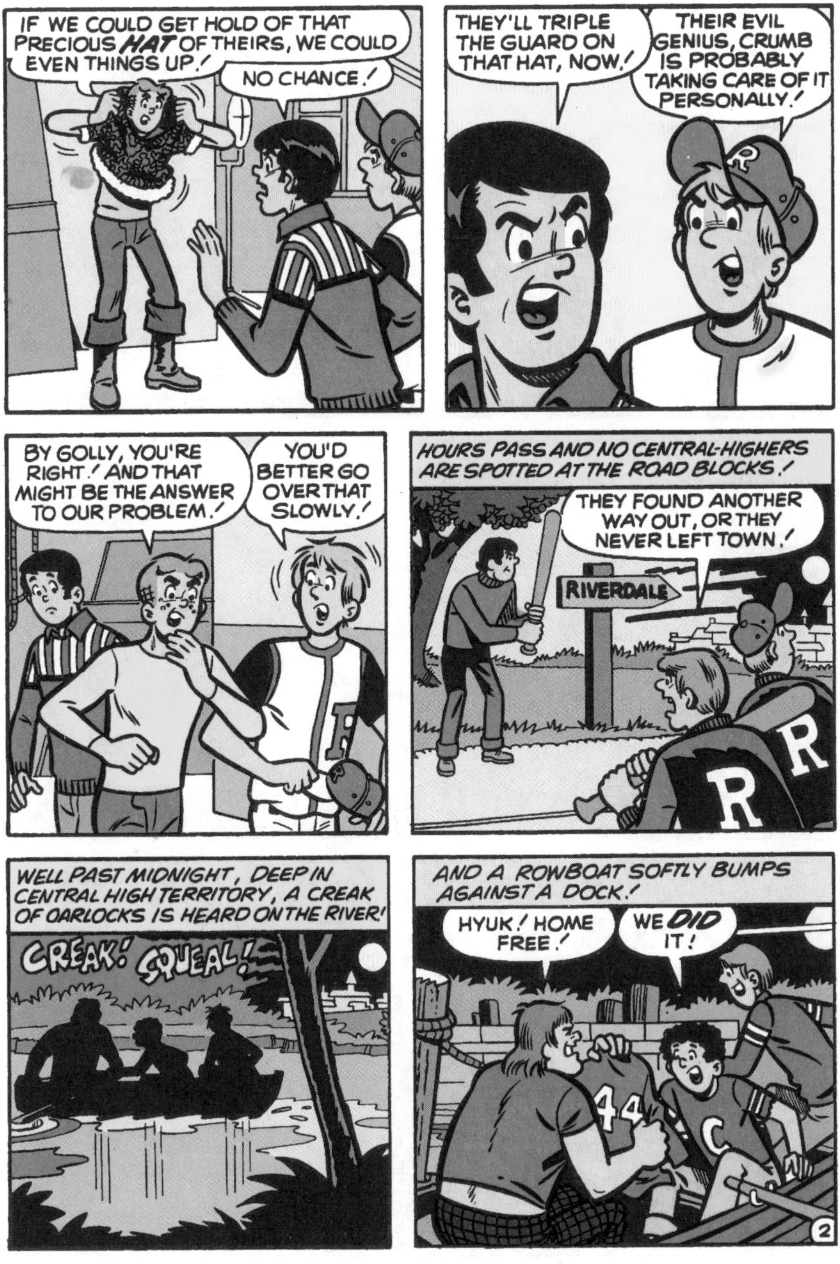
IF WE COULD GET HOLD OF THAT PRECIOUS HAT OF THEIRS, WE COULD EVEN THINGS UP!
NO CHANCE!
THEY'LL TRIPLE THE GUARD ON THAT HAT, NOW!
THEIR EVIL GENIUS, CRUMB IS PROBABLY TAKING CARE OF IT PERSONALLY!
BY GOLLY, YOU'RE RIGHT! AND THAT MIGHT BE THE ANSWER TO OUR PROBLEM!
YOU'D BETTER GO OVER THAT SLOWLY!
HOURS PASS AND NO CENTRAL-HIGHERS ARE SPOTTED AT THE ROAD BLOCKS!
THEY FOUND ANOTHER WAY OUT, OR THEY NEVER LEFT TOWN!
RIVERDALE
WELL PAST MIDNIGHT, DEEP IN CENTRAL HIGH TERRITORY, A CREAK OF OARLOCKS IS HEARD ON THE RIVER!
CREAK! SQUEAL!
AND A ROWBOAT SOFTLY BUMPS AGAINST A DOCK!
HYUK! HOME FREE!
WE DID IT!
2

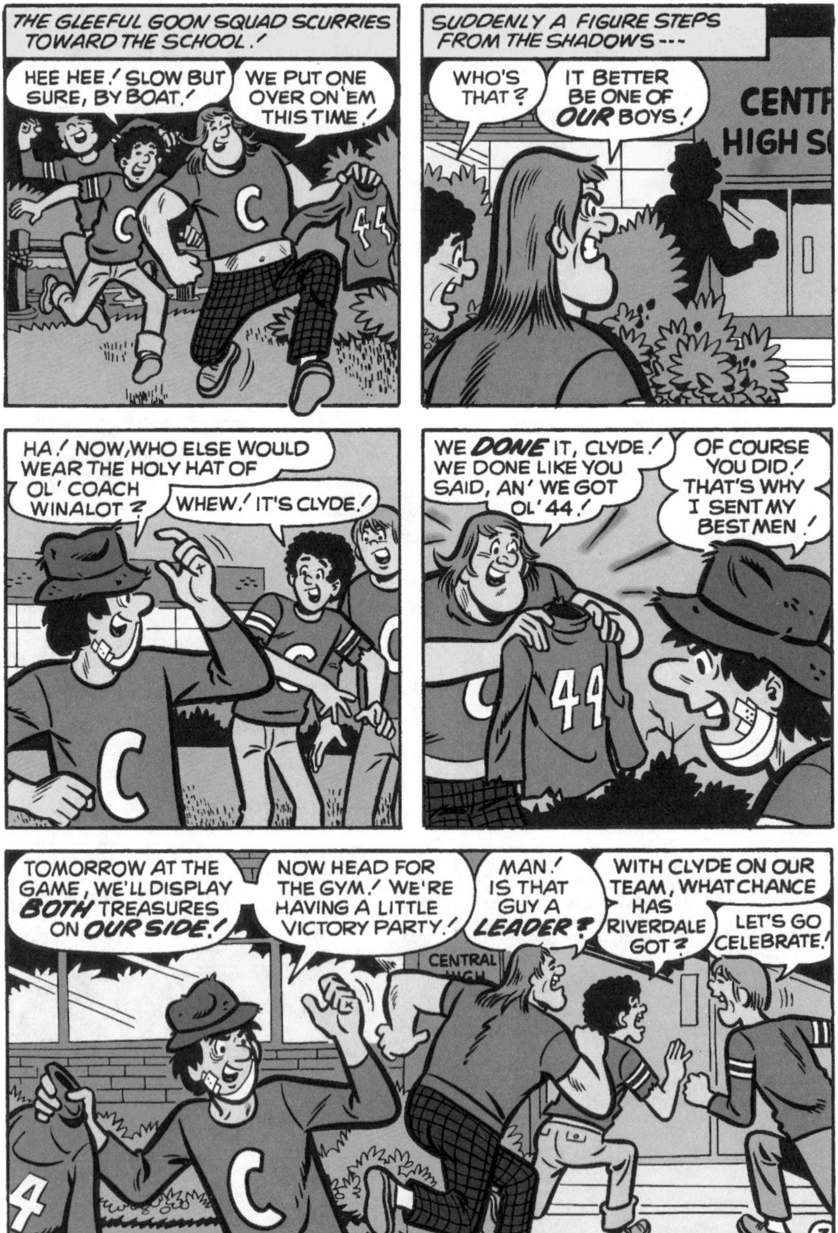
THE GLEEFUL GOON SQUAD SCURRIES TOWARD THE SCHOOL.!
HEE HEE.! SLOW BUT SURE, BY BOAT.!
WE PUT ONE OVER ON 'EM THIS TIME.!
44
SUDDENLY A FIGURE STEPS FROM THE SHADOWS---
WHO'S THAT?
IT BETTER BE ONE OF OUR BOYS.!
CENTR
HIGH S
HA.! NOW, WHO ELSE WOULD WEAR THE HOLY HAT OF OL' COACH WINALOT?
WHEW.! IT'S CLYDE.!
WE DONE IT, CLYDE.! WE DONE LIKE YOU SAID, AN' WE GOT OL' 44.!
OF COURSE YOU DID.! THAT'S WHY I SENT MY BEST MEN.!
44
TOMORROW AT THE GAME, WE'LL DISPLAY BOTH TREASURES ON OUR SIDE.!
NOW HEAD FOR THE GYM.! WE'RE HAVING A LITTLE VICTORY PARTY.!
MAN.! IS THAT GUY A LEADER?
WITH CLYDE ON OUR TEAM, WHAT CHANCE HAS RIVERDALE GOT?
LET'S GO CELEBRATE.!
CENTRAL
3

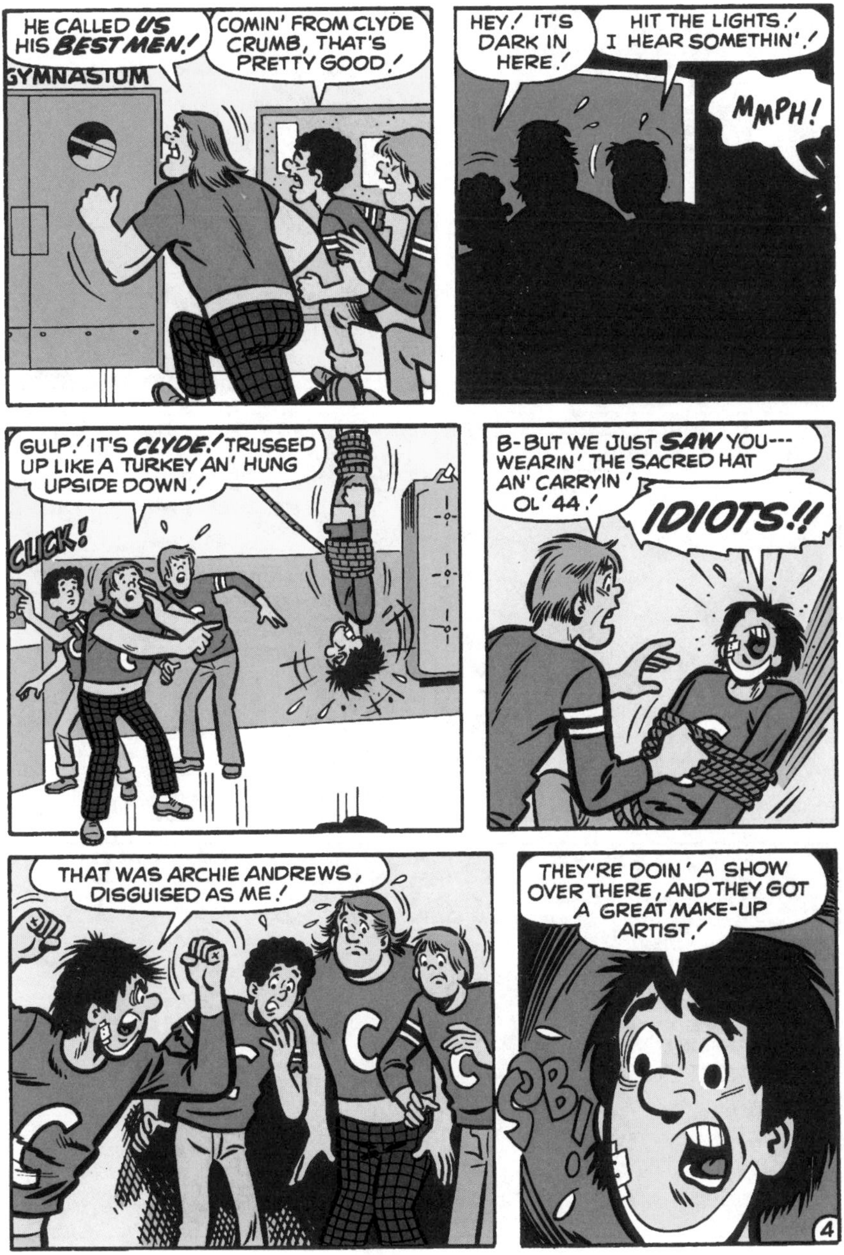
HE CALLED US HIS BEST MEN!
COMIN' FROM CLYDE CRUMB, THAT'S PRETTY GOOD!
GYMNASIUM
HEY! IT'S DARK IN HERE!
HIT THE LIGHTS! I HEAR SOMETHIN'!
MMPH!
GULP! IT'S CLYDE! TRUSSED UP LIKE A TURKEY AN' HUNG UPSIDE DOWN!
CLICK!
B-BUT WE JUST SAW YOU--- WEARIN' THE SACRED HAT AN' CARRYIN' OL' 44!
IDIOTS!!
THAT WAS ARCHIE ANDREWS, DISGUISED AS ME!
THEY'RE DOIN' A SHOW OVER THERE, AND THEY GOT A GREAT MAKE-UP ARTIST!
4

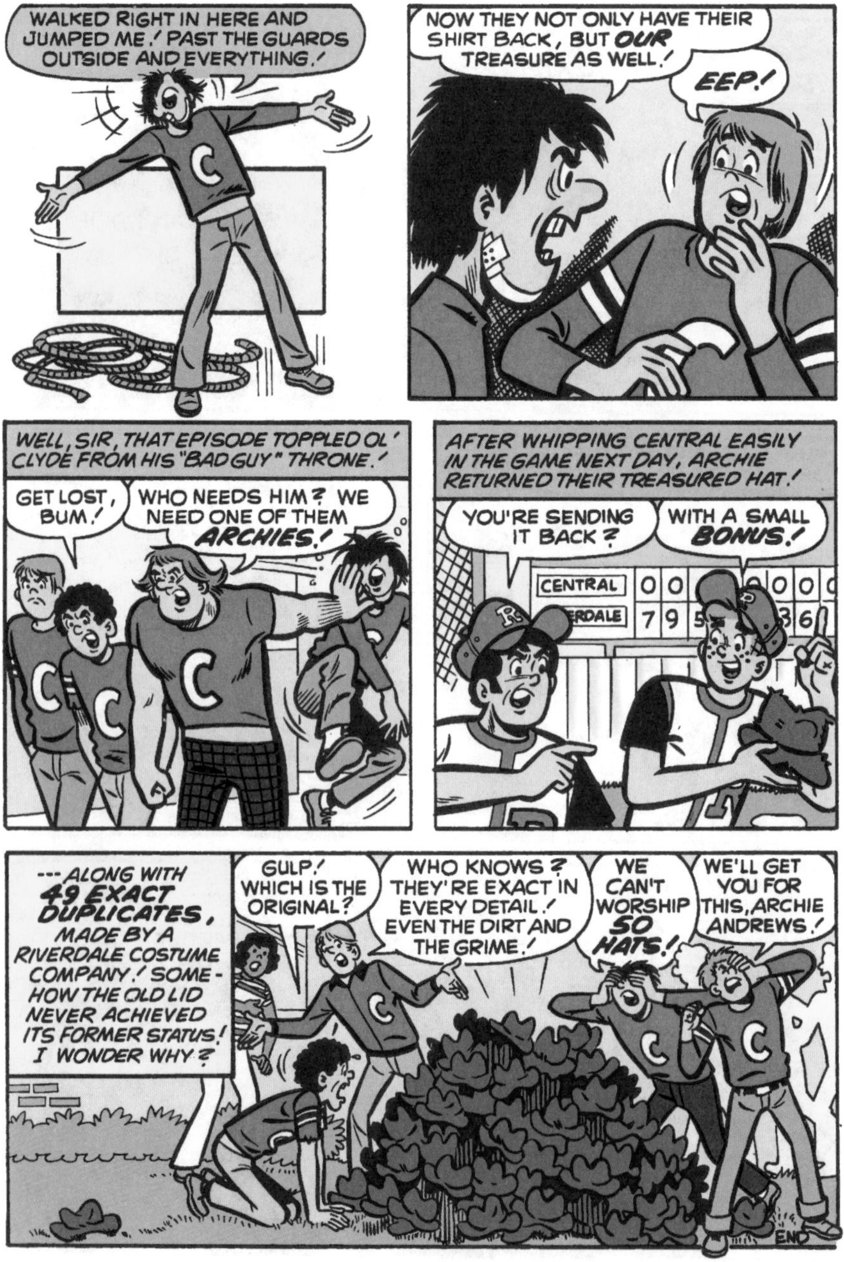
WALKED RIGHT IN HERE AND JUMPED ME.! PAST THE GUARDS OUTSIDE AND EVERYTHING.!
NOW THEY NOT ONLY HAVE THEIR SHIRT BACK, BUT OUR TREASURE AS WELL.!
EEP.!
WELL, SIR, THAT EPISODE TOPPLED OL' CLYDE FROM HIS "BAD GUY" THRONE.!
GET LOST, BUM.!
WHO NEEDS HIM? WE NEED ONE OF THEM ARCHIES.!
AFTER WHIPPING CENTRAL EASILY IN THE GAME NEXT DAY, ARCHIE RETURNED THEIR TREASURED HAT.!
YOU'RE SENDING IT BACK?
WITH A SMALL BONUS.!
CENTRAL
---ALONG WITH 49 EXACT DUPLICATES, MADE BY A RIVERDALE COSTUME COMPANY.! SOMEHOW THE OLD LID NEVER ACHIEVED ITS FORMER STATUS! I WONDER WHY?
GULP.! WHICH IS THE ORIGINAL?
WHO KNOWS? THEY'RE EXACT IN EVERY DETAIL.! EVEN THE DIRT AND THE GRIME.!
WE CAN'T WORSHIP SO HATS.!
WE'LL GET YOU FOR THIS, ARCHIE ANDREWS.!
END

Archie at Riverdale in "Double Header"

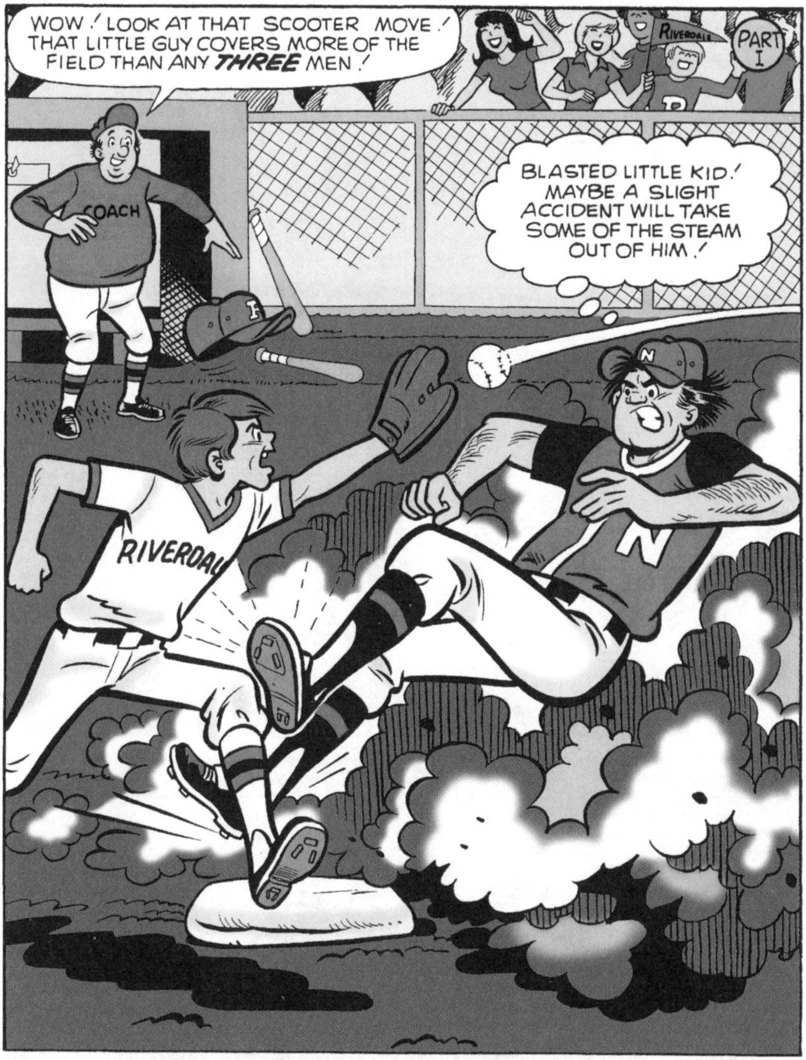
PART I
WOW! LOOK AT THAT SCOOTER MOVE! THAT LITTLE GUY COVERS MORE OF THE FIELD THAN ANY *THREE* MEN!
BLASTED LITTLE KID! MAYBE A SLIGHT ACCIDENT WILL TAKE SOME OF THE STEAM OUT OF HIM!
RIVERDALE
COACH
RIVERDALE
N
N

Story: Frank Doyle   Pencils: Stan Goldberg
Inks: Jon D'Agostino   Letters: Bill Yoshida   Colors: Barry Grossman

Originally printed in ARCHIE AT RIVERDALE HIGH #46, JULY 1977

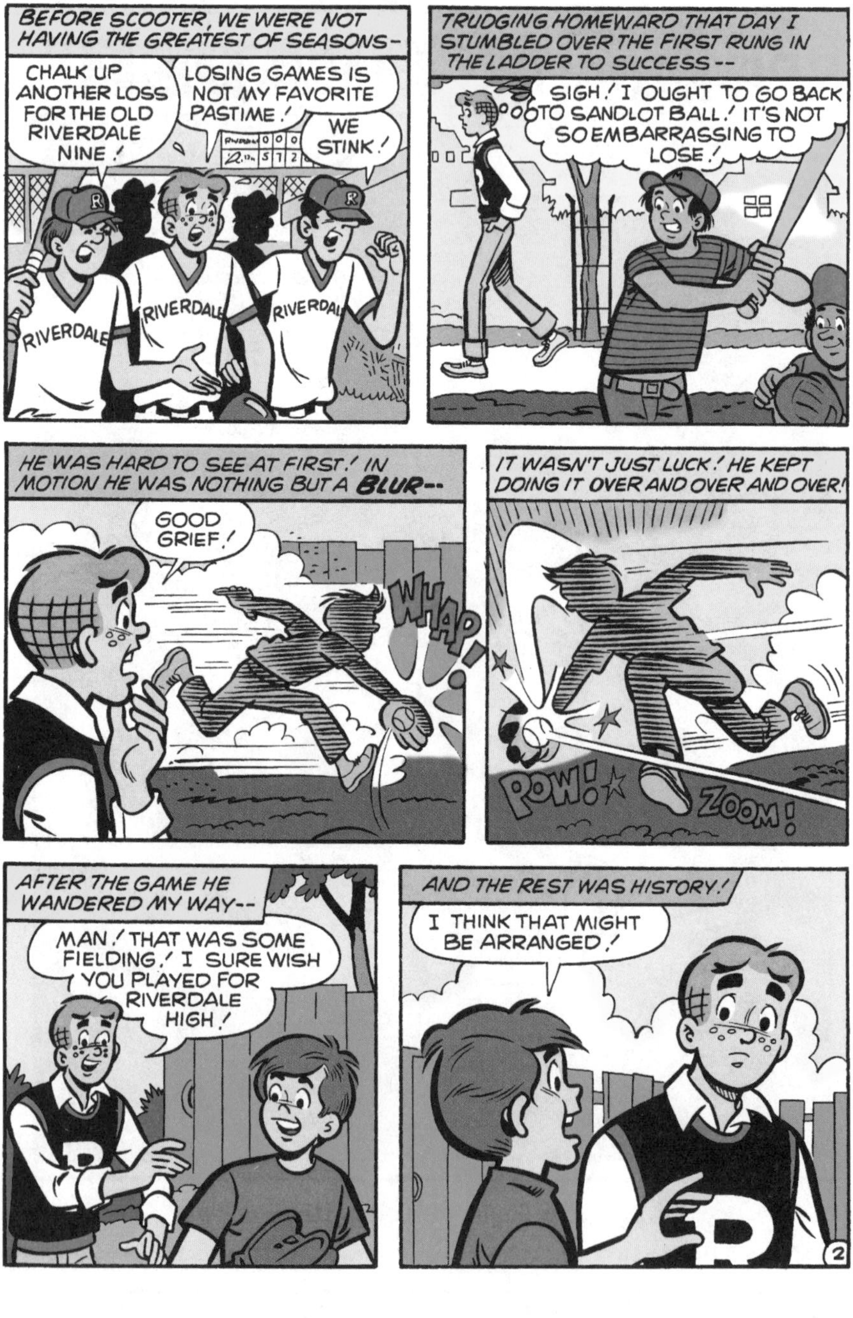
BEFORE SCOOTER, WE WERE NOT HAVING THE GREATEST OF SEASONS-
CHALK UP ANOTHER LOSS FOR THE OLD RIVERDALE NINE!
LOSING GAMES IS NOT MY FAVORITE PASTIME!
WE STINK!
RIVERDALE
RIVERDALE
RIVERDALE
TRUDGING HOMEWARD THAT DAY I STUMBLED OVER THE FIRST RUNG IN THE LADDER TO SUCCESS--
SIGH! I OUGHT TO GO BACK TO SANDLOT BALL! IT'S NOT SO EMBARRASSING TO LOSE!
HE WAS HARD TO SEE AT FIRST! IN MOTION HE WAS NOTHING BUT A BLUR--
GOOD GRIEF!
WHAP!
IT WASN'T JUST LUCK! HE KEPT DOING IT OVER AND OVER AND OVER!
POW!
ZOOM!
AFTER THE GAME HE WANDERED MY WAY--
MAN! THAT WAS SOME FIELDING! I SURE WISH YOU PLAYED FOR RIVERDALE HIGH!
AND THE REST WAS HISTORY!
I THINK THAT MIGHT BE ARRANGED!
2

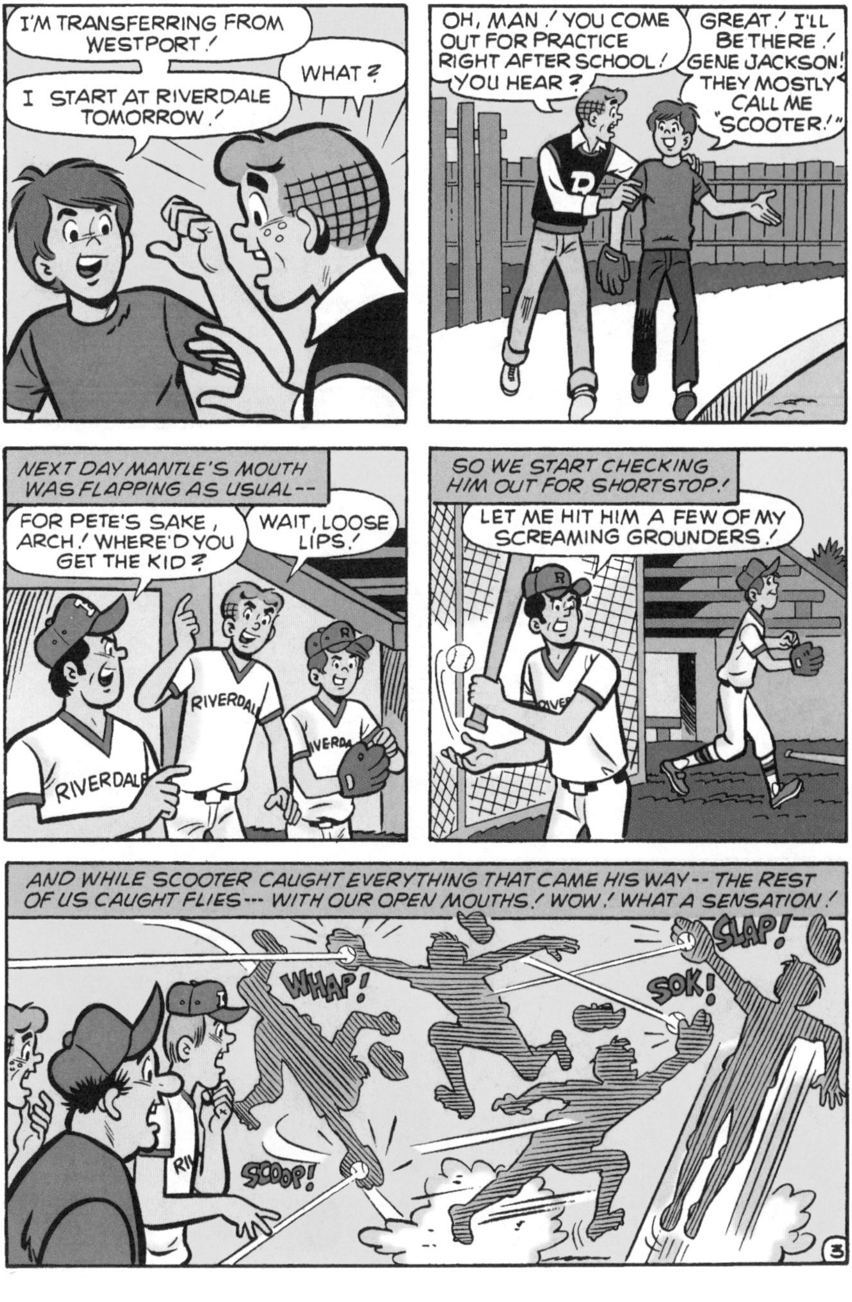
I'M TRANSFERRING FROM WESTPORT!
I START AT RIVERDALE TOMORROW!
WHAT?
OH, MAN! YOU COME OUT FOR PRACTICE RIGHT AFTER SCHOOL! YOU HEAR?
GREAT! I'LL BE THERE! GENE JACKSON! THEY MOSTLY CALL ME "SCOOTER!"
NEXT DAY MANTLE'S MOUTH WAS FLAPPING AS USUAL--
FOR PETE'S SAKE, ARCH! WHERE'D YOU GET THE KID?
WAIT, LOOSE LIPS!
RIVERDALE
SO WE START CHECKING HIM OUT FOR SHORTSTOP!
LET ME HIT HIM A FEW OF MY SCREAMING GROUNDERS!
AND WHILE SCOOTER CAUGHT EVERYTHING THAT CAME HIS WAY-- THE REST OF US CAUGHT FLIES--- WITH OUR OPEN MOUTHS! WOW! WHAT A SENSATION!
WHAP!
SLAP!
SOK!
SCOOP!
3

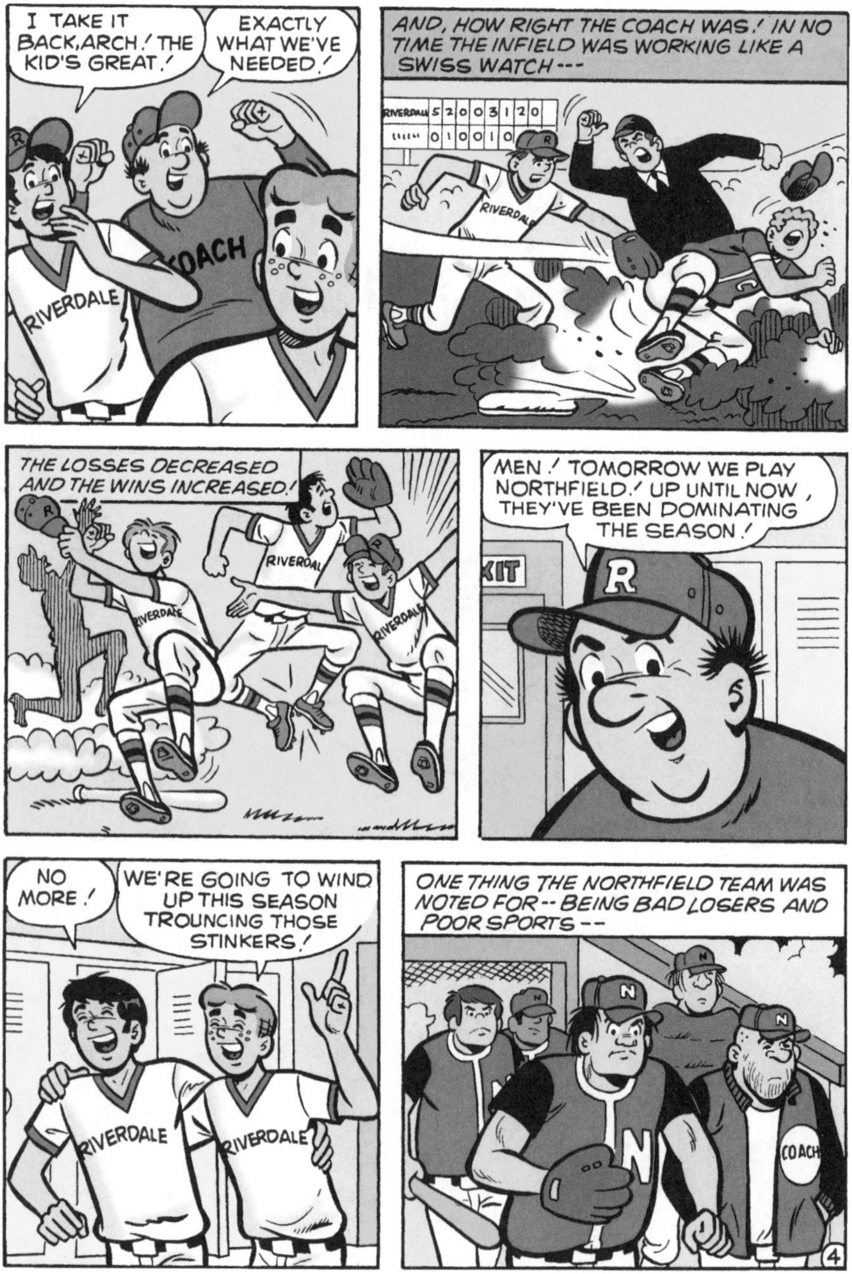
I TAKE IT BACK, ARCH! THE KID'S GREAT!
EXACTLY WHAT WE'VE NEEDED!
COACH
RIVERDALE
AND, HOW RIGHT THE COACH WAS! IN NO TIME THE INFIELD WAS WORKING LIKE A SWISS WATCH---
RIVERDALE
THE LOSSES DECREASED AND THE WINS INCREASED!
RIVERDALE
MEN! TOMORROW WE PLAY NORTHFIELD! UP UNTIL NOW, THEY'VE BEEN DOMINATING THE SEASON!
NO MORE!
WE'RE GOING TO WIND UP THIS SEASON TROUNCING THOSE STINKERS!
RIVERDALE
RIVERDALE
ONE THING THE NORTHFIELD TEAM WAS NOTED FOR -- BEING BAD LOSERS AND POOR SPORTS --
COACH
4

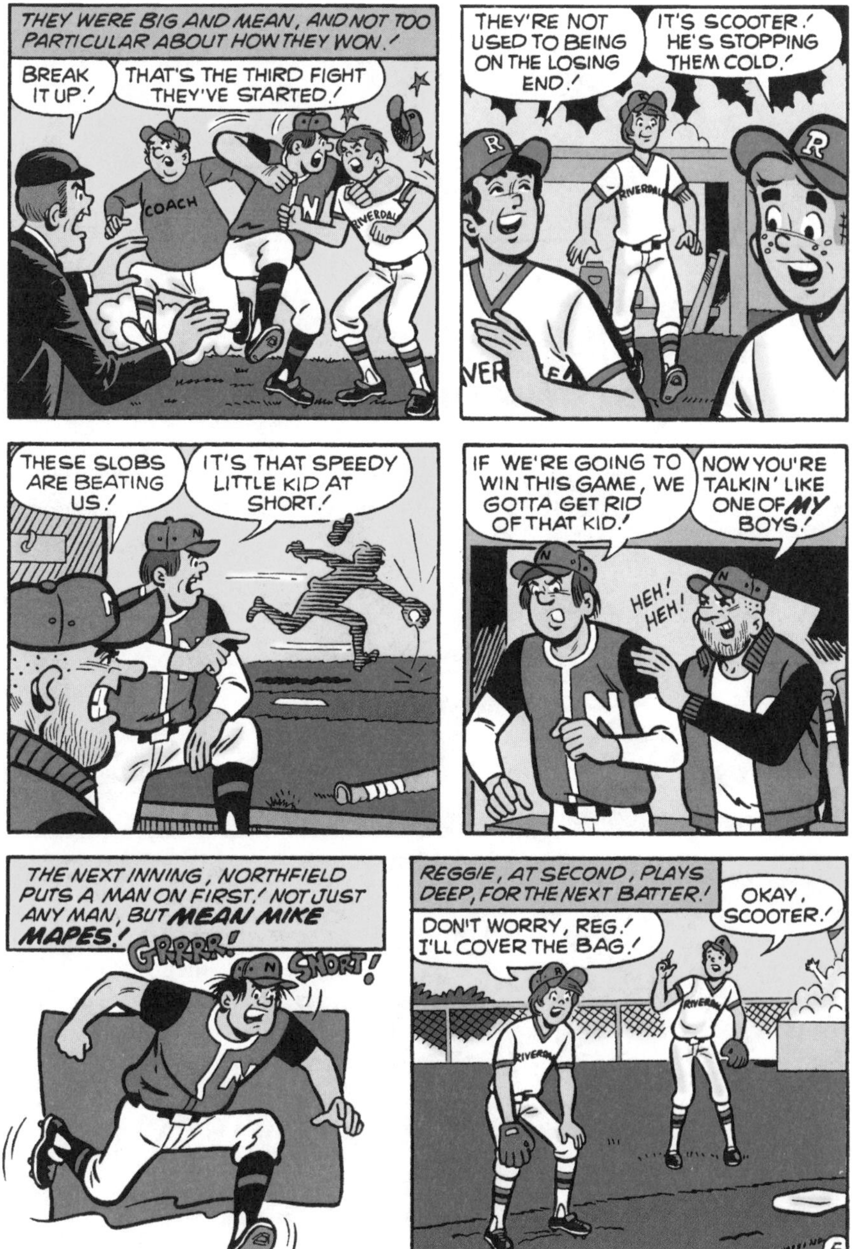
THEY WERE BIG AND MEAN, AND NOT TOO PARTICULAR ABOUT HOW THEY WON!
BREAK IT UP!
THAT'S THE THIRD FIGHT THEY'VE STARTED!
COACH
RIVERDALE
THEY'RE NOT USED TO BEING ON THE LOSING END!
IT'S SCOOTER! HE'S STOPPING THEM COLD!
R
RIVERDALE
R
THESE SLOBS ARE BEATING US!
IT'S THAT SPEEDY LITTLE KID AT SHORT!
IF WE'RE GOING TO WIN THIS GAME, WE GOTTA GET RID OF THAT KID!
NOW YOU'RE TALKIN' LIKE ONE OF MY BOYS!
HEH! HEH!
THE NEXT INNING, NORTHFIELD PUTS A MAN ON FIRST! NOT JUST ANY MAN, BUT MEAN MIKE MAPES!
GRRRR!
SNORT!
REGGIE, AT SECOND, PLAYS DEEP, FOR THE NEXT BATTER!
OKAY, SCOOTER!
DON'T WORRY, REG! I'LL COVER THE BAG!
5

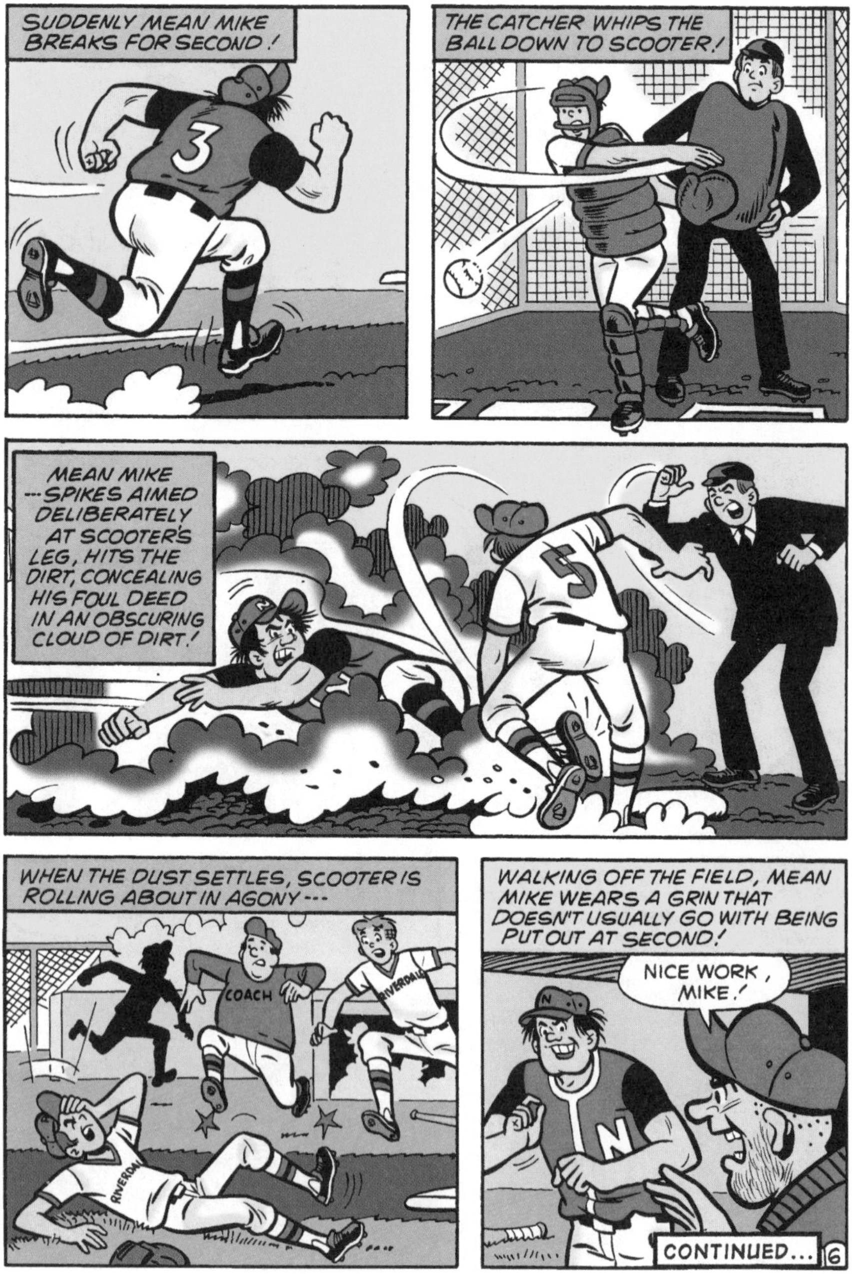
SUDDENLY MEAN MIKE BREAKS FOR SECOND!
3
THE CATCHER WHIPS THE BALL DOWN TO SCOOTER!
MEAN MIKE ---SPIKES AIMED DELIBERATELY AT SCOOTER'S LEG, HITS THE DIRT, CONCEALING HIS FOUL DEED IN AN OBSCURING CLOUD OF DIRT!
5
WHEN THE DUST SETTLES, SCOOTER IS ROLLING ABOUT IN AGONY ---
COACH
RIVERDALE
WALKING OFF THE FIELD, MEAN MIKE WEARS A GRIN THAT DOESN'T USUALLY GO WITH BEING PUT OUT AT SECOND!
NICE WORK, MIKE!
N
CONTINUED...
6

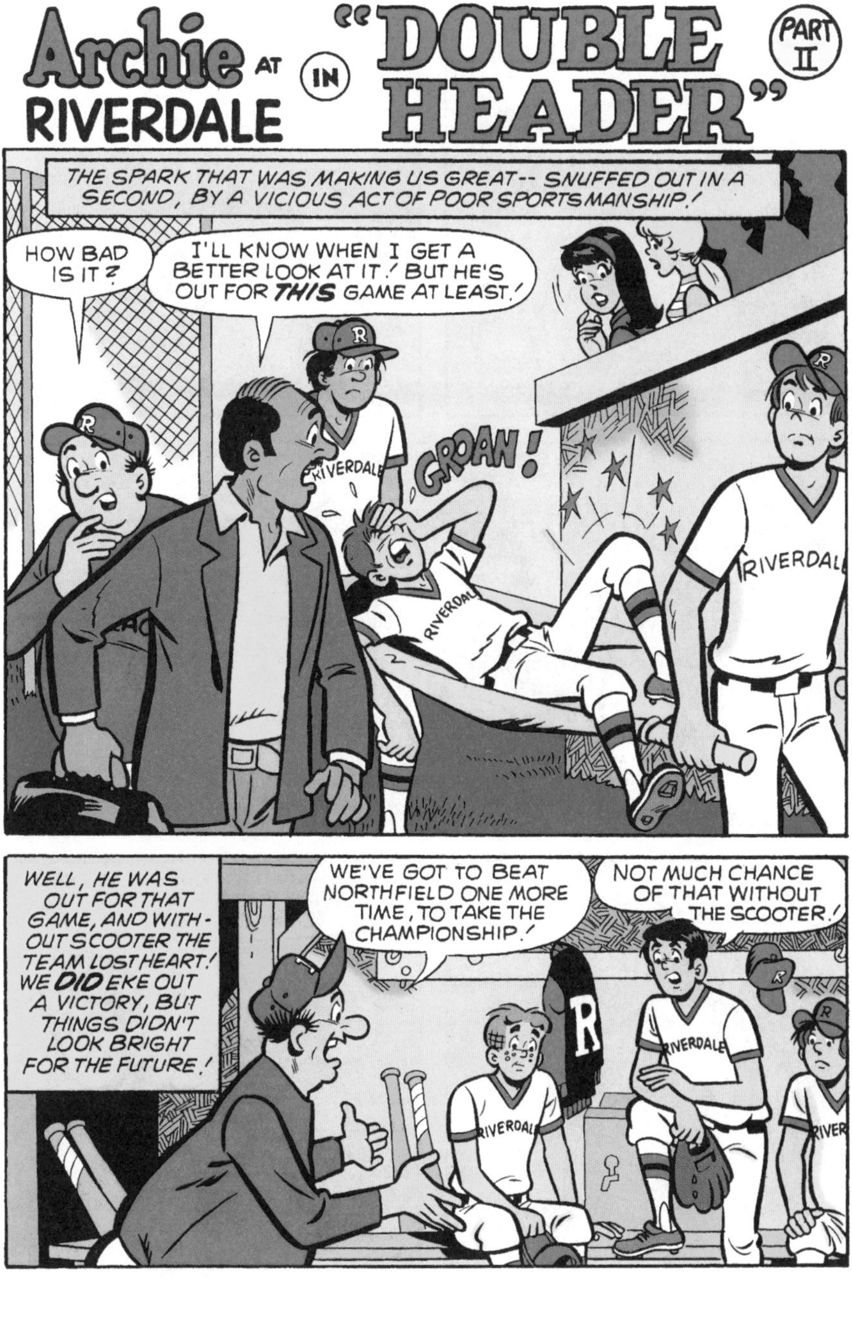
Archie AT RIVERDALE
IN
"DOUBLE HEADER"
PART II
THE SPARK THAT WAS MAKING US GREAT-- SNUFFED OUT IN A SECOND, BY A VICIOUS ACT OF POOR SPORTSMANSHIP!
HOW BAD IS IT?
I'LL KNOW WHEN I GET A BETTER LOOK AT IT! BUT HE'S OUT FOR THIS GAME AT LEAST!
GROAN!
WELL, HE WAS OUT FOR THAT GAME, AND WITH-OUT SCOOTER THE TEAM LOST HEART! WE DID EKE OUT A VICTORY, BUT THINGS DIDN'T LOOK BRIGHT FOR THE FUTURE!
WE'VE GOT TO BEAT NORTHFIELD ONE MORE TIME, TO TAKE THE CHAMPIONSHIP!
NOT MUCH CHANCE OF THAT WITHOUT THE SCOOTER!

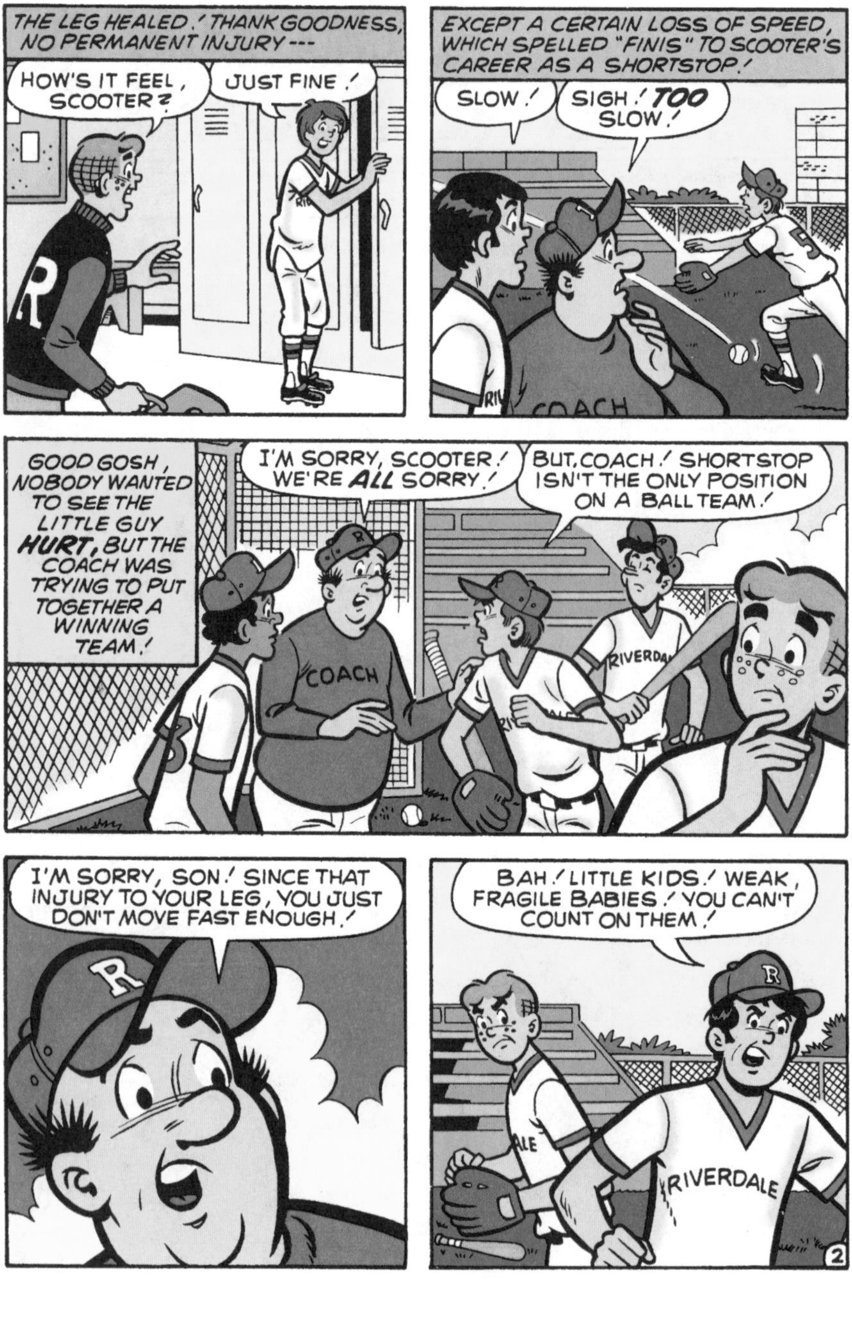
THE LEG HEALED! THANK GOODNESS, NO PERMANENT INJURY---
HOW'S IT FEEL, SCOOTER?
JUST FINE!
EXCEPT A CERTAIN LOSS OF SPEED, WHICH SPELLED "FINIS" TO SCOOTER'S CAREER AS A SHORTSTOP!
SLOW!
SIGH! TOO SLOW!
COACH
GOOD GOSH, NOBODY WANTED TO SEE THE LITTLE GUY HURT, BUT THE COACH WAS TRYING TO PUT TOGETHER A WINNING TEAM!
I'M SORRY, SCOOTER! WE'RE ALL SORRY!
BUT, COACH! SHORTSTOP ISN'T THE ONLY POSITION ON A BALL TEAM!
COACH
RIVERDAL
I'M SORRY, SON! SINCE THAT INJURY TO YOUR LEG, YOU JUST DON'T MOVE FAST ENOUGH!
BAH! LITTLE KIDS! WEAK, FRAGILE BABIES! YOU CAN'T COUNT ON THEM!
RIVERDALE
2

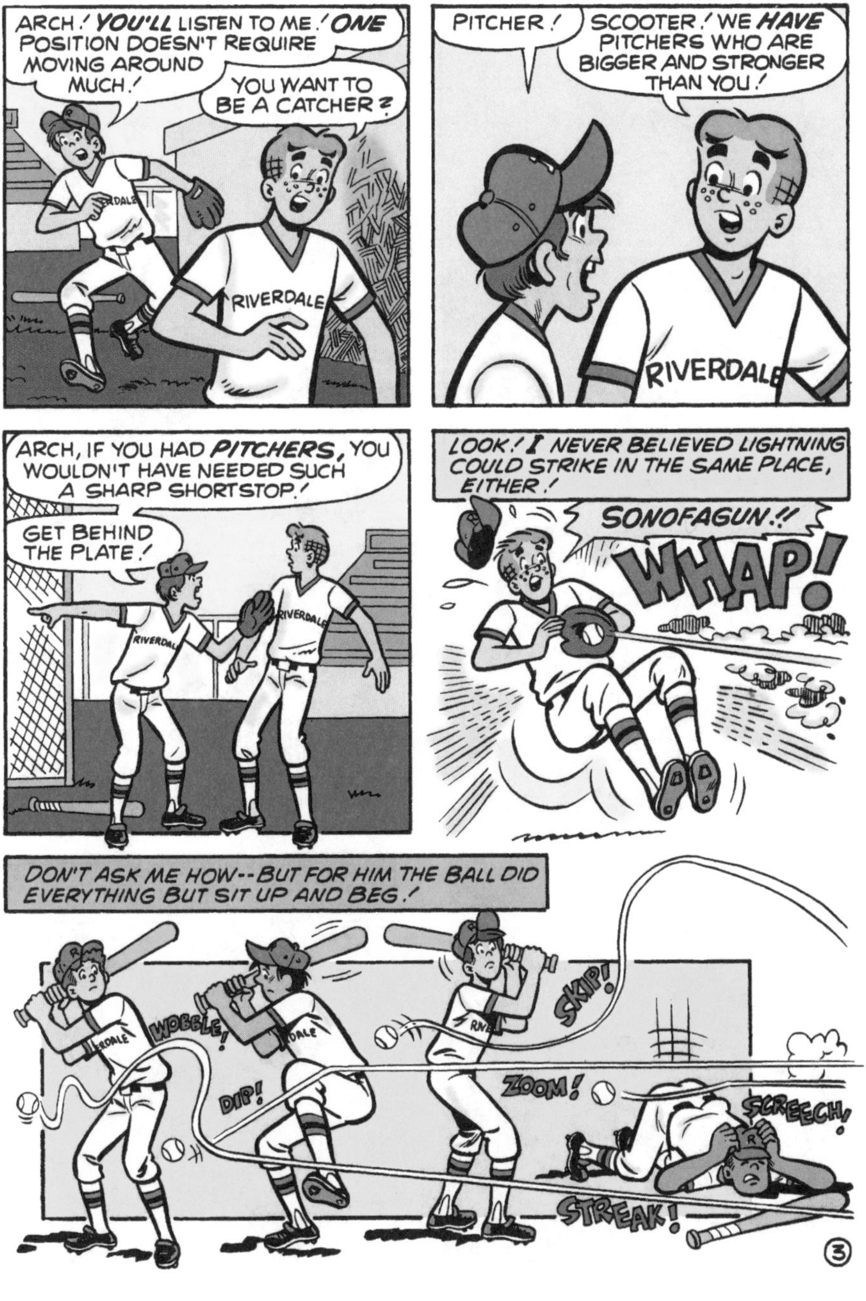
ARCH! YOU'LL LISTEN TO ME! ONE POSITION DOESN'T REQUIRE MOVING AROUND MUCH!
YOU WANT TO BE A CATCHER?
PITCHER!
SCOOTER! WE HAVE PITCHERS WHO ARE BIGGER AND STRONGER THAN YOU!
ARCH, IF YOU HAD PITCHERS, YOU WOULDN'T HAVE NEEDED SUCH A SHARP SHORTSTOP!
GET BEHIND THE PLATE!
LOOK! I NEVER BELIEVED LIGHTNING COULD STRIKE IN THE SAME PLACE, EITHER!
SONOFAGUN!!
WHAP!
DON'T ASK ME HOW--BUT FOR HIM THE BALL DID EVERYTHING BUT SIT UP AND BEG!
WOBBLE!
DIP!
SKIP!
ZOOM!
SCREECH!
STREAK!
3

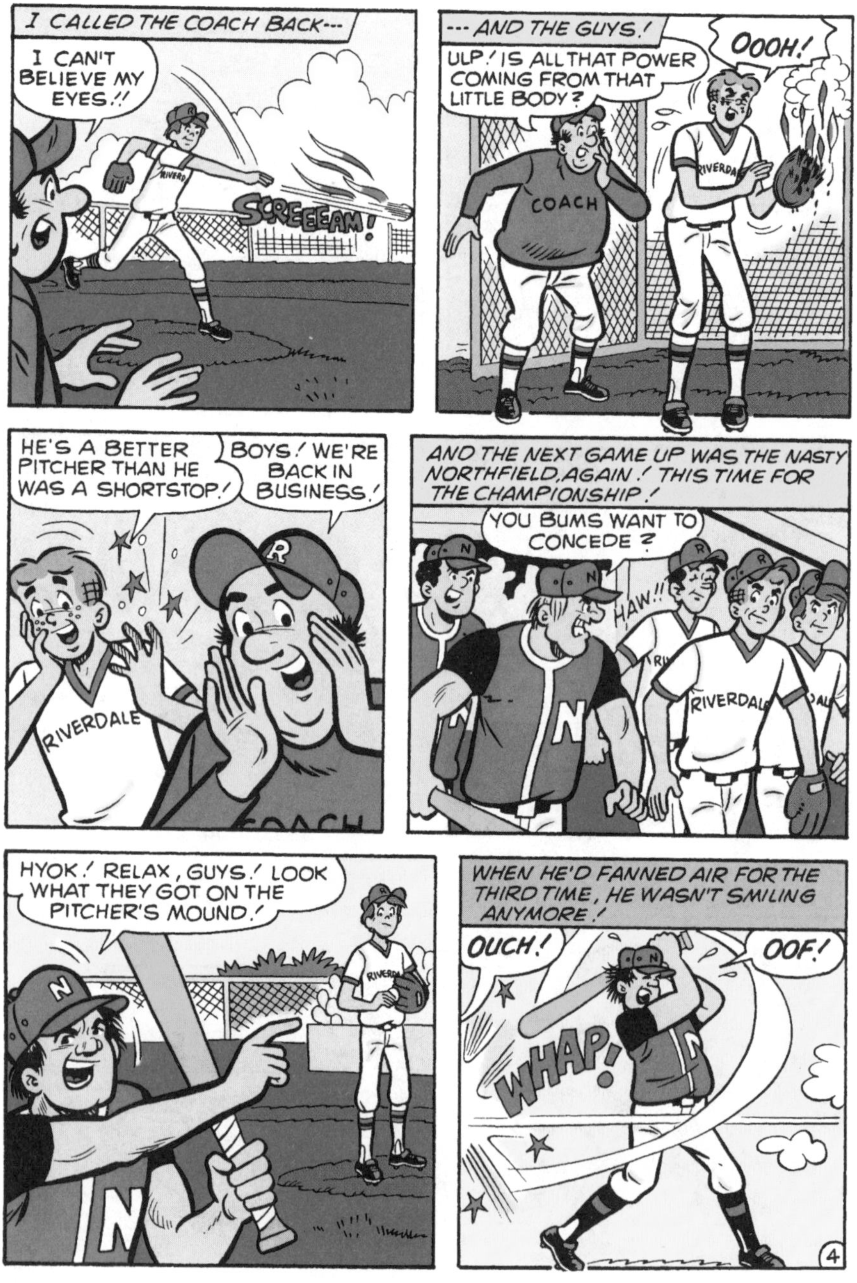
I CALLED THE COACH BACK---
I CAN'T BELIEVE MY EYES.!!
SCREEEEAM!
--- AND THE GUYS.!
ULP.! IS ALL THAT POWER COMING FROM THAT LITTLE BODY?
OOOH!
COACH
RIVERDALE
HE'S A BETTER PITCHER THAN HE WAS A SHORTSTOP.!
BOYS.! WE'RE BACK IN BUSINESS.!
RIVERDALE
AND THE NEXT GAME UP WAS THE NASTY NORTHFIELD, AGAIN.! THIS TIME FOR THE CHAMPIONSHIP.!
YOU BUMS WANT TO CONCEDE?
HAW!!
RIVERDALE
HYOK.! RELAX, GUYS.! LOOK WHAT THEY GOT ON THE PITCHER'S MOUND.!
WHEN HE'D FANNED AIR FOR THE THIRD TIME, HE WASN'T SMILING ANYMORE.!
OUCH!
OOF!
WHAP!
4

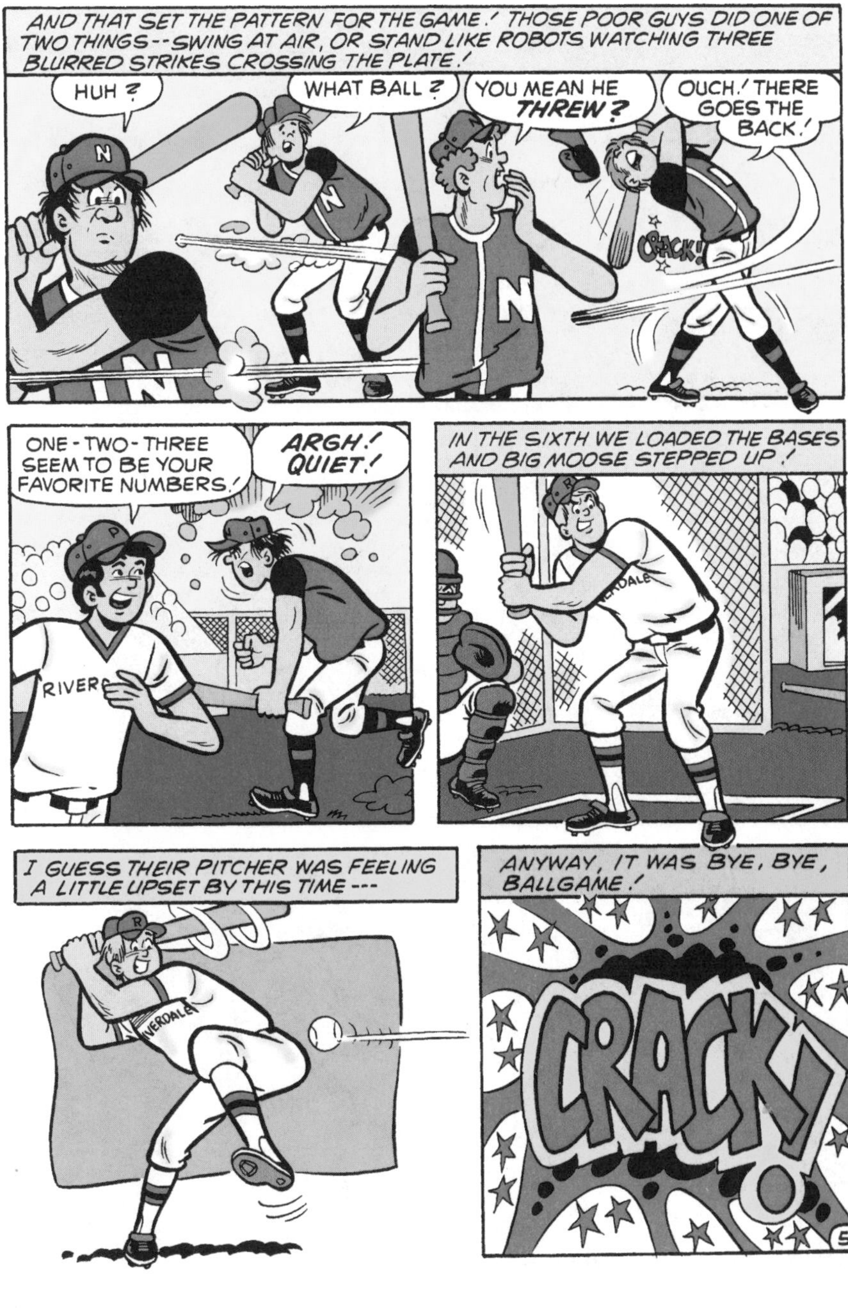
AND THAT SET THE PATTERN FOR THE GAME! THOSE POOR GUYS DID ONE OF TWO THINGS--SWING AT AIR, OR STAND LIKE ROBOTS WATCHING THREE BLURRED STRIKES CROSSING THE PLATE!
HUH?
WHAT BALL?
YOU MEAN HE THREW?
OUCH! THERE GOES THE BACK!
CRACK!
ONE-TWO-THREE SEEM TO BE YOUR FAVORITE NUMBERS!
ARGH! QUIET!
RIVER
IN THE SIXTH WE LOADED THE BASES AND BIG MOOSE STEPPED UP!
I GUESS THEIR PITCHER WAS FEELING A LITTLE UPSET BY THIS TIME ---
ANYWAY, IT WAS BYE, BYE, BALLGAME!
CRACK!
5

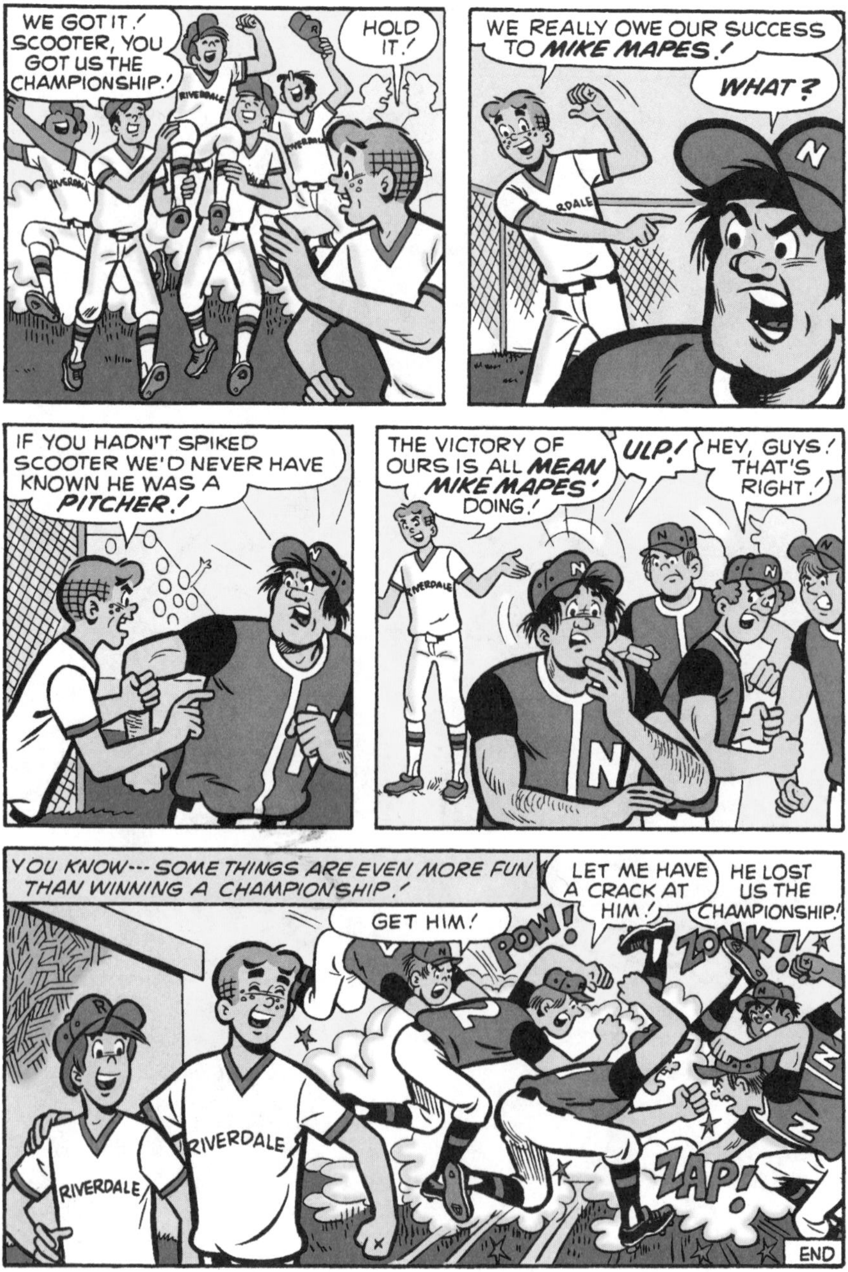
WE GOT IT! SCOOTER, YOU GOT US THE CHAMPIONSHIP!
HOLD IT!
WE REALLY OWE OUR SUCCESS TO MIKE MAPES!
WHAT?
IF YOU HADN'T SPIKED SCOOTER WE'D NEVER HAVE KNOWN HE WAS A PITCHER!
THE VICTORY OF OURS IS ALL MEAN MIKE MAPES' DOING!
ULP!
HEY, GUYS! THAT'S RIGHT!
YOU KNOW--- SOME THINGS ARE EVEN MORE FUN THAN WINNING A CHAMPIONSHIP!
GET HIM!
POW!
LET ME HAVE A CRACK AT HIM!
HE LOST US THE CHAMPIONSHIP!
ZONK!
ZAP!
END

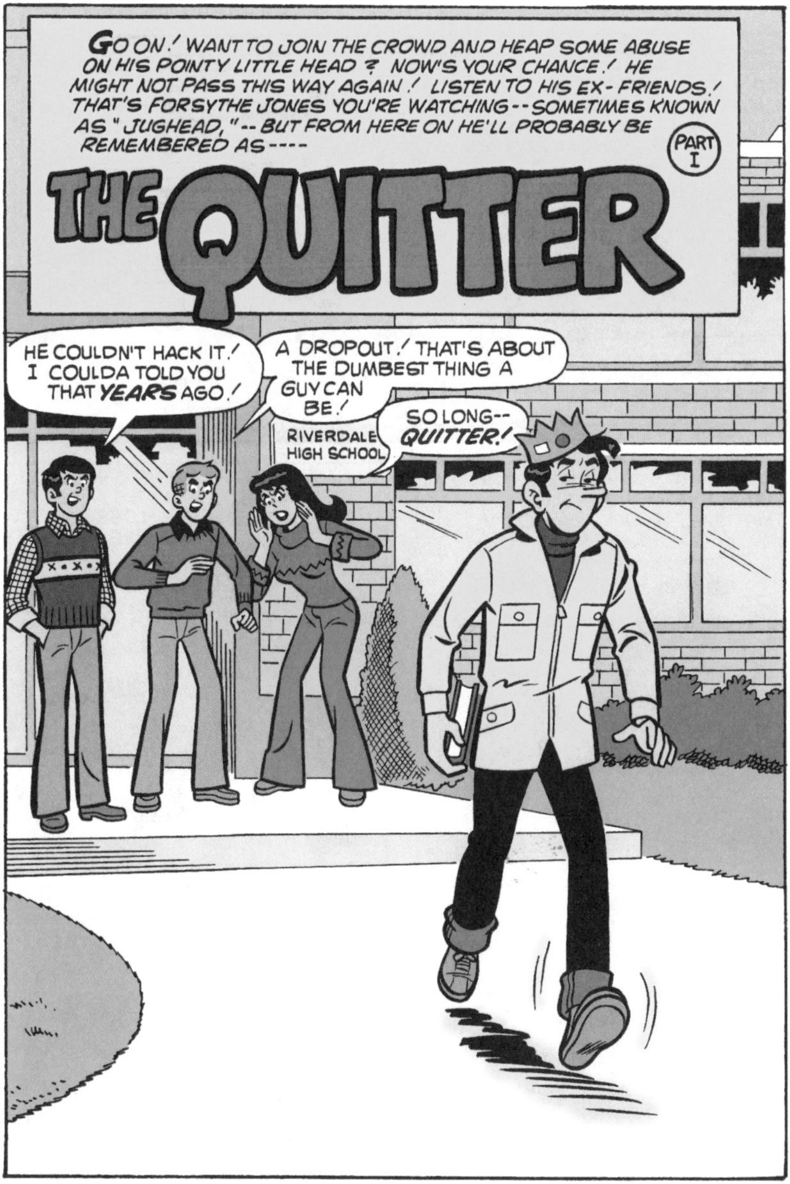
GO ON! WANT TO JOIN THE CROWD AND HEAP SOME ABUSE ON HIS POINTY LITTLE HEAD ? NOW'S YOUR CHANCE! HE MIGHT NOT PASS THIS WAY AGAIN! LISTEN TO HIS EX-FRIENDS! THAT'S FORSYTHE JONES YOU'RE WATCHING--SOMETIMES KNOWN AS "JUGHEAD," --BUT FROM HERE ON HE'LL PROBABLY BE REMEMBERED AS----
PART I
THE QUITTER
HE COULDN'T HACK IT! I COULDA TOLD YOU THAT YEARS AGO!
A DROPOUT! THAT'S ABOUT THE DUMBEST THING A GUY CAN BE!
RIVERDALE HIGH SCHOOL
SO LONG-- QUITTER!

Story: Frank Doyle Pencils: Stan Goldberg
Inks: Jon D'Agostino Letters: Bill Yoshida Colors: Barry Grossman

Originally printed in ARCHIE AT RIVERDALE HIGH #46, JULY 1977

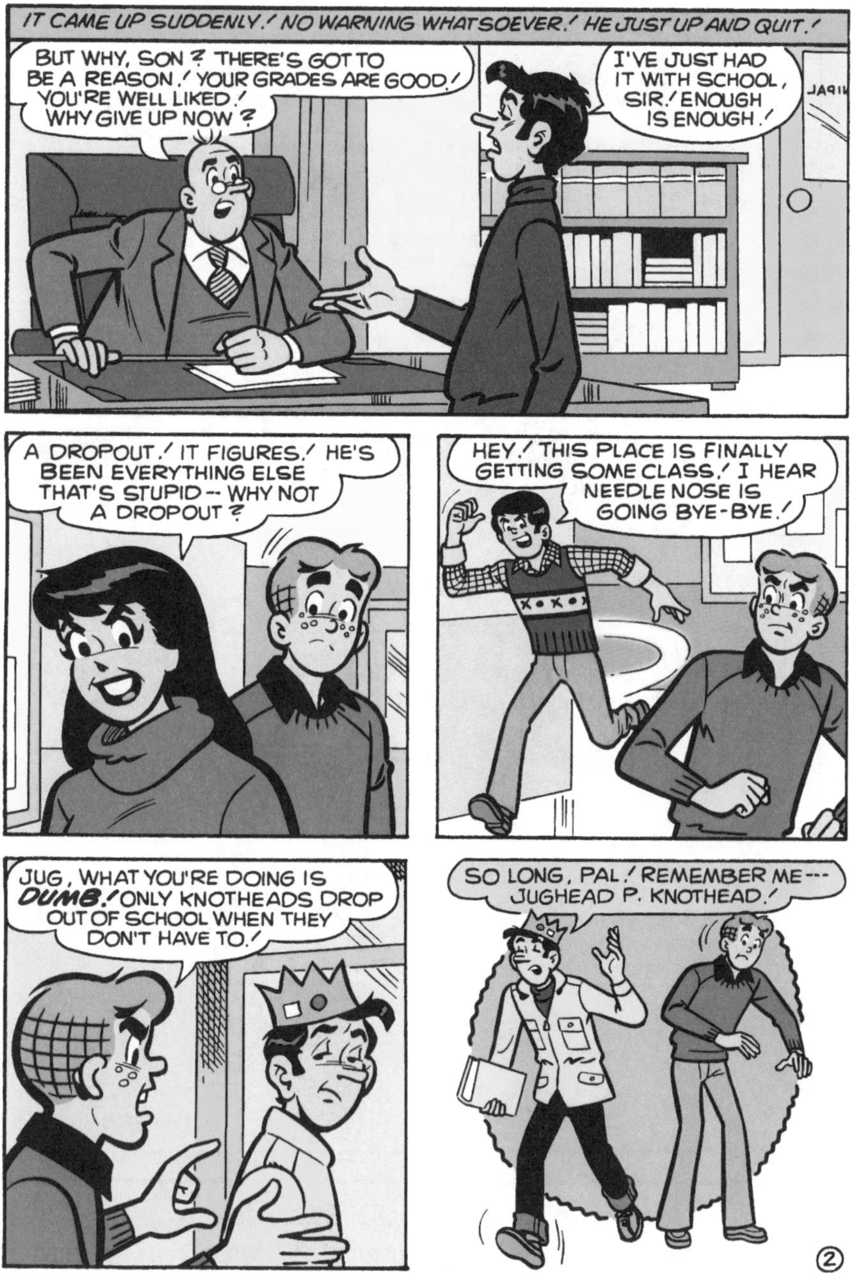
IT CAME UP SUDDENLY! NO WARNING WHATSOEVER! HE JUST UP AND QUIT!
BUT WHY, SON? THERE'S GOT TO BE A REASON! YOUR GRADES ARE GOOD! YOU'RE WELL LIKED! WHY GIVE UP NOW?
I'VE JUST HAD IT WITH SCHOOL, SIR! ENOUGH IS ENOUGH!
A DROPOUT! IT FIGURES! HE'S BEEN EVERYTHING ELSE THAT'S STUPID -- WHY NOT A DROPOUT?
HEY! THIS PLACE IS FINALLY GETTING SOME CLASS! I HEAR NEEDLE NOSE IS GOING BYE-BYE!
JUG, WHAT YOU'RE DOING IS DUMB! ONLY KNOTHEADS DROP OUT OF SCHOOL WHEN THEY DON'T HAVE TO!
SO LONG, PAL! REMEMBER ME--- JUGHEAD P. KNOTHEAD!
2

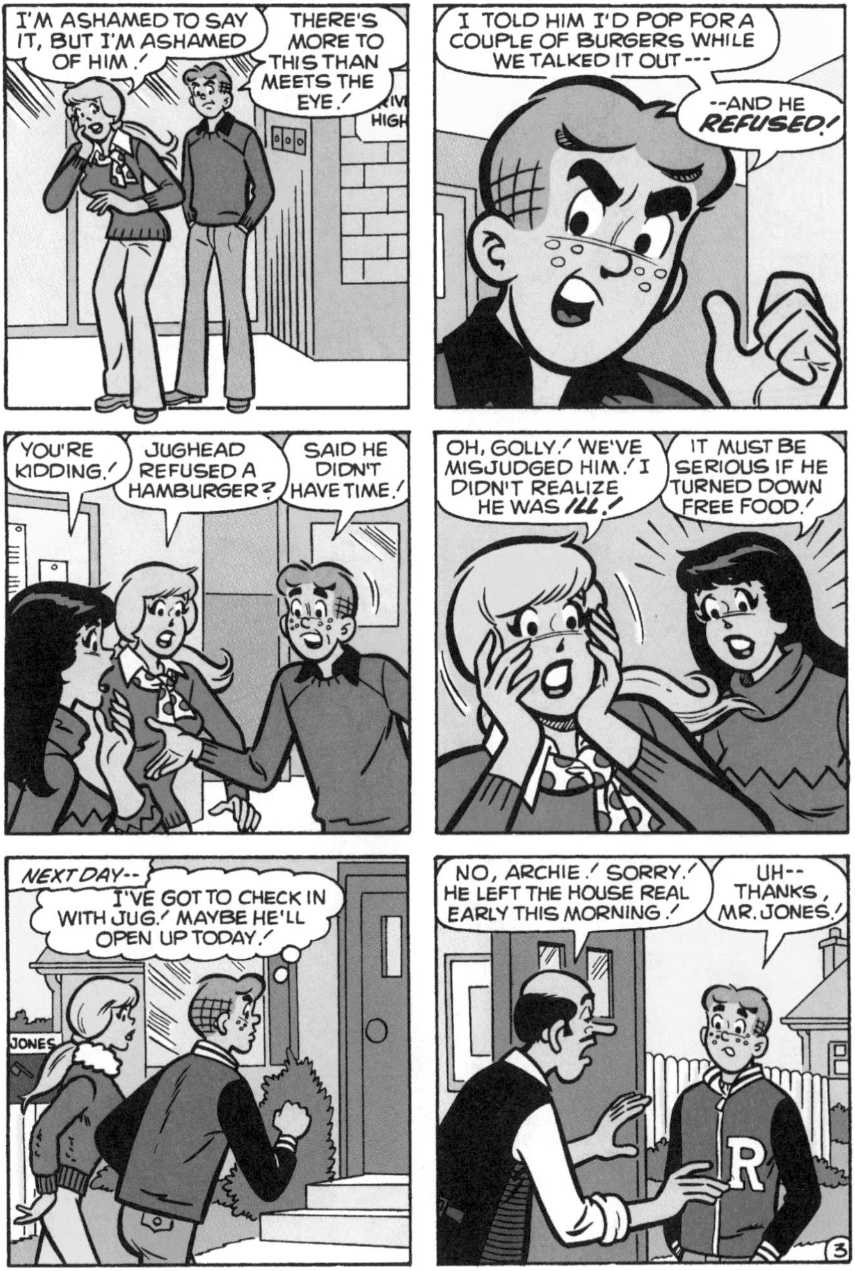
I'M ASHAMED TO SAY IT, BUT I'M ASHAMED OF HIM.!
THERE'S MORE TO THIS THAN MEETS THE EYE.!
I TOLD HIM I'D POP FOR A COUPLE OF BURGERS WHILE WE TALKED IT OUT---
--AND HE REFUSED!
YOU'RE KIDDING.!
JUGHEAD REFUSED A HAMBURGER?
SAID HE DIDN'T HAVE TIME.!
OH, GOLLY.! WE'VE MISJUDGED HIM.! I DIDN'T REALIZE HE WAS ILL!
IT MUST BE SERIOUS IF HE TURNED DOWN FREE FOOD.!
NEXT DAY--
I'VE GOT TO CHECK IN WITH JUG.! MAYBE HE'LL OPEN UP TODAY.!
JONES
NO, ARCHIE.! SORRY.! HE LEFT THE HOUSE REAL EARLY THIS MORNING.!
UH-- THANKS, MR. JONES.!
R
3

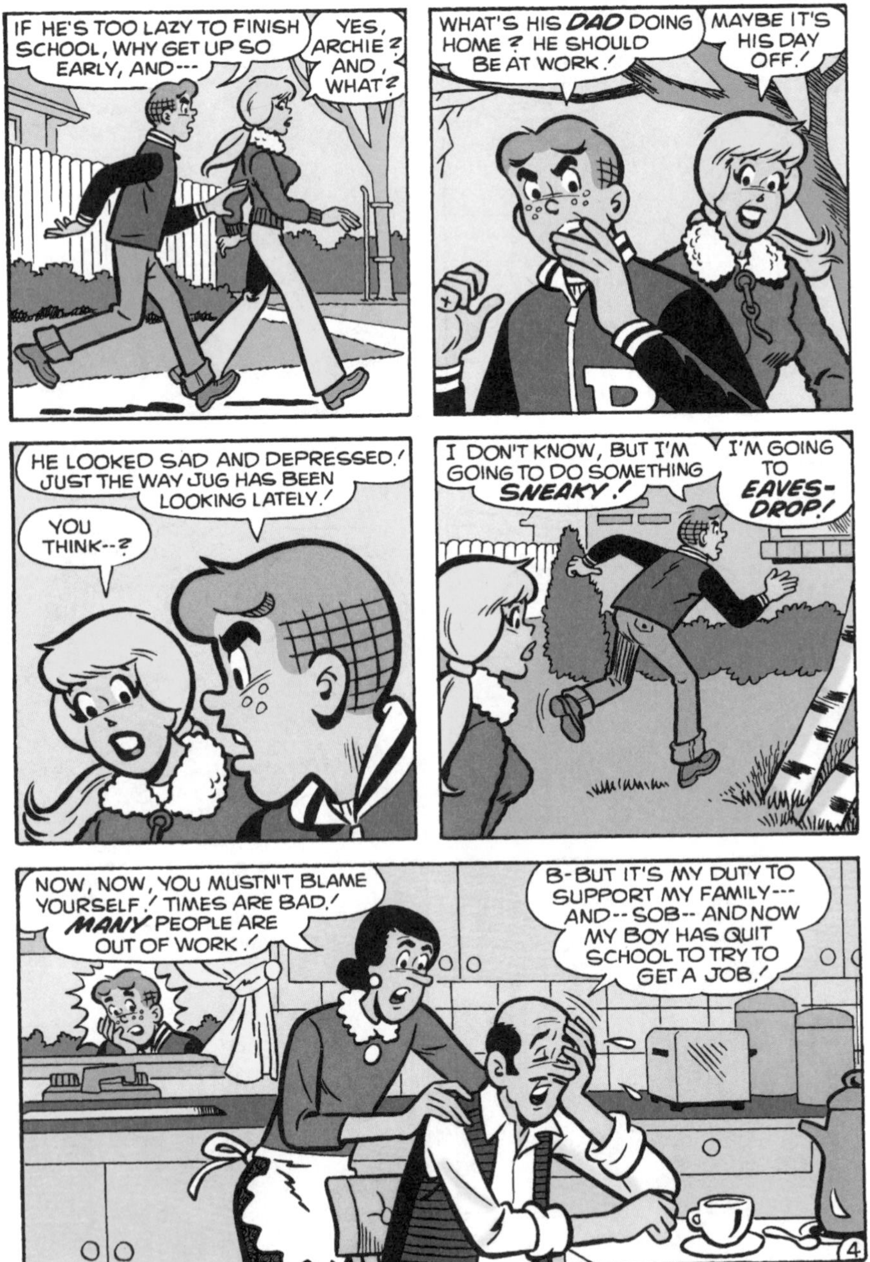
IF HE'S TOO LAZY TO FINISH SCHOOL, WHY GET UP SO EARLY, AND---
YES, ARCHIE? AND, WHAT?
WHAT'S HIS DAD DOING HOME? HE SHOULD BE AT WORK!
MAYBE IT'S HIS DAY OFF!
HE LOOKED SAD AND DEPRESSED! JUST THE WAY JUG HAS BEEN LOOKING LATELY!
YOU THINK--?
I DON'T KNOW, BUT I'M GOING TO DO SOMETHING SNEAKY!
I'M GOING TO EAVES-DROP!
NOW, NOW, YOU MUSTN'T BLAME YOURSELF! TIMES ARE BAD! MANY PEOPLE ARE OUT OF WORK!
B-BUT IT'S MY DUTY TO SUPPORT MY FAMILY--- AND--SOB-- AND NOW MY BOY HAS QUIT SCHOOL TO TRY TO GET A JOB!
4

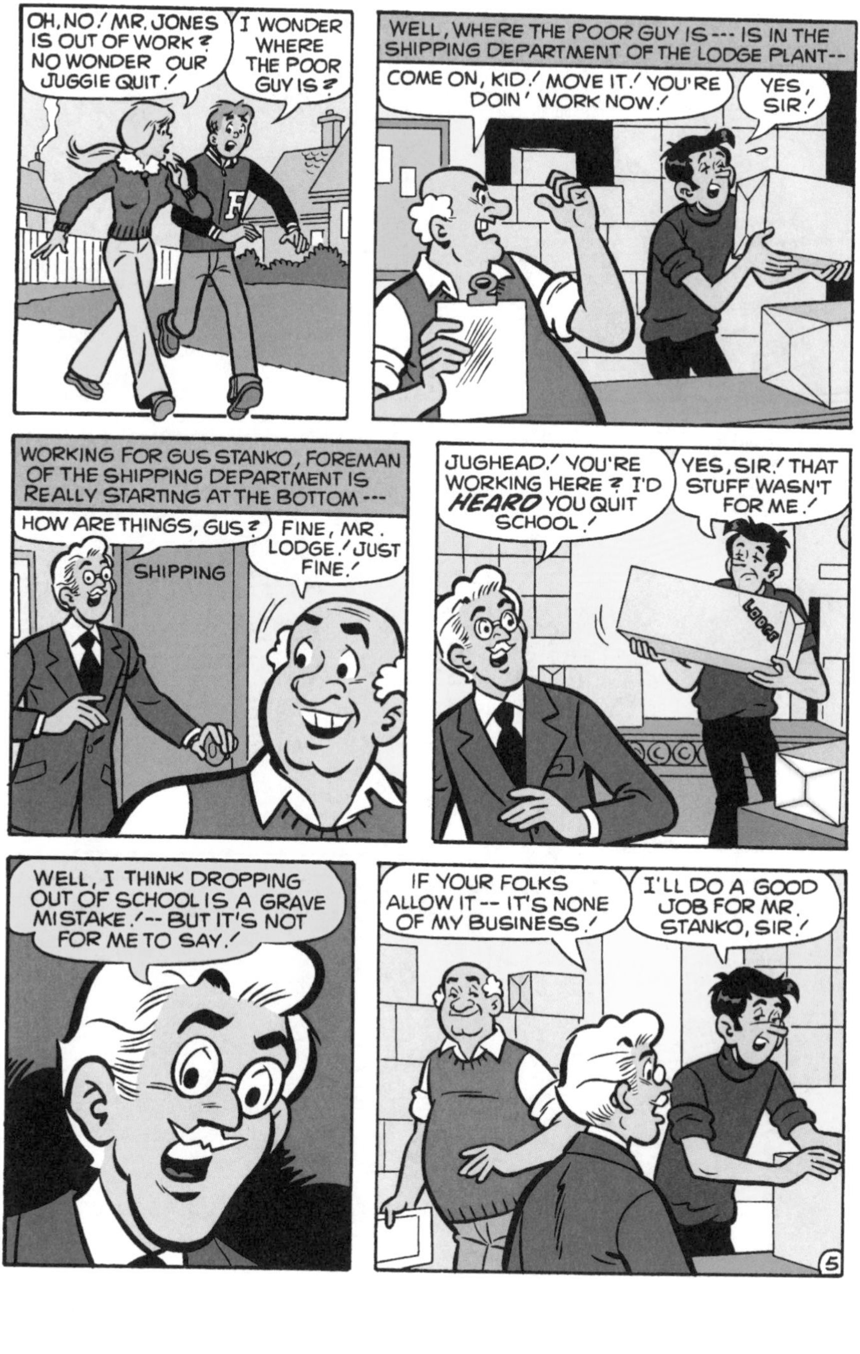
OH, NO! MR. JONES IS OUT OF WORK? NO WONDER OUR JUGGIE QUIT!
I WONDER WHERE THE POOR GUY IS?
WELL, WHERE THE POOR GUY IS --- IS IN THE SHIPPING DEPARTMENT OF THE LODGE PLANT--
COME ON, KID! MOVE IT! YOU'RE DOIN' WORK NOW!
YES, SIR!
WORKING FOR GUS STANKO, FOREMAN OF THE SHIPPING DEPARTMENT IS REALLY STARTING AT THE BOTTOM ---
HOW ARE THINGS, GUS?
SHIPPING
FINE, MR. LODGE! JUST FINE!
JUGHEAD! YOU'RE WORKING HERE? I'D HEARD YOU QUIT SCHOOL!
YES, SIR! THAT STUFF WASN'T FOR ME!
LODGE
WELL, I THINK DROPPING OUT OF SCHOOL IS A GRAVE MISTAKE! -- BUT IT'S NOT FOR ME TO SAY!
IF YOUR FOLKS ALLOW IT -- IT'S NONE OF MY BUSINESS!
I'LL DO A GOOD JOB FOR MR. STANKO, SIR!
5

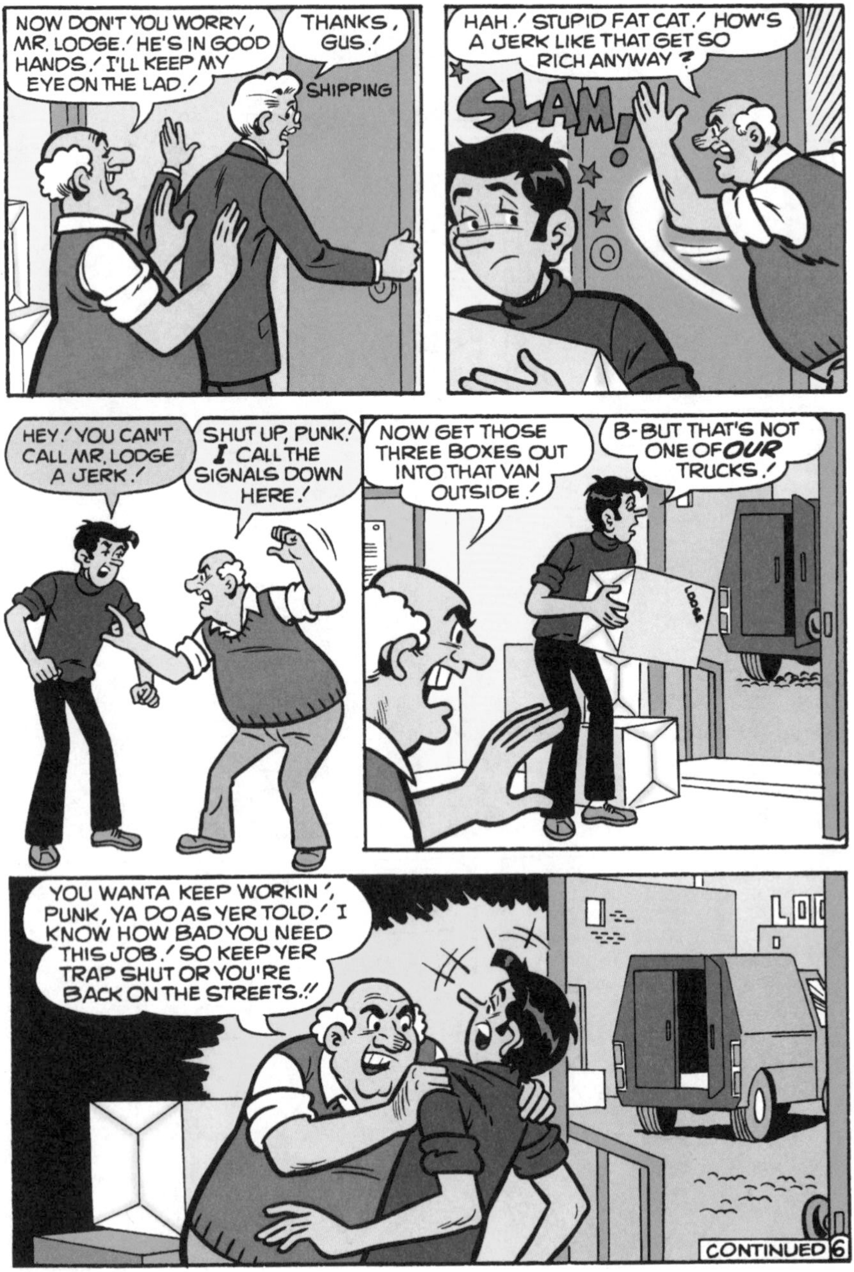
NOW DON'T YOU WORRY, MR. LODGE.' HE'S IN GOOD HANDS.' I'LL KEEP MY EYE ON THE LAD.'
THANKS, GUS.'
SHIPPING
HAH.' STUPID FAT CAT.' HOW'S A JERK LIKE THAT GET SO RICH ANYWAY?
SLAM!
HEY.' YOU CAN'T CALL MR. LODGE A JERK.'
SHUT UP, PUNK.' I CALL THE SIGNALS DOWN HERE.'
NOW GET THOSE THREE BOXES OUT INTO THAT VAN OUTSIDE.'
B-BUT THAT'S NOT ONE OF OUR TRUCKS.'
LODGE
YOU WANTA KEEP WORKIN', PUNK, YA DO AS YER TOLD.' I KNOW HOW BAD YOU NEED THIS JOB.' SO KEEP YER TRAP SHUT OR YOU'RE BACK ON THE STREETS.!!
CONTINUED 6

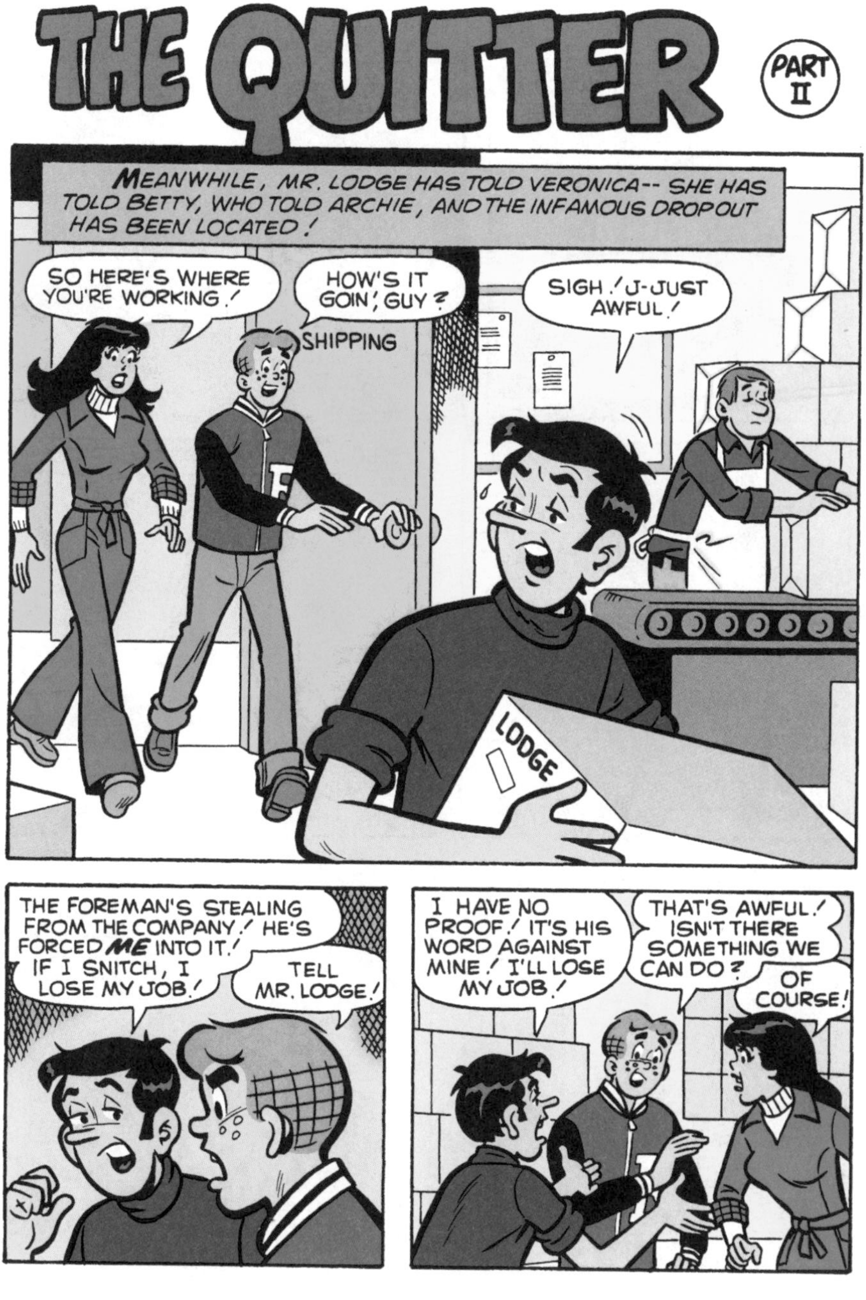
THE QUITTER
PART II
MEANWHILE, MR. LODGE HAS TOLD VERONICA-- SHE HAS TOLD BETTY, WHO TOLD ARCHIE, AND THE INFAMOUS DROPOUT HAS BEEN LOCATED!
SO HERE'S WHERE YOU'RE WORKING!
HOW'S IT GOIN', GUY?
SHIPPING
SIGH! J-JUST AWFUL!
LODGE
THE FOREMAN'S STEALING FROM THE COMPANY! HE'S FORCED ME INTO IT! IF I SNITCH, I LOSE MY JOB!
TELL MR. LODGE!
I HAVE NO PROOF! IT'S HIS WORD AGAINST MINE! I'LL LOSE MY JOB!
THAT'S AWFUL! ISN'T THERE SOMETHING WE CAN DO?
OF COURSE!

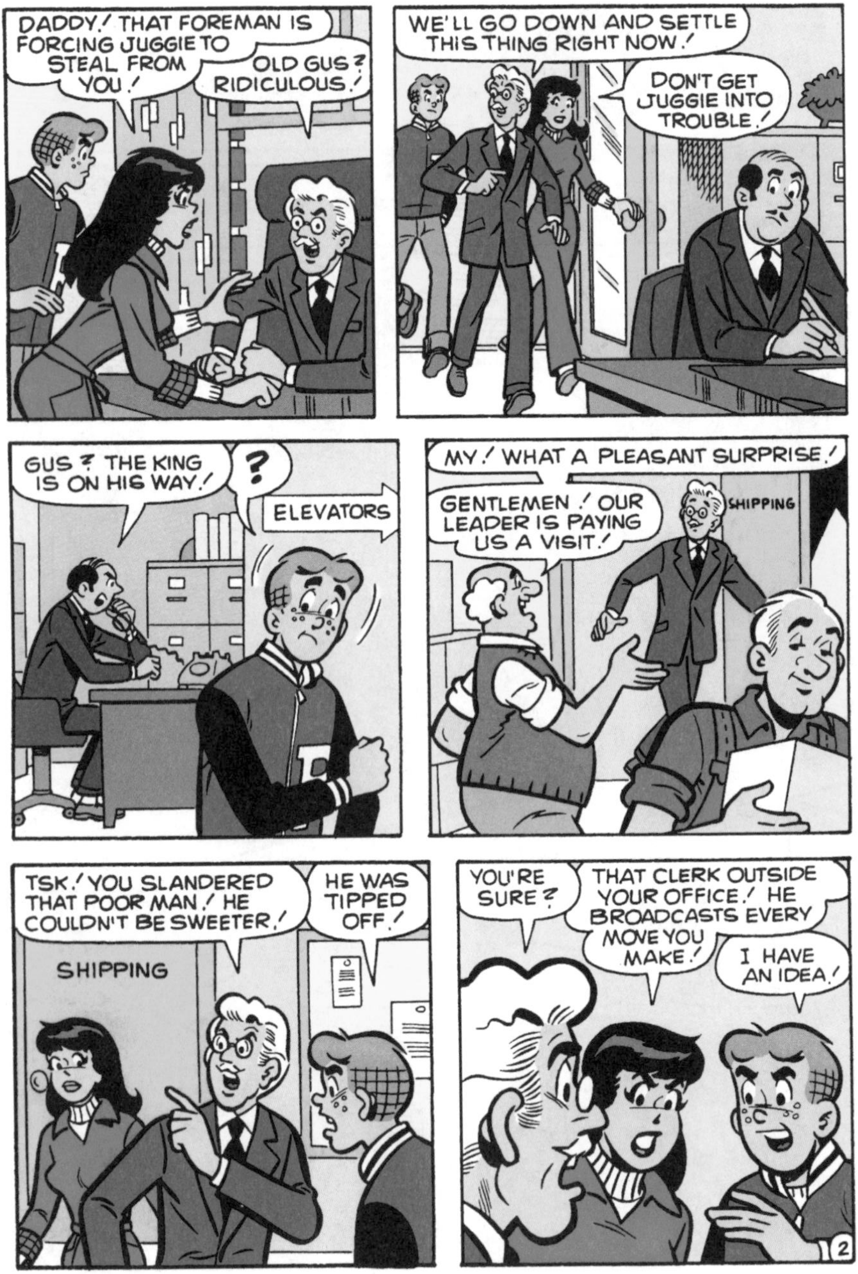
DADDY! THAT FOREMAN IS FORCING JUGGIE TO STEAL FROM YOU!
OLD GUS? RIDICULOUS!
WE'LL GO DOWN AND SETTLE THIS THING RIGHT NOW!
DON'T GET JUGGIE INTO TROUBLE!
GUS? THE KING IS ON HIS WAY!
?
ELEVATORS
MY! WHAT A PLEASANT SURPRISE!
GENTLEMEN! OUR LEADER IS PAYING US A VISIT!
SHIPPING
TSK! YOU SLANDERED THAT POOR MAN! HE COULDN'T BE SWEETER!
HE WAS TIPPED OFF!
SHIPPING
YOU'RE SURE?
THAT CLERK OUTSIDE YOUR OFFICE! HE BROADCASTS EVERY MOVE YOU MAKE!
I HAVE AN IDEA!
2

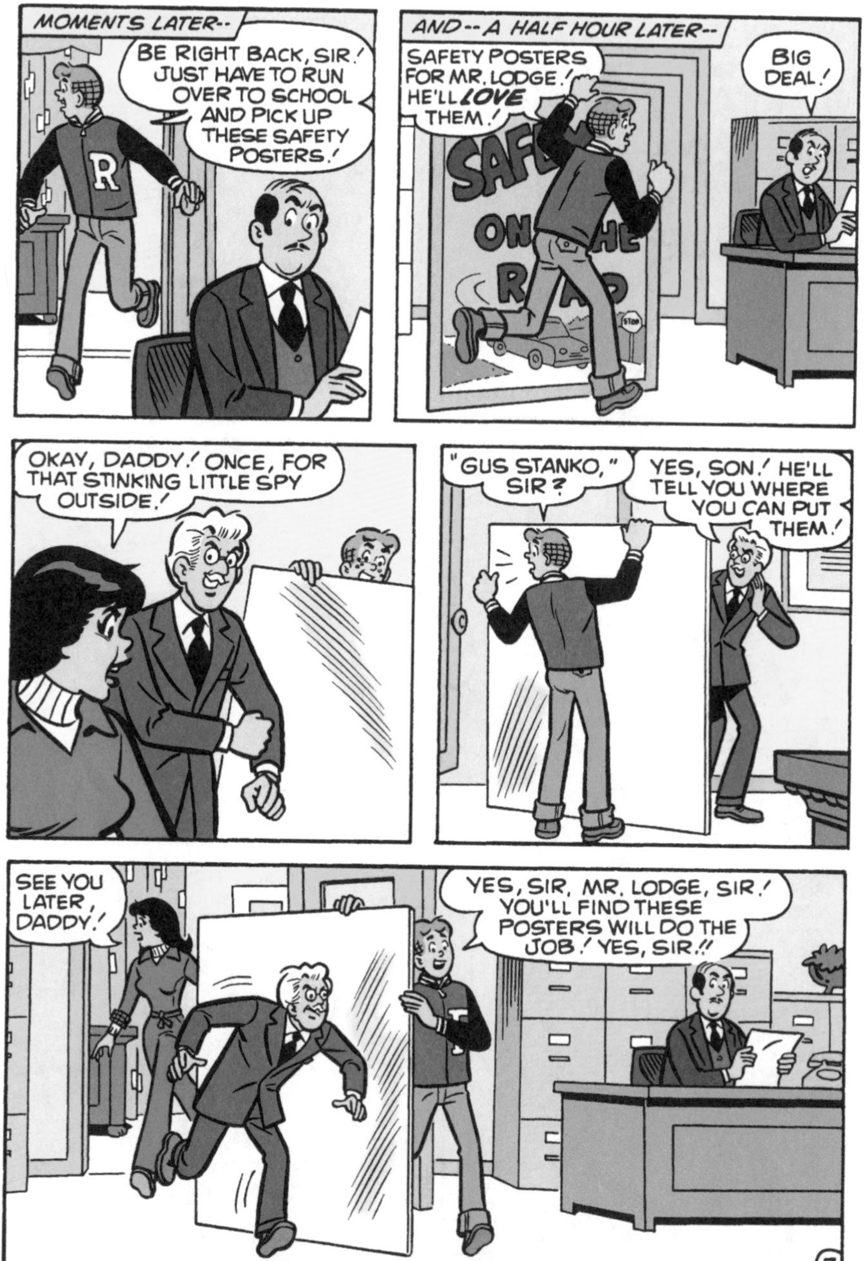
MOMENTS LATER--
BE RIGHT BACK, SIR! JUST HAVE TO RUN OVER TO SCHOOL AND PICK UP THESE SAFETY POSTERS!
AND--A HALF HOUR LATER--
SAFETY POSTERS FOR MR. LODGE! HE'LL LOVE THEM!
BIG DEAL!
OKAY, DADDY! ONCE, FOR THAT STINKING LITTLE SPY OUTSIDE!
"GUS STANKO," SIR?
YES, SON! HE'LL TELL YOU WHERE YOU CAN PUT THEM!
SEE YOU LATER, DADDY!
YES, SIR, MR. LODGE, SIR! YOU'LL FIND THESE POSTERS WILL DO THE JOB! YES, SIR!!
3

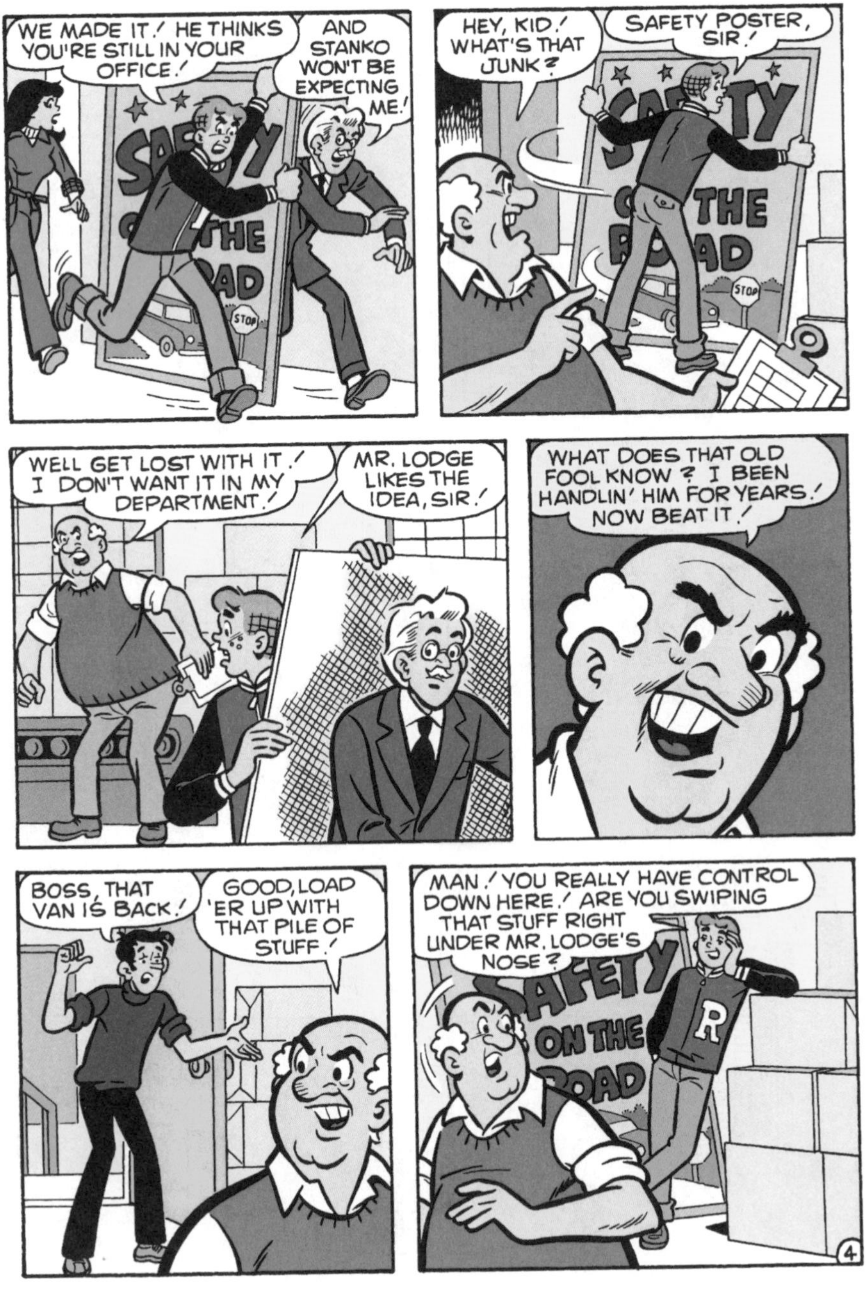
WE MADE IT! HE THINKS YOU'RE STILL IN YOUR OFFICE!
AND STANKO WON'T BE EXPECTING ME!
SAFETY ON THE ROAD
STOP
HEY, KID! WHAT'S THAT JUNK?
SAFETY POSTER, SIR!
WELL GET LOST WITH IT! I DON'T WANT IT IN MY DEPARTMENT!
MR. LODGE LIKES THE IDEA, SIR!
WHAT DOES THAT OLD FOOL KNOW? I BEEN HANDLIN' HIM FOR YEARS! NOW BEAT IT!
BOSS, THAT VAN IS BACK!
GOOD, LOAD 'ER UP WITH THAT PILE OF STUFF!
MAN! YOU REALLY HAVE CONTROL DOWN HERE! ARE YOU SWIPING THAT STUFF RIGHT UNDER MR. LODGE'S NOSE?
SAFETY ON THE ROAD
R
4

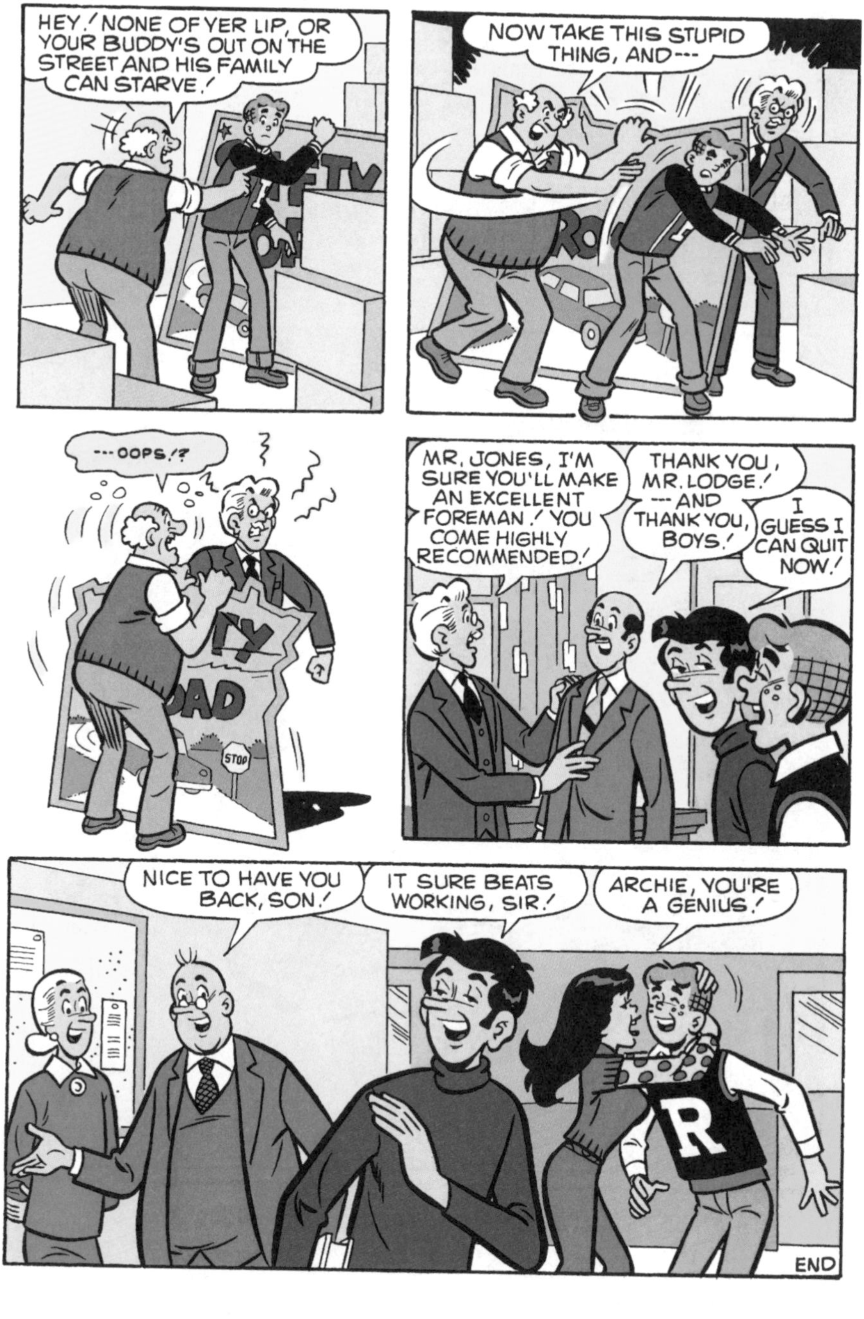
HEY! NONE OF YER LIP, OR YOUR BUDDY'S OUT ON THE STREET AND HIS FAMILY CAN STARVE!
NOW TAKE THIS STUPID THING, AND---
---OOPS!?
MR. JONES, I'M SURE YOU'LL MAKE AN EXCELLENT FOREMAN! YOU COME HIGHLY RECOMMENDED!
THANK YOU, MR. LODGE! --- AND THANK YOU, BOYS!
I GUESS I CAN QUIT NOW!
NICE TO HAVE YOU BACK, SON!
IT SURE BEATS WORKING, SIR!
ARCHIE, YOU'RE A GENIUS!
STOP
END

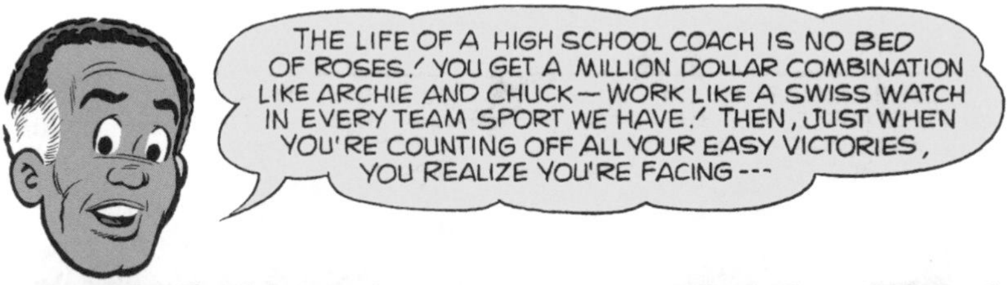
THE LIFE OF A HIGH SCHOOL COACH IS NO BED OF ROSES.! YOU GET A MILLION DOLLAR COMBINATION LIKE ARCHIE AND CHUCK— WORK LIKE A SWISS WATCH IN EVERY TEAM SPORT WE HAVE.! THEN, JUST WHEN YOU'RE COUNTING OFF ALL YOUR EASY VICTORIES, YOU REALIZE YOU'RE FACING---

DEFEAT FROM WITHIN

PART I

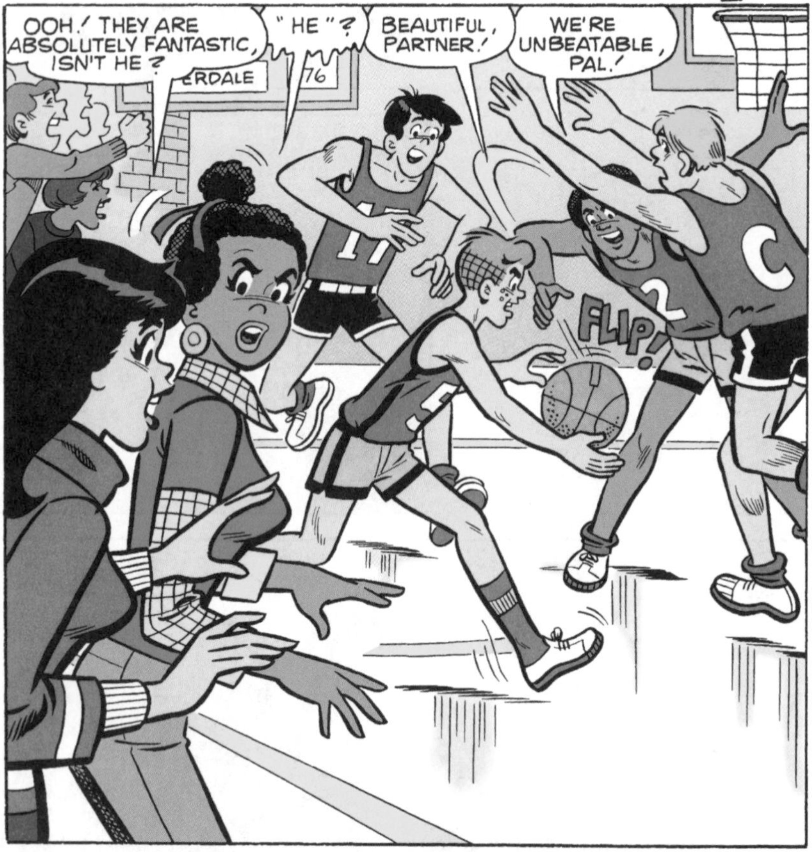
OOH.! THEY ARE ABSOLUTELY FANTASTIC, ISN'T HE ?
" HE "?
BEAUTIFUL, PARTNER.!
WE'RE UNBEATABLE, PAL.!
FLIP!

Story: Frank Doyle Pencils: Stan Goldberg
Inks: Jon D'Agostino Letters: Bill Yoshida

Originally printed in ARCHIE AT RIVERDALE HIGH #55, JULY 1978

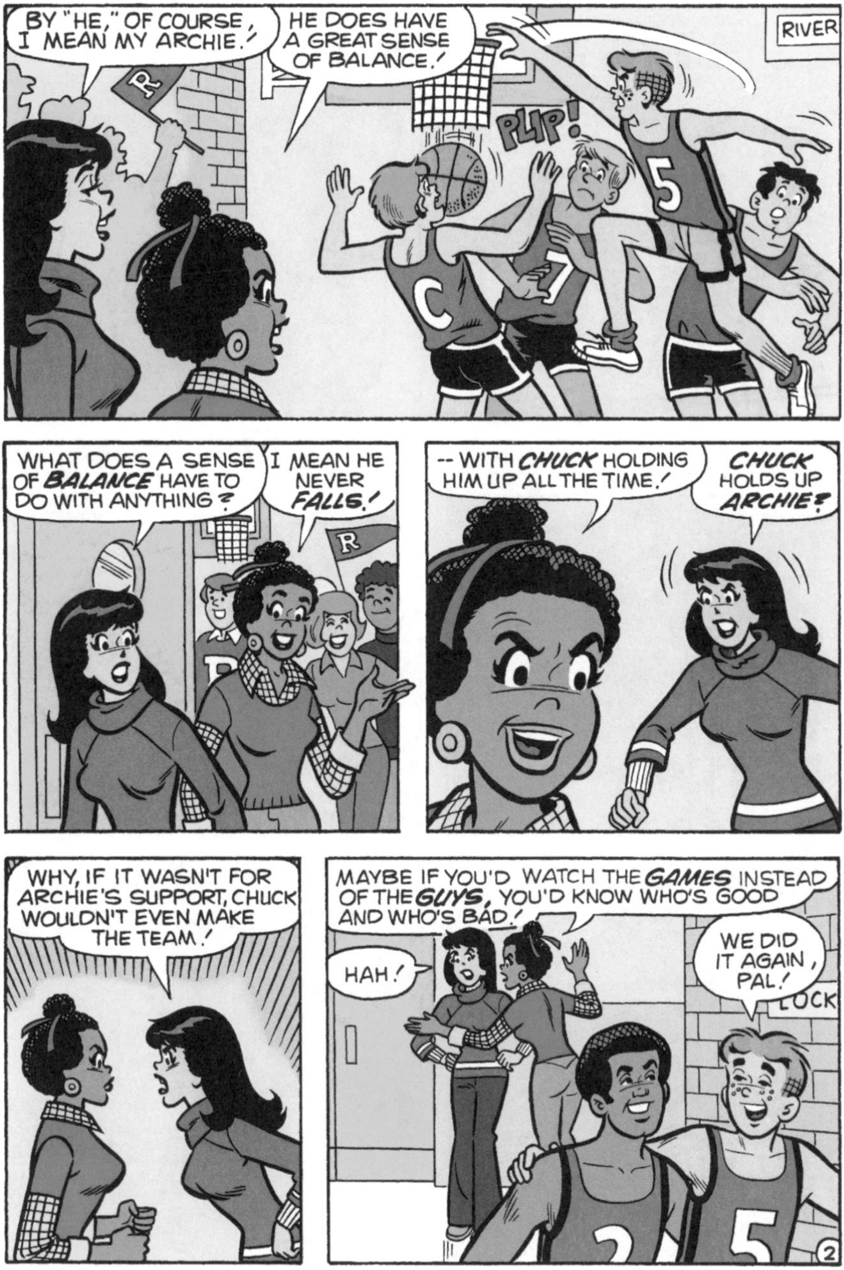
BY "HE," OF COURSE, I MEAN MY ARCHIE.!
HE DOES HAVE A GREAT SENSE OF BALANCE.!
RIVER
PLIP!
WHAT DOES A SENSE OF BALANCE HAVE TO DO WITH ANYTHING?
I MEAN HE NEVER FALLS.!
-- WITH CHUCK HOLDING HIM UP ALL THE TIME.!
CHUCK HOLDS UP ARCHIE?
WHY, IF IT WASN'T FOR ARCHIE'S SUPPORT, CHUCK WOULDN'T EVEN MAKE THE TEAM.!
MAYBE IF YOU'D WATCH THE GAMES INSTEAD OF THE GUYS, YOU'D KNOW WHO'S GOOD AND WHO'S BAD.!
HAH!
WE DID IT AGAIN, PAL!
LOCK
2

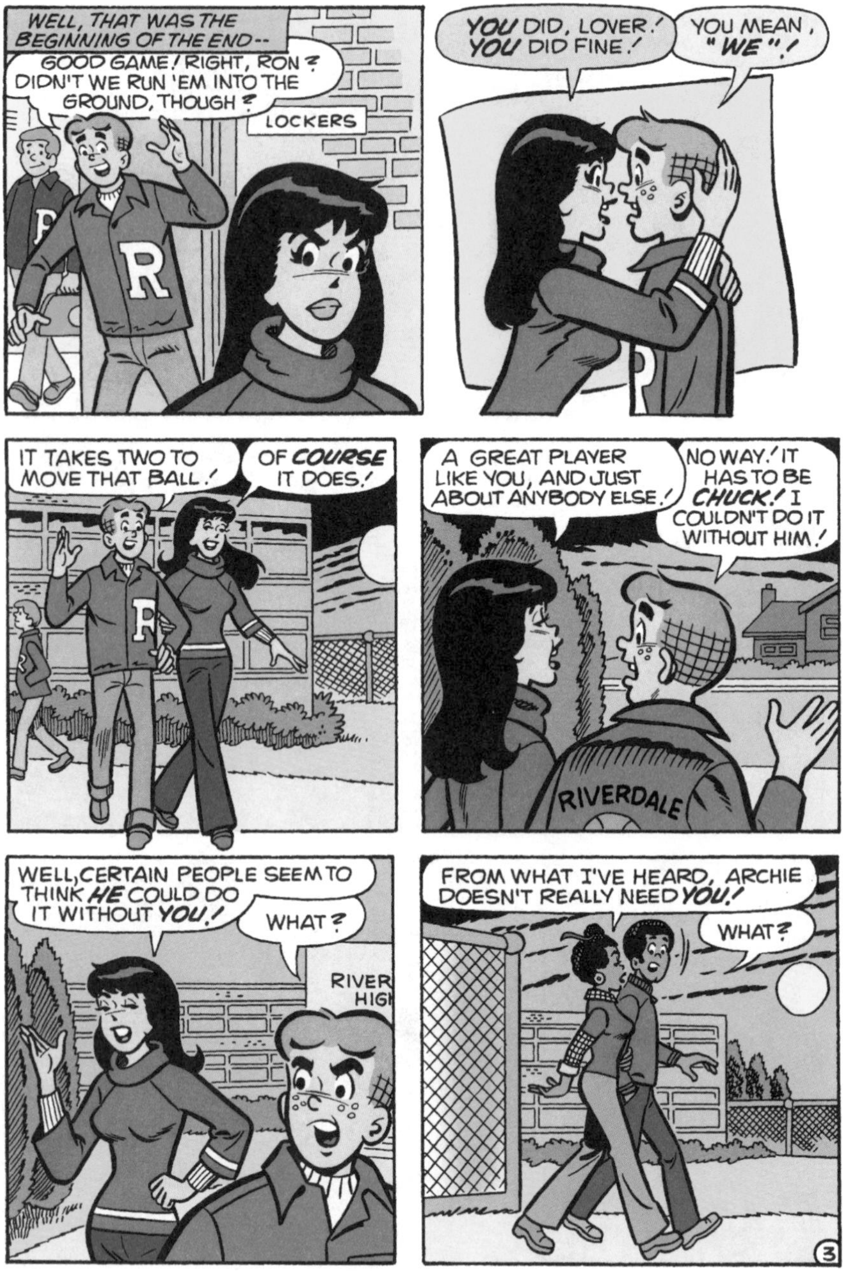
WELL, THAT WAS THE BEGINNING OF THE END--
GOOD GAME! RIGHT, RON? DIDN'T WE RUN 'EM INTO THE GROUND, THOUGH?
LOCKERS
YOU DID, LOVER! YOU DID FINE!
YOU MEAN, "WE"!
IT TAKES TWO TO MOVE THAT BALL!
OF COURSE IT DOES!
A GREAT PLAYER LIKE YOU, AND JUST ABOUT ANYBODY ELSE!
NO WAY! IT HAS TO BE CHUCK! I COULDN'T DO IT WITHOUT HIM!
RIVERDALE
WELL, CERTAIN PEOPLE SEEM TO THINK HE COULD DO IT WITHOUT YOU!
WHAT?
RIVER HIGH
FROM WHAT I'VE HEARD, ARCHIE DOESN'T REALLY NEED YOU!
WHAT?
3

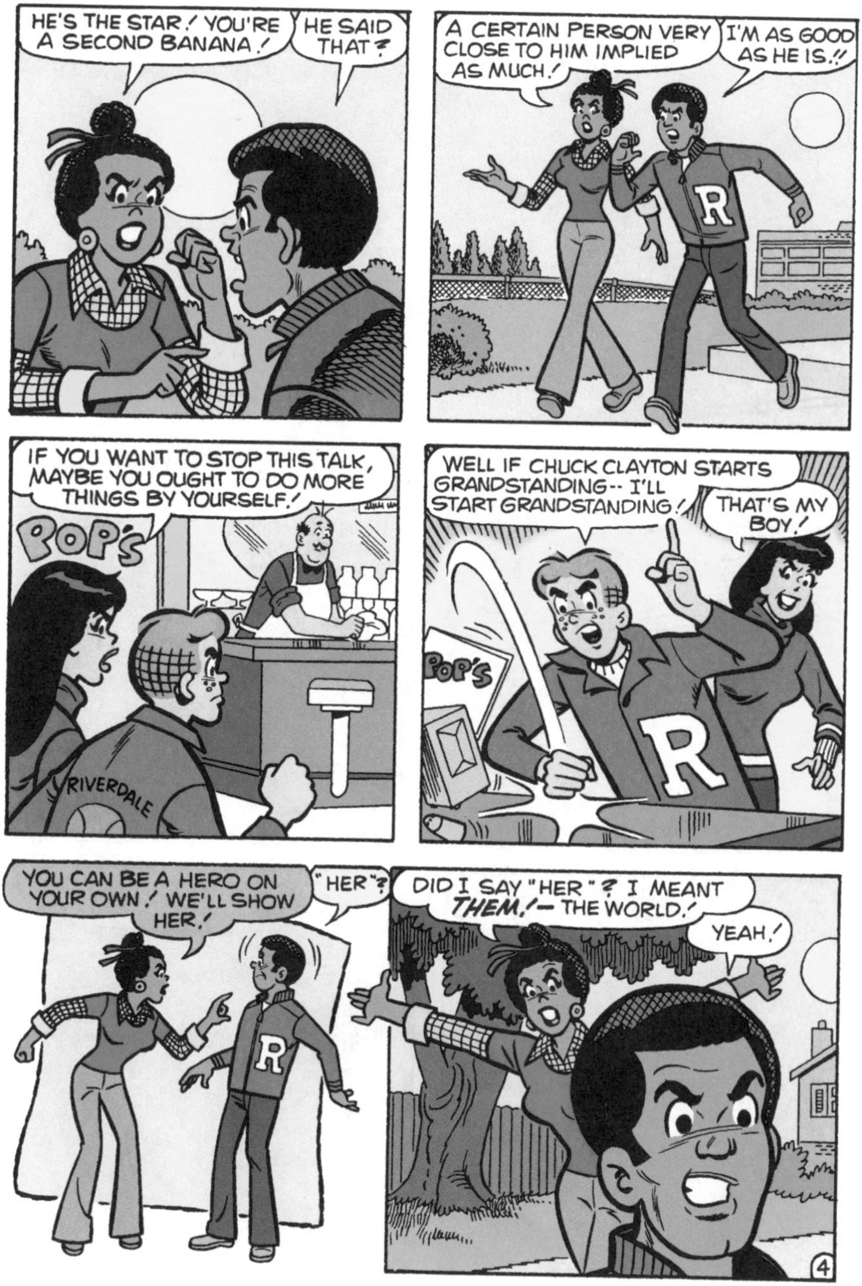
HE'S THE STAR! YOU'RE A SECOND BANANA!
HE SAID THAT?
A CERTAIN PERSON VERY CLOSE TO HIM IMPLIED AS MUCH!
I'M AS GOOD AS HE IS!!
IF YOU WANT TO STOP THIS TALK, MAYBE YOU OUGHT TO DO MORE THINGS BY YOURSELF!
POP'S
RIVERDALE
WELL IF CHUCK CLAYTON STARTS GRANDSTANDING-- I'LL START GRANDSTANDING!
THAT'S MY BOY!
POP'S
YOU CAN BE A HERO ON YOUR OWN! WE'LL SHOW HER!
"HER"?
DID I SAY "HER"? I MEANT *THEM!*— THE WORLD!
YEAH!
4

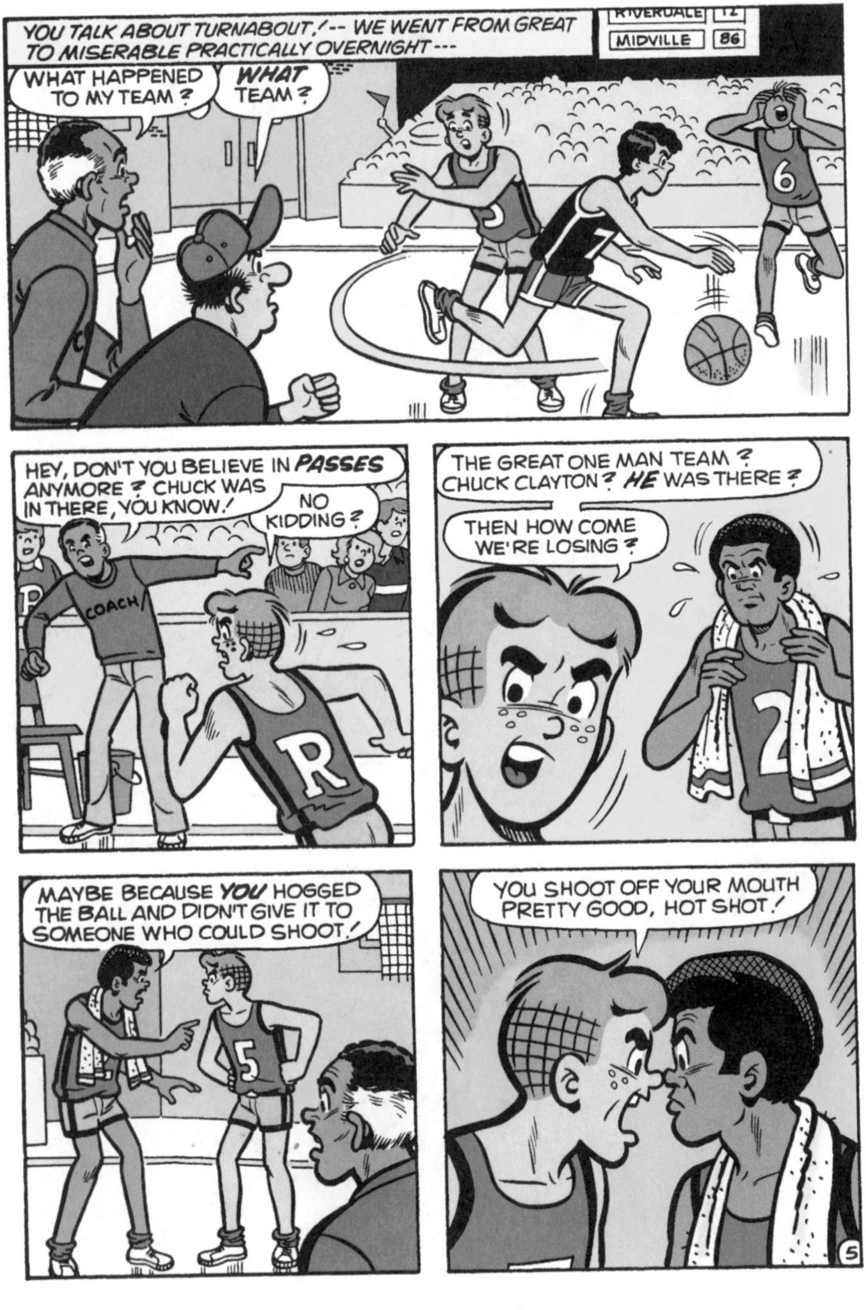
YOU TALK ABOUT TURNABOUT!-- WE WENT FROM GREAT TO MISERABLE PRACTICALLY OVERNIGHT---
MIDVILLE 86
WHAT HAPPENED TO MY TEAM?
WHAT TEAM?
COACH
HEY, DON'T YOU BELIEVE IN PASSES ANYMORE? CHUCK WAS IN THERE, YOU KNOW!
NO KIDDING?
THE GREAT ONE MAN TEAM? CHUCK CLAYTON? HE WAS THERE?
THEN HOW COME WE'RE LOSING?
MAYBE BECAUSE YOU HOGGED THE BALL AND DIDN'T GIVE IT TO SOMEONE WHO COULD SHOOT!
YOU SHOOT OFF YOUR MOUTH PRETTY GOOD, HOT SHOT!
5

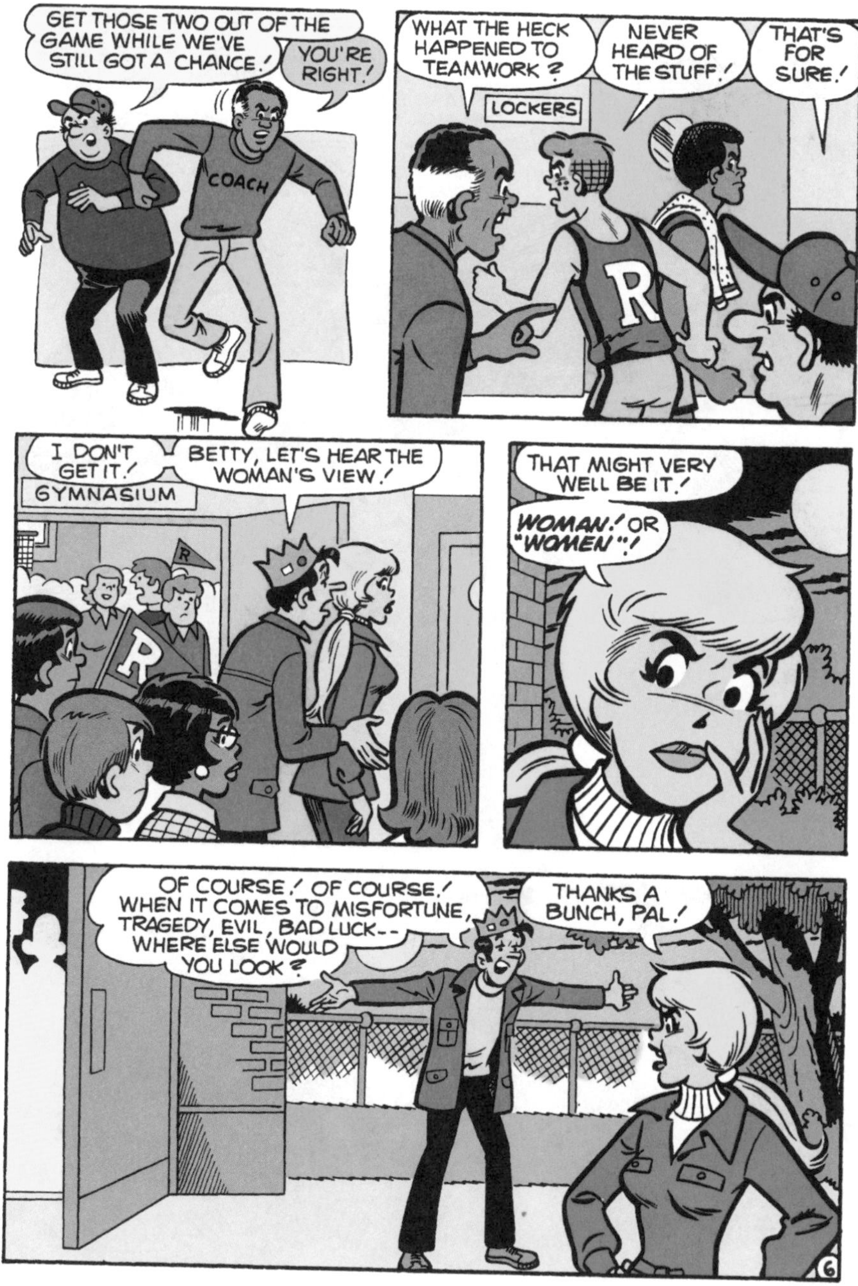
GET THOSE TWO OUT OF THE GAME WHILE WE'VE STILL GOT A CHANCE!
YOU'RE RIGHT!
COACH
WHAT THE HECK HAPPENED TO TEAMWORK?
LOCKERS
NEVER HEARD OF THE STUFF!
THAT'S FOR SURE!
R
I DON'T GET IT!
BETTY, LET'S HEAR THE WOMAN'S VIEW!
GYMNASIUM
R
R
THAT MIGHT VERY WELL BE IT!
WOMAN! OR "WOMEN"!
OF COURSE! OF COURSE! WHEN IT COMES TO MISFORTUNE, TRAGEDY, EVIL, BAD LUCK-- WHERE ELSE WOULD YOU LOOK?
THANKS A BUNCH, PAL!
6

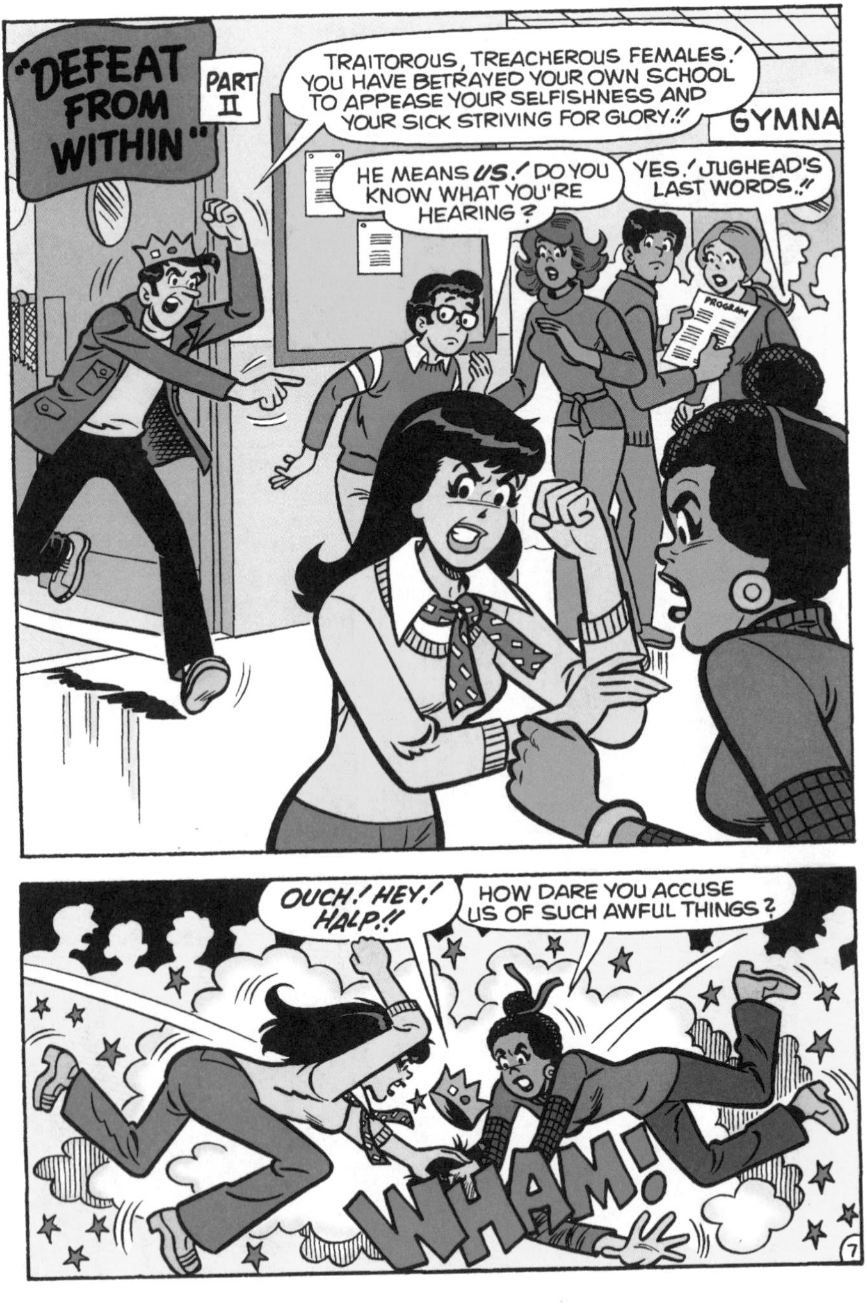
"DEFEAT FROM WITHIN"
PART II
TRAITOROUS, TREACHEROUS FEMALES! YOU HAVE BETRAYED YOUR OWN SCHOOL TO APPEASE YOUR SELFISHNESS AND YOUR SICK STRIVING FOR GLORY!!
GYMNA
HE MEANS US! DO YOU KNOW WHAT YOU'RE HEARING?
YES! JUGHEAD'S LAST WORDS!!
PROGRAM
OUCH! HEY! HALP!!
HOW DARE YOU ACCUSE US OF SUCH AWFUL THINGS?
WHAM!

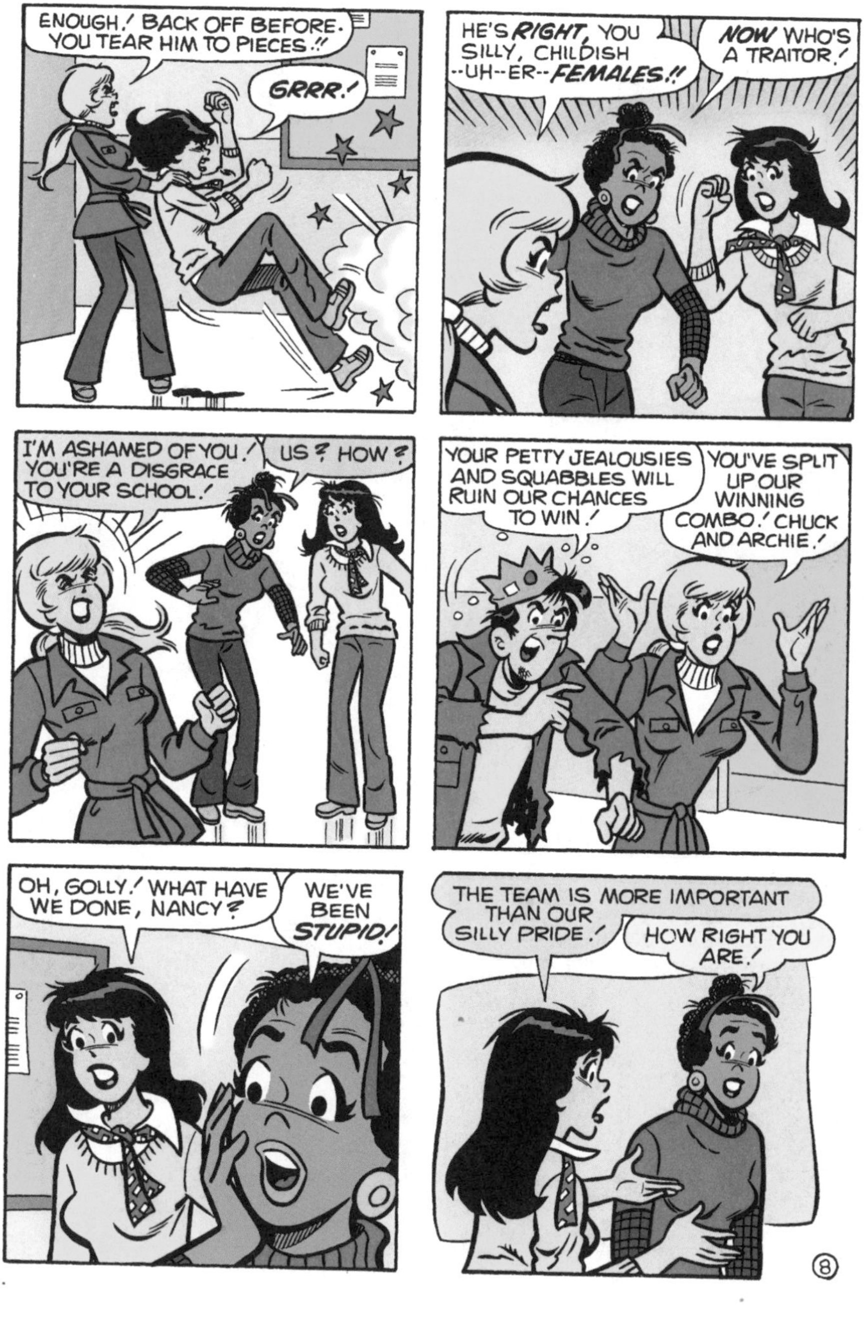
ENOUGH! BACK OFF BEFORE YOU TEAR HIM TO PIECES!!
GRRR!
HE'S RIGHT, YOU SILLY, CHILDISH --UH--ER--FEMALES!!
NOW WHO'S A TRAITOR!
I'M ASHAMED OF YOU! YOU'RE A DISGRACE TO YOUR SCHOOL!
US? HOW?
YOUR PETTY JEALOUSIES AND SQUABBLES WILL RUIN OUR CHANCES TO WIN!
YOU'VE SPLIT UP OUR WINNING COMBO! CHUCK AND ARCHIE!
OH, GOLLY! WHAT HAVE WE DONE, NANCY?
WE'VE BEEN STUPID!
THE TEAM IS MORE IMPORTANT THAN OUR SILLY PRIDE!
HOW RIGHT YOU ARE!
8

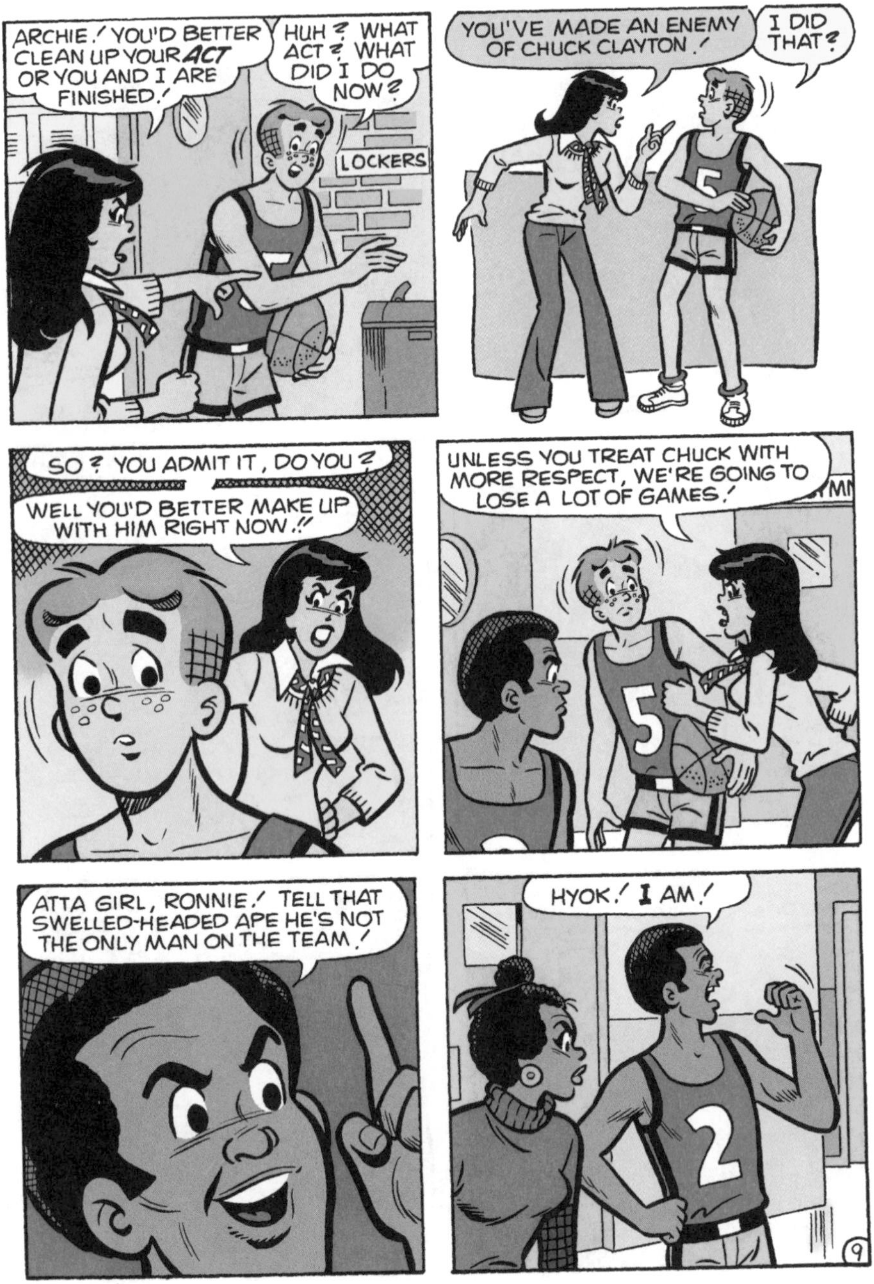
ARCHIE! YOU'D BETTER CLEAN UP YOUR ACT OR YOU AND I ARE FINISHED!
HUH? WHAT ACT? WHAT DID I DO NOW?
LOCKERS
YOU'VE MADE AN ENEMY OF CHUCK CLAYTON!
I DID THAT?
SO? YOU ADMIT IT, DO YOU?
WELL YOU'D BETTER MAKE UP WITH HIM RIGHT NOW!!
UNLESS YOU TREAT CHUCK WITH MORE RESPECT, WE'RE GOING TO LOSE A LOT OF GAMES!
5
ATTA GIRL, RONNIE! TELL THAT SWELLED-HEADED APE HE'S NOT THE ONLY MAN ON THE TEAM!
HYOK! I AM!
2
9

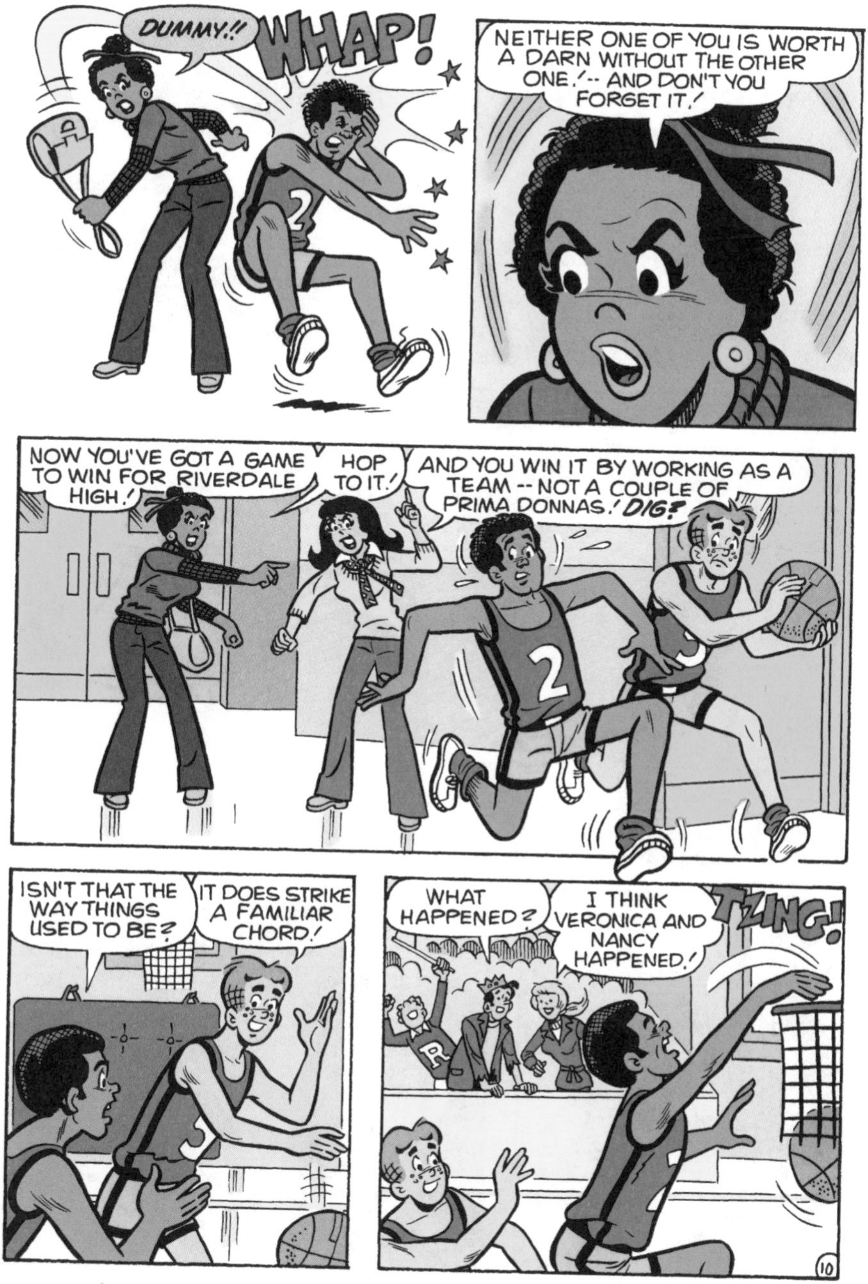
DUMMY.!!
WHAP!
NEITHER ONE OF YOU IS WORTH A DARN WITHOUT THE OTHER ONE.!-- AND DON'T YOU FORGET IT.!
NOW YOU'VE GOT A GAME TO WIN FOR RIVERDALE HIGH.!
HOP TO IT.!
AND YOU WIN IT BY WORKING AS A TEAM -- NOT A COUPLE OF PRIMA DONNAS.! DIG?
ISN'T THAT THE WAY THINGS USED TO BE?
IT DOES STRIKE A FAMILIAR CHORD.!
WHAT HAPPENED?
I THINK VERONICA AND NANCY HAPPENED.!
TZING!!
10

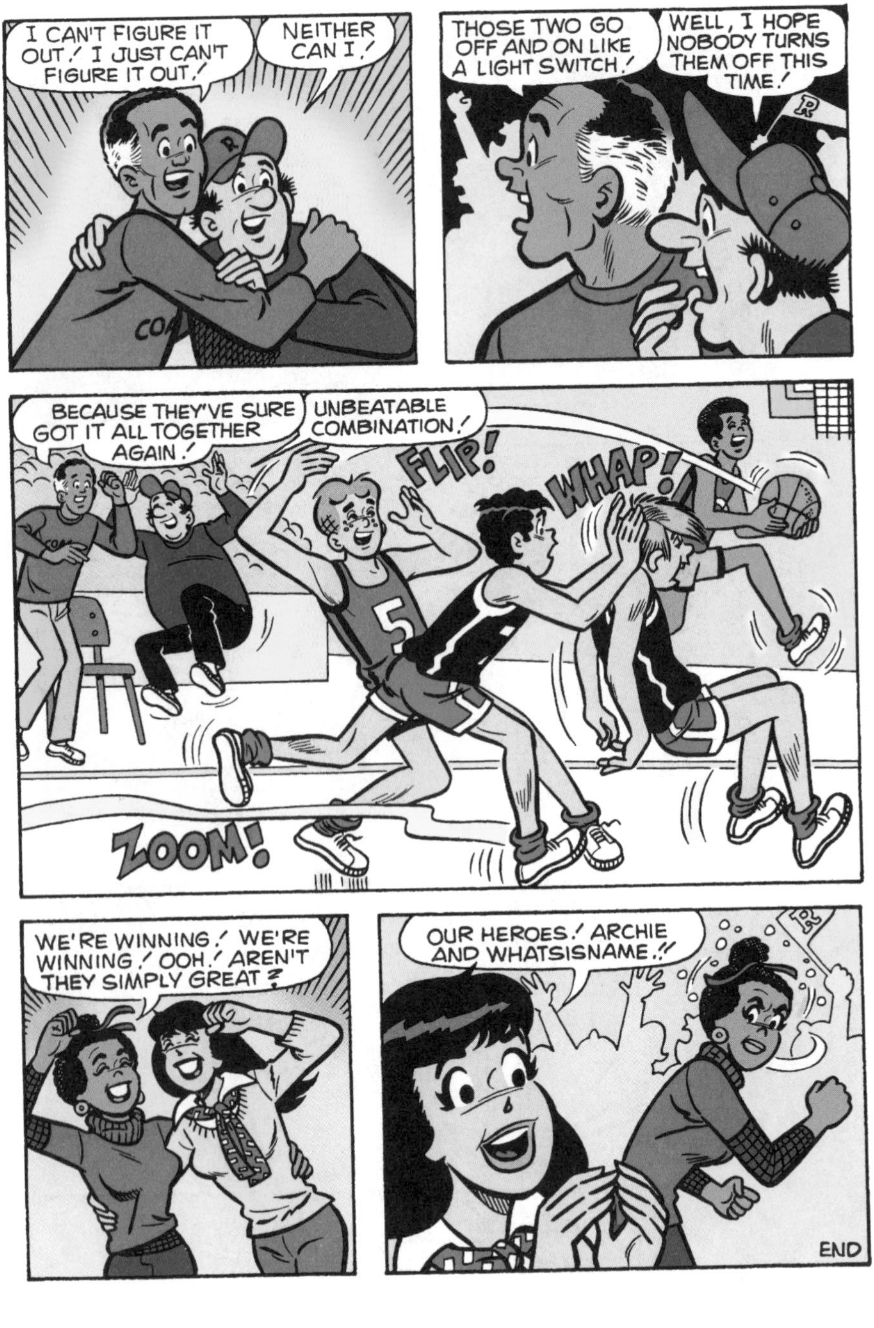
I CAN'T FIGURE IT OUT! I JUST CAN'T FIGURE IT OUT!
NEITHER CAN I!
THOSE TWO GO OFF AND ON LIKE A LIGHT SWITCH!
WELL, I HOPE NOBODY TURNS THEM OFF THIS TIME!
BECAUSE THEY'VE SURE GOT IT ALL TOGETHER AGAIN!
UNBEATABLE COMBINATION!
FLIP!
WHAP!
ZOOM!
WE'RE WINNING! WE'RE WINNING! OOH! AREN'T THEY SIMPLY GREAT?
OUR HEROES! ARCHIE AND WHATSISNAME!!
END

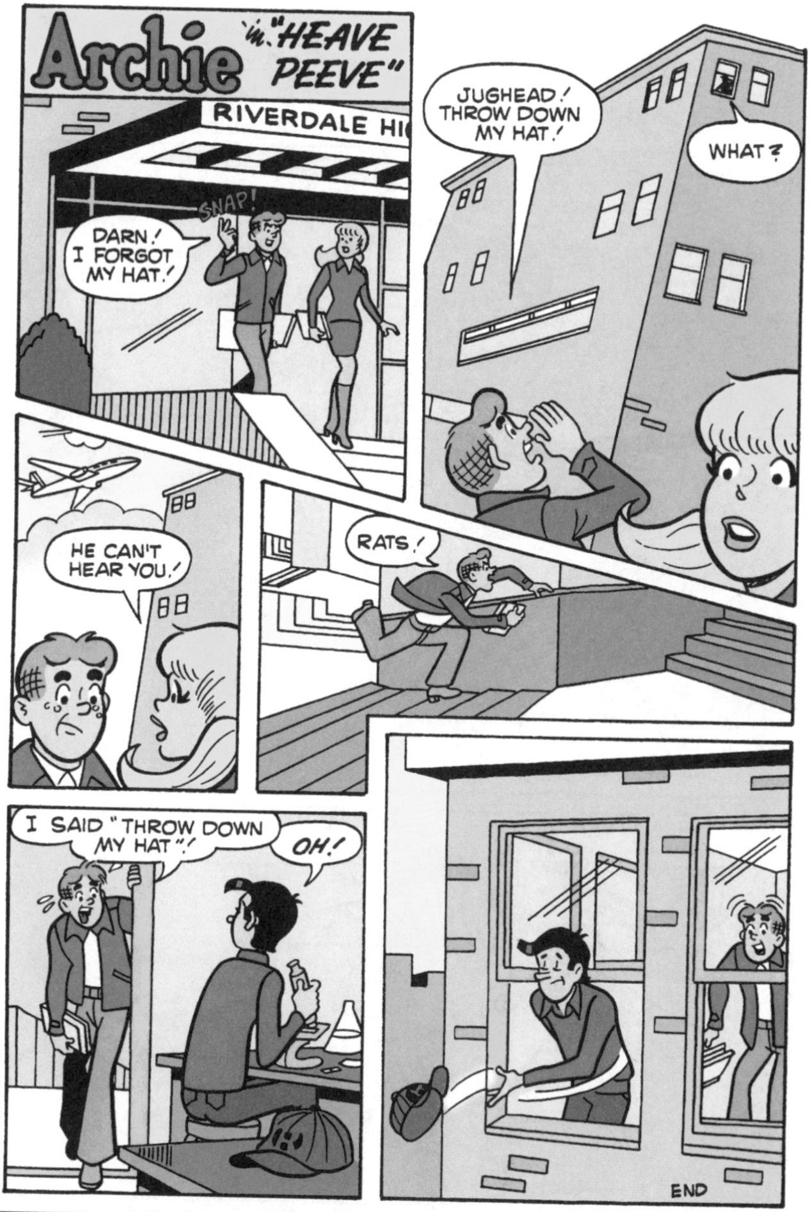
Archie in "HEAVE PEEVE"
RIVERDALE HIG
SNAP!
DARN! I FORGOT MY HAT!
JUGHEAD! THROW DOWN MY HAT!
WHAT?
HE CAN'T HEAR YOU!
RATS!
I SAID "THROW DOWN MY HAT"!
OH!
END

Story: George Gladir Pencils: Bob Bolling
Inks: Rudy Lapick Letters: Bill Yoshida

Originally printed in ARCHIE AT RIVERDALE HIGH #64, JULY 1979

Archie AT RIVERDALE "TWO FOR TEASE"

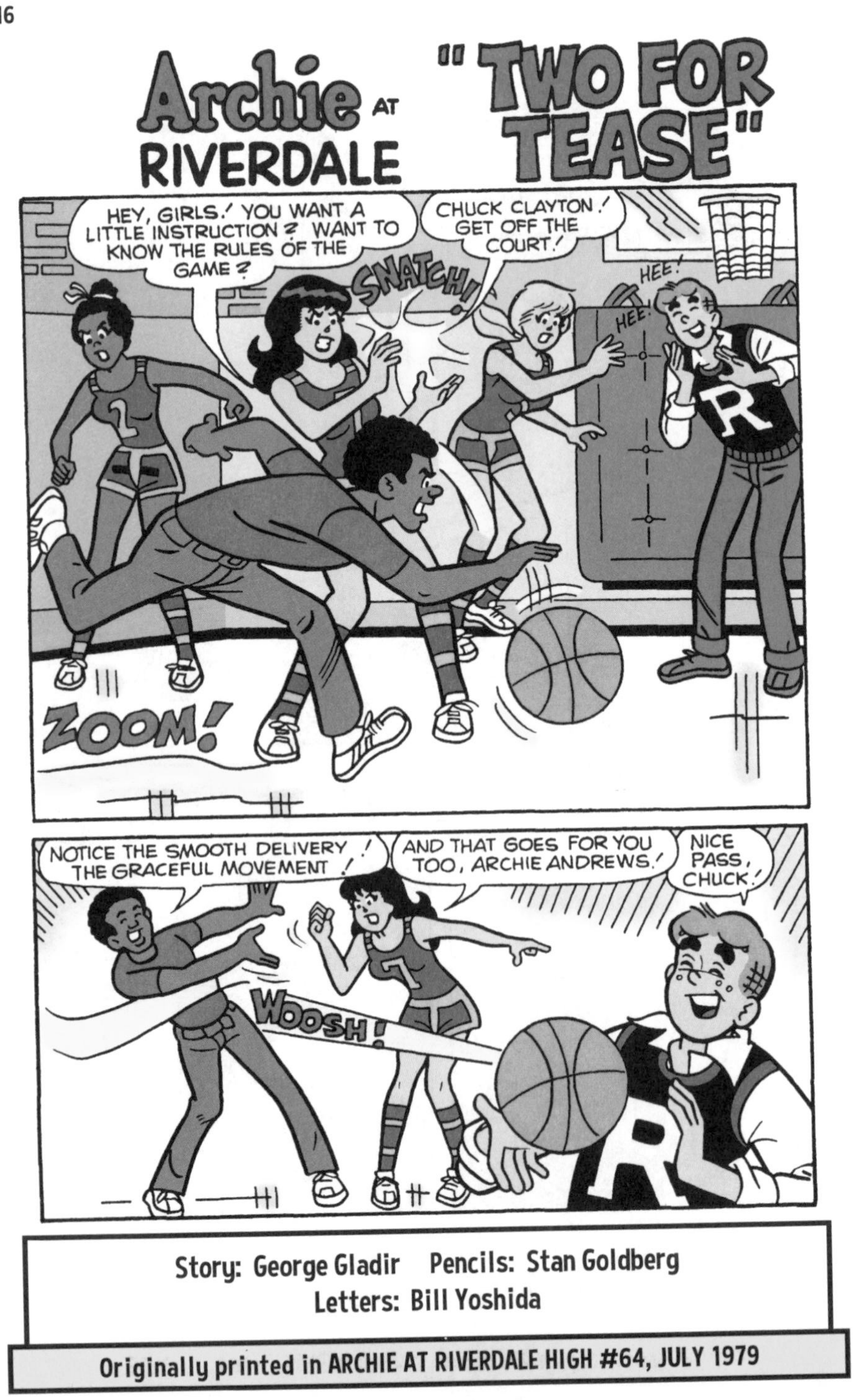
HEY, GIRLS! YOU WANT A LITTLE INSTRUCTION? WANT TO KNOW THE RULES OF THE GAME?
CHUCK CLAYTON! GET OFF THE COURT!
SNATCH!
HEE!
HEE!
ZOOM!
NOTICE THE SMOOTH DELIVERY! THE GRACEFUL MOVEMENT!
AND THAT GOES FOR YOU TOO, ARCHIE ANDREWS!
NICE PASS, CHUCK!
WOOSH!

Story: George Gladir Pencils: Stan Goldberg
Letters: Bill Yoshida

Originally printed in ARCHIE AT RIVERDALE HIGH #64, JULY 1979

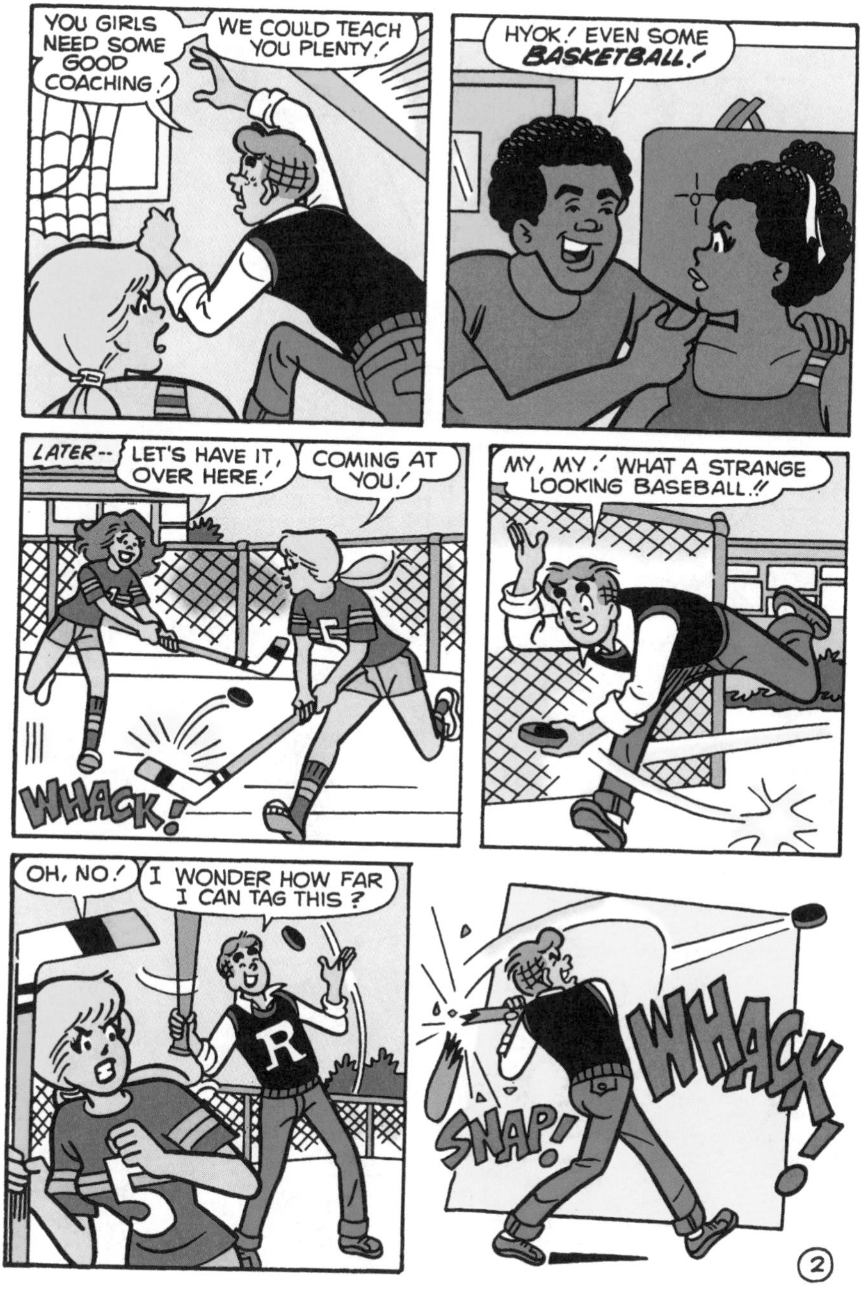
YOU GIRLS NEED SOME GOOD COACHING!
WE COULD TEACH YOU PLENTY!
HYOK! EVEN SOME BASKETBALL!
LATER--
LET'S HAVE IT, OVER HERE!
COMING AT YOU!
WHACK!
MY, MY! WHAT A STRANGE LOOKING BASEBALL!!
OH, NO!
I WONDER HOW FAR I CAN TAG THIS?
WHACK!
SNAP!
2

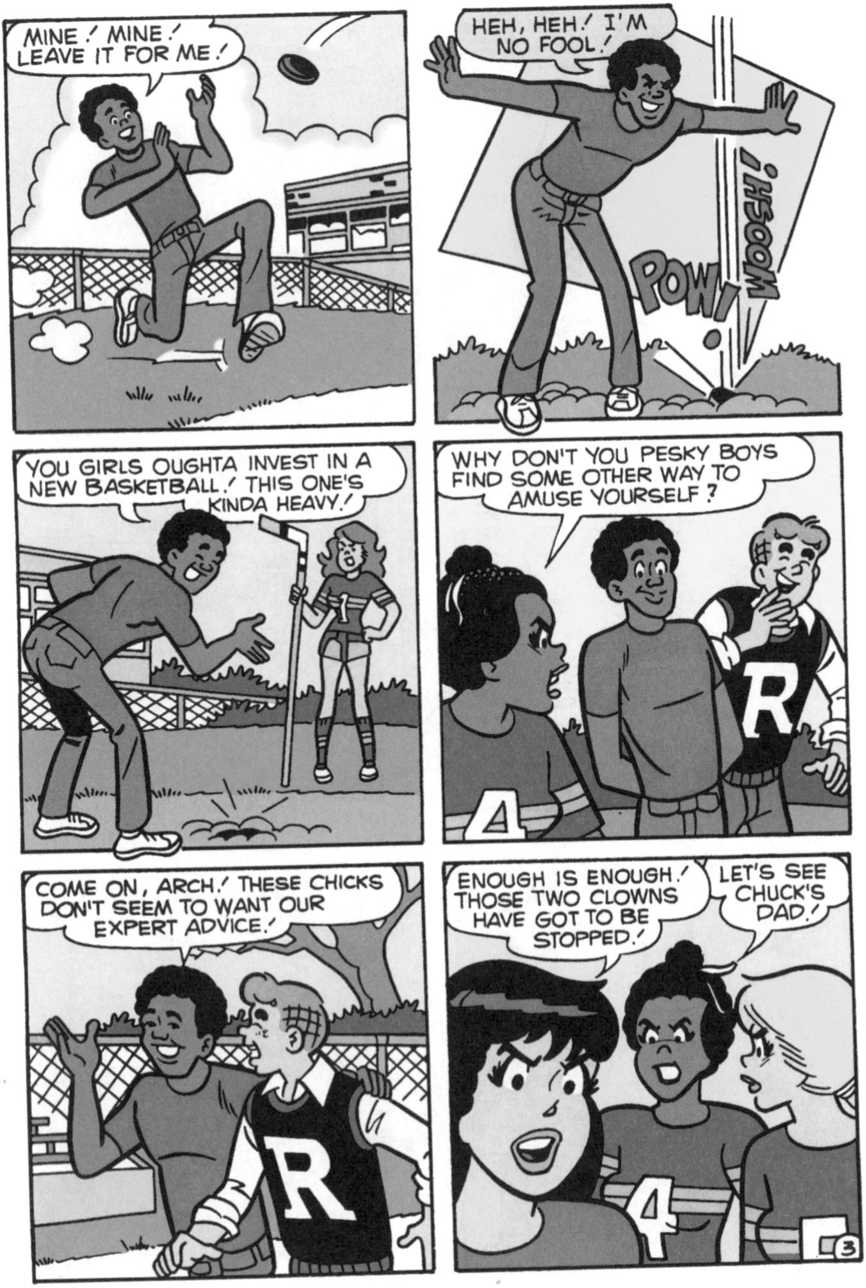
MINE! MINE! LEAVE IT FOR ME!
HEH, HEH! I'M NO FOOL!
WOOSH!
POW!
YOU GIRLS OUGHTA INVEST IN A NEW BASKETBALL! THIS ONE'S KINDA HEAVY!
WHY DON'T YOU PESKY BOYS FIND SOME OTHER WAY TO AMUSE YOURSELF?
COME ON, ARCH! THESE CHICKS DON'T SEEM TO WANT OUR EXPERT ADVICE!
ENOUGH IS ENOUGH! THOSE TWO CLOWNS HAVE GOT TO BE STOPPED!
LET'S SEE CHUCK'S DAD!
3

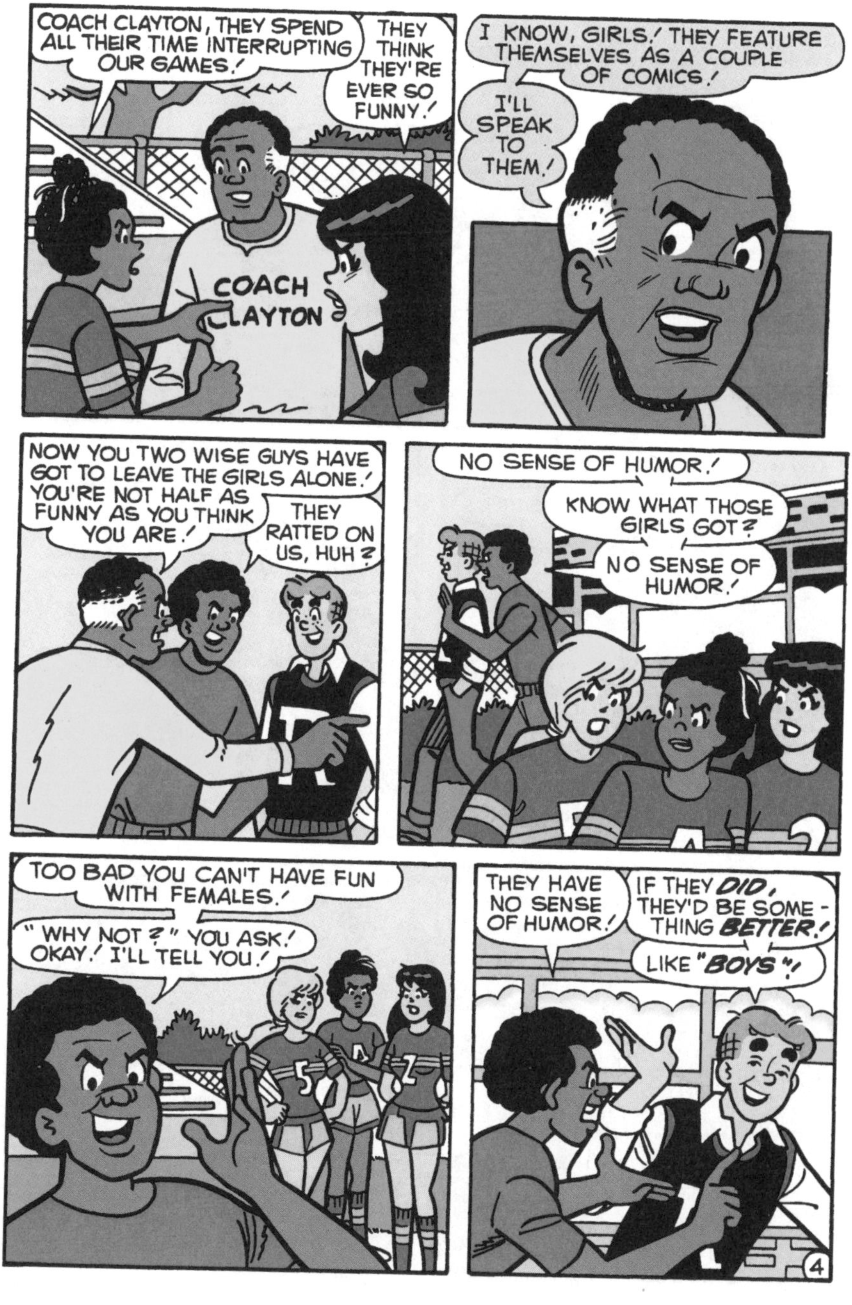
COACH CLAYTON, THEY SPEND ALL THEIR TIME INTERRUPTING OUR GAMES!
THEY THINK THEY'RE EVER SO FUNNY!
COACH CLAYTON
I KNOW, GIRLS! THEY FEATURE THEMSELVES AS A COUPLE OF COMICS!
I'LL SPEAK TO THEM!
NOW YOU TWO WISE GUYS HAVE GOT TO LEAVE THE GIRLS ALONE! YOU'RE NOT HALF AS FUNNY AS YOU THINK YOU ARE!
THEY RATTED ON US, HUH?
NO SENSE OF HUMOR!
KNOW WHAT THOSE GIRLS GOT?
NO SENSE OF HUMOR!
TOO BAD YOU CAN'T HAVE FUN WITH FEMALES!
"WHY NOT?" YOU ASK! OKAY! I'LL TELL YOU!
THEY HAVE NO SENSE OF HUMOR!
IF THEY *DID*, THEY'D BE SOME-THING *BETTER*!
LIKE "*BOYS*"!
4

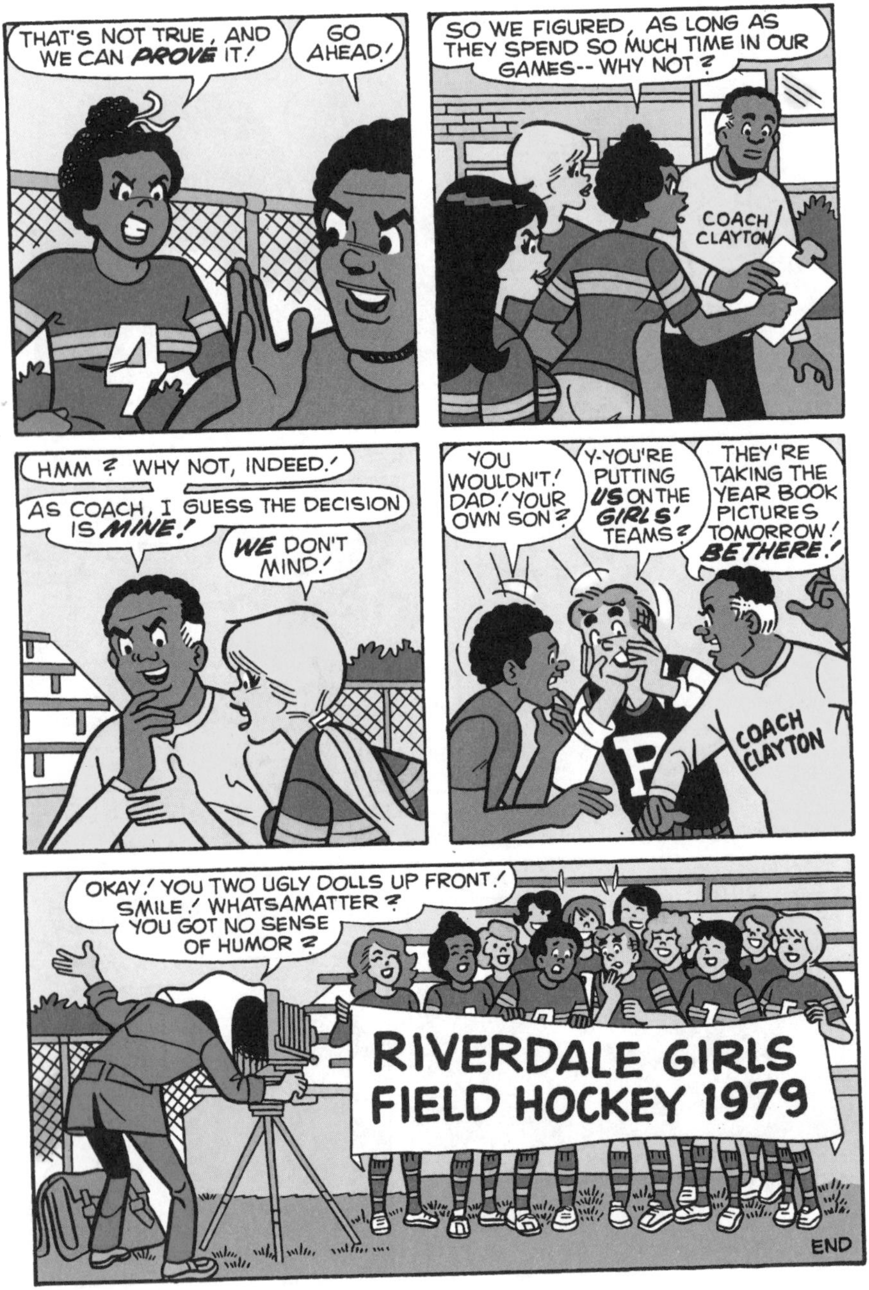
THAT'S NOT TRUE, AND WE CAN PROVE IT!
GO AHEAD!
SO WE FIGURED, AS LONG AS THEY SPEND SO MUCH TIME IN OUR GAMES-- WHY NOT?
COACH CLAYTON
HMM? WHY NOT, INDEED!
AS COACH, I GUESS THE DECISION IS MINE!
WE DON'T MIND!
YOU WOULDN'T! DAD! YOUR OWN SON?
Y-YOU'RE PUTTING US ON THE GIRLS' TEAMS?
THEY'RE TAKING THE YEAR BOOK PICTURES TOMORROW! BE THERE!
COACH CLAYTON
OKAY! YOU TWO UGLY DOLLS UP FRONT! SMILE! WHATSAMATTER? YOU GOT NO SENSE OF HUMOR?
RIVERDALE GIRLS FIELD HOCKEY 1979
END

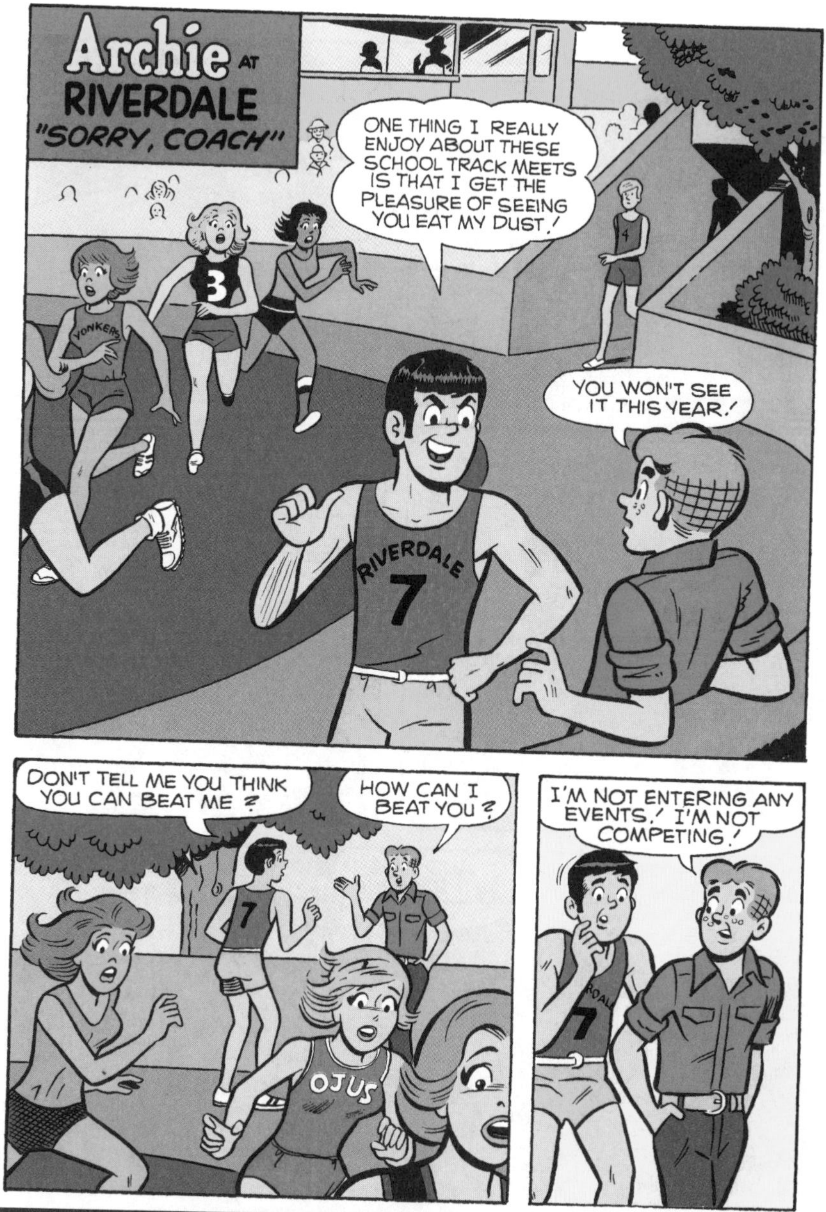
Archie AT RIVERDALE
"SORRY, COACH"
ONE THING I REALLY ENJOY ABOUT THESE SCHOOL TRACK MEETS IS THAT I GET THE PLEASURE OF SEEING YOU EAT MY DUST!
YOU WON'T SEE IT THIS YEAR!
YONKERS
3
4
RIVERDALE
7
DON'T TELL ME YOU THINK YOU CAN BEAT ME?
HOW CAN I BEAT YOU?
7
OJUS
I'M NOT ENTERING ANY EVENTS! I'M NOT COMPETING!

Story: Mike Pellowski Pencils: Bob Bolling
Inks: Rudy Lapick Letters: Bill Yoshida Colors: Barry Grossman

Originally printed in ARCHIE AT RIVERDALE HIGH #65, AUGUST 1979

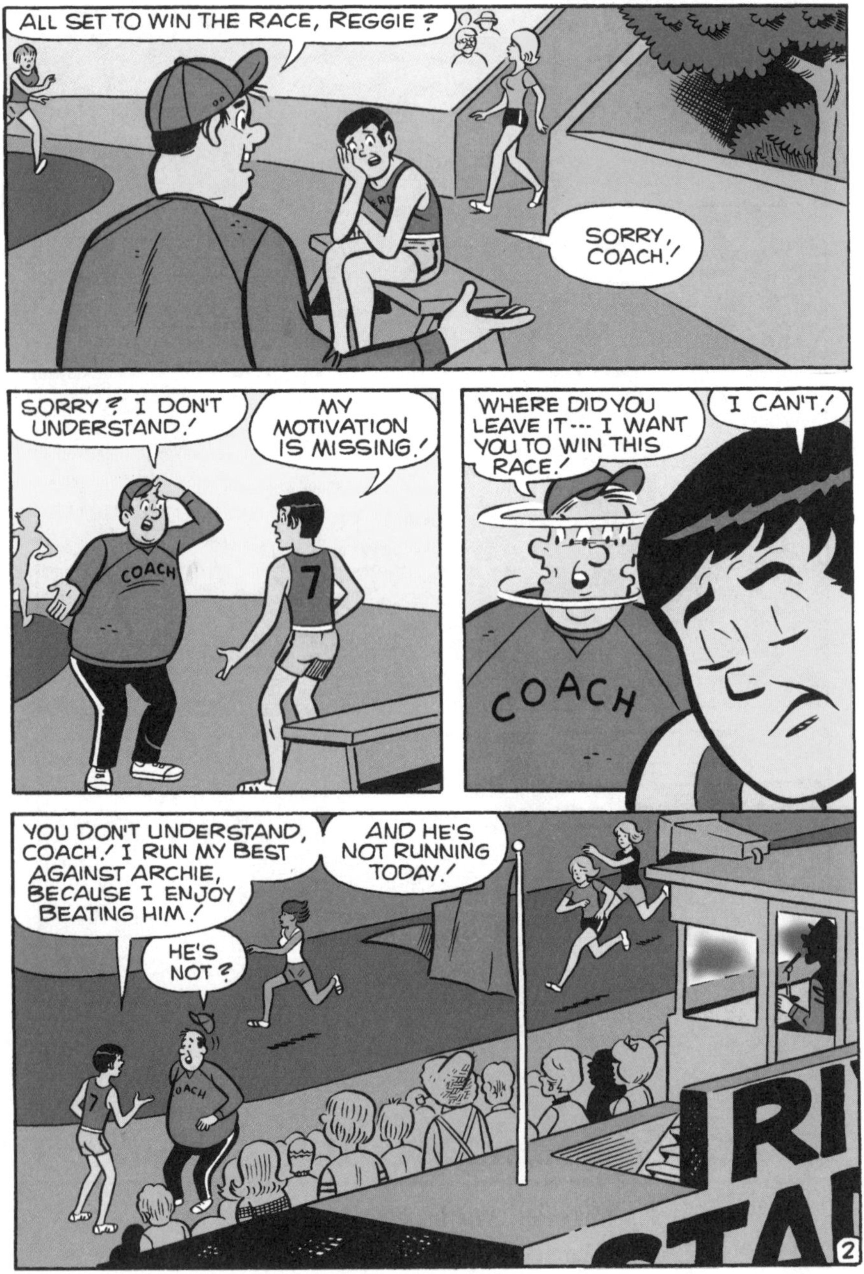
ALL SET TO WIN THE RACE, REGGIE?
SORRY, COACH!
SORRY? I DON'T UNDERSTAND!
MY MOTIVATION IS MISSING!
COACH
7
WHERE DID YOU LEAVE IT --- I WANT YOU TO WIN THIS RACE!
I CAN'T!
COACH
YOU DON'T UNDERSTAND, COACH! I RUN MY BEST AGAINST ARCHIE, BECAUSE I ENJOY BEATING HIM!
AND HE'S NOT RUNNING TODAY!
HE'S NOT?
2

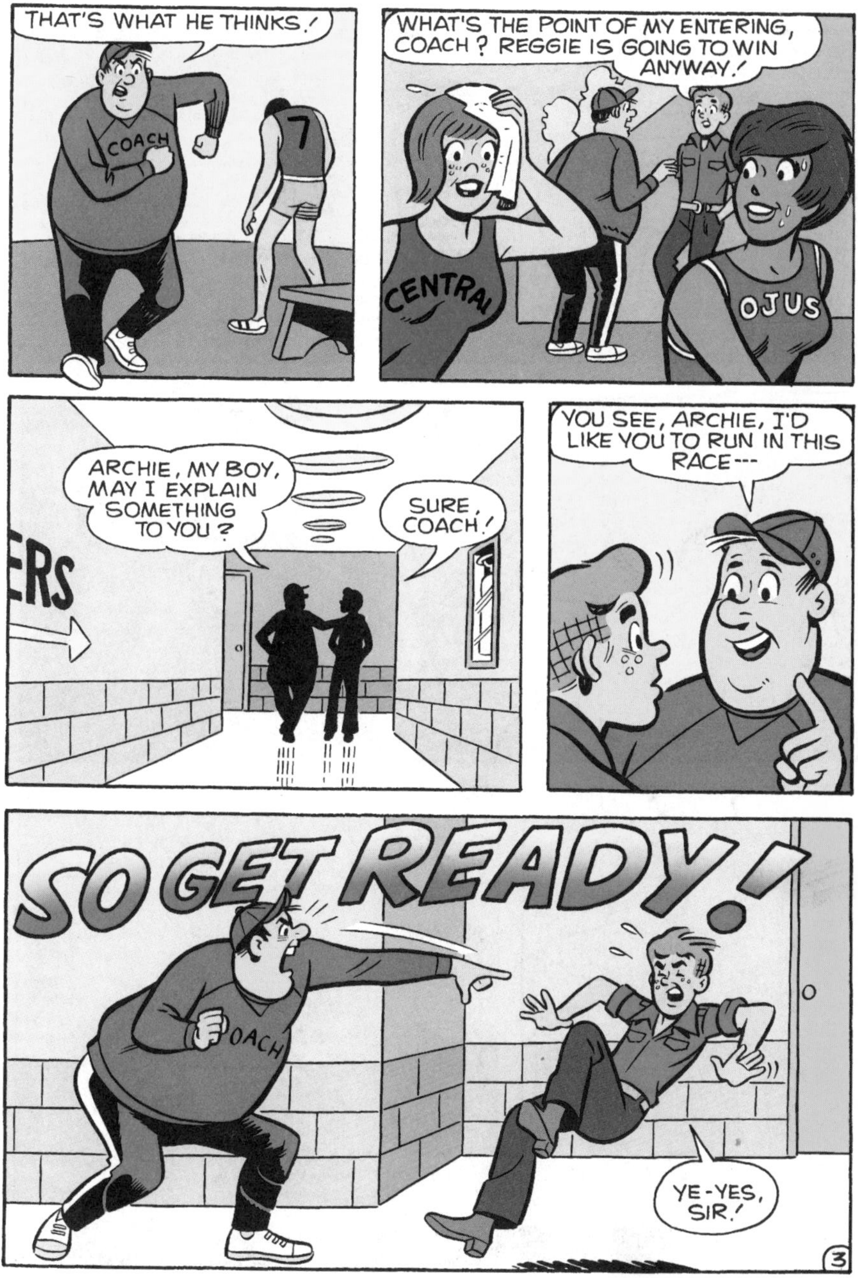
THAT'S WHAT HE THINKS.!
COACH
7
WHAT'S THE POINT OF MY ENTERING, COACH ? REGGIE IS GOING TO WIN ANYWAY.!
CENTRAL
OJUS
ARCHIE, MY BOY, MAY I EXPLAIN SOMETHING TO YOU ?
SURE, COACH.!
ERS
YOU SEE, ARCHIE, I'D LIKE YOU TO RUN IN THIS RACE---
SO GET READY!
OACH
YE-YES, SIR.!
3

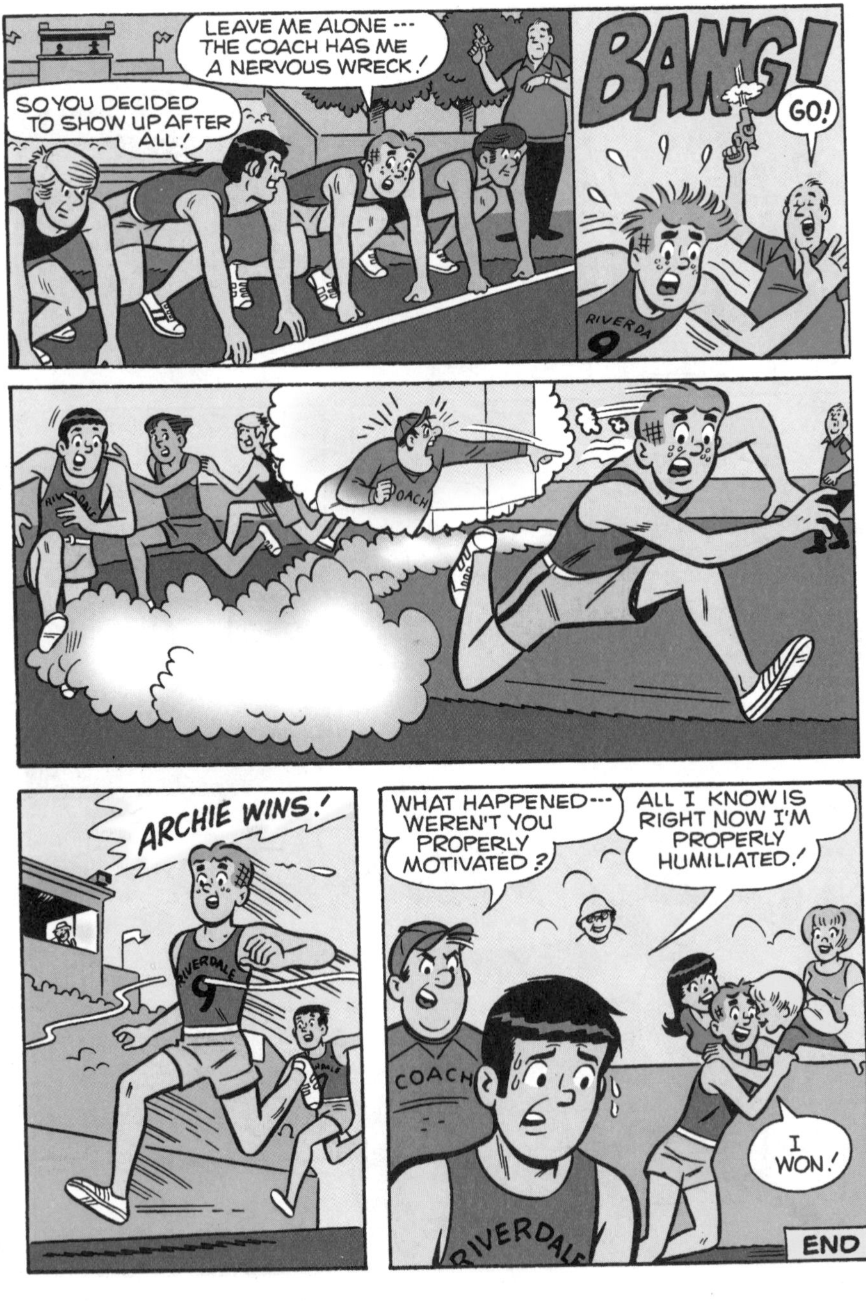
LEAVE ME ALONE --- THE COACH HAS ME A NERVOUS WRECK!
SO YOU DECIDED TO SHOW UP AFTER ALL!
BANG!
GO!
RIVERDA
COACH
ARCHIE WINS!
RIVERDALE
WHAT HAPPENED--- WEREN'T YOU PROPERLY MOTIVATED?
ALL I KNOW IS RIGHT NOW I'M PROPERLY HUMILIATED!
COACH
I WON!
RIVERDALE
END